HE WHO BREAKS THE EARTH

HE
WHO
BREAKS
THE
EARTH

CAITLIN SANGSTER

MARGARET K. McELDERRY BOOKS

New York   London   Toronto   Sydney   New   Delhi

MARGARET K. McELDERRY BOOKS
An imprint of Simon & Schuster Children's Publishing Division
1230 Avenue of the Americas, New York, New York 10020
This book is a work of fiction. Any references to historical events, real people, or real places are used fictitiously. Other names, characters, places, and events are products of the author's imagination, and any resemblance to actual events or places or persons, living or dead, is entirely coincidental.
Text © 2023 by Caitlin Sangster
Jacket illustration © 2023 by Carlos Quevedo
Jacket design by Greg Stadnyk © 2023 by Simon & Schuster, Inc.
MARGARET K. McELDERRY BOOKS is a trademark of Simon & Schuster, Inc.
For information about special discounts for bulk purchases, please contact Simon & Schuster Special Sales at 1-866-506-1949 or business@simonandschuster.com.
The Simon & Schuster Speakers Bureau can bring authors to your live event. For more information or to book an event, contact the Simon & Schuster Speakers Bureau at 1-866-248-3049 or visit our website at www.simonspeakers.com.
Interior design by Irene Metaxatos
The text for this book was set in ITC Galliard Std.
Manufactured in the United States of America
First Edition
10 9 8 7 6 5 4 3 2 1
Library of Congress Cataloging-in-Publication Data
Names: Sangster, Caitlin, author.
Title: He who breaks the earth / Caitlin Sangster.
Description: New York : Margaret K. McElderry Books, [2023] | Series: The gods-touched duology ; book 2 | Summary: "A sequel to the first book, four friends hunt down a murderous shapeshifter in a high-stakes heist"—Provided by publisher.
Identifiers: LCCN 2022023223 (print) | LCCN 2022023224 (ebook) | ISBN 9781534466142 (hardcover) | ISBN 9781534466166 (ebook)
Subjects: CYAC: Shapeshifting—Fiction. | Magic—Fiction. | Fantasy. | LCGFT: Fantasy fiction. | Novels. Classification: LCC PZ7.1.S263 He 2023 (print) | LCC PZ7.1.S263 (ebook) | DDC [Fic]—dc23
LC record available at https://lccn.loc.gov/2022023223
LC ebook record available at https://lccn.loc.gov/2022023224

To Mom and Dad, because you spent a lot of time and effort teaching me that the world and the people in it are much more than I can see from the outside

HE WHO BREAKS THE EARTH

CHAPTER 1

Sweet Rolls to Die For

When Mateo stepped out of his room at the inn, all he could feel was death. It was a scent coming off the scuffed wooden walls, from beneath the floorboards with their thread-bare carpet runners. Death was a shadow in the chatter of servants emerging from their rooms and a sour note in the scent of honey and cream-filled sweet rolls coming from the kitchen.

He took in a deep breath, as if he could latch on to the fleeing details of the world where he was alive instead of slowly rotting away into nothing. If he ignored it, maybe it would go away. His father had always made the nothing go away before.

I'm not *going away*, the nothing said. *I only just found you.*

Mateo started down the hallway, his humors churning with discomfort at the hollow voice. The nothing hadn't always *spoken* to him. It had started with a hiss just after he'd woken up in the carriage with his father, the dust of Patenga's collapsed tomb still on his coat. Now, even walking down the inn's narrow hallway felt as if he were trapped in a spotlight on a stage, hundreds of little eyes peering up at him from a darkness that had gnawed at his humors, his muscle and bone. Mateo had always believed that slow drain of energy had been wasting sickness burning through his aura, but now he couldn't un-know.

It was . . . a thing. A *nothing*.

A nothing that was suddenly aware of him, watching him, occasionally commenting on his choice of dress, and pushing energy *toward* him instead of sucking it away, lacing the air around him with rot.

Mateo wasn't sure it was a fair exchange if it meant he was already dead.

Mateo's toe caught on the stained rug just before he got to the stairs, almost sending him down them headfirst. Heart racing, he blinked at the narrow passage, harsh beams of morning light touching each stair he would have hit—his knees on that second stair, then his head and neck on the fourth, his spine on the tenth, as if the light itself wanted to break him into little pieces. Calsta, the sky goddess, set on destroying an abomination.

Chin thrust forward, he started down, shrugging off the light as it washed over him.

A month before Mateo had been at the edge of a new beginning, a new *life* to replace the one that had been gnawed to pieces. He and his father had finally located an undisturbed shapeshifter tomb with the Basist-made healing compound, caprenum, sitting at the bottom, just waiting to heal the wasting disease that plagued him and half the Warlord's Devoted.

They'd dug and dug, dodged traps, lost workers. Then his father had introduced him to Lia. Mateo had brought her down into the tomb with them the night they'd broken into the shapeshifter's burial chamber to get the caprenum—which turned out to be the shape shifter's very own sword.

Are you stomping? the voice asked. *Did the stairs do something to you, or are you always this delightful?*

Mateo caught himself stepping lightly onto the last stair, then made himself stomp the rest of the way to the kitchen, reveling in the feel of energy bursting inside him, then disgusted with himself because now he knew where that energy came from. He slammed open the kitchen door, the last barrier between him and the heavenly scents of Hilaria's cooking, and couldn't stop his mind ranging out to touch the bits of metal and stone in the room, like even more potential energy just waiting for his signal.

For the first time, using his power like this didn't make him dizzy. He didn't stumble, didn't faint. His feet were there, squarely in the world, and suddenly nothing could stop him from doing what he liked.

Not even the hole inside him come to life.

I'm not *a hole*, the voice whispered. *And I wasn't going to stop you eating your weight in sugar anyway.*

Even the sweet rolls smelled like decay.

Mateo gave the maid a dignified nod, then grabbed a plate from the rack of dishes she'd been drying, surprised when she gave a perturbed squeak and jumped out of his way. As if somehow, for the first time in his life, he was someone to be wary of.

"I'm so sorry, I didn't mean to frighten you." He gave her a flourishing little bow that would have made Lia smirk at him.

"No, of course not, sir." The maid shrank back against the wall, keeping one eye on him even as she continued drying dishes.

Mateo carefully checked the wide kitchen for Hilaria before stepping in any farther and only found raw fowl trussed and ready to be roasted on the wood-topped island at the center, the back counters filled with vegetables and roots for stew. Hilaria's tray of sweet rolls was shoved onto the counter just by the door out to the stables, topped with snowy cream and glistening with raspberry glaze.

Mateo slid two sweet rolls onto his plate.

Just as he began to lick his fingers, the door swung open and whacked him in the back of the legs.

"Mateo Montanne, you *entafolin!*" Hilaria was on him before he could run for the stairs, the maid blocking the door with both hands clamped over her mouth, looking between him and the terror Hilaria had probably made of her life for the two days their party had been camped at the inn. Hilaria swatted at Mateo's plate, knocking one of the sweet rolls back onto the tray, narrowly missing his shoulder. "You get your grubby hands away—"

Mateo ducked the next swat, pushing past her through the courtyard door, gratified that he'd managed to keep hold of the one sweet roll. Hilaria's food was to die for, but sometimes it seemed as if death was the only payment she'd accept for consuming it.

Once he made it through the door, Mateo snaked into the hubbub of servants carrying trunks, saddling horses, and hitching wagons and carriages. He ducked behind their head hostler, Harlan, even as Hilaria shouted from the kitchen door. Harlan cleared his throat, pushing Mateo down an inch lower as he scanned the organized mess with an absurdly casual air, as if he weren't trying to hide a young man and his stolen raspberry cream behind his spindly legs.

"She's going to gut you one of these days," the old hostler murmured once Hilaria had shouted her way across the courtyard, letting Mateo stand up. "But not today if you get into the carriage quick."

"You'd think she'd be flattered." Mateo lifted the roll to his mouth to take another bite, freezing when he caught sight of a small carriage out front, the door hanging open. A shock of coppery hair showed through the window, the occupant arguing loudly with the servant trying to close her inside. "Where's the other carriage, Harlan?"

Harlan's face didn't change, a little too close to read. "Master Montanne sent it on ahead of us the day we got here. Didn't you notice?"

Mateo swore, shoving another bite into his mouth and looking around for a place to hide. His stomach lurched as he looked down at his coat, the lacy front dribbled all over with glaze, the bright raspberry red dripping from his buttons like blood.

There had been a lot of blood down in the tomb. All from that boy on the ground, a sword in his gut, impaled just the way the shape-shifter's skeleton had been.

Knox, the voice hissed.

A sword just like the one they'd stolen from the tomb that Tual had bundled up and dragged behind his carriage in its own special wagon—a sword that was supposed to save Mateo's life. Mateo wasn't sure why the caprenum sword they'd stolen from Patenga's tomb needed a whole wagon to itself, but Tual had kept him and every-one else in their company from peeking under the tarp, as if touching the sword before the right time would ruin everything. But his father *couldn't* expect him to share a carriage with Aria Seystone. She was just like Lia, only smaller and slightly less good at violence.

Mateo shoved the last of the roll into his mouth, icing dribbling down his lip. "Saddle Bella for me, would you?" he mumbled to Har-lan around the lump of pastry.

Tual appeared at the inn's main doors, his sun hat tipped. He was all smiles and banter as he crossed to check under the tarp covering the wagon where the shapeshifter sword was. Once he'd resecured the canvas, Tual walked toward the little carriage, Aria growling insults from inside. Mateo ducked down even farther, his stomach swirling with bile.

". . . .riding alone probably isn't the best option." Harlan was still talking, and Mateo hadn't heard a word. "Didn't they tell you about the attacks, boy? That's why we stayed at the inn for two days despite your father being in a fury to get home. Even he couldn't brush off finding bodies in the road."

"Bodies?" Mateo turned to look at the hostler only to catch sight of Hilaria storming from the kitchen yet again, both her fists clenched around the tray of sweet rolls to offer to the company. She made straight for Tual despite servants grabbing at the tray left and right and presented him with the last one, which Tual took with a bow, then handed it in to the carriage's single occupant.

It flew back out quick enough, landing in the dirt at Hilaria's feet. Mateo cleared his throat, turning back to Harlan, vaguely horrified about the waste of a coveted sweet roll. "What do you mean they've been finding bodies?" His mind flicked back to the terrifying girl who'd been at the bottom of Patenga's tomb, the one who'd made vines burst out of the earth and grasp at him like snakes. Had she managed to follow them somehow? Father had said she might.

"The first night, it was . . . well, a *Devoted* of all things. On the road."

"Something killed a Devoted?" Mateo paused.

"Yes. Completely white and shriveled, he was, like he'd been drained of blood. And there were bites. . . ." Harlan looked down. "We thought it was a coincidence coming across him on the road. But then we started seeing animals in a similar condition near the camp. And then last night . . ."

"Last night *what*?" Mateo leaned forward.

"Well, Master Montanne's getting us out quick enough, but it won't bring back the kitchen boy."

Mateo's chest clenched a hair tighter. He looked just beyond the inn out into the dense wall of foliage, the road cutting through it like a wound. They'd be safe soon. They'd be back at home where no one could get to them.

No one except Lia, who'd stop at nothing to get her sister. A shudder trilled down his back. Lia Seystone was not above killing. The Beildan girl he'd seen at the dig wouldn't be either. Mateo's mind flashed again to the shadowy figure in the tomb, energy singing like poison in the air around her, Tual answering with a terrible magic that stank of murder . . . .

No. Mateo's jaw clenched. *No. She isn't my sister, and I'm not . . .*

You're not what? the little voice sang. *You're not like your father, the one person who loved you before I found you? If you weren't like him, then you'd be dead.*

Dead. The thought echoed in his head. He hadn't chosen to turn shapeshifter. He hadn't wanted it, didn't want it now. But that couldn't *change* the sacrifice Tual had helped him make, killing an innocent girl to save his own life, even if it had made him into . . .

A monster.

Mateo breathed the word in and then out again. People were the choices they made, not the labels other people gave them. He was what he was. He was alive. And he would make do with what life he had left.

No one could fault him that.

"Are . . . you all right?" Harlan's voice was concerned.

Mateo looked down to find the plate in shards between his two hands, blood on his fingers. He dropped the broken pieces like a dead snake, recoiling back a step. Hilaria was very animatedly speaking to his father by the carriage, and the barely contained glee on Tual's face made Mateo fairly certain that it had to do with a stolen sweet roll. His father turned a fraction and caught Mateo's eye across the courtyard, a guffaw so painfully held in that Mateo knew Tual would be cackling about it later.

He'd thought his father had finally decided to be open with him, to *stop* keeping secrets. How could Tual have known about these killings and not told him?

"Mateo?" Harlan was still standing there, worried.

"I'm fine." Mateo wiped his bloody fingers on his coat, flinching when red smeared across the fabric to match the raspberry. This coat had been his favorite back at the university—just the right number of ruffles to be interesting without being too much, the shade of green perfectly complementing his light brown skin. He started toward the stable, Harlan twitching along behind him as if he'd been attached with string. "I'm going to ride, Harlan. Nothing is going to attack us in broad daylight."

"They look almost like auroshe kills," Harlan murmured.

Mateo's stomach roiled, the sweet roll threatening to come back up.

"With the first body being a Devoted and . . . well, I think we both know auroshes don't roam free this far south. Honestly, I'm surprised we don't hear more tales of those monsters killing their riders. If you are determined to take Bella, keep your eyes open. There could be more of them following us."

"Devoted or feral auroshes?"

"Either." Harlan shrugged.

Mateo turned toward the open stable doors. It wasn't the Warlord he was worried about. She would at least try to talk to them before gutting him. The Warlord thought they had something she wanted: a cure to wasting sickness. Auroshe kills and dead Devoted on the road sounded more like Lia with her foul steed prowling after them. It wasn't enough that her actual job . . . magical calling . . . gods-given *purpose* in the world was to kill people like Mateo and his father. Tual had gone and kidnapped her younger sister.

Because he wants me to live. The words unspooled inside him, his own this time. *I want to live.*

Mateo strode into the light-starved stables, straight for Bella's stall. She gave an excited whinny when she saw him. He ran a hand down her neck, grateful when she buried her nose in his chest. His heart slowed a beat. But only the one.

If the kills out there weren't Lia's doing, he'd eat his own oversized sun hat. A sick feeling of betrayal welled deep in his chest.

Tual had blackmailed her into an engagement, encouraging Mateo to get to know her, to give her a chance. And Mateo had accidentally done it. He'd talked to her, almost been killed with her, stolen an auroshe with her, saved her from the Warlord, and then he'd thought that maybe . . .

He'd *wanted* to . . .

He'd even thought that *she* might want . . .

That someone could see past the many deaths of Mateo Montanne to *him* had always been an impossible thing until that day in his father's office with Lia. She'd stayed. She'd talked to him. She'd listened. She was smart. She was funny, she was beautiful, she was exactly what he . . .

Mateo forced the thought of Lia's burnished hair, her freckles, her blue eyes from his mind, turning to take the saddle from a hostler and place it on Bella's back. The maybes that surrounded Lia had been so new and unexpected and *hopeful* that they'd felt forbidden, secret, delicious. But then she'd seen the reliefs in Patenga's tomb the same moment he had.

She'd been Tual's plan all along—Lia *plus* a caprenum sword. All magic required sacrifice, and the sacrifice that had made Mateo into the creature he was had been botched, tearing a hole inside him instead of filling him to the brim with power. The magical caprenum he'd been searching for with his father for years was just the vessel—the knife, the sword, the ax to seal the sacrifice of the person you loved most.

Because that's what Mateo needed to survive—a new sacrifice to replace the old one that hadn't worked.

It put him in a difficult place. How could he fall in love with Lia Seystone knowing it was all to keep his own heart beating at the expense of hers? And how could he persuade her to love him back as the oaths required when she now knew *exactly* what the end would look like for her? Dead on the end of a shapeshifter's sword.

But without Lia, Mateo would continue to die bit by bit from the hole the transformation had left inside him, a hole that had to be filled with something. Some*one*.

All magic came from sacrifice. It was only in the last month that he understood it was sacrificed love—a love realized, bonded, solidified, then torn asunder—that could make something as powerful as a shapeshifter. And if Mateo wanted to live, he had to make that sacrifice himself, the right way.

Mateo finished pulling the buckles tight and stood. Lia would come, but it wouldn't be with an open heart. Maybe she'd already gone back to the Warlord and would come with an entire Devoted army.

She's not with the Warlord, the little voice giggled. *She's with your sister.*

Halfway to sticking his foot in the stirrup, Mateo faltered, falling forward. Bella snorted, her head twisting back to look at him reproachfully. *Lia's with . . . are you sure?*

I think they've formed the first official "I Hate Mateo Montanne" club.

Mateo's insides went cold. *Gods above, couldn't you have said something earlier?*

Why does Lia *scare you so much?* it said, ignoring his question. *Lia Seystone is just a girl. She's made of muscles and energy and toenails and hair, and worms will eat her face just as quickly as they would anyone else's. As fast as they would have eaten you if I hadn't been there.*

I didn't ask for my father to make me kill you, he thought furiously at the nothing, but then turned the fury back on himself for engaging with it at all.

I'm not nothing, and I'm not an it, the little voice hissed, and Mateo could feel the shape of her underneath the helpless whisper she'd been using with him, like a monstrous mass of sinew, bone, and claws flexing from behind its little-girl mask. *My name is Willow. And if you know what's good for you, you'd be worrying more about the other one.* Her voice broke. *Knox never would let me have her, even when I starved. She would have fixed everything, but she ruined it instead.*

I am worried about the other one. Mateo mounted Bella and steered her out into the courtyard, past the little carriage, the wagons, the life that had been so kind to him these last eight years. Running from the one he'd forgotten. Tual had told him in the carriage as they'd ridden away from the tomb that his sister had spent her whole life looking for him.

But even if that were true, how had *Willow* known?

Mateo cleared his throat, kicking Bella even faster, pushing the name away. The thing in his head didn't get a name. It didn't exist.

I'm so hungry, Willow sighed. Her voice quieted, shriveling down to almost nothing. *You're hungry too, so you know how it feels. You'll feed me, won't you, Mateo?*

Mateo shivered at the sound of his name made from thorns and ice. Because he did know how that hunger felt.

He did want to live.

And nothing was going to stop him, not Hilaria and her sweet rolls, not blood in the cuts on his hands, not Aria Seystone swearing when she thought people could see her and sobbing into her pillow when she thought they couldn't. Not his sister, whatever monstrous thing she'd become.

Not Lia and her red curls, her auroshe, and her sword.

If I tell you more about what they're doing, will you stop calling me a thing? Willow asked.

But Mateo couldn't let himself listen to a ghost—who even knew why she was inside him, what she wanted, and what she'd take from him? Because that's all people ever did. Take.

Keeping his eyes open for the rocky formations that marked the hidden path to the caves that would take him home, Mateo kicked Bella out onto the road, thinking only of the wind in his hair and the sun on his face because it was touching him, making him as real, as important, as *alive* as anyone else in the company, no matter the scent of death in his nose.

He wanted to live.

CHAPTER 2

An Indecent Portrait

N oa sat back in the wagon with her eyes closed, glad for the sun on her face. She could feel Altahn watching her as the wagon lurched across the street toward Castor's temple, the heckle and cry of Rentara's university district louder than any kind of applause. People were always louder when they were angry than when they were happy.

Everyone in this city was angry. Not as angry as Anwei, though Noa's friend hid it inside the carefully formed mask she'd made of her face. Not as angry as Lia, back at the camp sharpening her sword. But angry enough, as if every person on the road had looked out their window that morning and decided everything was going to go wrong.

It made Noa want to do a handstand on the boxboard, somersault down, and ignite her fire tethers in a fiery swirl. Maybe that would be enough to make *one* person in this city smile. That's what Noa was good at: making people smile. Anwei hadn't let her bring the fire tethers though—something about sneaking into a library not meshing well with flame. She'd had that awful mask of a smile on her face when she said it too, almost as if she thought fooling Noa would be as easy as fooling everyone else.

"Are you going to help me brace this thing, or are you just here to keep the wagon from blowing away?" Altahn called from the other side of the wagon.

"I thought that was why you brought that lizard with you every where." Cracking one eye open to look at the Trib, Noa got a full view of his firekey lizard instead, the little creature glaring at her from where its blunt nose stuck out from the back of Altahn's collar. Noa closed her eyes again, relishing the way Altahn's gaze just sank in deeper, as if he couldn't look away. Maybe it wasn't just making people smile she was good at. Catching people's attention wasn't hard—all it took was a little surprise, a little sparkle. *Keeping* attention required real talent. "Isn't Galerey supposed to help you with all the little things you can't do yourself?" she asked.

"Unfortunately, Galerey isn't up to keeping fifty pounds of inde-cent stained-glass portrait upright in this traffic." Altahn braced himself when the wagon jerked to a halt, Anwei swearing from the driver's bench. "She's better at burning people when they annoy me."

"He thinks I'm trying to annoy him," Noa said in Elantin to Anwei's back, the bright crimson scarf she'd help tie over the healer's long braids flapping in the wind like a flag. Altahn's long tail of hair with the short bits in the front was covered too, both of them styled to look like artists, hopefully the kind no one looked at twice because their scarves weren't knotted or braided to show rank. A Beildan healer and a Trib rider carrying a heavy load into Castor's temple like drudges would have caught a few too many eyes. "You think I should show him what it looks like when I'm *actually* trying to annoy someone?"

"A show I'd love to see, but it'll be hard to deliver that thing to the temple if it breaks in half on the way," Anwei called back in Noa's own language, the words bittersweet in Noa's ears. Noa missed the Elantin docks, the smell of the southern sea, the playhouses and the people who played in them. Though she didn't relish the thought of joining one now. It would just be an excuse to get out of a life that expected nothing of her except a good marriage and obedience. It was as if she were nothing more than a portrait herself, shrouded until someone impressive enough asked to admire her. Noa raised a hand to look at her extended fingers. She looked much better out here, in the sunlight.

"You can't just tell me I'm handsome in words I understand?" Altahn asked.

"I wanted to pretend we were *unrilthasen*." Noa sighed, leaning in to brace the portrait when the wagon lurched forward once again.

"I swear she can speak Common. She just *won't*." Altahn laughed. "I could start using only Trib, and then none of us would understand each other."

"I'd understand you," Anwei shot back, swearing when a silenbahk swung its tail just ahead of her, making their horse dance. Altahn's horse, really. Most of what they had was Altahn's. "She's saying she wanted to sneak into the scholar god's sky-cursed library as *fire dancers*."

"Don't help him, Anwei." Noa grinned. "He needs to learn he doesn't know everything."

"Really? Fire dancing?" Altahn peered at her from around the side of the ridiculous portrait. "I'd pay to see that."

"You wouldn't get to watch—Anwei only convinced me to deliver this glass in place of the special window the First Scholar ordered because we know how bad you are at dancing."

"I am *not* bad at dancing."

"You are holding the glass, right, Noa? Because we're—" Anwei's voice cut off when a horse reared directly in front of them.

Noa wrinkled her nose, bracing the shrouded glass pane tight against its ties. Over the top of the wagon sides, the temple facade of thirteen white columns stood out like jewels in an ebony frame, one of Castor's thirteen moon phases carved into each. Together, the columns made a sunburst that centered on the building's front steps, the entrance itself populated with a crowd of wrinkled acolytes in blue robes chanting about Castor's unending fight to rule the night sky. Why scholars chose such drab apparel, Noa would never know. Even the scholar god, Castor himself, knew how to put on a show, the moon a riot of blues and purples as he crossed the sky and danced with his brother moon, Jaxom. The scholars chanting on the steps looked, at best, very comfortable.

When Anwei turned the wagon down the little service road to the side of the temple, Noa eagerly looked past her to the university compound beyond it. She'd always wanted to come study in Rentara, but her father had said suitors in such places wanted more than a girl who knew how to shine, and that she wasn't suited to do anything else. The sight of the buildings sprawled past Jaxom's temple had walls of warped glass, all the different gods' halls like squat little frogs getting ready to do battle, with students scurrying between them like ants. Noa sighed and looked away. It wasn't that her father was correct—she could do more than shine—but the buildings here didn't look so different from the university in Chaol, and everyone there had seemed to agree with her father about what Noa should do with herself.

Jaxom's temple rose a full story above Castor's, blocking the scholar god's view of the rest of the temples. Trying to needle his brother, as usual. There were devotees on Jaxom's steps shouting back at the ones praising Castor, a war of words and wrinkles.

Noa touched Falan's flower in her hair, grateful her own goddess was much more amenable to fun. She could feel the goddess like a hand on her shoulder, Falan eager to see their mischief. "Why are all these old people out chanting at one another?"

"Starfall last month. Remember, right before we left Chaol?" Anwei didn't look back, pulling the horse to a halt and tying the reins to her bench. "They're still yelling about who lost the battle."

"I'm going to say it was us, since we have to listen to this racket." Noa stood, waiting until Altahn had undone the tethers holding the frame on his side before she knelt to untie the ones on hers. It felt like years, not weeks since the two moons had gone to war in the night sky, their arrows darting as flashes of light. She'd been standing on the governor's balcony, the boy to whom her father had deeded her facedown in his soup.

Anwei had given her the herbs to put Bear to sleep—to fight her own war in a swirl of light and fire, just like the moons in the sky—and it had been that moment she'd seen the way out. Noa had spent her life wrenching at the strings her father had fastened to her wrists and ankles, an unruly marionette that danced where she liked, until her father handed the controller to someone new. Bear wasn't so controlling, but his father, the governor, had thoughts about what his son's prospective wife should or shouldn't be doing. Wearing. Saying. *Being*.

So, the night Anwei had invited Noa to help haunt the governor's ballroom—nothing but little sparks of fire and some scary voices—Noa hadn't minded when things escalated after she set fire to the governor's prized Palashian drapes. It was slightly less amusing when the governor barred all the gates and locked her up right when Noa was supposed to be helping Anwei get out of the compound safely.

It wasn't until Noa overheard the governor yelling at his steward that she'd realized he hadn't locked the compound gates with all his guests still inside because of some burned drapes. A book had gone missing from his study. The lock jimmied, guards found collapsed on the floor.

The servants searched every guest, every servant, every hostler, every auroshe in the stables, probably. But somehow, despite the fact that Noa had seen Anwei on the ballroom floor right before the whole place had been shuttered, she and her little shadow friend, Knox, were nowhere to be found.

Standing there in the window, watching the swirl of agitation Anwei had left in her wake, Noa had realized the dance Anwei was performing was something wholly different from what she'd thought. It was on some other stage, in another version of life Noa had never seen before. Anwei wasn't even *dancing*: she was the puppeteer, twitching people this way and that until she got her way.

So Noa had climbed out the window to join her.

Which had led to helping Anwei set a shapeshifter excavation site on fire right in front of the sky-cursed Warlord herself. Hiding in a sugarcane field *shaking* as the auroshe calls came closer and closer. The ground rumbling under her feet and Devoted scampering in the other direction like scared little children. *Away* from the tomb, as if it weren't the Warlord's job to ensure the shapeshifter down in that hole stayed dead.

All except one Devoted had run.

Noa's mouth twisted at the thought of him—and what had happened to him. She wouldn't take back any of what she'd done for a single coin from her father, because out here, the things she did mattered. To her. And to everyone else.

"You've got your side?" Altahn's voice brought her back to the cobblestones. He peeked over the top of the glass, a smile still plastered across his face.

Altahn always smiled. It made Noa wonder what was beneath it.

"I don't carry anything that weighs more than I do." Noa stood up, stepping back from the glass. "My face would turn red, and my job is to be distracting in a *good* way."

He shook his head, laughing, and Noa looked away, worried there *wasn't* anything underneath his smile at all. That he was exactly what he looked like from the outside: a rich boy who had found a new and interesting place to spend his coin. Boys like that could be entertaining for days at a time, sometimes even weeks. Until they weren't anymore, because, in her experience, rich boys cared for nothing but what they wanted next.

Noa hopped out of the wagon, making room for Anwei to help Altahn slide the ungainly thing toward the wagon's lip. Patting the two loops of hair knotted just above her ear—Anwei had threaded them with gold before they left camp that morning—Noa walked up to the gate where the guard was staring curiously at them through the wrought iron bars.

"Would you please open this?" She gave the bars a slightly exasperated rattle. "You were supposed to be ready for us. Oh, and we'll need one of you to help carry the ladder and tools, of course."

"This gate is meant for gardeners." The guard cleared his throat, his eyes brushing the two knots that marked Noa as second khonin, then jumping down to the gold and crimson embroidery coiling up her skirt. "Which you clearly are not. How may I help you?"

"Gods above and below," Noa moaned. "They didn't tell you to expect us? The First Scholar herself ordered this piece." She gestured dramatically toward the shrouded glass Altahn and Anwei were sliding off the wagon bed. "She came to *me*. I *promised* her on my mother's life that I'd find something suitably dramatic and yet . . . subtle for her study." Drawing herself up, Noa gave the gate a rattle. "This is the only way to get such a large piece of art into the building without breaking it, and, frankly, you are *in our way*. Open this gate immediately."

The guard backed up a few steps, gesturing toward the main building. "I'll just check—"

"*Priceless art*. Commissioned by *the First herself*." Noa gave the glass an aggravated flick as Altahn drew up next to her, huffing. His arms looked quite nice in his Trib vest—they never saw the need to wear shirts under those things, which made sense because it was *hot*. "And it's heavy. One slip, and six months of painstaking work—" She slapped her hands together with a flourish. "The First has been waiting most impatiently to see this masterpiece I've created for her, and I don't like to think what could happen if we're made to stand out here a moment longer." Noa refrained from batting her eyes prettily. Anwei had advised against smiles since scholars at Castor's temple were much more likely to be moved by fear of politics rather than long eyelashes. A role she didn't usually play, but Noa didn't mind pretending to be a doltish rich lady. She'd done it often enough back in Chaol. "Perhaps you might tell me your name so I can bring it to the First's attention once we are finally allowed to deliver this one-of-a-kind, *highly* valuable, *extremely fragile*—"

"Fine." The guard extracted a set of wrought-iron keys from his coat pocket and jammed the largest of them into the lock. Anwei had brought Noa with her to scout the temple grounds two nights before to identify the entrances that would allow them to pass the fewest number of guards before they made it inside the temple itself. Normally, she said, they'd have snuck in at night, but according to her contact at the university, the scholars of Castor's great library doubled the guard at night and were more likely to be present at their desks and in the stacks during those dark hours. That wouldn't have been a terrible hurdle except that the restricted collections underground were locked up with iron and chain, three guards at each door. Since the underground collections were where they needed to go, Anwei had opted for something less stealthy.

Luckily, the First Scholar's real window was set to be delivered that very morning. Even more luckily, it had broken the night before due to an unfortunate incident with the apprentice glazier, two knuckles of malt, and a dropped hammer.

Noa had been the one who dropped the hammer.

The apprentice was probably waking up now, remembering nothing but the girl he'd met at the malthouse, not how the priceless work of art his master had only just finished had ended up in pieces on the shop floor. With any luck, he'd stew until the master glazier arrived after his midmorning tea to deliver it to the Holy First.

Just enough time for them to get inside and steal whatever it was Anwei wanted from the library's dusty old shelves—something that would lead them to her snake-tooth man and the cursed sword he'd managed to lift right out from under them at the tomb. Tual Montanne. The *shapeshifter*.

Prickles of excited horror bristled down Noa's arms at the thought. She gave the gate one last shake that sent it flying open and walked through. Watching Anwei with her puppet strings had been fascinating—Anwei was so wild and free, doing exactly as she pleased and getting everyone else to do as she pleased as well, almost like magic.

But Tual Montanne was the same. Lia Seystone, too. They were all made from the things they wanted. They were people who acted, who *did*, and the whole world held its breath as they passed. And pass they did, leaving whole cities hanging askew.

Each of them was running toward something, which was very different from running away. Noa had never been much good at anything more than making her father angry. She consoled herself that, at least on that front, she was probably doing rather well. But since running away, she'd found that defining herself as the dull ache behind her father's eyes seemed less and less meaningful.

The guard gave Noa a slightly anemic bow as she walked into the compound, reaching to pull back the glass's shroud as Anwei and Altahn passed. Anwei slapped his hand away just in time, the very picture of an artist lugging six months of work that she didn't mean to waste on someone who wouldn't appreciate it. "You honestly believe I'll let you look at this masterpiece before the Holy First herself gets to see it? You'd be lucky to set your eyes on this even after it's put in place."

"Right." The guard gritted his teeth, turning back to Noa. "A ladder, you said?"

"And the tools, yes, thank you. They're in the wagon bed. Oh, and bring the wood for the armature, of course." She started down the garden path, not bothering to look back at him.

The side entrance to the temple was only fifty feet back from the gate, the guards standing there already prepared to block her way, but Noa was ready with the honorable master glazier Fanilig Berstrom's seal (Anwei had snagged it after Noa had broken the window the night before). They opened the doors just in time for Anwei to "trip" over the top step so the glass swung wild again, Altahn shuffling to the side with a groan. One of the guards darted forward to steady it.

"Castor's *quills*," Anwei swore, and Noa was impressed by the hint of tears in her friend's voice. "You *heathen*, Marcus. I might never hold a grozing iron again after shaping this piece, and you choose today to *stumble?*"

Altahn didn't bite back because Galerey had chosen that moment to scuttle down the back of his shirt. Noa slid between him and the guards to block the sight of his tunic moving all on its own, wondering what little lizard claws felt like skittering down his spine. "Can you believe these two?" she whispered to the door guard, leaning a hair closer than was perhaps strictly necessary. Old habits. "Perhaps you could escort us so they don't destroy my masterpiece before it's been installed."

The guard's smile in return was hesitant, baring the temple's *v* house mark on his front canine. "I see there's a delivery scheduled from a Master Benedict later today. . . ."

"That's me." Altahn's voice sounded forced. He was a terrible actor *and* a terrible dancer.

"The First will be waiting for us. This window is possibly the most beautiful thing I've ever created." Noa lowered her voice. "Those two did the actual designing and cutting and painted the details and all that"—She flipped a hand toward Anwei and Altahn, the latter of whom seemed to be actually shaking, though if it were from laughter or strain from holding the glass window, Noa couldn't tell—"but the commission was *mine*. She sent two messengers just this morning to hurry us along, but I said no, you cannot rush an artist. I hadn't even had my breakfast."

The guard started to laugh, but then stopped himself, lowering his voice to match Noa's. "The First isn't even here." His smile came a little more naturally and he leaned forward a bit, and Noa knew she'd done the right thing. He undid the latch and propped the door open. "Given the circumstances, I suppose it's all right. I probably *shouldn't* let you in, but . . ."

"Oh, I agree. You probably shouldn't." Noa kept her smile, wide and full of teeth, as she gestured for Altahn and Anwei to come through. "But intelligent folk like you and me understand *true* urgency."

The temple's inside was all high ceilings and rows upon rows of bookshelves, the way into the main stacks blocked by a jeweled grate. They followed the guard up to the barrier, Noa letting him explain who they were to the woman in long scholar robes with a single khonin knot draped across her forehead. The scholar held a book in one hand, and the pinch between her eyebrows said that she'd rather be reading than conversing with real people. "The First isn't going to be here at all today, so any rubbish about messengers and fancy windows will not be tolerated." She turned her glare on Noa. "I suppose she was supposed to pay you upon receipt? Scholars are not fool enough to fall for such a story, girl. I'd be willing to bet there's nothing under that packing but bare wood."

"Bare *wood* . . . ?" Noa feigned shock, something Anwei had made her do in front of a mirror for an hour before she'd been satisfied. The First being absent was an eventuality they'd been anticipating, seeing how Anwei had poisoned the woman's tea that very morning. Just enough to make her ill, of course. "It's so difficult to move, and every moment it's unmounted is a moment of *risk*." She'd rehearsed this too with Anwei, liking the way it felt almost like a dance. "I'm not worried about being *paid*. True art transcends silver rounds."

Anwei made a good show of not agreeing.

"Maybe it's better the First isn't here?" Noa continued. "We could install it now before she returns. It was designed for the space in her office, so where else should her first sight of it be but *in that space*? Just think, the reveal." She put her hands up, looking toward the high ceiling. "The *drama*!"

The old scholar was clearly trying very hard not to roll her eyes. "Fine," she said. "If all you want is to leave that thing in her office, I can show you where to go. There will be no money, and you will not just be *set free* to roam the stacks. The time it will take to supervise this ridiculous scheme will set my precious studies back *ages*." She closed her book with a disgusted sniff and gestured for them to follow her past the gates.

The guard craned his neck to get a look under the glass's covering as Anwei and Altahn passed, but it was tied tight, thank the sky. Once they were through, the scholar led them down the aisles between shelves, bright beams of light coming from the blue-stained windows above to paint Castor's phases on the floor. Past thousands of books, past the scholars copying old manuscripts onto new vellum and illuminating the margins, all the way to the grand staircase Anwei had marked on their map of the temple that would take them up to the First Scholar's office.

The staircase was quite long. Noa felt very positive about her choice not to carry anything during this particular performance. By the time they got to the upper landing, the guard carrying the ladder was red in the face, and Altahn was sweating. The scholar went to a jeweled door, sunlight streaming through to cast a kaleidoscope of colors across the floor. Opening it, the scholar shooed them inside, Noa impressed by the imposing desk covered in books, a pane of glass behind it etched with Castor's moon so when the First sat there, it would frame her head like a corona. The scholar cast a sharp eye across the laced vellum tomes stacked neatly on the desk.

Maybe this was an opportunity for the scholar as much as it was for them. Noa gave her a moment to examine the books and bound papers piled on the desk before clearing her throat. "Perhaps you could give my artists some space to work?"

The scholar didn't even look up from inspecting the texts, wide-eyed with barely concealed awe as she picked one up. "I can't in good conscience leave you unattended, especially after the Warlord herself defiled the lower stacks earlier this week—"

Noa lurched toward her, grabbing hold of the scholar's arm and dragging her squawking from the room, the scholar clasping the book to her chest like a newborn child as if she expected Noa to wrench it from her hands. There was a reason Jaxom triumphed in every battle with Castor—scholars might believe words were enough, but it didn't stop people from pushing them around. Noa grabbed hold of the guard by the door, barely giving him time to deposit the tools and ladder before pulling both of them out onto the landing.

"Start with the hammer, Altahn," she called over her shoulder before letting it swing shut. She let go of the scholar, standing between her and the jeweled door. The guard looked with great uncertainty between the two of them. "Surely you, a seeker of knowledge, understand just how inappropriate it would be for you to see this window before the First does?"

"That is ridiculous—"

The scholar made to push past her, but Noa held her ground, maneuvering the old bat backward toward the stairs. "Perhaps this pride of yours is something I should speak to the First about when she returns? Or I could tell her the name of the book you stole from her office?" Noa snatched it away before the scholar could stop her. "*Surviving Reliefs That Reference the Nameless God.* Interesting."

The guard gasped, both hands over his mouth.

Noa held the book up. "*This* is what you take from the Holy First's office?" She wished this was the part where she could ignite her tethers, or the book, or *something*, and twirl in a circle of flame. Unfortunately, she was stuck with being judgmental, which was much less fun. "I didn't think such disrespect and blasphemy existed among Castor's scholars!"

"I did not take it from her office. *You* took *me* from her office and—"

The guard looked as if he meant to cry.

Shattering glass sounded from inside the office, and Noa's heart began to race, even as she blocked the scholar from pushing past her. She hadn't thought Altahn would be able to bring himself to do it. Laughter bubbled up inside her, and Noa wanted to pull open the door to see what Altahn looked like while defacing an ancient temple. But she had a job. "We all knew the old window would have to be broken—old traditions are meant to be documented. Remembered. But not kept on top of us, demanding we continue on. This is the beginning of something *new*."

"But—" The scholar's spindly fingers latched on to Noa's wrist, trying to wrench her out of the way.

"I'm going to go assist." Noa pulled free, tapping the book thoughtfully before turning back toward the door. "I'll have to think very carefully about what to say about what happened here to my aunt Vesper."

Vesper. One of the hundreds of useless old women draped in gold and jewels with whom the First was quite chummy. The very name caused both the guard and the scholar to blanch. Noa opened the jeweled door. "Don't interrupt us, please. Creating something new is a holy thing, is it not?"

She stepped through, pulling the door shut after her and setting the latch so it couldn't be opened from the outside. Altahn was perched at the top of the ladder, his whole face screwed up in horror at the gaping hole where the moon had been etched into the glass. Anwei was nowhere to be seen "Please tell me some god isn't going to smite me for this?" He reached up to tap at the glass with the hammer again, cringing when it cracked.

"The scholar god will probably just have people write nasty things about you." Noa began unwrapping the glass they'd brought. "Anwei found the way down?"

"Before the door even closed behind you."

Getting down to the restricted stacks was no easy feat when you didn't have a million keys hanging from your belt—only scholars would think to use keys as some kind of status symbol. The Holy First, however, had a special stairway set aside just for her use that led directly to them, which was why they'd had to get rid of her, then break into her office. Altahn finished cleaning out the last of the glass just in time to avert his eyes when Noa pulled away the last of the wrapping.

"I'm afraid if I look at it again, it'll be stuck in my head for the rest of my life. When I fall asleep, all I'll be able to think of is—"

"The Chaol shipping advisor missing his skivvies?" Noa shuddered as she looked over the glass, skillfully pieced together and painted with, perhaps, more detail than anyone could have wanted.

"Where did Anwei come by that thing, anyway?"

"It was in the load we brought from Chaol. I don't think she brought it on purpose, but apparently the shipping advisor paid her to steal it out of his mistress's apartment. She showed it off to some of the wrong people, I guess." Noa opened the bag of tools they'd taken from the glazier's shop. It was full of sharp things and heavy metal-looking things and jars of liquidy things that looked quite poisonous. She pulled out a small mallet and turned to face the gap in the framing over the First's desk. "I guess he didn't pay the rest of his fee, so Anwei kept it. I think she's glad to give it the attention it deserves now."

"You don't think Anwei actually wants us to put it up, do you? We only brought the shipping advisor because they wouldn't have believed we were installing a window if we had no window."

"But just think of the First's expression when she sees it! A whole day's worth of appointments where she'll have to sit with the shipping advisor looking over her shoulder before they can get a glazier to remove him." Noa took hold of the glass's frame and began dragging it toward the desk. "Anwei said we had at least ten minutes before we had to get out. Don't be a drag—this'll be fun."

Altahn sighed. Smiled. He always smiled. But then he picked up the other end, still averting his eyes. "I'm not sure fun is the right word."

❧

Anwei stole down the stairs, pulling up the hood of the scholar robe she'd snagged from the First's office, and stuffed the key that had been under the false bottom in her desk's top drawer into her pocket. It was hard to keep herself from running, the black pall Knox made at the back of her mind freezing and stabbing at her in turn.

The connection between them felt hot, warping the air around people walking by, as if suddenly she had a flicker of his Devoted aura-sight and a taste of his strength. Since saving him in the tomb, her sense of smell had blossomed larger, so even stone seemed to sing as she walked by, inviting her to touch it when before it had only moodily acknowledged her existence. Herbs were what she knew.

Now, with her aura all mixed together with Knox's, there was more.

More to worry about too. Although their minds were still connected, Knox had only come out of his sleep in fleeting moments since the snake-tooth man had stabbed him. Every day Knox's presence seemed to wane. He tossed in his sleep, thrashed when she forced food and water down his throat. Anwei had barely managed to keep him alive. She bit her lip, ready to demand godly help, to poison, fight, steal, *destroy*, if it meant saving him. There had to be a way to bring him back. She just had to *find* it like she'd found everything else she'd ever needed. But the snarl of ice and thorns that she felt in his mind worried her. She wasn't sure *who* he'd be if—*when*—he woke.

He'd been a ghost when he fell. A ghost who had been trying to kill her.

Anwei had reacted the way she always did—with her herbs. She'd thrown calistet at him, the poison no one could recover from, without thinking. As soon as she'd done it, the energy coursing through her had blazed bright, golden and hot, worse than the panic of realizing Knox would die the moment it hit him. With that energy, Anwei had managed to grab hold of the calistet with her mind midair to stop it from reaching him. All while wondering if she couldn't poison him, would he stab her?

Then the snake-tooth man had arrived to stab a sword through Knox's gut since he hadn't taken enough from her yet. Everything after that was a singular blur of pain, light, fire, and roots writhing like snakes all, the whole world fading to nothing as she tried to heal Knox's terrible wound.

The shapeshifter she'd been chasing for eight years, the one who was supposed to have murdered her brother, had been there. Right there within reach. And she'd let him go.

It was hard not to stomp, or yell, or run at the memory. But Anwei had to stay focused. She'd told Noa and Altahn they only had ten minutes in the temple before they needed to retrieve the wagon and meet her three streets over. She didn't have time to start hyperventilating.

Anwei reached the first floor a good thirty seconds ahead of schedule. The staircase let her out just behind the guards keeping people from wandering into the restricted stacks. Moving quickly, Anwei walked down the hall as her contact at the university had told her to. The hallway would end in a door—

Only it didn't. It turned a corner. Anwei slowed, taking in a breath. She smelled nothing but the dusty brown of aged vellum and old gray stone. No people. So she raced around the bend only to find a two-story picture window: a very large, very cross-looking scholar glaring down at her in white and red glass.

There was no door. Anwei's gut twisted. Ten minutes. She had already used one and a half of them. Inhaling again, she caught braised lamb and roasted greens slipping through the layers of color, closely followed by dusty blue-gray cotton, sweat, and the clammy scent of ink.

Anwei stared at the glass because the smells were somehow coming from inside it.

After a moment, she walked straight toward it, bracing for her nose to hit glass, but it never did because the picture was an optical illusion, the frame a doorway that lined up perfectly with the window at the far end of a hall. Leave it to scholars to try to trick people with their own minds.

Once she was through the opening, Anwei turned past the glass toward wrought-iron doors blocked by a dusty little scholar at a desk.

They'd been following the snake-tooth man for weeks when he'd suddenly disappeared from the road, almost as if he'd crumbled to nothing, setting Anwei into a panic. Until she remembered so many years before when she'd tried to learn which family marked their servants with a snake.

The scholars had written down her name that day. One had even scrawled a little picture of her, she'd thought, then told her the mark was associated with a specific estate, only the last family to live there had died seventy-five years earlier in a fire. That there was nothing else worth sharing And also to get her dirt-crusted hands away from his precious records.

But his mouth had been tight as he said it. Extra care taken as he checked her name again, almost as if he was addressing a letter at that moment to tell the snake-tooth man someone had come looking for him. There was information here. Hidden. An address, perhaps. Maps. Maybe even plans of the house where the snake-tooth man had taken Lia's younger sister and Patenga's cursed sword. A house where her brother had . . .

She strangled that thought. Her brother, who was not dead

Anwei fanned away the anger burning in her throat as she approached the desk. The scholar looked up from a very beautiful illustration of a tree he was embellishing with a little pot of gold paint. "Did you need something?" he asked. "You have to have direct orders to get something from these shelves—"

Nodding, Anwei pulled out a little bottle of malt from her bag, uncorked it, then held it out to the scholar. "Would you hold that please?"

He took it even as he protested. "What is—"

"Hold still now." She extracted the wooden funnel from its place in the bag's side pocket and jammed it into the bottle's open mouth, then poured in a little stream of powder. Stowing the packet of powder and the funnel, she took the bottle back and corked it, giving it a good shake. Flashing a smile at the scholar who was staring at her open-mouthed, she shook the bottle one more time, waiting for the harsh citrine smell to turn to fiery red. Little splatters of powder had gotten on the book, the scholar staring at the page with horror. "Sorry." She tried to sound it, though she wasn't particularly. "A bit time sensitive, this stuff. Thank you so much for your help."

It wasn't changing. She swirled the bottle around again, anger pricking inside her, her energy reaching out to touch the little bits of powder, the acrid white burn of malt. *You have to push it,* the thought came. *Just a little bit, to make it bond correctly . . .*

The scholar's yelling wasn't helping her concentrate, of course. "What in Calsta's name do you mean by—"

She breathed in again, pressing the smells together in her mind, and the liquid warmed her palms through the glass, the crimson scent dimming to a sickly gold. Perfect. Better than perfect. Anwei uncorked the bottle and emptied the liquid over the scholar's head.

"You sky-cursed *initiate's* pen nib of—" The scholar lurched back from the desk, half trying to save his precious illumination, half scrabbling at his face as the concoction dripped down. "Are you trying to destroy *years* of work on an irreplaceable—"

In her mind, she cheered the concoction on, and suddenly it snaked down his collar as if it were alive. Anwei's breath caught, the energy inside her *burning*. She'd never seen the compound do *that* before.

Grunting, the scholar fell facedown onto his vellum. He lay there, gold paint smeared across his cheek, and a dribble of saliva beading on his lips to drip onto the page under his chin

Anwei blinked, fear like a rotten pit in her core. It had taken her whole soul to stop the calistet from killing Knox down in the tomb, but this had just . . . happened. She grabbed the little lamp sitting next to the fallen scholar on the floor, lit the wick with her own flint and steel, then ran through the doors to the restricted stacks a little too quickly.

Books. I'm looking for books, pages, records about the estate that uses a snake house mark. The shelves were laid out in long rows that disappeared into the darkness, the air a dry, underground cold. Running into the first aisle, Anwei forced herself to calm, losing herself as she systematically checked for signs of the house mark. How much time did she have left? The guards outside wandered back to check on something about every eight minutes based on her observations the day before, and knocking out the scholar hadn't been timed the right way.

She had to hurry.

The air somehow breathed thicker between the ancient shelves, the scents of dust, cured hide, ink, and mold strangling Anwei. *The records are hidden down here,* she whispered to herself as she moved on to the next set of shelves. *He has scholars reporting on anyone who comes looking for them. I'll be able to see it, whatever it is. I have to.*

The family name, I remember the name they told me all those years ago—

She crashed between bookshelves crowded together like old gossips at the well, searching for a section with property records. When she found the right aisle, Anwei recoiled, something foul twitching in her nose.

There was a pot sitting in the middle of the aisle, its contents a slippery cinnamon red that reached for her, sticking in her lungs.

Aukincy. In Castor's library? Excitement surged in Anwei's gut. Aukincy was hardly an accepted practice. Scholars wouldn't allow it down among their precious records. Which meant that scholars hadn't put it there.

Keeping watch on records that referred to Tual's own history made sense to Anwei—a shapeshifter able to survive as long as he had to be monitoring who was asking questions about him and why. Anwei did the same herself, rewarding her contacts if they told her about anyone who came asking.

But aukincy in the restricted stacks themselves? Why bother? If the information was so dangerous he needed this kind of precaution, wouldn't he just destroy records? But then she smelled it. The awful scent of *nothing* that followed Tual everywhere he went, the reek of stolen soul.

She darted into the aisle, noting records about rogue Devoted, Basist collectives, crimes against children. All hidden in the dark to keep Devoted from destroying them like they had every other record of Basists from temple donation ledgers to property sales, no doubt. According to what Lia had learned in Patenga's tomb, the centuries of attempting to cleanse Basists of the nameless god's touch had been for nothing. It wasn't Basists that were dangerous; it was bonded pairs of gods-touched working together, the danger only coming when one betrayed the other.

The scars marking Anwei's arms and legs, her collarbones, and her back began to burn at the thought. A rush of anger seemed to wait inside her all the time now, looking for the tiniest trigger to flood her humors. All these years the Devoted had been protecting the Commonwealth from shapeshifters. Soul stealers. The creatures who made themselves gods, who stole energy from others instead of sacrificing for their own magic. Dirt witches. Basists.

But the shapeshifter tomb in Chaol hadn't belonged to a Basist. The shapeshifter king had been touched by Calsta. Lia had seen the reliefs with her own eyes showing a Devoted stabbing the man he loved most—a Basist—to take his life and power. *Any* gods-touched could become a shapeshifter so long as they were bonded with someone touched by a different god. A truth the first Warlord had hidden, eradicating the threat of future shapeshifters by destroying the kind of magic that wasn't hers. You needed both a Basist and a Devoted to make a shapeshifter, so if Basists were all dead, no new shapeshifters could emerge. Devoted still taught the horrible lies the first Warlord had used to make herself the Commonwealth's new leader. *If we don't destroy Basists, they'll eat our souls.*

Anwei tripped, the clatter of a metal pot against stone ringing in her ears, and a bloom of *something* clouded up toward her face. *Of all the ridiculous moments to get angry and stop looking properly for threats—* Anwei jerked back, but it was too late. Her vision had begun to warp.

No. She stumbled back, jamming a hand into her medicine bag, the smoke burrowing down her throat with ferocious glee that was too many colors. Her mind ticked through all the scents coming from her medicine bag, her fingers closing around a fistful of packets that would counter the poison before she . . .

Anwei suddenly found herself staring at the wall, one hand deep inside her medicine bag and her mind blank. Lost in thought when Anwei only had five minutes at *most* to find the information that would lead her to the snake-tooth man. *Maybe I'll have better luck in the next aisle.* Her legs shook as she squeezed between a gap in the shelves, her eyes settling on a pot . . .

A pot. Hadn't she seen a pot a moment ago? It had seemed so important.

She looked down at her hand inside the bag. One of her fingers was prickling with heat, knuckle-deep in a packet of belur stamens, the acid eating into her skin. When she pulled it out, two other packets came with it. Ground piphor scales and a dried husknut shell cut into neat strips. Taking an experimental step forward, Anwei held out the lantern and saw a single tendril of smoke spilling over the pot's lip, the smell of it pleasant, like herbs and—

The door at the entrance rattled, and Anwei jerked to life, her eyes tracing the same spot on the wall, her arms limp. She stumbled backward, the air around her no longer sweet. Light bled into the stacks, footsteps slapping against the stone. The guards must have found the incapacitated scholar. She was out of time.

Turning back to the row she'd been searching, she saw a pot.

A pot with a cloud of smoke *pouring* from it.

Her hand was once again thrust deep into her medicine bag, herbs burning her fingers. This was the second time she'd tried to take them out, the taste of them a perfect answer to the smoke. Holding her breath, Anwei tore the scarf from her hair and twisted the herbs inside it. She shoved the scarf against her nose, then ran into the cloud of smoke so thick she couldn't see through it anymore. Her skin, her mind, every inch of her *crawled* with the feel of magic trying to worm its way back in through her ears, her eyes, her mouth.

The herbs were there to stop someone. To delay them, to make sure they got caught. Perhaps so Tual could come himself to find out who had gone to such lengths to find him.

Anwei touched book after book, squinting at the spines, then going by feel until she stumbled over another pot. They were boxing in this section of shelf, belching smoke that roiled in poisonous waves, as if kicking over the first pot had triggered some kind of trap. Pressing the herbs tighter against her nose and mouth, Anwei turned back to search through the section again, gasping down a single lungful of herb-laced air.

Lantern light flashed past her, the shouts close now.

Anwei's lungs burned. She fell to her knees, pulling books from the shelves one after another, but she couldn't *smell*, not with aukincer smoke clouding around her head. Rage rose like a monster inside her. Anwei gulped down another orange-tinged breath through the scarf, lashing out toward the shelf where she'd smelled the nothing smell before, throwing all of the bound papers to the ground. None of it looked right, property records, edicts, books of history . . . Anwei's eyes began to fuzz at the edge, making her wobble. She caught herself on the top shelf.

And her fingers found leather. She pulled the object down, not a book but a folio jammed tight with papers. A snake had been tooled into the leather. It had been pulled from the shelf and left open on top as if someone had recently been reading it but had forgotten midsentence why they would want to be down in this dark, awful cave. There was nothing down here worth her attention, just useless books.

Grunting, Anwei wrenched herself free of the sticky thought and grabbed the folio in both hands. She took it and ran, upsetting the shelves behind her to stop the scholars from easily seeing what she'd taken. Shouts echoed up from all around her, closing in.

She was surrounded.

A guard stepped into the aisle just next to her, lantern held high. The smoke didn't seem to confuse him, and she had only a moment before he saw her over the tops of the books.

Drawing in another poison-tinged breath, Anwei threw herself up against the shelf, groaning with effort until it tipped. Books began to fall with sickly thuds into the aisle on the other side of the shelf, the wooden joints creaking until the shelf fell to the ground with a terrible crash of old leather and fluttering paper on top of the guard.

Figures appeared at both ends of the aisle, guards cautiously approaching. "Do not move!" one shouted, only thirty paces between them.

Thrusting the folio into her bag, Anwei's fingers closed around the calistet packet with its distinctive button. Flashes of Knox on the ground, of powder in the air—

—of energy being violently sucked out of her chest, the herbs burning in the air right before her eyes—

—the snake-tooth man holding Knox's sword—

"Grab her!" the guard shouted.

Anwei let go of the packet and grabbed the one filled with ground corta instead, sprinting for the pot billowing with smoke. Hands grabbed for her robe, but Anwei skidded down onto her knees, tore open the packet, and emptied half of it into the gushing smoke. Arms grabbed her around the ribs, lifting her off the ground, but Anwei had already twisted to grind the last of the orange powder directly into the guard's nose and mouth. Jerking back, he let go of Anwei, scrubbing his eyes with his hands.

Stumbling away from him, Anwei found the strength to run. She scooped up the pot as she passed it, corta granules bonding with the elements in the smoke to turn a sticky toxic red where it tried to push past the herbs protecting her breath. It made a cloak around her as she ran, any guards who came close clutching their throats and retching.

I said ten minutes. The herbs in her scarf were fading, one last breath all Anwei could gasp down. The weight of the folio seemed to drag against her shoulder, but Anwei was full of sunlight, of hope, excitement, and *vengeance* even as the smoke swirled out to catch another guard in the face. Whatever was in that folio, it was going to change everything. It had to.

Down the last aisle, up the stairs, through the door, smoke churning around her like a storm cloud. Past the desk and the scholar just beginning to blink his eyes open, and on to the grumpy man in the picture window to whom Anwei gave a cheeky salute.

But as she crossed into the main library, something in Anwei's mind gave a sharp twist.

Anwei stumbled past the two guards keeping people out of the restricted stacks, clutching the pot around the belly as she tried to find her balance. Her thoughts contracted around the spot at the back of her mind that was tied to Knox. A lightning burst cracked out from Knox's consciousness, and Anwei gasped, pitching forward onto her knees.

And then the pain was gone, leaving only Knox there, the warm touch of him pointing her back toward the camp. He was *awake*.

Fists grabbed hold of her robe, wrenching her up from the ground.

Anwei smashed the pot into the guard's head. The contents swirled up into the air in a poisonous, cinnabar sparkle. He let go of her, stumbling back even as Anwei gagged, a mouthful of poison and corta and only the nameless god knew what else was in that pot going down her throat.

Unwrapping the herbs tied into her scarf, Anwei shoved them directly into her mouth, the taste of them burning her tongue. She lurched past the stacks and the frozen scholars shouting with confusion, the herbs turning the angry red of the smoke to a breeze of yellows and blues. Shaking, she crashed through the door that opened onto the main steps, chanting scholars crying out with surprise as she stumbled through their midst, then heaved herself into a wagon full of palifruit.

The driver turned to shout at her, but Anwei wasn't listening, hopping out again once the guards had raced past. She rushed down the next few streets toward where Altahn and Noa were waiting.

Knox was awake. The thought sent a nauseating swirl of relief, excitement, and worry through Anwei's humors. But there was fear as well. Because if Knox was awake, then that meant Willow was too.

CHAPTER 3

The Wrong Kind of Veil

Lia sat under a tree with Vivi's head in her lap. Her veil pressed tight against her nose and chin, the front of it trapped under the auroshe's pointed snout. The crisp morning air prickled like needles across Lia's skin despite the thin veil fabric Noa had bought for her in the market. It covered her face, hair, and shoulders, shrouding her to the waist. Gold threads sewn through it teased light into her peripheral vision. Noa's interpretation of what "plain fabric" meant was different from any other person Lia had ever met.

Her hands worked fast on Vivi's mane, tying knot after fancy knot.

It didn't matter. Not the gold thread, not the braids, not anything. Lia could hardly *see*, her eyes glazed over with the last words she'd gotten from Tual Montanne, a note left on her front gate while her home burned with her parents inside. *Your sister misses you.*

Please. She thought it toward the sky goddess, stripes of pain across her ungloved hands as she pulled Vivi's coarse hair tight. *Please, I've been wearing this veil for weeks. You know what I want.*

That was the problem. Oaths weren't supposed to be about what people wanted but rather what the gods who touched them did. Lia had her aurasight, her first oath to Calsta restored in Chaol—it had been a relief, Calsta's power flowing through her despite the fact that she'd run away from the Devoted. The power that came from keeping her second oath—to own only things necessary to survive—had returned that morning, letting her see farther and hear better than she was supposed to. But she was still diminished. The goddess had yet to return Lia's strength, her ability to push against gravity and hide in broad daylight.

It was a difficult oath to keep, the third one. To love only the goddess. And the oaths that a veil and gloves should have brought back—the ability to track auras no matter where she was, and her view into people's thoughts and feelings—felt even more impossible.

Only you can stop him. You and Anwei and Knox. The memory of Calsta's voice burned through Lia, the Devoted thinking that for once she and Calsta had the same goal.

As soon as the thought came, Lia sent it away again, batting at it like a pesky bee intent on stinging her. The goddess had never been against her in the first place: that had been the masters. The seclusions. The Warlord, speaking for Calsta as if she had any right. Calsta didn't require those she touched to make Devoted oaths, didn't even require Devoted to hold those oaths their whole lives. It was the Warlord who had turned oaths into a prison Lia couldn't bear.

Choosing to make oaths in exchange for power was easier than being forced to make them. But, deep inside, Lia knew that she was following Tual because she wanted to save Aria, not because the goddess had told her to.

Lia wiped a hand across her forehead, annoyed when her palm met fabric instead of skin, smearing a trickle of sweat dripping down her temple. She'd chosen to wear the veil. Choosing to do as Calsta said *was* loving the goddess more than anyone else. Calsta had told her to destroy Tual. That was what she was doing. It didn't matter that Aria would be safe as a result, too. Did it?

She had to believe Calsta would see her sacrifice and reward it.

But she'd put on the veil weeks ago, and her powers hadn't returned. Frustration bubbled in Lia's gut, her hands shaking because she had to *do* something or it would boil over.

She *couldn't* wear the gloves, too. Couldn't. The veil was hard enough, surely Calsta could see that. They both wanted the same thing, so why wouldn't Calsta give her the tools she needed to destroy Tual Montanne and save Aria?

Knox's aura gave a sleepy churn inside the tent. Lia went absolutely still, focusing on the change. Vivi's hackles rose, a low growl scratching from his throat. *We can't leave Knox alone*, Anwei had whispered to Lia their first day on the road, far from where Altahn might overhear. *You saw what happened in the tomb.*

Indeed, she had. Lia reached out to touch the sword in the grass next to her, the tightness in her chest loosening only a hair when her fingers found metal. Finally, she had a weapon again. Borrowed, of course. Apparently, Trib clans respected the Warlord's decree that only Devoted could carry swords in the Commonwealth, but only so far as stashing their weapons where Devoted wouldn't see them.

Having a proper weapon felt like the *beginning* of doing something. Knox had come at her with a sword down in Patenga's tomb, teeth bared, his eyes stretched too wide, trying to fight right through her as if she were a wall between him and Anwei.

Tual Montanne had much to answer for—along with murdering her parents and kidnapping her sister, it was he who had killed Knox's sister and trapped the girl's soul inside a shapeshifter sword. Knox had been carrying her ghost around, letting her feed off his energy ever since. And, apparently, sometimes the ghost took him, mind, body, and soul, leaving nothing behind but an appetite for death.

Vivi's eye slid open, inky black staring up at her with reproach. Lia pulled her hand away from the sword to loosen the strands of hair she'd been tightly knotting and smoothed a hand down his serpentine neck. "Sorry," she whispered. "I didn't mean to hurt you."

He let his eye drift shut, mollified. Lia envied the way Vivi had settled into an unyielding calm, as if tromping through the undersides of the Commonwealth was all he ever could have wanted so long as she was on his back. As if Lia disappearing and Ewan bonding with him had never—

Putting a hand to her head, Lia clenched her eyes shut. *Ewan.* His blood watered a shapeshifter's tomb, his body food for scavengers. No matter how many times she thought of him limp on the ground, unable to hurt her anymore, the memory of him alive was twice as strong. His awful leer. His groping hands.

Only now, in her mind, his face had been replaced with Tual's.

Ewan had only wanted her body. Tual wanted her soul.

Standing, Lia fumbled with shaking hands to tie back her veil, then picked up the sword. Vivi bared his teeth from the ground in what passed for an auroshe laugh as she set her feet into a fighting stance, gripping the sword with both hands. "I'm rusty," she whispered to him. "They wouldn't let me touch a weapon while I was under the veil."

He snaked his head across the grass, rolling onto his back with his forefeet curled to his chest as if he meant to play like a dog.

"You want to put me through my paces?" She slid from the first stance to the second, the sword high over her head. The thought of Aria simmered through her. Her humors burned, each step coming faster and harder, the fan sweep, the lunge and parry, the—

Something in the tent moved.

Vivi gave a low squeal, rolling over abruptly to stare at the tent. Turning slowly to face the heavy flap, Lia let her sword tip drop. Her aurasight circled the tight globe of energy that marked Knox, swirls like mist beginning to roil inside it.

He was waking up.

Brow furrowing, Lia advanced on the tent, her veil blowing back against her face as she walked, the sword heavy in her hand. Knox had only stirred a few times since the night Tual had killed him and Anwei had . . .

Well. She'd done *something*. The skin prickled across Lia's arms as she took another step toward the waving tent flap, thinking of that night, a swirl of Basist power around Anwei like a brazen call to war. But Lia fought to put that thought away. It wasn't Basist magic itself that was bad. Mateo had shown her that.

An insight that still twitched uncomfortably inside Lia. She'd killed people for their purple gods-touched auras. The fact of it sat deep in her gut like a knife that would cut at the slightest movement. Mateo had made the argument that Basism was no better than Calsta's touch and that no one kind of magic should be banned. That anyone with power could do evil—it wasn't the power itself that was wrong. It had made sense when he said it, and then Anwei had proved it, using the nameless god's touch to save Knox's life.

But then Mateo had turned out to be a shapeshifter.

Those first few days Lia had wanted to pretend it wasn't possible. She'd even brought it up with Anwei. *He didn't do it. Whatever you're so angry about, it had to have been Tual. Mateo didn't know he was a shapeshifter. He doesn't remember he's your brother. I don't think he remembers you at all.*

Anwei had stopped when Lia had said that, a well of pure fury sparking in her eyes. The thief hadn't said another word for the rest of the day. *He doesn't remember you.*

He didn't remember Lia, either, it seemed. That was a better explanation than the one that was most likely, after weeks of her sister gone and no word.

Lia drew back the tent flap and found Knox sitting up, hand to his head. His aura was a clouded white instead of gold, his bond with Anwei somehow blocking Calsta's touch from Lia's aurasight.

Knox swiveled to look at her, his voice croaking. "Lia?" He blinked at the veil. "You're sparkly."

Lia dropped her sword, falling to her knees next to Knox on the pallet to wrap her arms around him. The breath whuffed out of him because she was squeezing his ribs too hard, but his arms circled her, pulling her close. Lia's eyes began to burn, and she couldn't let go. "I am so, so happy you are awake," she rasped. If Knox wasn't some ghost, then maybe Aria wasn't her only family left. *He'd* help face down Tual Montanne. Lia pulled back far enough to look Knox up and down, eyes stopping on the bulge of bandaging just under his ribs where Tual had stabbed him. "You sound like yourself. Are you . . . all right?"

"Why wouldn't I be myself?" Knox's hand crept up to touch the bandage. He closed his eyes, concentrating. "Where's Anwei? She's . . ." He looked east. Toward Rentara.

"Not here." The words came out abruptly, Lia not knowing what to say. *His* oaths were still intact even as he held Anwei's name in his mouth as if it belonged to him. Feelings off-limits for a Devoted.

"What happened?" Knox twisted back toward her. "I was in town, and that cranky, awful woman threw my sword at me—"

"Gulya?" The old apothecarist he and Anwei had lived with back in Chaol. Anwei hadn't been able to understand how Knox had come by the dangerous sword again after she'd hidden it. Apparently, Gulya had found it. "You don't remember anything else?"

Pressing his lips together, Knox looked down, letting Lia go. He *did* remember something. "When did you say Anwei was coming back? She's all right?" He put a hand up to his forehead. "Where are we? Whose tent is this? Why are you wearing a *veil?* I thought you weren't going back to the Devoted."

Lia paused at the sound of footsteps approaching the tent, an aura she recognized from Altahn's riders approaching. She pulled her veil back down over her face. "That is a lot of questions."

Knox was already looking toward the flap before a voice called from outside—no, Knox was definitely not diminished. "Miss Lia?"

"In here," she called. It was Gilesh, the one with calluses from the fiddle he played while others drummed and sang around the campfire. Lia knew him best because he was the only one who didn't stare at her veil, speaking to her and joking as if she were anyone else. He'd even laughed at her when she'd asked if they played music around the fire every night, only because she'd never heard people playing music except from a distance. Music and dancing, both too trivial for a Devoted. She'd liked the feel of it, those drums beating alongside her heart in her chest. Calsta hadn't seemed to mind either.

Gilesh's hand pushed the tent flap in. He froze when he found Knox and Lia both staring in his direction. "I, uh . . . sorry. I didn't mean to interrupt."

"You're not interrupting," she said coolly, standing to face him. "Did you need something?"

"Your friend is feeling better? Those stories they tell about Beildan healers really are true, aren't they?" Gilesh's eyebrows quirked when neither of them responded. "I came over to ask if you might finally let me cross blades with you. I saw you doing forms a moment ago, and Bane said—"

"You don't want to fight with Lia," Knox interrupted.

"I mean, I think I do?" He grinned. "It's not just Beildans I've heard stories about, but if I'm honest, the ones about Devoted are a little harder to believe."

Knox blinked. "Who is this?" he asked carefully.

"I need to oil my cuirass and leathers. I wouldn't be surprised if we ride out this afternoon." Lia stood, hoping Gilesh would take it as an invitation to go. "I'll come by the armorer's tent in a bit. Once I'm sure Knox is settled."

"That a yes?" Gilesh leaned forward, a gold-capped tooth flashing in his grin. Anwei had noticed it the same day they'd left Chaol and had stopped the whole caravan to check what was under it . . . somehow. With her magic? Her sense of smell, perhaps? Trib clans didn't use house marks, but Anwei didn't care what people usually did or didn't do.

"Don't say anything." Gilesh was grinning so wide he could hardly talk. "Bane will persuade you—you can't hide from us all the time. Either one of you. You're Devoted too, aren't you?" He looked eagerly toward Knox, though Knox looked nothing of the kind, thinned out and rangy, hollows in his cheeks and shadows under his eyes. "We'll let you recover before we push you into the training yards. Quite a wound you took, wasn't it? One of us untouched wouldn't have lived to see the other side of it."

Knox's hand went back to the bandages under his tunic.

"Right." Gilesh glanced once more between them both. "Well, you're both being incredibly awkward, so . . . I'll see you over there?"

He grinned, waiting for Lia to respond, but she wasn't sure what she was supposed to say. Nobody ever spoke to Devoted that way—no one except Mateo, who had almost seemed like he wanted someone to end his life before it ended all on its own. So, she tried smiling back. That's what Anwei and Noa both did, Anwei's smile ever charming and helpless, Noa's cutting like wire. "Sure. I'll show you which stories about Devoted are true."

Of course, he couldn't see her face through the veil, she realized.

It didn't seem to matter. Gilesh nodded eagerly. "I could show you a thing or two about Trib forms. Different style." He took a step toward them. "Very aggressive."

"I'm sure they are." Vexation simmered out through Lia's arms to her fingertips. She itched to grab hold of her sword. She *did* want to fight. Fighting had always dulled the pain. It was hard to remember how unhappy you were when you were sparring in a training yard or fighting for your life on the road, nothing but a saddle, a sword, and a goal to accomplish. Gilesh wouldn't put up that kind of fight—she'd have to pull her strikes, go slow. Lead him through forms like fighting trainees so new they could still remember the taste of sugar.

Lia swallowed the choking feeling of *Aria*, trying to replace it with *Knox awake*. Soon, Anwei would be back with the key to bringing Tual down, she'd said. But it wasn't enough to feed breath back into Lia's lungs as she tried to answer Gilesh. "Devoted forms are pretty aggressive, too. I've broken more than one opponent's sword."

"Sure, sure." Gilesh leaned toward Knox, lowering his voice. "We find the Commonwealth's tiniest Devoted, and somehow she still thinks she can take me." Turning, he walked out, giving them both a careless wave, though Lia didn't miss his flinch when Vivi snarled in his direction.

Knox's mouth hung open. "Where in Calsta's name are we?"

"A ten-minute ride outside Rentara. Tracking Tual Montanne, Anwei's snake-tooth man."

"With a Trib clan?"

"Weren't you working with Altahn before we went into the tomb? Anwei said he paid you to steal Patenga's sword."

"The pineapple?" Knox's brow creased.

"Pineapple?" Lia crouched next to him, impatience swelling in her chest like pus under a wound. Vivi trilled from outside as if he could feel it too through their bond. Knox didn't seem to be a danger to anyone, though she wasn't sure he was in his right mind. "Maybe you should rest. Wait until Anwei gets back to check you over before we get into everything. She should be here soon."

Shaking his head, Knox pushed the blankets off his legs. "No, if you're going to go fight some cocky Trib, there's no way I'm missing it. Are you going to do it in a veil, though?"

Lia looked down at herself, the light travel leathers and comfortable trousers Noa had been absolutely certain were too plain starkly contrasting to the floaty veil. "I need Calsta to be with me," she whispered.

"Why?" Knox reached out to pick up her sword from the ground but then didn't touch it, staring at the length of the blade with a grim sort of revulsion. "You aren't wearing gloves, and you hugged me just now. We both know oaths take time, and you're still diminished far below that veil. Plus, you *hate* wearing it."

"Because Tual has my sister, Knox." Lia leaned forward to pick up the sword herself. "It doesn't matter how much I hate wearing a veil. *I need Calsta*. I'll need everything she can give me to face him. You were too hurt to see—"

Knox flinched, his hand going to the bandaging again. Maybe he had seen some of it. "You can do whatever you want." He reached out to touch her arm. "We both know Calsta doesn't see oaths as penance. She doesn't exchange pain for power, so torturing yourself isn't going to make anything go faster."

Frustration erupted inside Lia like an army of ants. "I have to *do* something, Knox. I have to *fight*. Wearing this . . ." She tugged the end of the veil.

"You don't have to explain yourself to me," Knox said quietly when she trailed off. He had always been quiet, but it was a different sort of quiet now—one that didn't wait. He was not quite the boy she'd grown up with. Lia didn't like the idea of him changing, though she'd changed enough for the both of them. He looked up at her. "You want to fight? Let's fight."

"You just woke up."

"I'm *fine*." He held out a hand for her to pull him up. "You're not fine. Let's do this, you and me."

"You and me?" Lia's insides melted, tears pricking in her eyes because Knox knew her. He *knew*.

"Like old times."

It was the wrong thing to do, helping Knox up from the ground. Like Mateo had said that day they looked at the painting of the nameless god and Calsta reaching for each other: it was not who you were or which god chose you, it was *what* you chose. She knew it was wrong to lead Knox out of the tent toward the dry bit of ground the

Trib used to spar. She knew he was sick, knew Anwei was worried something inside him would snap, and then Knox would be gone.

But Anwei wasn't here.

He seemed normal. Familiar. The one person who knew Lia before she'd followed a shapeshifter and gotten her whole family killed. Lia *needed* familiar.

She needed her sword.

So, when Knox followed her out of the tent, she didn't argue.

CHAPTER 4

An Untouchable Weapon

K nox stepped out of the tent after Lia, his mind buzzing with fresh air and light and words and *life* as if
he hadn't been unconscious long enough to get halfway across the country. Anwei pulsed at the back of
his mind like a cord tethering him to the earth. And
Willow . . .

He felt around inside his mind, looking for her shadow, but
Anwei's presence there was too strong. Willow was gone. Knox ran a
few steps to catch up with Lia. "Do you know what happened to my
sword?"

Lia pressed fingers to her mouth through her veil and blew a kiss
toward Vivi lying under a tree a ways away from the tent. In return,
the thing threw back his head in a feral scream that was all teeth and
quivering gullet.

Anwei must have told Lia about the sword. About Willow and . . .
Knox's mind flashed back to the last thing he truly remembered: Gulya
slamming the pockmarked hilt of the cursed sword into his chest. After
that, there were only shaky blasts of memory, of pain, of darkness, of a
boy his age collapsed on the floor nearby. Willow shriveling inside him,
claw-deep in whatever kept him alive as she dragged him to oblivion

with her. And Anwei's hands, her energy burning bright as it flooded him. Calsta's voice telling him to reach for her.

"The sword melted." Lia's voice was quiet. "I don't know what Anwei did with it. But it's gone."

Knox breathed in slow, then out. Did that mean Willow was free? Released from her rotting prison to go in peace? That was all he'd ever wanted.

All I ever wanted. The thought sat in his head, catching on every syllable. Because there were new things he wanted now. The memory of Calsta's voice whispered through him. *A bond,* she'd said. What had happened between him and Anwei—the link that had joined their minds—was a magical bond. One that fit within the framework of Devotion. There were more oaths to make, Calsta had said, and saving Willow from the sword had hinged upon it . . . but Willow was gone.

It is not finished, Knox, Calsta's voice whispered through him. *You are not free of her.*

Of who? Anwei?

Your sister is not gone. Anwei is keeping her from taking control of you, but Willow found the other half of her corrupted bond, and she likes him better than you.

"Knox?" Lia had led him to a large circle of open ground past the tents, where the weeds had been stamped to bare dirt. Three Trib sat on old stumps next to it, strumming mandolins, taking turns picking out melodies and laughing at one another when they hit wrong notes. "Are you all right?" Lia's voice was tight, aurasparks glittering and skipping around her head like a crown. That *was* Lia. She'd always gathered up all the feelings she wasn't allowed to have and turned them into energy almost as if she were a goddess herself.

"I'm fine," he said.

"You're moving slowly. Is it your wound? Calsta above," she swore. "I shouldn't have let you get up."

"No." Knox's hand went to his side. A hard knot sat just under his ribs, which he'd felt when he first sat up but hadn't been sure what it was or how it came to be. It pulled on him as he walked, as if everything inside him was two or three degrees crooked. "I'm just trying to remember everything." He wanted Anwei to come back. She'd given up something; he could feel it. She'd made some oath, sacrificed something to save him from whatever had happened in the tomb. And it had solidified the bond between them.

She's frightened of you. Calsta's voice was scorching.

Frightened? Knox's fingers dug into the knot under his ribs before he could stop himself, flashes of Anwei's long braids in his face, Anwei threatening to spike his tea, Anwei's rosebud mouth turned up in a smile. Anwei limp in his arms as he ran toward the gate in the tomb compound, and Anwei's skin traced over in scars. *She was* angry *at me, but that's not the same thing. Did Willow do something...?*

Yes, Willow tried to kill her again, but that's not what I mean. Anwei is frightened of you.

Knox rolled his eyes—Calsta was in fine form, as always. Anwei had sworn at him, teased him. Confronted him when Willow's sword was in his hand. Even yelled at him the night he'd told her about Calsta's oaths. But there was no way Anwei was *afraid* of him.

He wasn't afraid of Anwei either, but Knox couldn't say that to Calsta. He didn't even know what he was allowed to say to the goddess anymore. Only that everything inside him that was twisted together with Anwei wasn't something he could step back from, even if he wanted to.

Which, in this moment of clarity, he very much did not want to.

You think I can't hear every one of those thoughts darting through your little mind, Knox? Knox shrugged away Calsta's amusement, then tensed as the Trib who'd come into the tent earlier appeared from what looked like a supply shelter erected next to the training field. Several others followed him out of the enclosure. Lia grabbed hold of her veil and pulled it off so quickly that it was over before Knox knew it was happening, Lia a mass of spangled white one moment and a snarl of red curls and freckles the next.

"Miss Lia, your face . . ." The Trib faltered.

"My veil isn't sewn on, Gilesh," Lia informed him. "You thought I was hiding something, right? Maybe a missing nose?"

Another of the Trib, much taller and with bangs that hung in his eyes, elbowed Gilesh. "I mean, we didn't take bets or anything, Miss Lia."

"Well, make them now, Bane." Lia let her veil drop to the grass. "And get Knox a sword."

"No!" Knox's stomach jolted, his palms suddenly sweaty. "Not a sword. Anything else would be fine."

"I thought *we* were going to spar." Gilesh pouted.

"It wouldn't be fair to you." She pushed past him, going into the tent.

Riders began to fill in around the field, coming to see what the hullabaloo was about. They crowded in behind Knox, pushing one another and yelling out taunts toward Gilesh. Knox ran an eye over the growing company, struggling to find a pattern to who carried what: knives, spears, axes, even one with a pair of bronze maces large enough to punch through plate armor. Lia emerged from the tent holding her sword in one hand and a long quarterstaff in the other. She pointed it at him. "Are you feeling the least bit ill? Light-headed? Tired?"

Knox wrenched the staff away from her for an answer. He ran into the circle of packed dirt, holding his arms wide toward Lia in a chal- lenge. Lia obviously needed a good spar, to sweat until she was tired enough to forget for a few minutes, but suddenly he wanted it for himself, too. He was *awake*. Full of energy, full of *life* instead of full of a ghost. He felt like *himself* instead of whatever the sword had made of him.

Willow's not gone, Knox. Calsta's reminder burned. But Knox didn't want to hear it. Didn't want to believe it with all this energy rushing through him and the sky clear.

"He's been on his back for a *month!*" Gilesh stepped toward Lia, hand on his weapon.

"She probably doesn't want to hurt any of you riders," Knox called back. He racked his brain for the Trib leader's name, the one who had managed to infiltrate the apothecary back in Chaol, then had spent his time there lying on the floor across from Anwei making explosives, as if they'd been playing marbles. "Altahn won't like it if she starts picking you off."

"You think Miss Lia won't hurt *you?*" Gilesh's smile had spread into a grin. "Or you think the kynate would rather she hurt you than me?"

"The second one." Knox leaned on the quarterstaff like a cane. He was still confused as to how they'd landed in a circle of Trib with Altahn at their head. That sneak had pretended to help them back in Chaol only to escape with all the information they'd gathered in order to break into the tomb. "Are you going to come out here or not, Lia?"

Lia walked deliberately into the circle, keeping her sword point low.

Everything went quiet—not the Trib, who had begun shouting from the edges of the circle, but Knox's mind as he breathed in, centering himself. His muscles felt soft, weak, but when he closed his eyes, Calsta's well of power was there inside him, waiting to be drawn. Lia was too diminished to have her strength back, so at least that made them somewhat even. Lifting the quarterstaff, Knox took half a step toward Lia, glorying in the familiar calm he'd learned at the seclusions. He wasn't a thief desperately trying to hide from his past, not a tool in Calsta's hands. And he wasn't the puppet that Willow had made of him.

A shard of ice came winging through his thoughts, quick like a startled bird and gone in a blink as it glanced off the barrier that Anwei and Calsta made in his head. Knox's side began to throb, the hairs on the back of his neck prickling.

Willow *was* still there.

Knox breathed in, trying to negate the background hiss she made inside him. *Go free, Willow! What do you want with me and this world?* The thoughts came in desperate gasps, the dark presence gathering thicker like a storm over the wall of magic protecting him. *The sword is gone. Just go!*

Lia settled into her stance across from Knox, letting the tip of her sword hover just above the dirt. Her cheeks had gone pink, her eyes flicking between him and his quarterstaff, and Knox could see that she needed to swing that sword into *something*, and it didn't matter who or what. A screech rang out over the camp followed by a long, shuddering auroshe squeal, as if Vivi could feel her agitation and couldn't stand to be left out of the fun. The gooseflesh down Knox's arms spread up his neck, his palms beginning to sweat, and a flash of unease stirred in his gut.

By now it seemed the whole camp had gathered to catcall and cheer. Gilesh and Bane tried to begin a synchronized clap, but it didn't catch. Lia's eyes ticked toward the sound, and in her moment of distraction, Knox threw himself forward, Calsta's energy singing through him as he slammed the quarterstaff down onto Lia's shoulder. It should have broken her collarbone—with a sword, it would have slit her from shoulder to navel—but Lia's sword was up before he got close, batting the quarterstaff away like a fly.

Knox twisted in midair, fending off Lia's return stab. When he landed, the riders were suddenly all very, very quiet.

Lia hesitated a second, as if to somehow acknowledge Knox's days abed, but then she was a wildfire. Stab after stab, swipe after swipe, Knox blocking and spinning, trying to fit in his attacks toward her feet, then her arms, then her head, but she blocked each one, coming faster and faster until her frown was gone and she was nothing but energy.

Each attack came stronger, Knox drawing in more of Calsta's energy to compensate for his leaden feet, the way he seemed to stick to the ground, turned too slow, and blocked a hair too long before returning an attack. Swipe, spin, stab, moving forward and backward and around until Lia spun up into the air, a kick swiping toward his face, then the full momentum of her sword slamming into the center of his quarterstaff when he blocked, slicing it in two.

Knox retreated, fending off her continued attack with the two severed pieces like twin swords, but then Lia hacked the one in his left hand in two and batted away the second when he threw it at her chest like a spear.

"Hey! Over here!" One of the riders held a mace out toward Knox. Knox rolled to the side to avoid another swipe from Lia's sword, jumping up to catch the mace when the man threw it, barely bringing it up in time to block Lia's sword.

Her eyes were wild, her teeth bared, and there was nothing in her but fight. Like so many years in training—with every frustration, every moment of anger and homesickness—Lia bled it dry on the practice field. This felt different, though, as if every blow, every form, every jump only stoked the raging bonfire inside her. She was raw. Out of control.

And she was coming for him.

Calsta help me, he swore, only to have the goddess laugh. *In this fight? Why?*

Lia leapt into a roll, her sword swiping a perfect arc toward his legs, forcing Knox to veer out of the way. He swung the mace toward her head, but Lia neatly slid beneath it, attacking with a barrage of kicks and stabs that left Knox off-center, forcing him to retreat toward the edge of the circle. The mace was too heavy to easily block her quick blows, and Knox felt as if he were moving in slow motion, the last swipe at him coming from underneath as Lia slipped inside his guard yet again. Turning the close proximity to his advantage, Knox landed a blow just above Lia's sword hilt, knocking the weapon from her hands.

Lia swore, slamming the palm of her hand into Knox's chin, then an elbow into his side, finishing with a cut toward Knox's windpipe that forced him to drop the mace so he could block her arm. She slithered away from him, kicking her sword up into the air, the point coming toward her instead of the hilt. Whipping off her coat, she caught the sword by its point with the fabric protecting her and swung the hilt toward Knox's head. He dodged, the split second he was on defense giving Lia an opening to flip the weapon up in the air and snag it by the hilt.

"Knox! Over here!"

Knox barely had time to wonder how the Trib knew his name before two objects were hurtling toward him. He jumped up to catch the first projectile, then spun low to grab the second. Trib knives.

They were too short to be much good against a sword, and Lia was rushing him, a feral scream on her lips. Vivi was screaming too, almost as if he were in pain.

Knox threw the first knife low, then the second one high, but Lia managed to strike the first one out of the air with her sword, then went down into a split to catch the second, sending it right back to him.

He swerved, and it flew into the swollen crowd of Trib, curses and laughter billowing out from their midst.

"Lia!" Knox yelled, ducking a blow from the sword. He whacked the flat of the sword away with his arm and grabbed her wrist. "Lia, you're going to hurt someone!"

She didn't seem to hear, clocking him in the stomach with the sword hilt just above the knot under his ribs. Pain arcing through him, Knox stumbled back. Another yell from the crowd. They were laughing, as if they couldn't see that she had completely lost control. "Here!" someone called, and another weapon was in the air.

Knox lurched forward to catch it, spinning to face Lia before he real-

Anwei wasn't helpless. She'd never been helpless. But the feeling made a hole inside him, stealing his breath and tightening his chest. The bond between them was electric. Anwei *felt* helpless, and so he was feeling it too. Helpless, and . . . afraid.

"You're here," he breathed.

There were tears—actual *tears* in Anwei's eyes. "Storms and *gods* and *broken skies*, Knox. What is wrong with you? I thought you were a goner."

He let out an incredulous breath, a laugh that wasn't a laugh at all. "I thought I was too."

Anwei crashed into him, her arms circling him tight. Her hands twisted into his tunic as they always did, as if she thought she was the only thing holding him fast to the ground. There were elbows and shoulders and shouts from the Trib jostling Knox from all sides. Adrenaline coursed through him, and his neck still tingled with the feel of Lia's sword swinging toward his neck. But all he cared about was Anwei's arms around him and her cheek pressed to his chest, her long braids trapped between them. He lifted her off the ground and spun her around, a laugh bursting out of him almost like pain.

Panic suddenly sparked inside him in the wake of his joy—his oaths, his goddess . . .

But Calsta didn't say a word.

"Wait—" Anwei pushed away, slipping out from his arms as if she were made of fog. But then she grabbed his hand and dragged him through the crowd. The bond between them was like a bright light in his head, Calsta's energy flowing around it—*through* it—and the swirling purple umbra of Anwei's energy gusted back toward Knox as if they shared an aura now too.

New oaths. More together than apart. They'd mixed somehow, and there was no separating them.

When they got to the tent, Anwei yanked him inside, then dropped his hand to pull open her medicine bag. She squared her shoulders,

ized that the weapon clutched in his hands was a sword. His

to blink out, his arms and hands adjusting automatically t

the familiarity, the *horror*. Willow's shadow reared up insid

He dropped it like a hot poker.

"Knox!" Anwei's voice was suddenly there. He hadn'

turn, his attention all on Lia. "Knox, *move!*"

Lia's sword was swiping toward his throat. Knox could

folding, the world slowed to a snail's crawl as Calsta's en

him. He could count the grass blades, hear each one as the

against one another in the wind, feel the shape of each v

from the crowd, the swish of leaves in the trees, Vivi's pani

ing, birds' wings overhead—

And his sword on the ground.

"Knox!"

Knox dropped down, jamming a fist into Lia's biceps,

blow knifing into her wrist.

The sword spun out of her hands and landed on the

stood there, chest heaving, tears trailing down her cheeks.

at Knox, then Anwei, who was standing inside the ring of

the hubbub of laughter and jeering rising every second. \

tears from her cheeks, Lia pushed past Knox into the crowd,

catcalls dying in awkward yowls at the sight of her tear-stain

"We're leaving!" Altahn's voice rang out over the noi

down and saddles up in the next hour!"

"Lia!" Knox took a step after Lia, but the sound of

spurred her faster. So he turned toward Anwei instead, h

sparking in his head. Riders were flooding the training circl

of mirth and back-slapping dimming to a background hu

Anwei pushed into sight. Knox's insides lurched. There we

under her eyes, her braids were all askew, and there were

of red that smelled like herbs across her face and neck. Sh

helpless somehow, staring up at him as if the world had sto

rosebud mouth open as her eyes darted down the length of him, and she inhaled. The purple haze around her corded into streams, thick and ropy as they began to circle her, and even as Knox felt her thoughts churn with it, he caught a whiff of something salty and sweet that he'd never smelled before.

Knox knew to trust Anwei's nose. But he was somehow *part* of it for a split second, the smell there, then gone in a flash, like a memory. Yet there wasn't anything Knox could have cared about less in that moment. He reached for her again.

Anwei's hand shot out, palm hitting his sternum and pushing him back onto the closed trunk next to her bedroll, forcing him to sit.

"What in Calsta's name is wrong with you?" She knelt beside him, her hand sliding down from his sternum to touch the hard knot under his ribs. "You roll out of bed and pick up a *sword?*"

Disappointment flared inside Knox, then a terrible twinge of embarrassment, which was worse because Anwei could probably feel it. This was *not* what he had expected when she dragged him into the tent. "Lia needed—"

"Lia didn't try to kill all of us, then *die* for a month. What happened?" She stood back up, agitation prickling their bond. "You *were* gone. There was hardly anything inside you. Just *Willow.*" She swept the braids back from her face, brow furrowing when her hand came away streaked with whatever herb coated her face and hair. Wiping her hand on her long skirts, she faced him again. "What did Lia do? How did she wake you up?"

"Lia didn't—"

"Where *is* Lia?" Anwei jerked around to look at the tent flap as if she had expected Lia to follow them and couldn't believe the Devoted was keeping her waiting. "Why was she fighting you? You just woke up from a coma! Why is her veil off? And Willow—I can still feel her inside you—" Her face crumpled, and she sank to the ground, hands covering her face.

Knox slid off the trunk and pulled Anwei close. Worry and confusion coursed through the place she'd claimed in his mind like notes vibrating from those Trib mandolins, each one out of tune. She let him gather her up, her forehead pressing into his shoulder—and Knox couldn't think. Not about anything but the way she was touching him.

Energy sparkled in the well inside him. There were no warnings, no bells tolling, no interjections from the goddess he wasn't thinking of even a little. Everything inside Knox began to twist, tighter and tighter until he couldn't breathe. Anwei went still in his arms. "Knox?" The words were barely a whisper. "You said—"

Knox smoothed a hand up Anwei's spine, the other circling her waist to pull her into his lap. He buried his face into her neck.

"You said this wasn't okay," she whispered against his cheek.

"I don't know what the rules are anymore," he said. And kissed her.

For that moment, the world seemed to break, the air nothing but a high, clear note in his head. Anwei's lips moved against his, and there *was* no Willow, no goddess, no wound in his side, no *world* because it could have all ended right then and he'd still be kissing Anwei.

Anwei's emotions swirled around him, relief and desire and excitement and *fear*.

Fear.

She's afraid of you, Calsta had said.

Knox paused. Then suddenly Anwei was pulling away, a movement so fast and ferocious that she fell backward, catching herself on one hand. Anwei's legs curled up under her, her hands closing into fists in her lap.

"Sorry." Knox swallowed, swiping a hand across his forehead. "I should have—"

"No. You don't need to apologize." Anwei didn't move, but the rush of feelings that had been so closely twined with his just moments before was shrinking back, leaving him cold. "I, um . . ." She cleared her throat but couldn't seem to come up with any words, the light brown of her cheeks tinged with pink. "I need to go." Getting onto her knees, Anwei pushed herself up from the ground. "Lia and the others need to see . . ." Her hands strayed to her bag, a corner of a leather folio full of documents sticking out. "You're all right?"

Knox blinked, confusion thicker than fog inside him. "I think so?"

"Then you stay here." She started to back away, pulling her sleeves down so they covered her to the knuckles, the hint of pink in her cheeks deepening when they went to the button at her throat, checking, as always, that her scars were covered. "I'll need to look at your side before we leave. It's not healing properly."

"What is happening here, Anwei?" Knox's insides wouldn't settle, his heart still pounding with the feel of Anwei pressed up against him where now there was only dead air.

"I found what we need to get to the snake-tooth man."

That wasn't at all what he meant, but Knox nodded anyway, waiting for her to continue.

"He tried to kill you. And my brother isn't dead. He belongs to Tual Montanne now." Anwei's heel caught on a messy bedroll, making her stumble to the side. She caught herself, a tense laugh squeezing out of her throat. "It's all gotten very complicated. But I think, maybe for the first time, I might be a step ahead of him. But that won't last if we don't get out of here."

"Wait, your brother is *alive?*" Knox swallowed. "And we're going to get him. And Lia's sister. And finally get rid of the snake-tooth man."

Anwei nodded, a strained smile touching her mouth.

"And you want me . . . to stay here? In the tent."

"Yes." She hugged the medicine bag tight to her chest, still backing away.

Knox stood, moving slowly. Feeling too large, ungainly, *wrong* somehow. "Why?"

Anwei bit her lip. "You trust me, don't you?"

"You know I do."

"Then stay here." She turned and walked out.

CHAPTER 5

The Most Terrifying Thing of All

ontanne Keep wasn't a real keep. Mateo's first sight of the white house on the lake with its three stories of bright windows sent a burst of energy through him. He brushed a hand down Bella's neck, the horse patiently standing beside him on the barge. "We're almost home," he whispered.

Bella shifted uneasily as the barge glided out of the cave and into the channel that fed the lake, exchanging dank darkness for light. Grabbing hold of Bella's lead, Mateo moved to the very edge of the barge, ready to run for the bridge that led from the shore to the island's stone-paved courtyard, suddenly grateful that when his father had rebuilt the house from the old one's dead ashes, he hadn't gone for thick walls, slitted windows, and a healthy population of rats under the beds as a true keep deserved.

Mateo didn't mind the misnomer, of course. "Montanne Keep" sounded quite fancy.

The moment the hostler manning the barge poles nosed the craft onto the channel shore, Mateo was already on Bella's back, trotting toward the bridge. The carriage was in the rear barge, and he didn't mean to dawdle until it disembarked. Aria would see him.

Tual had pulled him aside after everyone had gotten to the underground docks and the hostlers had begun readying the two flat barges that were the only safe way to get to the estate. "No, that wagon comes with me on the first barge!" Tual pointed to the wagon carrying the sword when one of the hostlers started pushing it toward the other boat, only turning back to Mateo when the hostler had managed to wrestle it around. "Miss Aria asked if we could ride with her today," he murmured.

"Miss Aria can stuff it," Mateo hissed back, doubting Aria had done any such thing.

"She's scared, Mateo." Tual put his hands on Mateo's shoulders, gripping him tight despite the easy smile on his face. "The two of you got on so well back in Chaol—she *likes* you. If you would just talk to her—"

Maybe Tual didn't mind that Aria's very existence in their party was a stain. Aria had a family—two parents, a sister—and somehow she was with Mateo and his father instead? Mateo shook the thought away, spurring Bella faster as Tual manipulated the controls to make the tunnel close off. No one could follow them into the keep through Basist-made traps and tunnels. Except for the people they allowed. Like Lia.

That was the plan, after all. To lure her here using her little sister. It rankled, even the idea of it, despite the fact that Mateo had agreed. Had helped plan the next steps, the ones that would make Lia want to stay once she arrived, would make her trust him again. But taking the first step down that path seemed much harder than writing everything down in nice bullet points with timelines and projected outcomes. Making nice with Aria Seystone would be taking that path at a *run*.

Clutching the drawing satchel at his side, Mateo tried to smooth out his thoughts, the energy prickling inside him like a thousand needles just waiting to gouge him from the inside out. He was an artist. An archeologist. A student. A scholar.

A shapeshifter.

A murderer?

He held the satchel tight, ducking closer to Bella. It had to be this way, at least if he wanted to live—and he very much did. But Mateo wasn't naive enough to think he was ready. Not yet.

Bella's hooves rang against the stone as they went over the bridge toward the tall white house with its red-tile roof. Home. Where everything would be comfortable and make sense again. The lake was an almost-perfect circle, with their island at the south end where the cliffs rose up behind it like a curtain. Ancient towers and long-fallen statues thrust up from the cliff top like fat fingers, each one so covered in vines and moss that it was difficult to tell them from the natural stone formations. A waterfall cut the cliff face in two, making a pretty picture: white house, red roof, gray cliffs, blue water, at least if you didn't look hard at the holes pockmarking the cliff face or the odd ripples marring the lake's surface.

Mateo urged Bella faster, flying by the watchtower that bloomed up over the gates at the far side of the bridge, the structure made without seams or mortar as if it had been raised whole from the depths below. Across the courtyard, past the gardens, straight to the newly thatched stables just past the tight U the house made on the south side of the island.

Reveling in the lake's quiet calm, Mateo dismounted and led Bella to her stall. Until he caught a whiff of decay among his home's comfortable scents, the ghost watching him from wherever it was she sat.

The rattle of carriage wheels on stone jarred him to action. Pulling Bella's saddle off, Mateo dumped it in the stable walkway where a hostler would be sure to see it. Waving a quick goodbye to Bella, Mateo sprinted for the house, swearing when the carriage pulled up between him and the grand entrance. Skidding to a stop, Mateo changed directions, praying the back doors were unlocked—and why wouldn't they be? No one but servants knew how to get to the island, and even they didn't know how to open and close the channels that led to the lake.

Grabbing hold of the kitchen door latch, Mateo swore when it didn't open. He went to the courtyard door—also locked. Then he tried his chances on one of the lower atrium windows, sending a prayer of gratitude up toward the sky when it pulled open. Barely managing to stuff himself through, Mateo stumbled through the plants and birds darting around the glassed-in atrium, then out to the servants' staircase, taking the steps three at a time until he got to the third floor.

His breath didn't catch. Not once. Not even when his mind went out to touch the unnaturally solid foundations of the place, the stones that made up the courtyard, the ones tiled across the walls. The glass making the atrium a swirl of light . . .

Mateo bit his lip, giving in to the flash of glory, of unbridled *glee*, despite the aftertaste of rot in everything his mind touched. No matter what the ghost wanted, his muscles, his body, his *magic*—they were *working*. He was somehow all right, as if his father killing the boy in the tomb had jarred something free, making it so his soul wasn't stretched across two people.

Three, really, Willow whispered. *We're family now, so I don't mind sharing.*

Mateo skidded to a stop at his own rooms, stumbling through the door and slamming it shut behind him. Leaning back against the gilded wood, Mateo breathed in deep, looking up at the familiar high ceiling of his sitting room, the gold trim, his books on archeology, history, and art lining the bookcases by the window. It smelled like home, pigments and resin, charcoal and vellum, like books and . . .

He swallowed hard. *Like rot.*

You can't have this, Mateo thought at the ghost in a panic. *This is my home.*

I'm so hungry, Mateo, she cried, her words icicles that only grew after they'd been spoken, sharpening like teeth.

Pushing off the door, Mateo darted into his sleeping chamber, almost tripping on the edge of the green Palashian carpet to land on his knees by the grand four-poster draped in salmon and cream. Mateo dove under the bed, rolled onto his back, and stared at the underside of the frame, the wood carved with trees and snakes.

This had always been his safe place when he was young, under this bed with his drawing pencils or a book. Lying under it was one of his first memories of the house. One of his first memories of Tual because his father had come in to hide with him, though Mateo couldn't remember what he'd been hiding from.

Maybe his family. The ones who had cut off his fingers, then nearly bled the life from his body. The sister who'd finally come after him, perhaps to finish the job?

Lia's with your sister, the ghost had said. How would that change their plans? Tual hadn't accounted for the murderous figment of Mateo's past tagging along with the murderous girl who was supposed to be his future.

Mateo glanced down at his fingers, whole and unmarked inside his riding gloves. *They cut off your fingers*, Tual had said, and yet there they were, whole and slim. Ready to draw as if Mateo had blinked into existence after his family had tried to murder him, nothing left in his mind of who he had been before.

He'd always believed it was because Tual had brought him to Montanne Keep as a young child—too young, too traumatized to remember. But it wasn't true. He'd watched Tual count on his fingers, lips pursed as he added up years that were all Mateo had left of his life. Eight. Eight years at Montanne Keep. Leaving the eleven years previous smudged and obscured.

Closing his eyes, Mateo tried to look into that dismal darkness, the before he didn't know he'd had. The ghost—Willow?—began to crackle and spit like a fire doused with oil, and something sliced through the black, sharp as broken glass.

A girl.

She was laughing. In her hands were a mortar and pestle. Her hair was an odd mix of coarse waves and braids. Half a Beildan.

Mateo's eyes burst open, and he couldn't breathe, the broken edges of the memory cutting him up and down. Gasping for air, he clutched the drawing satchel to his chest, curling around it as if somehow it could anchor him to the life he knew. The memory didn't fade as he hoped, only morphed into a taller girl. A girl with a full head of uneven Beildan coils, her expression murderous. Dark hair, tawny skin, the very freckles across her nose—it was like looking in a warped mirror.

Maybe I should have taken you both. Tual had said it in the carriage. *She's had a difficult life, Mateo.*

She'd been trying to save the other boy. The one Tual had killed in the tomb.

She's his family now! Willow rasped in an explosion of mental sound that had Mateo scrambling to cover his ears, as if it would block it out. But the ghost didn't scream again, the feel of her slamming shut inside his head, as if she were in a huff about something.

Mateo waited a moment. Had Willow gone? He breathed in slowly only to taste her death on his tongue.

"Mateo!" Tual's voice echoed outside in the hall. The door to his room opened and footsteps approached, stopping next to the bed. "What were you hoping to find under there?"

"Some dignity. Maybe a future that doesn't involve kidnapping or murder—"

"Miss Aria is sick to death of me, so coming out of hiding would serve that second goal." Tual bent down, his face appearing in the gap between the bed and the floor. "Our plan is going to work." He scratched at his beard. "Provided Aria doesn't strangle me with a hair ribbon or something. You trust me, don't you? You are my life, Mateo. I am going to set you right if it's the last thing I do."

Mateo stared at the underside of the bed, wondering at the shape of that sentence. His father had let him believe all sorts of things about himself, his life. None of those things had been true. But Tual had proved over and over again that what mattered most to him *was* Mateo. Letting his head turn so his cheek touched the floor, Mateo allowed himself to look at his father. "Harlan told me about the bodies. Why didn't you say something?"

Tual eased down to sit on the ground, silent for a moment. Finally, he sighed. "I guess I can't always keep the bad things away from you." He laughed, one helpless chuckle that was all the sadder for its attempt at cheer. "I've always tried to pretend that our lives are made from licorice and spun sugar."

"I don't like licorice." Mateo scrunched his eyes tight. "Are they auroshe kills? And if they are . . . what should I be worried about? Lia? Or . . . ?"

"I hope it *is* Lia." Tual cleared his throat, pulling a thin roll of vellum tied with a velvet ribbon from his coat. "My aurasight reaches farther than yours—when we've finished fixing you up, you won't only be able to see gods-touched. I can see every insignificant energy spark from here to the edge of the lake, and whoever it is out there is taking great care to stay out of range."

"You can see all auras, not just gods-touched?" Mateo thought back to the auras he'd seen—hundreds of different Devoted, Lia's, Ewan's, each somehow distinct and imprinted on his brain even more deeply than their individual names.

"People I know, yes. Instantly recognizing someone without knowing them is spiriter stuff, and I've never tried to develop that side of my abilities—Lia would have been able to do it. But I worry this is a more likely explanation for the attacks." He waved the roll of vellum. "It arrived in Kingsol by post this morning."

Mateo took the letter and untied the ribbon. Hastily glancing through the text, he skipped to the signature and sigil down at the bottom, two auroshes with their horns crossed. The Warlord was asking after her cure. Mateo let his head sink back down to the ground, pushing the roll of vellum back toward his father. "You think she followed us here and is . . . killing things and leaving them for us as a threat?"

"Maybe."

"How does she know where we live? How would she even go about getting here? No one knows how—"

"I wouldn't underestimate the Warlord. What happened at the tomb was a bit too dramatic for her to look the other direction any longer." Tual sat back on his haunches, clutching that ridiculous sun hat of his as he made room for Mateo to come out from under the bed. It wasn't actually ridiculous because Mateo had the same one, only in a tomatoey shade that brought out the warm undertones of his skin. He just wasn't feeling very kind. "Hiring an aukincer to cure her army was a stretch, even after she saw the results."

"A larger stretch than she realizes, considering you were the one causing the Devoted to get sick and lose their energy in the first place."

Tual chuckled. "Well, I don't think there's going to be any more stretching now that she thinks we've got what she wants. We'll either have to hand something over that looks like it can cure an entire religious order of terrible wasting sickness or be gutted in our sleep. She'll be here in the next few days."

"She'll lose half her company just getting here. Unless the forest is kinder to Devoted than the rest of us?" Mateo poked his head out from under the bed, then made himself slide the rest of the way out, leaving his safe haven for the cold air in the room. Most people who walked into the forest didn't come back out, eaten by snakes or other animals or falling into the underground channels made by long-dead Basists. "And it doesn't make sense that it would be one of her auroshes harrying us if she's days out. The first body *was* a Devoted."

"True." Tual hopped up from the floor. "Just in case some rogue predator has managed to follow us all the way here, would you keep an eye on Miss Aria? Show her the ropes, the lay of the land—"

"I don't want to get the lay of the land."

Mateo flinched at the sound of the girl's voice coming from his sitting room. He turned, wishing to Calsta herself that Aria was across the country, over the border in Lasei, on a pirate's ship—anywhere but glowering from his sleeping chamber door.

"I'm not going to be a good prisoner at *all*." Aria tipped up her chin as if she were going to snoot her way right out of the difficult situation she'd found herself in. Her freckles stood out against her pale cheeks like dirt, and beads of sweat dripped down her temples.

It must have been awful in the carriage. The heat. Wondering what had happened to her family . . .

"Why, Miss Aria, we were just talking about you." Tual smiled.

"I know. I heard you." The fact that she was standing there with bared fists instead of tears made her Lia's sister more than red hair and freckles ever could have. Mateo swallowed, looking away. She really did look just like her older sister, only more murderous, if that were possible. "I hope you know my sister is going to kill you," the little girl informed his father. "If I don't manage it before she gets here, anyway."

"As you've mentioned several times." Tual's smile only grew. "It was Lia herself who asked us to keep you safe after the Warlord—"

"That is a load of silenbahk dung. Lia had a plan to get us out. You were half the reason we had to *go*. You took me away from her and my mother and my father—"

"I don't know how to put this delicately, but Devoted came to your house not moments after I got you away and—"

"I don't think there's any reason to argue," Mateo interrupted, more for himself than for Aria's benefit. He didn't know what his father had or hadn't done to Lia's family. Lia's father may have even deserved a nasty end, what with his illegal shipments of salpowder going to foreign leaders and assassination plots and whatnot, but Mateo wanted to exist in ignorance. "You can murder me later for practice, Aria. My father will take a little more work, so you'll need it."

Aria leaned to the side to get a good look at him. "I'm going to find a sword and stab you."

"Get Harlan to show you to the armory. Only the Devoted are allowed to have swords, but you'll be able to find a nice machete, at least." Mateo gave her a ponderous bow from the ground, which took her scowl from murderous to positively genocidal. "That'll give me time to take a nap before you come for me. Otherwise I might faint in this heat, and then stabbing me wouldn't be nearly so satisfying."

"You're just as wimpy as Lia said."

Mateo nodded. "Absolutely, I am. Now go away. Last I checked, kidnapped girls were supposed to be shut up in their rooms."

"*Not* kidnapped. We are trying to help." Tual gestured grandly toward the doorway. "Let me show you to the gold room, Aria. I believe it will suit your taste. It's just next to Mateo's, so if you decide to kill him in his sleep, it will be quite convenient. There's even a rumor that there are secret passageways from this wing that lead all the way to the catacombs. . . ."

Aria didn't fight Tual, sticking her nose in the air and giving Mateo one last glare before allowing herself to be shepherded back into the hall. Mateo waited until his father's voice had faded before picking himself up from the ground to stare at the door after her, carved snakes curling up both sides of the frame.

Snakes like the one carved into his father's tooth. Mateo had never asked about it—it had always just been a part of Tual, same as his smile, his beard, the mischievous look in his eyes. But now, after everything, Mateo had questions.

He walked out into the hall, catching the tail end of something about where the poison was kept in the kitchen as Aria's flaming curls disappeared into her room. She slammed the door in Tual's face before he could follow her. Tual chuckled the whole way back to Mateo, rubbing a hand across his cheek to wipe away a tear of mirth. "I like her. I like the whole family. Now—" He clapped his hands together, rubbing them with gleeful anticipation. "We have some strategizing to do. Meet me in my office once you've had a chance to bathe?"

"We have more to plan? Because of the Warlord?"

"The Warlord will be easy to deal with. Unless she sees Aria."

Mateo stopped, turning to face him. "Because she'll realize Aria is Lia's sister? That Lia, the spiriter she's been trying to get her hands on for weeks now—"

"—disappeared the same time we arrived?" Tual nodded. "I have no doubt that if she puts the right pieces together, there will be more questions than we can answer comfortably, and I've grown a little too attached to this house over the years to just abandon it so I can spend the rest of my life running from gods-touched warriors."

"So what are we going to do? Drain them all down so far that they can't hurt us?" Looking out at the lake through the wavy glass made Mateo want to jump in and sink until all he could feel was water pressing in on him. Of course, he couldn't *actually* do that any more than Tual could drain a whole company of Devoted—the whole household knew better than to dangle so much as a toe in that lake without proper precautions. "You keep warning me that I might do it myself by accident—and that the energy I steal will just siphon down the hole I have where my soul is supposed to be."

Tual led Mateo down the stairs, heading for his office next to the atrium on the first floor. "Haven't you been feeling better? I didn't think killing off that boy would completely fix things, but you've been so healthy—"

"That's not what it is," Mateo grumped, opening his mouth to say something about ghosts. Voices. Power. The taste of death on his tongue . . . Slowly, he shut his mouth again, not wanting to make things worse by saying them out loud.

"I couldn't drain more than one Devoted in a day—at least enough to incapacitate them. For all the stories of shapeshifters, I don't know how they grew to be so much larger than life." They passed the antiquities room, artifacts Tual had found over the years and a few from Mateo on display, along with some of Mateo's sketches from inside tombs. Mateo caught a glimpse of something new through the glass door, the sight making his stomach curdle. A box.

The box. With Patenga's sword. The one he was supposed to use to kill Lia. After so many weeks of hiding it in the wagon, Tual was just going to put it out like a trophy for everyone to see?

". . . .I'm stronger than I ever have been before," Tual was musing. "But if the reliefs in Patenga's tomb are to be believed, he could suck the energy from an entire assembled gathering. I don't know where he put it all. There's no place for the energy to *go*." He opened his office door and hung up his coat just inside the doorway, his shelves of pots and jars, bowls and books built in against the window wall shared with the atrium. He sat down at his desk, brow furrowed. "There's a reason I've stayed away from all the various Warlords and Devoted cronies up until these last few years. Getting help from them wasn't worth the risk that I'd catch their attention. I could fight one, like I said. Two, *maybe* even three . . ." He trailed off, kicking himself around in a circle on the stool. "Ten? Twenty? Not so much. I don't know the whys or hows or *anything* useful about magic. I've only been able to take care of myself. And you, now that you've come along, but only barely."

"And you're *not* worried about the Warlord tracking us here and bringing Calsta knows how many swords with her?"

"Not yet." Tual kicked himself in one last circle before standing up. "Hiding is much easier than trying to fight an army when you've only one sword. We can still hide."

Anger boiled up inside Mateo at the idea. Hiding because of what he was, punishment looming for what he might do, not what he'd already done. Not for what he thought, what he wanted, but what he *could* be. What would they think of him once he became a true shape-shifter? he wondered.

We'll be immeasurable. Larger than any storm, deeper than any sea.

Your father doesn't know what he could do. But I do. Willow's voice grew darker. *We need the sword.*

Mateo swallowed, the imprint of Patenga's sword at the back of his mind like a knife waiting to stab him. "I'm worried. I'm not any of the things I need to be, Father," he whispered.

"You don't need to be anything but—"

"I don't even know what's true and what's not. I didn't know why we were at the tomb. I didn't know about being a sky-cursed *shape-shifter*. I didn't know I had a whole life before . . ." Mateo wrung his hands through his hair. "And a *sister*! What about her?"

"I didn't *lie* to you, Mateo." Tual's voice came out a little pinched, lines worrying his forehead. "I didn't want the burden to be on you. All of it—your sickness, *everything*, is my fault. I wanted to fix it without you having to shoulder the trauma of *why* it had to happen. Or how it had to be done."

Mateo paced across the room. "More sheltering? I'm the one who is supposed to stab the person I love most. Unless you were planning an elaborate sleepwalk, I think I would have figured it out eventually."

"And I'm going to be here, right by your side." Tual stood, easing around the books and papers already piled on his desk from their luggage. A bird chirped in the atrium, a flicker of life just on the other side of the glass. "We're going to do this together."

Mateo looked up at the little bird flitting from branch to branch.

"I didn't intend for you to find out the way you did. But would you have done anything differently now that you know?" Tual came up behind Mateo to grip his shoulders. "You want to live? This is how it happens. This is how everything changes."

"Everyone wants to live," Mateo breathed, full of angry words, but they wouldn't come. They stuck inside him like mud dried over the years of bitterness and anger at what he was: broken. Hunted. Condemned for no reason. Of course Mateo wanted to live. Maybe this was just how life was. If you had money, someone else didn't. If you had food, it had probably come from someone else's mouth. If you made decisions in your own favor, they were most likely hurting others.

Was this any different? Maybe there was a finite amount of life in the world, and he had the advantage of knowing how to secure his share.

He turned, brushing Tual's hand off his shoulders. This wasn't fair. He hadn't chosen to have a hole punched in his soul.

Not a thing or *a hole*, Willow growled.

Nor am I, he thought back. *I didn't ask for any of this. Don't I deserve to live?*

I did, I think. And I do still.

But I *didn't do any of this, so why should I be punished for it?* The thought was to himself, the edges tinged with decay. No different from the rage that had followed him throughout his whole life.

Tual stayed by the glass, back to the light as he looked up at the shelves of books and papers, the years of searching, digging, drawing, begging for information. "I can't lose you, Mateo. Not now. Are you having second thoughts about our plan?"

"No." Mateo slumped onto the sofa across from the desk. "I just need a stiff malt. And something impossibly scrumptious from Hilaria's kitchen." He deserved that much, at least.

Tual shook his head, spreading his hands wide. "There, I cannot help you. That woman terrifies me."

Altahn's voice outside the tent was muffled, Noa straining to hear as she sat down at the table in his tent. His riders were running helter-skelter in response to his careful instructions to pack up their belongings. When he finally came gusting through the tent flap, Galerey hissing on his shoulder like the little fusspot she was, Noa couldn't help but be a little impressed at the picture. Not *too* impressed, of course. Altahn was impressed enough with himself that he didn't need her.

"Where is our dear patron goddess of thieves? She hops into our wagon as wild-eyed as the nameless god himself, tells us we've found what we need, won't say a single word except to shout at the horses to go faster . . . and now that we're here, she disappears." Altahn sank down in the seat across the table, his customary smile gone, as if it were suddenly time to be serious.

"She's fine. I think they chased her out of the library, is all." Noa sat forward, wondering if the truth of him behind the smiles would now come crawling out.

"They almost chased *us* out, but my eyes weren't all red, and I didn't smell like death."

Noa shrugged. "Matter of opinion, I guess." She cleared her throat when Altahn cocked his head, not sure if she was insulting him. Which she had been. "Those herbs she rubbed all over her clothes got rid of it quick enough."

"Right." He grinned, but then it wilted into that same careful smile, as if Altahn realized he'd forgotten himself and needed to pretend that he was pleasant but not *too* pleasant. It was easy to see the game he thought he was playing with Anwei, but Noa loved the moments he slipped with her. "It *was* pretty close. That scholar saw me *touching* that awful glass."

Noa propped up her chin on both hands. "And that's how she'll always remember you. I know it's the picture of you I'll have lodged in my head: your hands full of someone just a little too manly for you to—"

"You can stop anytime now." Altahn laughed. Galerey scuttled down his arm to sit on the table in front of him. He had a nice laugh. "I shouldn't complain, I suppose. *Yaru* managed to pull it off in her typical singed hair, good-thing-no-one-thought-to-stab-us fashion like a true goddess."

"You don't like working with Anwei?" Noa extended a finger to Galerey, still delighted at the notion that Anwei had made up a goddess as a front to help her steal things and poison people. "She gets what she wants in the end."

"The problem is that I'm not sure she minds a few broken bones and lost limbs along the way." Altahn sighed, drawing a fanciful line across the little collapsible table, then frowning when Galerey sparked and licked at the spot, leaving whorls of ash in her wake.

Noa couldn't argue with that. She leaned forward to squint at the little burn marks the lizard had left on the table surface. It was the one concession to normal furniture in the whole camp. For all that Altahn's tent was the largest, it was simple, divided into a main receiving area and a personal area at the back with a canvas wall separating them. She'd never seen him go into his sleeping area, more often finding him sleeping under the stars with the other riders. The floor of the tent was strewn with carpets and pillows, giving them all places to sit as they talked and planned. There wasn't a single chair, no beds, not even proper silverware. Trib lived in their saddles, it seemed, needing nothing but a bedroll and a bit of canvas over their heads when it got too cold or too hot or too wet. It was a stark difference from the times Noa had traveled with her father over land, the trade caravan almost as opulent as her glittering rooms in Chaol with couches and screens, beds and a bathtub, along with people and wagons enough to carry them. That was only when her father couldn't justify traveling with his beloved riverboat fleet, goods taking up the space he and she should have on board.

Galerey's eyes narrowed on Noa's fingers extended toward her, little sparks igniting at her mouth when her tongue came flicking out. The little creature twisted to look up at her master. Altahn's brow furrowed, but then he nodded toward Noa. The lizard swiveled back, darting to nuzzle Noa's outstretched fingers.

Noa gasped, jerking away only to have Galerey follow her. The little lizard nestled in the cup of her hand, snuffling her knuckles, then nosed her hand over and sat on top like a falcon on her keeper's wrist.

"She likes you," Altahn said, a hint of annoyance flashing past the easy smile.

"She has good taste." Noa grinned, brushing her other hand down the lizard's crest and neck as she'd seen Altahn do, the creature closing her eyes, a soft rumble coming from her long torso like a cat's purr.

Altahn's fingers drummed relentlessly against the table. "You know *Yaru* better than I do. What did she need from the library, and why wouldn't she tell us? I can't work with a 'goddess' who only shares information she feels the rest of us mere mortals deserve. Tual Montanne already killed my father. I can't—"

"Anwei is no goddess. She's smart enough not to share everything when it means someone might run off with it all and leave the rest of us behind." Noa grinned when he looked up at her, the vague smile flagging a tiny bit. "You can't fault her after you stole all her information and tried to use her as a scapegoat in Chaol."

"She didn't tell you what we were after in Chaol any more than she's telling us now. She didn't even try to warn you that there was a full-fledged shapeshifter involved. Not until we were all neck-deep in vines."

"I wasn't down in the tomb." Noa looked toward the door, the flash she'd seen of Lia out in the training circle, sword raised, teeth bared, bringing back the awful memory of the last time she'd seen the girl's face before it was hidden under a veil. A hulking Devoted creeping toward her, awful desperation wearing Lia like a worn-out coat. Noa's fingers strayed up to touch Falan's flower at the end of the hair stick in her bun, the sharp prongs still feeling dirty, though it had been weeks since she'd cleaned the blood from them. "Lia should be coming in too, shouldn't she? Did you see where she went?"

"You mean after she riled up all my riders into shouting across the training circle like spectators at an auroshe fight?" He chuckled, covering his face with both hands. "We're supposed to be *hiding*."

"Some of us aren't suited for hiding." Noa looked back at the tent flap, wondering if she should go look for Lia. *Something* had happened while they were gone, but Lia didn't like being coddled and hugged. She would come to them. So Noa tickled Galerey's eye ridge, shrieking with delight when the lizard started climbing her sleeve. "Anwei's sorting it all out. You saw—her *belanvian* is feeling better." Normally, Noa started by liking people, because liking people was more fun than hating everyone and sitting alone at dinner. But she'd never quite warmed to Knox. Calling him a *belanvian* was the closest she could come to describing what she felt when she looked at him. *Belanvian* were legends of shadow in Elantia that waited under docks and in dark alleys to pull unsuspecting victims into their realm. No one who had actually seen one had survived to tell the tale, so far as Noa knew. Knox left her with that same feeling, that if she dug below the shadows that clung to him, she might not live to tell about it.

She had never seen anything like it before him, almost as if he were wearing a costume for everyone else. Falan saw through liars and bad actors clear as glass, and Noa was certain that seeing Knox's shadows was some kind of help from her goddess, no matter what all the priests said about lower gods not sharing power. Unfortunately, when she had explained her misgivings about Knox to Anwei, the healer had only giggled as if Noa were telling a joke.

Anwei had sat by Knox's bedside every night since the tomb, one hand around his wrist as if she thought letting go would mean his blood would stop pulsing, not a care about what would happen if his hands suddenly clutched back. He'd been pale under the light brown cast to his skin, barely breathing.

And now he was awake.

"What was *wrong* with him?" Altahn's voice broke through her thoughts. "Yaru wouldn't say a single word about it, only that he was injured in the tomb but he's important to what she's planning. Maybe . . . because Tual will trip over his limp body?"

"He wasn't so limp out there on the practice yard." Noa couldn't be surprised that Anwei's grumpy shadow friend had woken up with a weapon in his hand. "You'll see why Anwei wants to keep him around."

Altahn's fingers began to drum faster. "Oh, I've seen."

Pursing her lips, Noa brushed her hand down Galerey's scaly side, the lizard pulsing with internal heat that came out in little whisps of smoke from her nostrils. "We need him as much as we need you." She looked up, her smile stretching to a grin, trying to think how best to poke him out from that aggressively even keel. "Or you wouldn't be here."

"We?" Altahn's fingers stopped drumming, and he spread his hands forward across the table, stretching like a cat. "What are you doing with someone like Anwei, anyway?"

"Me?" Galerey darted up from Noa's shoulder into her hair, a laugh bursting from Noa's lips. "Why wouldn't I be with Anwei?"

"You think I don't know who you are?"

Noa frowned, but before she could respond, Bane—a favorite of Noa's among the riders—stuck his head in the tent flap. He shot Noa a grin that she returned in earnest despite the worry sinking through her humors. "We'll be ready to move out in an hour, like you asked, Altahn."

What did Altahn mean, he knew who she was? The thoughts swirled quicker and quicker as Noa listened to the Trib deliver his report. Had Altahn meant to accuse her of something? To *threaten her*? Noa hadn't left her father and his trading empire with permission, exactly. It was likely he was throwing open theaters and malthouses all across Chaol in search of the precious bauble he'd sold to the governor. Or perhaps he wasn't looking for her, fed up once and for all with Noa and the fact that she didn't act like a crate of goods. Noa wasn't sure which was worse.

"Are we going to stay off main roads as we have been up until now?" Bane took another step into the tent. "Because Mari's got her maps out and—"

"We're still discussing destinations." Altahn nodded to the canvas wall that divided the tent's gathering area from his bed and belongings. "Most of my things are still on the wagon, so you don't need to load them for me."

Noa glanced toward the divider. He hadn't even unpacked? The words he'd said about the shapeshifter came back to her: *he already killed my father*. Galerey twitched in the little spot she'd hidden at the nape of Noa's neck, the feel of her claws suddenly sharp.

This tent and all the things in that little room had probably belonged to Altahn's father. The former clan kynate. Was that why he wouldn't sleep back there?

Before she could think much more about it, Altahn continued. "We can start taking this tent down once I've had a chance to speak with our guests."

Bane hesitated a moment, but then flipped his hand up in a jaunty version of a Trib salute and backed out of the tent.

Galerey clambered up the side of Noa's head, her claws pulling on Noa's khonin knots to gain purchase. When Noa looked back at Altahn, he was watching her, not the firekey. "Are you going to answer my question? What are you doing here sleeping on dirt next to a thief instead of sitting on the governor's balcony letting your fiancé feed you grapes?"

Noa laughed, leaning into the table. "Why are *you* here, Altahn? Kynate of a Trib clan. Hundreds of miles from your own land, chasing after a meaningless—"

"My father died trying to return Patenga's sword to our family." He licked his lips, then pressed them together, something in his face hardening. The bland smile had somehow faded, looking more like regret. "And I'm the one who told him we needed to go after it."

"You . . ." Noa's smile ebbed, and she couldn't help but sit up a little straighter. "Why?"

"It doesn't really matter, does it? But you could see, maybe, why

I'd be a little concerned that the daughter of a very powerful man who deals in rare antiquities suddenly appeared among the thieves I paid to steal this sword?"

Noa's skin pebbled, Galerey's long tail slipping around to encircle her neck. "You spent all morning teasing me. You helped me hang a mostly naked man in a library for an old lady who is absolutely not going to appreciate the favor. And *this* is what you've been thinking the whole time? That I'm here"—laughter bubbled up from deep inside her—"I'm here to *betray* all of you?" She curved forward, hands to her stomach, the laugh biting as it came out. "Just to get my father a pretty *sword?*"

Altahn's brow furrowed, and she put up a hand in apology, trying to get the words out. "No, wait. Don't get angry." She reached up to extract Galerey from her hair, the lizard looking around wildly at the sudden movement and sound. Her belly warmed Noa's fingers as Noa set her gently on the table—she was *too* warm, as if those flames she could spark lived inside her all the time. Mirth still pulled Noa's mouth into a bitter grin. Unfortunate, because she loved to laugh, but some things were funny for the wrong reasons. "You've never met my father, have you?"

Anwei bustled through the tent flaps before Altahn could respond, the leather-bound folio she'd taken from the library in her hands. She was moving too fast and bumped into the table, jerking it forward a few inches. Just as fast, she pulled it back into place and set the folio down. "Where's Lia?" she asked, looking around. "We need to go through all this as quickly as we can."

"Weren't you bringing Knox?" Altahn asked. "He seemed much better."

Anwei pulled the folio open and began to spread the papers out. "It'll be better for him to rest—we can fill him in once we're on the road."

Noa eyed her friend. Anwei had spent almost every night since the tomb sitting up with Knox's still body, hollow-eyed and grim. But now that he was awake, the healer wore a sparkling smile that was so fake it hurt Noa to look at. Something was wrong. Anwei pushed the pages toward Noa. "I think I've managed to read through most of it."

Completely oblivious, Altahn sat forward, craning his neck to get a look at the top pages, all of them spotted with age and worn so thin that Noa could see through each one to the writing on its opposite side. It was all classical Elantin, the old script from before Elantia had joined the first Warlord to destroy shapeshifter kings. Focusing on the looping script, Noa picked up a sheet of vellum, her brain twisting to translate. She frowned, looking over the top of it at Anwei. "Are these . . . household records? Because that would be quite a story. The first shapeshifter in centuries, and the key to his downfall has something to do with hundred-year-old underclothing in need of a scrub."

Altahn stood, startling Galerey into scuttling up his sleeve in a shower of sparks. Swearing, he brushed at the little black marks on his hand and shirt where her fire had touched him before squeezing in next to Anwei, his arm carefully nudging Noa aside to make room. "You told us we were stealing information critical to locating and stealing the sword from this shapeshifter."

Noa nudged him back, knocking his shoulder into Anwei, who didn't seem to notice, just moving down the table to give him space. "I said it was critical information about Tual Montanne. I've been hunting him for eight years. One of the first things I did was go looking for a house that used a snake for its mark. The only place I found any hint the information existed was Castor's temple. When I went in, this old scholar pushed the lady helping me out of the way and dragged me off to a little room—said he knew exactly what I was looking for." She blinked twice. "I was thirteen and had spent enough time on the streets to know most people who say they want to help don't mean that at all, but I *had* to find the snake-tooth man. So, I sat there and he . . . started talking. Said something about a fire seventy-five years ago, and not to move, and kept starting and stopping and getting confused. At the time I just thought he was putting me off, so I stole two of his rings and ran off. I came back a few times, but it was always that same scholar, and he always seemed to find me. And I knew . . ." Anwei's voice cracked, and her eyes went down to the table. She pushed the top few papers back, looking for something. "I already knew the snake-tooth man could do things to people's memories."

"Anwei, what does this have to do with getting Patenga's sword?" Altahn said very, very calmly.

"You're saying Tual Montanne knew there were records at the library that could lead back to him somehow. And he set scholars on anyone who came looking?" Noa held up the household account. "Like, he thought it was important to hide . . . how many silver rounds he spends on blueberry scones?" She went to the next paper and the next, spreading them out in front of her, trying to piece together the old words. "Why is any of this in the restricted stacks anyway? It's just really old records from a particular estate like they have for all the old houses in the Commonwealth—it's all stored in Rentara. Names, birth dates, death dates. Gods-touched . . ." Noa shuffled through a few more papers. "I mean, this house changed hands a few times over the years, which isn't typical for an estate this size, I suppose. Most high khonin claimed their land at the end of the shapeshifter wars and haven't let it go. Still, it's not the kind of thing that scholars would lock away, is it?"

"How about an address?" Altahn looked over Noa's shoulder. "Do we even know this is Tual's house? Or that he's headed there now?"

"It's his." Anwei reached out for a sheet of vellum folded in half. Opening it, she smoothed out the outline of an island on a lake inked in blue. "And it's in the restricted stacks because Tual Montanne lives on the cursed bones of an old Basist fort."

"Cursed?" Noa eagerly pulled the map closer, the edges creased and fragile. "What do you mean?"

"He's an archeologist, so destroying the records wasn't a comfortable option. According to Lia, Mateo was *livid* at the idea of records featuring anything to do with the nameless god being destroyed—"

"*Curse*," Noa interjected. "Tell me about the curse!"

"But I'm guessing he left the documents there because it makes for a good trap. Anyone who knows enough to go looking in the restricted stacks for information about his house is someone Tual would want to know about. And there were certainly precautions in place." Anwei pointed to the pretty calligraphy on the map. "It was a Basist stronghold until the very end of the shapeshifter wars. By that time, Devoted were targeting them just as much as the shapeshifters. If you look at the map and the notes attached to it, there are apparently extensive and extremely dangerous defense systems that the Basists built around the entire lake, including into the back sides of these cliffs where most of them lived. And something about 'ways,' but it doesn't say what that is supposed to mean, only that people got killed in them if they didn't know how to use them properly."

Altahn looked up at that. "Where? Does it show any of it on the map?"

"No. A shapeshifter moved in at the end of the wars and killed everyone in the fort, so the people who knew didn't survive long enough to tell Devoted. Even in later documents it just says that the ways are closed and marks safe areas for roads to be built out past the estate's borders."

Noa pushed the papers away. "Anwei, I'm going to shrivel up and die if you don't get to the curse part *immediately*."

Anwei didn't break eye contact with Altahn. "Even Devoted couldn't crack whatever the Basists built around the fort. This shapeshifter was one of the last to fall at the end of the wars. All the records are here, the date the Warlord set out, the food requisitions, the number of horses and auroshes, the Roosters who walked on foot."

Huffing out an exasperated breath, Noa threw up her hands. "Okay, so they went, they got in somehow, and we can use the same

magic he can find and digging up shapeshifter bodies with his *son*." Her lips grew thin as she pressed them together.

Noa put a hand over Anwei's, the angry haze that had hovered around her friend since she went into the tomb sharpening. She wasn't sure exactly what Tual *had* done other than take her brother, but whatever it was had been curing too long inside her friend to be neutralized, like salpowder distilled to its most potent, and a single spark would be all it took for Anwei to explode. "We'll find him, Anwei."

Anwei swallowed, looking away. It wasn't the right thing to say, for some reason.

"Well, *Yaru*." Altahn finished scrawling and put down his quill. "These maps are from before the fire. You say there are Basist defenses and that the roads are gone, but at least we know where he'll be and sort of what we're up against. If there were no roads until high khonins bought the land, that means there's another way in. We'll have to find it—through the forest or the cliffs. . . ."

"Tual wants us to follow him. Otherwise, he wouldn't have kidnapped Lia's sister. We're going to have to approach this in a way that keeps him from finding us before we find a way to him. I think if we move quickly, we have two pathways forward: surveilling the area to find out how Tual gets in and out, then attacking him when he least expects it. That still puts us at a disadvantage because we'll be in his space and we have no idea what we'll find in there." Anwei tapped the map again. "Second pathway, we draw him out of the fort. Make him come to us."

"How?" Altahn's eyes glossed over the map again.

"My brother."

Noa sat back in her chair, the edge to Anwei's voice cutting deep. "What use would Mateo be?" she asked carefully.

"We have three goals." Anwei put up three fingers, ticking them off as she went. "You want Patenga's sword." Anwei pointed at Altahn. "Lia wants her sister back." The second finger went down. "I want

Tual dead" The third finger went down, making a fist of Anwei's hand. "My brother is the one thing Tual has consistently shown interest in, so if we kidnap him, Tual will come out of his fortress to save him, no?"

"Yes, but . . . isn't Mateo a shapeshifter as well?" Noa asked.

Anwei waved her hand dismissively. "Not a good one. I can make sure he won't hurt any of us while we keep him prisoner."

Altahn flinched, and Noa had to try very hard not to giggle. The time he'd spent tied up under Anwei's temple apparently still stung.

"If worst comes to worst, Mateo knows how to get into his own house." Anwei continued, and Noa couldn't help the trill of worry at the ice in her voice. "He'll know where Aria is. He'll know where the sword is being kept. Making people tell the truth isn't so hard."

"You have more gamtooth venom?" Noa sat forward when Anwei shook her head, discomfort an odd thing inside her. By Lia's account, Mateo Montanne was harmless, not interested in doing much but digging up old bones. Was there something more to him Anwei wasn't saying out loud because of Altahn? "Well, I have always wanted to throw a coat over someone's head and kidnap them," Noa said slowly, not sure if she should try to dig deeper or be distracting enough to keep Altahn from doing it.

Altahn's look of concern was reward enough regardless of what Anwei wanted. Whatever her friend's feelings toward Mateo, Noa suddenly wasn't sure Anwei's plan included him still breathing at the end of it. She'd thought of Anwei as a puppeteer, twitching the world to fit her favor like any good goddess would, but this was different. Anwei wasn't usually so cold.

"The tributaries coming off the river means it's probably near where the Felac empties into the ocean," Altahn interrupted her thoughts, Noa looking away from her friend's face to follow his fingers walking down to the edge of the map. By the time she turned back to Anwei, her friend had bent down to examine the stretch of river he was pointing to. "There's a town right on the river there, I think."

"Kingsol," Anwei supplied, her brow crinkling for some reason.

Noa cleared her throat, ready to play her role. The distraction. "Perfect. Didn't Lia say that Mateo likes sweets?" Rubbing her hands together, Noa gave an excited squeal. "We'll stake out every bakery in town."

"Did Lia say that?" Anwei went back to looking at the papers, her hand settled next to the shapeshifter's portrait, finger's resting beside the words under her feet: *I am the sword.*

CHAPTER 6

Both Helpful and Good
at Killing People

t took a while before Lia was calm enough to even think about walking back toward camp. She sat in the afternoon sun with her veil in one fist and nothing in the other, where her sword was supposed to be.

If she even deserved a sword. Lia tried to breathe, but the air wouldn't come, whistling at the back of her throat as she saw it over and over again: her sword swinging toward Knox's neck.

What is wrong *with me?*

She stared toward the road leading into Rentara, the little shops with people milling between them, the gangly shape of the university just over Rentara's walls, the smell of smoke and people and *life* on the wind, and all she could feel was *rage*.

Lia's parents were dead.

Her sister was in a monster's clutches.

And the world was sitting down to afternoon tea as if nothing at all had changed.

When Ewan had attacked her, she'd frozen. When her oldest friend had sparred with her to help her feel better, she'd tried to cut him in half. Maybe Tual didn't need to kill everyone she loved, because she was making a good stab at it herself.

Hand knotted through her hair, Lia tried to block it all out, replacing the thoughts with how she'd survived in Chaol. Ewan had been hunting her. The Warlord had been right behind him Tual had promised to kill her whole family. Calsta's oaths had hung over her like an ax. Through it all, her father had been there trying to fix things. Aria had been there to pour honey onto Lia's hairbrush and salt into her tea. *Mateo* had been there, a useless distraction who had nothing better to do than make her want to slap him across the face. And roll her eyes. And laugh, as if maybe there was still something inside her that could be a person, not a Devoted terrified of her own goddess.

The thought of Mateo only made Lia's chest clench tighter, as if she'd never breathe again. Her feet kicked back and forth, harder and harder, the veil tearing in her clutch.

An aura detached from the camp, coming toward her. Gilesh. Lia tensed as he came closer, wishing he were a thief, a warrior, a *murderer* for her to fight. It didn't matter that her sword was probably still lying in the trampled practice field grass. It was like every other moment in her life—at the seclusions, on the hunt for Basists, after she'd escaped Ewan in Chaol—moving, fighting, doing *something* because she couldn't do what she truly wanted. Only now it wasn't helping.

And now, unlike before, it wasn't Lia's life at stake.

Gilesh slowed, stopping a few strides behind her. "Miss Lia?" he asked.

She turned slowly, stretching her arms, her legs, every muscle that would listen, so they wouldn't snap into something violent and deadly. Gilesh noticed, but continued toward her anyway, a funny mix of concern and lack of self-preservation. "I just wanted to make sure you weren't hurt."

"I'm not hurt," she said stiffly, wondering which part of that was true.

"Miss Anwei whisked that boy you were fighting away quick enough, and we didn't realize . . ." He broke off, and Lia closed her eyes, the idea of having to explain what was going on inside her actually worse than feeling it, for some reason. "I mean, *are* you all right? I'd say you beat him fair and square, even if he managed to get you to drop your sword at the end."

"Very generous of you."

"You don't seem the type to cry because you lost a fight. Is there . . . something you want to say? I won't even listen if you don't want. I'll just stand here."

"What type am I, then?" Her feet kicked and kicked.

He eased closer, sitting next to her a few feet down the broken fence. "The type with freckles?"

"A telling character trait."

"Why'd you take off the veil?" She looked at him, and Gilesh put his hands up, shrinking back. "I'm just hoping if I ask enough questions, you'll slip up and give something away. We both know something bad happened to bring you to our clan. The same bad thing that killed Shale and has Altahn running so far south that I can hardly remember what snow looks like." When Lia didn't volunteer anything, he sighed, looking up at Castor's blocky silhouette rising from the afternoon horizon. "I've known Altahn since we were boys. He's not acting like himself. Now I've found you out here alone, minus your sword even though you've been glued to the thing since your first day in camp. You took off your scary veil. And now you're crying. I get the feeling you know more than I do about what's going on."

"You came out here to grill a crying girl for information?"

Gilesh let out a guffaw. "That is exactly what is happening, yes."

"Probably a good plan." Lia wiped her cheeks. "Knox is okay?"

"He seemed okay for someone who'd spent the last month lying in his bedroll." Gilesh shrugged, squinting down the road. "You know, it was Miss Anwei's fault you dropped the sword."

If she hadn't, Knox would be dead. Lia shivered, hugging her arms around her ribs. *Or maybe Anwei would have knit Knox back together like the last time someone stabbed him.* She slid off the fence and started back toward camp, Gilesh hopping off to follow a step behind as if he were guarding her back. Something she didn't need, but Lia was glad not to be alone. So many years as a Devoted and then a spiriter, she relished the feel of someone worrying about *her* rather than worrying if she were functional enough to fulfill her next assignment.

"You know I used to be able to see straight into people's minds?" Lia glanced back at the Trib. She wondered what the Warlord would say to her revealing something so specific to an untouched. Devoted were supposed to be mysterious and frightening—an easier reputation to maintain when people weren't quite sure what you were capable of.

Gilesh only grunted in response, as if seeing into people's minds wasn't quite as impressive as he would be when they finally crossed swords.

"I don't need it with you. You say everything you think out loud. And I like it." She pointed at Altahn's tent, the only one not yet stripped to a skeleton of poles. Altahn's, Noa's, and Anwei's auras were burning merrily inside. Knox was back in his own tent, though, away from the others. "They're planning whatever our next move is. Want to come in? We're stealing a sword."

"I guess I did know about the sword. It was more the rocks caving in and plants springing up from the ground to strangle us while we sleep that I was concerned about." Gilesh pursed his lips, eyeing the tent. "Altahn's been so quiet and withdrawn—I don't want to push him. Maybe we could just eavesdrop. Then, if he tries to kill me, you can do this stuff." He raised his hands into a fighting stance and threw a fake punch at Lia's shoulder.

"Give me a minute. You eavesdrop until I can get inside. We'll compare notes." Lia nodded as if a deal had been struck.

Bane came hurrying toward them from the flurry of tents being deconstructed. "You got her to talk to you?" It was the most accusatory question Lia had ever heard. "And you didn't bring me? Again?"

"She's going to help us eavesdrop on everything going on."

"Oh. Helpful *and* good at killing people." Bane nodded approvingly. "If you're forming a new little crew here, I'd really like to be part of it."

Lia pressed her eyes closed. "Right. I'll be back. You get started?"

Gilesh nodded enthusiastically. "Bane will get snacks."

Snacks. I wonder if he knows what Devoted eat. Lia watched Bane and Gilesh melt into the bustle of the camp before she walked toward Knox's aura. Vivi's head came up from his place outside the tent as she passed, baring all his teeth.

"I didn't leave you here because I don't want you, Vivi." She walked up to him, laughing when he rolled onto his feet, immediately snuffling her hands for a treat. "I don't have anything."

Vivi threw back his head with a mournful moan.

"Dramatic as ever. Your new braids look nice, though." Once she'd given him one last stroke, Lia turned back to the tent, steeling herself against the rage still molten inside her. Anwei was back. A path toward Tual meant there was a direction for that rage to flow. Not against Knox or Anwei or anyone else. Against Tual, because he was the one who deserved it.

It didn't change the fact Lia had lost control and attacked her dearest friend.

One more calming breath. No, two. Then she pushed through the flap to find Knox sitting on his bedroll, hands in fists.

"I'm really sorry," she said quietly. "I don't know what came over me. Are you all right?"

Knox stood up, rolling the shoulder she'd hit. "You're a lot less rusty than I expected after two years under that veil."

She blinked. "You're not mad? I almost *gutted* you."

"If you were going for my gut, then I take it back. Your aim is way off." His hand flitted up to touch his neck where she'd almost struck him. "Maybe it's fair after what must have happened in the tomb."

"Doesn't count when it's a ghost doing the stabbing."

"If only that were true." Knox's smile was a bit strained. "Anwei says she got what we need to find Tual. Once we're moving toward Aria and Anwei's got a plan to get us in, you'll feel less like stabbing people. This time we can actually fix things—not just push it down like you used to."

We're going to fix this. Lia's breath caught in her throat, the memory of smoke in her lungs. Some of it couldn't be fixed. Her parents weren't coming back. But Anwei had promised to fix the rest. A flush of determination put air in Lia's starved lungs. "What are you doing skulking around in here instead of planning with the others?" She grabbed Knox's arm and pulled him up. "Calsta above, I'm so glad you're awake. Noa tried to put beads in my hair."

He laughed, following her to the tent flap, but tugged free of her before she could lead him outside. "Noa has a short attention span. If she's bugging you, give her a dirty word to rhyme and she'll be occupied for hours."

Lia went through the flap, holding it open for him, but Knox still didn't follow. "You're not coming?"

"I can't. Anwei . . ." Knox's cheeks flushed a little.

"Anwei . . . *what?*" She gave his shoulder a push. "Come on!"

"I thought . . ." He scrubbed a hand through his hair, the ends curling at the nape of his neck. "Calsta's breath! I can't talk to you about this."

Lia frowned, clapping his shoulder again with her open hand. "Talk to me about what? Did Anwei miss healing something?" She jabbed a fist toward his ribs, but he moved too quickly, catching Lia's wrist before her knuckles could connect. "See? You're fine. Anwei could use a good dose of Devoted tactics to round out whatever she's planning. Spill whatever the problem is before I get annoyed."

"She just . . . *we* just . . ." Knox's mouth hung open a second. "I've only been conscious for less than an hour after weeks of . . . not? Maybe Anwei's worried about why or how or what changed. And things are weird with her. . . ." He looked around, hands helplessly gesturing to bundles of fabric and poles that had been tents a few minutes earlier. "I don't even know how we got here or what's supposed to happen next. She asked me to sit this out."

"And you just . . . do what she says?" Lia fell back a step, confusion blooming inside her. She looked toward Altahn's tent, where Anwei's aura shone out like a glistening white lie. "What is with you two? I've seen the way she looks at you—I saw it way more than *anyone* should have to over the last few weeks. Your aura is gone, but Calsta's still in there. It's like you don't even have to keep your oaths, and you're neck-deep in *herbs*." She jabbed his arm, and he flinched, rubbing the inside of his elbow where she'd poked him. "All I had to do was *touch* Ewan back in Chaol, and Calsta took every last drop of energy away from both of us."

Knox's cheeks flushed, and Lia could feel hers heating to match, because it was obvious that he *had* touched Anwei without the same consequences. But Lia didn't really want to think about it. She knew the rules weren't exactly what they'd been taught in the seclusions. Mateo had told her about what magical bonds were supposed to be— she'd *seen* it down in the tomb, all the reliefs with Patenga and the man he loved, both of them obviously still crammed to the gills with energy from the gods. Calsta wanted you to love only her, except for when she didn't, apparently.

But *Knox*? With a girl? With *anyone*? Much less *Anwei* of all people, who *reeked* of banned magic. It didn't square in Lia's mind with her friend, the Devoted who had been so steady, so dutiful, so . . . well, *devoted*.

She looked away, embarrassed, because even the way Knox held himself was different from before. He was her brother, the other half of her team. Lia didn't mind adding people to the team, but this wasn't the same. Knox really had changed, and it was *Anwei* who'd changed him.

Knox's hand slammed into Lia's shoulder, taking her by surprise. He pushed her hard enough to make her stumble into the path, rolling his eyes like he was twelve and she'd just given him a good flick between the eyes as the prize for being second up the seclusion training wall after her. "Just *go*. Fill me in later."

She went, feeling a tiny bit better.

Gilesh gave her a jaunty Trib salute from where he was loitering outside the tent, and she returned it with great solemnity before entering. Noa and Altahn both looked up from a pile of old papers when she walked in, Anwei standing up from the other side of the table. "There you are. Calsta's *breath*, Lia! What were you thinking, sparring with Knox?"

Lia sat down, not liking that Anwei thought she was in charge of Knox. "What did you find?"

"Knox has . . . been *sick*." Anwei didn't quite look at Altahn, who had gone back to sketching something on a piece of paper. "He needs to rest."

"He wanted to fight. He was trying to make me feel better. And he'd probably be pretty helpful planning things with us."

"I want to give him time to recover before—" Anwei suddenly went still, her eyes darting toward the tent where Lia had left Knox. She started running before Lia could extract herself from the low table, but Lia could see it too—Knox's aura frantically flashing. By the time she got to the doorway, he'd begun to drain.

Lia ran after the healer all the way to the tent. Anwei crashed to her knees next to Knox, who was lying on the ground, his eyes rolled back into his head.

"Calsta's *bastard son*." Anwei pulled open Knox's tunic, her hands frantic as she jerked the fabric back from his left side to expose the knob of twisted white skin where a gaping stab wound should have been.

"He was awake only a minute ago!" Lia's voice came out faint, her hands opening and closing because they were still empty. Useless. A single drop of blood welled at the center of the wound.

Anwei tore open her medicine bag and extracted a jar of salve Lia had seen her spread across the wound before. Her hands shook as she tried to undo the clamp. "You were here when he woke up. What happened?" she asked quietly.

"He just . . . woke up. He was *fine*. . . ." Lia licked her lips, the shine of Knox's aura thinning out, like a Devoted in the last throes of wasting sickness. She lowered her voice. "Anwei, *Mateo* had episodes kind of like this."

"He smells like *her*. The ghost." Anwei scrubbed a hand across her nose. Jerking back from Knox, she fumbled to unlock her trunk, almost bending the metal joinery to tear it open. Rooting through the contents, Anwei grabbed hold of something at the very bottom and went very, very still.

"What is it?" Lia rose onto her knees to see past Anwei into the trunk. Her fingers were clasped hard around something wrapped in a dirty blanket. "Is that . . . ?"

Anwei drew in a shuddering breath and pulled out a long blade of pockmarked caprenum. The sword that had killed Knox's sister. The one that had linked him to Willow. The one that had made him *attack* all of them in the tomb, and the one Tual had stabbed through him. Lia sank down next to Knox, her heart racing. "I thought that thing melted in the tomb! How did you . . .? *Why* did you bring that *with* us?"

"It *was* melted. It was just a hilt." Anwei's voice strung tight around her neck, each word choking. "I could still feel Willow inside him, and—"

"We need to get rid of it!"

"If melting it didn't get Willow out of him, then we have to figure out what will, Lia! We can't just leave it behind and hope it isn't a factor!" Anwei shoved the sword back into the trunk and locked it, wiping her hands down her tunic. "How could it have *grown back*? *When* did it grow back? Today? Is that why he woke up?"

Altahn burst through the tent flap, Noa a step behind him. Catching sight of Knox, Altahn slowed, hands full of papers he'd brought from the tent. Lia didn't miss the way his eyes stilled on the raised skin scarring Knox's side, the drop of blood now a runnel that pooled under him on the tent floor. "What happened?"

"He overextended himself, is all." Anwei picked the salve back up, her voice so calm Lia wouldn't have believed that only a moment ago she'd been panicking. She dipped two fingers into the oily salve and smeared it across the top of the scar, the blood sticky as if it was already solidifying into a scab. Noa's hand crept up to cover her mouth.

"You never told me how he was wounded." Altahn didn't come any closer, hovering just inside the tent flap.

"He'll be all right." Anwei wiped her oily fingers on a cloth from her bag, then closed the jar with sure hands.

"He *was* all right. I've never seen a wounded man act this way—is it . . . something unnatural? Did Tual do something—"

"Last I checked, shapeshifters don't suck your soul out through your stomach," Noa whispered. "Though I suppose I could be wrong."

Lia settled on Knox's other side, waiting for the healer to meet her eyes. When Anwei finally looked up, her expression was frighteningly easy. Like nothing at all had happened, and Knox was some patient with the sniffles, not a boy with a torn soul and a hole through his gut that shouldn't have healed.

Come to think of it, Anwei was all smiles *most* of the time. For a moment Lia caught herself wishing for gloves and her veil. Anwei was so different from her twin, who wore his thoughts and emotions like a fancy broach on his lapel.

"The fastest way down to Forge would be by river." Anwei stowed the salve in her bag and looked up at Altahn, continuing their conversation from the tent as if nothing was wrong. "If messengers travel by road, we could have a week before Tual gets word that we found the library records. I messed things up enough down in the stacks that it could be days before they realize the folio is gone. A boat would get us there in days."

"I can't take Vivi on a boat," Lia said quietly.

"Or my riders," Altahn interjected. "The horses, our wagons . . ."

"Lia, you'd move much more quickly than we could if you rode. You could even go cross-country."

"We can't leave my riders." Altahn's voice was firm.

"I wouldn't want Lia to go *alone*," Anwei purred. "A girl out in the forest on her own? Maybe she could take an escort of two or three riders?"

Lia's skin pebbled at her tone, the healer somehow frail and weak as she smiled bravely at Altahn. When he looked away, Anwei's expression morphed into something fierce. *"A little help?"* she mouthed at Lia.

"Yes, I would definitely love to let Vivi eat a few of your riders and their horses," Lia deadpanned.

Anwei's fists clenched for a second, but then she was inching sideways to make room for Noa, and Lia wondered if she'd imagined it. The dancer reached toward Knox as if she wanted to help, but stopped well short of touching him, her fingers clenching. Lia tried to see what was making her hesitate, but the high khonin only brushed her fingers across Falan's flower in her hair as if she were praying to the goddess. The same hair stick that had struck Ewan's neck, distracting him the split second Lia had needed to fight back.

Lia's breath hitched, and she forced her mind to focus wholly on Knox's chalky skin, willing the image to fade. Noa had guts—maybe more than any of them, facing down Ewan and Vivi together with nothing but a hair stick. Maybe there was something about Knox she could see the rest of them couldn't.

"If Tual Montanne doesn't know we're after him already—" Altahn was saying.

"He probably thinks he has more time before we find him," Anwei pointed out. "This is going to be our only chance to get close."

Forge. That was where Mateo had said he'd found the painting of the nameless god and Calsta together, but he'd neglected to mention that he'd grown up there.

"I . . . could follow." Lia's aurasight brushed over Gilesh, who was hovering just outside. "Horses will slow Vivi, but Anwei's right. One or two wouldn't be so bad if you feel like we need the numbers." She looked at Altahn, then Anwei, the agitation still present in the quickness of the healer's fingers. Lia let go of the clench in her stomach. Anwei had been keeping Knox alive all this time. Hiding him from the Warlord for a year. Knox trusted Anwei.

Anwei could take care of him, even if he was sick like Mateo. Or sick like something else.

So, she did what she knew Anwei wanted. "Even with extra riders, I'll probably beat you down there."

Noa grinned, nudging her with an elbow. "Boat versus auroshe? I'll take that bet."

"You'll have to bet with something I want, because Devoted don't take coin." Lia turned to Altahn. "I'm friends with Gilesh and Bane. Can they ride fast?"

Altahn's fingers were loose around the sheaf of papers he'd brought from the tent, but Lia suddenly noticed the muscles clenching in his shoulders. His eyes were hard, as if counting the people in the tent.

If he went with Anwei on the boat, he'd be outnumbered. Were things really so strained between them? Lia frowned, wondering how she'd missed it. Of course Altahn didn't want to leave behind his clan . . . but the entire Trib group being with them wouldn't be useful if the plan was to sneak in without Tual noticing. They couldn't go running through Forge with thirty Trib. Not unless they wanted to announce their presence with horns and fanfare.

Altahn bowed his head an inch, caving. "I suppose that makes sense, given the facts. I'll look into chartering a boat."

"I know someone with a boat near Rentara—an old friend who'll do it as a favor. He'll know to keep it quiet." Anwei smiled at Altahn's slow blink. "Benefits of working with a goddess."

To Altahn's credit, he only rolled his eyes a little. "So long as you're sure this is the best way to get to the sword. And to get rid of the monster." He turned to walk out, giving Knox one last worried look. "My father never meant to leave Trib land. The thought of him under all those rocks and trees . . ." The congenial expression he always wore flickered, something steely and determined peeking out between the gaps. "We couldn't even get to his body."

Anwei stood, touching his arm softly. "That sword can kill Tual. Shapeshifter blades are the only thing that can do it. We're going to find him and avenge your father."

Was that a hint of tears shining from her eyes? Lia blinked, wondering if she'd imagined it. But then Altahn seemed to soften, responding to whatever it was Anwei was doing. He covered Anwei's hand with his own. "Thank you. I hope Knox feels better once we're on the move." He gave her hand a cautious pat, then walked out.

Lia waited until he was gone to look up at Anwei. "He doesn't know it was you?"

Noa perked up. "What did Anwei do?"

Shooting an exasperated look at Lia, Anwei knelt back down to check Knox's pulse, then put an ear to his mouth to listen for breaths.

"Knox doesn't seem any worse than before. He should be stable enough to move. We'll need to watch him very closely."

Lia took hold of Knox from under the shoulders, helping drag his dead weight to his bedroll. She couldn't stop her mind from circling back to Altahn softening at Anwei's promise of vengeance. Because it had been *Anwei's* magic that had shaken the earth and collapsed the tunnel Altahn's father had been using to get into the tomb. She'd lost control down there—maybe she'd never had control in the first place—growing a whole forest with the violence of an attack as she tried to fix the hole Tual had made in Knox. As if all Anwei had been able to do in her panic was command Knox's ruptured humors to *grow*, and the spillover had torn the world apart.

"You can't just go *quiet*. Now it feels like there's a secret," Noa prodded when neither of them answered. "I like secrets! What did Anwei do? She gets away with everything."

"Not everything." Anwei smoothed the heavy down-filled blanket she'd procured for Knox. "Altahn originally hired me to steal Patenga's sword to take the blame for things missing from the dig. He and the dig director were going to use me as a scapegoat." Anwei smiled sweetly, and Lia wondered if Noa noticed that she hadn't answered her question. "We're on better terms now, is all."

"Are you? He keeps calling you 'Yaru' like you're going to start sprouting thief devotees who pray for silver rounds to multiply in their pockets." Noa giggled, turning to Lia. "But if you mean that Anwei's firing with a few more arrows than the rest of us, he definitely doesn't know."

Lia gave Knox's hollow cheeks one last worried look before going to pack up. "What do you mean?"

"You've got Calsta on your side. So does Knox. Anwei's got the nameless god." Noa shrugged when Anwei's head jerked up. "Wasn't that hard to figure out after you disappeared during the governor's ball when no one else could get out. There was a hole in the wall with ivy that wasn't there the day before growing through it. Then plants start growing out of the tomb, and somehow you're keeping Knox alive when he's obviously not supposed to be?" She took a quick breath, visibly steeling herself before gesturing to Knox, keeping her hands well away from him. Again, Lia wondered what it was she was so frightened of.

CHAPTER 7

Nicknames

Anwei stood at the railing of the *Plump Plum,* wind in her face and a lump in her throat. The sails were full, the shallow boat taking them downriver fast enough to have them in Kingsol in two days. The captain, Ellis Kent, was one of the most prolific smugglers of archipelago malt in the Commonwealth. The man himself stood there next to her, half a smile on his face, which was a quarter more than she'd seen him give anyone else. Unless he was about to slit someone's throat.

"You can be straight with me," he rasped. "I've been working with Yaru long enough to recognize the signs."

Anwei sighed. "I wouldn't dream to aspire."

"You *have* to be Yaru herself." He raised his hands. "I'm honored you chose my boat. Really, I am."

"I'm not." Anwei didn't know why she was bothering anymore. After what had happened in Chaol, Yaru was dead. She'd have to come up with another name, another front, another story. The boat rocked under her feet as she thought it, leaving her to wonder why she'd need a front once Tual was done for.

Unimpressed, Ellis leaned toward her conspiratorially. "Which name is *really* yours? We've been exchanging services for long enough that I think I deserve to know. Yaru? I think it was Moltoven a few years back. And before that it was Lily." When she didn't answer, he gave her another nudge. "You refuse to use my nickname, so it's only fair I get a real name."

"Your nickname is ridiculous."

"It does its job."

Anwei rolled her eyes. "I have some questions about Kingsol. Do you know anything about the tributaries that come off the Felac down there?"

"Why?" Ellis cocked his head, ready to glean anything he could. Just like any good contact would.

Anwei looked out over the water, choosing her words carefully. "That forest has always been a resource for healers—specimens of flora and fauna grow there that cannot be found anywhere else. Are the estates in the area friendly to Beildans?"

"What kind of *specimens* are you after?" Ellis's smile turned to a grin. "Rare plants of pure silver and gold?" But then his face turned serious. "I wouldn't try going out there if I were you. On this side of Kingsol, we hold our breath that whole length of the river, even inside the boat. I have heard of Beildans coming from the island to collect herbs, but only on the western side of Kingsol, down toward the Elantin port."

Anwei frowned, her heart beating a little faster. "Why?"

"The ground isn't stable anywhere else, I guess? There are underground waterways branching through the north and east clear to the Palashian coast. Rumors have it that some go deeper, farther. But it's dangerous out there—only snakes and spiders live in those trees. Kids dare each other to go exploring out on the tributaries. Enough of them don't come back that people whisper about curses."

Anwei shaded her eyes as she looked down the river, the words shivering through her. *Curses.* Underground *ways.* Like in the records she'd stolen from Castor's library?

Ellis gave her a companionable nudge. "I won't charge you for that piece of information, seeing how you're letting me talk to you direct and all, Yaru. It's my pleasure to share."

Anwei peeled a bit of paint off the rail and let it fall into the water. The shield she'd hidden under for so many years was so cracked that she didn't know why she was still holding it up. Anonymity had made working for the gangs in Chaol a little easier. It had stopped high khonin from following her back to Gulya's apothecary, using her services, then having her thrown in jail so they could take their money back. Mostly, though, hiding her identity had been to keep the snake-tooth man from knowing she was after him.

Not that it had mattered. Tual hadn't even recognized her. Had been mildly amused when he'd put together who she was, as if catching a little girl like her following him was adorable.

"I'm right then?" Ellis grinned again, little prickles going down Anwei's spine. "A *Beildan*? I never would have guessed. You know you're my favorite to work with, don't you? Years and years, and no one's done such a good job procuring the things that don't come so easy." He reached back to give the tiller a fond pat. It had been a while since Anwei had last heard from him, bringing her gossip and occasional supplies from the south in exchange for forged shipping manifests. Those hadn't been difficult to find, though the original vessel documents with his name on them had been her work as well. Long before she'd gotten to Chaol, she'd found them and the right harbormaster, allowing Ellis to sail from the harbor waving his hat days before the proper owner even noticed the ship was gone.

"You're putting me in danger just saying that," Anwei murmured. "What if one of your sailors hears and tells every lowlife in the Elantin port that he's found *the goddess*? Wardens will come after me. *Yaru* will come after me."

Ellis still grinned. "I have some information for the great goddess Yaru, but if you're not her—"

"I'm not. But I'll take a message if it's important."

"You've got greater access than the rest of us?"

"We're old friends is all."

"Sure." He winked. "There's salpowder up and down this whole river. Some fancy man up in Chaol got hold of some and gave it to anyone with coin to pay."

"Smugglers like you?" Anwei guessed. "You look happy enough. I'm wondering if any of the other boats got wind of the opportunity."

Ellis shrugged, lounging on the rail. "I'll admit, I've managed to expand my business a bit past smuggling in the last year with a little help from some redirected salpowder imports from the Trib up north. If Yaru's got more on her to-do list than harvesting leaves and spider legs for poison, I've got a fair bit of sway on these waters clear down to the southern archipelago." He leaned closer. "That boy you've got stashed in the cabin—I heard him asking for someone called 'Anwei.' Is that your real name?"

"I haven't tried to hide *my* name from you." Anwei's throat clenched. Knox was asking for her? She waved Ellis away with a smile that went no deeper than her lips. "I'll tell Yaru to send you a good dose of Chaol's plague if you don't stop it. Go bother Noa." She said it carefully—Ellis had a winning way about him, but she knew better than to tell him what to do on his own ship. His nickname wasn't *so* ridiculous based on stories she'd heard. "It might be good for everyone if you did, actually. If Noa gets bored, she might set something on fire."

"She's got enough eyes on her, I think." Ellis gestured toward the two sailors swabbing dirty mops across the deck below them, their chins tipped up toward the dancer where she sat in the crow's nest, her hair and skirts streaming behind her like a flag. "Stop looking up her skirt or I'll throw you all to the elsparn!" he shouted toward them, laughing when the boy closest jumped to attention, and the farther one looked around, slathered so thick with confusion, not even his own mother would have believed it.

Ellis switched back to squinting at Anwei. "You know she's the only one of you lot who's worth anything on deck. Not many high khonin know their way around a sail. Is she valuable?"

"Not particularly. She's a friend, and last I checked, you weren't the type to go back on a deal." Anwei held his gaze.

Ellis nodded in assent, but when he glanced back up at Noa, Anwei didn't care for the calculation in his eyes. According to Noa, her father didn't know she was gone, but based on Anwei's own contacts, he wouldn't be very happy once he did figure it out.

Altahn appeared in the stairwell that led to the hammocks below, his eyes finding Noa up in the sails. He looked away so violently that Anwei had to stop herself from laughing. The way Altahn had traded off between staring at Noa and trying not to stare since the first day he'd seen her was almost pitiable. Noa had jumped into the bay to stop Knox from being caught stealing salpowder. *Smuggled* salpowder.

Anwei tapped the railing in front of her, waiting for Ellis to give her his attention again. "How would salpowder give you more sway out here? You'd have to get onto another ship and light it on fire to burn anything. And it couldn't stop wardens from inspecting your cargo. Wouldn't they throw you in jail even if they found more than the diluted stuff performers use?"

"If only there were a way to shoot it like an arrow. Across the water and . . ." Ellis made a very unconvincing explosion noise, dramatically popping open his fists.

"If only." Anwei frowned. She'd made tiny salpowder packets that made frightening popping noises on impact for Noa and had timed a salpowder smoke bomb to scare people at the tomb excavation with Altahn, but that had been with very small quantities, and according to Altahn, it had been lucky they hadn't blown Gulya's shop halfway to Calsta's throne. The idea of *shooting* salpowder long distances to cause damage on impact seemed a bit far-fetched. "Can't imagine wardens would be happy to see such a thing."

"Oh, wardens don't like the idea at all." Ellis nodded. "But it's been hard to get Devoted out here to explore the situation, so mostly they try not to think about it—wave me on by like they're worried their imaginations will get sparked." He raised a finger, tapping it to his temple. "Merchants, though—most of them aren't afraid to really *envision* the damage such a thing could cause." He chuckled, pointing to the green circle of paint Anwei had noticed on the prow. "I've got my own little fleet these days shipping things up and down the river. Had to do quite a few favors shouldering extra business until things feel safer out here."

"That is very interesting. I'll have to—" Anwei's mind cracked, like a pick stabbing into a glass ball. She grabbed the rail, the world dipping sideways.

Knox was awake again.

"You all right?" Ellis cocked his head.

"Yes. Your business model does seem like something Yaru would be interested in." Anwei rubbed a hand across her forehead, trying to banish the crackle of broken glass and storm clouds swirling up from Knox's spot inside her. "You know she only corresponds in writing, so if there are any other details, write them down, and I'll get them to her."

He nodded, and she could feel his eyes on her back as she passed the sailors minding the sails. Sidling by Altahn, she lowered her voice so only he could hear. "Keep that firekey of yours out of sight."

Altahn froze, then leaned closer, not quite looking at her.

"He's using salpowder to control the trade on the Felac. Wouldn't want them to see Galerey and get ideas about producing their own." Anwei wasn't sure how Trib made salpowder. It was a secret the clans held close even when they weren't getting along with one another. But she didn't think Ellis would turn down the opportunity to find out more if a tame firekey lizard appeared on his deck. "Do you know anything about people using salpowder from far away? Like an arrow, Ellis said."

Altahn pulled away. "He said that?"

"We still have some salpowder from the smugglers in Chaol. I'm assuming you have some hidden in the trunk you brought as well?"

A slight nod from Altahn. Anwei hadn't assumed. She could smell its silver and charcoal bite wafting from Altahn whenever he walked by. "If you *do* know something about shooting off salpowder, it could come in handy once we get to Kingsol."

She left him looking contemplative, Galerey a quivering lump inside his sleeve. Down the stairs, past the warren of hammocks, some of the sailors snoring to the rhythm of the boat's slow roll, to the cabins at the back where Ellis had stuck Anwei and the others. Yaru's name had been enough for him to relocate three of his crew members to sleep on the deck. Knox's consciousness roiled inside her, his thoughts worried. At least he didn't smell of *nothing*.

He hadn't tried to find the pockmarked sword. Back in Chaol, Knox had looked for it without success, so she doubted he'd know where to look for it now, or even that they'd brought it with them. Willow didn't learn anything Knox himself didn't see or hear around him, based on what Anwei knew. She could feel the threads Willow had sewn through him, his soul grown to accommodate her in lumpy, diseased bits, like a tree trunk strangled with wire. She was still there, but not . . . here somehow. Like she'd decided to bother someone else for a while.

Anwei pushed through the door and found Knox standing with his face to the little window at the back of the cabin, the glass open to let the breeze ruffle his hair in its tie.

"You're awake again." Anwei's insides grated nastily against one another when he turned, his eyes blinking blearily as if he still wasn't used to light.

"I've been awake a few times. How long has it been this time?"

"Two days since you first woke up." Each time he'd woken since had been random moments of consciousness only lasting about five minutes.

"Where's Lia?"

"She's taking Vivi south on foot." She shut the door behind her, the feel of him inside her head swelling larger and larger even though he still wasn't quite looking at her.

It was close. Too close. Not close enough. She couldn't look at him without that moment in the tent flashing back through her, his lips pressed hard against hers, and the way she'd just . . .

Forgotten. Everything. And how she still wanted to.

⁂

Knox's space in her head seemed to flex, sparked with gold. He wasn't what Willow made him when she thirsted for blood, but he wasn't all the way himself, either. Calsta had made a cage around him.

Calsta, whispering which direction he should look, what he should say.

Maybe it had been Calsta who told him to wake up and kiss her.

Knox sat down on the bunk, stretching his legs out in front of him and arching his back, like a cat after a nap. She'd always liked that about him, that he was comfortable. He didn't sit up too straight, didn't say anything other than what he thought, and was quietly confident in his place at her side, as if he'd been born there. Not like her contacts, who needed constant petting and validation.

Knox just was. And now he was being quiet, waiting for her to speak.

"I need to look at your wound," she finally said. "It started bleeding again, and I haven't been able to see how it changes while you're awake."

"Sure." He lay back, every movement graceful and measured, his muscles constricting under his skin where the sleeveless tunic pulled against his movement.

Anwei moved to sit on the floor next to the bed, trying for a smile. The air felt so thick between them that she couldn't breathe. It didn't help the way he'd drawn tight inside her mind, like a bowstring waiting to release. "Can you imagine if I'd asked to look at a wound before all this?"

"You did ask. Every scratch, every time I stubbed my toe." He stretched his hands up to cushion his head so they'd be out of the way. Anwei stared at his tunic buttons, done up to his throat, but he didn't move.

Anwei pulled the medicine bag into her lap and undid the buckles, then fished inside for the salve she'd brewed. "A whole year of refusing so much as a cup of tea from me, and here we are." She pointed to his buttons. "And shy now too? I don't have enough fingers to count how many times you went parading through the apothecary half-naked."

He looked down, hesitating. Then began to undo them one by one. Anwei looked away, breathing in to get the measure of whether anything had changed, then immediately regretting it because it was worse. Much worse. Knox's smell was like a map of things they'd done over the last year. The things they'd stolen, the times he'd come to sit in her room and talk, the times Gulya had tried to poison his food while he was helping with chores. The time she'd pretended to kiss him in the governor's office, and Knox had almost jumped out a window to get away. Knox carrying her out of the excavation compound, his hands on her feet, tracing the line of her scars.

And two days before, when she'd come running into the camp worried that she'd find a ghost with a sword only to have him catch her up and spin her around as if nothing between them had ever gone wrong. He was himself. It had been his arms around her. His voice. *I don't know what the rules are anymore.*

But there *were* rules. *Calsta's* rules.

Breathing out fast, Anwei concentrated on the odd red and yellow thread that seemed to lace Knox together now, the same since the day Tual had stabbed him. Every time she tried to use her nose to match it to an herb or spice, a mineral or tincture as she did with all other wounds, it swelled up inside her head like an abscess, blocking everything out until it was all there was left of Knox. It wasn't any different now that he was awake, pulsing with a poisonous, dangerous heat.

When she looked back at him, Knox was pulling open the last button. He hunched up to look at the knot of scar tissue in his side, making his stomach flex.

Gods above, why is this so much easier when he's asleep? Anwei closed her eyes, trying to make herself think about Knox as a patient. A collection of skin, bones, muscles, and humors, the scar an ugly, raised arc of pale skin just under his ribs and the trail of dried blood from its center dried in crackled bits down his side. But then when she opened her eyes, he was watching her.

Their bond was probably telling him exactly how much of a lie her blank expression was.

Knox lay back again, rearranging his hands under his head and looking away as she pulled out the salve, jar cold between her fingers.

"You know," he said slowly. "This might be an awkward moment to bring it up, but back in the camp, I—"

"Yes. I was there." Anwei pressed her lips together.

He waited. And waited, something like hope, or excitement, or *nervousness* twisting her tighter than a spring. "I was going to say that I don't remember much of anything between Gulya handing me the sword and waking up in the tent two days ago. I mean, there were moments. Flashes of . . . things that happened when you were there and trying to help me. I know you saved me and that we . . ." He pulled a hand out from behind his head to circle a finger between them. "Changed because of it."

"When you're awake, I can see Calsta's energy around you. Around Lia, too. And . . ." Anwei looked down, a trickle of purple mist worming its way past her. "Right now I can see something around me, if I look really hard. But maybe it's only when you're paying attention. It happened in flashes a few times back in Chaol when we were . . ."

"Close?" Knox provided when she trailed off.

"That's probably accurate." When he'd almost died at the governor's mansion, when they'd joined together in the tomb to try to break open the burial chamber, the feel of him touching every inch of her though they hadn't been touching at all. And then after, in her room . . .

Face flooding with heat, Anwei jammed her thumbs into the jar's clamp, and it popped open so violently that it jumped from her hands and clattered to the floor. "Now it happens more often."

Knox's mouth quirked. "And sometimes I can smell things I couldn't before." He started to laugh. "Gods above, it only comes in fits, but I've never wanted to know less about the people around me. And I feel . . . crooked." Tipping his chin down again to look at the scar, Knox licked his lips. "Like I'm still in pieces, and sometimes they shift if I move too quickly."

"Well, you're not in pieces. You're healing just fine." Anwei grabbed the salve from the floor, wiping the rim where it had spilled. Dipping a finger into the jar, she pulled back the skin that had congealed on top. The scent of it twisted around her, reaching out to smooth the edge of sharp crimson issuing from Knox's impossible wound. It shouldn't have worked—none of it should have. Not their bond, not their magic knitting him into one piece, or the scents that had helped her cobble together medicine that soothed his wound that wouldn't quite heal. Anwei knew bodies and bones, humors and organs, and Knox's had been spilled all over the tomb floor. Yet here he was, his soul twisted together with hers. With Knox's magic inside her, Anwei could feel the impossibility of herself, the gods' hands reaching through her to change the world.

A god's touch left much larger scars than any sword or poison could.

"You know I'm not going to drink that, right?" Knox broke into her thoughts, laying a less than enthusiastic eye on the jar. "My faith in you only goes so far."

Anwei snorted. "It wasn't easy to put you back together, and I'm beginning to wonder if you're properly grateful."

Knox chuckled, eyes following her every move as she extracted a cloth from the bag and dipped it into the salve. Every bit of her sparking, she reached toward the wound.

He caught her hand. "Wait."

A thread of desperation wormed through her, wanting to be done with this. Knox flinched, looking down at her hand hovering over his torso. A bit of salve had dripped on him. "That stuff is really cold."

"Sorry about that." Anwei carefully extracted her hand and began to apply it to the twisted scar, only touching him with the cloth and trying to ignore the way his ribs moved at her touch.

He breathed in and looked up at the bunk above. "I'm really sorry about earlier."

Anwei paused, then smoothed the last of the salve across the wound. "About attacking me in the tomb? I don't think Willow was asking for permission."

"No, you and me in the tent." He shifted uncomfortably when she pulled away. "Are we going to talk about this? I'd be okay with *not* talking and just . . . moving on to whatever it is you want, Anwei. But I don't like . . . *this*." He circled a finger between them again. "Whatever it is. You're worried about something, and you ran away from me before, and I probably shouldn't have just kissed you, especially not after what Calsta said—"

"What Calsta said?" Anwei closed the jar with a snap, swearing when her fingertip got pinched in the clasp's wires. Wrenching it free, she tried to ignore the prickle of rage that had shadowed each of her steps since Tual had stabbed Knox. Now that he was awake, it had dulled into a sort of calm concentration. She knew what needed to change to make her world right, and she was going to do it. But that awful rage flared at the mention of the Sky Painter too, dribbling her messes all over unsuspecting humans as she always did. "Please share. What did your goddess have to say about me now?"

Knox's brow furrowed as if he knew mentioning Calsta had been a mistake. "She said you're afraid of me. If it's because of Willow . . . the sword is gone, isn't it? Willow's . . . trapped." Scrubbing a hand through his hair, Knox clenched his eyes shut for a second, hand pausing on his forehead. "It's like she's locked out because of you and Calsta. Lia told me a little about bonds the second time I woke up and you were . . . helping one of Altahn's riders with a toothache so you couldn't come see me. Anyway, I have a theory—"

"I'm not scared of you." Anwei shoved the salve into her bag and stood.

"You were." Knox sat up, shirt ballooning open, and a new bead of blood welled up through the salve. "When I kissed you. I could feel it. Like . . . at first you were there for it." He smiled, eyes crinkling at the corners. "And then you weren't."

Anwei's jaw clenched. "Please, tell me. Explain to me how I feel."

Eyes wide, Knox didn't speak, smart enough not to answer.

Pulling the bag's clasp tight, Anwei shook her head. "Sorry. I. . . . you said you have a theory about Willow? I'm worried about the way you keep blanking out. Lia said it's like what . . ." The rage, the awful loss of control after so many years of concentrated planning burned up her throat. "Like what happens to Mateo Montanne."

"Yes," Knox said slowly. "Calsta says Willow didn't know he was there before, so she just took from him by accident whenever I used Calsta's powers because I wasn't leaving enough energy for her to drain. Then, when we started getting closer, your bond with me began walling her off, so she started taking more and more from him—Lia said he started having terrible episodes after he got to Chaol. That was right when I. . . ."

"When you fell off the roof and our minds . . . joined." Anwei remembered that day, the first hint she'd had of the snake-tooth man in two years, and suddenly Knox was calling for help in her head. She'd turned away and ran to help him, leaving the clue behind.

Unease chilled her bones. That wasn't the only time Knox had drawn her away from her purpose.

Knox paused, looking up at her as if he'd felt it too. "What is it?"

She shook her head. "So Willow was taking power from Mateo by accident?"

Blinking, Knox stood, his shirt still hanging open and his feet bare. "Right. Willow started out begging for me to kill anyone. Basists especially. Every year she got more desperate, more unhinged, not like my sister, but like . . . something else. A ghost. Then I met you, and as we got closer, she fixated on you. She didn't want me to kill anyone; she wanted me to kill *you*."

Anwei's breath came out in a rush. She'd seen evidence enough of it not to be surprised. "And?"

"Calsta says Willow found Mateo and likes him better. I think Willow was always asking me to kill because she needed souls, *energy*. When she realized I couldn't take people's energy, she concentrated on Basists. Then when you and I formed an actual bond—"

"She wanted me," Anwei breathed. "Because if you killed *me* . . ."

"I'd turn into a shapeshifter." He pressed his lips together. "I'd be what she needed: someone who could drain other people's souls at will. And now she's found Mateo—"

"Who *can* drain souls. So she's with him." Anwei pinched a finger between her eyes, trying to think. "Like, the three of you only have enough soul for two." She didn't like that idea, the memory of Tual's voice ringing in her ears. *Knox was dead the moment he picked up the sword.* "So now she's stealing from *you* when *he* needs extra?"

"I guess?" Knox shrugged. "There are so many different things in my head, Anwei. Calsta, Willow. You. It's been that way for so long, maybe I'm just as latched on as Willow is, so when she leaves . . . the part of me that's awake does too. Now there's nothing left to hold me in my body except you." He shrugged again. "I know how my oaths work. I know how the Sky Painter does things—it's an exchange, almost. Or like qualifying for a job. Then she gives you the tools to do the job. Shapeshifters are the opposite, which is why they're so dangerous. They don't have to qualify; they don't have to give anything up. All they have to do is take."

"Which, right now, includes Willow and Mateo taking you?"

He shifted. "I guess? She can't do it all the way because of—"

"Me." Anwei said it too quickly, looking down. "And Calsta. Got it."

"I guess to find out more, we'd have to get hold of your brother."

Something inside Anwei twisted, sparking hot. "Mateo Montanne isn't my brother."

Knox cocked his head. "No?"

The anger bottled up inside Anwei pressed hard against her chest until the pressure began to crack, like steam tearing through any weakness it could find. "Knox, I have spent the last eight years of my life trying to find the man who killed my twin."

"But Tual didn't kill him. He—"

"*Eight years* of my life, Knox." She looked down at her hands because they'd started shaking, her heart beating like a drum call to battle. "Eight years of trying to avenge my brother's blood. Eight years of trying to *set the world right*. And do you know what Mateo Montanne was doing for those eight years?"

"I—"

"Mateo Montanne was sleeping in a comfortable bed. He was buying expensive clothes and eating his weight in cream and dried fruit. He learned calligraphy, sat in front of an easel and *painted*—"

"Anwei . . ." Knox took a step toward her; his voice was quiet.

"Eight years. We were best friends, two halves of the same *soul*, and he's never once even thought my name." There were tears in her eyes, and her throat was raw.

Knox's hands were on her shoulders, and Anwei couldn't help but look up at him, wanting the world to somehow change.

But the world didn't change. Not unless you made it.

"I understand why Lia wants to go after them." Knox's head dipped toward hers, his brown eyes wide. "Tual took her sister. And Altahn is obsessed with Patenga's sword." His brow creased. "But why are *you* following the shapeshifter? It's not for me, is it? Because I don't need vengeance. All I need is to get the last of Willow out of my head."

"No!" Anwei's voice rose, she couldn't help it, the things she'd kept in a stranglehold deep inside breaking free. "I *do* want to help you, Knox. I want to help *Willow* because it would help you. But I can't just . . . pretend the last eight years didn't happen. It's *gone*. I was so alone, just . . . wanting my family. Wanting *someone* to care about me—Tual was the one person who I thought *would*."

"You think Tual—"

"He took *everything* away from me." Her family. Her home. She'd had to learn how to *find* when she was supposed to be healing people in an apothecary with Arun. All of it was Tual's fault—Anwei wouldn't have broken the day Arun disappeared and destroyed her father's shop if not for Tual. She wouldn't have sailed into a storm in a leaky rowboat drenched in blood if not for Tual. She wouldn't have spent the last eight years looking sideways at every person she passed on the street, searching for a shapeshifter's scent if not for Tual. Then he'd tried to take Knox, and it was only *gods*—gods who seemed to prey on the desperate—that kept him alive. She could feel it now, Calsta reaching out through Knox to sink those long, monster claws into her mind to make their bond.

"I am going to take everything away from Tual Montanne that he took from me," Anwei said quietly. "He didn't just murder my brother. He murdered *me*." Knox's hands pressed into her arms, holding her up from the weight of everything that had been pressing on her since the moment she'd seen her brother in the tomb. "Arun was right there the whole time," she gasped. "He could have found me. He could have *looked*. He was half of who I was, and he didn't want me either, Knox. My whole life wasted on someone who didn't even think to say goodbye. He chose a *shapeshifter* instead."

It was too much. Anwei couldn't breathe because it was too big, too heavy: Arun had been her life. And the last eight years had been her last grasping moments to keep him there with her, in her heart, to prove that *she* had not forgotten.

But *he* had forgotten *her*. Just the way her family had forgotten so quickly that she was their daughter. Even the narmaidens infesting Patenga's tomb had known it, singing out her worst fears: *Please save me. I've done nothing wrong. They were* supposed *to love me . . .*

. . . but I wasn't enough. The last part was too hard even for a narmaiden to sing.

"Anwei, you're alive!" Knox was shaking too. "You are still breathing. You still have *choices*. What happened was wrong. Arun—Calsta's breath, Anwei, we don't even know what happened to him or why he didn't come looking for you. Lia says he doesn't remember being anything but *Mateo*."

"Tual made my whole town forget him, but he couldn't pry Arun out of *my* head. I remembered him when no one else could. Arun *knew*."

"Then stop looking for him. Stay with people who *do* love you. Noa would do anything for you." It was almost like shouting, Knox's arms tight around her. "*I* would do anything for you."

Everything inside her stopped, an eerie quiet that burned.

"This is why you're afraid." Knox's anguish for her came across their bond like a smear of salve on a wound that was far too deep to ever heal. "It's not Willow; it's *this*." He pulled back, looking her in the eyes, and gestured between them. "We're not going to leave you, Anwei. I am not going to leave you."

Anwei stiffened, bracing herself against the weight of such a blatant lie.

This was what had happened before. She'd allowed something new into her life. A partner. Then it had turned into something more: a friendship. Something that scared her a little because friendship meant trusting people. Relying on them. Leaning on someone who, one day, might decide not to be there anymore. Most of her relationships were like tools. Like Ellis—she needed information, and he had it. She needed a way to Kingsol, and he had one. When she needed a contact, she could pick it up just like any hammer or wheelbarrow, then put it down again until the next time. When tools broke or went missing, you got a new one.

Friendship was different. It was a comfortable chair that could hold you up when you were tired, catching you when you thought you were going to fall. Or sometimes *you* were the chair, taking turns as needed.

The problem was, if you went to sit and the chair wasn't there, or it *broke*, that left you on the ground, bruised and wondering how you got there. With Knox, she'd reasoned a few bruises might be worth the moments she'd been able to sit, held up by something other than her own two feet. If it broke, she'd stand up, brush herself off, and keep walking.

Until it hadn't been only that. It was just Knox in front of her. A person Anwei didn't want to disappear, to break, to go away. For the first time in eight years, Anwei had let herself take a step forward toward something *she* wanted—not a plan or a tool or a contact who could take her closer to the snake-tooth man's death. Knox and her together were something outside her bitter hunt, something sweet on her tongue when Anwei had forgotten she could taste.

But then Knox had said no, thank you.

Because of Calsta.

His goddess didn't—*couldn't*—approve of Knox being part of anything other than her godly designs. Which was when Anwei had realized that with Knox, their relationship wasn't a chair. It wasn't even a rope she could cling to. It was a cliff.

She'd stepped over the edge, and she was still falling.

Anwei drew in a thorny breath, willing herself not to be angry, but it was impossible. There was nothing but anger left inside her, everything burned away. "You know I love you, Knox."

He was very quiet for a moment, the air full of static, noise, of things unsaid. But then, when he finally spoke, she knew he understood. "Why do I get the feeling that means exactly the opposite of what I'm hoping for?"

"It means you can't promise me you won't leave." She pushed away from him, suddenly so, so tired. "And my soul's in too many pieces already to let you tear off more when you go."

"I'm not going to tear your soul like some shapeshifter."

Anwei backed away, then jolted in surprise when her back hit the door. "I can't share you with a goddess, Knox." If she were going to step off a cliff, she wanted to be falling *with* someone. But Calsta wouldn't allow Knox to fall.

Anwei had already jumped. But she couldn't let herself hit the ground. Not again.

"It's not sharing." Knox started laughing, a shocked sort of sound that left electricity blistering in the air between them. "The two of us are *fated*. A Basist and a Devoted forming the first bond in five hundred years. Right when a new shapeshifter rises?" He stepped forward, pausing when she put her hands up to stop him. "This is what *Calsta* wants. It just had to happen in the right order. Two gods-touched together is—"

"I am not interested in gods and their messes. I am not some hero people will write stories about. All I want is . . ."

"What?" He breathed when she didn't finish. "What do you *want*, Anwei?"

Anwei clenched her eyes shut. *To avenge* myself, she thought. *For Tual to suffer for destroying my life, then forgetting I existed. I want him to know who I am.*

And I want you, *Knox.*

Impossible things on an impossible list. But of all of them, Knox was the most impossible, standing there as if he didn't know it.

She fiddled with her medicine bag. "I don't want the nameless god's touch—I've spent my whole life trying to forget he's even there waiting for me to do something terrible again. I'm just a healer. A thief. I can't be what your goddess wants. And you will always choose her instead of me."

"It's not like that. I mean, not really." Knox swallowed, looking down. "I can't help who I am, Anwei. I can't help the commitments I made or where I came from before I met you. Calsta promised to help me find a way to help my sister go free, but she can only do that if I keep my oaths. You are a part of that promise."

"I am not the fulfillment of *any* god's promise," Anwei hissed.

"That's not what I mean. There's *room* in the oaths I've made for you. She led me to you, not because you're a *gift* for a faithful Devoted like me—that's disgusting. That's how Ewan treated Lia." Knox tipped forward, ducking his head to get her to look up at him, but Anwei could only stare down at his bare feet on the floor. "She led me to you because she thought we might fit. And we did. We're bonded because of *us*, Anwei. Not because of Calsta."

"For how long? The moment I don't suit Calsta's purposes, she'll send you off in another direction to fit with someone else, and I'll be—" *Alone again. Abandoned again. Forgotten. Again.*

"I'm not going anywhere." His voice went quieter. "What do you want from me? For me to say I'd break my oaths if you asked?"

"I don't want you to break your oaths. Your sister is still trapped, and the only way to fix it is for you to keep them—I would never ask you to . . . Gods above and below!" Anwei pulled her braids back from her face, twisting them up into a knot, feeling as if every inch of her was crawling. "You and me, we're . . . we're friends. We're business partners. We're two people who should have kept our lives separate—no history, no future, and no questions. No attachments. That was our agreement."

He shook his head. "The agreement evolved. I love you, Anwei."

Knox didn't even flinch as he said it, as if he'd been granted permission to use those words at long last. They burned in the air toward Anwei, glowing across the bond like a horrible invitation that she wanted to accept more than anything else in the world.

That was the problem.

Anwei's heart shivered in her chest, but there were too many other memories fluttering like torn paper inside her. Her parents, dead-eyed as they came for her, the magic inside her too strong for their love. Her twin, the other half of her *soul*, curled on the tomb floor looking like a man who'd grown up not needing her. And Knox in her room the night he'd almost kissed her, then turned away instead. *I have to keep my oath to love only Calsta,* he'd said. *And every day I'm with you, I break it.*

Knox stepped into Anwei, his hands pulling her close, sharing the warmth of him. His breath was on her neck, his hands soft on her back, and Anwei breathed him in, every inch of her wanting to lean into him and kiss him the way he'd kissed her, as if the world ended when they stopped. But Anwei's life was pinned so carefully that even one more torn edge would mean the end.

No god had ever hidden Anwei the way Calsta hid her Devoted. No god had ever fixed the world into a place that included her, only marked her as something inherently wrong.

She touched the scar above her collarbone, hidden for so many years. Gods asked for too much, then took even more. They were just like people—love went both ways. Unless it didn't. *Until* it didn't.

Knox had already shown her the path he meant to walk. And as much as Anwei wanted to walk a span with him, the idea of him walking on alone when his goddess asked was too much.

He belonged to Calsta, and goddesses *didn't* share.

Anwei forced herself to look at Knox, their faces so close she could only see parts: an eye, the curve of his cheek. His lips only inches from hers. Everything was wrong. But the words that came out were true, sharp as stars. "I am here. As myself. Not part of a divine plot, not a vigilante trying to rid the world of magic that could tear it apart, not a gods-touched. I'm just me, trying to turn my life into something that makes sense. Maybe someday . . . when we've sorted out Willow and you aren't . . ." She shook her head. "When *we're* enough, you and me, you let me know."

"You *are* all I want," he whispered.

"That's not true. It's not even what *I* want—no one should have to want only one thing. It's just that sometimes the things you want don't go together, and you have to choose."

She gently pulled away, opened the door, and walked out. She paused as soon as she crossed the threshold, stuck because she wanted him to come up with something that would allow them to fit—allow *her* to fit as she was.

But there *was* nothing. Not unless something changed.

Things will *change. You're on a path forward that will* make *the world change.* The thought pricked inside her like hope. But Knox just stared at her, tears like ash on his cheeks. *Can't there be room for both of you?*

But that sounded too much like a compromise that would break her at the hinges. Like the old Anwei she'd left bloody on Beilda's beaches. The one who waited too long when she saw the knife in her mother's hands because she didn't want to understand it.

So, Anwei turned toward the sun, leaving Knox there in the dark. But as she took her first step, the acid bubbling *black* of salpowder hit her nose.

"Anwei!" Knox grabbed hold of her, bracing against the wall, just in time for the boat to lurch sideways, the timbers shuddering with a bone-chilling *boom.*

CHAPTER 8

The Ones Who Don't Rely on Wishes

The sun was a blessing, as were the sound of wind in the sails, the rush of water, and the world open before Noa like a gift. She didn't want to come down from the low sail, a hidden platform just behind it as if the sailors on this ship needed to keep a clear view of the river without anyone getting a clear view of them. She stretched her bare toes and hummed the first few bars of her favorite song, a bawdy thing she'd skipped to through the streets singing at the top of her lungs with her dance troupe after performances, hoping her father would hear of it by morning.

The memory made Noa stop singing.

"This isn't your first time on a boat." The voice made Noa jump, and she looked down to find the captain, Ellis, just under her on the rigging. "None of Anwei's other friends know how to tie knots, hoist a sail, or operate a winch."

"Learning made my father angry." She grinned down at him. "So I did it as often as I could."

"A girl after my own heart."

"He has boats out here somewhere. Not as big as this one." She swept an eye appreciatively across the large vessel. It was not a pretty boat. Not even a *fast* boat. But sitting up at the top with a destination she'd chosen and no chance anyone would stop her felt like a whole new life.

Except for the shapeshifter. He might stop them. But Noa didn't mind that so much. Shapeshifters were crammed full of magic and death and teeth and claws, not silver rounds. "Maybe I'll end up on a boat like this, laughing at the world as it goes by."

"This boat doesn't care much what anyone thinks of it." Ellis squinted against the sun. "It seems a little like you, in that way." He pointed to the platform, some kind of metal tube on a strap hanging down his back. "Unfortunately, you'll have to go not care what people think deckside, because I need the platform."

"What for?" Noa slid over, grabbing hold of the crisscross of ropes around the short mast.

"Business." He climbed up and pulled the strap off his shoulder, setting up the tube on a sort of tripod. When she didn't climb down, Ellis propped a hand under his chin. "And you'd have to join up to the crew if you want more information than that."

"Are there open spots?" Noa asked. "I'll join up right now."

"Yaru won't appreciate me poaching her crew, and I prefer it when Yaru appreciates me." Shooing her with one hand, Ellis turned back to the tube, going up on his knees to peek up over the sail. "Now run along."

Noa ducked to peek through the gap between sails and caught sight of what had Ellis so excited. Downriver, a stocky little boat was headed in their direction. She stilled, staring at the familiar shape of it in the distance. "Falan's dice!" she hissed under her breath. Swinging backward off the beam, Noa tucked into a flip as she fell, landing on her feet.

"Fancy." Altahn was sitting at the prow. "Was that for my benefit, or do you always add in a little sparkle for anyone who might be watching you jump from fifteen feet below?"

"I can't help sparkling, Altahn." She pushed past him to the rail, squinting at the boat quickly approaching. It was a much smaller vessel than the one they were on, fitted for no more than five crew members at the most, the rest of the space jam-packed with crates. Noa's stomach twisted. Maybe her father *had* noticed that she'd gone.

"What's going on with the pirate?" Altahn's chin tipped up toward Ellis, the man's long hair in a simple braid down his back that didn't stop the bits round his face flying around his cheeks.

"Pirate?" Noa looked around frantically, wondering how in Calsta's name she could have missed such an interesting detail.

"The prow's painted green," Altahn provided, warily looking around as sailors ran up from the hammocks below to fit oars to the ship's low sides. "Pirates are the only ones who do that. Why are they so excited?"

"Be ready!" Ellis's voice rang down over them. "It's one of Russo's! Keep your knives at hand, lads!"

"Are we sailing into a *fight*?" Altahn scrubbed a hand across his face. "This is the last time I'm letting Anwei call in favors just to get us somewhere faster." He started for the passageway that led to the rooms. "Isn't Russo your—"

A terrible *boom* rocked the boat, a shower of ash and smoke blocking Ellis from view. Noa darted after Altahn as the sailors frantically ratcheted up sheets of metal that had been hinged to the rails. Noa saw it before she felt it: a crack of light bright as lightning. A split second later, the sound of it buzzed through her to the bone.

The whole boat lurched sideways, sailors cursing, Ellis yelling—

"What under Calsta's blue sky is going on?" Altahn roared, his placid smile finally forgotten.

"You're the one who said they were going to fight. What do you think this is?" Noa peeked out through the doorway, smoke billowing up into the air, but she couldn't tell from where.

"With your father?" Altahn ducked, stumbling to the ground and covering his head with his arms as the boat rocked again. "I guess I see now that if he wanted my sword, he would have been more direct. Seems like he's here to collect you, as well."

"Shut your mouth." Noa breathed in deep only for the smoke to come coughing back out.

Altahn slid over to her, patting her back. "Are you all right?"

Eyes watering, Noa started to laugh. "Are you really"—she coughed, gasping for air—"stupid enough to ask me that question right now?"

Anwei and Knox came running up the hallway, rushing past them without sparing them a glance. No more explosions or loud cracks tore through the air for a moment, and Noa hunched forward, hands to her chest as the last few coughs squeezed out of her. She put an arm over her nose to block out the awful smell of smoke.

"It won't help." Altahn covered his nose and mouth despite what he'd said. "This stuff smells like it came from the Belains. The oil cast to the smoke gets through everything. They charge extra for it."

"Another Trib clan?" Noa dragged him deeper into the corridor, jamming a shoulder into the locked cargo door. Altahn kicked it open and let her enter first, shutting the door once he was through. It was almost completely dark inside, the bare dribblings of light like lamps set to glimmer at the front of a stage.

At least the air tasted clean. Noa felt around until she found a low crate and sat on top of it, jumping when another muffled crack rang outside.

"I can't *believe* someone sold these twits a *salpowder carom*." Altahn's voice cut sharp, and Noa could hear him rustling around in agitation. "They're not supposed to leave Trib land. Calsta as my witness, heads are going to *roll* when I get back with Patenga's sword."

"A shapeshifter's sword is going to stop Ellis from shooting fire at people?" Noa braced herself against the crate, wondering when the next impact would come. "I think the narmaiden's already in the nursery, Altahn."

Altahn's footsteps thunked between crates, Noa's eyes beginning to pick out shapes in the darkness. "Maybe they just bought a single carom. No one in their right mind would sell the *plans*. . . ."

Noa stood, feeling her way after him. "Your father wouldn't be pleased with the snarl you've made of things, I guess?"

Altahn stopped. Turned. "What?"

"Haring off after a sword when it seems like the Trib clans are making trouble." Noa cocked her head. "I'm not trying to be *mean*. You're a what . . . a clan kinder-something. Doesn't that mean you're supposed to be in charge?"

He put a hand on the crate next to him, his knees bending with the roll of the ship as if he suddenly needed the support to stop himself from folding up. "Kynate."

"So fancy. *Sparkly*. Like me."

Shaking his head slowly, he started checking crates and looking under bags. "Maybe Anwei will know if he has any more of them; then I can take them all with us when we go. She'll . . . see the clues, or bend things together like she really is some kind of goddess. You know she did something to the salpowder back in Chaol that should have been impossible." Altahn threw a shadowy bundle from the stacks of goods onto the ground, then kicked it on his way to the next line of crates.

Noa slid between him and the row, her hands up. "Okay, first of all, if this guy really is a pirate, stop breaking his stuff. It's not like the shipping advisor this time. Ellis is *right here to notice* if you put a hole in the beautiful portrait he's just commissioned."

Altahn grunted. "You knew that was one of your father's boats. Is he looking for you? Are you leaving him clues or something? Is Anwei holding you hostage, and your way of crying out for help is continually referencing a naked shipping advisor I would prefer to forget?"

"I pray to Falan that my father isn't searching for me. I thought I had at least a month before he'd notice I was gone." Noa hopped onto a crate next to Altahn, eyeing the bag on the floor he'd kicked. It had made suspiciously shattery noises when it hit the ground. "But I'm beginning to wonder if leaving even matters. I was sitting up there in the wind thinking this was the last place he'd ever want me. And then wondering if I chose to come because of him. Is that really escaping, or is it just a different cage?"

Altahn didn't speak for a moment. Then slid onto the crate beside her. "My father wanted me to marry this girl."

Looking over, Noa wondered where Galerey had gotten to, Altahn's sleeves and collar unoccupied for the first time she'd ever seen. "Is she pretty, at least?"

"Who cares? I've always done everything he asked, even when it meant staying in every evening to read the codes instead of racing horses with my friends. Waking up with the sun every morning to properly reverence the Blue Lady, though we never actually *did* anything other than yawn a bit and shiver. Or leading riders on salpowder runs when every single one of them had been hunting firekey warrens since before I was born. Telling me to find some nice flowers for a bridal wreath before I'd even met the girl who was supposed to wear them was too much."

Noa hated the feeling bubbling up inside her: jealousy. Altahn's father had been training him to lead their clan. Every time she'd tried to look at travel routes or supply lists, her father swatted her away. She'd been one of the goods listed on his shipping manifests, not worth his notice beyond finding the right man to buy her. He didn't even care if she *liked* men.

She did. But he'd never thought to ask.

"I'm supposed to be on a trip choosing textiles for my wedding with my father's most recent . . ." She waved her hand indeterminately.

Mostly because there weren't clear words, only that her father's latest companion was sure, as they all were, that she was going to be the one that stuck. A sad naivete that Noa had long since learned to ignore because it didn't do to attach herself to her father's women—her own mother had lasted longer than most, by all reports. She hadn't been sent back to Elantia until Noa was three. "The woman was so excited that I entrusted the whole affair to her superior taste that she didn't realize leaving without me and not telling anyone was a bad idea."

"You're engaged?" Altahn looked up, realization dawning on his face. "The first time I saw you, you were with the governor's son."

"That's the one." Noa pressed her lips together. "Not the highest bidder, but the one with the best silver round to political power ratio. Father's been waiting *years* to cash in on his investment in raising a daughter. He got a respectable bride price for me, but the real prize was a connection to the man controlling the docks across the bay from Lasei." She turned a little, leaning toward Altahn. "Can you imagine the money he'll make selling under the table? He thinks if he wishes hard enough, the borders will stay closed forever except for the one little tunnel he's dug to Lasei."

"Men like your father don't rely on wishes."

Noa nodded because it was true. "What about you? Did your father need some extra . . . what do Trib pay for bride price? Cows?"

"Fathers pay dowry to ensure their daughters are taken care of among the clans. And yes. In *cows*. Because that's all we care about."

She rolled her eyes. "I was only—"

"I know." Altahn sighed, pressing back the long fringe of hair hanging down his cheek. "Everything was set though, cows included, before anyone thought to tell me about it."

"So technically you're engaged too? Wreaths and everything?"

"Technically. But I . . . . couldn't do it. Father said he understood, and I thought he meant that maybe I could have a say in that at least, but then he told me to take a few riders south, have a few laughs, and then be ready to do my duty when I got back." He took a deep breath. "So I went south. Heard about Tual looking for tombs. And . . . got obsessed. We knew where Patenga would have dug his tomb, and the legends about the sword put it with him inside. I stayed in the south for weeks, sent people to go looking for the tomb, greased the right palms. When they found the opening, I went home."

"Distraction tactics. I like it."

"No, the sword is important. It wasn't just a distraction. It was . . ." Altahn scrubbed his hands down his face. "It *has* to be important. My father knew it was or he wouldn't have let me convince him to go after it."

"So you're going to face down a shapeshifter to get it back?" Noa chuckled, nudging his shoulder. "I'll write a story about you for my troupe to perform when I get back to Chaol." A twinge of sadness rippled through her at the thought of them. She missed them. But she didn't miss them enough to want to go back. "The bridegroom who would rather fight monsters than wear flowers in his hair. Maybe she's beautiful. Maybe she's smart. Maybe—"

His head dipped. "It doesn't matter what she is, because now that my father is gone, it's worse. While he was here, I wanted to please him. Now, it's like the things he wanted matter *more*. Like I *have* to be the son he wanted now. I *have* to go find that girl and set a wreath on her head. I *have* to find this sword, because if I don't . . ." He trailed off, his voice nothing more than a ghost.

"If you don't, what will happen, Altahn?"

Altahn's chin tipped toward her, his eyes finding hers in the dark. "It was my fault he was in the tunnel."

"Guilt makes you more obedient than love?" Noa flinched at the words herself, almost wishing she hadn't said them. She turned away from him, her smile falling away. "I never was obedient. When

I realized being disobedient wouldn't force my father to see me as a person, I knew I had to get away. Yet somehow he's still in charge now. Everything still revolves around him. The things I think, the songs I sing, what I say, what I like, what I wear. Like all I've ever been was a thorn in his finger that he couldn't wait to pull out, but now that I've pulled myself out, all I am is a thorn. Not connected to anything."

Altahn looked down at her skirts, threaded through with gold and silver. "You're nice-looking for a thorn."

She laughed. It was quiet outside now, so whatever had happened was done, and none of her father's sailors were hammering on the door looking for her, which was a promising sign. "The question I'm trying to ask myself is what do I want. It sounds so easy, but it isn't." She glanced at him. "Unless you're already happy with what you've got. A bunch of cows?"

"Cows aren't so bad. At least I want to believe it. Why else would my father have worked so hard to get them?" Altahn's heels kicked against the crate. After a moment he slid off and bent to inspect the crate's label before moving to the next. "But I really do want the sword. Patenga stole it from us, and ever since, our clan hasn't had a single gods-touched. We've been unlucky, the mountains capped with snow, the firekeys hiding from us."

Gods-touched among Trib? Noa perked up at the thought, ideas about stories featuring the vast network of lies to hide their young from Devoted. There would be fighting, and dancing, and her fire tethers roaring to life . . .

"The idea always was to retrieve the sword in order to bring Calsta's favor back to us. My whole family for generations has spent at least one month every year giving up things they've seen Devoted refuse—the things Calsta requires, even if the Warlord won't share what the oaths are. Sugar, onions, spices—"

"So you *are* a Prin. . . ." The voice startled Noa even as it fumbled over the word. She turned to find a shadow approaching from the hold door. Her skin prickled at the way the darkness twisted around the form, too large to be a man. She slid off the crate, her heart beating faster.

Knox's mouth twisted in thought as he stepped closer, oblivious to her discomfort. He turned to look at Anwei, who'd followed him in. "Prina? That's not right. Priath? No, *pritha*."

"Did you just call me a pineapple?" Altahn's brow furrowed. "In my own language?"

Anwei's mouth curved into an unwilling smile as she grabbed hold of Noa's hand. "He means *priantia*. A holy one. Trib who sacrifice everything in the hopes that Calsta will notice them and touch them with her power."

"I know what *priantia* means." Altahn didn't follow as Anwei dragged Noa toward the door.

"Ellis is breathing fire, and he's on his way down here." Anwei's grip on Noa's hand was almost as tight as her voice as she led her between crates. "What in Calsta's name are you two doing breaking in here? That was literally his *one* condition, that we stay out of the hold." Noa craned her neck to keep one eye on Knox and his host of shadows, the idea of him lurking behind her as welcome as a spider crawling into her mouth.

"Altahn!" Anwei hissed. "Come, *now*."

"I have to find out if he has any other caroms down here. That other ship had one too. If Ellis is *selling* them—"

"Those salpowder tubes? The other ship didn't have one. I'm not exactly sure what happened, but—" Anwei let out an exasperated breath and gave Noa a push through the door. "Get out of here." She turned back to the darkness. "Knox? Hurry up. I have to fix the damage they did to the door and stop Altahn from stealing pirate booty."

"I can't let him keep them," Altahn hissed back. "Caroms belong to Trib and Trib alone, and the Commonwealth having them will change . . ." He looked up at Anwei, as if suddenly wondering how may words he'd said out loud and which ones would fetch the highest price.

"I can help you search." Anwei's whisper was hoarse. "I'll even help you get them out of here, but we can't take them until we're about to step off this boat."

"Is this the part of some new contract between us? You help me find the caroms, and suddenly I owe you extra salpowder?"

"Call it a kind deed, Altahn. Just get out of there!"

Altahn blinked, then nodded slowly. "Thank you."

"Come on." Knox swept into the hall, sending Noa scuttling toward the deck. He strode past her, moving faster at the sound of Ellis's voice grumbling down from above.

"What did the other ship do?" Noa forced herself to grab hold of Knox's sleeve. "It was one of my father's. They didn't try to board? Didn't know *I* was here, right?"

"You think he'd try to come after you?" Knox's brow furrowed. "Does Anwei know that?"

Noa shrugged. Ellis's voice was growing louder.

Knox shrugged. "Best tell her. Ellis shot something toward the other boat—I guess he has some kind of monopoly on river trade. But the other boat shot off some kind of warning. By the time I got up there, they were charging us, like they meant to ram our boat head-on. Ellis ordered the sailors to back off the second he saw Russo's house mark. We passed peaceably after that, so if your father is after you, he didn't know you were here."

"So, something's different about my father's boats. Ellis knows not to go after them." Noa's thoughts began to spark. Her father had stumbled across something to stop pirates like Ellis from blowing holes in his hull. Something to do with salpowder? Noa took an unwilling step toward the deck, the idea too interesting to stop the way it danced in her mind.

Knox paused, turning back toward her. "Please do not go spouting off about Russo's boats. If a man like Ellis finds out he has Russo's own daughter on board, it's not going to go well for us." He squinted at her. "You're all right, though?"

The words didn't enter Noa's mind at first, circling her twice before she understood what he was asking. A belanvian. A moody one. Concerned about her? ". . .Yes?" she said slowly.

"Not feeling sad about leaving your fancy bed and weird singing friends?"

Not concern, then. Noa grinned, stepping up to him and poking him directly in the chest, shuddering when the shadows around him billowed a little closer as if they were alive and wanted a good look at her. "You don't like me."

Knox's shrug came a beat too slow. "I almost died the last time you didn't come through. When we were at the governor's house, your distraction started too late, I got poisoned, and you didn't show up to get us out of the compound safely. Anwei and I both almost died." He waved her off as footsteps started toward them from the deck. "I guess I'm just waiting for the next time you forget that the rest of us aren't dressed in costumes, dancing around to entertain you."

CHAPTER 9

Other Things That Might Kill You

Mateo awoke to morning light and a terrible sheen of sweat. His dreams had been full of shapeshifter bones. Human phalanges ending in long claws, a skull with a protruding muzzle attached to a human neck and spine, human ribs next to swollen humerus, radius, and ulna, with femurs thick as clubs, as if Patenga's heart had been the only thing unchanged.

And magic. In the air, in his mouth, in his chest, in his mind. Mateo breathed in, the fullness of it intoxicating even as a memory, a dream. He'd been a fully fledged gods-touched, a force to be reckoned with down in the tomb that day when he drew in Lia's energy.

You liked that taste of her. Well, she's coming. She'll be here soon.

Mateo sat up fast, pushing his covers off with an angry swipe. *Normal* people—even gods-touched—were alone in their own heads. But he couldn't stop the tug of that power. The feeling of being *more*.

Think of what you want, Tual had said, *and then take it.* So different from what the gods asked for—all their rules and oaths and sacrifices. He could be more, enough to offset the sad, depleted existence Mateo had endured for most of his life.

Just take what you want.

Only now it was Willow's voice that said it, made of ice and rotting leaves. Mateo swung his feet over the edge of his bed, stomach churning. Morning light streamed through the window, turning the lake a beautiful turquoise, bubbles rising from the depths just near the white-pebbled beach. He went to his closet to choose the perfect tunic, jacket, and boots for a day spent avoiding a little girl. Salmon and cream, red and cream . . . perhaps a strong sage and cream with his paisley embroidered scarf? He went to the mirror by the window for the best light as he held the scarf up against his chosen tunic, only to catch sight of something moving on the beach below—a little girl walking toward the water . . .

A jolt of fear stabbed through Mateo's stomach. Did Aria not know to stay out of the water?

"Aria!" he yelled through the glass, fingers scrabbling to get it open.

Still she walked down to the white-pebbled shore, the contrast of blue water turning her copper hair to flame. He stumbled back from the window and ran, rushing through the keep, out across the courtyard, and down toward the lake. Mateo found her sitting on a rock with her little feet stuck out into the deep water because there were no shallows here.

"Aria, get out of there!" he shouted, and now his voice was far too loud. Aria startled, her eyes wide. She scuttled back from the water's edge just as something very large drifted up in a cloud of bubbles, a mass of segmented scales churning the water into a rush that lapped clear up to the paving stones.

Mateo bent over, breathing hard after his run, Aria goggling at the place where the scaly back had been only moments before. Willow boiled up inside him, excited and horrified all at once for some reason until the snake sank back down out of sight. *Ooooohhhhh,* she whispered.

Aria was too frightened for Mateo to wonder why a ghost would care about an ancient snake. "What in Calsta's name was *that?*" the little girl yelled, mortification flooding her face when the last bit came out in a squeak.

"It's . . . it's a she." Mateo cleared his throat, marveling at the fact that he'd run. That he could breathe at all. "Abendiza." Another shiver from Willow at the name set his teeth on edge. "Our snake. Well, not really ours. She's been here longer than father, even. The house is named for her. Didn't you see the carvings in the entryway? She ate my cat when I was little. I took the poor thing into town with me, and it was batting at elsparn and—"

"I saw the carvings, not a warning sign to *stay out of the water*." Aria's skirts were wet to the knee. "Your father said I could go anywhere I wanted. Only that it wasn't safe to leave the island."

Mateo tried very hard not to imagine his father thinking this through, watching Aria until she went to the inviting warmth of the water and saving her just before she was dragged to the bottom as a way of proving he was trustworthy. He twisted to look up at the windows overlooking the lake, half expecting Tual to be watching from inside.

Of course he wasn't there. Winning Aria over was the job his father had delegated to Mateo. That way, when Lia appeared with her sword, Aria would tell her to spare him.

But Mateo couldn't do it. From the first time he'd seen her sweaty in the closed carriage, holding tight to her insults and threats so she wouldn't cry, he couldn't—

"Glad you got here in time?" Aria's fists connected with his side, giving him a violent push that sent Mateo skittering sideways. "Give yourself a pat on the back and a treat."

"I apologize." Mateo gathered himself up, dodging backward when she started toward him again. "I assumed someone would warn you."

"Like maybe *you* should have? Since it was your job to show me around? And you didn't?" Aria glowered, advancing on him.

"You didn't *want* me to show you around." Mateo stopped retreating and glowered back, hands on his hips. "Remember?"

"Well, then leave me alone!" she spat at him. Then lowered her voice, looking sideways at the waves still washing up onto the little beach. "Unless there are more things that could eat me. Tell me about those and *then* leave me alone."

Something in Mateo melted even more at that hard exterior, squaring off against him because he was the easiest one to fight. He didn't like to think of how he would have fared at her age being taken from his home and—

Mateo frowned. That was exactly what *had* happened to him. He tried to tuck the thought out of sight, but it wouldn't go.

He liked Aria. They'd spent a whole afternoon throwing flour at each other with her sister back in Chaol, and Aria had taught him a new curse—probably one she'd made up, but she'd come up with a good story to go with it. His father had said that he liked the whole family, brash threats, clenched fists, and all.

Mateo thought of Lia and how he'd liked the same things. And how he didn't want to use Aria, didn't want to participate in what his father had done . . .

And how he had to anyway. So Mateo found a smile for her that made his teeth clench. "There is maybe *one* other thing that might kill you, I suppose," he said slowly.

Aria blanched, but her expression remained determined.

"But maybe not." He shrugged. "It's pretty interesting. Do you want to see?"

"No." Aria's brow puckered. "Maybe. What is it?"

"I'll tell you when we get there. First, let's go by the kitchen."

"For sweets and bread and picnic things?" Aria turned her glare on the house. "You can't make me like you by feeding me sweet rolls, Mateo. I'm old enough that it doesn't work."

"Who says the food is for you?" Mateo started climbing toward the back end of the house where the kitchen let out, both gratified and terrified by the patter of bare feet on paving stones behind him. "I haven't had breakfast yet."

It doesn't have to be for the plan. The thought felt flimsy even unspoken in his head. Willow began to laugh her spiked, torture-garden cackles, but Mateo didn't listen. He put a finger to his lips at the kitchen door, cracked it open, then gestured for little Aria Seystone to follow him into the danger zone.

By the time they emerged from the other side of the house, the knots tying up Mateo's insides had loosened a little. They'd done well—he'd ended up with one of Hilaria's sweet fig and apple rolls in one hand and a mug of camillia tea in the other (Aria had elected to forgo the tea to allow for a sweet roll in each hand).

Across the courtyard, a wagon was peeking out from just behind the stables, a tarp tied tight over the top of it. Mateo frowned. Wasn't that the same wagon his father had guarded so fiercely on the trip down? The one with Patenga's sword hidden in the bed. But the sword was in the antiquities room, so why was the wagon still out?

He swerved toward it, Aria skipping after him as she licked frosting from the top of her sweet rolls. Mateo peeked over the edge of the wagon where one corner of the tarp had been pulled up.

For some reason, Mateo's heart began to race. He glanced at Aria, suddenly unsure he wanted to know what was underneath the tarp, and doubly unsure he wanted to expose Aria to whatever it was. But then he shook the thought away. Ridiculous.

He set his tea down on the driver's bench and pulled the tarp back a little farther. The wagon bed was empty. Stained with some kind of white powder along with a few greasy-looking marks at the far end that looked uncomfortably human shaped. But that was all.

Breathing in a little too shakily, Mateo dropped the tarp and reclaimed his tea.

"You're angry smiling." Aria took a very large bite of her sweet roll, her mouth full enough that bits of it stuck out between her lips.

"I thought I was normal smiling." Mateo took a sip of tea and started toward the other end of the island.

"You look extra angry when you pretend to smile, like you're mad about whatever you're mad about *and* mad about having to smile." Aria skipped to catch up, licking the side of her sweet roll where the fig filling threatened to drip out. "What do *you* have to be so mad about?"

"I'm not mad. I'm scared you think I don't know about the knife you snuck out of the kitchen."

"I didn't take—" Aria twisted to look back toward the open door through which Mateo could still see Hilaria happily terrorizing the staff. She must have missed them an awful lot—she'd hardly noticed the two of them stealing pastries from her cooling tray. "Calsta's *teeth*, I should have thought of that."

"Well, there's always next time."

"Lia's probably most of the way here, so it doesn't matter." Aria took another bite, filling dribbling down her chin as she tried to talk with her mouth full. "I don't want her to save me, exactly, but I wouldn't mind having help getting out when it's time to go. Master Montanne isn't so scary, and you . . ." She rolled her eyes as if she didn't have to say out loud why Lia wouldn't find him much of an obstacle. She lowered her voice. "But the monster that followed us here was kind of scary. Is that what you meant about something else here that could kill me?"

"The monster that . . . followed us?" Mateo's arms prickled when she looked toward the bridge, her eyes wide. Had someone told her about the bodies on the road, or had she actually seen something?

"I really liked the auroshes I met back in Chaol. I let one out of its cage once, you know," Aria said importantly, turning her back on the waving leaves and branches, the far shore dark with shadows. "All of them liked me—I could see it in their eyes, almost like they were smiling through all those teeth. The one I let out didn't look at me twice, went straight for the meat I brought to bribe it out so I could distract everyone and get Lia away from that awful man. . . ."

Mateo bit his lip hard, not sure he could stop himself from interrupting with questions if pain wasn't involved. *Save Lia? From . . . Ewan?* Had Aria been there the day he attacked her? Lia's reaction to seeing the Devoted had always confused him since she had no trouble roughing up anyone else who looked at her crosswise, but he couldn't pretend to understand. Aria being there would have only made it worse. He tamped down the pity threatening to unfold inside him. *Monster. I need to know about the monster.*

". . . .But the one out there?" Aria shivered. "I'd wake up in the middle of the night and see it watching me through the carriage window. See it out in the trees as we passed, all bloody down its front, its horns torn off. And since we've been here I found . . ." She gulped. "A dead rat in my *bed*. Like it's warning me I'm next or something. It *wants* me for some reason. To make Aria cakes? Maybe Aria sweet rolls?"

"Aria soup, perhaps? I think auroshes tend to have a more savory palate." Mateo took another sip of tea, ignoring Aria's incredulous scowl as he breathed in the flowery scent. *Camillia. For anxiety and stress.* But he breathed out, letting the thought go with it. A ghost from the life he didn't remember as a Beildan healer. "A mangy auroshe, eh? You're the only one who managed to get a look at it. Father was worried it was your sister. Or the Warlord herself."

"If it had been Lia, both of you would be in pieces." Aria pointed at him. "But you knew about the monster? No one said anything. I had a nightmare about it biting right through the carriage window to get me. And when I woke up, there was blood dried along the bottom of the glass." She looked down at her hands. "It watched you too, you know. Probably would have eaten you up quick if not for your dad protecting you. It could probably smell easy prey clear from Chaol."

"It followed us from Chaol?" Mateo turned toward the watchtower, trying to leave the shivers behind him.

He knew which auroshe was stalking them.

The image of her blossomed in his mind, pink-tinged hide, matted hair. Lia's hand pressed between the creature's broken horns even as it bared its long, jagged teeth. *This will keep her from hunting you*, she had said. *She'll be safe here. We'll call her Rosie.*

The auroshe Lia had fought with her bare hands. The one they'd ridden out from the kennels like heroes, or maybe like the next big trend at the underground fighting ring. Person versus auroshe. At the time, Lia touching his hand and helping him bond with the auroshe had felt as if it was supposed to mean something. The two of them standing on the beach with scrapes from the battle and a stolen beast shared between them.

Now it felt like a much bloodier promise, because the thing had hunted him clear across the country. It was bonded to Lia, too—was that why it was interested in Aria?

Had Lia sent it? Could auroshes understand intent? Directions? Orders?

Mateo cursed himself for not paying attention enough to know. All Lia's talk about auroshes had been simpering over that foul mount of hers—*Vivi*, her voice rounding into a croon every time she said it, as if he were a kitten instead of a monster. They'd saved Rosie—*Rosie* was the name Lia came up with, of all things—from the fights by accident, but if anyone knew how to use an auroshe bond to do something like retrieve a kidnapped family member from a shapeshifter, it would be Lia Seystone.

"Mateo?" Aria's voice was cautious. "Is there a reason you're just standing here in front of these old doors?" She narrowed her eyes, looking up at the watchtower with obvious disappointment. "You're going to try to convince me that this is the other thing that could hurt me, aren't you? That the roof will fall in on my head or something."

Clearing his throat, Mateo pushed through the doors, the heavy stone sliding smoothly open as if they'd been hung and oiled the day before. "Ruins can be *very* dangerous."

"Calsta's teeth, you are the worst." Aria rolled her eyes, though the quiet awe that followed when she stepped in after him was gratifying enough. She tipped up her chin to gape at the ceiling five stories up, beams of light shooting down from the impossible windows above. The walls were cut through with balconies, each level housing the servants, hostlers, and guards who worked in the keep, with a mosaic that spanned the hall from top to bottom depicting a vine with fruits of all kinds blossoming at different levels and little mosaic people picking them and eating them.

Mateo did his best not to stare the way Aria was, though it was difficult. The tower was one of his favorite places, an ode to what he was supposed to be. What people like him had been, what they'd done, impossible to obscure or destroy, though Devoted had tried back during the first Warlord's time. It had always made him feel strong, as if eventually the world would have to acknowledge and accept Basists without prejudice. Energy rushing through his humors lit up the walls like rubies, diamonds, and emeralds, his magic touching each of the materials that had been shaped together to make this place into the beautiful haven it was. They'd been artists, just as he was.

But then his mind snagged on a trace of pain near the high, high ceiling. A spot in the mural too high to see clearly, but the feel of it jarred a breath from his lungs. This place had been lovingly formed, coaxed, shaped. But that one spot had been hacked away, with a new *wrong* stone jammed into the wound.

Just like he'd sensed in Patenga's tomb. The touch of a shapeshifter.

It hadn't been Devoted who had washed these floors with Basist blood. It had been a shapeshifter. One that had left her mark even on the building, apparently. His magic had been too weak to notice anything amiss until now.

Mateo turned from the light, from the bright colors, from the beauty and promise of it, his hands clenching around his teacup His long artist fingers, somehow still there after his family had cut them off, were just as *wrong* as whatever had been done up at the top of the tower.

"So, is this all?" Aria gave Mateo a push with her sticky hand, taking a bite from her second sweet roll and noisily chewing. "I don't see anything dangerous."

"You prefer auroshes watching you in the dark?" he sniped back, trying to wipe away the sticky spot she'd left on his sleeve.

Aria's expression darkened. "You think I'm making it up? Well, let me tell you, Mateo Montanne, I hope the auroshe comes in here and tears up all your pretty clothes right where you can see before it bites your head off. If it doesn't, I *am* going to get a knife from the kitchen, and I *am* going to wait in your room until it's dark, and then—"

"Don't mind us." Mateo nodded to the two maids descending the staircase, herding Aria away from their curious stares. The little girl's voice was echoing clear to the top floor. "She's . . . just a little excited."

"I am *not* excited, and you are *the worst*," she yelled, yanking her arm away from him, the maids startling and walking a little faster to get past them to the entrance.

"You're probably right about that." He put his hands up when Aria began to steam. "I do believe you about the auroshe. It's definitely a monster, definitely followed us, and definitely won't come over the bridge. That's why Abendiza is there. The snake? She keeps us safe. My father too, of course." He hoped.

"How could your father keep me safe from *himself*?" Aria shot back, resisting when he tried to lead her toward the underside of the stairs, the actual thing he'd brought her to see. "He's the only reason I'm in this position at all. Giant snakes. Wild auroshes who want to slurp up my insides. A stupid archeologist with fewer muscles than I've got in my little toe . . . !"

"Accurate. And I'm so sorry for the inconvenience, but if you'll just come over here—"

"So you can show me more mosaics?" Aria's voice echoed as she dodged away from him. From under the stairwell, a depiction of Abendiza stood taller than both of them, a newer addition made with tools, but still old enough that it had to have been done by one of the first high khonin families that moved in after the shapeshifter had been dealt with. It seemed impossible that Abendiza could be so old, but Mateo had never been able to think of another explanation.

"Lia said you were really fascinated by old paintings and stuff, but *normal* people aren't interested in boring stuff like that, Mateo," Aria called from across the open space, twirling in the light. "You promised me something that might *eat me*."

"You shouldn't trust people who kidnap you to keep promises." Mateo went to the stairs on his own, making a show of waiting for a guard descending from above to exit the hall before ducking into the hidden gap between the snake's jaws.

"Wait—Mateo?"

"Shhh!" He stuck his head back out, lowering his voice to a raspy whisper, which echoed even worse than speaking in full voice. "Do you want *everyone* to know about my secret door?"

Aria followed him into the hidden alcove, her eyes widening when he pressed the latch secreted between two stones. A section of wall swung inward to reveal a dark passage, crystals embedded into the ceiling giving off a soft glow for light. "Where does it go?" she asked, but then wrinkled her nose. "I guess I can't believe anything you say."

"How about we compromise, and I don't tell you." Mateo set down his teacup, wolfed down the sweet roll, then stepped into the cold light. The tunnel went down, the air cooling on Mateo's skin as he followed the narrow switchbacks. The crystals were set haphazardly in the ceiling, some of them dark or broken so the pattern they'd made originally was long lost. Mateo could still feel them singing with Basist magic. He licked the frosting off his fingers as he walked, trailing his other hand along the wall to touch the lines that had been chiseled after the Basists had been destroyed. Mostly simple pictures, each with a name carved beneath it.

This was the keep's mausoleum.

Many of the dead here were victims of the ridiculous "curse" on the keep. At least one death in the families who lived here every generation. Each family had fled, one after another when the supposed curse became too dear. He supposed it was easier to blame misfortune on the long-dead Basists who built the keep than to deal with the fact that people died and there was no logic to it or anything you could do about it.

Mateo couldn't help but scoff as he passed carving after carving, as if "unexplainable" deaths across the whole Commonwealth hadn't surged after all the Basist healers were killed. Basist books, Basist records, Basist schools, Basist art all burned to ash, then scattered to the wind. It had left a world used to magical healing scrambling to learn how bodies and illnesses worked.

When he passed a carving of a man who resembled a slightly drunken parchwolf, Mateo stopped looking, not wanting to read the names of all these people who had died hating those like him for no reason. But curse or no, the keep had claimed at least one soul every generation until the year the house had burned to the ground, killing the entire last family who lived here, along with their household.

No one had died since Mateo had lived there. That was the difference between reality and ignorance.

"Are these *graves?*" Aria whispered, shrinking back from the remembrances, though he didn't miss the thread of eagerness in her voice. "There are so many of them. Probably from whatever it is you're leading me to, right? You send people you don't like down here and the monster eats them? I bet that was your nursemaid." She aimed a kick at a column inscribed with *Sebastian Multoi Bolera* and a date about three hundred years after the last shapeshifter had been killed. "And this one was probably your cook after she made you something with no sugar," she said as she ran a hand along the next, *Isabella Gravis Bolera*, with a date about twenty years later.

Aria didn't seem to mind his silence as they continued on, keeping quiet herself until the path leveled out, stately columns carved halfway out of the rock framing the passage. Mateo could feel her thinking. Probably about stabbing things with kitchen knives or coming up with a story exciting enough to go with a secret door and a secret tunnel—

"Did Tual tell you why?" Her voice cut through his thoughts as the little glowing crystals ran out, the expanse beyond stabbed through with beams of light that only made the darkness between them and it all the darker. "The day he took me, I was teasing one of the auroshes the Warlord had quartered in our stables with a bit of steak. Suddenly Tual grabbed me around the middle and dragged me to that dratted carriage. The auroshe got the steak," she added solemnly, as if losing it was the worst travesty of that day.

Mateo stepped into the darkness. Usually, even when he thought he knew his father's plans, new details floated up like bodies long drowned in the river. "I don't know why my father does anything."

This time it wasn't true.

"He said my family wasn't safe. But he took me, not Father. Not Lia. Not Mother. Mother was too sick to go anywhere anyway. You saw her." The wobble in Aria's voice stabbed at Mateo's stomach, and he took another step into the darkness.

"Remember?" Aria's voice rustled like dead leaves. "It was a few days after we built forts in the kitchen, and you and Lia laughed and laughed. And you had honey in your hair and almost didn't care that I ruined your white coat with blueberry jam? You came running in, and you were all sick, and Father and Lia were there—"

Mateo remembered. He'd found Lia sitting by her mother's sickbed, tears in her eyes. He'd dragged her away because the Warlord was coming, minutes from discovering Lia hiding in her parents' house. It had almost felt heroic, riding to her house with a fit coming on, even if Lia had to hold him up the whole way back to the cliff house.

Now he knew he'd only exchanged one bloody ending for Lia for a different one.

"If you hadn't taken Lia away before the Warlord came, she would have been able to protect us." Aria's words clipped off. "And then you lost her somehow and took me instead."

Mateo pressed his hands to his eyes, the darkness around him complete. Why hadn't Mateo brought them *all* to the cliff manor that night? He'd known Lia's father was in trouble with the Warlord, that Lia's mother was ill. That Aria had nowhere to hide.

But he hadn't done it.

Then Aria had appeared in a carriage in their company headed south with no explanation and the smell of ash on Tual's hands.

He didn't have to know details in order to *know*. But Mateo didn't *want* to know.

He made for the light ahead, walking faster when the floor smoothed into glass. This was what he'd wanted to show Aria—an impossible transparent tunnel deep beneath the lake that connected the island to the cliffs. Beams of sunlight filtered in from the lake's surface above, touching the underwater rocks and roots, trailing vines, and little flickers of movement where fish darted past the thick glass. The ancient construction was like energy around him—*power* left behind by what felt like the gods themselves.

"Why did he do it?" Aria asked again.

"I don't know," Mateo rasped. "But I hope your sister murdering my father and me will be a proper recompense." The snarky response twisted out of his mouth before he could stop it, leaving his stomach churning. Though Mateo had spent much of his life hating Devoted for what they'd done to Basists like him, at that moment, he couldn't blame Lia for coming after Tual.

After *him*.

Mateo hadn't known that Tual's plan was for him to fall in love with Lia, then kill her. All he'd known was that Lia was funny and strong and interesting and worth talking to. She listened. She argued back. She was beautiful. She was *terrifying*.

And now, so was he.

Mateo reached for the light, and it struck him too bright, turning his arms and hands a ghostly white against the shadow he cast deep into the lake below. Little green glows crowded just below him, bioluminescent creatures hiding from the sun.

Aria followed him out onto the walkway, her feet tapping against the glass faster and faster until she was running, bowling past him until she reached the next beam of sunlight. It was wavery and blue, settling around her like an aura. It suited her; Aria didn't belong in darkness. The little green glows followed her, one thumping into the glass beneath her feet. "So where's the thing that's going to eat me?" she asked. "What ate everything else back in those graves?"

"Those things could do it." He nodded toward the glow of bioluminescence wriggling beneath her. "Elsparn. They're worse than Abendiza."

Aria flinched when another of the things tapped on the glass beneath her feet. "Can they see me?"

"Something like that. They're just not smart enough to figure out why they can't bite your toes off through the glass—"

Aria gasped, tripping out of the light when something whooshed past the glass, spiraling past Mateo only to dive back down into the darkness below. Too large to believe. Too quick to see clearly.

In the creature's wake, the little green lights had gone, and now Willow was doing something in the back of Mateo's mind. Foaming? Writhing?

"Was that . . . ?" Aria's hand was clamped over her mouth.

Mateo pushed Willow's weird fizzing in his head aside. "Abendiza, yes."

Aria shivered, hands pressing to the glass as she peered. "And the eels?"

"I think Abendiza eats them. They aren't really eels; they're . . . something." It tickled the back of Mateo's mind as he said it, as if once he'd known more than to avoid elsparn. Something to do with the smell of salt, slippery skin, and dried—

He cleared his throat and closed his mind. Whoever he was before— the boy who knew what to do with fishy, flesh-eating eel-things—he was that boy no longer. "They're in all the water channels in this area." Mateo gestured for Aria to follow him toward the far end of the walkway, where it connected to the cliffs. "There are plenty of things that could kill you up in the cliff passages, but the first chambers past the tunnel are safe enough. There are some fossils poking out from the wall like the Basists built the whole passageway just to show them off—they're eel-ish things like the ones in the water, but much bigger. Want to see?"

Aria was standing with her arms outstretched, looking up toward the lake's wavering surface. "You brought me down here to see *eel bones*?"

"Very scary carnivorous eels." He thought for a moment. "You could probably steal their fangs and use them to stab my eyes out or something, if that makes you feel better."

She spun around once, watching her shadow dance below her, looking for all the world like a butterfly of coppery red and green about to be pinned into a glass shadowbox. "Why are the passages in the cliffs dangerous?"

Mateo blinked away the image of the little girl stuck under glass. "They're full of old Basist traps. It's kind of a labyrinth with tunnels connecting down deep in the lake, some going out to the water channels in the forest, and all these underground rivers . . . it would be easy to get lost and drown. We know how to control a few of the channels, like the one we came here on and the one that takes us into town. The rest . . . Father says there are enough waterways to link this whole forest together—some huge system that Basists built long before the shapeshifter wars." He kept walking, rubbing a hand through his hair, then cursing himself because he'd taken the trouble to comb it into something nice, and now it probably was sticking out in all directions. "Other things that can hurt you, let me see . . . I mean, Father's office is probably one to stay away from. He's always brewing *something*, and half the time it's something that could eat the flesh right off your bones. Then there's the antiquities room—stuff we've dug up over the years. Father's got all sorts of protections up to keep people from letting too much light in or accidentally bumping into the artifacts. It's our life's work." He swallowed, the image of Patenga's sword so casually laid out on a table shuddering through him.

"Abendiza doesn't have enough eels to keep her fed in here. How does she eat?" Aria demanded, her breath fogging the glass.

I'm so hungry, Willow whispered.

Mateo rolled his eyes at the ghost, continuing toward the entrance to the cliffs. "Sometimes Abendiza disappears for a few days, so she knows the waterways better than we do, I guess. She can feed herself."

"Wait, Mateo—" Aria's feet tapped against the glass behind him, and

Mateo could feel Willow focus on the energy pulsing through Aria—*not a lot of energy, but it is there, and the little girl isn't really* using *it. . . .*

Mateo frowned, walking faster. Something was wrong. The tunnel was closing in around him. He needed to get out. "Keep up, if you're not too scared," he called over his shoulder, trying to sound nonchalant. "I was never allowed in the cliffs when I was young, so of course I came all the time—"

But then suddenly Willow was expanding in his head, the smell of death and ash, of endings and energy crackling in his nose. Mateo wobbled, her claws like ice around his mind, tightening as he struggled to push her away. *Willow!* he yelled inside his head. *What in Calsta's name is wrong with you?!*

"Mateo?" Aria's voice rang in his ears, a white light erupting over the girl's head while the rest of Mateo's world faded to black. An aura? But he couldn't see normal people's auras.

I'm so hungry, *Mateo,* Willow crooned.

It all happened so fast.

Willow took in a great, shuddering breath—

Mateo's vision exploded into white, a rush of energy bursting inside him, sending him staggering into the glass wall.

And then just as suddenly, the energy was gone. Mateo fell to his knees.

When his vision cleared, his eyes found Aria on the ground, crumpled like a discarded scarf. Her curls made a slash of bright red across the green glass, her eyes rolled back to show only white.

With a contented sigh, Willow relaxed her grip on Mateo. She pulled back to lick her chops after a good meal. *Thank you,* she whispered. *I couldn't do that with Knox.*

"I'm not—what is—I would *never*—" Mateo stumbled forward, falling to his knees next to the little girl. "Aria?" She didn't move, her skin tinged green by the watery light. "Aria Seystone, if this is a trick, I'll . . . !"

She didn't spring up at him with a knife or try to throw an arm around his throat to choke him to death. Aria Seystone had turned to nothing.

Mateo scooped up her limp body and started running. "Father!" he shouted, long before Tual would ever have been able to hear him. "Father, *help*!"

CHAPTER 10

A City of Waiting

It wasn't until Anwei caught sight of Kingsol's wide docks that she headed for Ellis's hold. Taking Altahn's salpowder tubes wouldn't be hard. It was getting away without Ellis noticing that would cause problems, but they had a plan. Altahn looked up from his trunk as she stuck her head in the cabin, Galerey pouting up at Anwei from her little swaddle of scarves inside.

"Just a little longer, all right?" Altahn murmured. "If the pirates see you, they'll try to cut you open." She gave a little annoyed chitter of sparks that set one of the scarves burning. Altahn swore, batting it out with his bare palm. He carefully closed the lid and looked up at Anwei. "Ready?"

Noa closed her trunk and started for the door. "Any tips on keeping Ellis's attention while I'm asking him for a job?"

"Lay it on thick—say something about being the last of six children and there being no money to back up those khonin knots of yours and"—Anwei shrugged—"needing to prove yourself, or something?"

"Crying or no crying?" Noa twisted her hair up into a bun and stabbed it through with her hair stick, ignoring Knox's perturbed expression from where he was sitting on the bunk. "You know him best."

"He's more susceptible to ambition than pity."

Noa gave a very inappropriate salute and sashayed out the door.

"You're a terrible influence, Anwei," Altahn grumbled.

"On Noa?" Anwei shot him a grin. "I didn't do any of that."

"Ellis is on the move." Knox slid off the bed, smoother than water. Anwei did not look at him as he picked up Noa's trunk, but she could feel him in the room. Feel how close he was and how the way he avoided looking at her wasn't quite natural. She let him and Altahn leave before she went to kneel before the narrow hold door. She waited to hear Noa's husky voice and Ellis's deep laugh coming from the deck before pulling out her lock picks.

Carefully inserting the two picks into the keyhole, Anwei probed until the mechanism clicked, then pulled the door open, frowning at the bowed latch and the splintered frame from Altahn kicking it in. Ellis probably wouldn't notice the damage unless he helped unload. He wouldn't notice he was missing anything until the cargo was all accounted for up on the deck. Hopefully. Anwei ghosted between stacked crates shrouded in oilcloth, past the rank supply of salpowder bolted to the ship's wooden floor, to where she and Altahn had found the heavy metal carom Ellis had shoved between bins.

Grabbing hold of the strap, Anwei swore, laboring to pull it over her shoulder. It weighed as much as a silenbakh and was twice as ungainly, turning her walk into more of a lurch as she headed back toward the door. *This is necessary*, she told herself as the door came into sight, somehow still too far away. *Dragging it out isn't a waste of time that I will regret. I need Altahn. Altahn needs this stupid tube.* Altahn wanted both stupid tubes, but the other one was stashed in Ellis's cabin. Lifting the one in the hold was trouble enough; she wasn't going to risk more than she already was, no matter how much it made Altahn's eye twitch.

Compromise. A word neither she nor Altahn cared for.

When she peeked out of the hold, Knox was down the hall holding their cabin's door ajar, blocking anyone looking down from the deck. Anwei grimaced the whole walk to the cabin, the carom strap cutting into her shoulder. Knox slipped in after her and helped her lift it into Altahn's trunk, Galerey sparking angrily at having to move aside to make room.

Anwei pulled the lid shut, trying to control the spike of concern when she noticed her own trunk was already missing from the room with Knox's cursed sword inside it. Knox must have carried it up while she was lugging the carom out.

So far as she knew, Knox hadn't even asked after it. Maybe he was finally safe from the awful thing.

And she could use it to do some good. All she needed to kill Tual Montanne was a shapeshifter sword. With Knox's safe in her trunk, she didn't need to worry about finding Patenga's sword before Tual found her.

"Get everything off the boat as fast as you can," she murmured to Knox as he picked up Altahn's trunk. He didn't even groan. The carom by itself probably weighed more than her, and the trunk wasn't even pulling his arms straight. "I have to meet my contact in Kingsol, but I'll hire the porter to take our things to the Sower's Path. That's where *Ellis* expects us to be. Oh, and keep an eye out for anyone following—"

"I know, Anwei."

"Then when you get to the Sower's Path, I'll need you to hire a different porter to take our things to the other inn. The Rigors. Ellis shouldn't be able to track us there if we lie low."

"We already talked through all of this." He paused in the doorway, and she tried not to be annoyed when he switched to holding the trunk under one arm. "We're okay, right? You and me?"

"Of course." She picked at her sleeves, making the mistake of breathing in deep to check that no one was coming. The air was a mouthful of yellow-green saltwater and seagrass's glassy blue.

Salt and seagrass smelled like *home.*

Knox looked down, making Anwei feel itchy and uncalm, as if now every time there was silence, they'd have to revisit her decision to be partners instead of whatever it was Calsta was lobbying for these days. But when he finally looked at her again, all he said was, "You've been here in Kingsol before, haven't you? That's why you're upset."

The question stuck in Anwei's gullet as she tried to swallow it down. "No, I haven't been here, exactly." She took the scarf wrapped around her neck and tied it over her braids with a jaunty knot that stuck out over her ear, then checked that the button at her collar was fastened and that her sleeves were covering her wrists.

"This is the closest port to Beilda."

"Yes." She walked out of the room. Knox followed her to the deck, carefully sliding Altahn's trunk to the pile of luggage they'd brought.

"Kingsol. The city of waiting." Ellis appeared with a melodramatic opening of arms, taking in the little city perched over the ocean. The docks had moorings enough for hundreds of boats, but Anwei could have counted the sails there on her hands and feet, which seemed odd. Not even one Beildan ferry decorated with blue swirls of paint was in sight, when the whole port should have been thick with them.

Kingsol squatted on the rolling hills past the docks, stocky and chinked into gaps in the stone, the whole of it braced for one of Calsta's storms. After so many years of Chaol's sky bridges between cays and towering halls, Kingsol felt too bright, too exposed, as if everyone in the city could see Anwei standing there.

"The city of waiting?" Knox asked. "What are people waiting for?"

"For passage to Beilda. Not so much anymore, of course." Ellis continued before Anwei could ask—no, she didn't *want* to know where all the ferries were. "Waiting to get all their nose growths ungrown, their bloody coughs scoured clean, and breech babies birthed. Just like I'll be waiting to hear from you, Anwei." Ellis grinned. "You and Yaru. I know how far your contacts go. I know the things you could make, if you wanted, the things we could sell. Just *think* what we could do."

Anwei forced a grin that hung tired on her face. "Sometimes all it takes is a new perspective. I'm sure Yaru will be excited by the prospect." She cast a look toward Noa, who was haughtily retwisting her hair into a bun, pointedly not looking in Ellis's direction. Anwei hadn't really expected Ellis to hire Noa—it would have been inconvenient if Ellis had—but the way she stabbed her hairstick into her bun made Anwei wonder if Ellis had said something to make Noa envision stabbing *him*. If he'd realized who she was—

"I assumed you aren't done with her, so I wasn't going to poach," Ellis said, following Anwei's gaze toward Noa. "When you are, let me know. She'd be an interesting addition to my crew." He winked and strode to the prow, shouting orders to the rowers as the boat rolled toward the dock.

Altahn was supposed to . . . Anwei's breath caught at the empty space next to Noa. The Trib wasn't in position.

Clearing her throat, Anwei casually turned to search the deck for the hard edge of silver that followed Altahn wherever he went only to have Knox brush her arm, jerking his head back toward Ellis's cabin. A note of panic sang through Anwei's humors as she turned away from the cabin door, sailors pulling the mooring lines taut. Altahn *couldn't* be idiot enough to—

Knox darted forward, lurching into Noa as if it were an accident. The high khonin gave a louder-than-warranted squawk, drawing attention when she turned to take a swipe at his shoulder, actual rancor in her eyes. "Grow some sea legs, you oaf!"

Just as Noa shouted, Altahn slipped out from Ellis's cabin, a box in his arms. He looked around as if he were being stealthy coming out of the *captain's cabin* in *broad daylight*, then hefted the thing onto their pile of trunks. The three of them had planned it. Without her.

"What in *Calsta's name*—" Anwei hissed.

"We're going to have to run fast," he whispered back.

"Gods and *monsters*, Altahn—"

Knox ducked away from Noa, who was still trying to swat at him, and picked up the box. He headed across the plank Ellis's sailors were steadying against the dock as if he wasn't carrying Ellis's prize weapon. Anwei grabbed hold of her own trunk's handle, and Altahn took the other side, the two of them moving fast to get all their belongings off the boat.

She hurried to the porters massed farther down the dock, and Noa flitted through the bustle after her like a butterfly, too colorful and fluttery to do much other than follow. Flipping a split copper to one of the porters, Anwei described Knox and the number of trunks, then hurried toward the stone archway that served as the entrance to the city.

She reached up to touch her braids through the scarf covering them. There would be other Beildans here. People from home. The thought stuck like a tick, sucking away at her.

"We need to go faster." Noa's words came in a breathless wheeze. The dancer linked an arm through Anwei's and gave her a sharp pull.

Anwei bristled. "Did Ellis—"

"No. *Faster*, Anwei. Away from the docks."

Anwei skipped a step to keep pace with Noa as they pressed through the crowd to pass under the arch. The wet ocean breeze picked at her scarf, whipping it across her face. The last time she'd seen these waters, they'd roiled and lashed, bulging and breaking across her bleeding shoulders, the sky a terrible scowl.

Was that you? she thought toward the empty heavens, wondering if Calsta only listened to Knox, or if she grasped at any human thought that bubbled up in her direction. *The lightning and thunder, the waves and the water in the bottom of my boat—it all should have killed me. Did I live just because you were saving me for your golden boy?*

Calsta did not answer.

I'm safe now. The thought growled out from the depths of her mind. *It doesn't matter what happened before or what any god wanted. I found Knox myself. I found Noa. I'll find Tual, too, and then all of this will be over.*

"Calsta's teeth!" Noa's face was pale, all the fun bled dry. She pulled Anwei past the canal that led directly into the markets past the docks, small enough that only skiffs and rowboats could pass. "Which way to your contact?"

"His name's Paran. I don't know exactly. I have to ask—" Noa jerked Anwei into an alleyway ripe with the cloying, potato-skin brown scent of rotting vegetables. Anwei extracted her arm and looked around. Had Noa seen something she'd missed? She felt frantically across the bond for Knox after days of trying to pull back—maybe Ellis had already found the carom gone? Reaching for Knox felt like slipping on a warm glove. Knox's flicker at the back of her head grew brighter, softer, as if he'd felt her reach and was tentatively reaching back.

He was fine. Not agitated or even *sweating* so far as she could tell. So it couldn't be Ellis that had Noa panicking. "Would you please tell me what is going on? You were fine five minutes ago."

"Knox said you'd know your way around here!" Noa sent a flustered look toward the market.

"I tried to come here once from Beilda, back when I was young. I lived just across the strait in a town called Belash Point." Anwei let Noa pull her into the crowd, past stalls of fish and shrimp, memories of her trip across the water sharp. "But my boat got caught in a storm. It blew me clear to the Elantin port."

"Which is why you speak like a goddess instead of a commoner," Noa replied in Elantin. "So we're lost, Ellis is going to kill Altahn and then kidnap me, and that's only if Knox doesn't kill me first. None of which matters because one of my father's boats is docked *right next to the porters.*"

Frowning, Anwei felt across the bond again, cringing back when, this time, Knox came flooding toward her like a question. She calmed herself, not wanting him to decide she was in trouble and come running. "Why is Knox on your list?"

"He doesn't think I'm trustworthy."

Anwei nodded slowly. That much she knew. "I'm happy to report that Knox doesn't kill people, so you don't need to worry." *Not anymore.* He'd never *wanted* to kill people so far as she could tell, but that didn't matter much when the Warlord had forced Devoted to hunt and kill Basists for five hundred years. It had only been working with Anwei that made Knox realize that Calsta and the Warlord didn't necessarily see eye to eye on what Devotion was for.

"Knox has shadows all around him, Anwei. Like a *belanvian*. It's not as bad as when we were in Chaol, but . . ." Noa closed her eyes.

"Shadows?" Anwei asked when Noa didn't continue. "His oaths make it so he can hide sometimes. Does Falan let you see past Devoted defenses?"

"No, it's not like that. It's . . . *shadows*, like some of him isn't *here*, and if we get too close, he'll drag us to wherever the rest of him went."

Anwei went cold. That was how Knox had described Willow— like she was gnawing on him, that some of him was *gone*. She took Noa's arm again, pulling her up to a palifruit stand to ask where to find Paran's street. With clear directions, Anwei found a path out of the market, lowering her voice so only Noa would hear over the babble of sellers calling about their wares. "Knox is not going to drag us anywhere. Now, what's this trouble with your father's boat?"

Noa's shoulders fell. "His sailors know me."

Anwei circled a hand, impatient. "And?"

"And they'll know I'm not supposed to be here and take me back to Chaol. I've been trying to go home to Elantia—to my mother, my old nursemaid, my friends from school—for years, Anwei. If they see me, they'll *know*." She dragged a hand down her cheek. "Knox said I should tell you that my father might come after me, but it didn't seem important at the time, so—"

"Right." Anwei kept the curse pressed behind her lips. They had to find her contact quickly. Get away from Ellis. And make sure Tual hadn't put the word out to look for them in Kingsol. She needed to know everything she could get from her contact about Tual, the estate, and where Mateo Montanne liked to go when he was in town, and then they needed to find someplace safe to make their plans.

"It's going to be all right. We don't have to go near the docks, and sailors aren't going to be staying in town. They won't see you." Anwei gave Noa a reassuring smile, though the extra complication stung. It would be fine. She would make it fine. Outside the market, Anwei walked faster, Noa skipping to keep up. She couldn't help the ugly starts of recognition at the familiar shapes of the buildings, the wood covered in moss and stone scored by ocean storms. Bright colors swabbed across anything that could be painted.

It looked just like home.

Which made her wonder: How could Arun live here, a place so very like where they grew up, and *not remember*?

CHAPTER 11

Only the Best Face Cream

oa's lungs didn't start working again until Anwei stopped in front of an apothecary.

How was she supposed to hide? Standing out was what Noa *did*. It wasn't on purpose. It was like some kind of inborn, personal magic. She couldn't turn it off at will.

Is this what your touch does, Falan? she asked when Anwei didn't go in immediately, eyeing the blue swirls painted on the door with suspicion. Scholars said that lower gods couldn't truly bestow powers the way Calsta and the nameless god could. But Noa didn't need some kind of magic to come bursting out of her to prove that Falan loved her just as much as stuffy old Calsta loved her bloody-fingered Devoted.

Ready to be out of sight, Noa pulled open the door. "Come on," she hissed, pulling her friend into the dark, low-ceilinged shop. Inside, mismatched jars of bones, dead snakes, and spiders glared at them, the dark clutter almost as menacing as Anwei's expression. Every surface was crowded with treasure. If you treasured fish eyeballs and dead caterpillars, anyway. Which Noa did.

The shelves jutted out at odd angles so the shop felt like a maze.

Flowers and dead leaves hung from the ceiling, and the air was muddy with spice.

Noa instantly liked the place.

The air almost seemed to hum around Anwei as she leaned back against the shop door, unwilling to go any farther, as if some of the things peering at them weren't all the way dead. "Something is not right in here." Anwei's nostrils flared. "The whole place stinks of aukincy."

"Should I expect all your contacts to be apothecarists with something not quite right about them?" Noa whispered.

"This isn't an apothecary." Anwei slid past her, a finger running along the bobbing host of distorted, bulbous animals stuffed inside their jars with no room to move. "Hello?" she called toward the back of the shop.

Noa followed quietly, excitedly looking over the shelves with this new bit of information. Tual Montanne was supposed to be an aukincer. The Warlord's very own, to be exact. But he was the real thing—an actual *shapeshifter*, not a poor imitation mixing poisons and herbs and hoping they'd come together to make magic without a god to help them change. Could the shop belong to him?

Most high khonin didn't mess around owning shops and such, but Noa could easily imagine a shapeshifter keeping a place like this, if only to occasionally pop out from behind the shelves to steal an unsuspecting customer's eyeball.

Something rustled at the back of the store. Anwei crept toward the sound, and Noa tiptoed close behind, excitement brewing inside her.

Anwei stopped to peer around a taxidermied cat, bits of fur coming off when Noah pressed a hand to its back in order to get a look over her friend's shoulder. Past the cat, Noa saw a counter nestled at the very back of the store. No one was there except for a gigantic fish skeleton that had been mounted on the wall, its bulbous eyes somehow still intact. Beneath the fish, a large purple curtain hid the wall, a breez rustling it from behind.

"Sorry, I heard you come in, but—" The curtain pushed open, and a man bustled through, hands full of a mortar and pestle. His dark hair was in long braids and twists just like Anwei's, all of them pulled back in a neat tie at the nape of his neck. Anwei's hand reached out to grab hold of Noa's wrist, her eyes on the yellow grains in his mortar bowl.

He paused, his face crinkling into a pained twist before sneezing quite impressively into the crook of his elbow. "Sorry," he repeated, setting the bowl of yellow powder on the counter. "I've been grinding this stuff all morning, and I'm beginning to think I'm allergic."

Noa wanted to squeal with delight—Anwei had to be missing her people as much as Noa missed her own place in the world—but she faltered at the grip Anwei kept on her. A smile flickered on her friend's face, a habit that could always save her, it seemed. No words came out, though, so Noa did what friends were supposed to. Lie.

"We were just wandering down the street and saw the blue door—my friend is low on herbs." Noa pulled her wrist free of Anwei's grip and walked up to lean on the counter, keeping well away from the yellow powder. "Do you have any of those?"

"Do I have . . . herbs?" The man licked his lips, looking up at the flowers and leaves hanging from the ceiling above her head. "Yes."

"A friend of mine recommended your shop." Anwei still hung back behind the shedding cat. "Paran?"

"Oh." The Beildan pulled a stool up to the counter and began grinding his yellow powder again, his nose twitching. "He's not in at the moment. We've got a shipment of face cream for nice young ladies such as yourselves"—he winked at Noa—"going out tonight. Getting it around those pirates hogging the Felac has been quite an adventure. Paran's out there yelling at people as we speak."

Anwei didn't quite look at the bowl, her nose twitching. "I'm sorry, I haven't even asked your name. I'm one of Yaru's messengers."

"I'm Cylus. Paran's lousy healer. And you?" He grinned when Anwei didn't respond, looking toward Noa. "All of Paran's friends are the same. A little bit unkempt, dirt under their fingernails, and they all seem to have forgotten their own names." He grinned toward Noa. "What about you?"

"Unkempt?" Noa straightened her back and gave him her best second khonin stare. "I beg your pardon?"

Cylus laughed, pushing the bowl aside to squint back toward Anwei. "You don't look old enough to have made it out of Beilda."

Anwei finally found the grin Noa knew so well, still not quite looking at the bowl that was now sitting between them on the counter. "Is that rinoe compound for part of your shipment, because contact with the skin can cause lesions and . . ." She gave a dainty sniff, then flinched back as if she'd gotten more than she'd bargained for. "Calsta's *breath*! What else is *in* there?"

Cylus put up his hands, not the least bit fazed. "Oh, I know. Honestly, I was skeptical too, at first. Aukincy in general tends to bring us more patients than it cures." He pulled the bowl a little closer. "But our local aukincer here can do miracles like I've never seen before."

"An aukincer. Here in town?" Anwei's face was a careful blank.

"No, he's got some kind of estate out in the jungle north of here. Not many are brave enough to venture out that way except kids daring each other to enter the caves. He always comes in on a boat, then sails out again, but I'm not sure where he goes, exactly. The tributaries are quite treacherous."

Noa knit her fingers in front of her on the counter, excitement an electric sting in her humors. This was truly living, clues coming up in a real conversation instead of as part of a script on stage. Even if the stage had more fireworks and nice music to set the mood. "The aukincer makes . . . face cream?"

"Comes in every few months with bricks for me to grind up," Cylus was saying. "All he asks in return is that Paran stock a few less traditional supplies—"

A bell on the door chimed.

"You've been so helpful." Anwei's smile spread wide across her face. "I'll come back when Paran—" Something changed in Anwei's face, her nostrils flaring. She grabbed hold of Noa's wrist again and dragged her behind the counter. Noa craned her neck to see who had come in but couldn't catch a glimpse through the maze of shelves. Cylus slid off his stool, confused.

"I'm fascinated by these bricks. Do you mind if I take a look?" Anwei swept the curtain back before Cylus could stop her, pulling Noa into to a workshop crowded with tables and broken chairs. There were shelves up on their sides with jars clustered on top and underneath dried insects in trays, messy piles of leaves and petals sorted by color. In the center of the room, there waas a heavy work table with a yellow brick of compressed powder on a tray square in the middle.

"Um . . . all right?" Cylus fumbled to hook the curtain open on the edge of the door, Anwei shrinking back to the far corner of the workroom, out of direct line of sight from the shop. "I've got another customer, so . . ." He turned to face the man who'd come in, Noa only catching sight of a suede sun hat. The customer seemed to be quite taken with what looked like a jar of dirt near the entrance, then began exclaiming over a blue bottle with something lumpy and clawed bobbing inside.

Anwei scuttled across the workroom to the back door, which opened with a squeak. "Don't touch anything," she whispered, sliding through to hide behind it. "He doesn't know you. Stall. No, watch him. No. *Hide.*"

"Anwei—" But the healer had already shut herself out of sight. *Watch Cylus?* Noa wondered. *He's not even the contact we were looking for.*

"We were just talking about you." Cylus called to the customer.

Edging around the table, Noa sat on the one unbroken chair, finally getting a clear view of the man who'd come in. He plunked the blue jar down on the counter and took off his hat. "Hopefully only good things. When did you get this little beauty in, Cylus? I ask specifically for rare specimens, and Paran puts this one out on the shelf for anyone to snap up?"

Tual Montanne.

Noa had never seen him in person, but she was certain it had to be him. She held her breath, drawing on every drop of stage training she had to present a calm exterior and sending a prayer up to Falan it would stick. This man looked so normal. Brown eyes. Light olive skin that could have matched just about any province in the Commonwealth. He had a beard, though, and Noa knew not to trust a man with a nicely shaped beard.

How could he have arrived at the shop at the same exact moment Anwei had come to meet her contact? In a stage production, such a coincidence never would have made it to the final script.

Noa's humors went cold as Tual bent down to peer through the jar, glass and water distorting his brown eyes as he stared at the unfortunate creature floating inside.

"We never know when you're going to be around, and you know Paran," Cylus was saying. "He's not going to say no to someone with silver rounds. Why anyone would want it is beyond me—it's not only foul, but I half expect *looking* at it to give me some terrible disease."

Tual grinned, standing up. "Foul and diseased, my two favorite words. I'll have something really special ready for you when the rest of the things I ordered come in."

"Noa!" Anwei was peeking through the shop door, a glimpse of a stairwell showing behind her. She mouthed the words rather than risk a whisper. "Get out of sight . . . *move!*"

But Noa couldn't move because Tual had looked past Cylus to where she was sitting at the table, a curious smile on his good-natured face. But when their eyes met, a chill spread through Noa, shadows dancing behind his eyes that were there one moment, then gone the next. Like Knox's shadows.

Falan seemed to rise inside her, pulling back Tual's costume until she could see the darkness in his wake, a thousand times deeper than the flickers around Knox, though it was better contained. Noa swallowed, willing herself not to show the fear fizzing up inside her.

Tual gave her a friendly wave. "Are you a new assistant?" But then he caught sight of her khonin knots and frowned. "Someone of your rank shouldn't be grinding up posies in the dark for an old coot like Cylus."

Noa grinned, her face feeling strained. Knox's stab wound. The plague in Chaol. Lia's parents burned up in their own home. All those things belonged to this man, and she could feel it in those shadows lurking behind his eyes. Tual Montanne had no right to look so genial and harmless. He was a *monster*. Noa floundered for something to say, suddenly wishing this *was* a stage, with lines written for her to say, and a set happy ending. "I can't just buy face creams willy-nilly. You're the one who makes this stuff he's mixing?"

When he nodded, Noa forced herself to gesture to the piles of dead plants on the table behind her. "My skin is extremely delicate. One wrong flower petal, and all this hard work . . ." She waved a hand across her face and snapped. "*Gone*."

"We wouldn't want that to happen—your skin's a veritable work of art." Tual's smile was too warm for someone missing a soul. Or holding too many, she supposed. "You'll put this old codger through his paces, but I think you won't be disappointed. Speaking of which, Cylus, when *are* my shipments coming in? Is Paran here?"

"He's, um . . ." Cylus glanced back at Noa apologetically, his eyes darting past her when he didn't see Anwei. He leaned forward, trying to look farther into the room to catch sight of her. "He's upstairs."

Noa had to stop herself from frowning. Cylus had said Paran wasn't there.

"There's a new shipment of *something* up there," Cylus continued. "He told me not to disturb him, but I think he'd want to know you're here." The healer walked into the little workroom, glancing around for Anwei. Noa's stomach lurched, but when she looked back, Anwei had somehow slipped back inside and was calmly inspecting bunches of thorny stalks in the far corner where Tual wouldn't be able to see her.

Cylus gave her an apologetic nod. As if his lie about Paran was the worst thing happening in the shop. "I'll be back in a moment. Don't touch anything, please."

Anwei hardly looked away from the stalks, nodding until he disappeared through the back door and up the stairs, which creaked with each step. The moment he was out of sight, she waved her arms wide, then pointed to the wall between them and the counter. Her eyes bulged in the most unskilled attempt at charades Noa had ever seen. Noa sighed, wondering if it was too late to teach Anwei the proper value of a good stage whisper.

Tual hummed tunelessly, tapping his fingers against the counter. "Your accent is Elantin, no? What brings you to our little town?"

"Oh, I was supposed to go upriver—my father's got a whole merchant fleet and promised me a trip to Rentara, but I guess there's some kind of hullabaloo about ships on the river. Father says it's unsafe, and I already fired every single apothecary in the port, so stopping was a bit of an emergency." She sighed, looking around the workroom, doing her best to mimic one of Father's little hangers-on. "I mean, this place *looks* like some kind of aukincer human sacrifice den, but everyone knows it's those secret backdoor shops no one talks about that produce the best products."

"I keep my favorite places secret too. That way I don't have to share." Tual didn't even have the decency to look condescending, lowering his voice as if they were sharing confidences.

Which Noa would have thought was charming. Except for the part where she knew he was a murderer who could turn his skin into scales at will. Or maybe it wasn't at will, just a by-product of doing blasphemous magic that killed the people around him. She'd have to ask Anwei later.

"Some of the shipment *was* yours," Cylus called from the stairs. Before he got to the bottom, Noa saw Anwei stiffen from the corner of her eye, her friend's nostrils flaring. She turned toward the stairs as if she expected an assassin to emerge with Cylus's severed head hung on his fist, but the Beildan emerged intact, two heavily reinforced bags made from oilcloth in his hands. He passed Noa with a smile.

"Paran is a wonder, isn't he?" Tual dug in his pockets and came up with five silver rounds that clattered on the counter when he dropped them. "Where's the rest of it?"

"He said we'll have it in the next few days. Send a pigeon, and we'll meet you at the docks?"

Tual replaced his hat with a flourish. "As always, a pleasure doing business with you. Miracle workers, both of you."

"The miracles are all yours." Cylus took up his mortar and pestle once again.

"I hope you find the cream to your liking." Tual gave Noa a friendly bow, stuffed the jar under his arm, and picked up the two packets. "I hope you'll be safe in your travels. The rumors about boats sinking on the river are enough to curdle blood much stronger than mine." He turned to point at Cylus. "Did you hear about the three boys—"

"That went missing." Cylus's brow furrowed. "Yes, and it wasn't river pirates that did it. Kids disappear every year."

"Well." Tual gave one last bow before heading to the shop's entrance. "Both of you stay safe."

When the door banged shut, Cylus turned back to the workroom, eagerly looking toward Anwei. "What do you think of my stores? Do I pass muster? Some of it I get from suppliers, but all the basic stuff I harvest myself."

"I'm actually quite impressed." Anwei had switched her panicked miming for a shy smile. "It's so good to see someone else from the island, and I'm so intrigued by this . . . compound?"

"You disappeared quick enough." Cylus spread his hands. "You could have asked the man himself. I can't tell you any more than you can see for yourself. It's like magic."

"Magic? Don't let any Devoted hear you say that." Anwei gathered her medicine bag. "Best of luck with your shipments and . . . fixing all the problems."

"You don't need any herbs now? Or to talk to Paran now that you know he's here?" A warning sparked inside Noa when Cylus leaned on the table, his lips pursed. "You mentioned that your father has boats in port right now, miss? Because we just received word the boat our shipment was supposed to go out on got marked by pirates not ten minutes ago—the pigeon came just as I went up to get that customer's supplies."

"Marked?" Noa stood up from the table, wondering if Cylus had mentioned the two of them to Paran.

"Sorry about Paran." He shrugged apologetically toward Anwei. "He's not usually so busy, and normally I know he'd want to talk to one of Yaru's messengers. But maybe if we could come to an arrangement that could get our shipment out on time, I could get Paran to come down for you?" He looked at Noa. "What was your father's name?"

Noa couldn't speak. She didn't want to give her real name. Didn't have a fake one to provide. She looked at Anwei for help, who shook her head regretfully. "Not possible, I'm afraid."

Cylus nodded, but his expression didn't change. He turned back to Noa. "Well, let me get you some of the cream, like you said." He went to one of the cabinets and took out a little glass jar, then spooned in something jiggly and white. He seemed to be going slowly now, drawing out each word he spoke. Maybe Paran wanted to get a look at Anwei? Or there was something else afoot, Tual and Paran working together to… what? Drain Anwei and Noa dry right there in the shop? He could have already done it if he'd recognized them. "I haven't seen new braids in Kingsol in years. Not since the ships stopped. Which town are you from?"

"Instav?" Anwei walked back out into the shop, not a single crinkle on her forehead. Maybe there was nothing to worry about. Noa followed her around the counter, trying to remember the town Anwei had mentioned before, fairly certain it hadn't been Instav.

"*Instav?*" Cylus followed them out of the workroom. "It's been abandoned for half a decade."

"Abandoned?" Noa asked just as Anwei said, "What do you mean?"

Cylus stopped, eyeing the both of them with something that looked like surprise. But then his face paled, and he sat back down on his stool, something like pity clouding his face. "You don't know about the massacre. Belash Point?"

"*What?*" Anwei's hand snaked down to grab hold of Noa's.

Belash Point. Recognition bled through Noa's thoughts. That was the name of Anwei's town. Noa's stomach churned at her friend's look, Anwei's eyes just a little too wide.

There could be a thousand reasons for Anwei to pretend she didn't know what Cylus was talking about, but Noa could see in her face that she knew. She knew about this massacre.

"Eight years ago. I thought everyone clear to Lasei knew. Forge and Elantia were up to their ears in Devoted. I was already here in Kingsol by then, but it wasn't the kind of mystery anyone could just ignore. We all know what happens to those kids who disappear looking for treasure up the waterways—those old caves aren't kind to anyone. But a whole town just . . . disappearing in the middle of a storm? All their clothing still in their closets, meals laid out to eat. The apothecary a mess, herb jars all smashed on the ground. Some of the buildings looked damaged from the storm, but there was no blood. No bodies. Every person in Belash Point was just . . . gone."

A million possibilities burst in bright colors through Noa's head. Ghosts. Sea monsters. Pirates. The shapeshifter . . .

"I've been on the mainland for a very, very long time," Anwei said faintly. "But my family . . Belash Point is *miles* from Instav. Whatever happened there couldn't have—"

That wasn't the right question, and Noa knew it "What happened?"

"People within a few miles of the Point started getting sick. They'd forget things—where they lived, who their children were, their own names. It happened in Lanat, Ventum." Cylus set the little jar of cream down on the counter next to the mortar bowl and pulled over a set of scales, glancing at Anwei. "Instav. Went on for more than a year before—" He put up his hands, eyes going wide. "Gods above and beneath, I'm telling this all wrong. I'm sure your family is fine. Most everyone was all right once they put some distance between themselves and the coast."

"Oh, thank Calsta," Anwei breathed.

Her family wasn't, though. Noa could feel it.

"You said massacre. How do you know they were killed if there weren't any bodies?" Noa asked, watching as he brought out a little set of tongs and pulled the mortar bowl close. He was moving so slowly.

"If it happened now, I'd say pirates, what with the Warlord pulling her Devoted back farther every year." Cylus carefully dropped a measure of powder onto the scale, then a bit more. "They've gotten bold these days, and I wouldn't be surprised if they've started trading in *people* outside the Commonwealth." He shook his head, carefully setting more weights in the opposite cup. "Back then all the stories said monsters must have come up out of the ocean and eaten them. Or a plague turned them to ash. Or maybe Calsta herself sent a burning chariot to ferry people into the sky."

"Hard to tell the difference between gods and monsters sometimes." Anwei's smile squeezed out like the last dregs of oil from a cloth. "We have another appointment, so I'll try Paran again in a few days. Noa can come back for her cream."

"Patience now, only a moment more and I'll be done. And I've got to finish my story before your little friend explodes, don't I?" Cylus shot Noa a smile as he tipped the powder into the little jar and started stirring. "The Warlord was certain it was a shapeshifter, but the proof didn't come until they started looking at the trees." Cylus tapped the spoon on the side of the jar, then clamped it shut. "Three copper rounds'll do it."

Anwei fumbled for money in her medicine bag, practically throwing the coins down once she'd extracted them, then started for the door. Noa took the cream, not sure where to put it. She wasn't a pockets person.

"Trees aren't so deadly, are they?" she said. "They just stand there. And if you don't like them, you can light them on fire."

"Trees had sprouted up all over town—in the middle of the street, growing through porches, blocking fields, through the docks. People who went in to investigate didn't realize they were new until they found bones sticking out of one of the trunks."

"Bones?" Noa couldn't find her voice. A real ghost story. A real shapeshifter, who had really murdered people. And trees, flowers, vines, a whole summer's worth of seeds growing up out of nowhere, like that day at the tomb.

Anwei had pushed open the door. "Are you coming, Noa?" she called.

"It was a hand and arm coming from *inside* the tree trunk, as if it had clawed its way out. They cut down the trees and instead of rings, they had skeletons inside of them."

"Skeletons," the word whispered out of Noa cold and hard. "Trapped inside the trees."

"That's why the ferries stopped, why Beildans haven't been letting anyone across the strait. Who could have done any of that except a dirt witch?" He leaned back, squinting at Noa. "Now, don't play the idiot with me. You and your friend here have got a few too many questions for girls looking for face cream. No names, dropping Yaru's like nothing, and you go haring off out of sight the moment our highest-paying customer walks in?" He cocked his head. "I've heard the requests for information, same as Paran." He edged out from behind the counter to look at Anwei where she stood by the door. "You think we don't know who you are? What exactly do you want with Tual Montanne, Yaru?"

CHAPTER 12

Skirts with No Pockets

P anic buzzed in Knox's head like a swarm of bees as he ran from the inn where Altahn had just slapped silver on the bar in exchange for slightly cleaner blankets. Something was happening. Something *terrible*. Anwei never panicked. Anwei—

Knox stumbled to a stop when the alleyway abruptly ended, forcing him to circle back to find another way. He knew where she was, her presence brighter than any aura, but he didn't know how to get across this sky-cursed town. There were hardly any water channels, and the alley ways twisted around one another like snakes. Knox jumped a low wall and took off running around the edge of a bustling market, silenbahks groaning at a watering station on the far side so loud they made the cobblestones tremble underfoot. Darting past a table covered in roasted fish and hopping a narrow channel that led to the docks, Knox threaded between trays of cakes, bolts of cloth, fruits, and a pickpocket with an aura just misty enough with malt it made Knox's stomach heave. Groping for Calsta's power almost made it worse, the noise of so many people bartering, arguing, sighing, and laughing like an assault. That was nothing compared to the haze of auras, all of them fading into one another and blending, a sea of people that could be hiding the one aura that mattered.

Knox turned down the first road that seemed to be leading in the right direction. Anwei was close. Not hurt, he didn't think, just *fleeing*—

A cheery blue-painted door at the end of the street opened, and Anwei came waltzing out, her braids loose and her face a breeze that said nothing of the panic sizzling in his gut. She caught sight of him and glided toward him, Noa bobbing behind her like a cork on a fishing line.

"What's wrong?" he gasped, meeting her in the center of the street.

"Keep walking, and keep your eyes open. We need to go."

"Go? What happened? We just barely got to The Rigors—"

"No inn. We can't stay at the inn. We can't stay anywhere in town—" Anwei was walking faster and faster, and Noa was not talking, which Knox hadn't realized was possible.

He took Anwei's arm and pulled her down a side street, where fewer people would be watching, then across to the back side of the market to stand behind a stall crowded with people eating fried something with too many legs. "What's going on?"

Anwei turned to Noa, pointing. "We need a boat. We can hide in the river tributaries everyone is so scared of. We'll watch for his boat—there's another shipment coming next week. That's what he said, right? We can still grab Mateo. It just might take a little longer—"

"Back at the tomb . . . ," Noa faltered, her face graver than Knox had ever seen. "That's not the first time you've made trees grow?"

Waving a hand between them, Knox couldn't stop the pulses of panic rushing through him. "Tell me what happened!"

"You knew about the massacre." Noa was talking like Knox wasn't there, something in her face making him prickle with wariness. "And you just told me you came from Belash Point. It happened when Tual took your brother, didn't it?"

"We don't have time to talk about this, Noa. Yes, Tual was there.

Yes, I was there. But just now, Tual Montanne was standing ten feet away from me. He must have recognized my aura . . . but he let Cylus ask what we want with him. It's like he's playing with us. Or really does see me as *nothing*." Her hands twisted together, more agitated than Knox had ever seen her, the now familiar bloom of anger rubbing like sandpaper across the bond. Some of it was for whatever had happened in the shop, but some of it was . . . because of Noa? Worry stabbed through her, the same way it did when she talked about Calsta and him.

She was worried Noa would leave.

"Wait." He waved a hand between Noa and Anwei, but neither of them looked away from the other. "Tual was in that shop with you?"

Noa stared at Anwei a second longer, her brow furrowed. But then she shrugged. "What did Tual buy? I know it was something nasty."

Anwei seemed to wilt with relief, her hand reaching out to grip Noa's. She groped for Knox too, holding both of them there, and he couldn't help the wave of sorrow that washed through him. In Chaol he'd never thought of her as afraid.

"Tual bought enough ulintis paranme to put half the Commonwealth to sleep." Anwei finally turned to Knox, the strained smile on her face gratitude he'd come so fast. "It's extremely rare, distilled from these flowers on the southern tip of the archipelago. Beildans use it to put people to sleep during painful healing procedures, but it's not something most people can get their hands on—every gram of it is kept track of by the school on Beilda. Dried into powder, it can be mixed into all sorts of nasty things." She swallowed. "Ever heard stories about Sleeping Death?"

Knox nodded, fairy tales about whole cities falling asleep during the shapeshifter wars a warning echo in his head.

"He bought it right there in front of us. Maybe he wanted us to see."

"So Tual does that creepy . . . energy sparkle sight, or whatever it's called? Where he can see people even if they're not in the same room?"

"Aurasight," Knox had to grit his teeth very hard not to keep from rolling his eyes.

"Lia says Mateo had aurasight. But not like you." Anwei looked at Knox. "He could only see gods-touched. Maybe he *didn't* know I was there? He's never met Noa. . . ." She shook her head and started into the market. "It doesn't change the fact that Paran and Cylus know who I am."

Noa tried to follow, and Knox took pity on her, shepherding her through the gaps that Anwei found in the crowd. "You think it's possible Tual walked into that store less than a minute after we did by coincidence?" the dancer asked.

"It doesn't matter. Either Tual saw us and knows we're here, or Paran and Cylus will tell him. Either way we have to leave." Anwei pulled at the scarf covering her braids. "He must have been feeding me false leads since the day we first connected." She stopped. "Could Paran be linked up with Ellis, too? Gods *above*! My network wasn't supposed to feed me to the same sky-touched murderer they were helping me find!"

Knox grabbed hold of her hand, lowering his voice when a woman behind a table of dripping fish turned to stare at them. "Let's have this conversation somewhere less crowded. We have to get Altahn, then we can plan."

"Even a boat is risky because Ellis will be looking for us too, and out on the river, we'll be . . ." Anwei's eyes widened, and she stopped again, grabbing hold of Noa's arm. "Your *father's* boat—"

Noa's head gave a wild shake, her khonin knots bobbing. "No, Anwei—"

"Ellis doesn't attack boats from the Russo fleet. All of them are small enough to go down those little tributaries—" She started walking again as if Noa hadn't spoken, then turned back to Knox. She didn't seem to see him, though, looking back in the direction they'd come. "Noa, you know where the inn is?"

"No—?"

"The Rigors. Take a rickshaw. Knox, will you take her?" Anwei pointed to the line of runners at the edge of the market with their little two-wheeled pull wagons. "Tell Altahn to sit tight and . . . stab anything that comes at you two. I'll meet you there in an hour." She pushed past Knox and started back toward the apothecary.

Knox didn't want to let her go, Anwei's panic still a sharp acid in his mouth. No matter how much Noa meant to her, he didn't want to babysit the high khonin if there was real work to be done. He forced himself to turn to the dancer. "Are you all right?"

Noa's face was pale, her jaw clenched as she stared at Anwei's back disappearing into the crowd. When she shifted to look at Knox, there was something new in her expression, sharp and curious. "You knew where we were."

He nodded slowly.

"You and Anwei . . . after she healed you, it changed something about the two of you." She swallowed. "Some of your shadows went away. But they're still all around you. They're trying to get *in*, aren't they?"

Knox's stomach twisted, wondering what that could mean. Shadows? The only thing that had gone away was Willow.

Her hand shot forward, latching on to his wrist. "I can tell Altahn that Tual found us. That Anwei's contact here is bad. You help her." Noa bit her lip. "I'm sorry about letting you down before. I didn't realize what would happen if I wasn't where Anwei asked me to be. I didn't realize how important any of this was until I saw him—Tual . . ." She shook her head. "I won't make that mistake again."

Knox stared down at her, incredulous. "You didn't know?"

Noa shrugged. "Nothing I've ever done has mattered, Knox. So long as I was wearing the right dress and saying the right things, I didn't matter. But here, all of us matter."

Knox's mind ran fast, trying to think of a response that was true. Anwei letting the dancer invade their rooms above Gulya's apothecary, Noa's loud laugh and raucous singing, her magpie caws over anything that sparkled, the way she flirted with Altahn—all of it rankled. All of it was an intrusion in the perfect team that Anwei-plus-Knox had been.

At least, that was what he'd thought before. But Noa was here. Anwei wanted her here. And he had to admit, since that first debacle at the governor's mansion, Noa had never again missed her cues. So he swallowed his pride, his annoyance, and the awful fear strung in hot beads across the bond. "You're part of the crew. You're part of Anwei's plan, so of course you matter. We need you."

She grinned. "Was that so hard to say?"

"Don't push it, Noa." He started to turn but paused. "You have coin for the rickshaw?"

Her brow furrowed. "I don't have *pockets*, Knox."

He pulled out a few copper rounds and flipped them in her direction, then pressed through the crowd after Anwei, trying not to enjoy Noa's flailing as she tried to catch them.

When he finally found Anwei, she was halfway back to the shop. She didn't look when he settled in a step behind her, only reaching for him to check their relative distance like any other time they'd been on a job in Chaol. She knew he'd be there.

"Why are you going back?" he murmured.

"If Tual's got Sleeping Death, then I need to brew an antidote. That means I need some of it to find a counter. Paran has more of it in his upstairs workroom." She checked behind them, then to both sides before walking into the street. "They decided I'm Yaru, just like Ellis did." She laughed a little. "Paran didn't even bother to come down and see my face. Years of work on that cover, and now it's gone."

The air seemed to hum around her, her aura thick with threads of deep purple that jerked and swelled around her as she walked. The bond shivered with fear, cold and dark and *poisonous* as if Anwei was remembering something he couldn't see. No thoughts from her had come directly across the bond since back in Chaol, but her *feelings* came through strong. A twitch of movement on the ground caught Knox's eye, and he had to look twice to be sure.

The grass between cobblestones was *growing*.

He put a hand on her shoulder. "Anwei. You need to calm down."

"I'm calm." She kept walking. "We need to find a way in, a way to distract him—"

"Anwei." Knox stopped, pressing a hand to each of her shoulders. "None of this is going to work if you're adding to the city garden as we walk."

She flinched, looking down to find the grass growing over the toes of her boots.

"We've done this a million times. Tual isn't going to jump out of the shadows and . . ." He shrugged. He hadn't actually been awake for whatever Tual *had* done. "If Tual knows we're here and this is his approach, he's underestimating you. Us. We have a good plan. Mateo is his weak spot. And knowing that he's brewing this Sleeping Death stuff sets us ahead."

"I don't know if that's true. But we're going to have to hope." She fell in next to him as they walked, her hand reaching out to touch his arm. It was almost like before. Before, when the world had been Knox, Anwei, and a ridiculously expensive bottle of malt in a Water Cay cellar, or a poorly judged love note under a high khonin pillow, or a set of candlesticks locked under the stairs.

But then Anwei recoiled, her hand jerking away from him, and her body tilted away.

The goddess sighed in his head. *You can't let her pull away. Not now.*

Relationships are between two people, Calsta, he shot back. *She's not* a broomstick. *I can't pick her up and drag her along after me whether she wants me to or not. If this is all she wants, then it's enough.*

It won't be enough. Bonds aren't meant for thieves, Knox.

When they got to the street with the apothecary's blue door, Anwei darted down an alleyway at the other end of the street, then counted until they came out behind it. There was a door cut into the weathered brick wall that was covered by a locked iron grate. Above it, there was a single glass-paned window. An aura burned in the body of the shop past the door, and another on the other side of the room from the window upstairs. "Do you have your lockpicks?" he asked.

Anwei nodded. "But going in that way would be too noisy." She looked up at Knox. "Unless Paran isn't up there anymore?"

"He's there. Could you pick the grate's lock from the inside if we need to get out that way?"

"Of course."

Tipping his chin up, Knox traced the line of the tile roof, catching sight of the false ceiling through the window that blocked off an attic space. Both of them ducked behind the wall when a bird came winging out of the window above.

Knox grabbed Anwei's hand. "Come on."

She followed, keeping close behind him as they passed the back doors to the next three shops until they got to a wall, the end of the last shop's roof dipped down on top of it to let rainwater stream down onto the street. Running at the wall, he jumped up and grabbed hold of the top, and pulled himself up.

Anwei walked up slower, her frown visible from ten feet up. "I was thinking you could pretend to be very, very sick, and I could take you in—"

"And you think Paran wouldn't notice Yaru trying to steal his expensive poison while you pretend to cry over my dead body?" He offered her a hand. "Come on."

"You know I hate you, right?"

"I can't help that you misspent your whole childhood not climbing things."

She took his hand and let him help her up, then moved to crouch behind the roof's peak. Knox started down the length of the roof, hopping the first gap between buildings and pretending the flare of Anwei's feelings wasn't there at the back of his head. It felt like a rhythm. Like normal. Like any other job. Steal dangerous flower dust. Easy.

He grinned at Anwei's whispered curse when she followed him across the gap. Anwei had been his best friend for over a year, which was what he'd missed most during their last weeks in Chaol, and missed even more since he'd woken up. He could pretend to be everything that had come before the tomb, before Lia had reappeared, before they'd found the snake-tooth man.

Everything before had been so easy.

Across the ceramic tile roof, one more jump to get to the next building (and another whispered curse from Anwei), and they were above the apothecary, Knox digging at the tile mortar about halfway up to pry one free. Anwei leaned down to sniff at the tile, then took out a bottle from her bag and poured a few drops across the mortar the next tile down, which immediately began to soften and bubble. She corked the bottle, then pulled the tile off. Once a large enough hole was made, Knox cut away the packed straw between rafters beneath.

Anwei hardly waited until he was done before she went in feet first. Knox followed, landing in the dark in a crouch that sent up a cloud of dust. Paran's aura was now on the first floor with the other bloom of white energy, the apothecarist Anwei had mentioned, he supposed.

"Is that dust from you, Knox?" Anwei prodded from the shadows. "You're losing your touch."

He sneezed, causing her to look around the dusty attic in a panic, as if a sneeze was worse than the noise they'd made jumping down.

The rafters made a peak overhead, the hole in the roof sending a stark beam of light down to the rough-hewn floor. Wooden crates were set in clusters clear to the edges, as if they'd been categorized and organized for easy access.

Anwei pointed down. What they needed was in the workroom itself. Knox checked all the bare patches of floor until he found the trapdoor that led downward. Paran's aura was still on the first floor, so he hooked a finger through the pull.

"Wait—" Anwei moved to grab his arm, but Knox had already wrenched it open. A bell sounded.

The auras below went still. Then one took off up the stairs toward them.

"You knew it was rigged?" Knox hissed, letting it drop to run for the larger boxes crowding the far corner of the attic. Anwei beat him to them, lodging herself into the triangle of space between one of the larger crates and the roof and pulling him in after her. He barely fit, every inch of him crammed against wall or box or Anwei's bony knees. "How do we feel about knocking him out?" he whispered.

"I don't want him to know anything is wrong."

"The bell already rang. I guess maybe it could have been a rat or something?" Knox looked up at the light streaming down through the hole in the roof, the aura in the office and climbing higher. "But I think at this point we'd have to pray pretty hard."

"*I'm* supposed to pray?" Anwei shifted behind him, her legs twisted up against his back. "I'd rather all the gods *burned*."

He contorted sideways trying to look back at her. "Keep your religious persecution down, would you? He's coming up the ladder now."

"Does it count as religious persecution when religious people persecute *you*?"

Knox snorted, covering his mouth and nose when the trapdoor

crashed open. Breathing in slow and letting it out even slower, Knox turned to the well of glimmering gold inside him. He drew it in, the feel of sunlight burning merrily through him. He willed the light around him to bend.

Darkness gathered around them like ink. Knox thought about hiding, about not being noticed, about the energy flare that was coming through the trapdoor walking right past them. Anwei squeezed in closer against his back, her heart beating hard enough he could feel it in his own chest.

Rider of Storms. The thought came automatically, deflecting the feel of Anwei against him. Paran walked closer, inspecting box after box until he was standing directly in front of the gap where Knox and Anwei were hiding. Anwei's breath was on Knox's neck. *Lady of Blue. Sky Painter.*

Friends. That's what they were. A friend wouldn't notice the spicy scent of herbs on Anwei's fingertips or the lavender oil she had used to retwist a few of her braids that morning on the boat. And so he didn't, concentrating on the shadow, on Paran. On the *First Smith, Wielder of Winds . . .*

The man stooped lower, peering into the shadows, his eyes not quite focusing on Knox less than a foot below him. After a moment, he swore, turning to check the boxes along the back side of the roof.

Anwei poked Knox in the ribs, and he moved, slowly extracting himself from the hiding place, using another grouping of crates as a shield. Paran moved on to another set of crates across the room, groaning to himself as he looked up at the missing tiles. Rats were a feature in the monologue, which seemed like a good sign.

Slipping past him, Anwei went for the open trapdoor. She was down the ladder in a breath, and Knox followed her, Paran turning just as Knox's head ducked below, the shadows still clinging to Knox, telling the man nothing was there.

Sliding down the ladder, Knox came out in a roll, almost crashing into a large wire cage fluttering with birds in little sectioned-off rectangles. There was a heavy wooden worktable next to it, half of it covered in oilcloth packages with languages from all across the Commonwealth on the labels. There were two barrels propped up at the end of the table, a desk, a counter covered in dishes and measures, and a scale loaded with little packets next to the barred window.

Anwei was hovering over the scale, shoving little packets into her bag with one hand and shielding her nose with the other, her eyes streaming tears. Papers were strewn across the table, a ledger with markings up and down it catching Knox's eye. He picked it up when he saw a notation marked with a capital *TM*. Tual Montanne?

Footsteps thunked toward the ladder from above.

Anwei ran for the stairs, arm still blocking her nose as she took them three at a time, Knox only a step behind around the curve that hid the first floor. She slid to her knees at the bottom in front of the heavy wooden door and wrenched it open, revealing the grate between them and the alley outside. She groped in her bag for her lockpicking tools.

The floor above them creaked.

"Fast would be good." Knox hummed through the cloudy scent of herbs coming from the workroom on the other side of the doorway. The aura above was coming toward the top of the stairs. For some reason, Paran's aura was flickering.

Tongue sticking out, Anwei slid one of the picks into the lock, and then a second.

Knox drew in a little more of Calsta's power, maintaining the bent light around them. Still, Paran was flickering in and out, as if Knox's aurasight was . . .

Knox's chest clenched, his lungs growing tight as the wound in his side pulled. He moaned, pressing a hand to the bandaging because he was cracking into pieces, the edges grating against one another. Willow—

Anwei was there, in his face, checking his pulse, his breath, curse words he didn't know the meaning of rapping out from her. "Hang on, Knox," she hissed. "Stay with me."

His hands began to shake as the gold scorching through his veins began to siphon away. *Willow!* he thought, but the wall that Anwei made between him and Willow was there, blocking the ghost from speaking. *Please,* he begged. *Don't do this to me now.*

But it was now. Willow couldn't speak, but she could *take.*

There was nothing to plug the hole inside him, energy sucking away as if his insides were riddled with leeches. Knox's lungs wouldn't inflate, his humors that had been rushing with adrenaline suddenly freezing into a stagnant mire. His knees buckled, sending him lurching into the wall, the ledger he'd accidentally brought from the office clattering to the floor.

All of Calsta's light bending around him winked out.

The footsteps in the office paused at the noise. Then started toward the stairs *fast.*

Somehow Anwei was supporting his weight and the grate was open, and Knox was limping into the alleyway. *You helped Anwei stop me from dying in the tomb, Calsta,* he pled. *You promised to help me fix Willow if I kept my oaths. How do I fix it? I can't fix it if I'm unconscious. Or dead.*

The goddess didn't see fit to answer.

Anwei's arm snaked around his waist, and they were in the street, people bumping into Knox from all sides. They stopped next to a shop with large clear windows full of flowers despite the sound of footsteps pounding after them. Perhaps Anwei had some concoction to throw at Paran to buy them time.

Knox's aurasight blinked in and out, Paran closer every time—

Which was when Anwei looked up at him, her hand snaking up into his hair.

"What are you—"

And it was like that night in the governor's office when he'd been poisoned. Anwei had come toward him, and he'd wanted to kiss her. He'd wanted it so much he'd almost fallen out of a window to get away, protecting his access to Calsta's energy like it was his soul. But this time Anwei moved slowly, looking up at him like the picture of a girl in love, her hand cupping his cheek.

She stretched up and kissed him.

And Knox forgot about the aura blundering toward them. He forgot he was about to fall over. He forgot about teasing Anwei and how well they worked together when they were *finding* things, he forgot about Calsta hovering behind him like the warrior goddess she was.

He forgot to think about anything else because Anwei's lips were moving against his and the bond was sparking like fireworks in his head.

"Hey! You, Beildan!"

Anwei broke away to face the man racing toward them, hand shooting up to cover her mouth, her cheeks pink. Heat climbed up Knox's neck.

Right. This was fake. It *was* just like in the governor's office. An act. Paran hadn't seen Anwei's face, so why not pretend?

"You, don't go any farther!" Paran stopped short of them, looking between Anwei and Knox with slowly dawning doubt.

"Did you . . . need something?" Anwei wrinkled her nose, smiling a little too big, a hand going to her mouth. She giggled, her arm still locked around Knox's waist to keep his knees from buckling. Willow had slowed, Knox's energy leaking in a drip instead of a roar. "Calsta above, this is embarrassing. We didn't mean to offend—"

Fake. It was all fake. He said it to himself again. Then another time, trying to breathe.

"You were in my shop." Paran's face had gone ruddy, though Knox couldn't see quite straight enough to know if it was with embarrassment or anger. "You were up there, and half my remaining supply is *gone*! Who told you—"

"I'm . . . sorry?" Anwei took a hesitant step toward the man, testing Knox's weight and then letting her hand drop from around his waist when he held himself upright. "My betrothed and I were just . . ." She looked self-consciously toward the window.

Flowers. They were braided into wreaths. Knox looked away. This was all set up just like everything else Anwei did, so she could pretend to be a real girl with a real betrothed and a real blush across her cheeks who could wilt like a pretty flower when Paran came growling after her. Anwei never had been the bouquet she pretended to be.

Knox knew what she was underneath. Steel.

But at the same time, he could feel her heart fluttering against him, her mind churning, the burn in her cheeks. The flowers, the window, the self-consciousness. All that was fake. But underneath, that blush was *real*.

The fireworks still sizzling in the back of his mind? Those were real.

Even Paran could see it, looking from her to Knox, then to the window. "Gods and monsters," he swore. "I apologize. Did you see anyone running down this street?"

"I mean, I wasn't really paying attention?" Anwei gave him an awkward grin and took Knox's hand, her fingers settling comfortably between his. Paran apologized again and walked away, and as soon as he'd turned his back, a thread of Anwei's anger slipped across the bond, bloody and red.

But before Knox could look down at Anwei, Willow was back and battering at his defenses. Knox's vision went hazy as the energy inside him began to drain. He gritted his teeth, jamming a hand to the pain in his ribs, his knees beginning to shake.

The last thoughts that pulled free as the darkness took him was that slip of anger, like teeth against his lip. Anwei loved him—not all sisterly and slightly violent like Lia, or condescending and annoying like Calsta. She loved him, *wanted* him, and it was only in that moment that he truly felt the slap that his words that night in Chaol had been for her.

When he'd told her that his Oaths to Calsta made the two of them impossible.

Anwei was drawing away rom their bond, and there was nothing Knox could do to stop her any more than he could stop Willow from drinking in the last dregs of him.

So he let go. Grateful that the last thing he felt, despite it all, was Anwei's arms catching him.

CHAPTER 13

The Butcher

t took longer than it should have for Anwei to get Knox to The Rigors. By the time Anwei got Knox back to the lines of rickshaws, both moons had risen high. She couldn't think of anything but Knox breathing, Knox being all right. Knox kissing her back. Anwei shut her eyes at that thought, which, of course, only made it worse.

When they rolled up to the inn, Anwei hopped out, flipping an extra coin to the runner to wait while she ran for help. Inside, the common room was crammed with people, the overwhelming smells of braised lamb, potatoes and cream, and sweat a welcome assault on her senses.

Noa was laughing from atop a table, a glass of malt in one hand and two men at her feet, teasing her into demonstrating some kind of fancy turn or jump. Incredulous, Anwei followed Altahn's silver and acid black scent to the bar. The Trib was tucked into the far corner against the wall, a plate of lamb, potatoes, and something vaguely green that must have been alive at some point in front of him. "Didn't Noa tell you—" She shook her head. They couldn't leave now, not with Knox down. "I need your help getting Knox upstairs."

Altahn stood, pushing his plate back. "What happened? You were supposed to be back hours ago."

"We'll talk once he's upstairs." She weaved back through the crowd and pushed out through the door. Knox hadn't moved in the rickshaw, the runner doing his best not to snicker as Anwei pulled his dead weight off the bench, her knees buckling under his weight.

He was heavy, his body pressed up against her. And Anwei was suddenly back in front of the flower shop, Knox's arms pressing her tight to him, and his lips . . . No. No lips. That was the danger of Knox. He fit her so well.

At least, he would have if the gods hadn't forged a bond between them like some kind of cage.

Altahn ran the last few steps to grab hold of Knox, pulling Knox's arm over his shoulder to take some of the weight from Anwei. Together they dragged him through the door, then up the stairwell to one of their rooms, where Altahn helped her deposit Knox on the closer bed.

The wound in Knox's side had begun to smell again, this time with new hues of yellow that hadn't been there before. Anwei pulled back his tunic to inspect the scar, gagging at the wave of sickly infected colors that came washing out. Steeling herself, Anwei untied the bandaging, her teeth clenched at the sight of the puckered skin somehow looking more fragile, as if a good bump would tear Knox open again.

Altahn dropped onto the other bed, watching quietly. "When are you going to tell me what is really wrong with him, Anwei?"

She glanced up at him, the pleasant tone a stark contrast to the words. "He just overexerted himself. You know he's sick."

"Sometimes."

"Yes, that's an accurate description." She sighed. "You were right—Tual is the one who hurt him, and herbs aren't doing everything they should. He's healing, but . . . not all the way." That much was true.

"Oh?" Altahn's voice shivered through her. "Noa came running back here with news that she'd seen Tual with her own eyes. That we have to leave, and something about a boat? But that he didn't even touch you."

Anwei looked up, her heart beating madly against her ribs.

"Don't think I haven't noticed your . . . extremely odd relationship with Knox." Altahn cocked his head at her. "I found you at the bottom of a tomb somehow alive after crossing a shapeshifter, and Knox . . ." He gestured. "Like this. Everything you've done so far, it seems like your partner here takes the brunt of it."

Anwei sat up straight, pulling her hands back from Knox. "You think I'm using Knox somehow? Like . . . an energy bank that I draw anytime I need it? Like a *shapeshifter*?"

Altahn didn't blink, staring her down.

She sat forward, cocking her head. "And you thought directly confronting me was the best way to *avoid* getting your soul sucked out?"

Reaching under the bed, Altahn drew out something long and thin from the trunk shoved underneath, the shroud of blankets not enough to hide Knox's pockmarked sword. Altahn pulled the blanket loose and let it fall, then set the naked blade across his knees. "Running with Lia Seystone has been educational. For one, now I know how to deal with a shapeshifter."

"I'm *not* . . . ." Anwei's muscles clenched, bile rising in her throat, the sword weeping with the nothing smell.

Carefully considering her situation—Knox in a dead faint, her medicine bag twisted up behind her, and faced with a shapeshifter sword—Anwei did the only thing she could.

She laughed. Hard and loud until she bent over, Knox's hand creeping over to take hold of her wrist as if somehow, even uncon- scious, he knew the sword was there. "Look at you," Anwei said, wip- ing a tear from her eye. "Rifling through my things like a real thief. You have learned quite a bit in the last few weeks, haven't you? Well." She craned to get a look at her trunk underneath, but Knox's grip on her wrist held her back. "Now that you've found my *secret weapon*, what are you going to do with it?"

"I want you to tell me the truth." Altahn raised the sword an inch from his knee, and Anwei's arms prickled when Knox's body shifted toward it, his eyes moving under their lids.

Anwei reached for her trunk. "Absolutely. Would you pull the rest of my things out, though? Knox's salve should be—"

"It's not melted anymore, Anwei." Altahn gripped the sword tighter, his knuckles turning white despite the measured calm of his voice. "I saw it on the ground completely destroyed. Who can manipulate metal . . . *grow back* a caprenum sword—something else Lia shared—other than a shapeshifter? You think you can just smile at me and I'll stop remembering?"

Anwei shivered, because that was exactly what the snake-tooth man had done to her whole village. She slid a foot under the bed to hook her trunk, Knox's grip on her wrist tightening. Turning a little, she slipped her free hand into her medicine bag where Altahn couldn't see it.

Her fingers touched corta leaves, then the tincture that needed to be mixed before it could knock someone out, then the other packets that could have immobilized Altahn, but Anwei knew none of them would work quickly enough if Altahn decided to stab her. Her fingers found the new oilcloth packages of Sleeping Death that she'd stolen from Paran, then moved past them because she didn't know how long it would last, how it would scatter, how much to give, or whether she could even safely touch it yet. Last of all, she found the calistet bag.

It was empty. After what had happened with the snake-tooth man and Knox down in the tomb, she'd left every grain of calistet behind in Chaol.

Calm. That was the most important thing.

Altahn still hadn't lowered the sword. "Tell me. Are you a shapeshifter? Are you stealing energy from Knox to ward off Tual's attacks somehow?" he asked. He didn't blink when she looked incredulously at him. "It's a simple question."

"No." Anwei pulled free of Knox and then dragged the trunk out the rest of the way. Altahn moved his legs to allow her room. "I'm not a shapeshifter, and you're not in love with me, so the only outcome from using that thing on me would be lots of blood for you to clean up." Her fingers closed around the little jar of salve, and she withdrew it, turning back toward Knox.

"I'm not in love with you? What is that supposed to mean?"

She chanced a look over her shoulder. "You're not, are you? Noa would probably poison my tea. She fancies you, I think."

"Noa doesn't fancy anything but doing exactly as she pleases, so far as I can tell. If it's not you doing it, then tell me what is wrong with him."

Unclasping the jar's lid, Anwei looked down at Knox. "You know how shapeshifters are made?"

"Something about these swords." Altahn looked down at the pock-marked blade.

"Two gods-touched, a Devoted and a Basist, can form a special bond that mixes their magic. It makes both of them stronger than they could be otherwise. But if one of them takes a caprenum sword and kills the other, the victim's soul and all their magic goes to the aggressor, turning them into a shapeshifter" Anwei dipped her fingers in the salve, the scent of the herbs dulling the awful smell of . . . whatever it was inside Knox. It felt oily and waxy at once as she carefully smeared the salve across Knox's wound. "Tual used that sword to kill a little Devoted girl to change . . . *Mateo* into a shapeshifter. There was no bond between the two kids, though, so it only partially worked. Knox ended up with the blade that killed her, and the girl's soul got stuck in there somehow. Now Knox and Mateo are joined with the dead girl's soul and . . . sometimes she takes too much of Knox's energy for him to stay conscious, I guess."

Altahn nodded slowly, as if that were an entirely plausible explanation. "Is that why Noa calls him a shadow man? Because of . . . the ghost?"

"I didn't know she called him that."

"And Tual tried to kill him? I saw all the blood from the wound that day, Anwei. Too much for someone to survive."

Anwei turned back to Knox, checking that the salve had covered everything before she replaced the bandage. "I . . . saved him." The memory of that terrible power shivered through her. Knox's eyes blinked open for a moment, his eyes unfocused as he stared up at her, his hand finding hers.

"Anwei?" Her name was honey on his lips.

Anwei's cheeks heated.

"Because you're . . . not just a healer; you're a dirt witch. And the two of you—" Altahn used the sword to point between them. "You've got that bond thing between you? Interesting."

"Thank you so much for saying so." She smiled politely, closing the salve with a snap.

He smiled a little, finally setting the sword down. "And Tual just so happening to be in that apothecary the same time as you?"

Stuffing the salve back into her bag, Anwei's hands stopped on a leather-bound ledger. Where had it come from? Pulling it out, she looked it over, vaguely remembering that Knox had picked it up in Paran's workroom. In the panic to get out, she must have shoved it into her bag after he dropped it in the stairwell. "I don't know what it means yet. Only that we can't stay here." Her eyes glossed across the smooth, loopy handwriting that seemed to be entries about shady activities taking place in Kingsol, notations about wardens and jurists. Paran keeping track of Kingsol like a crime lord's accountant. It paid to know what was happening around you.

"Would you mind putting that sword away? It's dangerous." She started to set the ledger aside but paused when her eyes caught on an entry near the bottom: *Kingsol harbor, dock thirty-three.* And a green circle. *Marked for fifth drum tomorrow.*

Green like the mark on Ellis's boat. *A pirate-marked ship*, Cylus had said. And Ellis, that morning: *I told Noa to stick around a few days. You never know what might come up.*

"What is that?" Altahn shifted forward to get a look, his firekey bursting out of his sleeve to hiss at Anwei before clawing her way up the Trib's collar to curl on his shoulder. The sword seemed to smolder next to him.

The panicky need to hide hummed inside Anwei's belly, the thought of Tual's distinctive scent of expensive soap and foods, dirt, and herbs rushing back at her, so different from the *nothing* she'd been chasing so long that she now knew had come from his victims. *A pirate-marked ship.* "Down at the bottom, Altahn—"

She stuttered to a halt when the window behind Altahn wrenched open from outside, a dark shape spilling through. Galerey hissed, and Altahn jumped up from the bed, grabbing for the knives in his vest. Anwei groped for her herbs until she saw the man's face.

She forced herself to relax, settling calmly onto the bed while Ellis finished climbing in before clearing her throat. Raising an eyebrow, she gave him an irritated wave of her hand. "Did you need something?"

"You took my salpowder tubes, you little wench." Ellis smiled, seating himself comfortably on the bed across from her. He gave Altahn a careless smile. "I knew she had to be Yaru. The gall! Took them right out from under my nose."

Altahn didn't move, knife tight in his hand as if he didn't know who to stab, Anwei or Ellis.

Ellis turned back to Anwei, head jerking toward the Trib. "Are you seeing this? It's like his face is frozen like that." Sighing, he drew a long knife from his coat and inspected the tip, polishing away some imagined blemish. "I'm not saying I'm disappointed to have found you so easily, but I guess I was expecting more?" He grinned, gesturing with the knife. "Don't kill my heroes, Anwei. I had Yaru built halfway to the sky."

Anwei smiled, fingers knuckle-deep in corta powder, but with Knox prone behind her and Altahn not sure if he was ready to defend or fight either one of them, making Ellis cough until his eyes turned red wasn't going to help the situation much. "They're called caroms, Ellis, and if you want them back, maybe you'll answer some questions for me. First: Did you notify Paran I was coming into town?"

He laid his long knife on the table between them like some kind of peace offering. "No."

"All right." Anwei wanted to believe it—that her contacts weren't all conspiring against her. And having Ellis's help could change things a bit—the bare bones of a plan were coming together in her head. She thought of Noa seizing up at the very idea of being seen by her father's sailors, the way she'd cried back in Chaol, begging to be taken in. "Second question." She held out the ledger. "Tell me about this boat you marked."

Ellis sat back, spreading his hands wide. "It's got the Elantin governor's copper bathtub on board. What can I say?"

"So, the crew, what? Hands over the bathtub, you all shake hands and go your merry way?"

"The crew rows outside the bay and abandons their ship instead of getting blown out of the water." He ran a finger down the blade of his long knife. "I don't want this to get ugly, Anwei. I could go through your rooms and just take the caroms. Dead people don't fight back." He shrugged, his voice going a little harder. "But I'm guessing you aren't stupid enough to have them here in your rooms, which means you need me for something. Dead people also can't tell me where my caroms are, I get it. I'm a busy man. Just tell me what you want."

Funny that he thought taking the caroms had been part of a scheme. Anwei held the ledger up. "I need a boat."

"You can't have that boat." He glanced at the ledger. "It's mine. And it's too big for four people to sail anyway."

"I don't want *this* boat." Anwei set the ledger down next to the knife. "One of Russo's little vessels is docked out there right now, small enough even for me to sail. You're not a fan of Russo and his fleet, are you?"

Altahn flinched, the first movement he'd made.

Ellis was gracious enough not to comment, his eyes narrowing with interest. "He rammed one of my ships and blew a huge hole in it with salpowder. He can't get his hands on caroms, so he rigged his holds with salpowder lines—willing to lose a whole ship if it keeps us off the rest of his fleet. He's even got some special agreement with the sailors—bonuses if they get hurt and more, so I hear. Trying to take that boat wouldn't go well for any of us."

"You know how quickly an impossible situation can turn given the right information." She leaned forward, ignoring the hiss of air coming out of Altahn. "For example: Did you know Russo has a daughter?"

Tual wasn't on the island. Mateo raced out to the docks with Aria limp in his arms only to find the boat gone. Eyes seemed to watch him from the forest as he carried Aria away from the dock, her whispers about a beast in the woods prickling across his arms. Mateo ran to hide her in Tual's office, his humors racing with energy and strength enough he could have carried the little girl's dead weight all the way up to the top of the abbey caves. Inside, Mateo placed Aria on the long couch, praying to someone, some*thing* that it wasn't *dead* weight because Aria couldn't be dead.

Please. Wasn't I supposed to be some kind of healer before. Why can't obscure flower names force their way into my thoughts now when I need them? The elsparn made me remember something—could they help? Please, I'm listening now!

Willow cackled in response, as if she thought he was praying to her. *You have everything you need, Mateo Montanne. You have me.*

Mateo pressed his hands to his ears trying to shut out her voice, gasping when something rough and cold touched his face that was not skin. Wrenching his hands out in front of him, Mateo fell off the couch, his lungs suddenly tight.

Because they weren't his hands anymore.

His wrists bulged out from his arms, his fingers swollen to twice their normal size like great sausages moldy with silver scales. His knuckles had turned knobbly, almost as if they could bend in too many directions, and long black nails jutted from his fingertips like claws. Mateo clenched his eyes shut, then opened them again, trying to dislodge whatever fear-induced hallucination had clogged his mind.

But the engorged wrists and knuckles, the scales, the *claws* were still there. He could feel them swelling larger, hot and stretched. Any moment his skin would split—

I made you better, Mateo! Willow sang. *You were too busy freaking out about that little morsel to notice.*

Little morsel. Heart racing, Mateo once again put an ear to Aria's mouth, frantic for a breath to say she was still there. When it didn't come, he went to her wrists for a pulse, tried sitting her up, laying her down, his hands dexterous and sinuous as they ran across her face, as if he'd had claws lurking inside him his whole life. Tears streamed down his cheeks because he had to find a way to save Aria, but he couldn't stop looking at his *hands*, his *beautiful artist fingers* that had turned to monstrosities. He had to pull them away from Aria, hide them behind his back as he sank onto the floor, sweat dripping down his jaw.

It had to be a dream. Waking up that morning, Abendiza, the tower, the flicker of movement out in the woods, the glass tunnel . . . all just a dream.

Mateo couldn't breathe. He couldn't think. He couldn't move. But still, his father's voice crept into his mind in an awful whisper. *Think of what you want,* his voice said.

Willow flexed inside Mateo at the thought, his swollen hands clenching along with her.

Bile burning up his throat, Mateo's whole body slick with sweat. But he closed his eyes and tried to concentrate on the little girl on the couch. *I want to fix her,* he thought. *Please help me fix her. That's all I want. I can feel all the energy you took, Willow.* It raged inside him, making him feel larger than life, like Patenga in his reliefs. *Put it back inside Aria!*

Willow only laughed.

Cursing, Mateo forced himself up from the floor, crying out at the terrible pain in his hands, but running toward the shelves anyway. He pulled down jar after jar, opening them to smell the contents only to throw them aside for the next, hints tickling at the back of his mind that he should know what each one was good for, only he didn't anymore. If Tual Montanne could swirl together plants and herbs and Calsta knew what else to bring people back to life with magic, why couldn't Mateo? Were they not the same?

He tried giving Aria herbs, took out salves, unscrewed spice jars, scattered shavings and petals and shriveled bug pieces, held resin blocks over her like incense. He even went to the jars with little creepy crawling things that skittered with excitement when he put them near Aria, then had to pull them away fast before they escaped. The smells, the shapes, the feel of them were more familiar with each panicked moment.

None of it restarted the breath in Aria's lungs.

Mateo threw the last jar down with a feral scream, the glass shattering across the marble floor, something with too many legs scurrying through the mess to hide under the desk. What good was being a shapeshifter if he couldn't *fix Aria?* He sagged to the floor by the couch and took Aria's hand in his two monstrous ones.

He didn't know how long he sat there, whispering, "Please, Aria. Please come back. I didn't mean to hurt you—*I* didn't hurt you, I just want you to come back. . . ." But it wasn't until the light had gone bruised that footsteps sounded in Mateo's ears.

Scrambling up from the floor, Mateo had no voice left to ask for help when Tual walked in, baskets strung over his arms. "Mateo, what are you . . .?"

But then he saw.

All the blood drained from Tual's face, and he was running. "Calia, Mateo. And the rinoe. The white one on the top shelf! Mateo, *move*!"

"Are those . . . herbs?" But Mateo darted toward the shelves, his hands—somehow now shrunk back to normal—moving faster than he could, finding the white jar, then going to the floor to pick bits of plants or dried bugs or whatever it was out from the shards of glass as if they remembered what calia or rinoe or whatever he was supposed to be searching for looked like when he couldn't.

Tual wrenched a pot free from under his desk and placed it over the little malt burner on its trivet before dumping everything Mateo brought to him into the pot's belly. He clapped a lid on top, then slid to his knees next to Aria to take her hand.

After a few moments, Tual turned to study Mateo. And then, with a nod to himself, he picked Aria up and left the room.

Mateo was too afraid to move, too afraid to acknowledge what he already knew. That it was too late. She wasn't breathing. People couldn't survive not breathing.

But soon Tual had come racing back into the room. He deposited Aria back on the couch, then checked the fire under the pot. There was a dusting of powdery white down her chin that wasn't any of the substances Mateo had gotten down for his father, but every question from Mateo, every entreaty, every demand for information Tual ignored until Mateo finally sank down into his father's desk chair and let his head rest against the wood as his father stirred and paced and swore. Tual's frenzied muttering and grinding of stone, bird, and beetle into a pot turned the room to steam that smelled of charcoal and lavender. As Tual stirred, Mateo tried to feel the change he knew had to happen as he felt energy drawing from *somewhere* into his father. But the medicine didn't knit into some miracle shape-shifter cure. It stayed lumpy and poisonous, a deathly stew.

Mateo couldn't move, and for once, it wasn't because he was tired or dizzy or sick—floppy, as Aria had said. He was stronger than he ever had been, Willow humming something that almost sounded happy at the back of his mind.

He had done this. No, *Willow* had done this. And even after Tual dripped medicine into Aria's mouth, she didn't move, as if whatever sparked the life inside her was now somehow inside Mateo instead.

But after a few minutes, Aria coughed. Mateo sat up, the shadows around her making her look pale and chalky, her hair a shade askew. But then Aria drew in one wet, gasping breath, and Mateo didn't care what she looked like.

Tual skidded to his knees by her side, spoon in hand, and Mateo willed himself to follow, but he couldn't force himself to go any closer to the little girl on the couch.

Aria inhaled again, a faint pink coming to her cheeks.

"She's all right?" Mateo gasped.

"Her state is very similar to your episodes. It mimics death, and it requires a specific antidote to come back. Which I think I've found." Tual rubbed a hand across his face, leaving a streak of the purple concoction he'd been spooning into Aria's mouth. There was no sign of the white powder he'd seen on her chin when Tual had first brought her in, but the hum of power was still in the air, making Mateo's head ache. The shadows around Aria looked too sharp, the girl herself almost fuzzy, as if she weren't real.

"You can't do this, Mateo," Tual whispered.

"*I* can't do this?" Mateo rasped, taking a step toward him. "I didn't do anything!"

"Don't come too close." Tual picked up the spoon once again.

"You have to be in control. Remember what I said at the tomb about you taking energy?" He stirred the pot three times, then drew another spoonful, holding his hand under it to keep it from dribbling onto the floor. "There isn't enough energy in the world to fill the hole inside you, Mateo. You *had* to take some down in the tomb because I can't manipulate rock. I needed you to open the burial chamber. But if you continue to draw energy from people around you, you'll be a drain—one I won't be able to *hide*. People will begin to notice the way death follows us."

Aria's face was pale, her eyes flicking this way and that behind her closed eyelids. Mateo looked away, because it was like looking at himself as he'd barely clung to life during those weeks in Chaol.

"I didn't do it. I was just standing there." Aria had been *dead*. Or almost dead, anyway. He hadn't been able to feel her heartbeat, the rush of her humors, no movement, no breath. She hadn't gone cold or stiff or anything, but she'd been gone. Mateo paced toward his father's shelves, the jars filled with mulch and pus and gods knew what. His father truly was a wonder. A god, even, bringing back life when there was none left. "I didn't try to take her energy. It was the ghost."

"You need to take responsibility for your own actions, son!" Tual gestured wearily toward the mess of glass glinting sharply amid the dried flora and fauna scattered across the floor. "You can't get angry and expect it to fill in the damage you've done. Aria isn't tethered to life the way you are—she isn't a shapeshifter. The hole inside you isn't going to go away until—"

"No, I mean the ghost is the one who *did* it. She tried to take Aria." Mateo turned with a groan, pacing past the desk, the shelves, the little burning pot. "*Did* take Aria."

Tual tipped the spoonful of steaming medicine into Aria's mouth, then rubbed her throat to make her swallow. He replaced the lid on the pot, put the spoon on top, then turned to face Mateo. "Please tell me what you mean."

"The girl who died—the one who made the hole. She's . . . *here*." Mateo flopped onto the couch next to Aria's head. She was still so pale and limp. *Drained.* Halfway to whatever afterlife Calsta had promised her.

"What do you mean, 'she's *here*'?" Tual began picking up the scattered jars and canisters, returning them to where they belonged.

"Her voice is in my head. She knows things about me, about you. About *Knox*, that boy you killed in the tomb. And Anwei—"

Mateo frowned. *Anwei.* The shape of the name was so familiar in his mouth, but he wasn't sure he'd heard it from Willow.

"The ghost should have died with the sword when it melted. With the boy it was attached to—he's the reason all this went wrong. Her soul was attached to you and that boy both, but there wasn't enough energy for three of you—"

Why does everyone keep saying I'm things I'm not? A thing. A hole. Now I'm dead? I'm right here.

"She's talking to me *right now*."

I was so hungry with Knox. Every day that girl was in front of us, ready to die so he'd feed me, but he wouldn't do it. Wouldn't share anything but what Calsta gave him. I wish I'd found you earlier. You and me, we're a pair. It's hard without the sword, though. Knox has it. Or maybe that girl does.

We are not a pair. I did not feed you, Mateo thought back. *You're the reason I'm dying.*

"Mateo, that isn't possible." Tual's voice rose. "I don't understand exactly how the sword latched onto that boy and kept from melting, but now things are right. He's dead. The sword was destroyed. The ghost's connection to you broke. You're stronger than you ever were before now that she's not sucking you dry." Tual swore as he accidentally knocked a canister down from the shelf, the container shattering when it hit the floor. He crouched, gathering up the bits of glass. "We just have to do the final steps to mend the hole she caused inside you."

Aria groaned, her head tipping to one side.

Mateo slid off the couch to kneel beside her, but Tual turned away, carefully gathering shards of glass up from the carpet and clearly gathering his thoughts just as delicately.

Tentatively, Mateo took Aria's hand. It was warm. The skin was a healthy pink now, practically glowing against the light brown of his own fingers. She wasn't dead.

"If caprenum was supposed to melt when it changed someone into a shapeshifter, then why was it scratched out of so many paintings and reliefs? Why was Patenga's sword *there* in his tomb? All the shapeshifters kept their weapons close." He groaned when Tual didn't answer him, brow furrowed as he continued to hunt for glass bits. "I'm telling you, the ghost is *in my head*. I took Aria to see the tunnels, and suddenly Willow was saying how hungry she was—"

"*Willow*? It has a name?"

"She always did, I'd guess. People have names. She reached out and . . ." Mateo gestured at Aria.

Tual stood, arms full of broken glass. "That is not possible."

"Well, it happened." Anger blossomed inside Mateo. Tual wasn't telling him everything, had *never* told him the whole story. If he could just goad his father into speaking—

Tual threw the bits of glass into a refuse bin, then dusted himself off before sitting in the desk chair. "Okay," he finally said. "Then this is uncharted territory. The only things I know about people like us are what I've stumbled into. So much of our history was destroyed long before you were born."

The swell of helplessness inside Mateo grew, and the rage grew with it, threatening to drown him. His unflappable father admitting that he *didn't* know something? How could someone with enough arrogance to believe he could bring his son back from the brink of death so long as Mateo was willing to take another life *not know*?

Was Mateo just another experiment? One that had gone horribly wrong because Tual had found himself invested in a specific outcome? Mateo with him, *alive*.

"Is Aria going to be all right?" Mateo whispered, her palm hot against his hands. His normal, non-swollen, non-monstrous hands. He shuddered, the memory of what they'd looked like twisting in his head until he couldn't recognize it. A hallucination. A stress nightmare.

"I think so." Tual sighed. "You always were. The Devoted always were, until we took too much. When I took from those who aren't gods-touched like Miss Aria here . . . well, they didn't always fare well, even if I only took a tiny bit." Tual didn't quite look at Aria, going instead to his desk and sitting down. He extracted a sheet of vellum from the top drawer, then picked up his quill and dipped it in his inkpot. "I've missed something, a part of the process, the magic. Whatever is happening to you is an opportunity to study. To learn something, so we can change our approach accordingly. So . . ." Tual cocked his head, quill at the ready. "How long has this ghost been talking to you? What does it say?"

Mateo tried to ignore Willow's breathing at the back of his head. "She says that she's a person? She seems to know what's going on around me, but it's limited to what I can see, what I hear, I think, but she also responds to thoughts. She says Knox—the boy who was connected to the sword—is alive. That he's with Lia and my sister."

Knox and that girl are in Kingsol, Willow hissed. *Lia isn't with them right now. She'll arrive soon, at least so long as she doesn't get eaten in the forest on her way down.*

Mateo choked on her words. Lia was in the forest? His sister was already in *Kingsol*? "She's talking right now. I guess most of them are in town." He bit his lip over Lia. There were things lurking in the forest, things even his father didn't want to face.

Tual blinked, and his quill paused. "If her perception is limited to what you see, hear, and think, then how would she know that?"

I told you I was going to keep an eye on them if you fed me. So I woke up Knox, of course. But then Willow's voice squeezed down small with rustlings and mutterings that were dark and wet, like decaying leaves on a forest floor. When she spoke again, her voice was too deep, wrong somehow. *That night in the tomb isn't the first time your father has tried to kill me. He still lacks the comprehension to understand what I am capable of.*

Lacks the comprehension? Mateo's brow furrowed. The little-girl mask Willow liked to wear was slipping. "It's not just . . . her in there, I don't think. Or maybe it isn't her at all, but something older. It *knows* you."

Not an it! the thing snarled.

"Mateo." Tual was shaking his head. "This sounds very . . . worrisome. I was just in town, and I think I would have noticed your sister and a boy with a mortal stab wound wandering around. At least, I *think* I would." He stopped, setting the quill down. "Though . . . I didn't recognize her at first in the tomb. Her aura looks so normal now, like ours."

"Normal like ours? You think she's turned shapeshifter? Killed someone so she can live forever?"

"She's killed before." Mateo didn't like the sad glint in his father's eye as he said it, an echo of horror rising as if her past was there inside him, just waiting to reveal itself like the name of an herb. And Tual's voice held a note of understanding Mateo didn't want to believe.

His sister. A shapeshifter? Father had said not many from their town had survived her escape from Beilda.

She's not like you, Mateo, Willow interrupted. *If she were, maybe I never would have found you.* It was Willow's voice again, the cloying, sweet tone twined together with rot. *Haven't you been listening?* she continued. *Knox and that girl already have that bond thing, like the one your father wants you to do with Lia so that you can get rid of me. But you wouldn't do that, would you, Mateo? I love you.*

They're bonded? Mateo asked.

She and Knox. Knox and her. She's the only thing keeping him alive now. If he'd killed her like I told him to, he'd be just fine. That's why you're my family now. He doesn't love me enough to feed me.

Tual leaned toward him. "She's talking to you now. What else has she said? Are there other effects? She stole the life right out of Aria without you being able to stop her?"

"And she made me shift. My hands . . ." Mateo clenched his long fingers into fists, the memory of claws scratching at his skin.

Blinking, Tual sat back in his chair. Shifting. That was something they hadn't talked about yet. That was what shapeshifter kings were famous for—like Patenga, with his reptilian head and parchwolf legs and feet. But Mateo, for once, didn't *want* to know. So he kept talking. "She's particularly interested in Abendiza, for some reason, but hasn't said why. And she's constantly saying that she's hungry. That Knox couldn't feed her because . . ." What was the difference between him and Knox? Mateo clutched himself around the middle, remembering the feeling of drawing in power, using it, and having that power do exactly as he asked. "I think she can take energy from other people because *I* can take energy from other people. Knox couldn't do that because he was only a Devoted, not a shapeshifter, so she had to survive on what she could drain from his connection to Calsta."

"And on what she drained from *you*, even if she didn't realize she was doing it."

"She doesn't like my sister. Or maybe she just wanted to eat her. It's hard to tell."

Your sister took Knox away from me.

Mateo suddenly remembered the relief he had copied showing Calsta and the nameless god together. "I saw the reliefs in the tomb— that bond you want me to make with Lia, that's where shapeshifters come from, right? *Our* auras are hidden. If that's what happens when Devoted and Basist magic mixes, maybe a bonded pair would get the same benefit." He paused. "But then I've never seen normal auras, only gods-touched."

"I assume if we fix you, you'll take on the rest of a Devoted's core abilities, though there are some distortions. This is all very interesting." Tual pointed at Mateo, his eyes flicking back and forth as he thought. "But it's only one out of a thousand things we don't understand. We have to approach this logically, like any other project we've done. How did the ghost latch on to you after so many years? What changed? And how are the environmental factors of your change different from when *I* turned?"

Aria began coughing again, curling sideways toward the edge of the couch. Mateo darted forward to stop her from falling off the edge. "Wake up, Aria," he whispered. "I can't let your sister find you sick like this. *I* don't want you to be sick." And the smaller voice inside him. *I don't want to kill anyone. Not you.*

Not Lia, either.

The thoughts felt like an anvil's weight pressing on his mind—if this was what it was to take a life by accident, then could he do it on purpose? If it was a choice between him and Lia . . .

Aria's slack mouth twitched, turning to a frown. Without opening her eyes, she spoke. "Mateo?"

Tual let Mateo help her sit up, watching them carefully. "The lake monster gave you quite a fright, didn't it, Miss Aria?"

"The snake?" Aria's eyes flickered open, her words coming out too slow and confused. "I don't remember a snake."

Mateo couldn't let go of her, Aria's lukewarm response almost more frightening than the pallor to her cheeks. "No digs about sweets or stealing swords?" His voice cracked, the words choking him.

Tual twitched, almost as if he meant to pull Mateo away, but he didn't, brow furrowing as Aria's slack expression turned into a glare. Another round of coughs bent her forward. "I bet you put something in those sweet rolls you fed me for breakfast," she gasped when she was done.

"I would *never* . . . And what do you mean, *I* fed you? You're the one who took *two*—"

"And all this stuff about not wanting me to die, not wanting Lia to hurt you. Who cares what *you* want?" Aria scowled.

"You should. I'm the one who feeds you." Mateo sat back, something in him unwinding. Aria wasn't broken. Aria was alive. His father had fixed it, just like he fixed everything.

"You should probably rest now, Miss Aria." Tual's smile was both calming and confident, as if he knew everything was going to be all right. "I'll call for a servant to help you to a special room to rest. Mateo and I have some business to attend to."

Aria didn't answer back the whole time Tual was gone fetching the maid, but Mateo figured she was probably too tired to harass him. A maid came and bundled her up into a rolling chair and took her out. Tual watched from the doorway, waiting until Aria had disappeared down the hallway before taking off in the other direction.

"Where are you going?" Mateo asked, following.

"You said Lia is coming, so we need to take care of some things before she gets here. The room Aria's going to be staying in will be hidden from aurasight. But there's more—"

Mateo's heart jangled against his ribs as he followed. "She wasn't supposed to come right now. Our whole plan—"

Tual slowed, eagerness flashing across his face. "I wish she *were* here already—with the Warlord only a day away, taking care of Lia first would have been much easier than her interrupting while Devoted are here."

"I hate to be the one to provide the barest sheen of reality here, but Lia and I haven't exactly been writing letters, Father." Stomach twisting, Mateo tried not to think about what the eagerness on his father's face was for. "What do you want me to do, send up smoke signals that say, 'Run faster! The convenient window for your attack is about to close'?"

"She's not going to attack us, Mateo." Tual slid to a stop in front of the pile of luggage in the entryway still slowly being put away from their long time away and began poking through the boxes until he found the archeological equipment. He grabbed one of the tool bags and headed for the door. "The whole point is that when Lia comes, you and Aria are going to leave with her. She's going to save both of you from me."

"Right." Mateo followed, his anger beginning to boil up inside him again. "She'll listen to Aria's story about getting sick in the tunnel and be twice as excited for me to run away with her. We'll be bonded before our first campfire, and I'll stab her over the egg tarts." The image stuck in Mateo's head as he followed his father outside and across the courtyard, and he immediately wished he hadn't said it out loud. Willow, however, seemed to glom on to the thought, playing it over and over in his head with a fiendish kind of hope.

Why would you want me to bond with Lia and then kill her? he thought at her savagely. *Didn't you just beg me not to get rid of you?*

Willow didn't answer, dark hunger unfolding around her in his head that felt somehow even worse than what she'd done to Aria.

"First of all, if you think egg tarts are what people on the run make over their campfires, the first few weeks on the road are going to be rough." Tual grinned over his shoulder. "Second, that's exactly why we planned for you to run away together. The two of you need more time to actually become attached. At this point, stabbing Lia would just make the hole inside you bigger—we know that now. Murdering an innocent instead of murdering the one you love doesn't work." Tual pulled open the heavy watchtower door and darted inside, going straight to the secret passage. "You could have *two* ghosts feeding on you instead of one if we do this wrong."

Mateo groaned, following his father into the darkness. "I guess you forgot to teach me the proper levels of devotion to achieve a shape-shifter sacrifice."

"Well, we've already got a proper start." Tual rounded the first switchback, past the rows and rows of monuments, names so small Mateo could hardly believe they belonged to people. So many, all blamed on a curse that didn't exist. "You like her enough that you don't want to kill her. Not even her little sister."

"I don't *want* to kill *anyone*."

They'd reached the glass walkway where Aria had collapsed only this morning. Tual turned back to look at Mateo, Castor's moonlight falling in slippery blue lines through the water that seemed to make the cliff tunnel at the end even darker. "That's true until it isn't anymore."

CHAPTER 14

Built for Slaughter and Survival

The air was heavy, the clouds above just waiting to pour rain down on Lia's head. She leaned in to pat Vivi's neck when he strained against the reins. As usual, the pat was enough to get him to sulkily settle into their less than brisk pace.

"I know you want to go faster," Lia murmured, raising a hand to push a branch out of her way. "These poor Trib horses can't keep up with you. Especially not on this little trail. They can't even tell where the ground starts to go brittle." She raised her voice a little for Gilesh and Bane to hear even as Vivi toed his way around a spot in the ground, as if he could feel the dirt thinning beneath his hooves. "They should have all gone back to Trib land like I said."

Gilesh gave her a cheeky wave when she looked back at him. "That thing would have eaten you a long time ago if it weren't for us watching your back, Miss Lia." Bane drew up behind him, keeping a good fifty feet between his horse and Vivi.

Ominous shapes fluttered in the trees as Lia led them toward the river that would take them to Kingsol, vines looking like snakes which looked like vines until Lia wasn't sure what she was looking at. There was an echoing roar of water from one of the many underground rivers in this place, the earth nothing but thin crust floating on what sounded like a long-forgotten ocean. The thinner the earth, the more Lia itched to turn Vivi directly south instead of southwest toward Kingsol. She wanted to find the lake. She wanted Aria.

But every time she started to turn Vivi's reins, the memory of standing in the tomb next to Mateo would come haunting back, the way her arms and legs had begun to shake, her muscles all quivering with fatigue after Mateo had stolen her energy . . .

It still rankled that he hadn't tried to contact her. Hadn't written or appeared on that little mare of his with Aria sitting behind him in the saddle. It jabbed at her, the thought of him doing *nothing*. At the very least, Lia had expected Mateo to *try*.

The first few days after Chaol, she'd missed his wry self-deprecation, missed the way he grudgingly did the right thing as soon as he figured out what it was, then surprised her by doing it again, and again, even when the right thing was hard.

When she'd gone out hunting for Tual's tracks, she'd looked for signs of him. Dropped sweet rolls or paintbrushes. That ridiculous hat with an arrow painted under the brim to point the way.

But every day, she'd found nothing. And every day, her hope tarnished a little more until it was a mottled, unrecognizable thing, a disappointment she couldn't bear to look at. How could she have hoped that Mateo, the boy raised by a shapeshifter—

The boy who thought he was going to die—

The boy who'd made her laugh when she'd wanted to crush the world between her fists—

The boy who'd stood between her and Ewan Hardcastle when the Devoted had been rabid, a sword in Ewan's hand and his oaths long forgotten.

The boy who'd come for her in the middle of one of his episodes to warn her the Warlord was coming, even though getting caught would have earned him a slit throat.

Lia had thought *that* boy would do something. She hoped that boy could still do something, even if he hadn't found a way to do it yet.

Lia locked her hope away into a box deep inside herself. Whatever Mateo wanted, *Tual* would have no scruples about stripping Lia of every drop of power she had, then forcing her to hold still for Mateo to stab her through the gut.

Lia couldn't go to the estate on her own. She needed a plan, and plans came from Anwei.

"We're going to get flooded out," Gilesh called. "Rain's going to start, and these cave openings will overflow. Then that *thing* you are riding will eat all of us to survive."

"Built for slaughter and survival. Just like me." She grinned back.

"You know I'm going to beat you when we spar."

"Your horse has spent this whole trip trying to run away, and we haven't even drawn swords." Lia turned forward in her saddle. "Pardon me if I don't spend any extra time practicing before our match—" The words stuck in her mouth as Vivi reared back, the auroshe barely managing to avoid going headfirst into a swollen channel of water that had been hidden by the foliage. Lia frowned at the water, which was flowing a little too quickly for something so flat. "Another one of those waterways."

"Miss Lia!" She looked up to find Bane on slightly higher ground in the trees to her left, boulders jutting up from the ground next to him. "The water just . . . stops."

Nudging Vivi to walk up the bank, Lia patted him consolingly when he lashed his tail. She had to tap his sides to get him to the rocks where Bane had stopped, the water oddly still and silent where it pooled beneath them. The rocks made an odd semi-circle opposite where the channel flowed out from it, each one jutting up almost unnaturally, like fingers clawing their way from the ground.

Dismounting, Lia pointed to the ground in front of Vivi's nose. "You'll stay?" she asked.

His neck twisted away from her, jabbering toward the trees. Probably a cat or a snake of some kind slinking away at the scent of a predator like Vivi. Knowing he'd obey regardless of temptation, Lia picked her way around the pool, circling up to the rocks, then back down, the water too still. It wasn't until she went back around that she saw it. A gap in the rocks.

When she took a step forward to get a better look, it disappeared, the rocks blending together to hide the opening.

Brow furrowed, Lia inched up to the tall rocks directly above where she'd thought she saw the hole, disappointed when there was nothing below her but water, brown rock, and . . .

A reflection. A tall, black reflection of an arch across the pool. A tunnel that led into the hillside.

Vivi gave an angry keen from below as raindrops began to fall. Lia could hear the slush of his hooves in mud, leaves brushing soft against one another, and something . . .

Lia closed her eyes, searching for the source of alarm fingering up her spine. Calsta had returned her ears and eyes, allowing Lia to hear and see better than the Trib. *There.* A rustling sound that felt measured. Exact, like a beast trying to walk as quietly as it could.

Something smarter than an average beast. And much larger. Lia climbed back down to Vivi, her mount balking when she reached for his reins, hackles raised as he peered into the darkness.

"Are you *sure* we're going in the right direction?" Bane asked from a safe distance down the channel. "These trees should all be cut down, if you ask me. No honest rocks and mountains—"

Lia put up a hand, which hushed him quick enough.

Vivi let out a hiss toward a clump of ferns grown so large that their long leaves were at Lia's eye level. Lia reached out to calm Vivi, edging closer to the trees, which was when she saw it: a flicker of gold at the very outside edge of her aurasight. Vivi jerked his head, pulling Lia forward, and the dusting of gold turned into a deluge. A *swarm* of aurasparks zipping this way and that.

Devoted.

Lia stumbled back, the gold rippling to nothing beyond the edge of her aurasight. She leapt onto Vivi's back and kicked him around. Her mind stretched as wide as it could for any auras that might have seen *her*.

"Move," she rasped, both Trib horses rearing when she charged Vivi toward them. "*Now.*"

⸎

Tual had always told Mateo to stay out of the abbey rooms hollowed from the cliff. Of course, Mateo had explored most of the floor level beyond the glass walkway anyway, but on various, slightly rebellious occasions, he had approached the stairs that led up into the ruins above, which he'd seen from the lake house, the empty windows like dead eyes staring down at him.

He'd never made it far.

The nameless god's touch had begun to blossom inside him even a few steps up, igniting the energy drain Willow had made of him. With no energy to take, he'd gone faint, sickly. But not enough to stop Mateo from feeling death in the walls.

Not just the taste of metal and gears, of false floors and unmarked tiles that would unleash the wrath of Basists on intruders in this place. It was the bones that stopped Mateo.

So as Tual passed through the end of the glass tunnel and immediately started up the stairs, Mateo hesitated, a taste of decay in his mouth that didn't belong to Willow. With the ghost burning inside him, Mateo's energy branched farther than it ever had before, sinking into the walls and touching stone, metal, and paint. He caught his breath when his energy didn't fizzle to nothing, tracing the shapes of rooms above and below him, clear down to the lake walls riddled with tunnels that branched out into the forest. All Basist made. Sealed for too many years to count since there were no Basists to operate them.

The tapping of boots on stone brought him back to the stairs, his father rushing up into the darkness Mateo had never braved. "Wait," Mateo called as Tual got near the top, something menacing waiting beneath the step. "*Wait!*"

But Tual hopped the stair as if he'd done it a thousand times. Insides twisting, Mateo trudged after him, stepping over the rigged stair.

According to Tual, the upper rooms were where most of the abbey children had stayed. There were training yards, a kitchen, lookouts, and sleeping chambers, the whole place peppered with traps that Basists could feel but no one else could, making it a safe place for those learning the nameless god's arts because it kept everyone else out. But then, toward the end of the shapeshifter wars, a monstrous shapeshifter king had come and killed them all. She'd stayed in their rabbit warren, drinking down their souls one by one until the first Warlord led a charge on the stronghold. Somehow, the Warlord had won, and Devoted had scratched every design from the walls, burned every remnant of the creature that had scurried through these tunnels . . . and every last hint of the people who'd lived and died there too. Every record of their learning, their history, even the fact of their existence.

Gone.

A massacre performed twice.

Death breathed out from these walls.

Tual ran down a walkway, narrowly dodging another trap before starting up a spiral staircase that burrowed directly into the rock above, the bag of tools bouncing against his side as he ran. Picking up speed, Mateo followed through glass passages, more stairs, through corridors and over a flowing channel of water that must have been connected to the waterfall, shouting a warning every time his mind snagged on something nasty lying in wait to catch his stone-blind father.

Somehow, Tual avoided every single one.

The higher they went, the thicker the smell of rot and bone layered in Mateo's nose. Willow had grown quiet in his mind. *I've been here*, she whispered. *I know this place.* Mateo ignored her.

Tual turned down a side corridor, glimpses of dusk over the back side of the cliffs away from the lake peering in at Mateo through the stone-cut windows. When Tual darted through yet another doorway, Mateo began to swear inside his head, sprinting to catch up, then almost tripped over his father, who had dropped to his knees just inside.

It was a large room, the ceiling arching more than two stories overhead with high pointed windows lining the left-hand wall, though the glass had either been broken out or had never been there to begin with. Through them, Mateo could see rolling hills covered in gently swaying trees, the sound of water whispering through the air. At the far end, opposite the openings facing the trees, there were more windows giving a view of the clear twilight sky over the lake.

The remains of what might have been a chandelier hung drunkenly from the center of the ceiling, smaller fixtures dripping broken strands of mud-coated lumps that might have been crystals around it. Mateo lowered himself onto the dirt-strewn floor, the outlines of broad black-and-white-checkered floor tiles showing through near where his father was kneeling, but obscured everywhere else, with what looked like bits of stone rubble poking through the dirt here and there.

Tual's ribs heaved as he tried to catch his breath, one hand to his chest. He pulled the tool bag from his shoulder and let it rest on the floor between them. "The air feels thicker up here."

It mostly felt cold to Mateo—unnaturally cold, as if the Basists who had lived here so long ago preferred the feel of living underground. The corners of the room were lashed with shadows and the walls rough, as if something had been violently torn from the side facing the lake.

Looking around, Mateo stood, suddenly understanding the rubble strewn throughout the room. Turning slowly, he tried to assess where the stone fragments had come from based on their current positions, trying not to step on any of the pieces when he walked a few steps closer to the center of the room. "Father, how have we never come up here? We'll have to categorize it like a tomb—these bits are from the *wall*. Is it possible these are what Devoted left when they tore this place apart?" He pulled out his shirt tail and used it to cover his hand, carefully dislodging one of the fragments. On the underside, there was a faint outline that looked like *paint.* "The top side's been exposed to the elements, but the rest of it—" Mateo's heart began to speed, excitement winding up inside him like a spring. The checkerboard floor would make it easy to map out where the pieces had fallen. If only he'd brought his drawing satchel. "This could be a huge find. A mural from a Basist abbey? This is *our history.*"

"No." Tual breathed, putting a tentative hand to the section of tile in front of him. "We can't disturb this place."

"It's not disturbing if you're trying to put it back together—"

"At least." Tual's voice was quiet, his eyes glazed. "We won't disturb it any more than we have to."

Mateo barely turned in time to see Tual raise a chisel from the bag of tools, then stab it into the tile.

"What are you *doing*?" Mateo jerked forward, hands outstretched to stop his father from breaking *every rule of archeology,* but Tual batted him away.

"I have to see." The hollow ring to his father's voice stopped him, as if his father was more ghost than Willow.

The spot Tual had chosen had less accumulated dirt, and he'd gouged the chisel into the seam between tiles, chipping the one closest to him. Grunting, Tual leveraged the thick marble square up with a muddy *crack.* He dragged it away from its spot in the floor with a groan, exposing dense clay beneath. Without looking up, he started after a second tile.

A jolt of uneasiness wormed through Mateo's chest at the sight of his father furiously clawing at the clay with his bare hands. "You made me *run up stairs* to watch you desecrate an important archeological site? What could *possibly* be under the tile that's more important than the mural Devoted tried to destroy?"

"You say your ghost came back. The sword came back when it wasn't supposed to." Tual bared his teeth as he leveraged the second tile back, leaving streaks of clay smudged across his hands. "You didn't even lose your breath on the way up here, and Miss Aria . . ." He groaned, sliding the tile onto the dirt next to the first. "Whatever is happening, it's changing you. The sword was supposed to melt, but if it didn't . . ." Groping for the tool bag, Tual extracted a trowel, the point wickedly sharp. He looked up at Mateo. "I have to find out if my dagger came back too." Tual stabbed the trowel point first into the black clay.

"Your dagger . . . the one you . . . it also melted?" Mateo knelt on the ground next to his father, careful of the bits of rock that needed to be categorized and pieced together but unable to look away from the hole his father was making in the ground. Willow held still inside him, her breath corroding the edges of his thoughts. *I know this place. I know these bodies.*

How could you know this place? Mateo shot back. *I've never been here.*

The rest of me knows it. They're louder now because they remember their deaths.

"If the weapon you used to turn shapeshifter melted, then what are you digging up?" A terrible thought bled into Mateo's mind. "Is *this* where you buried the person—"

"—who mattered most to me? Yes." Tual dropped the trowel and began digging with his hands. He went still, his fingers curving around something deep in the clay. "Honestly, I know almost nothing about what we are, what we can do, how it all works—but if my dagger came back, it would have come back here."

"But how could the body . . . ? It's under the *tiles*. . . ."

"I grew up here, Mateo. We learned where the traps were, one stupid, dead high khonin at a time—not all those graves under the watchtower are from the curse."

"There is no curse," Mateo said automatically. Then his gut twisted as Tual uncovered the first black-stained bone. "You were a servant here," he whispered. "You grew up in the tower? Your house mark—"

"It doesn't matter now."

But it did. "The cleared area with less dirt . . . You've pulled up this floor before."

Tual nodded as he dug, and bile rose in Mateo's throat as Tual unearthed the bottom of a rib cage, then a sternum, a clavicle. An upper arm and scapula. Next, the very tip of the widest part of a pelvis, as if this body had been buried on its side. There were threads of clothing, all decayed enough for a century to have passed. Perhaps two.

The rubble was just as old, based on the weathering and dirt.

Each bit of black-stained bone slowed Tual a little more, his breaths coming faster until he stopped, hunched over the grave.

"Father?" Mateo could feel him shuddering with each breath.

He threw the trowel aside and stared Mateo in the face. "I can't."

"You can't *what*?"

"I can't do this." Tual wouldn't look at the bones, his eyes glued to Mateo's. "I need you to do it with your energy. Look for my dagger."

"Who is she?" Mateo could see from the bones that she'd been female, an adolescent with hips that had borne no children. He placed his hands on the ground near the hole, then pulled them back again, trying to pretend that she was like Patenga. Like *any* of the other entombed bodies he'd helped excavate. A discovery. A clue to who he was.

But she wasn't.

She was his father's dead love, murdered by his hand.

"Beryl was my dearest friend. We grew up together like brother and sister. I would have died for her." Tual's voice cracked. He looked past Mateo to the cracks in the wall, his face pained.

Mateo bit his lip. Tual obviously *hadn't* died for her.

"It wasn't Devoted who broke that wall. It was a mistake after we found them buried down in the lowest caves. We brought them up here, not knowing what they were—"

"You found what? What are you talking about?"

"The caprenum blades. There were two of them. Devoted must not have known how to destroy them, so they hid them away." His head bowed.

"Two blades. The sword you used for me. And . . . ?"

"My dagger," Tual breathed. "Devoted didn't go looking quite so hard for gods-touched back then. They hadn't found . . . me."

"You?"

Tual met his eyes. "I was Calsta's. And Beryl belonged to the nameless god. I didn't know it until she found the blades. It was like she could feel them waiting down there. We brought them up here, and we argued."

"About . . . ?"

"What to do with them. She knew there was something wrong. We'd been all through the caves, seen everything the Devoted couldn't destroy. . . ." He swallowed. "I wanted to keep them. To study them— I'd always wanted to go to the university, and she'd always said maybe her parents would pay. . . ."

Mateo waited, Tual's head bowed. "You argued."

"It was a mistake. Well, it started as one. It was a terrible choice to have to make, Mateo. Her or me. It didn't have to be that way, but *she* decided it was—as if there is evil in an object, evil in me for touching them, wanting them. She made her choice, and I had to make mine." When Mateo didn't move, Tual took in another long breath and let it out again before forcing himself to look back down at the bones. "I wanted to live, not be killed for wanting to know more. Just like you, Mateo."

"To know *what?*"

"About the swords. About artifacts. About beings with so much power that they didn't need money, they didn't need family, or a university, or swords, or anything at all. They were free." The clay crumbled between his fists. "Healing was the first thing I tried to learn once she was gone and I had her powers. I would have used it to save her if I could, though it would have been the wrong decision." He looked down. "It was only a matter of time before someone reported something, before they came for her. This was a better death than the Warlord would have given her. So I've spent my life using her magic to do good. Healing. Changing the world. Saving *you.*"

Mateo couldn't breathe, the rubble around them, the dirt, the mud, the stone, the body itself too old, far too old. "How long ago, Father?"

Tual slowly raised his head. "Do you really want to know?"

Mateo shivered.

A curse. Willow sang in rotted notes, each vibrating deeper into Mateo's brain. *One soul stolen every generation, the energy stored away to gobble up when he needed it. How else could he have lived so long?*

You weren't here. You weren't even born, Mateo savaged back at her. *You don't know anything.*

"Please," Tual breathed. "Help me find it. A dagger made of caprenum."

Closing his eyes was as much to shut out Willow's awful keening as it was to shut out the open grave. Mateo placed his hands on the ground, his energy flowing out until he felt bones, so many bones—in the walls, in the floor. Everything inside him stuck. *You don't want to kill until you do.*

I didn't want to kill until he killed me. Willow's husky voice had thinned down to her girlish rasp. *But now I haven't much choice. Neither do you. Both of us are broken, and it takes blood to fix the holes.*

I was already broken before he broke you, Mateo wanted to argue.

The holes in his soul hadn't come from Tual. They'd come from his blood parents, from the village elders who'd found the nameless god's touch in his hands.

Mateo opened his eyes when Tual grabbed hold of his shoulders, bits of black clay from his fingers grinding into the fibers of Mateo's fine paisley coat. "You are all that matters now, Mateo. Your life. Our family." And Tual pulled him close.

The horror inside Mateo dulled, and he hugged his father back. This was his *true* father. The man who had carried him through life despite the extra risk it brought just to keep Mateo alive. If anyone loved him, it was Tual.

He'd always known his father was willing to do whatever it took to get the right things done. Sometimes that *meant* blood. Even Mateo knew that. His father was far braver than Patenga, who'd taken his own life instead of trying to fix what *he'd* broken.

So Mateo reached for the nameless god's energy inside him. Only it wasn't the nameless god's; it was *Aria's*.

He faltered, feeling sick. But then the room came alive in his mind. The stone walls whispered about how they fit together. The clay bed under the marble floor sang out a complicated combination of elements that were mixed together with the soft, slick feel of bone. Bones in the walls, in the floor, *so many bones* deeper than the ones his father had unearthed, generations' worth of the dead hidden from sight. There were more beyond this room too, dead in the stairwells below, dead in outcroppings and tunnels that wormed farther out past the abbey, unfortunates who had tried to come in and were denied.

All of it was quiet and cold, waiting the way Willow did at the back of his mind.

But there was something warm under the half-exposed skeleton in the clay before him.

As soon as Mateo's energy focused in on that warmth, goose bumps prickled down his arms. The object was, every molecule, *wrong*. The elements had been twined together like musical notes to form something perfect and beautiful, but then it had been corrupted, tortured, blasphemed.

Just like Patenga's sword in the artifact room, like the walls, the reliefs, the mosaics in his tomb. Like the spot of wrong at the top of the watchtower. This object was full of shapeshifter magic.

Energy rang in Mateo's ears, the corrupted metal calling to him. He wanted it out. And when he reached with his mind, the dagger was underground one second, then lying on the clay between jutting bones the next, absolutely clean as if it had been sitting there the whole time.

Just think of what you want, Tual said that night in the tomb. *Then take it.* The blade was pockmarked, like the sword Tual had stabbed the boy in the tomb with. Like Patenga's sword they'd taken from the burial chamber. Caprenum.

Tual reached out and grasped Mateo's shoulder. "You've never been able to do that before. Your control. Your *power,*" he breathed. "You *moved* it."

Aria Seystone did, anyway, Willow whispered.

Mateo recoiled, inching back from the hole, but death was inside him, rattling out with each breath. He could feel it twisting him into a new shape, one that wanted to reach for the dagger sitting so innocently on the clay floor, surrounded by rotting bones.

His hands felt tight, swollen. When he looked down, he froze, his carefully manicured nails bruised and black.

Lia kicked Vivi faster, but he keened, calling to the herd of auroshes they were leaving behind. He bent his head as if he meant to run back toward them, his serpentine neck twisting against the reins. Heart pounding like a beast caged inside her ribs, Lia spurred him deeper into the trees.

There had been ten Devoted right there on the edge of her

aurasight. If she'd taken another step, would she have seen more? Fifteen, twenty of Calsta's warriors, able to see her aura clear as an afternoon sky? Lia jabbed a hand into her saddlebags and pulled her veil out from where it was stowed to spread it across her lap in the saddle. Calsta hadn't restored her third oath yet, leaving her weak in the face of so many brimming with Calsta's strength. Surely the goddess would see her need for the third oath, then for the fourth to help her track auras, then the fifth, so she'd be able to see into Tual's and Mateo's minds when she got to them—to understand what was truly going on rather than making guesses. Her sister's life and her own depended on it.

What were so many Devoted doing in the middle of nowhere?

Lia sent up a prayer to the Sky Painter, the veil clutched in her hand. *I'm here. I'm trying to stop Tual, like you want. I'm keeping my oaths. I need my sister.* She fumbled to drape the veil over her head as Vivi stormed forward. When the folds had settled over her face, Lia breathed in, willing Calsta's energy inside her to change.

It didn't.

Batting a branch out of her face, Lia clung to Vivi with her knees as he jumped a fallen tree. Mateo had been excavating Patenga's tomb on the promise that some kind of wasting sickness cure would come out of it.

Could it be that the Devoted had come to collect? Or had they been *invited*?

"Lia?" Gilesh called from behind her. "Would you perhaps tell us what under Calsta's sky could spook a Devoted into stampeding a fully grown auroshe across unstable ground? Maybe let us know which direction this threat of yours is coming from and whether or not we should hide?"

Vivi tore the reins from Lia's hands, darting to the side and jumping a second felled log. Lia swore, her arms coming up to protect her face from the branches and leaves swatting by. "Vivi," she hissed. "If you don't—"

But then she saw it. A shape snaking through the trees after them. It was large, running with its head low as it darted after them: an auroshe.

"Don't follow me, Gilesh! Head for the river!" Lia let Vivi run, Gilesh's and Bane's auras winking out the moment they were out of range. Vivi snaked between trees and up a hill, not fleeing from the creature so much as testing it. Finally, Vivi swiveled around to rear just as the other auroshe overtook them and struck at the thing with his hooves. The other auroshe hissed, hackles all the way raised, but it didn't attack, as if it had seen one of its own, and despite the unfriendly welcome, couldn't bring itself to run away. Both its horns were broken, its teeth jagged, ribs showing like starvation itself.

"Vivi!" Lia coaxed her auroshe back onto all fours even as the feral auroshe made a play at charging—it was almost teasing, like a cat batting at a string. It shied off to the side long before it came within reach of Vivi's sharp horn, its eyes darting between Lia and her mount. Twisting to keep his eyes on the creature as it circled them, Vivi cried to be given permission to tear out its belly.

The other auroshe's hide held a familiar pink tinge.

Once Lia was certain Vivi was under control, she dismounted. "You stay," she whispered to Vivi, staring straight into his eyes and blowing into his nostrils. He lipped her veil, then threw his head back with a rebellious screech, but after a moment Vivi's horn dipped down to touch the forest floor. He'd stay.

Turning very slowly, Lia faced the half-starved auroshe. It had gone still, only the glow of its eyes visible in the darkness of the trees. "Rosie?" she whispered. "Is that you?"

The auroshe's head jerked forward into the light, wrinkled muzzle relaxing just a hair. Then its hackles began to lower, even when Vivi screamed, baring all forty-two of his sharp teeth. Lia gave Vivi a reassuring pat, then took a cautious step toward Rosie, the auroshe she'd freed from the fights in Chaol. She'd touched her horn and blown into her nostrils—the only way to bond to an auroshe—but Rosie wasn't trained the way Vivi was, so it was hard to know what the creature would do.

Rosie gamboled forward, her movements erratic and aggressive, but when Lia held a hand out toward her muzzle, the auroshe bent her head and rubbed up against Lia's palm, shivering when Lia stepped closer to blow into her nostrils through the veil to reaffirm their bond. Rosie's feet still danced, and her sides twitched, but her black eyes searched for Lia's through the thin fabric, unblinking.

"How did you get out here?" Lia whispered, scratching her behind the ears.

After rescuing Rosie from the fights, she'd left the auroshe on the beach beneath Mateo's house with plenty of fish and little beach creatures to eat.

Mateo's house. She didn't want to think of that night, of her pressing Mateo's hand to Rosie's forehead and bending him down to breathe into her nostrils as the first shots in Castor's and Jaxom's godly war streaked across the sky like runaway stars. Of shaking his hand and finding calluses, as if he'd done something worthwhile when she hadn't been looking.

Mateo had more to him than most people saw. At least . . . she'd thought he did. She bent down to press a cheek between Rosie's broken horns. "Did you follow him here?" she whispered. "And he left you out here like he'd never met you, either?"

Vivi screamed behind her, scaled nose pointing into the boulders beyond them.

Lia turned to look. They were very regular-looking boulders—so aggressively average that the formations seemed almost man-made.

A flash of aura showed above the trees. Not Calsta's gold—it was perfectly white and plain. The white light stuttered, then disappeared as quickly as it had come into being.

Lia took a cautious step forward, her senses singing. What could cause an aura to flash in and out of being like that?

The roar of water caught in her ears. A waterfall. Like the one next to Tual's house on the map Anwei had shown her.

She was close. Far, far too close.

Vivi chortled, making Lia jump. But before she could quiet him, the aura appeared again, a burst of light that once again extinguished almost immediately. This time, the flicker was enough to see the aura hiding in the rocks.

It was Mateo Montanne.

⟆⟇⟆

Hands shaking, Tual picked up the dagger from its cage of bones. A flower had been forged into the handle, the blade short with a decorative curve, as if it had been made to be looked at, not to kill. Pushing up from the tile, Tual turned away from the bones and held the weapon up to Castor's blue light—

And suddenly there was nothing in Mateo but hunger.

So *hungry*, Willow agreed. *Aria will help for a while, but it's not enough. We can sip from your staff, and maybe—*

Don't, Mateo growled back, but still his insides ached.

Where's my sword? Willow whispered. *It could make us all better.*

"How can this have returned?" Tual almost seemed to have forgotten Mateo, holding the dagger close to his face, then far away, his eyes squinted. "I don't know what it means. I *have* to know what it means. I always thought the shapeshifters' kings knew something I didn't to become so powerful. Conservation of energy could make an argument for the caprenum returning, but are the two related? Maybe Bettany's rule?"

"Isn't Bettany's rule about energy being split into two kinds of—"

"Shapeshifters are always depicted with their weapons in hand, Mateo!" Tual twisted to face Mateo, the dagger held out in front of him. "How many murals have we found with caprenum swords, knives, axes all scratched away? I always thought it was a symbol to show what they were, not an accurate depiction of how they *lived*. I've been blind." He moved toward the window at the far end of the hall, Jaxom's brighter gleam beckoning for him to hold the dagger high in the moon's light. It was as if the weapon had changed from a terrible memory into something precious in less time than it had taken Tual to inhale.

Mateo followed slowly, the world shaky under his feet. "What does it matter how it came back?"

Lowering the blade, Tual looked at his son. "That ghost latched on to her brother. Then, when you were all in the same room, she switched to you. Is the distance a problem? Has she told you to get the sword?"

Mateo nodded.

"The sword must matter, then. You're stronger now that she's with you, but she only knew she could switch to you because you were close to the sword. Her brother interfered in the original ritual, then kept the sword close all these years. . . ." But he shook his head, turning away again. "You aren't a representative sample. We know what went wrong with your turning, and I've never seen anything anywhere about a shapeshifter bond that included three people—"

An auroshe scream shattered the air, making Mateo jump back from the window, his hands shaking. Rosie had found him.

That was the only explanation. Rosie had followed him from Chaol, watched him and Aria in his sleep, and was now ready to tear him apart so Lia could retrieve her sister.

But then he saw it. A sparkle of gold through the gap in the windows, the stone walls blocking any other suggestion of godly power. Before he could think on that—the walls blocked auras?—he ran to the window openings facing the lake. It wasn't Rosie. There were three auroshes crossing the bridge onto the island below them, each one crowned with a golden aura "Father, she's here. The Warlord is the only aura I recognize, but there are two other Devoted with her."

"What?" Tual thrust the dagger into his belt, his voice uncharacteristically rough. He sprinted for the stairs, calling over his shoulder. "We were supposed to have another day! If she finds Aria, we're dead."

"I thought we couldn't die!" Mateo called after him, not feeling reassured by the way Tual ran from the room without answering. The lake was supposed to be safe. *He* was supposed to be safe. Heart drumming hard, Mateo pulled back from the window. It wasn't just Aria they needed to worry about. Evidence of what they were was easy enough to spot without a little freckled girl screaming about being kidnapped.

He held up a single hand, his artist fingers tipped in black, black nails.

～※～

Lia scrunched her eyes shut, as if straining would make Mateo's aura appear again. She stepped closer to the rocky horizon, the landscape dipping and bulging in odd places that made Lia remember something about Basist-built defense mechanisms around the whole lake. Vivi keened from behind her, Rosie screeching a challenge in response, but the ragged auroshe shrank back when Vivi reared. At least Vivi was still abiding by Lia's command to stay.

The sky was too dark to make out where the river turned into a waterfall, stars glaring down at her from between the two moons. Jaxom's orange glow seemed to egg Lia on, the warrior god mocking her for standing frozen when the answer to all their plans was nothing but a little climb up. *We're going to find Mateo,* Anwei had said, *and Tual will follow.*

One last step forward, and the aura shimmered into existence, Mateo's essence blazing back to life. Lia ran back to Vivi, hopped on his back, and unsheathed her sword.

～※～

Hiding his hands in folded arms, Mateo started toward the stairs, his mind full of traps, of swords, of bones and shapeshifter wrongness. But when he got to the door, something in his mind stilled, like a doe just before a parchwolf pounced.

She's here, Willow whispered.

I know the Warlord is here, so whatever you are doing, stop! Mateo started forward again, only to pause when another auroshe scream tore through the night from the forest behind him, far, far away from where the Warlord was gleefully conquering his home. Turning very slowly, he faced the windows that went out the back side of the cliff, the trees below a mask.

Were there more Devoted creeping up on them from behind? Not a friendly visit and demand for a cure to a terrible disease, but some kind of attack? Or maybe it *was* Rosie. Would the Basist traps keep out an animal, or had she finally found a way to get to him? No glass in the windows to keep her out, no hostlers, no Father—

The scream came again, the sound drawing Mateo up to the rough sill. A solitary aura sparked into existence down in the trees, crowned in gold.

She's here, Willow croaked.

Clapping hands over his mouth, Mateo darted back behind the wall, back slamming into the stone, then sliding down until he was on the floor. It was *Lia's* aura. Had she come with the Warlord?

Where's the sword? Willow rasped, the words lashing like talons. *We need the sword.*

The wall between him and Lia Seystone blocked the golden burst of light her aura made out in the trees—since when could stone walls block auras?—so much stronger than she'd been when they were in Chaol together. How many oaths did it take to make a Devoted glow like a little sun? Mateo's arms prickled with energy, and his palms began to sweat.

He'd yearned to talk to Lia. Thought about seeing her, what he'd say, what she'd say, then stopped thinking about it at all because what happy ending could there be to that conversation?

Peeking over the edge of the sill, Mateo caught sight of an open patch in the trees below, Jaxom's light turning the figure on auroshe-back below an unbecoming orange, a twirl of fabric blowing behind her like a flag.

She was *veiled*. Lia had pulled off the last of her face coverings right in front of him, swearing them off because she no longer had reason to be afraid. Now she was covered and holding a sword.

As he crunched back down onto the floor, Mateo's fists ached, his slightly too-long fingernails like blades to his palms. Swords were what Lia knew. *Calsta* and all her warrior nonsense were what Lia knew. He'd seen it time and time again back in Chaol. Lia's world was made of weapons and problems meant to be hacked into pieces until they were problems no longer.

Mateo tried to shove aside all the good things that had happened between himself and the shadow sprinting toward him. The sight of her red curls, the blaze of her aura returning, the look on her face when she'd finally taken off that awful blue scarf. The laughs they'd had. Rosie, because they'd saved her together. The way she'd looked him over when she found out he was a Basist and then shrugged it off, not afraid, not judgmental. She knew who he was and that magic didn't make him evil.

In that one moment, Mateo couldn't think of anything he wanted more than Lia.

She was made of flames, and Mateo wanted to stand next to her, to grow bright the way she was until she could look at him and see the flame he was too. That was why Tual had taken Aria—so that Mateo could return her and manipulate Lia into giving him a second chance.

And Mateo wanted to go. Not to pretend, not to lead Lia back to the lake and a shapeshifter's sword. Not to steal her energy to save himself.

He'd accepted his father's plan because underneath wanting to live, he wanted to see Lia again.

But, in the cracked moonlight, sitting in a chorus of bones, Mateo knew what a fantasy it had been. He knew who Lia was, and Lia

Seystone needed nothing, no man. She'd almost died rather than ask him for help, and the very idea that Mateo might be interested in more than friendship had made her sit so very straight that he'd taken it back before she'd even properly responded.

He knew. And by all the gods together in the sky, in the earth, in books, paintings, in the very air, that knowledge tore at him. Lia had chased after him, just the way he'd hoped. She'd found him, just as he'd hoped. But of course Lia had come brandishing a sword.

He'd known it from the first time he'd seen Lia in her father's study, covered from head to toe in blue. Mateo carried pencils, not weapons. Even after they'd fought together, laughed together, stolen the auroshe together, plotted to stand up to his father together, watched the stars fall from the sky together . . . when he'd finally got up the courage to really look at her, she'd looked the other way. And now it was going to have to be his father's plan or a choice of two deaths: death by ghost or death on the point of a sword.

It was a terrible choice to have to make, Mateo, Tual had said. *Her or me. She made her choice.*

I had to make mine.

And now Mateo had to make his.

She will never accept me as I am. We could never be. Not in a world that is true.

Mateo pulled himself up from the floor and stepped back from the window. Back from the blistering cloud of gold racing toward him and straight into the defenses old as the nameless god himself. Then he ran after his father.

CHAPTER 15

The Worst Mistake

Knox woke with a start at first morning light, feeling around for a sword that wasn't there.

His stomach churned the moment he realized what he was doing and he forced his hand to still. Out of everything in the Commonwealth, there wasn't a single thing he wanted less than Willow's sword.

Knox sat up and looked around. There was another bed in the room, the covers twisted around someone asleep. Two windows. The angle of the sun put them near dawn. He slid to the edge of the bed to get up and found Anwei.

She was curled up tight on the floorboards, as if even in sleep she had to protect herself. Her cheeks were pink, her braids spread across the blanket like coiled snakes.

A sick feeling washed over him. Anwei hadn't needed to sleep on the floor. He would have shared. A month ago, Anwei would have just stolen one of the pillows and pushed him over to make room. But then, he blushed. Because the last thing he remembered before waking up here was kissing Anwei. Really kissing her. Forgetting someone was chasing them, forgetting his body was attempting to turn off, hanging on to her for dear life. And he hated that now he was awake again that she'd felt the need to send him such a clear message. To look away.

So Knox looked away. It was only then that he paid attention to the muted auras in the room. There were two people in the other bed: Noa and *Lia*.

Lia's name was on his lips before he could think about whether waking her was a good idea or not. Her eyes opened before he'd crossed to the bed, her hands coming up to lash out at him before she saw him properly.

Lia rolled out of the bed, her curls standing out from her head in frizzy twirls. "I wasn't supposed to sleep this long."

"When did you get here? Does Anwei know? We've had some complications—"

"I spoke to her when I rode in last night, and I'm late. She wanted to talk to you first, so I'll meet you out there." Lia bundled her hair into a braid, pulled on her boots, and then went to the window. "There are Devoted in the forest outside Tual's estate. I don't know why they're there, but . . . don't take too long." She pushed open the window and climbed out.

"What?" Knox stood at the window, watching his friend make her way up the street. When he turned back toward the bed, Anwei's eyes were open, watching him. She sat up a little too fast, almost bumping her head on the side table, the bowl of wash water wobbling dangerously. "Good, you're awake," she croaked. "I need you."

"Did you see Lia? She just climbed out the window!" He pressed a hand to his side over the bandages, everything feeling just a little . . . off. "And yesterday . . . " Heat flooded his cheeks. Yesterday she'd kissed him. And he'd fainted.

"Go after Lia. We came up with a new plan last night, and she can fill you in." Anwei smoothed her rumpled tunic and skirts, checking her sleeve cuffs and high collar to be sure they were fastened. He caught a glimpse of a white scar on her ankle as she put on her shoes.

"You don't have to hide those, you know." He looked up from her feet. "I mean, not from me." A thread of warmth bled across their bond, but then forcefully pulled back like a breath stolen from Knox's lungs. "Sorry, I didn't mean—"

"It's fine. I'm glad you know." She stood up and slid past him, not a single hair of hers touching him. She sat on the bed and took Noa by the shoulders to give her a gentle shake. "It's time, Noa."

Knox closed his mouth. Opened it, but then let it close again. *Is this what you wanted, Calsta? To torture me? Giving permission for me to be with Anwei only once the possibility is gone?*

This is the opposite of what any god wants. Calsta's voice was amused. *Desperate youths aren't great at judgment, focus, or any kind of devotion when they're frustrated by love. Why do you think most Devoted are told to focus on me instead of the girls and boys they're sitting next to?*

Knox chose to ignore her. Again.

"Knox? Is your wound bothering you? You're not moving." Anwei had begun braiding Noa's hair despite the dancer's sleepy grumbling in Elantin, a hairpin sticking out from between her lips. She started to laugh in response to the unintelligible grousing, batting Noa over the shoulder. "You really think I'm going to believe Falan requires all her devotees to sleep in past a certain hour? Hold still so I can finish your knots." Anwei coiled the girl's dark hair around her finger, then looked back up at Knox expectantly.

"I'm fine." He smiled.

"Good." She shooed him toward the window as she pulled the pin from her mouth to set one of the knots of hair over Noa's ear. "One hour at the docks. Bring your goddess."

"I need a scone," Noa whimpered.

"You know about the Devoted—" Knox started.

"We know!" Anwei grinned at him. "*Go!*"

Knox went. Out the window, down the wall, full of energy as if Willow felt like sharing today. He wondered what Anwei's brother was doing—did Knox being awake mean Mateo was asleep? Willow could not comment, lurking outside the wall Anwei made around his mind.

Morning crowds had already begun moving toward the market square. Knox slipped between embroidered coats and lace-trimmed dresses until he caught sight of Lia's golden halo, Calsta's energy zipping across her aura like little fireflies. She didn't move to greet him, her face stony and a little gray. "Are you all right?" he asked, worry stabbing through him.

"I found Mateo." She looked up at him. "Sort of. He ran away from me."

The bitterness steeped in her words caught Knox by surprise. "Is that . . . not what you expected to happen?"

"I don't know. He's *always* been on Tual's side. I just hoped that learning what he was . . . and with Tual kidnapping Aria . . ." She grimaced, her hands making tight fists at her side. "Calsta above, why does it *matter*?"

"He's your friend." Knox flinched when she aggressively pushed past a man wearing two separate knives on his belt. "You didn't want him to run. He . . . didn't want anything from you and liked you anyway." He watched her from the corner of his eye, not sure how Lia would handle something like her trust, so fragile and tenuous, being shattered by some boy she'd just met. Everyone had always wanted a piece of Lia—to use her skills to their advantage, to best her in a fight, to take what she hadn't offered. Back in Chaol it had seemed like a little light had kindled inside her, a hope that maybe the world wasn't there to crush her.

A light that, if extinguished, would break something inside her.

What had happened while he was asleep to push her so close to the edge?

Lia's chin tipped up to look at him, her lips pressed together hard. "It sounds so ridiculous saying it out loud. Mateo doesn't matter at all now. Not as anything other than our way to get Aria, right?"

"It's not ridiculous." Knox took Lia's arm, pulling her into an alleyway. "We've been taught our whole lives to shun feeling for other people." He put his back to the wall, letting her stand there with her thoughts, hoping his presence at her side would be enough. Their relationship had never been forbidden—they'd been friends from the moment they met, watching each other's backs when no one else seemed to want to, not even Calsta. Was that not love? "Maybe it's not what you think?" He lowered his voice. "You won't know what he's doing until you actually talk to him. And you care about him, so why decide now when you don't have all the information?"

When she looked up, her face was hard. "I'm a Devoted. How could I have made this kind of mistake? To *care*."

The point of Devotion is to make that mistake over and over again, Calsta interjected. *You think I like watching people half starve and sleep in hard beds and give up everything they love? But what I'd like worse is my Devoted using their power with no sympathy for those it could hurt. Sympathy comes easier if you know what it is like to have nothing.*

"It's not a mistake to care about people, Lia," Knox breathed.

"It doesn't matter. Mateo ran." She shook her head, her hands still an awful knot. "And it was silly of me to think he'd stand up now when he . . ." Her lips twisted. "He did before. A few times. Just never against his father."

"It's a tall order, going against the person who loves you most."

"Like us going against Calsta, no?" She smiled grimly. "Regardless, we have a job to do this morning. Your pirate friend, Ellis, is helping us steal a boat."

"Ellis?" Knox blinked. "What boat? What's the plan? Did we ever figure out if Tual is—"

"I'll tell you on the way." Lia grabbed his hand and pulled him out of the alley. "But first, we need to cut your hair."

Mateo awoke to the sight of something watching him from the end of his bed, hollow black eyes and a mouth bared with sharp, jagged teeth.

He lurched back in horror, knocking his head against the bed and falling over the side, landing on his arm. Unable to care about the pain, Mateo froze there on the floor, waiting for the thing, whatever it was, to nose its way around the side of the bed. When nothing came, Mateo peeked up over the top of his mussed quilt.

There was nothing there. He stood, craning his neck to see over the edge just in case the thing was curled up beneath the foot of his bed, waiting to pop out and surprise him, but all he saw was a little brown shape on the floor.

He peered closer, stomach churning when he realized it was a dead mouse, arranged neatly where he was most likely to find it, like a present from a cat.

His cat used to do that, but then Abendiza had eaten her.

Slumping back down to the floor, Mateo tried to catch his breath. The house was quiet, sunlight streaming in through the windows. He couldn't smell anything from the kitchen, but Hilaria had probably outdone herself since . . .

Something on the floor below him flashed gold. Aurasparks gathered together like flies on the first floor. That's why he was having nightmares about monsters watching him sleep Who *wouldn't* have nightmares with Devoted sleeping down the hall?

He slowly stood and went around to the other side of his bed to put on his slippers, then kicked them off again in a fit of petulance. If Calsta herself appeared in a flurry of wind and lightning, she couldn't make him go down and break bread with the Warlord's murder-happy minions. The night before, they'd stayed up so long talking to Father in the dining hall, Mateo had actually skipped dinner rather than face them. After such a terrible evening and a nightmare, Mateo deserved a *bath*.

Ringing the bell for hot water, Mateo went into his lovely bathroom and pulled out his favorite scents. After a few moments, the mechanism in the tub faucet began to hiss, and Mateo turned it on, water gushing out in a wall of steam to mix with the soaps and oils he added to make foam. One of the many little things around the house that had been salvaged from Basist leavings.

Soon the bath was full, and when Mateo lowered himself into it, he wondered if maybe he could stay there until the Warlord left since this was the one place they weren't likely to come.

Which was, of course, when the door slammed open.

Hilaria came bustling in, her forehead and her lips both pinched. Mateo hunched down into the bubbles, frantically gathering them to cover himself, but Hilaria didn't notice. She gave the rose-scented air an incredulous sniff and stepped inside, closing the door behind her. "A fine time for a bubble bath, Master Mateo," she said in the most accusatory tone possible, as if he'd tempered the water by drowning someone before he got in.

"I hate to be a bother, Hilaria, but would you please remove yourself? Now?"

"There's a dead mouse on your floor—did you know that? Who killed it? They got blood all over the Palatian carpet and just *left* it—"

"Hilaria, get *out*!"

He splashed some water at her and immediately regretted it when her eyes narrowed into a truly terrifying scowl. "The Warlord has been asking for you since the sun came up, young man, and if you don't get down there, it'll be *her* seeing all these bubbles." She clicked her tongue in disgust. "When you go into town today, I need blueberries and yuzul from the market. Don't forget."

Mateo carefully gathered a mound of pink bubbles to cover himself more thoroughly. "You interrupted my bath to ask me to run an errand? For blueberries."

"And yuzul. *She* won't let us leave. I promised young Aria a special dessert tonight."

Aria. The name fuzzed in Mateo's brain. It was important for some reason. Someone he was supposed to talk to? Or maybe some-one who . . . needed him. He pressed a hand to his forehead, setting the thought aside so he could deal with the cook invading his bath. "I wasn't planning on going to town, but I'd prefer to discuss this downstairs."

"The Warlord can't keep you here. I need yuzul and blueberries. So, yes, you are going to town." Hilaria went to the door, pausing to shake a finger at him before pulling it open. "You keep your head about you. That old harpy wants something she isn't saying out loud, and I don't like it. And make sure you have someone see about that mouse!"

"Would you close the door—" Mateo rolled his eyes when she walked away without heeding his request, a draft now washing in from the open window in his bedroom. He settled even lower, but then the auras below suddenly began to move. If the Warlord had been asking for him since dawn, he doubted she'd wait too much longer before seeking him out. He'd had enough old ladies in the bathroom to last him the rest of the day.

By the time he was dressed and standing outside the dining room's arched door, Mateo was still too grumbly to go inside, con-tented to think about it and pick at the filigree on the wainscotting instead.

Two Devoted at his table. All the world's ills—or at least the Commonwealth's—just sitting there eating what looked like raw grain with silver spoons.

Mateo lurched back when one paused in consuming his pathetic excuse for breakfast to glance in his direction. The night before, Mateo had come blustering out of the watchtower only to find the sky-cursed Warlord sitting peacefully at that very table with a stalk of celery in one hand and a cup of plain water in the other. The two ogres she'd brought with her had been inspecting the gardens, leaving Tual to sit at her feet, bowing ever so nicely as she took bite after bite of celery.

His father hadn't even blinked once as the Warlord took control of the whole house, directing the hostlers, the maids. Apparently that included Hilaria too, which meant there were no scones, sweet rolls, *or* muffins for breakfast.

You already spoiled the whole Commonwealth for anyone with magic, he wanted to yell toward the blue morning sky. *Did you have to take my breakfast, too?* Instead, Mateo sniffed just loud enough for the Devoted to hear, readjusted his drawing satchel, and headed toward his father's study with his nose in the air. The two of them probably couldn't string more than three syllables together, much less . . .

Mateo blinked, sure he'd been walking. *Positive* he'd been headed toward the cheery office with the birdcalls and the jars of whatever, but his feet hadn't moved, the dining room door there in front of him. Willow was at the back of his head, panting.

They're so bright, she wheezed. *Surely we could take just a little?*

The two auras shone from inside the dining room, bright even through the wall. Mateo rolled his eyes at himself, realizing they'd been able to see him standing there dithering about whether to enter for as long as he'd been there. The walls here didn't block auras, not like in the abbey with Lia's.

A trill of worry thrummed through him at the thought of her, and he wondered where his father had taken Aria.

Aria.

Mateo slammed a hand to his forehead, pulling at his hair. Of course he knew Aria's name. How could he have forgotten it? She'd almost *died.* He could still feel the sick pull of power, her cold skin, and the relief when she'd finally choked out a breath. Father had said she had to be moved somewhere safe. He peeked around the doorway once again, hoping for a glimpse of Hilaria. *She* wouldn't stand for this rabbit food nonsense, would she? If he was going to find Aria, he needed *muffins.*

"Mateo Montanne?"

Mateo jumped in surprise at the voice, accidentally jamming an elbow into the wainscotting. "Great Calsta's swollen left—"

He broke off, teeth bared, mid-furious elbow rub at the sight of the Warlord standing behind him, her head cocked as if she very much wanted to hear the end of his sentence. Unlike Lia's wild curls, the Warlord's hair had been shaved at the sides to show her oath scars, the top cut short so her wiry, graying curls stood out like springs. Her eyes and forehead were deeply lined and her lips pinched. She looked as if her armor had grown too large for her, or perhaps as if she'd dried up like a parched shrub, leaving nothing but shriveled leaves behind in her pot.

Wasn't the Warlord a little old and frail to be riding auroshes and blustering into someone's home to steal everything including the celery? Clearing his throat, Mateo dropped a half bow that was at least five degrees too shallow for her rank, but with his heart beating so quickly and his stomach empty, Mateo couldn't muster much better. "I'm so sorry, I didn't see you there."

"An honor I am not often granted." Her amusement seemed much less natural than the sword strapped between her shoulder blades. "I rather liked that little spin you did just now."

"I save my entertainment routines for the really important guests." Mateo returned her smile as best he could. He pointed to the sword. "Did you find our table's silverware wanting last night and decide to supplement?"

The smile turned to a grin. "I've lived long enough to know when a situation requires a little supplementing, I suppose."

Willow's breaths were coming in quick pants that felt marginally indecent. *Stop it*, he thought at her.

Do you not see how much there is to eat? the ghost hissed. *Whoever took a bite of her left more than enough for us.*

Mateo blinked at the woman's aura, the golden sparks swirling over her head like a crown a little dull and sluggish. Was it possible her wrinkles and sagging muscles, her armor seeming too large . . . could they be symptoms of *wasting sickness*?

That would mean his father had already been at work draining her. Which seemed like an insane risk, sucking life from the very woman sworn to root out magic like theirs and destroy it.

Trying to cover his agitation, Mateo bowed again, this time to the proper depth, though the last flourish at the end was not strictly necessary. "I don't believe we've ever been formally introduced."

"Your principal purpose in life is to dig things up and then draw them." The Warlord leaned forward an inch, squinting at the whorls and flowers embroidered across his lapels before grabbing hold of one. "I don't believe an introduction was warranted until now."

It was a little awkward, standing there with her fingers knotted around his lapel. Perhaps someone so bent on keeping the Commonwealth under her control couldn't help but clutch at anything within reach. She'd employed an aukincer when most thought that aukincers were no better than the dirt witches they emulated. She'd put a veil on Lia's head and set a monster on her in the hopes of producing more little monsters.

She had freckles across her nose and scars across her knuckles.

"Well." Mateo pulled back, and she let him go, leaving him free to bow yet again. "It's an honor you're wasting time on me now, even if it wasn't warranted before. I don't suppose I could interest you in some breakfast?" He nodded toward the dining room. "I believe that's what they're calling that stuff on the table, anyway."

"If you hold that thing any tighter, you'll ruin your charcoals." The Warlord nodded toward his hands.

Looking down, Mateo found his fingers clutched tightly around his drawing satchel. He forced his hand to relax. It was hard for Mateo to breathe so close to a woman with so many deaths to her name.

She tucked her hand into the crook of his elbow and nudged him into the dining room. Inside, Tual sat at the head of the table, a plate of something drenched in cream in front of him. Mateo waved only a little frantically, and Tual started to stand, carefully dabbing his mouth with a napkin. "Mateo! I wondered when you would finally get up the nerve to come in here."

"Where did you get that food?" Mateo hissed.

"Hilaria likes me." Tual grinned, licking a bit of cream from his lip. "I have something very important to show you! You remember the guest we've been expecting?"

"Um, yes?" Mateo's nerves all trilled together. What game was his father playing *now*, bringing up Lia right in front of the assembled murder crew? What's more, why was he sitting at the head of the table, the place the Warlord should have claimed?

"Well, I've made some progress on the research we meant to do before she arrived, and I can't wait to get your opinion." Tual's hand snaked down to touch the dagger, which Mateo hadn't noticed sheathed at Tual's hip. A grim satisfaction dripped into his thoughts from Willow. *Not many shapeshifters managed to take caprenum blades from other shapeshifters.* Her voice crinkled at the edges, sounding like the ghostly death she was. *Of course I managed it. I managed it a lot. They were my trophies.*

What are you even talking about? Is it safe for him to be carrying that? The Warlord could see, not to mention— he thought back at her, then stopped, wondering what was wrong with him, asking *Willow* for advice. Mateo pulled away from the Warlord—he tried, anyway, but her fingers clutched his arm tight, unwilling to let go. "Um . . . would you excuse me? I think you know we're working on the artifacts we found in the tomb, or you wouldn't have come here—"

"That great ugly sword in your trophy room? I think it can wait. Tual's the . . ." She cleared her throat. "The *aukincer*. You'd just be in his way, and I think we all know just how important it is to get wasting sickness resolved once and for all." She turned to Tual. "You can do it, can't you?"

Tual gave her a cocky salute, and Mateo couldn't help but stare again. His father wasn't even trying to be deferential. "We've got everything we need. Now it's just a matter of experimenting with the materials we managed to preserve."

And he was lying through his teeth. She'd know in a few days that they had no cure. It was rash and poorly planned—two things Tual was never guilty of. Unless, of course, Tual's plans had changed.

"Good." The Warlord didn't notice Mateo's chagrin, her fingernails digging into his arm as she dragged him toward the kitchen door. "You don't mind if I borrow your son for a few hours, then, do you, Tual?"

"Be my guest." Tual gave a gracious bow. Mateo flapped a hand, making a bigger gesture when Tual didn't seem to notice him begging to be saved. "Where are you taking him?"

"I want him to show me around Kingsol. If I take you, you'll give me the whole history starting from before the shapeshifter wars, and I just want to know where the fresh apples are." The Warlord gave Mateo's arm an affectionate pat, then violently jerked open the kitchen door. "Cath? Berrum?" She gave a fond smile to the two Devoted who stood up from the table, their plates still partly full. "It'll be nice for you to be with someone your own age after so many months locked in rooms with books and bones, right, Mateo?"

Mateo swallowed hard as she whisked him through the kitchen door, the two Devoted following behind, positively bristling with weapons.

"Your father has always been so accommodating." The Warlord's smile faded as she led him past the long prep table covered in raw vegetables, of all things, sharp knives laid out to properly desecrate them. A perfect day for Aria to sneak one, and Mateo wished he could have found her room to let her know. Hilaria was yelling at someone from inside the pantry, too far to appeal for help. Or even a muffin. "Running straight to outbreaks the moment they happened, dropping his whole life to stop this terrible disease."

An ironic thing to say, considering Tual had created the illness he was credited with healing.

"Accommodating is my father's middle name." Mateo cleared his throat again, trying not to mind the way the Warlord's lackeys hovered just outside his peripheral vision as they headed for the door that led to the courtyard. "It, um, caused some problems during his years teaching at the university. The head scholar thought for sure he was trying to make some kind of joke in the paperwork."

The Warlord didn't even chuckle as she swept him into the gardens toward the watchtower. It wasn't until the bridge that he managed to pull himself free. "I'm so sorry." Mateo stumbled a few steps back, rubbing his arm where the Warlord had been digging her fingers into his skin. "I haven't even had breakfast yet, and I'm terrible company when I'm in this state."

"Your father said we could use his boat while we're here," the Warlord said, ignoring him. "Isn't it docked under the bridge?" She headed in that direction when he nodded slowly.

Mateo looked around for a way to hide. Escape. Find a plausible excuse like washing his many coats or feeding the giant snake. But the two Devoted waited behind him until he tripped after the Warlord toward the little dock where Tual's boat bobbed in all its turquoise glory. One of Mateo's first memories was helping choose that vibrant greenish-blue. He picked up a rock from the beach before going up the gangplank, tossing it up and catching it as he walked.

It wasn't until he was in his accustomed seat in the middle of the boat that he saw the male Devoted's eyes darting over him and the female one concentrating as if she were trying to hear something too quiet for the rest of them to detect. The Warlord herself even stepped carefully, as if there were invisible threads pulling tense between the three of them with him at the center. Which made absolutely no sense. Mateo propped up his boots on the bench in front of him, wondering if they'd stab him then or wait until they'd got out of the lake basin.

"This boat is too big for two people to row. Are you sure you don't want me to call a few servants?" he croaked.

"Cath and Berrum will be just fine." The Warlord sat in Tual's favorite chair kitty-corner from Mateo, the cushions bunching around her as if they didn't fancy touching her any more than she seemed to want to touch them. "Are you planning to hit me over the head with that and flee?" She eyed the rock he'd snagged from the beach.

"Would it do any good?" he joked, tossing it up in the air, then flailing to catch it when the boat began to move. "It's for opening the channel."

The male Devoted installed himself at the back of the ship, ready with a paddle, and the female Devoted, a squarish specimen with a long blond braid and roses on her sword handle, settled two benches ahead of him, tying a sun hat over her hair before she began unknotting the mooring line.

"Well?" the Warlord asked. "Show us what to do."

"You don't need my help with that, do you? There are cliffs to the south that you can't climb. Waterways block the foothills down below us. There are no roads, and there are beasts in the woods who like the kind of prey that puts up a fight." Mateo shrugged, leaning back in his chair. "You wouldn't be here if you didn't know how to open the channel."

The Warlord smiled with all her teeth. "The goddess favors her Devoted, Mateo Montanne. It was not an easy journey, nor one I could ask many Devoted to risk." There was a tightness to her jaw, as if somehow *she* were frightened to be sitting in the boat with *him*. "I'm very excited to learn the easy way."

Mateo let his feet drop, his chest tightening. She hadn't known about the channel before Tual had mentioned it. Was that why she wanted to go into town? To learn the secret so that she could bring in her murderous horde and clean the place out from cliff top to lake bottom? The blond Devoted turned to look at him over her shoulder, her paddle ready.

They didn't even *need* swords.

Neither do you, Willow whispered.

Mateo pointed toward the far side of the bridge. "The channel's behind that boulder."

The Devoted turned to contemplate the jagged edge to the bowl around the lake, the point he'd indicated as solid-looking as the rest of it.

The Warlord gestured for the Devoted to row before turning back to him. "Why settle here? It's so difficult to access."

Gripping the side rail when the boat began to move, Mateo shrugged. "I can't speak for my father. He bought it before I was born. He likes to be left alone with his experiments, I suppose." When they drew near to the boulder, he tossed the stone up again and caught it, trying to remember where the trigger to open the gate was exactly. It was a little tricky getting it right, but . . .

Tricky? For you? Willow giggled. *You don't really need a rock, do you? Use your mind.*

Bristling, Mateo stared up at the boulder, sure he'd only ever seen his father set off the mechanism using a rock, a boot, *some* thrown object. But just like Willow said, he could feel the shape of gears and springs in his mind, connected to an external trigger for people who couldn't feel the rock. Exultation flowed through him, victory, because he'd never been able to—

The Warlord was staring. So Mateo cleared his throat, took what felt like an athletic sort of stance. Even if Willow was right and he didn't really need to use the rock, opening it with his power would probably not be the best idea at the moment. Focusing on the trigger spot, Mateo threw his rock.

The stone barely made it to the boulder's base, *plink*ing against the stone, then splashing into the lake below with an embarrassing *ploop.* The three Devoted watched the boulder expectantly.

Go on, Willow hummed. *Using the trigger is for little bugs who walk the earth with no energy in their humors.*

I can't use magic right in front of the Warlord. Mateo's heart began to thump, something deep inside his chest stirring as Willow pressed him toward the warm spot on the boulder.

She won't know. They never know until it's too late.

Energy burst out from Mateo's mind in a bilious wave. The magic touched the mechanism inside the boulder, and his hands began to swell and burn. A section in the rock shuddered, then turned, the water from the lake mixing with the channel through the narrow gap that appeared. Frozen, Mateo waited for swords to come out of their sheaths. But instead, the Warlord nodded for her Devoted to continue rowing. Mateo's hands balled into fists, nails too sharp to be his digging into his palms.

The Warlord settled back into her chair as they passed into the tunnel, looking up with interest at the soft blue lights glowing in the ceiling to illuminate their way. It only lasted a few minutes before the other end of the path opened to let them through to the other side. Beyond was a little tributary that led to the Felac, a wide river choked with vines and hundreds of other little offshoots, a maze Mateo would not care to be lost in.

He kept his hands clenched in his lap even after the feel of claws in his skin receded.

"Basist wonders never break, do they?" the Warlord mused once they were through. "I've heard this was once a great fortress. Now it only protects an aukincer and his disappointing son."

"I do know you could get that cuirass fitted, if that would help?" Mateo forced his voice to remain polite even as the anger began to boil inside him.

The Warlord looked down at the armor dwarfing her shrunken torso, the double auroshe crest tooled into the spot over her heart. She smiled softly, leaning back in the chair. "I think you're acquainted with Lia Scystone?"

Mateo's heart made more than a few undignified skips. "Sorry?"

"You met Lia in Chaol. I need you to tell me what you did to her."

"What I did to . . . ?" Mateo shook his head, trying to find words. Words were what he did. He could do words. And he *hadn't* done anything to Lia, so it wasn't difficult to feign confusion. "Seystone . . . ? Are you talking about *Valas* Seystone? I never had the pleasure of meeting his wife . . . unless you mean their young daughter, Aria? She's quite *uncharming*, but I wouldn't call arguing as *doing* something to her—"

"Lia Seystone is Valas Seystone's oldest daughter, one of my spiriters, and a very valuable member of the Devoted order. Red hair, freckles. Very sentimental about her auroshe? She's about your age." When Mateo shrugged, the Warlord pursed her lips. "You and your father were meant to play a very specific role in Chaol: to dig up a dirt witch's grave and wrest an ancient cure from his dusty old claws. Instead, I have a missing spiriter, a tomb that was meant to be our last hope destroyed, and your father dancing around me with a sword and sparkly potions like he isn't even trying anymore." She waited until Mateo met her gaze. "You think I didn't hear all the reports that put you with Lia at the center of all that?"

Mateo wished he had a mouthful of tea to spray out, but like the muffins, he hadn't yet had any tea for the morning either. "No offense, but I've sort of gone out of my way to avoid your order. I'm an archeologist, not a warrior, and quite frankly, the lot of you make me uncomfortable. I spent every moment I wasn't asleep underground painting things. The tomb's destruction was one of the worst travesties of modern history."

"If you spent all your time at the tomb, you must have met Lia's partner, Ewan Hardcastle?" The Warlord drew the sword sheathed at her back. Mateo's stomach jolted. The blade was familiar, the hilt tooled with a design burned into his brain because the last time he'd seen it, he'd been hanging six inches off the ground with the blade to his throat.

Yes, Mateo had met Ewan Hardcastle.

A thread of surprised glee needled through Mateo at the sight of the blade minus its owner, because if the Warlord had it, then Ewan didn't. If Ewan had been relieved of his sword, did that mean he'd been kicked out of the Devoted? Or—

"He was found dead at the tomb, Mateo. Gored through by his own auroshe." The Warlord looked down the flat of the blade, turning it to examine the edge before switching her gaze to Mateo's face, watching for a reaction.

"I'm afraid I didn't pay much attention to the Roosters patrolling the site." Mateo kept his expression as blank as he knew how, a hot rush of satisfaction making his cheeks go pink. Then he remembered his father's voice: *You don't want to kill until you do.*

Perhaps he was right.

"You know he wasn't a Rooster. Let's not play games, you and me." The Warlord let the sword's tip sink to the boat's wooden floor inches from Mateo's silver-tooled boot. "The valas's wife was one of hundreds with the plague in Chaol. There were some odd symptoms— truth telling? Surely you helped your father tend victims?" The Warlord waited for him to nod before continuing. "But the later stages were very familiar, don't you think? All these years Tual has assured me wasting sickness was an energy imbalance due to Calsta's touch." She sat forward. "But it's funny, because we didn't have a single case of wasting sickness until you appeared with Tual in Rentara."

"My father only *went* to Rentara to help treat—"

"And the plague in Chaol didn't start until they day you arrived in town."

Mateo pulled his feet back from the sword's tip, panic like a live animal jumping inside him. The wasting sickness *was* because of him. The plague in Chaol *was* his fault, even if he hadn't been the one extracting energy. But that truth sounded more than a little fantastical. Causation and correlation were not the same thing, and the Warlord hand no *proof* of anything. No one did.

So, he furrowed his brow and licked his lips. "I don't think I understand what you're trying to say."

"The plague came with you. Then, days later, one of my most valued spiriters disappears. A few days after that, a girl with her face and hair covered stole an auroshe from the illegal fights and rode out with a boy behind her—a boy with a drawing satchel and a few too many words for his own good."

"I fail to see any connection to—"

"Days after that, the stolen auroshe was spotted fishing on the beaches directly beneath the house your father rented outside of Chaol. *You* were seen at the dig with a girl whose face was covered. In fact, Ewan, before he died, told me specifically that he had seen her with you and that you'd lied to prevent him from finding her."

Mateo tried very hard not to remember just how good Devoted ears were. Could they hear his heart beating out of his chest? "I guess I'm just as disappointingly unintelligent as you thought. Are you telling me that after the destruction of an incredibly valuable find by *shapeshifter* magic—yes, I think we ought to say it out loud—despite the fact my father managed to salvage what you need to preserve your army, you're concentrating on what? A completely baseless theory about me spreading a *plague*?" He gave a dismissive wave. "You do know how sickness is spread, I hope? Because if it were me, my whole household would be in the ground already. *I* would be dead. And how is any of this related to your spiriter?"

"Lia Seystone." The Warlord's voice was hard as stone, the trees behind her riffling with a cold breeze. The air was far too quiet. "One of my Roosters was killed, and his auroshe was sent to the fights. Only a Devoted or a *shapeshifter* could manage that, and he disappeared from *your house*. Lia wouldn't have done that in her right mind. In her right mind, she wouldn't have run away at all—"

"What in Calsta's name are you suggesting?" Mateo's cheeks burned. "That my father, after devoting his entire life to curing your little minions, is a *shapeshifter*?"

"No. That's not what I'm suggesting at all." The Warlord licked her lips. "In fact, I've been quite sure since I left Chaol that the shapeshifter is *you*."

⚜

Knox felt naked before he'd made it even a street closer to the docks. A woman picked up her young child to get out of his way, the boy gawking. Lia had cut Knox's hair clear to the skin on both sides and braided the top back, his oaths to Calsta now on full display. Lia hovered at his shoulder as they walked, ignoring people pushing to make way like the wolf she was. Devoted were supposed to draw attention, but after a year of no one caring who he was, all Knox wanted was to go back to the shadows.

Altahn was waiting just inside the archway that led to the docks, holding out a sword like a greeting. Knox waved it away, narrowing his eyes over the Trib kynate's hair, the loose tail he usually wore switched for a Rooster's three tight underbraids.

Lia broke the spell when she started laughing, dancing forward to circle the two Trib riders standing behind Altahn, their long tails also swapped for lopsided underbraids. She grabbed hold of the smaller, wider one's arm to bend him down so she could fix one of the plaits. "Don't *you* look handsome," she said, grinning as he tried to bat her hands away.

"We're not Commonwealth trollops," the taller one grumbled. "Have you never seen Calsta's statues in her temple? Her hair is *free*."

Mateo wasn't the only friend she'd made, as if taking off that veil had untied something else inside Lia. Knox couldn't help but love the sight of her, so angry and sad and worried and unhappy most of the time he'd known her, now grinning up at the lanky Trib. "You think Calsta's hair is free under that helmet she wears?" she asked.

Friends who weren't Devoted had never been allowed.

Theat isn't true, though, he thought, the feel of Anwei at the back of his head. *Why have we been denied normal relationships for so long?*

It's the Warlord who doesn't like you consorting with outsiders, Calsta's voice guttered. *She's afraid they'd like you instead of fear you.*

Why haven't you stopped her? he asked. *Why haven't you stopped any of the Warlords from holding those you touch like prisoners?*

Because gods need their devoted, and there weren't any other choices. I'm trying to change things now—there's a window, and you're in it. Don't fail me.

"Obviously Calsta understands not wanting hair blowing in our faces, Miss Lia," the lanky rider was saying with an exaggerated eye roll to go with it. "Why do you think we tie our hair back? It's all these *braids.* So you can judge who is above you and who is below just by looking at each other. Even Devoted do this blasphemy, *shaving* the sides to show off their oath scars." He shot a nervous glance at Knox and loudly cleared his throat. "The two of you Devoted excepted, of course. You're only doing it for the plan. Like Miss Lia and her veil."

"It's only for a few hours, Bane." Lia's smile was suddenly faint, one hand straying to the bag looped beneath her sword. She pulled the tie from one of his braids. "I'll fix it so you don't look like a little boy in a costume."

"I understand why we have to . . ." Bane shut his eyes tight as she began to plait. "Just promise you won't tell anyone."

"You'll need this." Altahn held out one of the cast iron tubes that had caused him so much anguish back on Ellis's boat. The anguish seemed to have returned because it took the Trib a moment to let go when Knox grabbed hold of it.

"Salpowder?" Knox asked, looking down the hole, odd striations disappearing into its belly. When he looked up, Altahn was biting his lip. But he handed over a bag that looked far too small, opening it to show Knox the leather-wrapped packets inside. "So I just . . . strike a flame? With flint?"

Altahn held out his arm, and Knox didn't understand what was happening until Galerey's frilled head popped out, her scaly little body launching toward him. He startled back, swiping at the feel of little prickly claws scrabbling across his body.

When he glared toward Altahn, the Trib only smiled. "She'll help you."

"Where is the other carom?" Knox asked, skin prickling as Galerey nuzzled her way down the back of his tunic.

"Anwei gave it back to Ellis." Altahn's smile seemed fixed in place. He turned away, gesturing for Bane and Gilesh to follow him. "But she said she'd get it back."

Knox hefted the carom's strap over his shoulder, watching Altahn walk into the crowds. Lia sighed, fingering her sword hilt and checking the sun. "We'll give him a few minutes head start?"

Knox nodded. "What did Bane mean about you only wearing your veil for the plan?".

"He thinks I put it on to scare Mateo last night. Veiled Devoted are scary, I guess."

"Did you?"

"No." Lia put a hand to her forehead. "I need to get Aria."

"What does that have to do with your veil?"

"I need everything Calsta can give me."

"You can't stand keeping it on long enough for her to give the oaths back." Knox shook his head. "I can't think it counts if you're wearing it only to get your sister back. We don't need you to be a spiriter. We can track people without your extended aurasight, and I think we all know what Tual's thinking."

"But we don't know what Mateo's thinking."

"That's a personal conflict, not a big picture one. You have to earn answers just like you have to earn Calsta's power. You never wanted to be Devoted. Why lean on her now? Being gods-touched is what's making you a target, Lia. Can Mateo turn you into a sacrifice or whatever it is if you aren't keeping oaths?"

There has to be a bond before someone can betray it and become a shapeshifter, Calsta whispered, almost eagerly. *I give power to those who sacrifice, but it hurts me to see sacrifices offered that are too much.*

"You don't have to be everything, to do all of it. I don't think Calsta even *wants* you to do all of it. Some fights can't be won with a sword." Knox didn't like the way Lia bit her lip, her hands twitching at her sides. "Your sister is going to need you as yourself, not a spiriter. I promised I'd help. Anwei promised—"

"Anwei makes a lot of promises, doesn't she?" Lia interrupted. "She promised to help get the carom back. To help you fix the sword. To save my sister." She looked away when he blinked. "I'm beginning to see why she made such a good underworld crimey sort of person."

Knox turned his gaze back to the gap in the buildings and the muddle of people, horses, and wagons washing by just past it. "Because she keeps her promises?"

"No. Because we all believe she will." Lia squared her shoulders and strode out into the street, looking as if she meant to destroy something.

Which, they did.

Knox followed a little more slowly, turning over what she'd said in his mind. *We all believe she will.* The crowd split before them as he followed Lia's blaze of curls toward the marked ship she'd told him about, people falling quiet when they saw Lia's sword hilt and Knox's oath scars bared to the sun. He caught sight of Anwei down the dock, her hands gripping Noa's tightly as the two talked.

Why wouldn't we believe Anwei's promises? He shook his head, wondering what pebble had got into Lia's shoe. *Anwei always comes through.*

Striding up the gangplank, Lia ignored the half-hearted protest from the man standing guard. "Bring me the captain," she said to no one in particular on the deck, and three sailors jumped to obey her, casting nervous looks over Knox as he followed her up the ramp.

The captain came out in a flurry of annoyance and bluster, at least until he set eyes on Lia's sword. "What . . . what can I help you with,

Devoted?" he stuttered. "We're already having an unlucky sort of day, and—"

"We're going to kill the pirates who marked your ship." Lia went to the tiller. "Get this boat off its moorings. Now."

When the captain went shouting down the deck, Lia inclined her head toward Knox, glaring at a sailor swabbing the deck behind him until the man took his mop and ran "Is that how you say it?" she whispered. "Get the boat . . . off its moorings?"

Knox shrugged. "I have no idea."

⁂

Noa's bracelets felt like shackles. She tried not to groan as Anwei pulled her toward the docks. They passed under the city's arched gate, and Noa's eyes found the low, ugly boat that belonged to her father's fleet at the end of the dock. Her stomach erupted in worms.

She dug in her heels, bringing Anwei to a stuttering stop. The healer had twined all her braids into one long plait that fell down her back, her long skirts exchanged for trousers and riding leathers like a Devoted. The most convincing part of the costume was the sword sheathed between her shoulderblades. Noa itched for a weapon, for a costume, to be anything but the part she was meant to play: herself.

"What's the matter?" Anwei asked, pretending she'd stopped on purpose to check her vest's buckles. The linen shirt she wore underneath was buttoned primly to her chin, the sleeves pulled down to cover her wrists.

"You know," Noa looked back toward the city with longing. "Pretending to be fire dancers wouldn't be a stretch this time. There aren't even any books to set on fire. *Everyone* would stop and watch, and when word spreads, Mateo will come, and—"

"We can't be fire dancers this time, Noa. Not with Paran on the hunt and Tual himself wandering through town." Anwei smoothed down the leather tunic, her chin dipping as her eyes caught on something behind Noa.

Noa turned to look and found Altahn, Bane, and Gilesh hulking between them and the little dumpy trade boat, Noa's house mark bright red on the prow. Altahn looked quite dashing with a sword at his shoulder, though the braids seemed a bit much. All their trunks were in a pile behind the Trib, somewhat spoiling the effect. "Let's think this through, Anwei," she said. "If Tual hears about a pretty show in town, maybe he'll come see for himself. We can grab him instead of Mateo! Cut out the middleman." Noa twirled a few steps, ending in a perfect bow, missing only her fire tethers. "It's much simpler than Ellis and pirates and boats and—"

Anwei sighed, squaring off between Noa and the boat. "I know you don't want to do this."

"No. I don't want to do this. If anything goes wrong, I'll be—" Noa swallowed, panic rising in her like a malt-doused fire. Either her father's lackeys would catch her or Ellis would, and both would take her right back to the cage in Chaol.

"Nothing is going to go wrong. Gods above!" Anwei looked down. "I wish this weren't the only way. We came here thinking we were miles ahead of Tual, and instead he's brewing Sleeping Death, and there are pirates, and *Devoted* assembling in the forest? We have to get out of sight before . . . I don't know, another shapeshifter arrives in a golden chariot with two swords and a halo made of ears."

Noa nodded eagerly. "No one ever figured out what happened to that curse lady, so it's possible—"

Anwei shook her head. "This isn't a story to brainstorm into a new fire dancing routine. Aria Seystone is trapped. Altahn's sword, the man who made my whole family go crazy—they're all at the old Basist fort. Tual is dangerous. Devoted are dangerous. And if we don't get out of sight, we're not going to end up with Aria, the sword, or any of it. We'll just end up dead."

The boat wouldn't disappear from its place at the dock no matter how many times Noa blinked. She could see a man standing up on the covered deck, his white hair in a long braid. Captain Loren. Bracing herself, Noa slid one step closer, then stopped, scuttling backward.

Anwei took both her hands. "I will *not* let them take you," she said in Elantin. "And if it all goes to plan, your father will never come looking for you again."

Noa swallowed down ideas still boiling up in her thoughts—that they could let the Devoted destroy Tual for them, that they could steal any other boat, like the rowboat left completely unattended less than ten feet away, for example. Anwei anchored her there, making her want to believe.

"I won't force you to do this." Anwei's hands squeezed hers. "If you can't, I understand. We'll find something else."

"Really?"

The nod came too slowly, and Anwei's head dropped. "I can't see another way. But you don't belong to me, Noa. Our crew—it only works if everyone wants to be here."

"You made me prove myself before you let me stay with you at the apothecary, then again to help at the tomb. I set fire to the excavation barriers right in front of the Warlord herself because you told me to." Noa hadn't known what she was getting into when she first followed Anwei home, only that it was somehow outside the walls her father had built around her. It had started as a game. An escape. A yearning for home, because Anwei spoke her language and, though Noa hadn't understood it at the time, knew what it was to be trapped. But this was asking too much. "Is this what it means to be in your crew, proving myself over and over again?"

"You know who I am." Anwei met Noa's eyes. "Being in my crew means there will be fires. But some of them will be the fires I set for *you*." She gripped her hands hard. "I will *not let them take you*," she said again, her gaze fierce. "If we do this, you'll finally be free."

Noa swallowed, gripping Anwei back, remembering Knox from the day before saying she mattered—all the more true because he hadn't *wanted* to say it but still grudgingly acknowledged her place among them. "You won't let them take me," she repeated, the feel of her own language like a balm on her tongue. "And . . ." This was the much more frightening question, the one she hadn't even wanted to acknowledge to herself. "If Loren doesn't care when he sees me? Or if Ellis sent a pigeon to my father and all he gets back is a note that says, 'Let her drown'?"

Anwei pulled Noa close, wrapping her arms around her tight. "Noa, the people who are supposed to love us do the worst job. That's why you have me. I chose you, and you chose me."

"But you're the one who is making me risk shackles and a boring husband," Noa sniffed, holding Anwei back as if not letting go meant she wouldn't have to face the ugly little boat behind her. "And if I disappear, you'll still have your shadow man."

"No shadow man is enough. Not when I can have you too." Pulling back, Anwei pointed to the docks. "He's waiting for you on the other boat with Lia. They're better than I am at taking care of people, and their job is to protect you from Ellis, Loren, sea monsters, and the Warlord herself if she comes floating down the river. We're all behind you."

Noa breathed the words in. If she became the flag that started this fight, it would be because she wanted to, not because her father told her not to. If Anwei, Lia, and Knox protected her, it wasn't because she was worth more without scars.

It was because she was one of them.

"What do *you* want, Noa?" Anwei whispered.

The one question no one ever asked her.

When Noa turned toward her own house mark, toward Captain Loren with his pockets full of silver and the threat of her father roiling in her head like storm clouds, it didn't feel like she was on some jaunt south or running away.

She wasn't running away. She was running toward something better.

So Noa let go of Anwei and took a step toward the boat. Then another.

Loren caught sight of Noa long before she got to the end of the dock. Dropping a rope he'd been tying, he vaulted over the rail and started down the gangplank, arms open toward her like she were some long-lost child. "Noa? Sky Painter protect you! Do you remember me? Fancy meeting *you* here!"

At the sound of her name, two other sailors on the ship bobbed up from pushing crates. Noa's skin pebbled at the way they immediately climbed up to the gangplank, not looking away. Her father knew she was gone, then, and had told his crews to watch for her.

"May she keep her storms far from us!" Noa shouted the second half of the Elantin greeting, stumbling to a stop farther away than she'd meant to. "I . . . I need help. You can't tell my father."

"Finally running, are you?" Loren didn't stop walking toward her. "I always wondered when you'd try it."

From the corner of her eye, Noa saw the pirate-marked ship begin untying its lines, Lia a burst of fire at the prow and Knox a shadow behind her.

The two sailors closed in behind Loren. Noa backed away, one of her shoulders bumping into a passing sailor. "You and I were always friends, Loren. I saw the house mark—"

He grinned, a gap in his teeth where he'd pried out the tooth that marked him as some other house before coming to work for her father. "I'm touched." And lunged at her.

Over on the pirate-marked ship, oars dipped into the water, inching it away from the dock. Lia drew her sword, pointing it toward the bay like some kind of hero. The signal to move.

Noa dodged Loren's widespread arms, gasping when arms clasped about her middle from behind, because she'd forgotten to watch the other sailors. Pivoting the way Lia had taught her, Noa smashed a fistful of Anwei's foul-smelling leaves into his face. The sailor cried out, letting go, and Noa ran toward the water.

⚜

Knox grabbed hold of the ship's rail as they lurched away from the dock. Lia stepped up to the prow and drew her sword to signal Noa.

Knox cast his sight out, searching for Noa's aura. Anwei was out there, a bluster of purple, but Noa . . . ? "Where is she?" Knox gritted his teeth, frustration lancing through him. "Are we going to have to start a fight on deck to stall them?"

Lia focused on the crowd. "Noa will come."

"Seriously? The sparkle girl?"

"She'll come."

Which was the moment Noa came crashing through the crowd. She slammed into a man with a basket of palifruit, sending fruits rolling down the dock. Hopping over a box of leather slippers, Noa tripped into a bushel of red blooms that cascaded into the water like blood. Noa kept stumbling toward them, though, her eyes glued to Lia and her sword. But the boat had already pulled too far from the dock for her to jump aboard. Three men rushed after her, one tripping over a rogue palifruit as they gave chase.

"She's not going to make it." Knox looked up at the sails, trying not to be annoyed that even rumpled and running for her life, Noa had somehow found a way to glitter. The dancer gracefully leapt from the end of the dock in a perfect dive, looking all the world like a swinging fire tether.

CHAPTER 16

Not One Part That Is True

Anwei watched Noa dive into the water after Lia's and Knox's boat, several people in the crowd clapping as if it were part of a street show. Captain Loren stumbled to a confused stop, then pushed one of the sailors in after, shouting at him to bring Noa back. Breath like a knife in her throat, Anwei grabbed Altahn's arm. "Let's go."

"She isn't on the boat. She was supposed to jump *onto* the boat!" Altahn started toward the water after Noa, but then Noa's head popped up on the surface, and she started swimming toward the ship. Lia sent sailors scrambling for a rope, and by the time Anwei's boots hit Loren's deck, Noa had been pulled on board the other ship. Altahn grudgingly picking up his trunk, Gilesh and Bane following with the rest of their things.

Loren pushed his way back through the crowd (some of whom were cheering for Noa, others shouting for the sailor to swim faster) toward them, his eyes bulging when he saw Anwei untying his mooring lines. "Hey!" he yelled, making a ridiculous leap across just as the wind filled the sail. He hit the side of the boat, grabbing hold of the rail with ropy arms, then clawing the rest of the way onto the deck. "Don't you know whose ship this is? Anton Russo will destroy anyone who so much as touches—

Bane and Gilesh threw down the trunks to draw their swords, pointing them toward the little captain

"You're going to blow up a Devoted and three Roosters?" Anwei asked calmly. "Or did you want our help getting Noa Russo back from that ship before the Butcher figures out who she is and gets to her first?"

Altahn froze where he was sneaking down the ramp that led to the hold. *"The Butcher?"* he mouthed. Anwei ignored him. Names were more frightening than the people attached to them, oftentimes. Ellis was no butcher, but the name had served him well over the years.

"The Butcher . . . ?" Loren echoed, pushing Gilesh off. He stood slowly, staring past her to the boat. "Half the harbor knew that ship was marked. He's here? In person?"

"You think I came here for you and your little boat?" Anwei gestured for Bane to make the ship go faster, though she wasn't sure if that were possible. "We're here to stop the salpowder war from clogging up the Felac. Are you going to fight us the whole way there? Just think what Russo will say when he gets the order for all his boats to be searched for illegal salpowder stores."

"You know what the Butcher can *do*, don't you?" Loren rasped. "He's sunk four boats in the last year with those salpowder arrows of his and marked five others. He doesn't bother fighting anymore; he just takes what he wants."

"You and the others in Russo's fleet have been quite effective in avoiding him. There are two Devoted planted on the marked ship." Anwei turned to look at him. "Why do you think we chose your boat to bring the rest of us?"

Loren glanced toward the harbor's edge, the marked ship ahead putting distance between them. His hands clenched and unclenched as if weighing the prospect of danger with the silver rounds he could get from Russo for taking out the Butcher. When he finally turned back to Anwei, his eyes were shrewd. "These trunks you've brought are some kind of plan?"

She glanced at the trunks, nothing but herbs, Noa's clothes, Calsta-knew-what in Altahn's things, and a cursed shapeshifter sword in them. "We're prepared."

"And you'll let me take Noa back to her father safely once the Butcher is sucking narmaiden skeepoo?"

"Please. Take her back to the people who love her. Calsta is merciful even to merchants like Anton Russo." Anwei couldn't help the way her mouth twisted over those words. She turned to stare into the water ahead, looking for Ellis's ship beyond the harbor. He'd promised to make the fight flashy enough to draw out the harbor wardens and had agreed that the caroms and Noa were worth losing a new ship for the fleet he was building.

He did pout for a full five minutes over missing out on the governor's copper bathtub.

Of course, Anwei's real plan would leave him with nothing.

Anwei meant to steal Loren's boat while the rest of the harbor was fixated on the fake pirate fight happening out in the harbor. Wardens wouldn't have time for complaints or descriptions from Loren until they were long gone. Anwei had agreed to keep Loren on the boat just long enough to watch Noa dramatically die in the pirate battle. That way he could carry word to her father that his daughter was dead. Then no one would be looking for Noa in Forge, Elantia, on pirate ships, in theaters, or anywhere else but among the eels and narmaidens deep in Kingsol's bay.

The boat veered sideways, almost knocking Anwei into the water. Getting Noa away from Ellis was going to be easy, what with Knox and Lia there to fend him off. But getting Altahn's other carom, well . . . Anwei hadn't quite come up with a plan for that yet. She had great confidence that between the four of them, they'd find an opportunity and take it.

Anwei tried very hard to hold back her grin when the boat lurched again and Loren began shouting at Gilesh and Bane to tie things off and move things and turn the rudder, suddenly quite content to be running with a Rooster crew.

People were so easy.

⌘

The Devoted steered out of the little channel hidden on the banks of the Felac onto the main river, the current pulling them downstream. Mateo's fists clenched hard in his lap, the Warlord observing him like a bird would a worm. The tense triangle the Warlord and her two Devoted had made around him after isolating him from his father suddenly made sense. A shapeshifter. She thought *he* was a shapeshifter?

She was right, of course. But how, when Tual Montanne was right there, could she have been suspicious of the sickly, harmless *artist*?

Clearing his throat, Mateo kept his voice absolutely measured when he met the Warlord's gaze. "You're *convinced* I'm a shape-shifter?" He looked around with wonder. "Isn't it your job to know for sure? Your influence and control in the Commonwealth are entirely based on the idea that you can tell the difference between gods-touched and everyone else. I've been around your lot long enough to know you can *see* the nameless god's touch on dirt witches." The slur burned like a mouthful of acid. "If I had even a whiff of him about me, you'd have stabbed me years ago. So what exactly are you trying to accuse me of?"

The Warlord sighed, her dark brown eyes flicking back and forth as she watched the trees pass behind him. Moments ago she'd been worried he'd steal her soul, now it seemed she was confident enough that Mateo didn't even merit her direct attention. "There's been something amiss in the Commonwealth for quite some time now. Something *new* that we can't see. We didn't make the connection to you until we found Lia's family . . . murdered in their home."

Mateo swallowed, the next incredulous sentence to build his case flaking away to ash on his tongue. Murdered in their home? He didn't *want* to know what had happened to Lia's family, didn't want to know why a woman responsible for so many deaths could pause over whatever she'd found—

"The whole compound was burned to the ground with the valas and his wife inside it." Her eyes flicked over him—she was watching him for a reaction. "Their *uncharming* young daughter, as you describe her, is still unaccounted for. That same day, less than an hour after you and Lia were sighted at the excavation, the tomb *caved in*. Trees sprouted from the sea cliffs clear to Chaol's bridge. Lia has since disappeared. Two other Devoted from my party tasked with investigating the site were lost." Her voice rose with each event. "And Ewan Hardcastle was found just outside the compound with a hole in his chest."

Trying to ignore the sickness unfolding in his lungs, Mateo couldn't help but grab hold of the rail, his knees wobbling. He'd known his father had done *something* to Lia's family, but burning her house with her parents still inside? Why?

You don't want to kill until you do.

"I am very sorry to hear that. I didn't know the Seystone family well, but . . ." Swallowing hard, Mateo rubbed his eyes with the heels of his hands, grasping for something. Anything. This was his life, his father's life. They were right on the cusp of being able to sink back into the shadows, to retreat from the risks they'd been taking to heal Mateo. He couldn't give any quarter to the Warlord's belief, even if she wasn't all the way wrong. So he did what he always did when he accidentally glimpsed the dark underside to one of his father's plans.

It was him or the Devoted. His father or the Warlord.

It didn't have to be that way. But they'd made the world impossible for the Montannes to exist in peacefully, and sometimes there were no other choices.

He said it to himself twice. Three times. Then again before he could find any more words for the Warlord. "It seems like the evidence points toward your spiriter torching her own house in a bid to escape from you. I'm nothing more than a student of archeology. An artist." He shrugged, smoothing down his lapels. "I mean, I know I look very debonair—I can see why you might think me qualified to help you untangle this mess. Unfortunately, I don't think my understanding is deep enough to comment on this . . . internal matter? Frankly, I thought that was the point of Devoted—you give up sweets and pretty clothes so that Calsta will give you the ability to solve problems like your spiriter for the rest of us."

"Lia Seystone is an exemplary Devoted. The behavior I have described would have been impossible, unless . . ."

Mateo licked his lips once. "Unless what?"

"We've seen evidence of . . . memory problems across the channel from here. People forgetting parts of who they are. Acting oddly." Her hand darted out to grab his wrist, and she cocked her head at him, the very picture of an old woman questioning her grandson, if only she weren't trying to break his arm. "And the plants in Chaol—weren't the Beildans all crying shapeshifter when every person in the town directly across the water from here got *eaten by trees*?"

An echo sounded inside him. *Trees. Eaten by trees.* A terrible hum filled Mateo's mind, Willow squeaking with dismay. If such a terrible thing had happened so near his home, how could he not have known? But the echo wouldn't go away, the taste of it like metal and herbs and sharp sap, waiting for him to remember.

I don't know what she's talking about, he whispered to himself. *I don't know. I don't want to know.*

"We never found even a hint of Basist magic," the Warlord continued over his thoughts, "But according to reports, those trees erupted out of the ground the same year your father appears to have purchased this estate—the same year you appeared in his household." Her fingers tightened on his arm, though not so tight as Willow's claws. "The history of this estate is riddled with mysterious deaths, stories of people drawn from Kingsol by some inexplicable force toward the lake only to drown in underwater caves. There's a giant snake guarding this place like no animal should. And all of that was buried so deep in the records that somehow no Devoted had ever heard of it. Scholars were set to guard against any mention of these records from leaving their library, though none of them could remember why or who had told them to hide something so mundane as property records in the protected stacks. I went to the library to get directions to this place, and I've never seen such a flurry of confused, panicked messages being sent, pathetic misdirection, and even outright lying from the First Scholar herself. She tried to deny the records existed while they were *in her hands*."

"You think I magicked a bunch of scholars into hiding my father's property records? Why not burn them if they're so incriminating? Why not burn the whole library?" Mateo's voice cracked over the darkness rising inside him. Something from his past fighting for purchase in his memories, more monstrous than the random appearances of root and herb names.

". . . . It wasn't until Lia's disappearance and erratic behavior and the deaths of her family members"—the Warlord was *still* talking, her fingers on his arm like a vise—"that I drew the connection between your presence and minds being altered in your general vicinity. Sickness just like *yours* trailing along after you across the Commonwealth. Even your father couldn't explain completely where you'd come from, only that he loves you so much that he gave up whatever he was before you appeared to search for an answer to your disease—don't try to deny it. I know his help treating wasting sickness is nothing more than an experiment meant ultimately to save *you*." Her teeth were bared in a terrible smile. "None of it makes sense, Mateo. The world around you doesn't make sense."

Her breath caught over the words, and for the first time, Mateo saw her fear. Drawing him away from his father, from the town, from everyone—this was an act of desperation. His heart began to pound, the sword point so casually resting on the floorboards etched into his mind.

Just think of what you want. The thought burned through him, his father's voice like a weapon. Mateo's stomach lurched as Willow seemed to grow inside him. What was it Willow had done before when Aria had been standing there healthy and hale one moment, near dead the next? He envisioned the Warlord shriveling away, leaving nothing but a pile of ash inside that ridiculous armor. He thought about how much more energy he'd have by taking from a Warlord rather than a little girl.

He thought about Lia and how much she hated this woman.

A sword isn't enough to destroy you and me, Willow whispered. *But taking the Warlord's magic won't stop the other two from trying to kill us.* Mateo could smell the rot inside him, the death. It wasn't a warning so much as an invitation. He wouldn't have to stop with the Warlord. He could suck the life from every Devoted on this boat to stop them from stabbing anything ever again.

Willow could see it. She ached for this fight. To take the energy swirling just out of reach—but then she lurched inside him, clearly frustrated. *It's too much right now, Mateo. We need the rest of me. We can't fight them all. Not without the sword.*

The words rang like a frozen bell, sending tendrils of ice through Mateo. *The sword.*

The ghost was right to caution him, but he didn't see how having the sword would help. Not even Tual Montanne could face down a host of Devoted head-on, sword or no.

That was why they planned. Why they schemed and hid. Fighting the Warlord would only make things worse. But in that moment he wanted to destroy the Devoted more than he'd ever wanted anything.

Why hadn't they attacked? Just as Mateo refocused on the Warlord's face, a frightened sort of satisfaction bloomed in her expression. She wrenched him closer, their faces inches apart.

"You haven't swollen yourself up into a lizard or a wolf. You haven't drained me dry or made the trees reach out to strangle us. Which means I was right."

"That makes you *right*?" Mateo laughed. There was nothing else he could do.

"We haven't had fully realized shapeshifters in the Commonwealth for generations. Centuries. We don't know what they're capable of." She let go of him, pushing him back into his chair. "And I don't think you do either. You can't control your power"

"This is ridiculous." Mateo kept laughing, burying his face in his hands. "You say we have a shapeshifter on the loose? And you choose *me*? You think I ensnared my own father into fixing my illness, did something odd and unexplainable to Beilda for no reason, hid records about my house that have no bearing on anything important, then *seduced* your lost spiriter whom I've never met and—"

"I didn't say seduced." The Warlord stood and went to the railing, squinting down the curve of the river ahead. "Lia has oaths to keep and . . . better taste, I'd hope."

Mateo flushed, heat rising in his cheeks. "All right. Let's say I broke her mind then, tricked her into going on a rampage through the city, killing Devoted and auroshes left and right, we destroyed the tomb together right in front of you, and then I abandoned her somewhere between here and Chaol and led you straight back to my lair here at the lake. What would any of that accomplish?"

"It got you the sword, of course. You are fixated on those shapeshifter weapons. They call to you. You even whispered it just now, something about a sword." The Warlord rounded on him, and Mateo couldn't help but flinch back, his hands coming up in defense before he could think clearly. He glanced over his fingertips, grateful to see that whatever using his power to open the channel had done to his hands, the effects were gone. "You need that sword to heal yourself, but instead Tual's going to use it to destroy the last crumbs of wasting sickness in our ranks."

Wasting sickness. Tual. One death every generation—had his father blamed Beryl's death on the curse? How much longer had he survived there in the old house, praying to a god who hated him to let him make amends, before he'd given up on forgiveness and burned everything to the ground? Mateo's mouth went dry, thinking of flame. Of Lia's fancy fountain and foyer blackened with soot, of her mother's body a pile of ash on the bed.

Of Aria lying still in the glass passageway, her face so, so white.

No. Mateo's eyes pinched shut as he replaced the fuzzy memory of Aria falling with the one where she opened her eyes again, then insulted him. Aria was going to be just fine. He *hadn't* killed her.

But still, the image of his father knuckle-deep in black clay, bones splayed around him tried to flood through the cracks in Mateo's mind. He thrust it away. His father had done what he had to.

He'd *always* done what he'd had to. To keep himself alive. To keep Mateo alive. To protect Mateo from having to do the hard things.

It wasn't Mateo's fault Willow lived inside him. It wasn't his fault his family had tried to kill him or that Tual Montanne had stepped in to save him, resulting in *whatever* had happened back on Beilda. Mateo's head began to ache again, the empty space sharp inside him where his childhood should have been.

He was on a path that only went forward. Survival wasn't something you could pray for, hoping some god would listen. Survival was something you had to take.

His father knew it. *Lia* knew it. When something came at her, she fought with whatever she could lay hands on. Pencils. A skirt. A satchel. A razor. An auroshe, ready to bite.

He knew who had killed Ewan Hardcastle.

Mateo wasn't evil. He wanted to live, just the way Lia did. That was what made him most human of all, wasn't it?

But what could *he* do?

Willow cackled inside him, the sound ringing deep. *I like you. There's not one part of you that's true.*

The Warlord flinched when Mateo looked up at her. He spread his hands wide and gave her the best smirk he had in his arsenal. Angry smiling. Mad, and mad about having to smile. "If this is truly what you think is going on, then why don't you kill me now? That's why you brought me out here, isn't it?" He stood, gesturing to the water, the forest, the world wide open and waiting to swallow him. "If your theory holds true, my father will forget I existed, and everything will go back to normal. Here." He pulled the drawing satchel off his shoulder and offered it to her. "I'll even let you keep my charcoals as a trophy to show the governors just how dangerous a threat you've extinguished."

The Warlord's smile split wider. Then she started to laugh, pressing back into the chair and hugging her arms around her, the sword like a pin stuck into a cushion, only the cushion was her. "Mateo Montanne, you can't goad me into bringing your power forward. You've demonstrated what happens when people try to get rid of you. Who was it who first tried to snuff you out when they realized what you were? Your parents? You suffocated them to death inside a tree."

Suffocate. Inside trees? Mateo's eyes burned.

"You talk just like the scholars whose memories you stole. You still have a sunburn from working in the tomb complex that you then caved in before I could enter, still have the stink of spoiled oaths you took from my spiriter. You left a whole city suffering from plague and stole bits of my Devoted, letting us and the peace in this great country waste away." She laughed again. "You ought to thank Cath and Berrum for coming—risking themselves to test how dangerous you are." She turned to look at the girl with the braid and the flowery sword. "This has been instructive. I don't think he can act unless he's triggered somehow. Why else invite violence now?"

The Devoted gave a sharp nod, not looking away from the river ahead as she paddled.

Turning back to Mateo, the Warlord heaved a great sigh. "We'll isolate you until we learn how to dispose of you safely. Who knows, maybe we can learn how to help you before that becomes necessary, Mateo."

Mateo squeezed his eyes shut. He reached out with his energy, feeling the stones on shore whisk by, the tree roots, the dirt, living creatures flicking back and forth beneath the boat, their heartbeats like little gears ticking away that he couldn't remember feeling before. He couldn't run. If he managed to get away, where would he go? Back to his father? That would only make things worse.

To Lia, then. It had to be to Lia. Only she'd come to him with a sword.

"You were sick. The caprenum sword is part of it." The Warlord gave a decisive nod. "We'll go to Kingsol for supplies as planned—there's an apothecarist there who has done some very interesting exchanges with your father—"

An unnameable trill worse than discomfort stung in Mateo's chest. His father never made him go into apothecaries when he went for herbs. He vaguely remembered going in a blue-painted door once—not what had happened, only that he'd run out quick enough and hidden under the carriage seat shaking while Tual tried to calm him.

"—he'll be helpful in restraining you until we can bring Tual over to our side," the Warlord was saying. "I don't think we can bring in the others of our company safely until we've incapacitated you completely, of course."

"Lovely." Mateo pushed off the feeling of dread and made a show of slumping back in his chair, propping his feet up on the bench in front of him. Wanting to laugh because she had it both so right and so wrong. "I'll be sure to lock myself in one of the monastery cells while you and my father brew poison to kill me. Oh," he snapped, pointing to the Warlord. "Buy some blueberries for Hilaria, would you? She'd probably kill me before you can if we don't come back with some. That woman takes her muffins very seriously."

The Warlord closed her eyes, putting her face to the wind so it ruffled her curls. "I always have enjoyed spoiled little children. They cry the hardest when they realize everything they love has been taken away from them. Tual is reasonable. He'll see this. I know he will." She settled back into her seat. "With his help, I'll rid the south of your blasphemy and reestablish the need to support Devoted in one go."

"A scapegoat to prove your relevance?" Mateo crossed his arms moodily, his mind racing. He could just jump out of the boat. Those ticking gears beneath him were those glowing eely-fish things that ate people. No Devoted would come after him if it meant losing body parts. If they thought he was already dead.

Mateo reached for Willow. *You're sure I can't die?*

You would have a long time ago if not for me.

She wasn't saying that he'd still have fingers and toes at the end of it, of course. Mateo looked at his long artist fingers, then to the water rushing past the boat. It was the only choice. And if he went to Lia . . .

She'd come with a sword.

But he knew her.

He did.

She'd listen.

Knox survived worse than Lia Seystone. Just think what we can do when we're all together, Willow whispered. Only there was something in her voice. A secret, something so terrible she couldn't help but think it.

The ghost gave a pathetic little mewl, as if their link went both ways and he could look inside her for a split second the way she always watched him. Which was when Mateo remembered his sister.

With Lia.

Anwei was the reason he was in this mess. *She* was the one who had whisked Lia away at the tomb. *She'd* been the one to bring down the walls with her roots and trees.

The darkness in his mind flashed again, the sounds of wood cracking, swelling, roots twisting, breaking—

Mateo's eyes burst open, the thoughts gone as fast as they'd come. His palms were sweaty, as if he'd been holding the sword. *Find it,* Willow cried. *Please. Before she finds us.*

He wiped his hands against his coat and stood, looking down the river for a likely spot to jump. They were one bend in the river away from the ocean, the gaps between the trees sparkling with open water.

"Look out!" Berrum cried out from the back of the boat. A bloom of red Mateo didn't quite understand bled up into the sky over the treetops. Fire?

Suddenly everything was too quiet: the river, the forest, the oars in the water. Then the boat jerked to one side, sending Mateo careening back into his chair as the boat rounded the last bend and the ocean's horizon opened before them.

There was a boat out in the bay—no, *two* boats, fire flinging through the air and water pitching as if it had turned to salpowder.

A deep *boom* shattered Mateo's ears, reverberating in his chest. He ducked down behind his chair, his flimsy, paper-thin aurasight reach floundering out to touch the battle

Something inside him jolted as his aurasight touched the nearer boat. Mateo peered around the chair to find a little figure on the prow, ethereal and fluttering with copper. Wreathed in an aura of violence and gold—Calsta's gold.

Mateo's gulped down air to shout a warning, but it was already too late. The two Devoted rowing had picked up speed, the Warlord at the prow staring out at the flaming ship with eagerness, her sword drawn.

It would be moments before they got within normal aurasight range, and then the Warlord and her lackeys would see Lia there, plain as the sun in the sky. They would take her.

And that would be the end. The world the Warlord described—the one where Mateo didn't deserve to live—would be all that was left.

And so Mateo did something.

He flipped the boat.

CHAPTER 17

A Prize Bathtub

The crew had not been particularly happy about Lia storming onto the boat and demanding they fight pirates. They'd been even less happy when Noa had dragged herself sopping wet over the railing like a narmaiden that had somehow grown a face as beautiful as its voice. But peak unhappiness was achieved when the pirate, whatever his name was, climbed up above his little sail and started shooting trails of smoke and fire into the water around them, splashing the rails with saltwater that smelled of acid and char.

To be perfectly honest, Lia wasn't particularly happy about it herself.

"You said you had a plan!" the captain screamed from where he huddled just below deck. "We could have jumped ship and rowed away safe like we were supposed to, but now—" He ducked as another blast flew toward them and clipped the forward prow, sending chips of wood zipping through the air.

"He missed," Knox breathed, adjusting the carom on his shoulder. He set the edge of it on the prow, Galerey climbing down into its belly with one of the salpowder packets in her mouth.

"He's so upset!" Noa breathed, but Lia could see her white-knuckling the edge of the bench. Knox braced the tube against the rail, unprepared when it kicked back in a sputter of smoke and flames, sending a ball of flame into the air with an unhealthy whine. It came down between the two boats, fizzing as it went underwater. After a moment, a dull boom churned up through the water, making the boat pitch backward. Ellis's ship continued its approach, threading its way toward their side exposed to the ocean.

The smoke from Knox's carom came out acrid, stealing Lia's breath. She hunched down, coughing until she could breathe again. Another explosion ignited on the other boat, sending something small and black lancing toward them. It struck the mast, splintering wood and sail.

"I think Ellis is getting impatient?" Lia breathed. She pointed toward the Russo boat making its way toward them and the little trail of smaller crafts racing out from the harbor, bristling with bows, knives, and spears. The harbormaster's own boat was at the very back, obviously not interested in being the one to face Ellis's carom. "That's our cue, I think. Knox, would you untie a rowboat?" She raised her voice, crowing like an auroshe. "Abandon ship!"

"Thanks all the gods," Noa breathed, hopping up from her seat to assist Knox in untying the ropes.

Lia joined her, letting the ship twist in the waves, a spectacle for anyone watching. The harbormaster probably had money tied up on this ship, and it wasn't going to last long enough for him to save much of any of it. The sailors would be picked up, though.

Lia heaved one of the boats into the water, then helped Noa over the rail before she felt Knox go stiff next to her. "What is—"

But then she felt it too. Golden sparks at the very edge of her aurasight. She looked around wildly. There had been Devoted at the lake, so many Devoted— *There.* Three auras, all in the water at the mouth of the river, clutching the turquoise hull of an overturned boat.

And one of them belonged to the Warlord herself.

Lia strained her sight and found one terribly blank white aura at the center of gold. Mateo.

"Calsta's breath." Lia *couldn't* breathe, the feeling of Ewan's fingers closing around her throat, her muscles crawling with then need to *run*. She wouldn't go back to the Devoted.

She couldn't.

Knox reached out to grab hold of her, as if he meant to steady them both. Form a united front against the woman who would never stop hunting them.

"We're within aurasight." Lia choked on the words, looking all around. There was no escape, only water on all sides, and the Devoted were already swimming toward them. "I manage to stay out of range in Chaol for weeks, and they sail right into our fake pirate battle here in *Kingsol?*"

"What's going on?" Noa yelled, the wind whipping her hair across her face.

"It's not too late." Knox grabbed hold of Lia's shoulders. "We're here to kill Noa, right?"

"Wait, *what?*" Noa squawked.

"Pretend! *Pretend* kill!" Knox waved her off. "What if we kill you too, Lia? They've spotted you, but if the Warlord watches you *die*—"

"If I'm dead . . . she won't chase me anymore." The words flapped through Lia, her eyes glazing over the sight of the turquoise boat, the Warlord, *Mateo*. Had he told the Warlord she was here? Brought the Warlord after her once he'd seen her aura the night before?

"*What in the name of Falan's squatty sidekick is going on?*" Noa's voice cracked, her fingers locked around the canoe's bow. A sailor jerked it away from her and pulled the lashings free, splashing it down into the water. "Anwei said that we were only going to *pretend* to let Ellis take us, not *actually let him take us!*" She pointed frantically toward the boat drawing even with them. Ellis climbed down from his perch with the carom tethered to his back.

Knox held up the bag of compressed salpowder packets. "They burn underwater. All we have to do is make it look good, then swim down until out of aurasight range. They'll think you drowned."

Lia's heart swelled, hope a poisonous thing inside her. "You trust Anwei to find us before we *actually* drown?"

"Of course." He twitched, face screwing up as Galerey popped out of his tunic front. "She still needs us."

Noa began swearing in Elantin when a hook flew over the rail and drew tight, pulling Ellis's boat closer. Lia's heart sank, the feel of golden auras ever closer. They were swimming fast, like fish in the water, because Devoted had Calsta to lend them extra breath.

Something Noa couldn't do.

Noa couldn't hold her breath long enough to fake drowning. Energy crackled through Lia, the spark of needing to act striking inside her over and over. She could feel Knox's hands go slack around the salpowder packets as he looked toward Noa, realizing what she just had. Noa couldn't hold her breath long enough to pull this off, and they couldn't leave her behind.

But Lia couldn't stay. Another projectile fell short of the rail and fell into the water below, air bubbling out from under it as it sank. Her mind went to the hold. They just needed to find some way to breathe under water. Drawing her sword, she slashed the ropes connecting their boat to Ellis's. "Give me some of that." She grabbed one of the salpowder packets from Knox, the acrid smell like vomit. "We can take Noa down with us. I have a plan."

"What do I need to do?"

Lia took Noa's hand and ran toward the hold, hollering at Knox over her shoulder. "Rig things up here to explode before Ellis can get on board, then come below."

The Devoted auras pricked in her mind, stroking closer every moment.

The stairs that led below were slippery—slippery like the odds this would work.

"Tell me what we're doing," Noa gasped, wrenching her hand free.

The Devoted were only fifty paces away.

"Stay close." Lia grunted as something above them gave an ear-bending crack, and then a boom that shook the whole boat. "I need you to help me find the governor's prize bathtub."

❧

About halfway to the ship, Anwei felt something go wrong.

It had all been perfect, the flashes of fire, smoke bleeding into the air so thick they could hardly see the boats, Loren white-knuckling the tiller, asking every two minutes if Noa truly would be safe.

One moment, everything was going perfectly, and the next, something in Anwei's mind changed. She staggered forward, grabbing hold of the rail. The touch Knox left at the back of her mind, the one she'd been pushing away, went from exhilarated to . . .

Terrified.

"She's worth quite a bit of money. To you too, if we get her unharmed, is all I'm saying." Loren was still talking. "If you'd just let me take us a little faster—"

The pirate-marked ship rocked to the side, smoke and flame erupting from where Knox, Lia, and Noa were supposed to be standing on the deck. A moment later, an earsplitting roar tore over. Flames burst out from the side, and the craft began to list. Knox was a flame in her head, reaching for her as she reached for him. Her mind bent, and suddenly she could see auras the way Knox did, Noa, Knox, and Lia, all somehow below. Trapped inside the foundering hull.

Anwei drew her sword—or tried, almost losing it halfway when it caught in the sheath, but Loren was too busy gasping obscenities to notice. "You said—*you said*—"

She held the tip to Loren's throat, her brain twisting into curls of panic that were not all her own. "Get us over there right now."

His eyes bulged. "It's too *late*—"

"Next time, before letting *Devoted* onto your ship, you should remember that anyone can have braided hair. We only marked one boat. Now we have two. If you don't get me over there, I will cut off your ears and feed them to you one by one."

Loren stared at her. Then slammed the sword away from his throat. He dove to the deck, groping for the salpowder trigger Ellis had warned them about. Fingers clawing, Loren pulled so hard that it came away in his hand.

No explosion came, of course. Altahn had dismantled the salpowder trigger before they'd been ten strides from the dock. Anwei advanced on Loren, pinning him to the rail with the sword even though the weight dragged at her wrist. "Get off my boat. The girl you wanted is dead, and you're going to join her if you don't jump now."

Both of them flinched at the sound of another explosion. Anwei looked up to see the ship burst out in flames. It rolled completely over, belly up in the water. Knox was still *there*, alive and . . . in control somehow. Knox seemed to grow inside her mind, stretching out past the little spot he usually stayed.

You're going to have to move fast. His voice was *in her head*, fully formed, like he was standing right next to her. *Meet down the coast, well past the river mouth.*

Altahn cried out, "Anwei!"

She dropped the sword, wrenching free the packet of corta stashed in her coat, the fabric tearing, knowing Loren's hands were coming for her throat before she even saw them.

The eruption of powder fountaining from the torn packet lit up in Anwei's mind like a beacon, each particle crying out to be *guided*.

It happened so fast she hardly understood it, each individual particle of powder changing directions at the same moment, like a flock of sparrows. With a nudge from her, they shot straight into Loren's face, and he staggered backwards over the rail.

She didn't bother checking to see if Loren surfaced again, her eyes full of the burning ship. "Get me closer," she yelled. "Around the back side and up the coast. Get us over there *now*."

But then she saw it. A turquoise boat.

Anwei clutched her medicine bag, frozen. Shimmers of light erupted across it as she watched, some flickering with gold and one that looked familiar. Her hands clenched on the railing, stuck as she stared toward it, the tomb flashing in her mind, the body on the floor swapping power between Knox and—

Arun. No, *Mateo*, the monster he'd become when he left her to die on the island for his new monster family. He was right there in the water, ripe for the taking.

Knox's connection to her flared with panic, and he suddenly was sinking, the little flare of Noa and Lia to either side of them.

Hurry. Knox's voice was quieter. *Up the shore.*

Ellis was backing off, her friends' energy was flickering, and the bond between her and Knox stretching tight. But Mateo was *right there*.

"Anwei?" Altahn's voice rapped out. He coughed, the smoke rolling over them. "Everything is *on fire*. My carom—"

Knox's aura winked out.

Anwei tore her eyes away from the turquoise boat. "Bane and Gilesh, stay with the boat. Take it up the Felac like we planned. Altahn, you and I are going to take the two canoes up past the river."

"But Ellis still has—" Altahn yelled over the roar of waves and fire.

Anwei swiped the sword through the ropes tethering the rowboats under the back rail of the ship, dropping it with a clang when the boats splashed into the water. "I'm not leaving them."

Altahn hesitated only a second before he ran past her, vaulting over the railing into the first boat. "I'm with you."

Knox could feel the Devoted when they boarded the boat. It was the closest he'd been to gods-touched outside of Lia and Anwei in more than a year.

The explosion had gone to plan, two holes in the same side of the hull that had water gushing up to his knees before the boat began to list. It didn't stop the sparkle of aurasparks from heading for the ramp that led down to them. Noa had gotten hold of one of his hands and was squeezing his fingers far harder than was warranted. Lia was on his other side, ready to move.

The two auras came closer. Closer.

But then something broke, a spurt of seawater flooding the boat so it was suddenly up to Knox's chest, the floor tipping out from under his feet, and the tub—

"Move out of the way, Noa!" Knox warned.

She let go of his hand and pushed to the edge of the quickly filling room just as the boat turned fully on its side. Lia pushed from the top of the now steeply sloped floor and Knox pulled from the bottom, the copper monstrosity turning upside down into the water with a slap over his head, trapping air inside. Ensuring the carom was firmly strapped to his shoulder, Knox dove under the lip to get back out from under the tub, surfacing to find Noa wide-eyed and whispering something in Elantin that sounded like a prayer.

"Quick, Noa! It's sinking!" The bathtub was extremely heavy, cast iron with a copper coating that made it sluggish in the brackish bay water. Knox tried to hold it steady, bracing himself to keep the bathtub from going down and the carom from dragging him with it. Lia was on the other side, face pained as she tried to keep the other side of it from sinking into the hole they'd made in the side of the boat. The water gushed in faster and faster, the pocket of air above their heads shrinking. "You need to get under it, Noa. There's air trapped inside the bathtub for you to breathe until we get you back up to the surface, we'll be right there with you—"

"Knox, I . . . ." Noa's gaze was terrified.

"Noa." He took both her hands, looking her straight in the eyes. "Anwei promised you she'd get you out, right?"

The Devoted had reached the top of the sideways staircase.

Noa closed her eyes. "I dance and make fun of people, shadow man. I'm not supposed to—"

"Listen to me. Anwei and I are partners, and her promise is mine. Maybe you and I don't get along, exactly, but I'm going to keep you safe."

Noa sniffled once. Then nodded, her panic palpable. Something crawled at the back of Knox's neck, wriggling out from under his shirt. He yelled, slapping at the writhing only to have Galerey scramble out, hopping from him to the top of Noa's head. She started laughing, gathering in the lizard and holding it close. "I've got you, little terror." She took one last look at Knox's face, then took a deep breath. "Hold your breath, Galerey," she whispered, then ducked under the water, coming back up under the bathtub.

"Lia Seystone?" a voice called. Knox didn't recognize the auras trying to pick their way past the rubble, water up to his chin. The boat gave a sudden lurch, turning the rest of the way over. Knox strained to keep the bathtub poised over the hole.

The ship was sinking fast now, taking Knox, Lia, and Noa with it like fish caught in a current. The auras above climbed up, back to the open air. Knox took in one last deep breath as the water level bubbled up to fill the room, the hum of the goddess's fire making him feel as if he didn't even need air. He braced himself against the side of the hole they'd made as the water pressure from below lessened, the bathtub beginning to dip down toward the hole. Knox and Lia struggled to hold it steady, waiting until the auras above them winked out entirely.

The moment they disappeared, Knox launched off the side of the boat, Lia helping him guide the tub down through the hole, then they both kicked hard, pushing the bathtub and its unhappy passenger out from under the boat.

Anwei was a warm hand on the back of his neck—she was frantically looking for him, smoke and confusion in her lungs. She couldn't see.

Down the shore, he thought. *Past the river.*

She was *close*. Not physically, but close inside his head, her presence threaded through him just like it had down in the tomb. Brought together by *panic*. She couldn't see what was happening with the ships or the pirates, but she did know the ship had gone down. She knew he was underwater, she—

Something changed, Anwei tearing back for a moment. The air in Knox's lungs suddenly burned, Calsta a fire around him, and his side—

But then Anwei was back, the weight of the tub, the pressure of water sucking at the boat's wreckage was all dragging them down, down—Knox could feel the energy coursing through him, more than just his own like other moments they'd reached out for each other. Lia, so graceful in the water beside him, was sketched out in a new kind of light that wasn't her aura. Knox could suddenly see everything inside her working together to move the tub across the bay. She had a blister from her sword sheath, the feel of it a distinct color in Knox's mind that he couldn't quite describe, Anwei's magic mixing with his as she reached out and he reached back.

Kicking harder, they came out from under the ship's shadow, and Knox dropped the carom's extra weight, watching the heavy tube disappear into the darkness below. *Sorry, Altahn. At least Ellis won't be able to get it.* He reached out farther with Anwei's power and found Noa under the tub, her muscles and bones moving together in ways he didn't understand, her fingers latched to under the tub's lip with a viselike grip, her lungs—

Something about her lungs was . . . *wrong.*

Knox pushed faster with a stab of panic, trying to gauge the distance to the surface. He couldn't see the auras above them, couldn't see the boats any longer, pirate or otherwise, but he could feel Anwei. She was up there, and *she* would know how to fix whatever was happening to Noa.

Lia caught his panic as the air trapped in Knox's lungs began to burn, not even Calsta's power enough to keep them under much longer. He ducked down under the tub and grabbed hold of Noa, hoping she knew to take in one last breath. He dragged her out into the water and started swimming toward the surface, leaving the bathtub.

Noa was light and limp as he kicked up into the blue, finally seeing the outlines of little boats on the surface.

Ten feet. Three. And then he was on the surface, gasping for breath, and Altahn was dragging Noa out of his arms into the boat.

"She's not breathing!" Altahn yelled toward the other boat. "*Anwei?*"

Knox climbed onto the canoe, remembering what he'd seen Anwei do when one of her patients had stopped breathing. He tipped up her chin and blew air into Noa's mouth, hard and forceful.

Hand seized his shoulders, Altahn's angry voice filling his ears.

"Altahn, keep the boat steady!" Anwei's voice shouted over the water, fading as the waves pushed them apart. "You have to breathe for her, Knox, just like that!"

Knox blew air into her mouth, panic unfolding inside him when she stayed pale and cold like a corpse. *Her heart—it's not beating.*

Noa needed a heartbeat. Anwei's presence, her magic, all of her twisted tight inside him, and he could almost feel her hands over his hands, moving them to press down on Noa's chest to match the beat ticking in his own chest. Anwei's boat swept farther away, and Lia, who'd been picked up by Anwei, was madly trying to row them closer as Altahn fought the pull of the waves drawing them toward to shore. *More breaths,* Anwei whispered inside Knox. *Then her heart again.*

Knox kept going, breathing, then beating Noa's heart, then breathing, then the beating heart, then breathing—

Suddenly, Noa's eyes bugged open, and she choked. Knox pushed her onto her side as water spewed out of her mouth. She was crying, and Altahn was yelling, and the boat pitched violently under them as it hit the beach. Knox grabbed hold of Noa, dragging her until the sand under his feet was dry. He fell down next to her, his whole body burning and tears streaming down his cheeks. "Noa?" he gasped. "Noa, are you all right?"

She was coughing, her hands pressing hard against her chest as she curled in the sand, the dry grains sticking to her face and hair. "Gods above, I hate you," she gasped. "And I feel sorry for Anwei if that's how you kiss girls."

"You are the worst." He couldn't help but laugh, flopping down in the sand next to her.

Noa's hand nudged his shoulder, almost like a pat. "*You* are the worst."

Altahn staggered up the beach, his Rooster braids matted against his forehead. He fell to his knees between them, an oar forgotten in one hand. "Noa?"

"Leave me alone," she rasped, waving him off. "I'll let you take care of me later when I don't actually feel like I'm about to die."

Slumping down on her other side, Altahn clenched his eyes closed and nodded. "Don't die. We traded saving the carom for saving you. If you die, I'll have gotten nothing out of this."

Knox squinted out toward the bay. "I think Ellis's boat is on fire, if that's any consolation."

"He'll soon have it out." Altahn's lips pursed. "But I guess that does make me feel a *little* better."

CHAPTER 18

The Yuzulfruit Supply Chain

Considering Mateo only half hoped that tipping the boat would work, he was quite surprised to find himself in the churning water, his boots and coat dragging at him as the river current pushed him one way and the ocean waves pushed him back.

I helped, of course, Willow crowed, even as the Warlord pulled the buckles free on her oversized cuirass and sword, letting them sink, then swam at him like a river rat. Mateo kicked backward in a panic and hit the boat's overturned hull just as an ear-shattering explosion rocked the water.

He twisted to see the spot where Lia had been a moment before now spouting white flames high into the sky.

"You see her?" The Warlord's voice was faint, but Cath and Berrum seemed to hear just fine, their heavy things already off as they streaked through the water toward the flames. Grabbing hold of the boat, Mateo stubbornly kept his boots and coat on despite the way they dragged him down deeper into the waves. Saltwater lapped at his chin.

Aurasight stretching farther than it should have with the taste of Aria Seystone's energy on his tongue, Mateo found Lia inside the tall ship. A boat full of slightly dirty-looking sailors were closing in on one side, and a host of boats were approaching from the Kingsol harbor. The largest boat was close enough he could see a figure jumping into a canoe alongside it—

A girl with braids.

He blinked. Clenched his eyes shut as a wave surged under him, his ears clogged with water. Something inside him twisted again, that darkness in the cracks of his memory waiting. He pushed it away.

"Help me, you little nuisance!" The Warlord's voice cracked across the waves, and he turned to find her on the other side of the boat. "You push on your side. I'll lift."

He obeyed, but by the time the boat was flipped back over, they'd drifted clear into Kingsol harbor. By the time he was dripping soggily in his chair, the hideous explosions had stopped, the smoke blocking his view of the two boats. His aurasight still strained farther than normal, but Lia was nowhere to be found.

Neither was Berrum.

Cath, however, was slowly making for them through the water. She emerged from the smoke, her sun hat still somehow tied to the ribbon around her throat. Smaller boats from the harbor were just now catching up, wardens shouting for information. Ignoring them, Cath clawed her way onto the turquoise boat, somehow managing not to look bedraggled in the least, as if she drew more power than ever from being soaked to the bone.

"What happened?" he demanded. "You can't blame this one on me—that was salpowder and fire and—"

"Runaway spiriters?"

He turned slowly to face the Warlord.

"Interesting that she's here and *you're* here. . . ." The Warlord raised her eyebrows as if inviting some kind of confession. "And that you upset our boat just as we saw her."

Mateo spread his hands. "What in Calsta's name are you even talking about?"

"The ship went down," Cath said quietly. "Berrum took one of the boats and started searching up shore. We lost her aura as it sank."

"You think she drowned?"

Mateo's breath went in with an awful quiver. Even if that boat went down, Lia couldn't have gone down with it. She was just outside aura range or . . .

He had felt her sinking and flicker out. Willow seemed to slick across his thoughts. *This was all her plan, you know.*

Whose plan? His sister's? Something inside Mateo seemed to harden and crack.

The Warlord flagged down a boat. "I'm taking this," she informed the three wardens inside it. "You take these two to the docks now."

They didn't say a word, practically shaking as they moved over onto Tual's boat, then held theirs steady for the Warlord to climb in. "Don't let him out of your sight," was all she said to Cath before she rowed off into the smoke.

The boat was very quiet as Cath and the wardens rowed toward the docks, Kingsol a familiar shape that should have been comfortable and happy. Home. How many times had Mateo come here to help his father buy herbs, to buy new charcoals, pigments, and stretched skins and canvas on which to paint?

"You all right, Mateo?" Cath asked, looking over her shoulder at him from behind her oar.

"You're not scared of the loose shapeshifter?" his voice croaked, water pooling around him like blood. Her mouth quirked, and he couldn't stand to look at it because it was a smile, as if he were ridiculous. "All I'm worried about is getting a sunburn. You dragged me out here without letting me get my hat."

Cath pulled her oar out of the water and stood, brandishing it in place of her sword, and Mateo flinched back, wondering if she even needed a sharp edge to skewer him through. But then she put down the paddle, untied the ribbon around her neck, and offered him her dripping hat. The three wardens stared straight ahead, pretending they were alone on the turquoise boat if it meant they didn't have to join in an argument with a Devoted.

"Why are you being nice to me?" Mateo snapped.

"Why aren't you being nice to me?" She cocked her head, holding out the hat until she took it. "One of the Devoted that disappeared from our company in Chaol was a close friend of mine. If you do know what happened to them, I'd appreciate knowing."

Mateo flopped the hat onto his head. "I have no idea what you're talking about." But then he remembered a wagon with the tarp tied down tight. He remembered a glimmer of aura.

A body Harlan found in the woods. *A Devoted with bites taken out of it.*

And stains on the wagon bed that were shaped like a human. And Mateo remembered energy flowing into his father, with no idea where it was coming from. He gritted his teeth, adjusting the hat so it blocked his view of Cath.

He didn't *know* anything about it. There was no reason to fabricate fanciful stories to fit the one the Warlord had come up with. Though . . . not all of the Warlord's theory was exactly untrue.

Once the boat was tied at the dock and the wardens had climbed off, Mateo still didn't move from his seat, not sure what the Warlord had meant Cath to do with him. "The Warlord said . . . there were some things she needed to buy in town?" Something from the apothecary to keep him subdued until they slit his throat. Maybe some more awful ingredients for an awful dinner? "I'd be happy to show you where the most disgusting and tasteless food is sold in town, though perhaps you'd like to visit the tailor first, now you've lost your . . ." He glanced from her plain undertunic down to her bare feet. "Everything? I wouldn't want your less-than-formal appearance to tarnish Calsta's good name."

Cath smiled sweetly. "Try not to choke on your own smarm, Mateo."

"Yes, I meant to see someone about that." He scratched his head, looking down the docks toward the market, though everyone seemed to have retreated into their chalk-colored homes. "Well, if you're not feeling a pressing need for normal clothing, I've been given an extremely important and sensitive task by our cook."

"We just watched pirates set fire to a boat and sink it. Even if you somehow aren't involved with Lia Seystone, doesn't the idea of her drowning bother you at all? You're still worried about muffins?"

Mateo's mouth was already dry, his stomach twisting. "Who else was on that ship?" Maybe his sister had gone down with it too. Or Knox—

No. He's alive. All of them are, Willow hissed.

The knot in Mateo's chest came free in a terrible snap. *You knew Lia was here all along. You knew she was in the bay, and you know where they are now. Why not* tell *me?*

I don't know everything, *Mateo. Only what they let me see. Knox was being so* boring *yesterday, but I think I know where the apothecary is, if you want to go get some of that Sleeping Death stuff your father already bought.*

Did you find out something useful, at least? Mateo shot back.

They stole a boat? And they're going to hide in the waterways. Oh, and kidnap you, I think. I only caught a little bit about that.

Kidnap *me? Why?* Panic bloomed in Mateo, and when Willow didn't have anything to add, he shoved her away, trying not to hyperventilate. His sister and Lia and only Calsta knew who else were trying to *kidnap* him—maybe to kill him off the way Tual had tried to do to Knox?

They can't do it now. Willow almost seemed to be rolling her eyes, like a little girl Aria's age. *They just stole a boat. You should look for my sword. Maybe they left it in Kingsol.*

"Hey, Montanne!"

He looked up to find Cath tapping her foot on the dock.

"You just going to sit there whispering to yourself?" She waited a moment before making a half-decent bow, inviting him to follow, which Mateo almost appreciated until he realized she was making fun of him. "If you run, I will kill you," she said when he joined her on the deck.

"Lovely. You can hold my bags." Mateo climbed onto the dock and walked toward the archway that led into Kingsol, his legs still shaking. He kicked at a cobblestone and almost tripped, determinedly not noticing the way his caretaker Devoted's hand went to her mouth, covering yet another laugh. It was people like her who had decided Mateo was an abomination. Not fit to live. So really, all of this was *her fault.*

"You said Hilaria needed blueberries?" Cath asked.

"Yes," Mateo said cautiously, only vaguely remembering that he'd mentioned blueberries on the trip down. "And something else that started with . . . ." He breathed out in a huff. "Something."

"Yuzul. I heard her asking you after she broke into your bath. I was just trying to be polite and pretend we couldn't hear you singing in the tub and then muttering outside the dining room about how much you hate all of us."

Mateo walked past her, not making eye contact. "I didn't realize Devoted spent their time eavesdropping." Lia hadn't been so terrible, had she?

Why do you like that red-haired Devoted so much? Willow burst into his thoughts again.

Mateo stumbled, almost knocking into a wagon full of cabbages. *I don't feel the need to discuss this with you.*

I think I used to like boys. Knox always remembered me liking boys. But I couldn't eat them, so it doesn't make sense.

Cath didn't feel the need to speak for the rest of the walk to the fruit stands at the far side of the market canal. The crates piled on the boats made an explosion of color that had Mateo groping for his drawing satchel only to find it wasn't there. He looked back at the bay, a tide of anger rising in him at the sight of the waves that had swallowed something so dear.

It was one of the first things Mateo could remember Tual buying for him—he'd been staring at it, too afraid to ask for money, not believing he deserved anything so beautiful. And then Tual had surprised him with it when they got home, spreading out a new selection of charcoals and inks. He still had that first bound book of sketches and paintings he'd done, as if his hands had long been practicing though he never remembered having picked up a paintbrush before—

The darkness flashed, Willow's hackles rising.

Mateo forced himself to walk up to the fruit stand, his eyes fuzzing when he tried to focus on the seller. She was about his age. Her dark hair was in two braids that were pinned like a crown across her forehead as many of the shopkeepers wore. "I'm looking for blueberries and . . . yuzul? And for someone to be nice to me, because I've had a terrible morning. People get so angry when you try to push them directly into elsparn-infested water."

"Looks like it." The girl cleared her throat, eyeing the drips still running down from his coat and Cath's bare feet behind her. But then her eyes widened, and she looked down, tension pulling her voice tight. "Blueberries are over there behind the fenela, but I haven't been able to get yuzul in ages. Hopefully your presence here will help." She nodded to Cath, not quite meeting her eye.

Mateo moodily moved to where the boxes of blueberries were piled and chose one, cursing Cath's oath scars. "Why would this inconveniently large person behind me change whether or not you can get yuzul?"

"Well, because of . . . you know." The girl nodded vaguely toward the docks.

"Pirates in the harbor?" Mateo looked over his shoulder but found nothing out of the ordinary other than the Devoted cleaning her nails with a knife. He shivered, wondering where she'd been keeping it. "Yes, I believe she killed a few just this morning."

"Oh, I meant because yuzul comes off the north end of Beilda. Pirates don't help, but Beildans haven't been growing as much ever since . . ."

Mateo picked up a small box of blueberries, wondering what she could possibly be hinting at. Why couldn't people just say what they meant instead of making him guess? He'd spent most of his life sick, not obtuse, but that didn't mean he *wanted* to guess the entire yuzul-fruit supply chain.

"No yuzul," she finally said. "What you have there costs a split copper."

Mateo handed over the coin and took the berries, wondering how to escape. Back on the boat, running to Lia had seemed best. But if she and his sister were planning to kidnap him—

"Sometimes you can substitute bethl powder in baking when fresh yuzul isn't available," Cath offered, interrupting his thoughts. "I was a chef's apprentice before joining the seclusions. There's probably an apothecary—"

"I know what you want from the apothecary," Mateo interrupted. "Something to subdue my very, very dangerous shopping." Another flash of dread washed over him at the thought of his first and only visit to the local apothecary. Trying to cover it up, he held out the box of berries. "Be sure not to squish any. Your goddess might think you're trying to consume them via smell." He paused. "Do nostrils count when it comes to consuming things?" He picked up one of the blueberries, eyeing the little thing. "Just think. Ranks upon ranks of Devoted out just like *that*." He squished the berry between his fingers, the tart smell making his tongue water.

"I like blueberries," the Devoted said with perhaps a little more patience than Mateo had expected from someone who'd so recently lost her sword. It was very annoying. "But I'd rather jump back in the bay than carry them for you."

"Pity." He stumbled to catch up when she strode into the crowd, narrowly avoiding a chicken that suddenly took off in front of him in a flurry of squawks. "You know where the apothecary is? Have you been here before?"

"I don't know which one the Warlord was talking about, but all these towns are set up the same at the center. Market. Apothecary. Fish sellers, flower sellers, clothiers, haberdashers, cordwainers. We can find you some bethl." Cath sent him a shrewd look as she drew even with him. "Or a tailor, if you wanted to remove that enormous auroshe insignia on your back before it spontaneously lights on fire."

"People tend to look a little less harshly at the aukincer's son when I'm wearing the Warlord's insignia."

"Seems like it isn't working anymore. Didn't you see the way that girl flinched when she realized who you are?"

"You think my *coat* made her mad?" Mateo raised his arms, holding the blueberries out and almost losing a few when he gave a little spin. "How could this glorious thing cause any feelings but unadulterated joy?"

"It may have taken some kind of divine intervention for the Warlord to cut through whatever magical nonsense you put up to keep us from discovering where you live, but the people *here* know you're living on shapeshifter land, idiot. That girl probably has some ancestor lying dead under the foundation of your house." Cath gestured at the people milling around them, their hands clutched tight around baskets and bags of food, hoping the big scary Devoted wouldn't notice them. "You think any of these people don't remember?"

"Something that happened five hundred years ago?" Mateo popped another blueberry into his mouth.

"The townspeople across the strait got eaten by trees only a few years ago. Your father's an aukincer, for Calsta's sake. Do you really think people don't worry—"

Mateo's stomach lurched. "Weird references to trees again? And I'm sorry, but you don't seem to have a problem with my *aukincer* father when he's curing your mangy goddess disease." Mateo picked out one last blueberry—it had to be the last, or Hilaria would know somehow he'd stolen from her berries and would murder him. Probably *with* the blueberries.

The Devoted drew herself up, tipping her chin back to look at the sky and taking in a long, slow breath, as if calling on Calsta for more than her usual kind of strength. "No. I had a bout of wasting sickness last year. If not for your father, I'd be dead."

"Great." Mateo saw the blue door before Cath did and pushed past her, dread bubbling up in his stomach. "Let's be friends."

"How can you pretend not to know about the attack on Belash Point?" Cath followed, her bare feet patting against the paving stone, grass grown a little long in the gaps between them. "Kingsol is *dying* because of that massacre. People used to come here to wait for cures, and now there aren't any. The ports are almost completely closed. I've only seen one set of Beildan braids in the last four years, and she was back in Chaol trying to cure the plague."

Mateo's skin prickled at the mention of the girl with braids. The trees eating people, the plague. His sister had been following them a long time, according to his father, but he hadn't known she'd been messing around with Devoted.

Didn't she know Devoted *killed* people like them?

Willow came to attention in his head. *What do you mean? You and that girl aren't the same.*

The words sat inside Mateo next to the ones he'd been thinking: *my sister.* An odd feeling of protectiveness had somehow fizzed up inside him alongside the revulsion, two feelings existing together instead of destroying each other. *The trees eating people.*

"Trees . . . like the ones at the dig in Chaol." Even as he said it, that echo of terror in his mind returned, like a narmaiden's song.

He stopped outside the apothecary door, staring at his hand on the latch. Willing his fingers to pull it, but it felt shadowy and dark, like a nest of huddled, hungry creatures made of claws and teeth. "What possible reason could anyone have to attack a bunch of healers? Unless they stopped shipping yuzul back then and Hilaria went after them?"

"*Why* is a very scary thing. It's what stopped the ships. It's the reason that shopkeeper girl looked sideways at you. Sad, because there are things enough in this world worthy of fear without her wasting hers on you."

"You are not very subtle." Mateo let go of the latch, and even that distance sighed through him like relief. "I thought Devoted were supposed to be elusive and refined."

"Yes, that's why we carry swords on our backs." She pulled the door open for him. When he didn't immediately walk through, she gestured impatiently. "Well, go on, then. I have a name, and it's not 'Devoted.' I'm Cath, if you were eventually planning to ask."

Mateo's cheeks warmed a little. "I know your name." He forced his feet to move, steeling himself. Inside, there were jars stacked on shelves clear to the ceiling, creatures floating in glass prisons. Mateo tried staring at his hands, at the dingy, crowded ceiling, and then at the floor, but it didn't stop his eyes fuzzing and the acidic buzzing sound growing in his ears. When he caught sight of the man standing behind the counter, he stumbled, almost knocking over a stack of empty glass bowls. The healer had braids. A hundred braids exactly, one for each of the heavenly herbs.

How do I know that? Mateo squinched his eyes shut when Willow immediately responded with, *How in Calsta's name should I know, Mateo?*

Cath had gone tense, looking around for the threat that had made him stumble, and he considered telling her the preserved snake staring down from a jar on the highest shelf had begun talking to him. A shiver ran through him at the thought, though, and he held his tongue, because the lie wouldn't have been so far from the truth.

Mateo marched up to the counter, not looking at the Beildan's braids, not thinking of that girl in the tomb who'd been wearing the same kind, or of himself. His own past. *I was a healer. I'd be wearing braids too if not for my father.*

No, I'd be dead. They tried to kill me on Beilda.

The trees grew around the same time you joined your father's household. The hidden part of Mateo tried to peer through the cracks in his soul, pulsing just out of reach. He didn't want to reach for it. He just wanted it to go away.

"Can I help you?" the Beildan asked, continuing to grind something that looked very much like sticky centipede guts in a bowl.

What if Mateo *had* done it? And it was one of the many things from his memories that his father had taken away?

"I need . . . something." Looking around helplessly at the jars, Mateo willed his mind to open and give him back the tiny thing Cath had said could be substituted for yuzul so that he could get out of this cursed shop.

But as he searched his mind, it began to catch on the colors, shapes, smells, and impressions coming faster than he could shove them away. Lilia and corta petals in jars of glass, trebulay powder with a waxed lid to keep the smell from—

—and then Mateo couldn't move, the hairs on the back of his neck standing on end, that awful buzzing growing louder with every second he stared at the jars of dead leaves and hair and insect bits until he couldn't think, couldn't feel.

Belash Point. Trees eating people. The attack right across the strait from his home.

He grew woozy as Willow darted this way and that inside his head, suddenly frantic. And then—

Click.

A house on the beach. Waves crashing. A shop full of smells that were meant to soothe but were taught to him by a man who didn't know what the meaning of "soothe" was.

Click.

A panic. People all around him, hurting him. And his sister, so far away. Her braids, the last one newly tied. He was supposed to tie it.

Click.

A storm.

Click.

A boat. High waves. And a beach he couldn't go back to, trees growing like blades of grass right out of the ground. His sister left behind.

Click. Click. Click.

Trees growing. Like blades.

Click.

"Mateo Montanne, if you don't wake up right now, I'm going to tear up that fancy coat of yours and use it to *clean my sword—*"

Mateo forced his eyes open. Somehow he was on the floor, and everything hurt as if he'd fallen and no one had taken the trouble to try to catch him. The feel of hands behind his head made Mateo grateful at least someone was trying to help, until he sat up and saw it was Cath.

"Calsta above," she swore. "They told me you were delicate. Not that you would *expire* at the tiniest hint of pressure."

"Beilda." He looked past Cath to the healer hovering just behind her, his arms full of little packets he'd probably meant to sprinkle over Mateo one by one. "What really happened on Beilda? There was a ceremony that went wrong. Something bad happened."

His *sister* had happened. Mateo remembered seeing the way she'd closed her eyes as she talked to a patient, inhaling slowly before turning to face the family's herb jars. The way her hands went straight to the right cures, even the ones she shouldn't have known yet. He'd tried to help her. To mess her up. To make her go slow.

She didn't know what she was. But he knew.

She didn't know the elders suspected him of the same witchery and that they were right, not from herbs but because of the way his paints blended together, because he could find lapis for blue paint when there wasn't any on the island, and because his pencils were always sharp.

His sister hadn't known that day when he tried to stop her last braid from being tied that the elders had told him to stay back. They'd wanted to preserve her innocence, taking care of her nasty, corrupted brother in a moment she'd be sure to be looking in the other direction.

"Mateo. *Mateo!*" Cath's voice, far away. "He has episodes like this every now and then. We need to get him back to his father." She turned to look at the Beildan. "Can you help me—"

"Beilda." Mateo forced the name out, his eyes feeling swollen as he looked up at Cath. "The people . . . they were found swallowed by trees. Trapped until they suffocated. Starved to death and rotted."

The look Cath was giving him was a mix of frustration and puzzled curiosity. "Don't move, all right? When Tual treated me last year, he said I couldn't move."

"Excuse me, if you wouldn't mind. I am, in fact, a healer." The Beildan gently nudged Cath out of his way and knelt by Mateo on the ground.

Mateo batted the Beildan's hands away and leveraged himself up from the floor. Trees. Like the ones that had popped up around the tomb.

Because of his sister.

Not many survived, his father had said of her escape from the village. She was worse than a shapeshifter, because she hadn't done it for power, not for energy, not for immortality. It was just death, slow and terrible, as if she'd meant them to suffer.

She'd done it because of him.

He remembered the apothecary they had meant to start together on the mainland with cupcakes and beautiful jars and no father to tell them they were worthless. He remembered his mother with the few braids she'd earned, the rest of her hair long with beautiful curls. He remembered the dock boy who had found them shells to make into wind chimes. He remembered *Anwei,* her hand in his, staring out at the world as if she meant to fight anyone who got in their way.

She'd killed them all.

There's something wrong with that girl, Willow whispered. *Something wrong. I always tried to fix it, but Knox wouldn't let me. She's mad at you because you were supposed to be dead, but instead you're alive and forgot about her.*

All I wanted was for her to be alive too. I wanted them to leave her alone.

He swallowed hard, trembling all over. Wishing he didn't remember. *Anwei.*

She's coming for you. She's mad, Mateo. Aren't I a good girl, finding out for you?

How could he have forgotten his twin? And how could his twin have *destroyed their entire village?* Mateo's bones felt as if they were sharpening, elongating, as if his natural shape wasn't enough to deal with such grief. He closed his eyes, willing his body to *stop.*

Was this what it was to be a shapeshifter? Unsure whether your bones would hold together?

Get the sword, and none of it will matter. We can eat up Lia and your sister both. Then you won't creak. You'll be forever, just like me.

"Cath," he gasped, reaching out to grab the Devoted's sleeve. She didn't pull away, helping to hold him up. "All of this stuff that has happened around me. I think I know who is doing it." He scrubbed a hand across his face. "I need to talk to my father. We are all in a great deal of danger."

CHAPTER 19

Meaty Things in the Water

L ia dug her paddle into the water, her heart still lurching at the sight of Altahn pulling Noa's limp body out of the water and Anwei screaming directions for how best to keep her alive. A current had caught them, swirling the two boats apart, but after a few minutes, Anwei had announced that Noa was all right.

She's all right. Lia breathed through the words, trying to replace the image of Noa's limp body. *Knox was all right after we fought. I didn't kill anyone.*

I'm all right. The Warlord won't find me out here. I'm alive and free to save Aria. That's all that matters.

"This inlet here," Anwei called, jabbing a finger toward a thin stream of water cutting into the sand. Not their river. Not where they needed to go.

Vines hung down over the little stream from the trees above. Lia angled the boat alongside a wave, Anwei paddling to ride it up into the little channel. "You're sure?" Lia asked, shivering as the vines seemed to close behind them like a curtain.

"This will connect to the main river upstream. We're meeting Bane and Gilesh at the tributary you showed us on the map—this will get us there without Ellis scooping us up and cooking us slowly over a bonfire made from all that's left of his ship."

"We had to blow up the boat. Ellis getting caught in the explosion wasn't on purpose. The Warlord was there. And Mateo."

Anwei dug in her paddle a little too deep at the sound of her brother's name, the silence like poison.

Lia wanted to say something. But also, she didn't. "What do you plan to do with your br—" Lia stopped short, something glimmering at the edge of her aurasight.

"What is it?" Anwei's paddle dragged in the water.

Lia blinked, then blinked again, the flicker of gold disappearing over the edge of her aurasight. She pulled her paddle out of the water and set it across her lap, closing her eyes. Anwei stilled behind her, waiting.

The aura cruised into her sight almost immediately, tearing up the little tributary after them. "Stormy skies!" she swore, stabbing her paddle back into the water and pulling with all her might. Anwei matched her, still waiting. "One of the Devoted from the bay is following us." Eyes glossing over the bank and forest beyond, Lia tried to think of a way she could hide, but there wasn't much she could do but paddle faster. "The Warlord won't believe I'm dead unless someone drags my bloated corpse to her feet."

"Which probably isn't feasible for us to accomplish," Anwei agreed. "Finding a body match is complicated even with lots of notice."

Lia couldn't spare the energy to properly grimace at Anwei, though the healer must have noticed a change because her voice was a little defensive when she spoke again. "I'm not a miracle worker, Lia. My only contact in this region is compromised."

"Oh, well, if your contacts are compromised—"

"How many Devoted?" Anwei interrupted, digging her paddle in to turn the boat around a sharp curve in the channel, Lia ducking under some trailing vines. "And how long do we have before they catch up?"

"Only one. There are two of us so we can row faster, but he's lighter, and . . ." Lia gulped. He was lighter, and he had Calsta's third oath burning inside him, making him stronger than she or Anwei could be together. "Maybe ten minutes?"

"But you've seen him, so that means he's already seen you and knows you're still alive and *here*. So why are we running?" Lia glanced back at her, incredulous, and Anwei shrugged. "Fine. *Paddling*."

"It's not your choice of verbs I'm wondering about, Anwei."

"If we paddle our hearts out and get away, the Devoted will report back to the Warlord, and then the whole camp you saw last night will be after you." She was quiet for a moment, and frustration sparked inside Lia as she felt the healer's paddle begin to drag. The golden aura loomed closer.

"Where's Vivi?" Anwei asked after a moment.

"A mile outside of Kingsol on the other side of the Felac." Lia ducked another vine, swearing when it clipped the top of her head. It wasn't loose, but woody and stiff, like a branch.

"Too far to be a resource. And you're not strong yet?"

"Knox told you about the oaths?"

"No, but I'm not blind. I did live a few feet away from Knox for a year. The Devoted is gaining on us because he's"—Anwei gestured awkwardly—"whatever you call it when Calsta thinks you're obedient enough to let you kill people more easily."

Lia started to laugh. "Exactly that, Anwei."

"So a direct fight isn't a good idea."

"I can fight—"

"Yes, I've seen. But he'll be easier to get rid of if he's confused." Anwei dug in her paddle, and the canoe lurched toward the shore. "You get out of the boat. I'll take care of this."

"I don't want to *kill* him." Lia kept rowing, her muscles burning as she fought Anwei's steering, the familiar feeling of helplessness kinking in her spine. She hadn't wanted to kill the Rooster she'd accidentally pushed to his death. And Ewan—

Ewan she hadn't wanted to kill either, for all he'd done. She'd wanted him to end. To cease to be a threat. And he hadn't agreed, so there had only been one path forward. Something she, Noa, and Vivi had all seen, the three of them coming together to make Ewan *stop*.

As they rowed farther up the inlet, trees loomed overhead, blocking out Calsta's sun. *Where are you, Calsta?* Lia thought. *If taking Tual down is so important, couldn't you have just kept the Warlord away from us? Couldn't you take away my aura sparks or take away that Devoted's power so he can't see me?*

Calsta had only spoken to Lia once, the memory of the goddess's voice like a spot of char in her mind. Lia knew Sky Painter wouldn't just take a Devoted's power. The one behind them had made the proper oaths. He'd made the sacrifices. Oaths went two ways. Ewan hadn't gotten his power back after he had attacked Lia, though. Surely that meant there was *something* Calsta could do.

"Help me find a good place to destroy the boat," Anwei interrupted her thoughts.

"A good spot to *what*?"

"Do you trust me, Lia?" Anwei placidly continued to row.

"I mean . . ." Lia swallowed, thinking of Noa lying still at the bottom of the boat. That had been Lia's fault. It had been Anwei who had given Knox the help he needed to bring her gasping back to life.

Of course, it had been Anwei's plan that put Noa on the boat in the first place. But it was also Anwei's plan that was going to get them into Tual's house. Knox trusted her. *She still needs us.*

"I guess I kind of trust you?" Lia still didn't stop rowing.

"Why don't you pretend to be a little more confident about it for a few minutes." Anwei flashed a smile at Lia when she glanced back at the healer. *That* smile—it had always bothered her because it was familiar, and just then she realized why: Anwei had been wearing it the day she and Lia had met.

The Beildan had been holding some kind of poison behind her back, ready to throw it at any moment even as she'd talked Lia through a panic attack.

"Look! This is perfect." Anwei was already turning the boat into a gap in the trees, roots twisting up out of the water clear to the rocky shore and vines hanging from the branches spread over the river like a curtain. "You get out of aurasight range. Don't leave any footprints."

"What are you going to do? Throw *herbs* at him?" Because that's what Knox said she did. She brought herbs to a sword fight.

"Something like that. Maybe stay close enough that you can help if things go terribly—" When Lia looked away from the shore to see why Anwei had stopped, the healer was bending over the boat's edge, her hand splayed out less than an inch above the water's surface. Suddenly, something writhed up from the murky water, then splashed back down before Lia could see what it was.

"Calsta's *teeth*," Anwei swore.

"What is it?" Lia hefted the paddle, wishing to Calsta her sword hadn't sunk to the bottom of the bay with Ellis's carom. In the deeper shadows she could see little spots glowing in the water.

"Elsparn." Anwei sniffed her wet fingers and recoiled, her nose twitching. "Don't touch the water—they'll strip anything alive to the bone." She pointed to the vines. "You'll have to climb. Go quick, or this isn't going to work."

Anwei brought the canoe as near to shore as they could with the roots sticking up from the water like dead fingers. Lia tested the strength of the closest cluster, the stiff curls holding when she prodded them with her toe. Transferring her weight from the wobbly canoe, Lia held on to the woody vines for balance, then started up the sturdiest one like a rope, climbing hand over hand until she got to the thick branch overhead. Once she'd pulled herself up, she climbed over to the main trunk, chancing a look down once she got there. Anwei was balanced on the same root Lia had used, clinging to one of the vines with one hand and to her medicine bag with the other. The boat was turned nose-down, halfway submerged, and trapped against the roots. When the healer caught Lia looking, she gestured violently toward the forest. *"Go!"*

Lia climbed higher, the burn of aurasparks out of sight for the moment. She edged down to where the tree's branches twined with the branches of the next tree over and climbed across. Once she was well past the shore, she jumped out of the tree and ran back from the bank, swearing at the hollow echo her feet made, little cracks forming in the moss as she went. It was one of those thin areas where the river continued beneath the ground as if the land was nothing more than skin on cold soup.

Panic and adrenaline buzzed inside her. What could Anwei do? Smiling and joking with a Devoted weren't going to stop him any more than flower petals.

Still, Lia ran until Anwei's aura winked out of sight behind her. She curved around to hide behind one of the thick trees. Just as she started to peek out, hoping to at least be able to *see* what was going on, a pitiful cry reached her goddess-enhanced ears. *"Help!"*

Lia went still. It was Anwei.

"Please!" the healer's voice pled. "My boat turned over, and there's *something* in the water—"

Even from where Lia was standing more than a hundred yards away, she could see the glint of Calsta's sun on the Devoted's blade as his boat slid into view.

When the Devoted spoke, his voice was quiet, but it left all Lia's senses firing. "How did you come to be here, healer?"

"Didn't you see the ship burning? I managed to get off, but"— here, Anwei's voice took a pathetically fetching rasp—"then something came out of the water and tried to bite me—it's still there, circling. All I want is to get back to Beilda. Please, do you have any water?"

Lia could not imagine a world where she would have let Anwei into her boat, but the Devoted put out a hand to help her down from the vines. He even helped her sit and patted her back consolingly as she sniffled into her palms. "Thank you. With all the ports being closed, I'd finally found someone willing to take me close to Beilda—"

"There was someone on your boat before it sank. Small, with curly red hair. Did you happen to see her after you escaped?" the Devoted asked.

"I didn't really see anyone but the captain. Most everyone went below, and then that other boat started *shooting fire*. I've never seen anything so horrible." She gasped down a sob. "Please, if you have water, may I have some? I inhaled smoke from the fire, and when I dipped my hands into the water, those *things* down there—"

"Yes, of course." He looked around the boat, picking up the waterskin Anwei must have seen as she climbed in. "There were a few boats that managed to escape the ship—did you happen to notice anyone else on the river here? I saw the red-haired girl in a canoe just like this one. There was a woman with her. With Beildan braids."

Lia went very still.

Anwei didn't seem to register the threat, her tears coming even faster. "There was another healer? Was she trying to help the sailors who were burned in the fire? I feel like such a fraud. I just *left*. I was so scared—"

Lia started running, the trees blocking her view as her humors filled with Calsta's energy. Of course he let Anwei into his boat. Of course he knew from the beginning who Anwei was. Of course—

Her foot punched through the thin crust of brittle earth, and suddenly she was knee-deep in water, flailing to get free. The forest was so, so quiet by the time she managed to extract her foot through the hole and limp toward the river, and when she finally got a clear view of the boat between trees there was only one figure standing there.

Lia's eyes seemed to blur, and it took a moment for her to realize they were *tears*. It was too late. She should run. She should—Lia tore through the foliage toward the Devoted.

What could she do without Anwei? Storm Tual's house on her own? With the Warlord, Mateo, and Tual Montanne all waiting for her? Aria was in the grip of a *shapeshifter*, the most conniving, immoral, *inhuman* person she'd ever met.

She *needed* Anwei if she wanted to save Aria.

"Lia?" The voice struck out like lightning.

Furious, awful tears burned down her cheeks as she charged toward the boat, rage like fuel inside her—she didn't need a sword; she didn't need any weapon but her own two hands—

"Lia?" The voice again. "*Lia, stop!*"

It was only the last shout as Lia ran into the shallows that stopped her. Pain stabbed into her calf, teeth digging into the skin.

Lia bit down hard, hurling herself back from the water and swiping toward the long, bluish-gray *thing* clamped to her leg. Her fingers peeled it back, digging into an eye and squeezing until it let go.

It writhed for a moment, purple blood seeping out from the eye socket down its floppy body until it lay still in the mud.

She looked up to find Anwei contemplating her from the boat, the unconscious Devoted's arms gathered in her lap while she tied his wrists together with a torn-off strip from her tunic. Anwei pursed her lips. "You are the most intelligent person I know."

Lia pressed a hand to the wound in her leg, sighing in relief to see it wasn't too deep. "I don't need you to make fun of me."

"I'm not. Would you collect that specimen while I finish up here?" Anwei nodded to the slimy gray thing, then turned back to her job. "I'm afraid I don't know the long-term effect of Sleeping Death when used in this particular form"—she gestured to the Devoted that she'd knocked out—"but uncertain side effects seemed a better alternative than letting him break my arm." She gave the lump of a shoulder visible over the side of the canoe a satisfied pat. "He should be out for a day at least."

Lia still couldn't breathe. She pressed a hand to her stomach as she tried to inhale. "I thought he *stabbed* you."

Anwei frowned. "Stabbing me wouldn't make any sense. He needed to know where you were."

"You have too much faith—"

Anwei swung her head around to look at Lia, an abrupt movement that made Lia's hand clench unconsciously for a weapon. "I have *no* faith in humans, Lia. Which is why we're going to leave this man for the animals to find. Or the Devoted. Or whoever. He won't remember what happened when he wakes up, so we'll let Falan and her luck decide." She gave a resigned sigh. "I guess we can leave him in the boat so nothing has too easy a time eating him."

Lia slowly stood. "It's all about control, isn't it. You telling us all what to do, where to go. But you make promises you can't keep."

"Which promises haven't I kept?"

"You've kept them so far because of luck, not because your plans were engineered to keep any of us safe. All of us are relying on you, Anwei. Noa was relying on you, Knox is relying on you, *I'm* relying on you, and you just climbed into that Devoted's boat like it was nothing. You run fool-headed into situations without thinking things through! People with knives in their gut *can still talk*. If you die, where will the rest of us be?"

"I know what I'm doing, Lia. You and I don't look at things the same way because we have different strengths." She shrugged. "People know exactly what you are because you hide nothing. For me, it's people *thinking* they know exactly what I am that lets me do things like jam a waterskin laced with Sleeping Death down their throats, then make them swallow."

"What about us? The people on your crew, Anwei. What are we supposed to see in you?"

"You *know* what I am, so you don't have to worry, do you?" Anwei grabbed hold of one of the vines and carefully pulled herself up, maneuvering the Devoted's little boat closer to theirs. She grabbed hold of the upturned hull of their canoe and pulled, gasping when the wood cracked. "Calsta *take* these awful elsparn—the seats just *smelled* like us and they gnawed them to pieces!" She let it fall with a disgusted groan. "I don't think this is salvageable. We'll have to walk."

Lia turned back toward the forest, rage still rushing through her deeper than any river, more voracious and destructive than any elsparn, and there was nowhere for it to go. It choked in her throat and begged to be screamed up toward the sky. Who was she angry at? The Devoted who hadn't killed Anwei? Anwei, who'd taken care of the problem exactly as she'd told Lia she would?

Grabbing the floating paddle from the water, she forced herself to breathe in deep the way they'd taught her at the seclusions. She'd lost control. Like when she'd sparred with Knox. She couldn't do it again. It would get someone killed.

If she lost control, it could get *Aria* killed.

But how could she let go of the rage that sliced so deep?

Anwei reached for the nearest vine, tied the Devoted's boat to it, then stumbled out onto the roots, her medicine bag swinging haphazardly at her hip. She gave the boat a good kick so that it stuck between roots, then picked her way to shore. Lia ignored her, concentrating on the forest, the leaves, the wind on her face. And then on Anwei's hand on her shoulder. Lia resisted at first but then finally met Anwei's gaze.

In the healer's eyes, she saw understanding there that she didn't expect to find. "You have to focus your anger," Anwei said. "Choose something to direct it at, or it'll take who you are. Poison inside you will kill you just as fast as any sword."

"Is that what you do when . . . there's *nothing* you can do?" Lia couldn't look away from Anwei's steady gaze, desperate for an answer, because Anwei was nothing but control after losing so much. "I wanted so badly to be free that I let people I loved die for it."

"Nobody died because of you, Lia." Extracting a jar from her bag, Anwei emptied out something cottony and studded with dead leaves. "They died because Tual Montanne killed them."

"But Aria—"

"Is alive. We're going to get her. She isn't going to be the next bloody exchange Tual makes to get what he wants. He steals from the rest of us instead of making his own sacrifices, but no more. This *is* us doing something."

"It'll never be enough." That was the truth bleeding inside Lia. The one that made her eyes blur and her fists clench, that made her scream until her throat was raw and swing at anything that moved. "*I* can't be enough. I can't do this anymore, can't have this inside me—"

"You have to do it, and it has to be enough. What *could* be enough? We have to settle for what we can take." Anwei knelt down by the dead fishy thing, her eyelashes dark against her cheek until she finally looked up. "Now, are you going to help me or not?"

Anwei's answer cut the hole inside Lia deeper, Aria like the one spot of color flying over the burned-out remains of a shining future Lia had imagined with her family in Chaol. Killing the man who'd set the fire wouldn't give the charred skeleton of that dream breath again, wouldn't grow back muscle and bone. *Nothing* she could do would bring her family back. Not even a confession, an apology, *remorse* could change the past. But Anwei was right—Aria was still alive. Lia could still save one thing.

So, as she held the jar for the elsparn's severed head, its ribs, and its long strings of guts, Lia promised herself that once she'd reclaimed the one thing left of what she'd wanted before, she was going to take Aria and build a new house. A new dream. A new life.

Whatever that was.

It felt like an impossible goal, like building as solid shelter from rotted wood, or sewing the disemboweled elsparn back together, but Lia forced herself to swear she'd find more than an ending.

An ending wasn't enough.

⚜

"I have a plan," Anwei said when they finally got to the shore across from the tributary Lia had scouted, Knox coming out in a boat to ferry them across.

"This isn't the channel that leads to the house," Knox said, reaching out to help her into the boat. "We walked part of the way carrying the canoe to avoid Ellis, and I saw Mateo and one of the Devoted come up the river. They . . . went through a rock somehow. I didn't understand it. But I know where it is."

Anwei didn't take his hand as she climbed in, the sound of Mateo's name like a razor pressed to her neck. He'd been *right there*.

And she'd been where Knox and the others needed her instead of doing what she'd set out to do.

Again.

There would be other chances to get hold of him. She had to believe it—that's what plans were for. She wouldn't be distracted again.

When Knox had rowed them across and into the little tributary, Anwei was impressed by how they'd managed to hide the boat, secreted by a screen of trees. But when she saw Noa upright and cackling over something with Gilesh, Anwei stopped thinking about hiding. She climbed aboard while Knox was still tying the canoe and ran to her friend, scooping her up in a hug that made Noa cough and squirm to be let free. Anwei inhaled quickly before letting go, sensing a thread of a chalky puce hugging one of Noa's left ribs—cracked while Knox had been making her heart beat. But otherwise, Noa was fine. Anwei sat down, arm still looped around Noa's waist as the dancer told a story about a copper-coated bathtub and fish getting caught in her skirts and Galerey being a model firekey, not sparking once as she picked sand out of her hair. Like almost dying in a bathtub was a theatrical production with colored lanterns, fire tethers, and a full orchestra. Not a promise nearly broken.

Because that's what promises were: weak. Subject to currents in the bay, the fire scatter of a salpowder carom, the whim of a god. Anwei's people had come through—Knox and Lia, if their goddess was on your side, were the people you could trust to make a promise come true. She loved the way Knox was laughing at the story, as if listening to Noa speak didn't make him want to throw her whole trunkful of skirts overboard, and Noa was letting him tell some of it, as if she wasn't scared of him. Altahn even told them about pushing Loren off his own boat. Gilesh crowded close when Lia gave a terse recollection of their brush with the Devoted and then poked at her until she laughed. Bane enthusiastically handed her a strip of what looked like dried meat that he must have gotten from the crates of goods in the hold. Lia showed them the bite marks on her leg—which were fine after Anwei spread a little eretrin and carbile from her trunk across them to combat the poison. Not worth as much attention as Lia hiding the dried meat behind her back when Bane wasn't looking, as if she didn't want to hurt his feelings.

Anwei loved sitting there in their little circle on a boat they'd *found* fair and square. But Anwei also knew that the moment each of them got what they wanted, they'd move on. Calsta would take Knox and Lia; Noa would find somewhere else to sparkle. Altahn, Gilesh, and Bane would go north with their prize, seeking the favor of a goddess who only blessed her Devoted with lives that no longer belonged to them.

And she knew, whatever happened, she couldn't let any of them take *her* ending.

"I have a plan," she said again when all the stories had been told. "Mateo was out in a boat today like nothing was wrong."

"With . . . three Devoted." Knox pursed his lips. "One of whom was the Warlord."

Anwei waved the objection away and took out the jar with the elsparn. "We don't need to worry about the Devoted. Right when they come out of the channel, we'll overturn the boat. With everyone in the water, it'll be easy to dose Mateo with some of the Sleeping Death powder we stole, once I've formulated the right proportions in a tincture, of course—"

"Oh, of course." Lia started to laugh. "How long did you say that Devoted would be out?"

"I'm not sure, which is why more exact measurements are necessary. We drag Mateo upriver, sit tight on the tributary until we get the information we need, then we trade him for Aria, the sword . . . and then double-cross Tual and kill him."

Knox's leg had begun to shake, his eyes going a little glassy, as if he wasn't the only one in his mind present to take part in the conversation. "Wait a second—"

"Yes, I have some questions," Noa piped up just as Altahn said, "We can get back to 'we don't have to worry about the Devoted trying to hunt us down' a little later, but—"

"First of all, Mateo can see gods-touched auras, no?" Knox looked around, the glazed moment over. "So that means Lia's out. And I don't think we can take on two or three full Devoted without her, especially if the others lurking around are watching the channel too."

Anwei stuck a hand behind Lia and pulled out the little stick of meat, waving it a bit to get everyone's attention before dropping it over the side of the boat.

"Exactly!" Noa pointed to it, ignoring confused looks from the Trib and Knox. "Elsparn infest all the rivers through Forge and Elantia. Even Ellis warned us about them."

"The *Butcher*," Altahn muttered, shuddering. "Who still has my carom, by the way."

"So just *swimming out* and tipping the boat over . . . ," Noa continued, words slowing as she craned her neck to watch the meat sink. "Maybe this stretch of the river is okay—"

The water began to churn violently, dark shapes with little glowing spots writhing just beneath the surface of the water. The meat jerked this way and that, the elsparn tearing it to pieces. "Never mind, not okay." Noa breathed.

Anwei pulled the jar full of flayed elsparn from her bag. "Lia, hold up your hand."

Lia looked around, her blue eyes confused as she slowly raised her sword hand.

"The other one."

She shifted, putting up both hands, the second stained purple, smears of purple blood and viscera from throttling the elsparn bright against her pink skin.

"Put it in the water, would you?"

"Put it . . ." Lia narrowed her eyes. But after a moment, she lowered it to just above the water. Hesitated for a second, then plunged it in. The elsparn, already riled up and fighting over the meat, immediately swarmed around her arm.

Noa cried out, reaching forward to pull Lia's arm from the water, but Lia fended her off, leaving her hand submerged. "They're not biting me."

Holding up the jar, Anwei gave it a shake, the one-eyed, detached head giving a gruesome wobble. She wrinkled her nose a little at the stink of it seeping past the tightly clamped lid. "It died under traumatic circum—you can take your arm out of the water now, Lia."

Lia looked up, laughing a little when Knox pulled her away from the boat's rail. "It's uncomfortable to watch, is all," he said, then pushed her away from him when she smeared river water and eel guts across his tunic. "What are those things, Anwei?"

"Elsparn, like Noa said. They're carnivorous and find food

using . . . it's like scent, I guess? That's how they know when something meaty falls in the water. When one dies in a violent sort of way, it exudes a specific kind of smell that warns all the other elsparn away. Fishers use it on their bait to keep elsparn from taking it. They'll even kill elsparn and nail them to the docks to keep them out of ports."

Knox's head cocked to the side. His eyes weren't quite focused on anything again, as if something no one else could hear was talking to him. Anwei's skin pebbled, but she forced herself to look away. Maybe it was Calsta speaking to him, which was none of her business. He'd said Willow was blocked out, but she couldn't help but think of the sword sitting at the bottom of her things, well within his reach.

"Wait a moment, the goddess . . ." He trailed off. Anwei didn't look up, not particularly interested in Calsta's opinion.

Noa frowned. She'd clearly never heard of elsparn being nailed to anything but wasn't about to admit it. She had a slight wrinkle in her nose as if this plan did not inspire her at all.

Anwei braced herself for Noa to bring up something about fire dancing.

"So you smear elsparn guts all over us." Altahn sat forward, eyeing the jar. Knox's back straightened next to him, his eyes glassier than ever. "Then, we . . . what?"

"Upset Mateo's boat," Anwei provided.

"So when Mateo and the Devoted fall in the water, they're not protected, but we are? They'll be too preoccupied with getting bitten to fight us off." He nodded slowly. "When were you thinking of trying?"

"Wait." Knox put a hand up.

"We'll set up a watch on the channel." Anwei placed the elsparn next to her on the bench. "I can make this into an ointment—it's already sort of water resistant, but I don't know how long the effects will last, so I need to do some testing to make it as effective as we can. If I work on it tonight, we'll have something by tomorrow morning,

I'd think. So we could pick him up the next time he comes out of the channel. Tomorrow, even."

"Elsparn won't stop them from chasing us once we're—" Gilesh started.

"Wait!" Knox jumped up, his hands raised. "Stop. Stop talking about this."

"Knox?" Lia asked. "Are you all right?"

"No more planning." The words barely squeezed out between his clenched teeth, and he picked his way out of the circle, stepping over Altahn's outstretched legs and past Anwei's chair.

"What is the matter?" Anwei frowned, tentatively turning her attention to the part of her mind that belong to him. "Did you get hurt on the boat or—"

There was something building inside Knox, a fire she could feel despite how far she'd pushed him back in her head. It beat like a warning even as he fumbled for words, his eyes clenching shut.

Then Anwei felt it, the subtle aftertaste of ice and thorns inside him. Hiding.

Willow?

"She's blocked." Anwei jumped up, ready to run, or grab a weapon, or yell, but Knox just stared at her, heartbroken. "You said she was blocked off."

"Calsta kept nudging me, not saying it—" He shook his head.

Anwei pressed her hands to her forehead, pulling her braids back from her face. "You woke up the day we broke into the restricted stacks. The day we figured out where Tual lived. And you've blanked out in between . . . when we weren't planning or talking. . . ."

He clawed a finger through his hair, the ends curling out from their tie.

Lia stood. "Oh, Knox."

"What is going on?" Gilesh asked pleasantly.

"Calsta would never say anything outright before—about bonds or magic. Shapeshifters. The nameless god. She still won't unless it's there glaring us in the face." Knox's voice burned down to ash. "Because she was afraid of who might be *listening*." He swallowed. "He can feed her, Anwei. She's going to choose him. She already has."

Anwei slumped back onto the chair, pulling the dead elsparn jar into her lap and staring down at it. She looked up at Altahn's voice. "I'm very confused at the moment—it's almost like Knox is reminiscing about a terrible former . . . lover? If that's what this is, it seems sort of off topic."

"That would be better news," Noa said slowly. "Tell me if I'm wrong, but Knox is being haunted by the same ghost as Mateo Montanne. And the ghost just listened to our whole plan."

CHAPTER 20

The Stone That Waits

The moment Knox was safely shut in the hold, Anwei upended her medicine bag, spilling the jar with the dead elsparn and packets of white death scattered through the other smells of camillia, elor, and rie. Hands shaking, she extracted her mortar and pestle from their pocket and a bottle of clear malt, setting them both within easy reach.

Noa slid to her knees, looking worriedly at the dead elsparn. "What do I do? What do any of us do?"

"Lia?" Anwei looked up. "How close is Vivi?"

"I could get him and be back in a few hours."

"Right. Do that."

"If there's a ghost reporting everything we're doing . . . everything we've done . . ." Altahn was still sitting over by the boat railing, staring out into the rustling trees. "Then that's it. Tual went to the apothecary because he knew you'd head in that direction. Mateo brought the Warlord to the bay because he knew we'd be there on the boat. If this ghost can understand everything Knox sees, everything he hears—I mean, she could know where we are right now." He stood up slowly. "How could this have happened? How could you not have told me—"

"Knox being haunted by the dead ghost of his sister wasn't relevant, Altahn," Anwei said, fumbling to bring out the little packet of oelia and parshan leaves, the smells dulling the acrid burst of color Sleeping Death made in her nose.

"What are you doing?" he asked, squatting down next to her mess.

"If Tual thinks we're grabbing Mateo from the channel, then he doesn't think we're going to storm the place tonight," she hissed. "Which means I need to have an antidote to Sleeping Death, because that's what he's got loads of in that place."

"Anwei." Lia knelt down next to her. "We don't have a way in. We don't know what's in there. We don't—"

"We do know. We have a map. We know waterways go in. We have a boat." She pointed down the tributary. "You said the water goes into a tunnel right underneath the fortifications around Tual's house. Where else would it go?"

"A little direct for a fortress, don't you think?" Noa interjected. "We've never even seen inside the cave. And you heard Cylus talking about those kids searching for treasure in the waterways. They're dangerous. It could be a dead end. Or a sinkhole, or—"

"A trap." Lia licked her lips. "You said it yourself. Not even the first Warlord with all her Devoted could get in."

"None of them were *Basists*." The word burst out of Anwei like a confession, and she felt a glow of something in her chest like relief that she *hated*. "I . . . can see why you are concerned. Altahn?" The Trib looked up from tracing lines through a bit of ground lilia that had escaped its packet. "Will you come with me to explore the cave? We'll take the canoe and some salpowder to use as a signal if we need help. If we don't find anything, then that's the end of it. If we find a way through, we go in."

Altahn gave a hesitant nod.

"Lia," she said, switching to the Devoted. "If we do find a way through, I have an idea of how we might be able to cause a distraction while we're there that will give us the time we'd need to look for your sister."

"We're not just trying to get Mateo now?" Noa asked.

"No, we still want to get Mateo. If there's even a chance we'll have to confront Tual himself tonight . . ." Anwei looked up at Lia, the shuddery feeling of something going missing inside her like it had in the tomb when Tual had been standing over her, the sword jammed deep into Knox's gut. "We need Mateo as bait. As a *shield*."

"You keep talking about him like he's an object. Bait. A shield. A prize you mean to *find* like any of the other jobs you've done." Lia's words were carefully aimed toward a question Anwei didn't want to have to answer, but she got to it before Anwei could stop her. "What do you plan to do with Mateo, Anwei? He's your brother, but you won't talk about him."

Panic rose inside Anwei. "I can't. I can't think. . . ." She breathed in, calming herself with the scent of river water and wood and sails. "What do you want me to do with him, Lia?"

The boy who'd forgotten her. Anwei couldn't fit the idea in her mind. He'd escaped and left her behind. The voice in her mind was small, so small she could almost ignore it.

Vengeance, if it was to be had, belonged to her, didn't it?

It didn't matter how small the voice was because when she looked at Lia, the Devoted was watching, concern twitching across her face. "You think he deserves to die." It came out flat.

"I don't know."

"If he's part of what happened to Aria . . ." Lia swallowed, looking down.

Anwei sat forward, the words fitting inside her a little too well.

"What if Mateo is just another victim in all this? That's possible, isn't it?" There was an awful kind of hope in Lia's voice. The kind of hope Anwei had abandoned before her leaky rowboat had gotten her to shore all those years ago.

So, she moved on. "Leaving Aria on the island when we're already going in doesn't make sense. She's in danger every second she's there."

"We'll talk about this later, I guess." Lia was already walking toward the edge of the boat. "I'll be back with him soon."

"Meet us at that pool you told us about, by the cave entrance. You two know the way?" Anwei looked at Gilesh and Bane, the former nodding enthusiastically and starting toward one of the paddling benches. Bane rolled his eyes, pulling another strip of dried meat from his coat, but he went to the other side and picked up the oar.

"What about me?" Noa asked, a hand pressed just under her damaged rib.

Anwei dug into her bag and produced a packet of fulamia stamens and the iridescent powder made from a dried coocoo beetle shell, eyes, and thorax. Pulling out an empty pouch, she measured out a bit of each and began to mix them. "You need to stay here and make a big enough ruckus that Knox thinks were all still here this afternoon. But not big enough anyone comes to investigate the noise." She pressed the pouch into her friend's hand. "Take a pinch of that with water. It'll dull the pain in your ribs." She kept hold of Noa's hands. "I need you to think of something sparkly. Something big and flashy so that when we let Knox out, he'll believe nothing is going on."

Noa gave a curt nod, clutching the packet. "Knox is locked in the cabin at the back of the hold, yes? I'll see if there's anything useful in the cargo."

Altahn didn't move from his crouch next to Anwei when she turned back to the assortment of packets shimmering red and purple and green in her mind. Drawing in the scents, she closed her eyes, swapping packets around the Sleeping Death, taking some out, putting others back in, swearing when the bloom of colors wouldn't quite balance. *Go slow*, she reminded herself. *Being frantic never served you well in the past. Think it through; plan it out. You just need the right combination, and it will all come together.* The thoughts calmed her as they always did, because healing wasn't a race any more than hunting or thieving was. It was an equation. A science. All she needed were the correct components and a plan.

Knox hadn't ruined her chances to finally put things right. There were always more chances. She *made* more chances, and she always had.

"Anwei." Altahn still hadn't moved, his voice quiet. "Is there anything else you haven't told me?"

"Does it really matter now?" Anwei stared at the little packet of Sleeping Death. Then pushed it away. She could almost taste the shape of the antidote, but there was something missing she couldn't quite place. Better to set it aside to let her nose work it through. She turned toward the elsparn jar instead, wrenching it open and spilling the slimy pieces onto the deck. "If Tual realizes we're coming in tonight, we'll have to start over. We can't risk what happened at the tomb again." The memory of energy tearing free from her chest burned inside Anwei, the glow of calistet charring midair. Tual had swatted away the most dangerous weapon she had, using the energy from Anwei's own aura, destroying it with no more thought than he would have an annoying fly.

Galerey popped out from Altahn's collar, calmly observing Anwei. When Altahn spoke, it was slow, probing. "My father was dead before we even knew anyone else was in the tomb, Anwei. Roots started growing out of the tunnel walls, making half the ceiling cave in. It was a miracle I got out unscathed." When she looked up, he was watching her. "We didn't know what we were up against back then."

"We do now." Breath caught between her teeth, Anwei set the elsparn's severed head into a shallow dish from her bag and picked up her tweezers, the pulse of Knox's bond like gold, stretching toward her.

She shrank away from it, trying to pull back every thread of her that touched him, but it was impossible. Knox twisted through her like a disease. Did that mean Willow could read her thoughts too? That

Calsta could? Her stomach churned at the thought, none of it worse than the idea of the nameless god stirring deep in the earth, his attention creaking toward her.

His hand reaching, like it had that day on the beach—blood and bones and sand.

She swallowed, not looking at the Trib. "All I know is I don't want it to happen again."

That much was true.

⁂

Altahn had gathered together an interesting assortment of tubes and packets by the time Anwei had finished composing the salve to ward off elsparn. They'd gotten to the still pool Lia had told them about, and Anwei sent Gilesh and Bane down to the hold with Noa to cause a ruckus while she and Altahn explored the tunnel. Across the still water, the tall stones beckoned. Rocks and minerals didn't speak to Anwei the way herbs did, but she could feel the bare outlines of the rock where it bent back from the water, almost like a sculpture fabricated to hide the narrow waterway that led into the stone.

Anwei had mixed the elsparn essence with oily ointment and malt in two separate jars, leaving one on the boat and taking the other. She gave it a regretful look before popping it open and sticking a finger into the purple ooze, then began to mark her sleeves and chest. It would have been much more effective with time to steep.

As Anwei smeared ointment down her skirt and then onto her ankles and shoes, she toed the larger salpowder packets Altahn had cannibalized from the ship's hold, inhaling slowly as he began strapping some of the smaller ones to his vest. "This one has some kind of resin?" she said as he shoved one into a pocket. "And this one"—she pointed to the one in his other hand—"copper salt?"

"It's a flare to mark where we are if we need help." He buttoned his pocket, stooping to bundle the rest of it into a crate he'd brought from below. "The one with resin creates a slower burn, so we could set salpowder lines to a bigger explosion, then get far enough back for it to blast through something without us getting hurt." He took one of the larger packets and set it in the boat, then stopped to give Galerey a fond stroke down her neck. "If this waterway does go through and we get caught, hopefully Galerey will be able to head them off."

"Galerey . . ." Anwei climbed over the rail into the boat, smearing the elsparn goo down her sleeves and across her hands, then up her neck and across her face. "Knox said she steals your aura sometimes. Is that what you mean?"

He didn't answer for a moment, climbing into the boat before he met her question with a shrug. "It's not just caroms that Trib have sworn not to share."

"Fair enough." Anwei smeared a few last dabs of salve down her arms, hoping it was unnecessary, but not sure what they'd find in the cave. She handed over the salve and took up the paddle. "So long as she doesn't try to burn me like when we first met in Chaol, I don't have any complaints."

Altahn shrugged again. "Don't try to choke me out like you did that night, and she won't either."

"You say 'try' like you didn't spend the next two days unconscious." Anwei pushed away from the boat with the oar and began to paddle toward the water foaming white. Elsparn gathered below them like little sparks of color in her mind.

Altahn took up the other oar, waiting for her to begin the rhythm of rowing before he joined in steering the boat out of the natural current that pushed away from the entrance. "Why aren't we trying to go in where Knox saw Mateo's boat?"

"A back way is always worth exploring. Especially if Tual doesn't know about it."

"And we're sure this is a back way in and not, say, an underground waterfall with sharp rocks at the bottom?"

Anwei breathed in as they fought out of the current and drew up to the rock face. She dug in her paddle, and suddenly they were facing a large, dark arch, the top of it mirrored down in the water like a great mouth. A gush of warm air breathed out from it, ruffling Anwei's braids.

The shape of the tunnel beyond this open maw teased out in her mind, the stones themselves awakening to greet her as if she were a long-lost friend. But the air in the tunnel was tinged with *nothing*.

Anwei shivered. "We'll have to see, I guess."

"Well, that's comforting. Lead on, Yaru." Altahn waited for her to dip in her paddle, then matched it, sliding them through the mouth and into the darkness.

Hot, wet air settled like mold across Anwei's skin as she paddled, not wanting to reach for the lantern they'd brought to hang from the bough until they lost the light from outside. Except that one moment she could feel sunlight on her back, and the next it was *gone*, the darkness around them complete, as if they had rowed through a portal into the underworld.

Altahn fumbled for the lamp, but she touched his arm to stop him, because the walls had begun to glow. Not like the sun or even the stars, but more like elsparn, the faint light forming patterns on the ceiling far above their heads.

It was pretty, a design of loops, leaves, and flowers that pointed them on. She opened her mind to the water, the rocks, the odd glow above. But in doing so, her connection to Knox burned at the back of her head, and drops of him swirled through her, making her jump.

"What is it?" Altahn tried to steady the rocking boat.

"Nothing." But it wasn't nothing. A white glimmer had appeared over Altahn's head. And when Anwei continued paddling, threads of purple spooled across her vision. The *wrongness* Knox had seen in her aura from the first moment they'd met, now hidden from everyone else by their bond like a dirty secret.

Their bond seemed to flower up inside Anwei even as she tried to tamp it down, her head aching with smells far too many and too strong—more than the muck growing on the walls. The cave felt like a puzzle, the pieces she never could have seen without Knox's power inside her snapping into place. It was like her herbs, the stone waiting for her to take hold of it. To make it into something new.

Bonds allow gods-touched to do more . . . Legends of miraculous healings and foundations growing up from the earth, castles built without hands like the islands in Chaol with their glass walkways sat in the back of Anwei's head like an invitation. As if with Knox glowing through her, she was something much larger to reckon with. She could feel more in the cave than rocks fit together at odd angles. More than the fluttering heartbeats below them in the water, hungry elsparn with their lights glowing bright.

She could feel that there was something waiting in the tunnel ahead.

"Anwei, talk to me." Altahn's whisper echoed down the tunnel as he stuck the paddle back into the water.

"Wait." Ahead, there was a chartreuse spike of scents edged with a glistening silver in her mind. "*Wait.* Help me stop the boat, Altahn," she whispered. "There's a trap."

Altahn shoved his paddle deep into the water, forcing the canoe to veer toward the side of the tunnel. Groping out for the wall, Anwei's palm hit a stalagmite's smooth tip. She carefully stood, making the boat rock, then stepped out of the boat onto the narrow shelf of stone littered with lumps of accumulated minerals. "If I scream, come after me, all right?"

Notably, Altahn didn't answer when Anwei grabbed the lantern from the canoe's curved nose, then struck the flint and steel starter to light the wick. Lifting the lantern, Anwei cast light over a forest of stalagmites and stalactites bristling down the length of the tunnel like teeth right before a curve in the passage. Inching down the narrow ledge between stalagmites toward the odd combinations of smells, Anwei gasped when one of them broke away in her hands, barely managing to stop herself from tipping into the water. Right when she rounded the corner, something ahead of her moved in the darkness. Anwei froze, breathing in deep.

When she lifted the lamp, the light fell on a column at the center of the waterway—no, not a column, a *statue*. It was a stone woman kneeling on the surface of the water, the current lapping up over the folds of her dress where it trailed into the deep. Her arms were spread wide to either side of her, head drooped so locks of hair hung over her face, the weight of the ceiling balanced upon her shoulders and back. The water parted to either side of her, and Anwei could smell the brownish green of rot coming from the wreckage of a boat caught in the spillway to the statue's right. Below, though Anwei shouldn't have been able to smell through water, she could taste the chalky grayish yellow of bone.

"Anwei?" Altahn hissed.

Anwei reached farther, drawing in even more of Knox so he seemed to sit inside her. The shape of the statue glowed in her mind. "It's a gate," she whispered.

It beckoned to her, asking for entrance into her mind, whispering that if she was the wrong shape, she wouldn't make it to the other side.

I am the right shape, she thought. *This place is the nameless god's.*

The words in her head didn't sit well even as her confidence grew. She opened her mind a sliver and the *something* flooded inside her, took a good look around, and was satisfied.

The statue creaked, and suddenly the walls and the ceiling were groaning as waves rippled down through stone. Altahn yelled from the tunnel behind her, but then the statue was standing instead of kneeling, her hands holding the ceiling high up over her head. Slits in the rock opened up, letting in jets of light from above that pierced the darkness like stars.

The statue's eyes were empty, watching Anwei. Her hair was made of vines. A hundred braids.

Anwei drew in a shuddering breath and got a full mouthful of *nothing* that billowed out through the newly opened tunnel beyond the statue. In her mind she could see another statue farther down the tunnel, and a room at the end, one great black pool with a mechanism that flared bright in her mind, as easy to open as any calistet jar, so long as you knew how. And beyond that, caves in a cliff.

A path made of water into a lake, to an island and a house made of stone.

"How big of an explosion could you make with the salpowder packets we brought?" she asked when she got back to Altahn and the boat.

"Did we find a way through? Does this connect?"

"Yes." She stared at him, waiting.

"An explosion . . . for what?" he finally asked. "You want to break down a wall, burn up a wooden structure—"

"I want to make it look like we're trying to destroy the cliffs where Lia saw Mateo—like we're trying to get through that way."

"Oh, just that." Altahn took the lamp. "More flash than cracked stone? Because I don't know how salpowder will hold up against anything Basist made. I'd probably need the rest of the stuff from the boat to make it look serious."

Anwei got back into the canoe and started paddling toward the statue. As they rounded the corner, Altahn's paddle dragged as he caught sight of the stone woman, then the bits of broken wood sticking out from the water at her feet.

"This is safe?" he asked.

"Yes." Anwei was sure. "We both need to be back on the boat later to show Knox what we gave up for the night. How much can you get done if I leave you the lamp?"

The cabin at the back of the hold was small. Too small for anyone, really, but definitely too small for Knox, the ceiling too low for him to stand straight and the bunks too short for him to lie down. Too small to pace, too small to do anything other than brace himself as the boat moved. He tried to draw his aurasight in as close as it would come to deprive Willow of whatever information she was gleaning by keeping him awake, but he couldn't stop himself from noticing when Anwei left the boat and came back again later. Things outside the room banged around, and people yelled and talked and laughed outside, and Knox was trapped in another world. On another path, another plane.

As he always had been. But for the first time, he was angry about it.

I have spent my whole life trying to save Willow, his thoughts roared toward Calsta. *I became a Devoted, gave my life to setting her free.* He could hardly remember her as she was, a girl who spent weeks crocheting lace to edge a dress she was making with their mother, who'd blushed pink and twirled for days when she first put it on, then paraded up the street past the forge so the blacksmith's apprentice might catch sight of her.

He still thought of her as taller than he was. As someone who got *him* out of confessing he'd broken the miller's window when he'd been pretending to be a Devoted, throwing rocks up and batting them out of the air like arrows. Willow had taken the blame.

And she would have *hated* being a Devoted, giving up all her lace and pretty skirts, the ribbons she braided into two plaits, then pinned across her head like a crown. So when the Devoted had come for them—

Knox slammed a fist into the wall, swearing when it did nothing but make his knuckles ache. "Calsta!" he yelled. "Why didn't you tell me sooner? Why couldn't you have just made me stay asleep until it was done? You said keeping my oaths would let me save her, but that's not what's happening. Now I'm trying to save myself and everyone else I care about *from* her, and I'm *losing*."

I tried to warn you. The goddess breathed fire in his head, but it was faint, far away, making him want to punch the wall again, to tear out the built-in bunk, to break down the door between him and the only people he had in life.

"You haven't tried hard enough! Why not just say it? Why not—"

Because I don't want some little girl neck-deep in shapeshifter putrescence to stop me from fixing what has been done to me and my love, Knox.

"Your *love*?" He was shouting now at the ceiling. "The nameless god? He must be alive, or Anwei wouldn't be stained purple. I wouldn't be bonded to her, and there would be no such thing as shapeshifters. But if I can't stop Willow, the people *I* love might not be lucky enough to survive. Just tell me how to fix her! The sword is gone, but she's still claw-deep in my chest and won't leave. How do I *make her go?*"

I don't know, Knox.

"You don't *know?*" The words opened a terrible hole inside him, deeper even than the one Willow had made. "So is that . . . it then? Anwei is right about you, that you just . . . lie to people so you can *use* them and—"

Knox! her voice blasted into his mind, larger and wider and hotter than he could hold. He fell back on the bunk, fingers digging into his temples. *It was never about saving Willow. It was about saving you. Detaching her from you. None of them have ever gone, just been turned into monsters alongside the shapeshifters who killed them. The oaths kept you safe from it, and now Anwei is keeping you safe. Somehow even Willow is still partly there—that's something new that could fix things. But it's also all the more dangerous because she could make things so, so much worse.*

"You lied to me," he whispered.

I have never lied to you. We can release her. I know it. I just don't know how yet. I need my love. When he is more awake—

"You'll finally tell me everything, Calsta?" Knox leaned back against the wall. "You told me I could save my sister, not the whole gods-cursed world."

Gods-cursed? She was silent for a moment, then began to laugh, louder and louder until the peals seemed to fall around him in a shower of embers. *Sometimes I think I should just let myself die, take back my oaths and fizzle into nothing when no one remembers my name. Then maybe you humans will stop taking power meant to help people and using it to hurt people instead. We gave you oaths because we knew humans were selfish, but that they could be more given the right incentives. Still you've figured out how to destroy everything. I am so sick of you all.*

"Is that how gods work? You feed on people's pain for power? How is that different from a shapeshifter, Calsta? Willow always goes on about being fed. What do *you* eat, Calsta?"

The hearts of men. Well, women too. People. I'm not picky.

The hair on Knox's arms stood up. He drew in a shaky breath, unable to say it out loud after so many years of his life spent trying to please the sky goddess. *So you* are *the same.*

Shapeshifters take souls to make themselves more powerful. I take hearts, which are given willingly, and teach them to grow larger, Knox. Her voice had gone from a salpowder roar to a thin gutter of flame. *You will be the last to know the answers. Otherwise, that little girl gnawing on your soul will have all the weapons she needs to come back. Which will let the rest of them out.*

"Come back?" Knox dug his fingers into his hair, his head aching.

But Calsta was already gone.

Willow could come back somehow? He thought of her screams and cries, her pleas for him to kill, to *feed.* If she'd gotten him to kill Anwei and turn into a shapeshifter, would that have been only the first step, the first thing she needed before . . . what?

The cabin door rattled, and Anwei burst through. Her mouth was hung heavy with a smile, but their bond seemed to shrivel as she looked at him.

The wound in his side twinged.

"Are you all right?" she asked, pulling him out of the cramped cabin. "There was yelling."

"Of course I'm not all right." He extracted his arm from her hand and backed away. "I can't come out. I need to . . . leave? Or—"

"Actually—" she broke in.

"No, I can't see . . . anything. What's in these crates, where you moved the boat, nothing—"

"Knox. It's all okay. We're fine." Anwei took his arm once again, pulling him gently between crates. "We're going to take a few days to reassess. Everyone is tired after this morning." She shrugged, leading him toward the ramp onto the deck. "And it's too dark for you to see where we are anyway. So we're—"

"We're having a *dance party*!" Noa pushed Anwei out of the way, dragging Knox the rest of the way onto the deck. "To celebrate me not being dead and the two of us not kissing ever again—"

"I did not kiss you!" Knox interjected, covering his face to block out anything Willow might not have seen yet.

"I agree! That was hardly a kiss. Then you broke my ribs. But we're friends now!" Noa gave a shout that echoed up into the sky, twilight just sitting on the horizon. "So, *dance party*."

Anwei cleared her throat, gently pulling Knox's hands away from his eyes. "*Noa* is having a dance party."

"No, *all* of us are. There were drums in the hold, and Bane promised to play, and *you* promised me—"

"Yes, yes, all right." Anwei gently pushed Noa out of the way, a harried smile on her face—a smile Knox didn't understand, so peaceful and calm on the outside with something much angrier, faster, more *terrifying* raging under the surface.

"Sorry we locked you in the cabin," she said quietly. There was a smear of something purple crusted to the side of her neck beneath the long braids. Looking down self-consciously at his scru tiny, Anwei shrugged. "Testing elsparn salve is going well—Willow can't do anything with that, can she?" She grinned, squeezing his arm. "We'll just . . . not plan things in front of you from now on."

"Or let me come when you go after Tual? Unless I'm blindfolded?" he said slowly, heart thumping to the beat of the panic inside Anwei.

She smirked. "Lia went to get Vivi, so if you're going to come up with weird training yard flexes like a blindfold to go with your stabbing practice, you'll have to wait until she gets back. Until then . . ." She spread her hands wide, taking in the darkening sky, the little lanterns Bane was lighting and a drum Noa was arranging in front of one of the paddle benches. "I think we can take one night to rest. Gilesh made food, and I think you can eat some of it."

Something was wrong, Knox could feel it. The curtain between him and Anwei remained solidly in place. Tension was strung tight across everyone else on board. Gilesh and Bane whispered to each other behind a table covered in food, and Noa trying to pry open a crate despite her splintered rib. The little forced laugh that came out of her when Bane shooed her away to sit down. But when Knox looked back at Anwei, she was just standing there watching him, the bond between them softening. "You look like you're about to kick something in the head. Please do it to someone who is not me, because you know I'm not above retribution. Maybe Altahn?"

"Thanks a lot, Anwei." The Trib pushed past Knox, dragging another crate from down in the hold. "Where did you want this one, Noa?"

It was only moments before Bane was sitting at a drum and Altahn was at the other, the two of them slapping out a beat that sounded quick as Noa's laugh, Gilesh pulling out one of the Trib mandolins he'd brought to strum a melody. In no time Knox was sitting on a bench with some kind of dried vegetables and barley in a bowl, Noa turning and stomping, Anwei clapping along and laughing next to him. He wanted to believe it. Wanted to rest, wanted to sit there next to Anwei. Wanted to believe it was real.

Noa ran up to Anwei, grabbing hold of both her hands. "You *promised* there would be dancing!" she sang.

"You can't dance, can you, Anwei?" Knox teased. Excitement seemed to have leeched out of Noa, taking root into all the empty spaces inside Knox like some sort of disease. The evening felt like an invitation to step into another world where Calsta's fiery laugh didn't exist. Where there were no closed doors between him and the rest of the crew. Where Willow had died and was painting clouds somewhere with the goddess in peace

Because down in the cabin, he hadn't been able to breathe.

But up here, there was nothing but laughter, the steady drums, the stars starting to wink down from the sky, and the golden glow of lanterns against the night.

"Don't let her try, Noa." Knox grinned. "Or you'll end up with more broken bones. She's stepped on me enough times—"

"Says the man who inhaled poison to avoid even *entering* a ballroom a few weeks ago," Anwei countered.

"Yes, I knew the poison was in the governor's drawer *before* wrenching it open for you and stuck my face right over the jet. All so I could avoid a waltz."

Anwei spun to point at Altahn. "He was the one who was supposed to prove he could dance, so why is everyone piling on me?"

"We'll settle it now." Noa grabbed Anwei's hand and dragged her over to Altahn, who shook his head so wildly, Noa had to move the drum aside to get him to leave it. She arranged Anwei and Altahn in the small open space on the deck and started yelling directions to Bane so he'd drum the way she wanted, Gilesh's picking coming faster and faster.

Knox didn't want to look away when Anwei raised her arms to match Noa's, stomping along to the beat of the drum. She was terrible. But Altahn was even worse, the two of them jerking like fish bobs in the water. Noa showed them some kind of arm-flaily jump that made Noa look like a wind goddess and Altahn as if he were having a seizure. Anwei was laughing so hard that her attempt didn't even make it into the air. When she spun around, her eyes landed on Knox, her smile wide enough for three.

Knox looked down. That was the rule, wasn't it? The one she'd reinstated first on Ellis's boat, then again after she'd kissed him. When they got too close to each other, they looked away. Closing his eyes, Knox willed himself to let the fog of carefree joy be enough for him.

Lia's aura appeared in the trees, and in a moment she was climbing on deck, her brow pinched with confusion. When she saw Knox, it pinched even more. Approaching cautiously, Lia slid down next to him on the bench, watching the others as she might some kind of enemy formation. "What in Calsta's name is going on?"

"I don't know."

"We're forgetting everything for a few hours, Lia!" Anwei called, a spark of caution rippling across the bond which didn't show on her face. "Come dance with us!"

Lia shrank down on the bench next to him, as if folding herself small enough would be enough to stop them from sucking her into Noa's shenanigans, and suddenly Knox felt like the dark frame to a bright picture. He liked the look of Anwei out there on the deck, her face free of worry. He liked the idea of fitting into that picture with Anwei, Altahn, and Noa, the former two trying so hard to follow the latter that Gilesh and Bane had bent over their instruments, laughing so hard tears were streaming down their cheeks. No swords, no magic, just people who liked each other.

Lia grabbed hold of his arm as if she could feel it too, the pull to join. "It's like I can feel the Warlord watching me," she whispered. "Old Master Tracy telling us that every moment we spent playing instead of training was a moment stolen from a goddess."

"There are times when that is true," Knox murmured back, the words sticking like pinesap in his teeth. "We are what we are."

And, for some reason, Lia flinched. Then she stood and stepped into the light.

As he watched her walk toward the others, it was almost as if he were in that other realm again, alone. Lia had always been beside him before. Being a Devoted had been like diving headfirst into deep water for Knox, and Lia had been the one to hold him up when he was too tired to swim. That was different from dancing badly with Anwei and Noa because it looked fun. Lia was already doing it, as if this was a battle she'd already wrestled to the ground, and Calsta had conceded. And when he looked at Anwei . . .

You are not the same as a normal person. Calsta's voice cut through his thoughts and sank in deep, and suddenly the glitter of the evening was gone. *I need you to focus.*

Knox swallowed, feeling himself shrivel back from the warmth and laughter. From the sight of Anwei smiling and twirling across the deck, because he didn't fit into that picture. *You said you were sick of me earlier. Have I ever told you I'm sick of you too?*

I didn't say this can't *be yours. Someday, when this is over, maybe it can. The Warlord made you think you're only valuable as a weapon. Yet another unfortunate imbalance. You can be more than one thing, Knox. Don't blame* everything *on me.* She paused, considering. *I've trusted you this long. Remember your oaths. We can't afford for any of this to go wrong.*

His eyes found Anwei's again, and she laughed, doing another horrible spin. "Are you just going to mock us from your chair?" she called to him.

He didn't want to be the frame, to be the one in another world. So, Knox slid into the light, toward Anwei's terrible dancing and the beat of the drum. She met him halfway, something sparking in her eye that was none of her normal calculation, no storm hidden by clouds, and none of the measured distance she'd put between them, as if she'd been afraid that touching him might burn her.

When Noa pulled him into line behind her, Anwei stood next to him, leaning into him when she laughed as Gilesh tried his feet in a leap and then almost fell over the rail into the water. She sat close to him on the bench later, her shoulder pressed into his side and his arm on the bench behind her, so like all the times he'd touched her when they were pretending, ducking guards, looking into each other's eyes as if they loved each other because people chasing thieves didn't believe thieves were human enough to love.

Now the almost-touch felt like a risk, as if he were putting all of himself out between them. A question in the air she'd already answered more than once, but this time Anwei wasn't moving away.

When she looked up at him, she didn't look away.

Tonight, in this other existence, this other world so disconnected from the real one, maybe Anwei *wanted* to be burned.

By the time the sky above was cold and dark, Lia was sitting by Gilesh behind the drums so he could show her how to play, Noa was giggling into a bowl of rice between Bane and Altahn, and Knox's shoulders began to sag. He blinked stinging eyes, willing his spine to straighten, for the fatigue, the *emptiness* to hold off just for a few hours. A few minutes.

I know you don't care about this, Willow, he pled. *But please don't take me away.*

It didn't stop his eyelids from drooping, and Knox braced a hand against the bench to stop himself from falling. Anwei looked up from where she was spooning something too sugary for him to eat into a bowl, a flash of concern across her face. She picked up a cup from the table and held it out to him. "Willow doesn't like dancing, eh?"

He closed his eyes. "I don't want to talk about Willow."

"I'll get you something else to eat. Maybe that will help."

Knox reached out and took the cup, his stomach twisting as he took her hand with it. "I don't want you to get me some food," he said quietly.

She smiled. "Drink it. You'll feel better."

He took a sip from the cup, trying to decide what kind of fruit came with such a clouded taste. It burned a little as it went down, and something inside him began to beat a steady, frantic rhythm, like the drum tower in Chaol before a storm.

"Knox?" Anwei's hand was on his arm, and suddenly he was tipping forward, his muscles all shivering. "Help! Someone, please!" Her voice warbled as if Knox was half underwater.

Another set of hands gripped Knox's other arm, sliding him off the bench because Knox couldn't stand, couldn't even sit, his whole body dead weight. "Is he all right?" a voice asked—Altahn, Knox thought.

"Help me get him down to the cabin," Anwei whispered, the curtain between them pulsing with worry and a tinge of fear. He wanted to tell her not to bother, but then she and Altahn were hoisting him up by the shoulders, and Knox was stumbling down the ramp. They took him through the hold, and Anwei helped fold him onto the bed that was too small. Altahn started to pull off his boots.

"Go on—" Anwei waved him away. "I'll be up in a second."

And before Altahn's footsteps had even made it to the ramp, Anwei had grabbed handfuls of the front of Knox's tunic. The air seemed to burn between them.

"I don't want to go back to normal," he whispered, the words coming out in a garbled drawl. "Can't *this* be how easy it is . . . ?"

But then Anwei's long braids were all around him and he could only smell river and herbs, her cheek against his and her heart beating fast as her arms pulled him up against her. Their bond sparked, touching her and circling back around so he wasn't sure if it was her feeling it or him. He couldn't breathe, every inch of him *alive* and waiting for her to move. But she was frozen, holding so, so still as his hands explored her back, the feel of her through the thin layer of cloth. "What do you want, Anwei?" he whispered.

The last time he asked, she'd walked away from him.

This time her fingers dug into his skin through his tunic and her breath caught in her throat, her heart drumming faster and faster. A taste of anger flowed across the bond, of unfairness, of *rage*, but then her mouth pressed hard against his, and her tongue brushed across his lip, and he forgot anything had come before or what might come after.

Everything except for her fists, twisted tight in his tunic as he slowly faded, gripping him hard as if she could keep him there no matter what Willow wanted. But as everything went gray and Knox's arms began to go slack, the last thing Knox felt were those hands slowly loosening and letting go.

CHAPTER 21

Not Much of a Romantic

"We have a new problem. And a sort of solution. And a bigger problem." Mateo spilled into his father's office. His basket of berries skidded as he set it down on Tual's desk and the little packet of bethl powder tumbled off.

His father wasn't there, a few of the glass jars from the shelves open on his desk and the pot over his little trivet still warm.

Aria. The thought bubbled up like air pockets escaping sludge. Aria was still recovering from what had happened under the lake. His father must have taken her more medicine. Mateo racked his brain, the thought of Aria unresponsive replaying over and over—the way she'd fallen in the tunnel, then the sight of her gasping awake. The night before, when they'd first spotted Devoted auras out in the trees, Tual had rushed to put her away where the Warlord wouldn't be able to see her aura. Maybe in the abbey where auras were blocked?

Mateo grabbed hold of the packages and ran for the entryway, not slowing until he got to the tower doors. There was no way Aria was hidden in the cliff rooms. It was dangerous up there, for one, but more importantly, the Warlord had already been on the island by the time Mateo had gotten back the night before. His father hadn't reentered the cliffs, and Aria had already been hidden, so that meant she was somewhere on the island out of aurasight. Furrowing his brow, he felt for that fluttering, scrappy aurasight that Willow had pushed out for him while they'd been on the river, letting him find Lia before the Warlord had. Breathing in slow, he thought of what he wanted.

And instead, he felt eyes watching him. Mateo turned to the bridge and stared into the trees on the other side of the water, and thought he saw . . .

Willow pressed into the edges of his mind, pulling him away from the thing in the woods to spread his aurasight like a length of ragged silk flapping in the wind. It covered the island from end to end, and up . . .

Up to the top floor of the tower, just barely tall enough that it would be outside a Devoted's range. He couldn't see anything—Aria wasn't a gods-touched, after all—but he ran for the stairs anyway, knowing he was right.

Bursting into the single room at the very top of the tower, Mateo found Tual sitting with his legs crossed at the ankle, nose-deep in the pages of *A Thousand Nights in Urilia*. The room was darkness itself for a split second, deep circles under Tual's eyes.

"Father—" Mateo stumbled into the room, and suddenly it was bright and cheery, a lamp lit next to Aria, who was propped up in a bed by the window, and a taste of energy in the air. "Where have you been?" she demanded. "Your dad made a bunch of horsey-smelling people drag me here, and you haven't come to visit *once*."

Mateo froze, looking from her to his father. Tual looked up from the book with a hint of concern. "Are you all right?" his father asked.

"Yes, I . . ." Mateo blinked, the memory of darkness, of his father hulking in the chair and a lifeless lump under the covers where Aria was now.

She glared at him. "Don't tell me you're pretending to be even sicker than me now?" The breath she drew in shivered through Mateo's mind, flashing back to her falling in the glass tunnel. But then Aria picked up a scone from a dish sitting on the covers and dipped it in the bowl of cream next to it. Taking a messy bite, she kept talking, crumbs falling from her mouth. "You were supposed to come visit me a long time ago. There aren't any weapons up here."

"That's exactly why we moved you, Miss Aria." Tual had gone back to the book. "I'm afraid you'll chop Abendiza into little bits and make Hilaria cook them for supper."

Mateo hadn't seen his father since breakfast—not that he'd had any breakfast or lunch for that matter—and once again, his eyes slid to the dagger at Tual's belt, the air around it almost blurred. Willow went still inside him.

But then his stomach grumbled, and Mateo only had eyes for the crumbly scones on Aria's plate. "Can I have one of those?" he asked, reaching for one.

She grabbed it away, holding it over her head. "I don't share with people who don't remember to visit me."

"You'd keep a scone back even from someone who is actively starving?"

"There's plenty of food down in the kitchen. I've seen it. Next to the knives," she said importantly.

Mateo frowned, watching the plate as she set it out of reach on her other side before turning back to his father. "I only came up here to tell you that the Warlord has decided I'm a shapeshifter, Father." His hands were still full of bethl and berries because he'd forgotten to leave them in the kitchen for Hilaria, and now she would probably try to kill him too.

Aria sat up a little taller in the bed, Tual's eyes flicking up to meet Mateo's. But then they went back down to *Thousand Nights*. "Give me a moment. I'm reading to Aria."

"From *that*?" Mateo goggled at the book's shiny cover.

"The fighting parts. Honestly, the story is ruined by all that other stuff—it's not even foreshadowed. Arben Trislight had a fabulous sense of story, but he wasn't much of a romantic."

"You're not concerned about the Warlord? Why didn't you tell me about Belash Point? Or the *plague* in Chaol? Why didn't you tell me my sister is a murderous tree-growing Basist *murderer*?"

Tual finally looked up from the pages again. "Did you just use murder twice in one sentence?"

"You have a sister?" It took Mateo a moment to look at Aria, her eyes wide. After a moment, her lips pressed together, and she looked down. "And being awful runs in the family, I guess? My sister'll take care of that. She'll slit all your throats like bananas."

Mateo frowned. "Bananas?"

"Bananas are skinny and either too sweet or not sweet enough." Aria's voice struck a defensive chord. "Which is exactly like all of you."

Something's happening, Willow whispered, breaking into Mateo's thoughts before he could make fun of such a terrible simile. *I don't know what it is. They locked Knox in a closet to stop me from listening anymore, and all I can hear is that loud dancer girl singing a song I don't understand about a girl with no elbows.*

Heat bled through Mateo's cheeks. *You mean the one about the girl with no knees?*

Is there a difference?

He cleared his throat, pushing Willow away. "Why didn't you tell me what happened to my family?" he asked Tual.

Tual closed the book with a snap, his fingers curving around the dagger's sheath like a claw. "Why all these questions, Mateo?"

Willow suddenly unfolded inside Mateo's mind with an animal roar, and Mateo couldn't look away from his father's hand on the weapon for a moment, almost as if his father had *changed*. Shifted. Like an actual shapeshifter was supposed to. But when he forced his eyes to focus, his father's hands were the same as they'd ever been.

"They're coming, aren't they?" Tual jumped up from his chair, excited. "You know what to do?"

"I knew what to do for Lia." Mateo swallowed. "All our plans accounted for *Lia*, not *Belash Point*. I told Cath—one of the Devoted—that it was my sister, that all the things they pinned to me were because of her following us around, and I think she believes me. The Warlord isn't back yet, so—"

"She is back, and that is a perfect deflection." Tual went to the door, glancing down at Aria, who was still being uncharacteristically quiet, her breaths coming too quickly. "I'll go tell her to expect an attack from our rogue shapeshifting stalker, and you concentrate on your part of the plan. Everything will be fine."

His fingers stroked the dagger, and the air seemed to negate around him, coalescing above his head like a crown. Then he left, a sort of glimmer remaining in the room where he'd been.

Mateo fell back into the chair Tual had vacated, shivers down his spine.

"Is she a shapeshifter? Your sister?" Aria's face was gray, her jaw set with such fierce loyalty it made him ache. Had that been what he was to his sister before? Ready to live, die, kill for each other? "And do you really hate her so much?"

"I didn't grow up with her, and she's . . . made some poor decisions since then, I guess." Mateo couldn't stop the prickling in his arms, his ears roaring with the sound of wood cracking and growing, roots splitting the earth, and screams—

I wasn't there. I couldn't have been there. The thought was a drumbeat in his head. *Was I there? Is that why Father took my memories? To spare me?*

"I didn't grow up with my sister, either," Aria interrupted. "I just always knew she was there. Protecting us. She was more than us. I wanted to be like her."

The ache in him grew. There were many worse people to turn out like than Lia Seystone. "I hope you are like her."

"Because you are madly in love with her, I know—that's why you're so mean all the time, because she thinks you're worse than snake poo."

Mateo's stomach sank. But he only shrugged. "You're probably right."

"I'll tell her you're all right, okay?" Aria mimed swiping a blade through the air, only to have her hands fall back to her blankets, sapped of energy, and Mateo's chest ached even more. "You can read to me until she gets here. Finish the part about the Ivy King climbing into the black witch's tower."

Mateo's fingers halfway to the book on the bedside table, he looked at her in horror. "The *tower*? I thought he was just reading the fighting parts?"

"Well, yeah. And the Ivy King is about to take the witch down!" Aria's brow puckered.

Clearing his throat, Mateo picked up the book and turned a few pages, then a few pages more pages, the heat in his cheeks growing until he found something he could read about the Ivy King with his scaled armor and the witch with her diamond firekey. Willow was shifting uncomfortably in his head. *Tual's right,* she whispered. *Your red-haired swordy-girl. She could be coming. And your sister, too. I'll keep checking.*

Mateo gritted his teeth, the book heavy between his hands. *If they come, then we'll stick to the plan,* he responded. *Father's plans never fail.*

When Knox woke, everything was dark.

His room. The hold beyond the open door. Even the ship, only covered by slumbering, white auras. For a moment, panic jolted through Knox's chest, memories of other times he'd suddenly awoken with no memory of how he'd gotten to where he was like a pall in his mind. Of the tomb, of Anwei bleeding on the ground—

But then he saw aurasparks on the deck. Anwei. Awake and headed toward the canoes. Frowning, Knox sat up. Usually the bond pointed him right toward Anwei, but it felt cold.

Had something happened to make her pull back? He ran a hand down his face only to freeze on a grainy bit of dried paste stuck to his cheek. It smelled of river.

Knox pressed his hands to his cheeks. Anwei had been in here. Anwei had been in his bed. She'd kissed him. . . .

He stood, heart pounding as he went to the ramp and up onto the deck to where her aura was next to the boat's rail. Pausing behind one of the discarded crates, he watched her, Jaxom's angry orange light making her only a silhouette against the rocks—

The boat had moved. He looked around at the trees, the pool, the rocky outcroppings. Then back to Anwei, who was opening her trunk where it had been left by the drums. He started to step out until he saw what was in her hands.

At once, horror and *wanting* broke out inside him because she was holding the pockmarked sword. Whole again. There, right in front of him. He took a hesitant step forward, Willow's presence charging at him, stronger than ever as if she could taste holes in the barrier Anwei made around him and was checking every single one.

Anwei looked up, falling back a step when she saw him. The bond hadn't been pointing her to him either, or she'd have known he was watching. Which was when he remembered the end of the dancing, the cup of something he didn't recognize burning down his throat. "You're awake," she whispered, her husky voice too soft.

The canoe bobbed on the other side of the railing.

He'd gone dizzy right before Willow had pulled him under. He hadn't been dizzy or clouded any of the other times, had he? Knox's insides seemed to curl up in protest, in *revulsion*.

"Anwei . . ." He started across the deck, and her hands went deep into her medicine bag, her aura swirling thicker. Knox stopped, the bond a wilted thing that hung slack between them. "Anwei," he tried again. "I'm . . . going back below. . . ." But he didn't. "Why did you do it? You know how I feel about . . ." Herbs. How he'd always felt about her magic. It wasn't fair to say it that way—before it had always been because he knew it was Basism and Basism was supposed to be bad, but now his skin crawled in a new sort of horror. Anwei had poisoned him to get him out of the way.

She'd kissed him while he was fading to make sure he didn't notice what she'd done, because then Willow would have understood what was happening.

Anwei didn't move, frozen.

But then she smiled. "Go back to bed," she said as if there wasn't a canoe floating in the water behind her. As if the shapeshifter sword that held his sister wasn't there in her hands. "We didn't put you in the watch rotations because I was worried Willow would try to drop you and let someone get into the boat."

The evening was playing out in his mind in slow motion, Anwei laughing with him, sitting by him, pressing against him. As if they were different people, people with no gods or goddesses, no shapeshifters, no ghosts of the dead standing between them. Like another life.

It hadn't been fake. He'd felt it so clearly across the bond. But at the end, she'd been so *angry*—

Anwei stepped into Jaxom's moonlight, her face a smile that was using all the wrong muscles. "Go back to bed, Knox."

You can't let her pull away, Knox. Calsta's voice was distant. Fighting against Willow, who loomed so large he could almost feel the brush of her claws. "Please tell me you didn't—" he started. There was nothing but air between them, the words hanging in it as if they couldn't go away now that he'd said them out loud. "I would have just gone to bed if you'd asked me. I would have walked into the forest without looking back if you'd asked me."

"Stop." Anwei swallowed, then looked up at Castor's glow higher in the sky. "Please go back to bed. Please. You shouldn't have woken up."

"Devoted heal faster than normal people." The words tore out of him like a blade. "We're partners, right?"

She nodded, the sword bristling from her hands like an unkept promise.

"Partners don't lie, Anwei. Partners don't . . ." The last moments between them flashed through his mind, and he couldn't let them go. *Don't let her push you away*, Calsta whispered again, farther than ever, but Knox didn't want to be the one sacrificing this time.

Don't let *her* push *him* away? He was the one with reason to be angry.

"I can't believe you poisoned me, and then—"

"I can't do this right now." Anwei kicked one foot over the rail.

"Do you care at all what I want, Anwei?" Knox stepped closer, his whole body buzzing. "We have always trusted each other—that means knowing the other person is going to be there, but it also means not having to check your own drink for noxious herbs." He looked at the sword, despair like a knife in his gut. "I've been pleading with Calsta to tell me how to let Willow go because I didn't understand how the sword could be gone with Willow still here. Have you had it this whole time?"

"I didn't mean—" More heat flared in Anwei's face than he expected, and he fell back a step as she kicked her other foot over the rail and landed in the boat. "The last time we got into a scrape, you tried to *impale* me with this sword. The time before that, you tried to strangle me. This sword makes you hurt me, Knox."

"You know that wasn't—"

"On purpose. I know. You talk about barriers and bonds and magic and Willow being too close but far away. How was I supposed to know that this time the sword wasn't going to steal you the same way it used to? It was luck that kept me alive before, and we need more than luck going forward." Anwei pulled the mooring line free.

"At least I do. *She* just needs you to keep breathing."

"I don't even want the sword anymore. Our bond blocks her from controlling me. That was the whole point of us being together, Anwei. You protect me from her."

"Well, I'm glad you're getting something from our bond." Anwei picked up the paddle, the threads of their connection fraying as she turned toward the rocks. "But I think we're all just a little hazy on what exactly it covers, which is why you need to *go back to bed*."

He put a hand to his ribs unconsciously, something in his side twinging. "You're choosing something different now. Different than in the tomb, or earlier today when we sank the ship, even when you were off doing Calsta-knows-what when I was locked in the cabin." The gaps in his mind from that evening started to solidify, ending with her lips against his and starting again here with Anwei holding the sword that had broken his soul as if she meant to use it like a weapon. "I'm not useful anymore."

Anwei's head gave an angry shake. "Don't be ridiculous—"

"You said you can't be with me because you can't stomach sharing me with Calsta, but that's not it. You *can't* choose me because being with me would be an oath. It would mean doing what the nameless god and Calsta want."

One second Anwei was staring at him, and the next the sword was out of its sheath. Knox's insides contorted, and his heart began to pound at the sight of the pockmarked metal, the truth of what he'd said like an anchor rusting at the bottom of his stomach.

"I do not make oaths," she said quietly, letting the point of the sword rest on the deck. "You wanted this sword fixed. The only reason you stayed with me was that you thought I could help you do it."

"And then I fell in love with you." The words came out before he could even think, truer even than the sword she was holding. Willow lurked at the back of his mind, but she didn't ask him to take it, didn't ask him to kill Anwei as she'd always done. "I dedicated my life to Calsta, and she showed me how you could still be a part of it because I love you. Which wasn't enough for you." The words choked inside him. "You say you haven't made oaths? You've dedicated your life to a *shapeshifter*, Anwei. At least gods give something back."

"You have the gall to—" Anwei spun around, and Knox hated the way her armor looked broken and that he'd been the one who had done it. She put a hand on that medicine bag of hers once again, but she didn't open it. "This is *my choice*. This is *my war*. And like I said back when all this started, you are *not invited*."

"Because you can't stand to lose another person you love?"

"Because you will *make me lose*!" Anwei shouted. She set the sword down in the boat and picked up the paddle. "My whole family is dead. Everything I was supposed to be is *dead*."

"Killing Tual isn't going to fix what happened to you. It won't change the choices Mateo made, the choices your family made."

"It will be a fair ending." She dug the paddle into the water and started into the darkness. "You can't take that away from me. I won't let you. I'm finished with being bonded if it means I have to give up everything I want. I'm *done*."

The bond tensed.

Knox couldn't move, Calsta a swell of panic inside him. She pushed at him, yelled in her little guttering words to *fix this*. As if even this one corner of his life couldn't belong to him.

But it was too late to fix anything, because Anwei was already gone, nothing left of her but a ripple in the water.

Which was when his side began to burn. The anger scorching him from across the bond flared, and then the bond itself began to char. *Don't let her shut you out.* Calsta's voice was suddenly *loud*, the undercurrent of panic turning to desperation, as if she couldn't find words fast enough to tell him what to do. *Not all oaths are spoken out loud. She cannot break this one. She cannot break this one, Knox, she cannot!*

She doesn't want it, Calsta! His head was spinning, the wound in his stomach suddenly wet and raw. The sickness that had been pressing up inside him burrowed out through his skin. Anwei was unspooling him, as if he were nothing but an old scarf and Anwei the string, pulling him apart knot by knot. Their scorched bond began to fray.

Willow flickered like mad at the back of his head, her claws pressing through the holes forming in the wall between him and the ghost. "Anwei?" Knox rasped. He lurched forward, off-balance, and hit the rail. Unable to catch himself, he fell forward into the river, the shock of cold water on his skin dulled and remote. He swam toward where the boat had gone, his breath smoldering like panic in his lungs.

But Anwei did not stop. Anwei was gone.

And then the water around him began to boil.

CHAPTER 22

Bells Are for Gods

Lia held herself absolutely straight in the saddle as Vivi picked through the trees toward the Montanne estate. He stopped to snuffle at the ground, pieces of earth falling in at the edge of where his cloven hooves had dug in.

A blue flare means the plan is off, she told herself, staring at the night sky. *A blue flare. Light it, Altahn. Send it up.*

The sky stayed black.

Anwei's plan—the one she hadn't said out loud until Knox was safely asleep below—stuck like needles down Lia's spine, every step jarring them deeper. *We need a diversion. What do the Warlord and Tual both want?*

Lia. They wanted Lia.

And just as Noa had found herself running toward her father's boat, Lia was riding through the trees toward Tual's lake alone, aura blazing, practically shouting for the Warlord to get her veil ready. "You tell them we're coming," Anwei had said as the healer bent over a bush with leaves that spiked out menacingly with large bursts of pink flowers sheltered inside. "I'll find Mateo and your sister while they're staring at you. You tell them I'm a Basist, a murderer, a shapeshifter, even, and that I'm coming for the sword. When Altahn sets off the salpowder explosion, you lead the charge into the cliffs to fight the attack. In the confusion, you can follow my aura to the tunnel we opened, and I'll close it once you're through." She sniffed again, nodding slowly as she extracted a pair of tweezers and a small, empty oilcloth packet from her bag.

"What about Tual?" Lia asked, stepping up closer only to shy away when Anwei shooed her back from the plant's spiky leaves. "The shapeshifter who wants to slit my throat? You know, so his son can eat my soul?" When Anwei didn't look up from the plant, Lia couldn't help the tinge of rancor sharpening her voice. "What in Calsta's name are you doing?"

"Something that has recently become extremely important." Anwei's brow furrowed as she leaned toward the little cluster of flowers sheltering under the leaves. "It's in the hibintia family—perfect for bonding humor markers to a tincture. Relatively common plants, though this particular variety is quite poisonous."

Lia fought to keep her hands from shaking. "Your plan is for me to walk directly into the trap Tual set and just hope he's not in the mood to spring it? And you are harvesting *herbs*?"

"Of course not." Anwei leaned forward, tweezers peeling back one of the bright pink petals to reveal a crawling mass of black. "I'm harvesting the ants. They digest the plant structure, and the process nullifies the poison. Ants give me the properties of a hibintia plant without this one's unfortunate bite—"

"Anwei." Lia did her best to school her voice into something that didn't sound murderous. "I can't do this. I'll end up dead, and so will Aria."

The healer's tweezers darted into the cluster of ants, pinching one free. Lia's stomach lurched at the sight, frustration like oil boiling in all of her limbs, demanding she move. Anwei didn't seem to notice, depositing the unfortunate insect into the oilcloth, then going back to the bloom for more. *Is that how she sees the rest of us? Like curious little creatures that might fit well into one of her tinctures?* But Lia banished the thought immediately. Anwei had been right about everything so far, and she'd done it gently, even waiting for Knox to bore Willow into putting him to sleep before beginning the heist.

"If Tual was ready to reveal he's a soul-sucking shapeshifter to the Warlord herself, don't you think he would have done it already?" Anwei picked another ant off the flower. "I'll get there long before you do—we'll call everything off if there's even a chance that things will go wrong. We can warn you away with one of Altahn's flares before you get close to the island." She'd buttoned the little pouch and started back toward the boat, leaving Lia behind in the darkness.

Too much faith. That was what Anwei had. Too much faith in her own observations, as if she were incapable of getting anything wrong. Too much faith in herself that everyone would follow, clustered like those little ants, ready to be sacrificed for whatever remedy Anwei had decided was worth their lives.

But Aria was there, inside the lake house.

No matter how many times Lia thought through the plan, it felt like panic. Like Ewan Hardcastle's teeth against her lip, like her cold seclusion room, like no one in the world cared who she was or what she wanted, not even the goddess who was supposed to love her.

But Calsta was with her now. Lia clung to the feel of gold glowing from her humors. The goddess *did* care. The goddess wanted her to succeed.

The goddess just . . . didn't want to give her any extra power to do it, keeping back the third oath that would give her enough strength to match the Warlord.

Do you trust me? Anwei had said.

Knox did. Altahn did. Noa did. And Lia had no choice but to do the same, the thought of Aria's little face like an arrow pointing her on. *Calsta* did, or she never would have brought Knox to Anwei.

The problem was, Lia wasn't sure Anwei understood what she

was asking. Walking into an arena with Tual and the soul-stealing sword he'd taken from Patenga on one side and the Warlord with her soul-stealing interpretation of Devotion on the other was worse than Lia finding herself trapped in an arena facing down an angry auroshe.

Do you trust me, Lia? Calsta's voice seemed to echo from the sky. Whatever Anwei's faults, the goddess knew exactly what she was asking. This was acting. This was *moving*. Fighting. Doing.

Wasn't that what Lia had wanted all along? The sword Gilesh had let her borrow to replace the one she'd lost in the bay felt heavy against her spine.

Vivi snorted, twisting to look off into the trees. He shook his head and continued on at Lia's kick, but not before she'd seen the hulking beast silhouetted against the moon on the rocks above them. Ahead of them, just beneath the shadow, an extremely large cat lay half-eaten on the ground.

Rosie. Why was she here? She hadn't followed Lia to town, she'd stayed here by the lake, as if Mateo was what she truly wanted. But if that were the case, then why hadn't she swum to the island? Lia's stomach twinged with pity at the thought of the injured auroshe out here alone, trying so hard to find the ones who had bonded with her, then carelessly forgotten her.

Perhaps Aria wasn't the only one who could use saving from the Montanne family.

When the lake finally came into sight, Lia forced herself to keep riding toward the shore, then across the spindly bridge that led to the island, her eyes fixed on the house silhouetted against the cliffs. No one stopped them, a white aura appearing in Lia's sight at the far edge of the bridge, but when she got to the island's shore, the guard only gave her a polite bow, gesturing for her to ride on.

Vivi gave the guard an interested sniff, but Lia kicked him on before he could try to nip her. A tower hulked just past the bridge, slumbering auras bright on the first and second floors. The third floor was empty, and Lia couldn't see the fourth or fifth because her aurasight couldn't reach. She rode past, Vivi trotting through the courtyard beyond it with his head down and his hackles up, bristling with every step. Into a garden, the house like a specter on the far side of the island, candles glowing like feral eyes in the windows. The waterfall spewing over the cliffs glowed a ghostly orange in Jaxom's light. There was no sign of Aria.

Lia forced her fingers clenching the reins to relax. Anwei was coming. *This is going to be fine.*

She thought it hard, like a prayer. The healer had promised.

And Lia believed her.

Fine fortress this is. And what a fine distraction I am. Will I have to ring the bell before anyone notices me? Lia stopped the moment her aurasight touched gold and dismounted. The Warlord was on the top floor of the house, her aura parched as if something had taken a sip from her golden light. There was one other Devoted aura present, and it was moving with purpose toward Lia from around the side of the house. Standing straight, Lia set her chin high, unease a knife in her stomach. Tual's aura slumbered calmly at the back of the house, but Mateo was nowhere to be seen.

The Devoted rounded the hedges and started toward Lia, a sedate smile on her face and a sword at her back, taking in the sight of Lia unveiled calmly as if Lia had written ahead to announce her arrival.

"Lia Seystone." She barely glanced at Vivi when he snapped at her. "I'm Cath. I don't believe we had the pleasure of meeting back in the seclusions."

Lia dipped her head in acknowledgment, heart hammering. "I'm looking for Tual Montanne. And the Warlord. And my sister. Not in that order."

"Your sister?" Cath's eyes trailed down from Lia's uncovered head, past the boiled-leather cuirass she'd haggled for outside of Chaol at a great loss to Altahn since she didn't know how to haggle properly. "You're not here to see Mateo, then?"

"Why would I be here to see Mateo?" Lia pulled on the mantle her oath scars were supposed to give, her tone sharp. "I came to warn the Warlord and the Montannes that there's an attack planned against the island this evening."

"An . . . attack." Cath's eyes narrowed. "How is your aura intact? You ran away in Chaol."

Lia licked her lips. "I serve the goddess, as you do. Leaving Chaol was the only way to warn . . ." She cleared her throat. "I came to prove . . . m-my . . . l-loyalty." The words stuttered out as the Warlord's aura twisted itself free from the snarl of candlelight coming from the top floor. She was far away then close with moments, appearing in the doorway like a spider at the center of this web. "We . . . are all . . . we're all in very great danger."

Lia's hands clenched at her sides. This was what she'd come to do.

Face her.

Lie to her.

Distract her.

But now she couldn't breathe, panicked gasps bubbling up like they had the first day Lia had climbed into Anwei's garden. Flashes of memory burst through her in quick succession: her mother waving as Lia had ridden away behind a Rooster, pretending to smile when Lia could see the tears plain in her eyes. *Flash.* Her scalp burning as the first oath was branded into her, marking her as a goddess's property. *Flash.* A veil dripping down over her head. *Flash.* Ewan riding behind her as they approached Chaol, the Warlord's words ringing in her ears as his terrible thoughts about her ran like oil into her vision, impossible to scrub away. *It's your choice, of course, who your bond will be with. But Ewan is one of our best Devoted. We need more gods-touched as strong as him. As strong as you both.*

The buzz of Calsta's energy shot through Lia like lightning. Years of loneliness, of sadness, of feeling as if she were no more than a sword, a veil, a *thing* to be moved where the goddess chose—it hadn't been Calsta doing it.

It had been the Warlord.

And now the Warlord was coming for her.

Vivi's reins tight in her grip, Lia turned to meet her, mind gobbling up every new aura in range as she came closer to the house. No Aria.

When the Warlord stepped into the courtyard, she held out her arms as if she meant to gather Lia to her like a lost child. "Lia, my dear girl. You've come back to me."

Lia looked the Warlord straight in the eye as she hadn't been able to do for the last two years with a veil between her and the world. She stepped back a pace, putting Vivi between her and Cath, ready to draw her sword at any moment. "A Basist is coming tonight. She's after Tual Montanne's sword."

"Interesting. That's exactly what Mateo said. You know Mateo, of course?" The Warlord waited expectantly. "What did he do to you, child?"

What did Mateo do to me? Lia's breath caught in her chest, rage like a wave inside her threatening to drown her. *Mateo did nothing but try to help me!* She wanted to yell. *It was you who locked me in a room with Ewan. It was you who took me from my parents. It was you who switched out my dolls for a sword, then took my sword when it became a comfort and gave me a veil. Mateo was on my side even when he didn't want to be.* She gritted her teeth, forcing her hands to stay at her sides. Vivi gave an eager screech. He could smell the blood in her thoughts and wanted to spill it out where everyone could appreciate it.

But Lia knew she had to keep herself together long enough for Anwei to get in. Keep the Warlord's attention long enough for the healer to locate Aria and Mateo. Long enough that Altahn could set off his explosions to cover their escape.

So she drew her sword. "They're coming. I don't know how Mateo knew, but I can't let them hurt you."

"You know I can see your energy flaring as you use it," the Warlord's low, husky voice drawled out from the house's fancy portico. She stepped into the moonlight, looking much smaller than the woman Lia remembered from the seclusions. "What exactly did Mateo bring you here for, Lia Seystone?"

Gritting her teeth, Lia stepped out in front of Vivi, the weight of her sword too comfortable in her hand. "I am not here on anyone's behalf but my own."

The Warlord squinted down the length of the weapon, unconcerned. "Interesting words for a Devoted."

<hr>

Mateo grimaced at his cards, glancing over them at Aria. She was twelve. *Twelve.* How in Calsta's name was she beating him at scales? "Whoever decided these suits must have been color-blind, because the complementary color to green is—"

"I noticed you rearranging your cards when you drew spears." Despite her pallor, Aria still managed to make her boredom sound like a weapon. She yawned, covering her mouth with her cards, and she seemed to blur at the edges, something still and dark at her center. Mateo blinked, wondering if the extra energy Willow had taken was making him forget how tired his body was. He blinked the sleep out of his eyes, willing his sight to go clear. "You have a queen and at least three stones. Complaining about the card colors isn't going to change the fact that I am going to destroy you."

"I thought you were sick. Why aren't you sick in a way that helps me?" Mateo tried to think of a swear word Aria wouldn't know so he could use it, which would do a better job distracting her than—

Lia's golden sparks flared in Mateo's stretched-out aurasight. He jumped up from his chair to look out the window, his cards fluttering to the floor in a forgotten pile. *Lia's here. Lia is here on the island.* The words choked inside him, Willow swelling up inside him to look too. *You didn't know. How come you didn't know?*

"You can't pretend to have an episode to get out of your bad hand, Mateo," Aria chided. "You're not *that* poor of a loser, are you?"

"Oh, I'm the *worst* kind of loser," he breathed, trying to imagine a world where Lia's aura below didn't come straight to him, sword ready to stab before he got to explain.

It won't matter if she stabs you, Willow whispered. Then suddenly she went still. *Mateo,* her voice crackled and deepened. *Your sister. Your sister has the sword. Get the sword. We need the sword.*

Goose bumps broke out across Mateo's arms.

"Mateo?" Aria's voice was a little too sharp, fear she didn't want to show poking through. "You aren't really having an episode, are you?"

"No. I'm—" He jerked back from the door—how had he got to the door? "I just thought I saw something outside. No, don't you go look—" He crossed the room again and stood in front of the leaded glass, though there was little chance Aria would be able to see her sister below in the courtyard. All he could see was her aura.

The sword. The sword. The sword. Lia Seystone. Willow swelled inside him. *We need to take it. We need all of it. All of them. All the energy. I'm hungry. FEED ME.*

Wait! That's not the plan. Mateo's thoughts barely penetrated, his skin feeling as if it were going to burst. Willow twisted inside him— twisted *him,* this *thing* he'd been talking to in his head as if she were a little girl and not an abomination. A monster. *Willow, wait!* he cried as the ghost clouded the world around him, everything going gray and smelling of bone and rot.

"Mateo! I'm scared. You're scaring me!" Aria had started to cry.

You aren't big enough to hold me, Willow crooned. *It's all right. Let me take care of you, Mateo.*

Then it was Mateo screaming because his arms and legs, his shoulders, his feet, his fingers—the ones Tual said had been cut off—all began to grow.

❧❧

Anwei's heart raced as she paddled the canoe away from the boat, away from Knox, away from everything that could ruin this night. *I'm done,* she'd said.

And his spot in her head dimmed. Broke down to almost nothing, plucking him free from her mind. The line tethering them together splintered. A cry shattered her thoughts: *Anwei!*

It hurt, uprooting the ties between her and Knox, like pulling teeth. She slowed, her eyes clenching shut over the awful promises of what could have been—an evening where nothing mattered. When she'd let herself forget everything and pretend nothing existed but the boat and the music and her friends. What could have been if she were a different person, and he was too. If they'd met in a market or a malt shop or class at the university. Maybe in the apothecary she'd dreamed of starting with her brother, smiling at Knox from across the counter and seeing his true smile the first time he ever looked at her rather than months later, the weight of a goddess dragging him to the earth.

But there were no malt houses, no markets, no apothecaries. There was no life to fit him into. Calsta and the snake-tooth man had made sure of that. And so had Anwei when she'd put the tiny dose of Sleeping Death in his drink, terrified it would be too much.

Any was too much. She'd broken the perfect evening to ensure that the second half of it wouldn't be interrupted. Because that was what it all had been for.

At least, that was what she'd thought until she started kissing him in that other world where nothing mattered, so there had been no reason to stop.

Anwei cut off the thought. Left it with everything else he'd said to drown in the water behind her. Into the cave's mouth. Around the bend, past the statue of stone consigned to holding up the sky. Into the deep water beyond, the walls glowing blue, the smell of elsparn on her clothes mixing with the overwhelming odor of lost souls. None of it was strong enough to counter how much she wanted to turn around. Knox left bleeding gashes in her thought, and her head felt as if it were being pulled to pieces.

Anwei! His voice gave one last, sad shout in her mind, then receded, leaving a space that felt like a shadow. A ghost. A tear tracked down her cheek.

She kept paddling.

Past the second statue she and Altahn had found, all the way to an impossible whirlpool in the water that led to the bottom of the lake, allowing them to row to one of the many underwater passages connected into the cliffs completely dry. She'd taken Altahn across to set up lines of salpowder, going up hundreds of stairs and skipping the ones that seemed to breathe poison into the air. They'd found banks of windows that looked down over the lake, and that was where Anwei left Altahn to pipe wet, oil lines between packets of salpowder. Once they'd come back through, they'd agreed that Altahn should remain in the waterway ready to set off the flare through the vents in the ceiling while Anwei went back for the last things they needed: a shapeshift-er-killing sword, packets of Sleeping Death in the old calistet bag with its special button, and the antidote brewed in a hasty tincture with the ants she'd harvested.

How did you find the exact ingredient you needed so close to the boat? That seems awfully lucky, Lia had said. But Anwei didn't need luck, not when the plants practically spoke to her, gushing with colors to show their every attribute. The ants had found her.

When Anwei paddled into the final chamber with the impossible whirlpool leading into the lake, something scrabbled across the ceiling over her head, the sound of claws on stone skittering across Anwei's skin. She breathed in, searching for the scent of what it could be, her hand dipping into her medicine bag.

But just as the last bit of warmth bled from Knox's place in her head, Anwei's whole mind went cold. Anwei gasped, pitching forward as the space where he'd been cracked open, splitting her in half. She breathed in, then breathed in again, searching for the scent of what could be wrong with her.

Nothing.

Shoving a hand into her medicine bag, she gulped down lungfuls of air, groping for the answer to her convulsing heart and splitting skull.

The packets didn't smell of anything at all.

Anwei sucked down another panicked breath, shoving her face into the mouth of her bag and frantically searching for the scents she knew so well—corta, lilia, linereed, and cottonflower, *Sleeping Death*—but they were now only faint imitations, their colors faded to gray.

Anwei almost fell as she lunged to grasp the pockmarked blade sitting there at the bottom of the canoe, one smell that would never pale. The *nothing*.

Usually touching the sword was enough to make her gag, but this time, it was only an uneasy feeling of wrong, a bad taste in her mouth instead of the full bite of rotten meat it was.

A bright light flashed overhead, and Anwei clapped hands over her ears, not understanding the high-pitched squeal that went with it until it ended in an echoing crack somewhere high above the cave.

The flare. She remembered the scrabbling sound of claws and looked around for Galerey. They'd had her lodge the flare up there in the vent, ready to go off at the slightest hint of trouble. Why had Altahn had sent her up there to ignite it now?

Where *was* he?

But then the place where Knox had been uprooted began to crack. Anwei lost her balance—her sight, her smell, her ears all screaming with something terrible. A part of her own mind seemed to be breaking free, leaving a gaping hole. *Calsta above.* Anwei choked on her own breath, on the tears streaming down her cheeks as she looked around for something—anything to use as a weapon or a medicine or—

I am not Calsta, a voice rang in her head, clearer than any bell. It was familiar, the same flavor as her own thoughts, like a voice she'd heard a thousand times before. It sat in the shadows of sicknesses she smelled, prickled with the herbs that itched to be combined to treat them.

It was her. Her healing, her magic. The voice of color, the one that led her to the ants.

But now it *spoke*. And it wasn't her at all. It was something foreign and *nameless*—

I am not nameless. The voice was tortured and faint, like one last, gasping breath. *And I have tolerated much from you, Anwei.*

Something clapped in her head, like lightning and thunder, only worse, because it smelled like fire and stone and herbs and water and everything in the world. *I've justified you as long as I can.*

And then everything—even the last hint of plague from the sword—*disappeared.*

This can't be for you, the voice croaked.

The moss, the water, the smell of *nothing* billowing from the cave. All the scents were there one moment, then gone the next—not blown away or thinned out, but *nonexistent*, as if the fabric of the world, the colors, the shapes, the touch and taste had blinked out of being.

Anwei retched, the paddle dropping from her slack fingers into the current. An energy inside her that she'd never known was anything but hers was draining away through the crack Knox had left in her head, leaving her dry. She lifted her head searching for *any* scent— the ruddy smell of the elsparn salve, the honey aroma of stone, the sediment-threaded water, the *elsparn*, for Calsta sake. Anwei knew they were there, lurking under the water with their little death lantern eyes watching her.

They were there, but their smells were gone.

Ahead of her, something very, very large streaking up through the opening to the lake, headed right for the boat.

⚜

Lia held her sword steady as Cath drew her own weapon.

"You can't shelter Mateo Montanne, little one." The Warlord's voice was so gentle, consoling. "I can help you. You're safe now. Whatever he did, it was wrong, stealing parts of you like only the nameless god can. How did he persuade you to run away and put this power over you? Tell me, and all will be forgiven, child."

"You know Mateo is . . . . ?" Lia flinched when Vivi snarled, snaking up to glower over her shoulder because Cath had moved too close. "You can't be serious. Mateo would rather copy reliefs than talk to actual people. He has *fainting spells*." Rage filled her like acid. She pointed her sword at the Warlord's exposed throat. "I ran away because of you!"

"That's hardly—"

"You told Ewan Hardcastle I needed a bonded mate, that we needed more little spiriters and that it was my job to produce them, then sent us to the farthest corner of the Commonwealth where no one would stop him from making sure he was the one who got to help!"

The Warlord's eyes widened, her sword lowering an inch.

"You sent him with me on purpose like I was a *reward*." Lia advanced a step, her skin hot enough to catch fire, forgetting everything but the woman in front of her. *Aria,* a voice at the back of her head sang. *You're here for Aria.* But Lia was shaking, the *something* she'd been wanting to do—to the Warlord, to the masters, to Tual Montanne and every other person who had told her to obey no matter the damage—was before her like a challenge on the training yard. The feel of the sword in her hands was the only thing that was *right*. "You knew what Ewan was, and you let him stay in the seclusions. You told him—"

"You know better than this, Lia." The Warlord hadn't moved,

hadn't even acknowledged the threat of Lia's sword pointed at her throat. Cath's aura sang with Calsta's power, and Lia didn't need to look to know she'd circled behind, forcing Vivi to move behind Lia to stay between them. "You were blessed above almost all other Devoted, studied under Master Helan, who has progressed farther in the oaths than any other Devoted in a hundred years. You tarnish your oaths by claiming to have heard thoughts like these from *my* mind?"

"By the time you got to Chaol, I couldn't read thoughts anymore! What did *you* think happened when you found me gone and Ewan diminished when you got to Chaol? Calsta knew what had happened. She didn't restore his oaths. But *you* let him keep his armor and his sword. You let him force my auroshe to bond with him—"

"You blame me? You blame *him*?" The Warlord shrugged one shoulder. "For *your* desertion of the goddess? If you didn't want him near you, why didn't you stab him through the heart, Lia? I've never once seen you struggle in the training yards."

Lia's insides roared, the words in her mouth far too bland for this woman who thought she was a goddess. Vivi screeched, eager for the blood spilling from Lia's thoughts as she lunged forward, sword hacking toward the Warlord's exposed neck. Cath was there quicker than lightning, sparks flying as her sword bit into Lia's, thrusting it away.

Something screamed into the night air overhead, a shower of sparks flying up from behind the cliffs. Lia's heart stopped, her sword grating against Cath's, unable to stop herself from glancing up.

It exploded with a deafening crack, raining ash and fire of bright azure blue.

Altahn's signal not to come.

There was a split second of quiet, the blast ringing in Lia's ears, the Warlord's freckles washed over in blue light. Then auras all over the compound exploded to life, faded with sleep one moment and burning bright the next, like an army of suns rising across the island. Tual Montanne's aura burst all over in bright lights, shining white as the sun.

Lia snapped back to reality, the one where she was trapped on an island, the distraction for a heist that was apparently not going to happen, her sword drawn and fire in her blood, but not the kind that would let her win against two full Devoted with Calsta's third oath roiling through them.

But the moment she had the thought, Calsta's energy rushed into Lia. She spun toward the Warlord, a torrent of energy filling her humors as it hadn't since she'd first arrived in Chaol, her arms growing strong and the earth steady under her feet.

Calsta? she breathed, and then there was no time to think because the Warlord was moving. Vivi moved at the same time, his horn spearing to block Cath as Lia dodged behind the Warlord and grabbed the woman's sword before she could reach for it. Vivi slammed his shoulder into Cath, knocking her to the ground just as Lia spun to face the Warlord, crossing the Warlord's sword and her own at the woman's throat. Energy crackled inside Lia, making the air around her sing, the heartbeat of every live person on the island thumping loud in her ears. Vivi screamed, charging Cath, who threw herself away from the Warlord to avoid his long, twisted horn.

"You are determined to betray your goddess, then?" The Warlord's voice was dead calm despite the blades pressed against the pulse fluttering in her neck. "You're nothing but your own wants. Why don't you just kill me? Let Calsta see what you really are."

"Calsta is with me *right now.*" Lia's muscles shook with rage, the blades pressing hard even as Aria's name played through her head, but then a blaze of caution threaded through her. She wanted nothing more than to lop off the Warlord's head, and her arms shook with the effort to be still as if Calsta herself had reached down from the sky to put a staying hand on Lia's shoulder.

I do not excuse her. But I still need her, Lia. There are Devoted in the forest who Tual will kill if you dispose of her now.

The voice *burned*, but not half as hot as Lia's rage. *Aria. Aria.*

Aria. Her sister's name twisted through her like a narmaiden's song, fear fanning the sparks inside her to a firestorm she couldn't contain.

If you lose yourself, Tual will win. Lia's knees buckled with the weight of Calsta's voice. The Warlord's chin tilted up as if daring Lia to kill her, Cath fighting to get past Vivi. *He is coming,* Calsta said. *Get out* now.

But Aria! Lia felt as if she'd been lost since the day she climbed down from the tower thinking somehow she could be free. Tual's aura sliced like a sword toward her, sprinting along an upstairs hall, then down a set of stairs and into the foyer.

Go! Calsta flamed, the feel of it building inside Lia to a terrible scream. Lia slammed her hilt into the Warlord's head and shot toward the bridge without waiting to watch her drop. The whole world seemed to tip sideways as Lia ran, Vivi leaving Cath to lope giddily behind her as if he'd missed this sort of thing, blood from Calsta knew where dripping down his muzzle. Cath's aura speared toward the Warlord behind them, then arced around to chase Lia toward the bridge.

Where is Aria, Calsta? Lia yelled in her head. *Just tell me. No more games.*

Get out! The goddess sputtered and disappeared, a candle blown out. Her energy raged inside Lia, not like panic or frustration or loss, but like *power* as she passed the tower's massive double doors. Looking up, Lia stalled a step as her eyes crossed to the higher floors, a candle burning in one of the high windows.

There was one place she hadn't been able to touch with her aurasight.

Vivi screeched in pain just behind her, jerking her back to the moment, to Cath with blood on her sword, and the auroshe's teeth bared in rage. Lia pivoted past him, twisting one shoulder back to dodge Cath's sword stabbing toward her chest, deflecting the blow with her own sword, then spinning to slice the Warlord's toward the Devoted's neck. Cath ducked and rolled past Lia, then jumped back to her feet.

Tual's aura was there in the courtyard behind them, less than twenty feet away. The energy inside Lia roared, and she could almost feel him roaring in answer, ready to take everything she was, to drink her down the way Mateo had accidentally done that night in the tomb.

An arrow sang through the air—the bridge guard, yelling as she sent it toward them. The wind of it caught Lia's cheek as she spun out of the way and dropped her sword to catch it, then threw it like a spear toward Tual's belly. Cath slammed into Lia, taking her to the flagstones. Lia's spine ground into the stone as she tried to curve out from under Cath's weight as the Devoted pressed her forearm to Lia's airway, sword arm pinned under the heavier warrior's knee. Flashes of pain struck Lia in quick succession, of Ewan's breath on her neck, of turning to stone, of Tual with his sword in Knox's stomach, of *life* being stolen right from her chest.

But suddenly Cath's arm across Lia's neck went slack, and the Devoted fell like a dead weight across Lia. The golden aura crowning her head guttered, flecks of energy streaming toward—

Toward—

Tual's aura glistened like a bonfire and starlight and Calsta herself in the sky as Cath's aura drained into him. The Warlord lay at his feet, deathly pale.

Lia pushed Cath off her and lurched to her feet, eyes on the tower. Sheathing the Warlord's sword, she heaved herself up onto the vines clinging to the stone, climbing up, up, away from the horrible silence where there had just been clamor. Not true silence, but the quiet of voices cut off, of bodies falling to the ground. The guard at the bridge. The flurry of white auras that had woken up at the sound of Altahn's flare, cooks, maids, guards, hostlers, all of them dimmed to almost nothing in Lia's head. Tual was sucking them dry.

Vivi screamed a challenge, and Lia suddenly remembered lying on the ground and Vivi not helping her, an impossibility unless he was hurt. Restrained.

Could shapeshifters drain animals?

Lia jammed her fingers between cracks in the unnatural tower wall, tears streaming down her cheeks as her boots slipped on vines, her heart refusing to beat to any rhythm but *Aria, Aria, Aria.* The next floor flooded into her aurasight as she heaved herself into a dark, empty window. Not a single soul was there.

Panic and power like terrible creatures inside her, Lia scrambled up to stand atop the arched window's upper frame. The top floor opened like a blossom inside her mind, two familiar auras flickering into being: Aria and Mateo Montanne.

⚬⁓⊸⁓⚬

Lia was coming.

Lia was coming, and Mateo was full of magic, his fingers claws of black. He couldn't breathe, and Aria had the blanket over her head to cover her scream, and the window crashed inward with a ferocity of golden aurasparks and broken glass. . . .

It's going to work. It's going to work! Willow trilled. *All we need is—* Her voice, which had been growing stronger every moment, seemed to thin, faltering.

Lia slid through the window, sword in hand.

Something is wrong. Knox is . . . Willow's voice went high and scared, almost as if she were the little girl she was pretending to be. *Something is wrong. Something is wrong. Something is wrong. Something is wrong. . . .*

Mateo stumbled back, trying to block out Willow's high keen, shielding his face with monstrous hands where his artist fingers had been. His throat started to close, his whole body shaking, as if Willow's panic was his own. "Aria . . ." He barely managed to get the name out from between his teeth clenching involuntarily down. There was a plan. He had to follow the plan. "Lia! Get Aria downstairs. There's a way out—the tunnel—"

Aria was still screaming, the blanket over her head. He couldn't see her, and she was too still, the scream echoing like he was down in the tunnel again, her body on the ground, and the sound was somehow coming from him.

Willow pulsed large in his head, filling Mateo until he began to split at the seams. He fell forward, groaning as Lia caught him, her grip like iron manacles. But Mateo couldn't focus, couldn't *care* because the thing in his head was *pulling free*. She was the bone and he the muscle, he the puppet, she the strings. It was like teeth being pulled from his gums, only throughout his whole body, as if his insides were made from ghost, and she was extracting herself in one ghastly wrench.

In that breath, Willow was gone. In the next, so was he.

⚜

Noa was dancing with Falan in her dream. The goddess was in her masculine form, and they were both all in gold and—

Something groaned outside the dream, pulling her back to the boat, to the coppery smell of elsparn salve and Gilesh snoring. Noa swore groggily, looking around for whatever had woken up. A groan that was still shuddering out until it rose to a scream.

Before Noa could move, it cut off in a terrible gurgle of water that sent Noa flopping from her hammock onto the floor. She tripped over her long skirts getting to the lamp still burning on its hook by the ramp, Gilesh and Bane falling from their hammocks to sprint past her on to the deck.

I was supposed to be awake. It came like a panicked lightning strike as she rushed after them, slamming into the rail where something was thrashing in the water. *I don't even remember lying down! I was supposed to keep watch.* She held out the lamp with shaky hands and—

"It's Knox!" Gilesh shouted.

Anwei's *belanvian* was flailing as if he'd forgotten how to swim between now and early that morning, little shapes wriggling all around him in the water. Dropping the lantern, Noa grabbed the bowl of

Anwei's dead elsparn entrails and smeared them down her arms and legs, then dove into the water.

Quick strokes took her to Knox, little slimy bodies squirming around her, but nothing bit. She grabbed hold of his arm, and Knox's whole body seemed to go limp as she dragged him back toward the boat. The elsparn swirled around them, catching in her skirts and darting in to nip at her shoulders and back, mouths gaping wide.

But then she was at the railing. Gilesh groped into the water to grab her hand and dragged her out of the water, Noa's shoulder screaming. Bane took hold of Knox and towed him onto the deck, Knox splaying out like dead weight. Heaving herself over the railing, Noa spilled onto the deck in a puddle, rolling up onto her knees by Knox's side. He was streaming blood, little bite marks all down his arms, but that wasn't the problem. Blood was seeping out of his side, the pool spreading fast around him. Noa lifted his tunic to find the wound in his side weeping with red. "Falan help me," she gasped. "Of all the things I can pretend, being a healer isn't one of them. Gilesh, get me a blanket. Bane, how about some bandages?"

"We don't speak Elantin, Noa—" Gilesh was pulling an elsparn off Knox's leg, the thing's hooked jaw wildly snapping at him.

"Bandages! Blankets!" she yelled in Common. She slid over to Knox's head, pushing his wet hair back from his face. "Knox? Knox, honey, I need you to wake up. I know exactly how easy it would be for Anwei to kill me, and if she finds you like this—"

His eyelids jerked open, and a guttural roar exploded from his mouth. Knox's back arched up from the deck, and he twisted toward her, mouth opening as if he meant to *bite*. Shadows erupted all down his body.

Noa screamed, skittering back until she hit the rail, only it was over before her voice hit the air, Knox limp and quiet as if she'd imagined it.

The shadows, though. Those didn't go away, thicker than ever.

Bane and Gilesh had both jumped back as well, an elsparn weakly writhing on the deck near their feet. "What do we do now?" Gilesh whispered.

Knox's head slowly swiveled to look at Noa. "He needs Anwei," he rasped.

The voice wasn't his. Even the blank, gray stare didn't belong to Knox, as if there were something *else* inside him, wearing him like a skin.

Noa shrank back. Not a shadow man, she told herself. *Not* darkness, not a *belanvian* waiting to drag her into Falan knew where.

One of Knox's arms jerked awkwardly as he tried to push himself up from the deck. "What are any of these muscles good for if they don't *work*? Why is he so *heavy*?" Knox's voice was worse than any ghostly caterwaul Noa had ever practiced. His head turned toward her again with a sudden jerk. "Help him! I mean help . . . me. *I need Anwei*. I can't die yet. Not like this."

His wounds bled and bled and bled . . .

Overhead something screeched up from the rocks, ending in a loud crack of blue. The flare.

Sweet Falan's broken feet. That wasn't supposed to happen now.

The flare couldn't happen *now*. Not when Noa was the one who needed help.

She couldn't move, frozen, because someone else was supposed to be making the decisions. Noa didn't know what to do when things went wrong or when people were bleeding or when shadows were curling toward her feet. She was the thing that *made* things go wrong, the diversion to make an audience look away while Anwei and the others made magic. She was the *sparkle*.

"Dump him overboard, Bane." Gilesh was moving toward the oars, his eyes up on the flare. "That's not Knox. We can't—"

"No," Noa's voice croaked, because even if she didn't know how to be in charge, that wasn't the right decision. Bane didn't listen though, circling carefully out of Knox's line of sight before moving closer, hand on his knife.

"No!" She yelled it this time, hopping up from the rail to push Bane back from Knox. "Knox needs us. Anwei and Altahn need us. *Everyone* needs us, so we're going to *go*."

"Miss Noa, with all due respect, I've seen that boy with a sword, and with all this talk of ghosts . . ." Bane edged around her toward Knox, who had started giggling, waving his fingers above his face even as he whispered Anwei's name over and over again.

"Get to your oar, *now*!" Noa pretended to be Lia with her no-nonsense rasp, or Altahn with his casual armor of control and authority. She manufactured a cajoling smile like Anwei's but lost it the moment she thought of how Anwei would break when she found Knox empty of everything but a ghost. This wasn't a part to play, and Noa couldn't magically have a plan like Anwei or threaten and stab like Lia. She couldn't be Altahn with his salpowder and vain title. So, digging deep, Noa found something of her own, like the crackle of fire tethers in her hands, her hands spread wide before an audience. "Snap to it, sailors, or it'll be *you* going in with the elsparn."

Anwei couldn't breathe, her nose blank of smells, her head full of a voice that wasn't hers, and something huge and black racing toward her.

"Anwei, *get out of the water*!" Altahn's voice rang out, only he was much higher than when she'd left him on the shelf of rock, clinging to the vines halfway up the cave wall.

She only had time to grab her medicine bag before the creature swished under the boat, rocking it sideways in a burst of water. It circled back through the tunnel, the top of a knobbly black head surfacing to knock into the side of the boat, sending waves cascading out in all directions.

Anwei tore open her bag, gasping for clues as to how to fight this creature. A *snake*, just like the snake-tooth man. Was it *him* inside that gnarled skin? She rifled through her packets, tears prickling in her eyes when none of it made any sense anymore, not the herbs, not the cave, the snake's scales, muscles, and humors, not the white clouding over the creature's eyes, not the bits of rot around its nostrils as it started toward her. It felt like standing on a bloody beach, her parents and the elders advancing with their knives while she had nothing, because all the weapons she'd found were sitting in unmarked packets. She'd always been able to tell them apart without looking, without *thought*. Now they were nothing more than different colors of powder.

Her mind was an empty cup, her years of healing, her training, everything draining out through the crack made by that *god*. She could still feel him there, watching, as if he meant to be sure she failed, no matter what she tried. Hand groping in the bag again, her fingers closed around one last hope: the fancy button that marked the packet of Sleeping Death.

"Anwei, *get out of there!*" Altahn yelled.

The snake was coming around again, racing toward her with its open maw gaping up above the water, a body too big, too old, too *much* for something so small as a packet of herbs.

"*Anwei!*"

Something hit the boat, and suddenly Anwei was underwater, the sword dragging her down.

The sword. She had a *sword*. But the current dragged it one way and wrenched her medicine bag in the opposite direction. Water pressed against every inch of her body as Anwei frantically groped through the darkness trying to find which way was up. Twisting to look for light and air and life, all she could see were black scales, black tongue, black teeth gaping toward her—

Something jetted down into the water between Anwei and the snake, exploding in a shower of bubbles and flame between them. The water roiled with the burst of burning salpowder, and the snake darted away in a cloud of black blood.

Anwei kicked up to the surface, greedily gulping down a mouthful of acrid air. She heaved the sword from the water, the metal clattering across stone.

"*Get up here!*" Altahn swore, a packet of salpowder in his fist, but he didn't light it. He jumped down from where he was perched halfway up the wall. "It can't reach this high!"

Water slopped over Anwei's head as she tried to pull herself up onto the rocky shelf. The current sucked at her long skirts, and she could barely keep her chin above the surface, little elsparn wriggling toward her and then away again. Altahn dashed down to grab hold of her wrists, hauling her up onto the rocks. Coughing, Anwei stumbled onto her feet and followed him to the wall, only pausing to grab the sword before she clawed her way up the vines to the rocky outcropping where Altahn had been hiding. As she pulled herself onto the platform, Galerey skittered down from the ceiling. The snake broke the surface again, the blunt tip of its nose following Galerey's progress as she hopped from vine to vine to land on Altahn's shoulder in a sparking, scrabbling heap. Galerey dropped something onto the ground next to Altahn, but he didn't pick it up, pulling Anwei back from the edge instead. "We have to get out of here. We're not going to be able to set off the salpowder distraction with that thing after us."

Only, their warning flare had already gone off, so Lia wouldn't be on the island to distract the Warlord and Tual until the main explosions in the caves ignited. Anwei's mouth was full of lake water and bile. They had to run. To hide *again*. Her plan to finally get to Tual Montanne, snake-tooth man, murderer of her life, was dead.

It *couldn't* be dead. Anwei felt scraped clean inside, the gashes where the nameless god had sat inside her still bleeding. She didn't *have* another plan, and she didn't have anything else to give up.

The sword sat dull at her feet like a question.

Anwei reached out to touch it just as Galerey hopped off the outcropping, Altahn running down with her. The lizard went one way, and he went the other, Altahn bending to swipe something out of the water before sprinting back toward the wall. Galerey circled around, the snake bursting out of the water toward her little form and slamming into the wall, barely missing. Galerey scrambled up through the vines and leaves past their outcropping until she was out of reach. The snake circled again, sending the canoe—upside down and aimlessly spinning—out into the middle of the swirling water.

Altahn climbed back onto the outcropping, his chest heaving. He was holding the oar. "What do you think, Yaru? Do you have a plan that will get us out of here before Tual Montanne realizes his pet snake found some intruders?"

The snake circled back lightning fast, ignoring the boat to strike up toward Galerey again. Its coils seemed to tangle when they lashed into the canoe. It turned, bumping the canoe with its blunt snout and recoiling with a dull thrum of distress, as if it hadn't expected to meet an obstacle.

White film across the eyes. Cataracts. The snake was *blind*. So how did it know where Galerey was hiding? Anwei reached out to pick up the object Galerey had dropped earlier: a little handle with flint and steel that, when you squeezed it, struck a flame. "Does Galerey have your aura right now?"

Altahn nodded, dropping the oar next to her. "You have that sword, and I have one more salpowder packet—it was meant to blow up the bigger packets, but—"

"Altahn, the snake can see *auras*. Probably has some kind of capacity to sense things near it or it would bump into walls, but it can't actually *see*." Anwei stood up, still hugging the sword close. It felt nice against her skin, like a plan. "Look. Come down."

"I'm not going down there just to experiment—"

But Anwei was already sliding off the outcropping. She stumbled as she landed, going farther down than she'd meant to. The snake darted out of the water toward her, teeth glistening. Anwei scrambled back up toward the ledge where she was still in sight but out of reach, her bag catching on a vine as she tried to pull herself back to safety. "Watch her!" she yelled.

"*Her*?" Altahn grabbed her hand and pulled her up the rest of the way. Behind them, the snake went still, its head cocking to one side and then the other as if listening to the echoes of their voices.

Rolling onto the ledge, Anwei stared down at the creature turning back toward Galerey. "Oh, she's obviously female."

"Great. Tell me how we escape the *giant female snake*."

"When you went down there with Galerey, the snake went for Galerey. And now that I'm out of range, she's after your firekey again, like we're not even here." She smoothed a hand over the rock, remembering Knox back at the tomb saying that the rock somehow blocked his aurasight. This stone was doing the same thing, blocking her aura from the snake's sight.

Altahn nodded slowly and dug into his open vest. The pockets were a soggy mess of salpowder, but he extracted one that was still intact, wrapped three times over in oilcloth. "This is all I've got. Show me your magic, goddess. We just need to get out of this chamber. I think the waterway is too shallow for the snake."

Anwei's eyes followed the snake's ripples as it went into the next passage with the statue, but then abruptly turned back.

Magic. Plans. Anwei's mind wouldn't work, the place the nameless god had been gaping like a newly pulled tooth. And Knox—

Anwei shivered despite the dense heat coming off the water and choking the air. She felt cold and small. Hollow. The sword sat there in front of her, the thing that had been eating away at him for so long. She picked up the sword and hugged it to her chest, her mind filling with finger stumps under the bed and blood soaked into her skirts. Of her mother with a knife, her father not even looking. A storm on the beach, and a life empty as hunger.

She hugged the sword closer. There would be time enough after everything was done to fix things with Knox. "We need the boat to get to the island," Anwei whispered, ideas beginning to crystallize in her mind.

"Get to the *island*?" Altahn started laughing. "No, no, no. G*iant snake,* Anwei. Flare already set off. I think they might know we're coming."

"I can't give up." Anwei's grip on the sword tightened, her fingers pressing so hard they felt melded to the sheath. So many years of searching a waste if they didn't go *now*. She stepped out onto the rocky outcropping and peered past the overgrown statue. "You shot salpowder through the water to get it away from me—will that last packet you have do that? It doesn't matter if it gets wet?"

"I can't shoot anything without a carom. All it did before was surprise the snake."

"But salpowder will burn underwater," Anwei pressed. "I saw it."

He put his hands up to ward her off. "Yes, if it's dry when it ignites. It's that distilled, crystalized kind left over from that stuff Knox stole off the docks in Chaol."

"The docks!" She tore open her bag and started pulling out vials from their sleeves along the side of the bag. In Chaol, Anwei had given Knox an acid to eat through the salpowder barrels, and it had caused a reaction with the crystalized salpowder, exploding the whole dock. Spreading the vials out with shaking hands, Anwei uncorked one and then the next, swearing when neither said anything back to her.

It had been clear. She separated out the ones that were clear, looking up when Galerey sent out a mournful chitter that echoed across the cave. Four vials. Acid. It had been strong enough to eat through wood in seconds, simmered over a slow fire under the temple in Chaol for weeks to achieve potency. "We'll break the acid vial in the outer layer of oilcloth."

"So the powder would still be dry inside all the layers after we threw it into the water, and the acid would set it off. . . ." Altahn looked down as the snake came thrumming up out of the water toward

Galerey, sending a wave of water over the boat. It had begun to dip down in the water. "How does that help us?"

"We'll make her swallow it." Anwei uncorked the first vial. Bracing herself, she poured a drop over her little finger. It was some kind of oil. She set it aside. "The acid will take a bit to react as it slowly leaks into the inner salpowder packets—"

"So it'll be in her stomach when it explodes and blow her in half." Altahn was already moving. "I'll get that started."

He called to Galerey something about moving, but Anwei didn't look to see what he was doing, opening the next vial. Biting her lip, she dripped it onto her skin. It burned a little, leaving a red welt, but then it was gone. Not the right one.

Third vial. Galerey sparked as she scrambled faster and faster through the vines, the snake roaring up to bite at her. Anwei opened the vial, gritted her teeth, and—

Burning. Anwei bit back a scream, dashing her fingers through the puddle of water at her feet, then wiping it across her wet tunic. Tears in her eyes, she recorked the vial and snapped for Altahn to hand her the salpowder. "Someone will have to go down there."

"Down . . . in the water?" Altahn's voice faltered.

"She swims with her mouth open, and with the way she's circling now we can see exactly where she's going. Galerey has your aura, so the snake won't see you. Jump in the water, break the vial, and make sure it goes down her throat." Anwei stood, holding out the packet. "I'll get the boat."

Altahn stared up at her.

She gave him a playful nudge. "I'll tell Noa all about it when we get back. You saving my life."

"Will I be alive for that conversation?" he asked quietly.

"Yes, and I would really prefer to keep you in one piece. We need you." The words came out easily, and Anwei suddenly realized they were true. Not because they'd need salpowder once they got to the snake-tooth man, or because they needed Altahn's horses or his wagon or his money, but because she'd come to like him. His calm exterior, his joking with Noa, Galerey, even . . . Anwei cared if he got hurt. The same way she'd come to care about Noa. About Lia some of the time. And Knox. Most of all Knox.

She bit her tongue to stop her face crumpling, the tears that wanted to come. Anwei didn't have room to care. Getting to Mateo and the snake-tooth man was all there could be until it was done, because everyone else kept getting in the way.

Anwei grabbed her medicine bag, then took up the sword. Altahn still hadn't moved, but she couldn't quite look at him, another person she'd somehow attached herself to when Anwei could only trust herself. "It's either die up here and let the snake-tooth man have our bones or die trying to get past this thing, Altahn."

Altahn frowned. But then he took the salpowder packet and pointed at her. "I want very specific descriptions. Lots of heroics."

"You actually like her, don't you?" Anwei laughed, but it was hollow like the rest of her as she forced her eyes toward the boat behind him. She pulled out the elsparn salve and smeared some extra down his arms while Altahn caked it across his neck and face. She hadn't seen many of them since the snake appeared, but avoiding the big snake just to be eaten by the little ones seemed like a poor trade.

Sticking the sword and the paddle through the medicine bag's straps, Anwei held her breath when Altahn jumped down from the ledge. The snake continued following Galerey's excited chittering. But when Anwei reached out to climb toward the boat halfway underwater on the other side of the cavern, the snake slowed, nose turning toward Anwei. Freezing, Anwei swore at herself, reaching the vines above to climb higher, her heart jumping when one tore away in her hand, leaving her dangling above the water.

Galerey gave a great squeal and dove into the water. The snake lashed to the side, darting toward the spot Galerey entered the water.

Moving as fast as she could, Anwei kept one eye on the boat, wishing she could see Altahn. It was too loud and too quiet in the cave all at once, water echoing off the walls, but not a single voice other than her own breath to keep her company. When she finally got to where the boat was pressed against the far wall, she tipped it to the side to empty out the water, then looked around for Altahn.

He hadn't come up for air, so far as she could tell. And the spot he'd gone under was laced through with a predatory glow, elsparn circling in a frantic dance.

Which was when the snake surfaced again, then dove toward the ruckus. Anwei swore—the snake probably *ate* elsparn, the disturbance they made in the water sending vibrations she didn't need eyes to see. She jumped into the boat and pulled out the paddle, thrashing around in the water just as Galerey did the same on the other side of the pool.

The snake didn't change course, moving faster around the edge of the cave toward Altahn. A flurry of prayers touched Anwei's tongue, like some terrible knee-jerk reaction to reach for the beings who had so blatantly shown her they weren't on her side. To Calsta, who claimed souls like the worst sort of shapeshifter, or the nameless god, who'd grown inside her like a choking vine, infecting her humors and thoughts, waiting for the right moment to strike.

And there was a voice, repeating the same thing he'd said earlier before he ripped her world out from under her.

It can't be for you.

How is this for me? she snarled in response. Her free hand flapped toward her medicine bag as if somehow it could help now and found the sword instead. She pulled the medicine bag free of her shoulder and let it drop like the dead weight it was and stood up, thrashing the water with the oar.

The snake swirled around, going deep down beneath the cluster of elsparn around Altahn. There was no way the salpowder was in its gut. There was no way Altahn could have held his breath so long, elsparn darting close, then away, but not letting him surface.

The spindly little voice didn't seem to care. You *put that man down in the water with an ancient terror holding nothing but a bit of salpowder. You sent Lia to face her worst fear, promising to get her out, then didn't show up. You poisoned your bonded partner and left him to die because he didn't agree with what you wanted. You'll do the same to me if you feel it's right in the moment.*

"I did not *hurt* Knox." The words tore from her, and Anwei let go of the vines as the snake circled beneath her, following Galerey. The elsparn suddenly moved together in one great shift, the snake turning to contemplate this development. "All I wanted was his goddess and his ghost out of my head!"

It was your bond holding him together, Anwei. What do you think happened when you broke it?

The snake had finally turned, the ripples heading for Anwei's boat. Her shoulder felt bare without the medicine bag, and she suddenly couldn't remember a time it hadn't been there, a solid weight that meant she wasn't powerless. That she wasn't standing bloody on a beach, knives drawn over her head.

That was what the god had been feeding her all these years. *Herbs.* To fight Tual Montanne, the shape of him more gargantuan and deadly than any snake. The ripples rushed at her, and Anwei grabbed for the only sure answer that had trumped any god: the pockmarked sword.

It burned in her grip as she held it tight between her hands, because suddenly she didn't need anything else. She never had. Only herself, and a proper weapon to kill a snake.

Before the snake's ripples hit the boat, something slammed into the prow, and arms grabbed hold of Anwei, Altahn's long hair streaming all around him in the water. He dragged her down, Anwei fighting hard, the sword burning in her hand as the snake streaked toward them.

And then, everything exploded.

Aria was there. Aria was screaming. Aria wouldn't let Lia pull the blanket from her head, so Lia grabbed her around the middle and hefted her over one shoulder, energy burning like fire.

She'd found her sister.

Lia ran for the door, cringing as she stepped over Mateo, who had melted to the floor like a puddle, his eyelids fluttering and his chest still. Not clawed, shadowed, *distorted* the way she must have imagined seeing through the window before kicking the glass in.

She paused, looking down at him, hiding up here despite his obvious sickness, almost as if he'd been waiting for her.

Maybe it's not what you think, Knox had said.

The fire in her humors wanted to roar and tamp down all at once. Anwei needed Mateo. That was why Anwei had really wanted to come. With Mateo they could stop Tual from killing anyone else.

Dipping down, Lia grabbed hold of his collar and dragged him out the door. Aria was wriggling so hard that Lia lurched into the railing, almost dropping her. "Aria!" she hissed, letting go of Mateo to set her sister on her feet and drag the blanket off her head. Her sister's aura looked wrong somehow, not quite the right shape or shade, as if she were sick. "I'm here! Why are you—"

The words swelled up in her throat, choking her. It wasn't just Aria's aura that looked wrong. Her sister's face was the wrong color, her hair in odd, sandpapery braids. Everything about her looked . . . off. There wasn't another word for it, but then Aria was grabbing her around the middle, arms too tight. "I knew you would come," she croaked against Lia's ribs. She grabbed Lia's hand and dragged her toward the stairs. "I know how to get out. We have to go fast!"

Lia lurched after her sister, dragging Mateo's dead weight. Her aura-sight combed over Aria's trying to find the source of *wrong* around her, but her sister looked healthy, rested . . .

"I knew you'd come." Aria bent to pull one of Mateo's arms over her shoulder, foot tapping madly as Lia took the other. "Come on! Quickly now!" She started down the staircase, Lia hobbling along, Mateo too heavy as if Aria wasn't holding any of his weight. There was a servant collapsed on the next landing and two guards splayed on the stairs below, their auras watery and thin.

More auras glowed to life in Lia's aurasight as they descended, each bled to the last drops. The Warlord flickered into Lia's aurasight in the same place outside the tower where Lia had seen her fall, gold flecks buzzing around her like flies on a corpse. And Tual. . . .

Tual was there too. In the courtyard, his aura thick enough to be a lightning storm. It towered over him, dimming everything else and growing every moment. He was out in the courtyard where she'd left the Warlord, aura so large it burned away even the thought of anyone else out there.

He wasn't moving. Why wasn't he moving?

"Which way, Aria?" Lia cried, stumbling down the last steps. She almost lost her grip on Mateo, his feet dragging down the steps after her.

Aria veered under the staircase into a shadowy niche. "You have to press those tiles—"

Lia dumped Mateo to the floor, and he fell like the bags of potatoes he was. She followed Aria's directions with shaking hands. "There's a passageway and a glass tunnel and some stairs and a way out past that—" Her voice came faster and faster as Tual's aura flared bright as a fallen sun just outside the tower.

"How do you know?" Lia hopped back as the door swung open. "They showed you the way out? Why did you stay here?"

"Mateo did—he always made sure I was all right. But then I got sick. Tual healed me, I guess, but probably only because Mateo told him to." Aria tried to lift Mateo, but he was too heavy, lying limp as if she hadn't touched him at all. Lia dragged him through the door with a curse.

And then Tual moved. He streaked toward them, outside one moment, then bursting through the tower doors the next, his aura like a war, lives swirling around him in a terrible flare. Dropping Mateo, Lia ratcheted the door shut and pulled the Warlord's sword to smash the latch. She sheathed the sword, grabbed Aria's hand, and ran into the tunnel.

"Wait, what about Mateo!" Aria dug in her heels, skittering along after her like an auroshe getting its first taste of a halter. *We need Mateo.*

There's a passage, he'd tried to say before collapsing. And Aria's little voice crowded in right after the thought: *Mateo made sure I was all right.* And Anwei's: *We need him as bait.*

Maybe it's not what you think, Knox had said.

Lia kept running. She needed Aria more than she needed Mateo, no matter if he was the boy she'd come to know in Chaol or something much darker. Aria's voice rose to a feral scream that echoed off the low tunnel ceiling as she fought Lia's grip, her fingernails digging into Lia's wrist. "We can't leave him there!" she screamed.

"We're out of time, Aria!" Lia cried. "Mateo is too heavy to carry. Tual will catch us if we try to bring him." She looked one last time at his still form on the ground before the passage turned, a pang of regret and hope like a seed planted deep inside her. But she didn't stop to let it grow or wither or burn. She dragged Aria around the corner, shivering when all the auras above her suddenly winked out.

Solemn statues and columns stood sentinel along the passageway, and Aria tried to cling to every one as they passed, crying for Mateo as if she'd forgotten what waited above if they didn't escape. It wasn't until Lia's boots hit glass that she heard Tual's voice.

"Lia Seystone." It hissed out from the passage behind her.

Aria tried to stop, but Lia dragged her into the glass passage, her sister's bare feet sliding frantically across the slick floor.

The terrible aura appeared in the corridor in a fury of fire and light.

Mateo's was there too, guttering like a dying candle in Tual's arms. "Please. Don't go this way, Lia." Tual's voice was terribly calm. "You'll die."

Aria's fingers were digging straight to Lia's bones, though Aria herself seemed to flicker and twist like she were made of smoke. "This is where I got sick. I was okay one second, and the next . . ." Aria began shivering. "Lia, it can't happen again. It can't happen to *you*. You can't go this way. Not without Mateo." Her voice echoed up and down the tube, glimmers of moonlight all around them.

They'd made it halfway across, the rocks of the island dark, and little glimmers of beasts in the water gaping toward her. Lia's muscles cried out even as Calsta fed them gold, giving her the strength to keep going. But Aria was shaking so hard she couldn't walk, jerking to one side and then the other as if she meant to knock Lia over. "We're almost to where it happened. Please stop, Lia!"

"You said it was a way out just a few minutes ago!"

"That was when we had Mateo to help us! Please, Lia, we need him. I can't leave him here!"

"A sky-cursed shapeshifter is holding Mateo, Aria! And if he could get you out, he would have done it the first day you got here." But Aria had collapsed, curling into a ball of shakes and muttering whispers. Lia fell to her knees next to her sister, trying to pick her up, trying not to think of her mother, skin of paper and thread. Of the burned remnants of their home on the Water Cay. And the terrible note. *Your sister misses you.* "Aria?" she cried, but Aria was wrong. Everything about this was wrong. Tual had promised to destroy her and everyone she loved if she went against him. And he didn't seem like a man who would go back on his word. "Aria, what is the matter?"

They were almost to the end of the tunnel, the opening a gaping black mouth.

"If you don't value your own life, at least let your sister live." Tual's voice crept across the glass toward her like frost.

Lia pulled Aria into her lap, heart beating like a battering ram as she hugged her close. Then she set her sister behind her, stood, and drew the Warlord's sword.

The sword wasn't enough. Not to face Tual Montanne. But if Tual had wanted Lia dead, he would have reached a fist right into her chest and taken every bit of her the way he had everyone else on the island.

When Tual stepped into the glass tunnel, it wasn't just his aura that had swollen too large. His body hardly fit, too big and too thin all at once, his head ducked over his son in his arms like a mantis with a meal in its clutches. When his head cocked toward her, Lia's whole body shuddered over the curve of Tual's nose and the beady black bleeding into the white of his eyes, none of him quite human. Mateo drooped in his father's claws, the ridiculous flowered jacket he was wearing hanging limp as wet butterfly wings.

Horror skittered through Lia even as her anger tried to fight it, and she found herself falling back a step. But then Tual held Mateo out like an offering, concern creasing his lined forehead. "What have you done to my son?"

"What have you done to my sister?" Lia croaked.

Tual's auraflare sparked like a campfire's abrupt snap, burning logs poised to crack and fall. Another step toward her, his mouth growing wide as he spoke, teeth poking out in jagged lines like an auroshe. "We are your family now, Lia."

"What did you do to her?" Lia repeated, stepping between him and Aria's huddled form. At least with Tual, she wasn't frozen. With Tual, she had a voice. "How do I fix it?"

"Come back upstairs with us, and I'll help her." He slid forward another step, his movements oddly jerky and skittering as if no part of him left was human at all. "Unless you want to stay here, trapped in this tomb." Mateo twitched in his arms.

Lia could feel her sister's aura flickering like a heartbeat behind her, like nothing she'd ever seen. Tual could have drained her and Aria both, could have taken Mateo to his pots and jars and fixed him rather than standing here talking. "Are you going to let me go, or are you going to kill me, Tual?"

"No one wants you to die." His voice lolled like a lullaby. "I can't *make* you stay. You'd never forgive Mateo. All I want is for you to love him so he can live."

"I know what you did with your own bond. What you already did to Mateo," Lia snarled.

"I won't force you to stay." Darkness slipped across his features, leaving only pinpoints of light where his eyes were. "But I'm not above providing incentive. Your sister will die if you take her away from me now."

Lia didn't want to break her gaze from Tual to check on Aria behind her. She held the sword up—it could hurt him. Distract him, at the very least. That much she knew from their fight in the tomb. She eased sideways an inch, gauging the distance between them.

Mateo's eyes snapped open. "Run, Lia!"

Run? In the split second before Tual moved, Lia felt Mateo's already guttering aura dim, and something in the glass around her seemed to contract, taking the air from Lia's lungs. She sheathed the sword, lunging toward Aria to scoop her up, only to stumble when the tube began to shift under her feet.

Hairline cracks spidered across the glass tunnel's floor.

"Run!" Mateo croaked. "Get to the other side!"

Lia lunged for Aria again, but Aria's tightly curled form guttered out like a candle's last gasp. Dropping to her knees, Lia pressed her hands to the glass, trying to find the hole Aria had fallen into. She had been *right there*. Where *was* she? Water welled like blood in the tunnel's cracks, spreading out from where Aria had been huddled, drops snaking down the walls.

A huge fissure splintered through the thick glass between Lia's feet, and the tunnel groaned, dipping at the center so Lia began to slide backward. Water sloshed around her ankles, and everything was so dark—

"Calsta above! *Run*!" Mateo screamed.

Lia ran.

She was up to her knees in water and then to her waist. The end of the tunnel gaped, the darkness calling all the names of the gods. The water sucked at her clothes, pulling Lia back from the escape, her hands grasping across the stone. But the rock came away in her hands, and suddenly Lia was underwater surrounded by shards of thick glass, the current sucking her down into the dark depths of the lake.

⚜

Water pressed in on all sides around Anwei, twisting and turning her in the wake of the explosion until she couldn't tell which way was up. She clutched the sword, refusing to let it pull her one way or another, her fingers wrapped around it numb. The water churned, and something large whooshed by. The snake was *angry*. Disoriented, Anwei stabbed the blade toward it and found flesh.

The creature writhed, wrenching the sword from her hands.

Lungs burning, and with one last, desperate kick, Anwei's face broke the surface, and she gasped down a breath of stale, rotten air. The water pushed her this way and that, the current from the snake's frantic movements seizing Anwei like a leaf caught in a stream. Blood ran like a river through the pool, stray hunks of flesh and scales knocking into Anwei as the water roiled around her.

The creature reared up out of the water over her, milky eyes pink with blood, black tongue flicking out from its mouth. Despite the sickly black holes in the side of its throat from the salpowder, it wound up, ready to strike.

Anwei screamed up at the snake, swallowing down her regrets, her anger, everything she had because she wouldn't bow.

Which was when the snake began to shrink. The scales on the end of its blunt nose twisted up into the nostrils, it's wide eye ridges and hooked jaws folding in on themselves like a hinge. Elsparn were massing around the snake, latching on to the bits of flesh and blood rifting through the water, swirling around Anwei's legs. One of them nipped at her, as if the elsparn salve had washed away. It probably had.

The snake was shrinking faster and faster now, but Anwei was occupied with kicking away from the swarm of elsparn. The creatures crowded under her as she tried to float on her back and stroke out of the cave.

Teeth found her leg, then her right foot, then her shoulder, little bites that tore through her. She kept swimming as something dark and wrong unfolded at the back of her mind, like a rot of her own to match Knox's. It was muddy, like a boil swollen hot and large in her mind, taking up space she didn't want to give.

You left him to die—that awful voice had said it, but it wasn't true. *You were the only thing holding him together.*

Her stomach roiled at the thought, worse than the elsparn gnawing at her fingers, her elbow, her back. *I only wanted to leave. I didn't want to hurt him. Did I hurt him?*

Did I do what the nameless god said? Did I kill Knox? A bite tore into her side and she cried out, wondering if this was some kind of gods-conjured punishment. Death one bite at a time for the girl who wouldn't do what they wanted. Even if it meant they didn't get what they wanted either: Tual would live.

Her head hit something in the water, and Anwei rolled out of her frantic stroke. Noa's ugly little ship? Hands grabbed hold of her, hoisting her onto the deck. They peeled the slimy bodies back, voices shouting for bandages. The deck was hard against her back, and another set of hands softly pulled her head up into a lap, a voice she didn't quite recognize filtering in through her ears as if they'd been clogged with water. Bandages were pressed to her wounds, and feet pounded across the deck.

Overhead, a sea of stars came into view. Anwei breathed out in one gush. She wasn't going to die alone in a cave, then.

Noa's face popped into her vision, the dancer's eyebrows knotted. "I know you must be in pain right now. . . ." She swallowed, hands reaching for her, then pulling back. Anwei shifted, wondering who was holding her so softly, tying bandage after bandage. "But we need you."

"It's worse than needing." That voice again. The one that wasn't Lia or Noa, not any of the Trib. It wasn't Knox. She inhaled, searching for clues, but only air came inside. "Get up, girl," the voice said.

Anwei sat up very slowly, the feel of blood slick against her skin. An old woman was sitting next to her, chin-length gray hair wet with water and completely loose. Not a single braid or twist or tail to say what she was. Her eyes were shadowed, and what looked like an old scar flowered from the corner of her mouth and down her neck.

There was something terrible inside this woman. Anwei could feel it. Something she recognized, like the beat of a heart she'd listened to a thousand times.

"Where's Altahn?" she said very carefully, not looking away from the woman.

"Here, Anwei. Galerey's all right too." His voice came from behind her.

"Where's Knox?" she breathed, the nameless god's words echoing through her mind.

The old woman's chin dipped, and she looked behind Anwei.

Skin crawling, Anwei followed her gaze.

Knox was lying on the deck.

No, *not* Knox.

A smile that was not his own twisted Knox's lips, and there was nothing of him in his black eyes. "I knew you'd come back for him," he croaked in his not-voice, Willow peeking out through all the cracks.

His eyes rolled back in his head, and he collapsed on the deck.

"Gods and monsters—" Anwei crawled toward him, unable to go

any faster, the feel of a sword in her hand where her medicine bag should have been. There was blood everywhere, his tunic soaked with it. "I need—Noa, Altahn, my things. Where are they?"

"I'll get your trunk." Noa ran, the others a blur as the forest went by, the oars moving fast.

"You want to save him." It was almost a question, the old woman's voice croaking out like dust from a grave. "I suppose we'll see how long that lasts."

Anwei ignored her, pulling back Knox's tunic to find the wound open, his insides muddled. Her hands began to shake as she stared down at the awful wound, Noa dragging the last of the herbs to sit next to her. "I need . . ." She faltered, her nose, her smell, her *magic* an empty corpse inside her.

"*What* do you need? I'll help you find it." Noa tipped the trunk over onto the deck, spilling the packets inside, useless every one. She couldn't discern one from the next, except for the one from Paran's shop, marked so everyone would know to stay away. Sleeping Death.

Anwei's hands dug into her braids. "I don't . . . I don't know. I can't . . ." She shut her eyes, speaking to the voice in her head. *Please. Whatever you are. I'm sorry. I didn't mean to do this.*

And then, like a solidifying sheet of glass, she felt a presence in her head, a little stronger than it had been before, as if being acknowledged somehow solidified its existence. But it said only one word: *No.*

It was a voice Anwei knew. A voice she *hated* that she knew, disgusted that for so many years, she'd mixed her own thoughts up with those of a god.

Anwei groped for Knox's buttons, then let go, not sure what she should do. Before, in the tomb, she'd only touched him, willing the parts that had been severed to grow back together. *Don't you gods have some kind of plan that involves both me and Knox? Help me fix him, or—*

Threats were exactly what I expected next, Anwei Ruezi.

A bitter shock ran through Anwei at the sound of her name connected to that other name. The one she'd shed so many years ago as if escaping it would mean she could escape the clutching memories of those who'd given it to her. She'd been nothing but Anwei since the day she stepped into that leaky rowboat under a lightning-cast storm, like a goddess. Calsta. Yaru. Anwei. They didn't need family names. Just one was enough to make their enemies shake.

Knox twisted under her hands, and something sparked in her mind. Part of him was still there, a thread caught on an exposed nail. "You're not helping him," the ghost whispered through his lips. "Why aren't you helping him? You love him."

"You're still connected to him. Is that why—" The old woman's voice vibrated like thunder, like earthquakes, like a storm—

"Anwei, please." Hands pressed into Anwei's shoulders, Noa's face blurring in Anwei's vision as she bent beside her. "What's wrong? Something is terribly—"

Names have power, Anwei. I know yours. I know who and what you are. The nameless god grew louder with each word, blocking everything else out. It solidified inside Anwei, like the rock and roots he was made of, strong as pain or hunger or hate, as if her sudden acknowledgment of his presence had built him into something tangible inside her. *Names tell you the shape of things. That's why the first Warlord worked so hard to take mine. Without my name I was a formless memory she could twist into anything she wanted. A worse evil than what people had seen or experienced with their own bodies. The nameless power, the nameless evil, the nameless* one, *so monstrous, words fail to quantify—*

"Shut *up!*" Anwei's fingers were digging into her temples, and the boat was swinging side to side, making her sick, and Knox wasn't breathing. He wasn't *breathing.* "Skip the history lesson and help me *fix this!* I'll do whatever you want. I know you can help me heal him, so *do it.* This is obviously not for me. It's for *Knox,* your friend Calsta's golden *toy.*"

The woman chuckled. "It's too late. The god doesn't even know it."

I know exactly who this is for, Anwei. The nameless god's voice was heavy, ropy, full of flowers and glass, the very depths of water and sharp treetops all at once, speaking only to her as if he hadn't heard the old woman's voice. *All these years I've given you the benefit of the doubt. You used my power to right wrongs, to cure the sick, to stop a corrupt society from loving their things too much. But tonight you showed me it is out of pain, out of trauma, out of a need for revenge. Your brother is alive, not dead, and that knowledge has changed nothing inside you. You mean to kill him too.*

He forgot *me!* Anwei screamed, not wanting to listen to the words. She hadn't thought about killing him, not directly. But the truth of it burned deep in her heart. *He didn't love me. Just like everyone else! You're the one who made me kill my family, the one who shook the whole earth and killed Altahn's father!*

The earth shook because you have no control—you used what I gave you to save Knox and brought down the whole world at the same time. Knox loves you. You would have been better off with his help tonight, but you chose to hurt him instead.

Anwei fell down next to Knox and tried to prop Knox up beside her like a banner because she was trying *now*. She hadn't understood before, and fixing it was what she wanted now. *I love Knox, too, but not because of you.* Anwei felt hard planks against her back, the place the sword was supposed to be pinched between her shoulder blades. Knox's arm flopped lifelessly onto her stomach because Noa was trying to move him. She couldn't tell if the words were inside her or out, if she was speaking out loud or if it was something else entirely, only that the one thing she always knew she could rely on deep inside herself was gone.

Which left . . . what?

I don't care who you love, Anwei Ruezi, Anwei the healer, Yaru the goddess, or whoever you think you are now. I care about who you actually are. Magic is power to heal or power to hurt. Power to build or power to destroy. Calsta's strength on one side of a relationship too easily turns foul, which is why her Devoted abstain until they return Calsta's oaths to her. There are exceptions only for those who come to the center from both sides of the magical sphere. For humans who have proved themselves to me and to Calsta time and time again, who we can trust to balance each other out. To bring their sacrifices together to represent all who they could serve. People who can listen to each other, trust each other, and see the world as a larger place as a result of who they are together. And tonight you chose yourself. *You chose* murder. *You chose your own plan over the good of everyone else. You have shown me who you are.*

Anwei twisted on the deck, Noa's hands on her shoulders, the world a tumult she couldn't hear, couldn't smell, could only feel as if her head had been sucked into some new world, leaving her suspended between the reality she knew and this new one until the nameless god spat her back out. She fought, pulling as hard as she could despite the anchors he had inside her, weighing her down. *Your system has worked out so very well in the past, hasn't it!* she snarled when he wouldn't let her go. *The shapeshifter wars and the five hundred years of Devoted murdering Basists are a wonderful example of how people with the power you can offer treat one another. My scars belong to* you.

The presence hooked into her brain seemed to shift, a terrible sadness growing like a vine around her heart. *Magic from two gods is great power. You can see clearly why there is a higher call, a higher accountability because of what you're capable of.*

I did not choose this, Anwei hissed.

I did not want to choose you either. The world is going to come apart, and we tried to stop it. The nameless god's voice seemed to delve deeper inside her, judging every last humor from which she was made. *Removing your power hurts* me. *It will hurt* Calsta. *It will hurt all in the Commonwealth who would like to breathe without fear, because without you and Knox bound together, Tual Montanne will rise. But with Knox dead and you untouched, it will be terrible.*

Anwei tried to find words that would persuade him, that could stop him, to bring him to her side, but he wasn't listening to words. He was inside her and had even less faith in her than she did. *I helped create the bonds that were meant to elevate you humans and gods into something greater. In doing so, I opened the door for something foul, twisted, and monstrous. I tried to bring the orders together to stop shape-shifters from destroying all that was good and failed. I tried to stop the injustice being done to the Commonwealth and failed. I tried to stop Tual Montanne, but I failed.*

His voice seemed to pry into her entire being, looking one last time. *At last I have learned to be wary.* You *I can stop. Goodbye, Anwei.*

And the world was silent, and dark, nothing but stars above her and Knox too still beside her.

Something reared up in her field of vision, blocking the pinpoints of light. "Your god is angry. He did not even see me here. Rude, after all our years together." The woman's husky laugh sent needlepoints down Anwei's skin, every word twisted by an accent she'd never heard in all her travels. "He commands as if he has not already failed with you two. There is a chance, I suppose. If it weren't possible to fix, I would have killed you already."

Anwei looked down the length of the boat, suddenly wondering where this old crone had come from, where Noa and the others had gone. They were there, all four of them rowing. Even Noa, though Anwei had never seen her pick up an oar once in her entire life. The boat was moving fast down the tributary, all of them perfectly in sync with one another as if they couldn't hear or see anything but the river before them, which had to be conquered. Her skin prickled, and she looked back toward the old woman, holding their minds like little parchwolf pups on a leash.

She sat up slowly, fitting the shape of the snake from the cave into this little woman's body. A snake like the one carved into Tual's tooth. Her hands clenched, missing the shapeshifter blade.

The woman stepped back, a littering of unused bandages around her feet. "Don't embarrass yourself, Anwei. Do I look like that bratty little shapeshifter who's barely learned to blow his own nose?"

Anwei cringed at the sound of her name, the nameless god's awful accusations like a stone in her chest. "You can read my thoughts?"

"Many who have betrayed the oaths can. There's quite a bit of variation, of course—it depends on our strengths pre-caprenum and that of our bondmate. Tual Montanne and I can both hear thoughts, and introduce new ones too, provided we have enough energy. Create triggers in someone's mind so new memories come forward when old ones interfere. We can even change what people see right in front of their eyes." Her head turned toward Altahn and the others at the oars. "Though I only nudge, these days. Little enough I don't hurt anyone."

The old woman tipped her chin up to look at the stars, light falling over her white cataract-dusted eyes, but Anwei could feel her attention like a vise closing around her. "No matter what that old god tells you, you're already like me." She sat down in front of Anwei and clasped her hands in her lap. "It hurts, I know. But there's something different here, which is perhaps why he cannot see it." Even as Anwei watched, the flowering scars at her mouth and down her neck—right where the salpowder had burned the snake—began to fade. "Tell me how you managed to put this boy in my sword without killing him all the way." She nodded toward Knox, her eyes narrowing a hair. "Tell me how the girl who was already inside my sword still clings to life. They both live when it should be impossible. Tell me. Then maybe we'll be able to help each other."

CHAPTER 23

Like a God

Mateo could hardly see, his heartbeat a far-off rumble, like an avalanche that would bury him forever if he didn't run. Water from the broken walkway swirled over them, deep enough that Mateo felt his father sway as he frantically tried to set Mateo back on his own feet.

Bits of stone and glass from the ruptured tunnel slashed Mateo's skin as the water swelled up higher into the catacombs. The rush of energy Tual had pushed at him in the tunnel was gone, and Mateo was a hole to nowhere, a break in the fabric of the world fit only to suck away the life all around him.

"Close this off, son! Think of what you want, then *take it*!" Tual yelled. It almost seemed gleeful despite the danger. "I can share with you. Take from me!"

Mateo could feel the glass trying to repair itself, but it wasn't growing fast enough. He reached out into the stone, begging it to close off the tunnel before they drowned. The water was up to his chest, splatters on his face making him choke, but Tual's hands were on his shoulders and a rush of energy flowed into him, his father like a bonfire behind him, brighter than any person had any right to be. Like a god.

The stone creaked.

Water up to his neck.

Tual's energy tore through him, the stubborn, Basist-made walls refusing to budge until Mateo screamed, *Move!*

The wall snapped into place in front of him, the fabric of stone trembling. And Mateo could feel it. The wrongness of the wall he'd just made to block the water, the stone contorted and straining to do his will.

The water in the passageway went still as if there had never been a hole leading into the lake, there'd never been anything but this solid wall and a pool of still water, the sudden lack of sound like a new kind of emptiness inside Mateo. The world glimmered around him like something to be undone, power that would all someday drain through him to the nothing on the other side.

"That was *perfect*—" Tual was all jubilation, his arms gripping around Mateo's middle to pull him up from the water. Mateo could hardly move, couldn't help as his father laid him out on the ground, cold, wet stone pressing against his cheek. But then Tual's hands were on his shoulders again, and another rush of energy burst through Mateo, sending him coughing and spasming up from the floor. He breathed in, his lungs filling in ways they never had after his father's infusions before.

It was direct. Like when Willow had taken Aria's life between her teeth and bitten down.

"Lia," he gasped. "I broke the glass like you said, but I was supposed to get to her before she fell through. We were supposed to get out together so I could protect her from Abendiza—pretend to protect her from you!" His knees buckled, his arms limp as boiled cabbage. He was supposed to be strong. He *had* been strong.

"No, it was perfect, *perfect*, Mateo!" Tual was pulling him up from the ground, his voice echoing up the tunnel like a ghost's warbling cry. "Abendiza went out into the waterways today, so I'm sure Lia's fine."

"But how can Lia get back out? The Warlord was right there, and the rest of the people Lia came with were trying to get in. Something happened to Knox . . . and my sister . . ." Something else. Someone else. Mateo's brain was fuzzy with swords and Lia and the blank space where Willow was supposed to be.

The thought of a little girl rippled through him, an unholy smile and a sweet roll sticky in her hand. A little girl Lia had been dragging down the tunnel who'd been shouting his name as if she didn't want to stab him through the heart . . .

Aria. Mateo's breath caught. How could he forget? "Where is Lia's sister? She was here—"

"Don't worry about Aria." Tual pulled Mateo close into a hug, and the thought of Aria melted away. "This is all going to work out. You're going to go out there and tell Lia what a monster I am and get her to escape with you. Once you're truly bonded, you'll be able to bring her home." The smile sat tired in his voice, stretching out into something hollow and small. "I don't want you to go, Mateo. I'll miss you too much."

Mateo gripped his father tight, like he was the anchor, the one solid thing in his life. Tual Montanne had done nothing but protect him, heal him, *save* him, and Mateo wanted to go back to that space. To pretend there were no plans to play out, no gods waiting to destroy them, no bones to be dug up. That it was just him and Tual against the world.

But there was too much.

"Willow is gone," Mateo gasped. "Something happened, and she just *left*. Right after trying to *eat Lia*. And she keeps going on about the sword—"

"What do you mean she's gone?" Tual pulled away, looking at his son.

"I mean one second she was trying to control me," Mateo wheezed. "Bursting out of me like a monster. You never told me that shapeshifting wasn't a *choice*—"

"Isn't a choice?" Tual's brow quirked. "I suppose it's a side effect of using magic sometimes. It can change you. But it can be intentional—as easy as sculpting your face to look rounder or fuller, the length of your spine. Some of those old shifters did it enough that the more extreme changes stuck, or maybe they liked their new forms—"

"No, Willow *did it* to me. It wasn't some side effect; she saw Lia and just went berserk. And then something happened with Knox and she went back to him." Mateo stumbled as his father tried to pull him up, the energy Tual had pushed into him holding. But Mateo could feel it leaking, one drop at a time.

"You're going to need infusions consistently again. Like in Chaol." Tual was already nodding as if this were no big thing. A slow burn of anger rose inside Mateo at the memory of the ghost swelling up inside him at the sight of Lia. Lia wasn't some prey to be eaten, not a quarry to hunt down. Willow had said—Willow had made him *believe* Lia was nothing more than a bauble to steal for a few moments. A set of clothes to don.

He pressed his hands to his face, the grainy feel of shattered stone rough against his skin, and the memory of death and rot on his tongue. That had been how he was thinking about Lia. Like a hunk of caprenum at the bottom of a tomb. Not as someone of flesh and bone and blood and warmth and wit and—she didn't belong pinned to a shadowbox and mounted on the wall next to Patenga's sword in the artifact room. She was fire and sharp smiles and fury and *life*.

That was why he'd liked her in the first place.

Lia hadn't even looked at him when she'd come through the window. All she'd wanted was Aria.

And Mateo was suddenly back in that last day in Chaol, staring at his ceiling, wondering how the world could have dealt him a hand where his life depended on a girl like Lia Seystone falling in love with him. She didn't care that he *existed*, it seemed. And . . .

With all the swords and kidnapping and forced betrothals and death, it wasn't so hard to see why. Mateo's fingers pressed harder and harder into his skin, human and smooth instead of clawed. Lia didn't need him, but he needed her. His body had never been his own, but now even his mind was shared space. Willow's absence was like losing all the bones from his body, but at least it was all *him* inside there now.

The feel of energy in the tunnel was like salpowder blasts and the full might of Calsta's sun. It had been burning around Tual like a crown, strong and terrible and *too much*. Which was when he realized his father had stopped walking, his arm around Mateo limp, and his other hand grasped tight to the dagger at his waist. And he was whispering.

Mateo slowed, horror squirming like worms burrowing deep in Mateo's stomach when Tual didn't seem to notice, continuing on down the passage. Muttering to himself with his eyes closed. "Father?"

Tual's eyes sprang open. "I think . . . yes. If you're going to need constant infusions, then I'll need to show you how to take bits of energy in a controlled fashion. You'll need a constant source of energy. The Warlord suspects you already so the seclusions won't be a good idea." He started up the tunnel, hands clasped behind his back, pausing to be sure Mateo could follow. " . . .Perhaps the Warlord herself has already provided a source for us to use."

"An energy source? What do you mean?" Mateo's legs were still wobbly as he tried to keep up, passing grave marker after grave marker, names sticking in his head as he walked. *Alfonso. Gabriela. Ivo.*

Tual was practically running by the time he got to the hidden door. He slowed to frown at the shattered latch before pulling it open and striding out into the tower. "We can change the plan a little and have the two of you stay here. I'll need energy to make that work, of course. She won't want to believe that I'm someone she can trust. Not after everything. So, we'll have to come up with a story she does want to believe. Maybe that I'm dead? That she killed me?" He shook his head as he got to the front doors, a grimace on his face. "I don't like the idea of hiding in my own home, but needs must, I suppose?" Hand on the door, he looked back at Mateo. "How long do you think it will take for the two of you to establish a firm bond? Weeks? Months? A year or more?"

"What are you talking about?" Mateo stepped into the moons' light, Jaxom and Castor mixed in a grayish puddle on the floor. "How could I bring Lia here? *What* resource? And the Warlord is *here* and already thinks I'm a shapeshifter, and if we don't give her a cure—"

"Oh, I'm not worried about the Warlord." Tual pushed out through the doors. "And the answer is, of course, what it always has been. Lia will believe what she wants to believe with a little help from me. It would have been too much for me to handle before, but now, with this—" He pulled the dagger free. "I can do anything."

Mateo's skin pebbled with cold. "You mean you can make her . . . not remember. You can—"

"I made her see Aria tonight, didn't I?"

Mateo's mouth hung open, his tongue dry. *He'd* seen Aria tonight. Had none of it been real? The questions about the Ivy King? The game of scales? The screams?

"Lia wanted to find her sister here, so it was easy to make sure she did," Tual continued. "Just like your family wanted to forget you. All except your sister. Her mind wouldn't stick." Tual held up the dagger, staring at the dulled edge. "With the dagger. I can see how to target it, how to shape things. There has to be some kernel of *wanting* for it to take, but it won't be like trying to strike one heart with a hundred arrows like back on your island. I messed that one up. There's still a wave of energy I left behind in Belash Point, taking people who walk through."

"On Belash Point. My sister . . ." The darkness seemed to bead on Mateo's skin, heavy where it touched him. *There has to be some kernel of wanting for it to take.* What had his father taken from him?

Why had he wanted to forget?

Did he still want to forget? Was that why things were creeping back in through the holes in his mind?

"Why did you make me forget my family?" he whispered. "Everything from before?"

Tual stared at the blade a moment longer, then let it drop. "I didn't make you do anything. You knew what they were, what they meant to do to you, and you didn't want it inside you either. You didn't *need* it, Mateo."

"And my sister? You said she was a victim too. That she fought back, that it was her who—" Cracking wood and screams and snapping bones . . . Mateo closed his eyes, willing for it all to go away. "It was her who killed all those people on Belash Point. I didn't know before, didn't even know it *happened*. Why do I know now?"

Stepping up to him, Tual pulled Mateo close again. "Memories are tricky things, Mateo. But I don't blame you for not wanting to remember them. For wanting a new life with someone who loves you without the stain of an old one to ruin it." He pulled back to hold Mateo's gaze. "You and me. Against the world."

Mateo nodded shakily. Not wanting to remember. Not wanting to think of any of it. The Warlord and Cath lurking somewhere on the island, the Devoted out there in the trees. Of Anwei and Knox and whoever else was in their crew.

Tual took hold of Mateo's arm and led him all the way back to the antiquities room, where things of stone, clay, bronze, and steel stared at him like old bones of the past no one wanted to remember, the Warlord removing every last hint she could find. Patenga's sword seemed to drink in the light seeping through the window, even the moons looking away from the dull memory of Patenga's blasphemy. It had been an act of violence for the first Warlord to erase the whole Commonwealth's memory. Even the bad parts.

And, as the image of a little girl with half her hair in braids flicked through his mind, Mateo wondered whether forgetting was really what he wanted.

"So, a story we could tell her." Tual stared up at the sword.

"One to bring all of them here. I'm learning that it isn't just any caprenum sword, but your specific sword that matters— That boy, the one I killed who didn't die—does he have it?"

"I don't know." Willow was too far away to tell him.

"If he hasn't brought it with him, then it's probably still in Patenga's tomb." Tual rubbed his hands together. "We'll need it eventually. But until then, your sister came for me out of some kind of revenge, I guess. Why not give me to her? Tell Lia and the rest of them that you'll show them some secret way in—the channel is a little straightforward, but perhaps one of the other waterways? Tell them I'm everything they fear and worse." Tual started for the door, going toward the stairs, gaining speed and excitement as he went. "Some of them will fall in the attack, leaving you and Lia here with Hilaria to cook for you and tuck you in at night—"

"Just the two of us here?"

"And her auroshe. I already put Vivi in a stall while you were all coming down the stairs. Far enough from Bella that she won't be scared, I promise." Mateo felt him pause in the entryway, his voice a thing of bright afternoons and cozy evenings tucked away with a sweet roll, charcoals, and a fresh sheet of vellum. "Lia will love it here—it'll be safe. Away from everything she's lost. She already likes you, Mateo. It'll be easy."

Mateo turned away from the sword, looking out into the light dusting over the entryway of this place he loved, his father crackling with energy on the stairs. Thinking of that last day in Chaol, Lia sitting in his kitchen with a cup of tea on the table before her as if she belonged. How she'd looked among his father's books and listened when he spoke, answering back with real thoughts and arguments, the two of them poring over the old paintings together as if they fit.

They *had* fit. And he wanted it again. The idea of Lia being here, not with a sword but with that smile he'd only gotten to see for one afternoon, glowed inside him. He'd show her the beaches where he'd painted, the high rocks on the far side where you could see Abendiza in the deep making ripples across the whole lake. The window where Hilaria left pies to cool as if she didn't know Mateo would take one, then rearrange the others to cover the gap. The channel with its trick to get in and out, the turquoise boat he'd painted with Tual. They'd walk through the streets of Kingsol, past the shops where he'd bought coats and shoes tooled with silver and pigments and vellum. The glass tunnel—

The tunnel, which had broken to pieces all around Lia, her hair a snarl, sword sharp as the gleam of murder and panic in her eyes. The tunnel where Aria had fallen, the feel of her slippery in his mind.

Willow had done it. *She* was the dangerous one. She was the one who had hurt . . . *Aria*. Even her name was hard to keep hold of, wriggling in his grasp. "What about Aria?" he called before he could lose hold of her, her name clenched tight behind his teeth. "Where is she?"

Tual smiled, and something in Mateo twisted hard for some reason, knowing whatever his father said next was going to be a lie. "Aria's just fine. You rest. I'll go pack some things for you—we don't have much time."

He ran the rest of the way up the stairs, disappearing in a flare of light as if he couldn't see the shimmery glass of Mateo's dream shattering. Because if he persuaded Lia to stay on the island, he wanted the things here to be *true*.

There's not one part of you that's true. The memory of Willow's cackle was enough to set Mateo walking out the front door to stare out over this place that had been his haven. Which was when he saw it.

The tiny fluttering of gold specks between him and the tower.

Mateo strode down the steps before he could look away from the Warlord lying on the ground, one arm under her at an odd angle as if she'd fallen on it. The sight of her prone with her aura gathered like a swarm of flies made the anger rise in him like a serpent rearing up. He was glad she'd fallen. He was *glad*—

But then he caught sight of a humanish lump on the ground behind her. Mateo stopped. Not wanting to know, not *wanting*—

A long blond braid lay limp next to the body. Cath. Not a single spark of gods-touched energy left to dance above what was left of her.

The sun hat he'd borrowed from her was still sitting in the tower by Aria's bed.

Something prickled up his neck, as if somehow Cath was watching him. Tual had said the Warlord brought them the energy source they needed. Were there more Devoted somewhere nearby, their energy, their souls of lightning and thunder waiting to be taken?

The world needs to change. The old refrain breathed in his mind, waiting for him to take it up. *They killed us for centuries, weeding out any last hint that the nameless god still existed. We were going to show them different. That's why we started looking for tombs, why we entered the Warlord's circle to help cure wasting sickness. . . .*

But that *wasn't* why. The feeling of being watched had turned from prickles to knives, the air taut, and the trees too silent, as if every Devoted ever drained was hovering there watching to see what he'd do next. Mateo's *father* was the cause of wasting sickness. Entering the Warlord's circle had been for access to their energy. And all of what Mateo thought he'd been trying to accomplish was a lie.

One thing was certain: now that Tual had his dagger, he could take everything he needed, just like Willow wanted Mateo to do. He wasn't concerned with hiding any longer.

Turning away from the Warlord's lingering aurasparks, Mateo froze at the sight of something moving across the bridge. Raised hackles, bloody scales, a mouthful of broken teeth, and eyes just for Mateo.

It hadn't been Cath or any ghost watching him.

It had been Rosie.

The auroshe's nostrils flared, and she started toward him—no, toward the two Devoted lying still on the grass between Mateo and the bridge, the Warlord's softly beating heart an easy prize to claim. Mateo ran to stop her. "Rosie!" he yelled, trying not to think of the stripped bones they'd found on the trail. Of his own bones stripped the same.

Of the eyes on him while he slept, the dead mouse. Aria shuddering as she looked into the woods.

"Rosie!" His heart began to trip, his knees wobbling as he fell before her on the path, the last thing between her and easy meat. "Please," he coughed, groping for a stone, a bit of dirt to throw, even his drawing supplies gone. "I probably couldn't stop you, and I don't know why I think you're reasonable—" The auroshe slunk past the two Devoted, crooning dangerously. Her black eyes didn't blink, focused hard on him. "This was a terrible mistake, wasn't it?" he breathed.

Rosie charged toward him, Mateo's hands coming up as if that were some kind of defense against fangs. He clenched all his muscles tight and shut his eyes, waiting for her to tear into him. Instead, something knocked into his shoulder, pressing hard enough to knock him out of a crouch onto the ground.

He opened his eyes to find Rosie nuzzling him, little crooning noises coming from between those long, jagged teeth, her inky black eyes closed as she bumped him again like a little puppy.

Hands shaking, Mateo put a palm to the spot between her broken horns, remembering Lia's hands on his. *We'll call her Rosie.* Rosie chortled, jerking back abruptly, Mateo bracing for the feel of jagged teeth against his throat. But the auroshe twisted her long, serpentine neck toward the tower.

The monster watching through the carriage window, Aria had said. She looked just like Lia. They shared the same blood. Was it possible Rosie could feel it and had been trying to look out for her? Staring in her windows at night, watching from the other side of the bridge.

Not just the other side of the bridge. Mateo thought of the bloody mouse on his floor, like an offering from a cat. Aria had found one in her room too.

Rosie keened, throwing her head back and ending in a terrible screech. *Aria's fine,* Tual had said.

Mateo stumbled back from the tower, heading for the stables. Harlan would know where Tual had put Aria if she wasn't in the house. He could visit Bella—Bella always calmed him. But the moment Mateo passed the courtyard, he caught sight of the stable doors cockeyed, something dark lying between them.

And he couldn't look.

He turned toward the house, suddenly wondering at how empty it had been, the kitchen windows open this late at night. And there was Hilaria inside.

Unmoving.

A terrible cry wrenched free from Mateo's throat, and he was running, slamming through the kitchen door, and there she was, Hilaria as rumpled and frizzy as ever, facedown in the bowl of blueberries he'd brought from town, a little pile of green ones set aside as if she'd been picking through them in the middle of the night. Grabbing hold of her wrist, Mateo pulled her off the counter, sinking to the floor with her as he felt for a heartbeat. He sat there, afraid to even breathe until he found the slow tick of her heart, as if it had been waiting for a safe moment to come out.

She was alive. Barely.

Someone had borrowed her energy when he came up short.

Something chittered at the kitchen window, and Mateo looked up to find Rosie at the glass. Waiting.

He carefully laid Hilaria faceup on the floor and stood. The first step was hard, but then the others that followed went too quickly. Mateo followed the auroshe across the courtyard to the tower doors. Up the stairs to the tower's highest floor, Rosie climbing the steps as daintily as a mountain goat kid. He couldn't breathe, and it wasn't because of the hole inside him. It wasn't because of Willow.

Mateo pushed open the door.

And there was Aria. Up where no one would stumble across her by accident.

Rosie gave a horrible screech, slithering toward the bed. It was just as it had been the night before: *One Thousand Nights in Urilia* bookmarked on the bedside table. A plate of scones, stale, without a single bite missing. A hand of cards on the table, dealt down and untouched.

Glass on the floor from the broken window was scattered across the bed and over the figure lying still under her blankets. Her eyes blank, her mouth open, her skin too white, just as it had been down in the tube when she'd first fallen.

Aria was dead.

Mateo sank to the floor, fingers tearing at his hair. The world fuzzed around him, the chair, the bed, the broken window, the body, the *body*—

No. Mateo went over it in his mind. He'd held Aria until his father came home, and Tual had done something, some shapeshifter miracle to bring her back. He'd seen her wake up. There had been white powder on her chin, powder like the stuff stuck to her now. . . .

But every moment after she woke up, Aria had been fuzzy in his mind. Shadowed, not quite right. Melting away so Mateo hardly remembered what he'd done, that she was ill, that she was on the island at all.

I deserve to live, Willow had said. The energy she's taken from Aria was proof she wasn't waiting for someone else to give her permission.

Was it possible that Tual hadn't healed Aria with a miraculous herbal tincture? Aria wasn't a ghost like Mateo and Willow, both clinging to the underside of life like ticks, fat and healthy so long as there were souls to eat.

Rosie chortled, snuffling her way toward the bed, which was when Mateo saw a bulge in the bed skirt, as if something was hidden under the bed. He pulled up the fabric to find a Devoted. Shaved. Scarred. Shriveled. Dead.

There had been bits of aura and energy around Aria that Mateo hadn't been able to understand all the way back to the caravan down to the island. Energy Tual used to show Mateo the reality he wanted to believe. A reality that didn't involve Tual kidnapping ready souls to suck. There'd been the wagon with the tarp tied down tight. One abandoned in the road to be picked at by animals once he was dry. The other . . .

Mateo dry-heaved, unable to look. Not at the Devoted. Not at Aria's still form, the dusting of white around her mouth, just like the white in the wagon bed. Aria's fate had been sealed the moment she'd fallen.

He'd known it when he picked her up in the tunnel. He'd known it while he held her slowly dying body, and he'd known it when his father whisked her away and brought her back to miraculously wake.

Mateo had known it and hadn't wanted it to be true just the way he hadn't wanted to think about Lia. And so Tual had given him something else to believe. And Mateo had believed it. Because he wanted to.

Rosie's pointed nose nuzzled against his arm, the auroshe giving a high-pitched whimper. Shaking, Mateo reached out to touch her neck, her hair crusted with dirt. "We have to go," he whispered.

Knox woke with a gasp. Ice crusted across his face and down his arms and legs, burning with cold. He put a hand to his head, looking around at a velvety darkness that seemed to be all that was left of the world. Pinching his eyes shut, he tried to remember. There had been pain and lights and dark and voices and Calsta crying and *Anwei*, but now there was nothing. He could breathe, so he wasn't dead. But it didn't change the nagging feeling that he *was not*.

Or rather, that he *was no longer*.

Calsta promised endless skies after death, but this place, whatever it was, was not endless. Knox stood up and found he had legs, reached out to touch the darkness to find he still possessed arms and hands. The black around him wasn't exactly shadow. It was tangible, like wool that had been spun into darkness. Soft, but vaguely menacing.

Knox paced the length of the circle of light around him, only it seemed to pace with him, keeping him near to the center. When he looked up, feeling for Calsta's power, there was no ceiling, and no sky, and none of the goddess's energy inside him. There were only shadows, or perhaps a star-broken night up there, or maybe it was nothing. A *between* where all lost things ended up.

"Anwei?" He coughed, choking on the air, which was dusky and purpled, making it hard to see more than a few feet around him. Anwei had left, and it had pulled him apart.

But she wasn't . . . gone? There was a thin thread, just one single trail that seemed to point out of this nowhere. The moment he discovered it, the thread ignited, burning like salpowder in his chest.

"Knox?" a voice whispered.

Knox froze, the sound of his name made from bone dust and rot prickling down his spine. It was a voice he knew well. He turned very, very slowly.

The little girl standing behind him hadn't been there before. She was wearing a white nightgown and a blank stare, both of which Knox thought he should remember but couldn't. Her hair was dark, her eyes dark too. Lace decorated the bottom of her nightgown that looked so familiar. Like the bits of lace Willow had made for a dress when they were young.

Knox swallowed when the girl stepped into the half-light around him, blinking as if she had been in darkness a long, long time. "You finally came," she whispered, her voice wet with tears.

The shape of her wouldn't hold steady in Knox's mind, this little girl who he'd always thought of as bigger than him, the one he'd found dead, a pockmarked sword shoved through her heart. And he couldn't hold it in—his arms stretched out to touch her, comfort her, wanting desperately for her to be real. . . .

This was the girl he'd set out to save. The one who'd been so frightened in his mind, crying for her brother.

Tears ran down her cheeks, and she ran toward him, her arms out. "Knox! I knew you'd help me. I knew—"

Which was when he saw the ash-gray claws gripping her shoulders.

Knox fell back a step. The shadows followed Willow toward him, a haze of shimmering *nothing* that shrouded the rest of the creature holding her tight. She faltered, sagging to a stop when his arms dropped. The bond inside him a thin string of fire pulled so tight he feared it would snap. It was the only warmth in the misty cold.

Willow's head drooped. "I thought you came for me."

The claws at her shoulders dug in, and she stumbled, the shadows following, folding over her to turn the nightgown to shreds and her insides to rotting bone. Her face contorted as she fell into shadow, her eyes growing large, her bones growing and shifting. "Are you giving up now, after all this time? They said you had to take your love and then maybe I could . . . go back out there with you. I want to come out because then maybe they'll go away."

"Who will go away?" Knox rasped. His whole body wouldn't unclench.

"It's too late, isn't it?" Her eyes swelled up to twice their size, the pupils narrowing to slits. Her voice lowered just a little, the words slipping out as if they were her own, but all Knox's hair stood on end at the dissonance threaded through her, a chorus trying to imitate one little girl. "You waited too long. She took the sword, and then she took you."

Willow stumbled forward into the light, and her eyes went back to brown. Her long braids were suddenly pinned neatly across her head, a beaded headband appearing to hold them in place, then twisting into a clip with jeweled butterfly wings that glittered and flapped when she moved. The nightdress shifted so it was longer, dragging on the floor behind her like a train. "I can think better now that you're here."

Knox's mind raced, only it was the race of something tired and flustered, wanted to shy away from what she was saying. But Knox didn't know how to shy away from anything, so he looked at it straight on, even the thing hunched behind his sister, its claws threaded through her hair. *Willow was in the sword.*

Which means either she's out—he looked around again at the not-room with its not-walls and dusky not-air—*or I'm inside the sword too. Anwei walked away from me when I needed her. She severed the bond between us.*

She killed me.

And now I'm in a shapeshifter's sword.

Which means . . . Alarm trilled through him, remembering every strand of purple that slunk through Anwei's aura, every sideways look, every lie she told, a smile on her face begging to be believed. *Caprenum is how shapeshifters are made. Kill the one you love. Steal their power.*

But she'd *taken* the sword, not stabbed him with it. And their bond, he could still feel *the last thread*—

The darkness behind Willow shifted, and she moved again, the clawed fingers gripping her shoulders tighter as if she were the puppet and it the strings. Knox braced himself, running through forms, attacks, and training exercises in his head as it observed him from the safety of its shadows with a glint of needlepoint teeth and a glimmer of malice in more than one set of eyes.

But it was Willow there. The girl he'd almost forgotten. His heart tore at the sight of her off-center, the little clip's wings fluttering madly as the shadow made her reach for his hand. "We're special, you know. You and me. And it makes them excited."

"Don't touch me." Knox cringed away, reaching across the bond for Anwei. When he concentrated, he could hear her saying his name, as if somehow that would bring him out of this place. But she didn't appear, and he didn't leave, the not-walls staying firmly around him. He reached for Calsta. He reached for the sword—

The sword he was inside—

There was nowhere to hide. Willow tipped up her chin to look at him, but it was the *thing* holding her out, offering her to Knox like a slice of cake.

Knox did not eat cake.

"It's been so long since you've let me talk to you," she whispered in her own voice, but there were still a few stray discordant notes. She scratched her shoulder as if she could feel the press of claws against them.

"Was it you talking?" he whispered. So many years of raging and crying and begging to be fed, of spurring him on to kill.

She looked down. "I tried to talk. They can't swallow me like they're supposed to. I know I shouldn't be glad you are here, but I missed you."

"I missed you too." The words shook as they came out of his mouth, and they were true, so very true. "Who wants to swallow you?"

Willow squinted at him, the same expression she'd worn so many times when they were children and he was annoying her. She waved a hand at the darkness. "Them. There are too many of us alive ones. The dead ones just eat each other, but we don't fit right. Mateo. You. Anwei. And someone else too who gets *so mad* that I'm not in here right." Hope brightened her eyes. "Maybe she'll get mad at you too because you're not in here right either. You're still all light. Lighter than me."

When Knox squinted, the shape of his sister turned ropy and dark, joining the hulking mass behind her. Was she really here, or was it some kind of trick? A sock puppet sewed together of memories to . . .

To what? What did the thing *want*?

"Where's Mateo?" he rasped, inching back when she reached for him again, her dress growing a collar of pearls. "Is everyone else all right?"

"I don't know. You were my thread." Willow's eyes traced the line of fire inside Knox that led out toward Anwei. She sighed, looking down at her feet. Only, it wasn't her feet she was looking at; there was a line strung between Willow and Knox, the dim gray of old bone and sorrow.

Was this part of the web he and Mateo had made that pinned Willow to life because her death hadn't been a real sacrifice? Knox *had* loved his sister. When he pulled the sword from her body, did his love for her keep her from getting fully trapped inside it? And if that were the case, and if Knox still had a connection like that to Anwei . . .

If you truly are *in the sword like Willow, then Anwei is the one who put you here.*

The thought felt poisonous inside Knox. Anwei would *never* have done this, not on purpose—

But there in his mind he could see the cup she'd given him. The poison. The way she'd taken him down to the hold and kissed him even as she'd waited for him to wink out. And then there was Anwei in the canoe, the last of her fluttering petal disguise gone, nothing left but steel down to her heart. The terrible things he'd said, and she'd said them back.

Then she had paddled away into the night while he fell apart.

The light in him flickered, darkness inching closer around him.

"Don't!" Willow's hands came up in a panicked entreaty. "Don't let it go!" She reached for him—

The air went still, Willow freezing with her hands—were they *claws?*—stretched toward Knox. The thread between them sparked, and Willow was shaking, tendrils of shadow crawling all over her, making her teeth pointed and her bones stretch, her skin grow fur and scales, then shed.

"Willow, are you all right? What is happening?" Knox stepped forward, then back again, not certain how to help.

The tendons in Willow's neck began to cord, the muscles in her arms and legs shuddering. One foot slid back. Away from Knox.

Knox's whole body was ready to fight, but his mind was looking at his sister caught on some creature's claws. How she groaned, forcing her body to back away inch by inch into the darkness. "I can't keep you safe," she muttered, almost too low for him to hear. "I can't. You couldn't. I can't. I can't."

CHAPTER 24

What Devoted Do to Shapeshifters

Lia clung to a fragment of wood, river water gushing all around her. She wasn't sure where the scrap had come from, only that it floated, and when she held on to it, she floated too. Apparently, Calsta could only lend her breath for so long—Lia coughed up half the lake as she drifted downstream. Her throat and chest burned, but Lia could only think of Aria. The way she'd lain there in the tunnel. How she hadn't been real.

Mateo cracking the tunnel's glass—ancient, Basist constructed, and supposedly *unbreakable*—so she could escape his father. He likely knew where Aria really was.

He'd probably show her. Maybe he would have if she'd waited. Tried talking to him instead of . . .

Lia's eyes clenched shut, every breath a knife. She'd lost control again. She hadn't thought things through. Her sword had been in her hand, and she'd felt that insatiable pull to *jump* as if Ewan were still coming after her. So she'd jumped.

It had been the wrong thing. *Don't lose yourself,* Calsta had cried, but maybe Lia was already lost.

Maybe Aria was paying for it at that very moment.

Something slipped past Lia's leg, wriggling up to her side, then darted away. *Elsparn.* The word sounded off in her mind, as if it were supposed to be important. Elsparn. *Not biting. Because of . . .*

Because of something Anwei did. Lia couldn't remember and didn't care. All she knew was that Anwei was supposed to have been the one to get Aria. Anwei was supposed to be there. She'd *promised.*

Something that was much larger than a fish bumped Lia's driftwood, almost knocking her into the water. Lia swore, her hands shaking as she reached for the sword weighing heavy between her shoulder blades, barely noticing that someone else was swearing too. Hands grasped her shoulders and heaved her onto a canoe. Lia twisted away, managing to pull the sword free, but cried out and dropped it into the canoe when her leg hit the side, pain a fire in her ankle, the bones grinding against each other.

"Miss Lia!" The hands laid her gently onto a wet wooden bench, and Lia peered blearily up at Gilesh. "You've exchanged your auroshe for this . . . extremely sexy form of transport?" He inspected the water logged plank before laying it next to her with just a little too much reverence for it to be genuine. "It's beautiful."

"Oh, shove off. Get us back to the boat. We found her, like Abendiza said," Noa's voice interceded, and softer hands helped her to sit up. Lia breathed in tentatively, worried her lungs would leak after so long underwater. "Are you hurt?"

"Where in *Calsta's wind-cracked name* are Anwei and Altahn?" Lia wheezed.

She didn't understand the flurry of movement that happened as they drew near to the boat or the gray of Anwei's face when she came into sight. There was something wrong with her aura, but Lia hardly saw that much before the healer was pushing her flat onto the deck, groping for a bag that wasn't there. "Lie still. Don't move," Anwei rasped, her movements jerky and unsure somehow. "You're hurt?"

"You didn't come." Lia's whole body shook with cold as Anwei began pressing fingers along her collarbone, then down her ribs. "You sent me into that place alone and—" She gasped when Anwei got to her leg.

"Altahn set off the flare. You weren't supposed to—"

"The flare came after I was already face-to-face with the Warlord!" Lia exploded, curling up from the deck. "*Where were you?* He drained the Warlord *right before my eyes.* She just . . . flopped over, like there was nothing left inside her. I saw my sister, and she . . . she—" A sob burned through the words, charring her tongue. Aria hadn't been there. Tual had said she wouldn't survive outside the keep—

Tual said all sorts of things. But Mateo would know the truth. Mateo would tell her.

"I . . . I am so sorry, Lia." Anwei's voice was wooden, a far cry from the manufactured tones Lia had come to expect from her, modified to exact specifications depending on who she was talking to and what she wanted. It was as if whatever she was made of had shriveled to dust, leaving nothing but herbs and two fingers mercilessly jabbing at her lower leg. "I think the bones here are broken."

"Let me."

A voice—an *aura*—Lia didn't recognize bloomed into existence. She skittered back from the foreign presence looming toward her, the woman's outline jagged as driftwood and broken swords. "Who are *you*—"

The woman knelt beside her and softly touched her knee. Calsta's power flared bright inside Lia's chest, the golden burn racing down to her ankle hot as molten metal.

Crying out, Lia jerked back from the woman's touch, the hurt there and then gone, leaving a scorched path through her everywhere it had gone. The woman slunk back into the shadows, nothing but the glint of eyes in the darkness.

Anwei didn't move, her hands limp at her sides. "Did you get anything of value? Could you draw me a map? Tell me where Patenga's sword is being kept? Where Tual's rooms are—"

"Who in Calsta's name is *that*?" Lia stared down at her ankle, the feel of grinding bones gone.

"What did you see in there?" Anwei asked. "I'm sorry things went wrong, but if there's anything you can tell me—"

"Anwei, *who is*—" But as she pushed toward the woman with her aurasight, Lia caught a glimpse of an awful, guttering aura from the belly of the ship.

Pushing Anwei off her, Lia wrenched herself up from the deck and ran down the ramp, her ankle hardly twinging as she zigzagged between crates to the back cabin where Anwei had taken Knox. Only now his aura was like the last breath before a candle went out. Slamming the door open, Lia fell hard to her knees next to the cot to find Knox's eyes closed and his skin gray as old candlewax.

"What happened?" Lia demanded. "Is he—"

"Dead?" It wasn't Anwei who had followed her down. The strange old woman's teeth clacked against one another. "Just about. Your friend up there killed him."

Lia grabbed his hands, but they were cold. She touched his face, but it was cold. She was crying, but her tears were cold, and she couldn't feel anything because Knox was all she had. Knox. And Aria. "No." It came out in a croak. "He still has an aura."

"Just a thread. It'll soon break."

A scream boiled up inside Lia. "He's not *dead*," she wheezed. "Anwei's aura is still white. She's still bonded to him—"

"My aura is white, child." The old woman chuckled. "Just like Tual Montanne."

Just like Tual Montanne. Like a *shapeshifter*. Goose bumps prickled out from Lia's arms. She pushed herself up from the cot, unable to process the old woman, only that *Anwei's* aura was white. Anwei was still there, and Knox was—

Lia ran. Through the maze of crates, up the ramp, away from the crooked tilt to Knox's neck, the slack line of his jaw. She ran to the deck, to the canoe, where the Warlord's sword sat like a dark promise.

Anwei was still kneeling on the deck, her hands clasped about her ribs as if she'd lost more than her medicine bag. "It was an accident," she whispered.

"The first thing you asked me when I came back here was what I found in that place." Lia's hands both gripped the sword. "You took Altahn's father and Calsta only knows how many other people when you brought down the tomb. You almost took Noa, letting her run into danger. You almost let me get taken, but thanks to your *shapeshifter brother*, I'm still alive." The words came louder and louder, liquid acid burning all the way up her throat. "Now you take Knox?"

Anwei's shoulders slumped. "I'm trying to fix it, Lia."

"*How can you fix it?*" Lia advanced on the healer, sword shivering in her hands. "You've smiled and petted us and told us each we were the prettiest one. Even Knox, the boy who *loves* you, could only be sure you'd come save us from drowning because *you still needed him.*"

Lia felt auras loom closer behind her as if they meant to stop her. Noa and Bane and Gilesh. Altahn was frozen, Galerey bursting from his collar and sparking like a bonfire. "What did you say about my father?" he hissed.

But Lia couldn't care, not about Altahn, not about the other messes Anwei had made, the other people she'd lied to, then destroyed. "How could you do this?" she cried. "How could Calsta have chosen *you* to fix whatever went wrong with Devoted and Basists? All you are is a fake goddess. A thief. A liar. A *murderer.* You were supposed to love Knox, and now he's *dead.*" The words kept spilling out, Lia's hands shaking so hard her knuckles had begun to hurt, her muscles too tight to do anything but shout. "The girl who collects *ants* while people die around her! I should have seen what you were the first time I saw you lie to Altahn. The first time Mateo's name crossed your lips. Your own brother—he's next, isn't he, Anwei? Use him, then dispose of him, like the rest of us?"

Anwei hadn't moved, her voice fluttering like ash. "I'm going to *fix it*."

"Did you kill Knox *on purpose?* Drink him in so you'd have enough power to finally face your snake-tooth man? You don't fix things, Anwei! You break them!" Lia lunged forward, but a voice cried out and something slammed into her before she could swing the sword. Noa stumbled into view, dropping the paddle she'd used to deflect Lia's sword to put her hands up, bracing herself for the next blow.

"You are worth more than this, Noa," Lia snarled.

But then Lia caught sight of the sword in her hand, Anwei a blur beyond it.

The Warlord's sword . . . *No.* She shivered as she looked down its length, nausea bubbling up inside her like poison. It was *Ewan Hardcastle's* sword.

Don't lose yourself, Calsta had whispered. Like the Warlord had. Like the Devoted had. So frightened they'd committed *genocide* rather than try to work through the horrors that shapeshifters had perpetrated. Like Ewan had, so obsessed with getting what he wanted that he forgot everything that mattered.

She froze, thinking of Aria, still trapped with a monster because Lia had been too busy trying to keep moving to notice Tual doing something to her brain. And Knox at the point of her sword in the Trib camp. Lia let the sword tip fall and backed away a step. Then another, her legs hitting the railing. Anwei stared up at her, tears rolling down her cheeks and her braids dripping, and that awful white aura flashing above her like a flag. *My aura is white, too, just like Tual Montanne's.* The old woman's eyes glinted from the darkness of the hold.

But in the cold moonlight, Lia didn't know. Not what was right or wrong or who had done what, only that anger was a live thing inside her—and she didn't want to be this person. She stared down at her hand on the sword. Ewan's sword. The very sword he'd brandished at her when all she had was a shovel to fight him off.

Ewan held this sword the same way the Warlord did. Like a right. Like a threat. Like anger and a surety they were right, with no reason to hold back.

That wasn't who Lia wanted to be. Fingers shaking, she dropped the sword, the blade splashing down into the river. She hated the way she still shook, as if she couldn't trust her own hands. "Fix it," she rasped.

Anwei's head came up, her cheeks wet.

"You owe me. You owe *him.* You owe all of us. Fix it, or I'll . . ." Lia swallowed, her voice broken glass. "I'll be back when. . . ." Grabbing hold of the rail, her fingers still wanted to tear, to wring, strangle, *destroy.* "You know what Devoted do to shapeshifters."

Anwei's eyes narrowed, but it was Noa's look that cut Lia through, the fear Lia had seen the day she'd faced down Ewan Hardcastle like a memory across the girl's face. Only now she was afraid of *Lia.*

Unable to stand it, Lia vaulted over the rail. When she hit the water, cold enveloped her, but that did nothing to douse the fire raging inside her. *How could you let this happen, Calsta?* she screamed inside her head. *Knox was how we get Aria back! Knox was supposed to be a part of destroying Tual!*

It wasn't until she'd clawed her way onto the muddy shore that Lia felt the sear of the goddess's reply. *I can't stop you humans from hurting one another. I give power to people I hope will do good, but in the end, the choices you make are yours.*

The words stung like a slap. Lia wanted choices. But she hadn't wanted *this*. Reconciling the two seemed impossible, a conundrum with no answer, only a deep dark hole down which she was falling alone.

She just had to get away before she did something terrible she couldn't take back. Lia set out between the trees, the thin ground crackling with every step. She couldn't lose herself because that would mean she'd also lose the only thing that mattered to her now.

Aria.

Without Anwei's plans, her manipulations, her lies . . . Lia walked faster, her hands twitching toward her sword. Anwei who brought a shapeshifter onto the boat. Who sat on the deck while Knox lay beneath. His pale face sat in Lia's mind like a chunk of coal waiting to ignite again, those last strings attaching him to Anwei—

Something skittered through the leaves behind Lia. She spun around, a scream already in her throat, the last of her control, her hope lost in the sea of nothing she had become. Running at the sound, Calsta was a force of gravity inside her, a force of wind, a force of *power* too big for her to hold, so when she launched into the air, sword raised to strike, Lia *was* the storm.

"*Lia!*" the voice had called a hundred times or maybe a thousand, familiar like poison and regret and the worst of all things in the world. And when Lia finally managed to focus on the shape ahead, all she could see was an auroshe of gristle and bone, worn away like the skeleton she was. A rider sat on her back with absolutely no aura hovering around him as if he were more skeleton than the auroshe, devoid of any soul: Mateo Montanne.

Lia strode toward the boy, following the sound of her name like a trap she couldn't stop herself from walking into. The auroshe skittered back as she advanced on them, Mateo shrinking down in the saddle at the sight of her.

"You'd better *run*," Lia choked out, groping for the sword only to find it gone. She started toward him, rage a monster unfolding inside her. She didn't need a sword to hurt someone who had hurt so much. "Hide. *Die* before I catch you, because it'll be better than the death you can expect from me."

The auroshe reared, Mateo holding his seat as Rosie struck at her. "Lia, *stop*!"

"Is this the next stage to becoming a shapeshifter? You completely lose your aura when your humanity is gone?" Lia dodged Rosie's hooves, spinning away to put a tree between herself and the auroshe. Thinking of Aria. Of cracking glass, and the feel of magic all around her, none of it hers. Of Mateo, who had managed to creep up on her because he had no aura.

None. Not even the thin mist that was all he had left of an aura in that tunnel. Lia didn't have it in her to care. She pulled the sheath from her back and gripped the hardened leather and metal like a sword, waiting for the sound of cloven hooves that would tell her where Rosie was, the sound of his breathing, the beat of his heart—

"A fight between us wouldn't be fair, you know." Mateo's voice cracked.

"Shut up, Mateo." Lia spun out from behind the tree, running at Rosie's flank. She was not sure if he meant that she would surely kill him or that he could squeeze her soul from her like oil from a rag. Rosie leapt over a fallen tree and swiveled to face Lia with a scream.

"Let me explain! I only need one second!" he cried. "Okay, maybe two seconds."

Lia tripped, landing on her knees. She breathed in deep, trying to remember her training.

Don't lose yourself.

There was one thing Anwei had right. Standing very slowly, Lia kept her sword point down, ready to move if Rosie charged. The auroshe gamboled around the edge of the trunk instead, as if she wasn't sure if this was a game or a battle. When Lia didn't move, Rosie skipped forward with a happy croon, butting into Lia's shoulder with the soft part of her forehead. Lia's chest was steel and bone and stone, nothing that breathed, or lived, or loved. But when Rosie began to nuzzle into her, Lia could feel her warmth.

Mateo, a bit too slowly, perhaps, swung his leg over her back in a fancy dismount, Rosie spoiling it when she danced to the side, making him trip on the way down. Once he'd recovered himself, he drew himself up. "I'm here."

"Where is Aria?" Lia didn't look away from the skeletal bridge to Rosie's nose, the skin pulled tight over the scaly ridges that protected her eyes and pointed snout. She rubbed a finger along the sharp lines of Rosie's powerful jaw, concentrating hard on not destroying the world. She raised the sword to point it at him. "If she's not with you, then this is all I have for you."

Mateo stayed well behind Rosie's withers, keeping the auroshe's cloven hooves and teeth firmly between them. "I don't have her, so I guess you might as well stab me."

"When you're done hiding behind fifteen hundred pounds of auroshe?"

"I want to help," he said quietly.

"With *what*?" she yelled. "All you ever do is sit very still and hope you don't get hit by a stray blow while fights happen all around you. If you want to help, you're going to have to actually *do* something. Helping means choosing between good and bad, not showing up here and hoping your father hasn't noticed you missing from your morning bath." Lia took a step toward him, and Rosie's hackles bristled up from her back, the auroshe giving a dangerous squeal.

"How could I come before, Lia?" he yelled back over Rosie's head. "We both know what my father wants with you. Calsta above, *I* wanted you, and you knew it. Anything I did before would have looked like I was going along with his plan—the one where you end up dead and I end up with an extra soul to patch up the hole in mine. You were there with me when I realized what being bonded to a . . . . . .a *shapeshifter* means."

The word tore out of him like a curse. Like a plea, a prayer, and a scream, all at once.

"I don't want to die, Lia." His voice broke. "And yes, I realize that coming here now without Aria makes it look like all I want is to die young, but that's not so different from what's going to happen to me if I stay on the island. So I thought I'd come do something good instead."

Lia waited, Rosie's low growl sending ripples of goose bumps down her neck. After a moment, the auroshe curved around to look at Mateo for assurance, as if she couldn't quite believe Lia was the thing he was so scared of. Mateo gave her a soft scratch behind the ears, wilting like the little flower he was as he pulled off his ridiculous tomato-colored sun hat.

His hair had grown out into little curls all over his head. It made Lia suddenly remember another moment Mateo had looked away with such embarrassment, worry, and an undercurrent of despair. He'd been wearing a bathrobe and slippers, surrounded by books about dead herbs with a new hope that somehow he wouldn't join them. *I like you*, he'd said. *I hadn't expected that.*

Mateo's voice shook. "I'm . . . I'm *not* here to help."

The emptiness inside Lia yawned wide, and she braced herself, waiting for him to take from her, just like everyone else in this world. The Warlord. Ewan. Tual. Anwei. They'd all *taken* everything they could, but Mateo could do worse than all of them put together despite his thin frame, his fidgeting hands, the erratic beat of his heart.

"I'm here to beg for *your* help, Lia," Mateo's voice rasped. "You want to talk about choices between good and bad? My father loves me. He's saved me from being murdered by my own family just because the wrong god touched me. I love him, even if . . . even if he made me into what I am now." Mateo was shaking all over, hat in his hand, nothing between him and her makeshift weapon, but he didn't look away from her eyes. "But he's gone too far. He's gone too far, and . . . I think it's only going to get worse. I need your help to stop him, Lia." He thrust a hand into his pocket and pulled something free from the soggy, dirty fabric, then held it out to her. A rock. "My aura is gone because of this. I think it would hide yours too, so I brought it for you."

CHAPTER 25

Like Some Hero

Anwei sat on the deck of the ship she had stolen, unable to move. Lia was gone. Altahn and his riders were gone. Knox was nothing but a faint stain inside her, and fading more every moment. *Knox,* she thought. *Willow could talk to you. Why won't you talk to me? Help me fix this!*

Footsteps padded across the deck, Abendiza's voice grumbling like an auroshe's growl. "There's a litter of Calsta's little burners in these woods. I wonder what will happen when your friends wander into their camp."

"Who?" Noa's voice was breathless, afraid. "Lia? She'll know to stay away from Devoted."

"No, your Trib friends who left in a huff when they found out that you killed the young one's father." Anwei opened her eyes to find Abendiza shrugging. "They're headed straight for the camp."

"You're the one from the records we stole, aren't you?" Noa breathed, all raptures and delight at the idea of a curse gone from her voice. "'The world is cursed to bleed—'"

"And I am the sword." Abendiza nodded. "I convinced myself that I was sacrificing my own soul to fight the abominations destroying the world. So many of us became shapeshifters for reasons that made sense—power was needed to fight power. But most of us only caused greater tribulation." She nudged Anwei with her toe. "You're going to sit here and mope while your friends are killed, I suppose?"

"Altahn came here to help his people regain Calsta's favor," Anwei whispered. "To kill the shapeshifter who took his father. To reclaim the sword that killed his father's . . . father's father's father . . ."

"Don't hurt yourself, dear." Abendiza's voice was a little too polite.

Anwei looked up. "But *I'm* the shapeshifter who killed *his* father. If I go after him, he'll kill me."

She flinched when Noa stood up. "Where are they?"

Abendiza waved vaguely toward the trees, holding Anwei's gaze. "Altahn knows what you are now, so you count him an enemy instead of a friend. Another enemy stands in his path, and thus the threat he poses is neutralized, all without a single bit of energy expelled from your system. Very neat. Let your nothing friend here try to stop it. She'll try to be a hero, but then she'll have to come running back to you—"

"I might not have whatever has let you grow so *very* old." Noa thrust herself between Anwei and the old woman, but then she kept walking toward the hold. "Maybe I can't fight like Knox and Lia, or grow trees and new body parts for people like Anwei, but that doesn't make me nothing."

So Noa was going, too, then.

"You're touched by a trickster." Abendiza's laugh rubbed like snake scales and poisonberry leaves. "May she give you her own luck."

They were all gone. *Knox.* Anwei's thoughts cracked into jagged shards. *I didn't mean to. Please—*

"Oh, be quiet," the old woman responded to the thought. "You *did* mean to, even if you hadn't let yourself look at the consequences. You put your own goals ahead of everyone else's, and gods-may-care what happened to the others so long as you got what you wanted."

"You're reading my mind like a spiriter?"

"Interesting, because I shouldn't be able to, given the oaths you've broken. Shifters' minds are usually shielded, even to other shifters. Taking a soul for ourselves makes us more than any gods-touched could ever be," the woman's voice croaked. "You, however, are changed, yet not changed—an open book when you should not be. Your magic should be a weapon instead of the boon it was meant to be, but you're not like me for some reason. Not like your enemy Tual, hurting his enemies and friends alike."

Anwei opened her eyes to glare up at the woman. "He—"

"Hurt *you*. The first time, yes." Abendiza went to the sails and began tying them down, one knot after another. "Then you spent the rest of your life hurting yourself. He didn't do it. Your brother is out there waiting for you—"

"He *forgot* me."

"Is your soul really worth those three words? Your life? The lives of your friends? You'd rather be remembered, respected, *feared* than spend even one second *happy*?" Abendiza pointed at Anwei's forehead, her gnarled finger stretching to press gently between her eyes. "The bond between you and that boy still isn't broken, though it should be. Is your pain really wrapped up so tight inside you that there isn't room for a life?" She climbed up to the second tier of canvas flapping madly in the wind and began to tie them down. "Because the life you think you are taking will only put you in the sword."

"What do you mean?" Anwei rasped.

"You become a shapeshifter when you bond with another, then kill them. But since you're tied together, that bond drags half your soul into the caprenum blade along with the one you love." The old woman stopped her knots a moment to stare down the channel. "Then when you finally die, the rest of you gets dragged inside to molder for all eternity."

"Is that why shapeshifters can only be killed with shapeshifter blades?" Noa came up from the hold, a bag over her shoulder with bits of broken wood sticking up from the top.

"Shapeshifters can only be killed by the blade they used to turn shapeshifter. I claimed a few caprenum weapons myself, for experiments, of course." Anwei's skin pebbled at the cold in those words as Abendiza climbed down to check the anchor. "It took a long time, lifetimes over lifetimes, before my research came clear: there is no escape from the fate of endless corruption and suffering inside a caprenum blade. At least, that was what I thought." Abendiza pushed the gangplank out on its hinges, the far end toppling lopsided onto shore. She checked that it was stable before giving Noa a gracious bow, as if she'd played a fanfare and thrown rose petals for Noa to walk upon. "I gave up. Stayed here in the lake where no one knew to hunt me, using so little life force I had enough stored up to last me centuries without having to destroy anyone new. Until I found you."

"You didn't kill anyone else?" Noa scoffed. "What about the Basists massacred when you took over this abbey? What about the *curse*?"

"I am not the one who destroyed the abbey, though I am the one who killed the shapeshifter who did. Tual arrived with the high khonin family who came to claim the island once the Warlord took power." Abendiza turned an eye on Noa. "It astounds me that he learned little more than to extend his own life by taking from his masters year after year. Hiding in the shadows like a little spider, hoping they wouldn't notice the corpses piling up around him." She pointed at Anwei. "But something changed when he took my sword and tried to use it to turn Mateo into a shapeshifter. Something broke."

"Where are Altahn and the others?" Noa asked, patience gone.

"Go find them. They're out there." Abendiza waved her away, uncaring. "Caprenum is unbreakable. If you use it to kill someone, all that happens is they die. If a gods-touched tries to sacrifice someone they don't love with it, it cracks their own soul in two instead of the victims'. But with Tual and Mateo . . ." Abendiza shook her head slowly. "Something new happened. Out of his love for Mateo, Tual helped Mateo murder that girl, and it broke something. The girl's soul went into the sword whole. Then someone who loved *her* took it up. That love latched onto her somehow. Made a bond strong enough to keep her here. I don't know if it was because of Tual, or because the girl was whole and unbroken when she went in, or because the sword already had an active shapeshifter attached to it—*me*. But whatever happened, instead of a single bond, it made a . . . . a *web*."

Knox. Anwei's throat clenched. *Knox picked up the sword, and Willow's soul clung to him.*

"It took me a long time to feel it—to understand what Tual had done with my sword. But just now, when you sent your little boyfriend into the sword without stabbing him at all, it destabilized even further. It's weak. Fragile in a way I have never seen caprenum before."

Anwei put her hands over her ears, not wanting to hear the analytical breakdown of what she'd done to Knox.

"I'm going," Noa interrupted. "Are you coming with me, Anwei? We have to stop them from falling into trouble."

"More trouble than they'd be in if a fire dancer and two shapeshifters showed up to save them?" The word curled on Anwei's tongue. *Shapeshifter.* That's what the snake-tooth man was.

What she was now.

"I love you, Anwei." Noa set down her bag to pull Anwei into a hug. Anwei couldn't move, her whole body slowly turning to stone. Noa was the last thing between her and alone. "I'm going to go help them."

"Noa, you can't go out there." Anwei was ashamed of the way her voice broke. "There are sinkholes and earth that will break the moment you step on it and spiders and animals and *Devoted*, Noa! You're just a dancer, not some hero!"

"And you're just a thief, Anwei." Noa let go of Anwei, and Anwei was somehow even colder than she'd been before. The dancer picked up her bag and started for the rail, the bits of splintered wooden crate sticking out from under the flap. "Sinkholes and spiders and Devoted are nothing to losing a friend. Stay here with . . . *that* if you want to." She cast a glance toward Abendiza, who was grinning from the top of the gangplank. "Keep her from eating Knox until I get back. Then we'll come up with what we need to do next. But it's my turn to save someone instead of being spectacularly saved. That's what friends do."

Friends. The word hurt as much as Noa flitting down the gangplank and into the trees, the first morning light touching her wild waves of hair, khonin knots a tangle over her ear.

Anwei stood, hands shaking as she felt for her medicine bag, but it was gone. The sword was gone too, lost to the water. She knocked over the box of herbs Noa had brought when Lia had dragged herself on board, but the envelopes of powder, leaves, and flower petals meant nothing to her dead nose.

Her fingers found the two specially marked packets. When Anwei pulled them out, her stomach twinged, because one was half gone. She'd poured it into Knox's drink.

Sleeping Death.

Anwei dropped them. Then picked them up again and stuffed them into her tunic pocket. Knees shaking, she stood and turned toward the forest. *Friends. Friends help each other even when they aren't wanted.*

"The sword isn't stable anymore," Abendiza's voice croaked, and Anwei turned to find the old woman looking straight through her, eyes clouded but her mind sharp. "Which means we might be able to destroy it."

"I don't care." Anwei started down the gangplank, the shape of Noa already lost in the trees ahead. "Not about swords or—"

"No, you need to listen to me." Abendiza followed her, effortlessly keeping pace when Anwei began to run despite the feel of the ground shifting under her feet. "A shapeshifter's soul, since it exists half inside the blade and half outside, holds open a tiny hole between our world and a place we can store someone's talents, their magic, their memories. But this web between Mateo, Knox, and the girl is making the hole bigger than it is supposed to be."

Anwei swore when her foot broke through a thin spot in the ground, making her stumble. "Which way did Noa go?"

"Knox and Mateo should never have been able to bond to the same girl." Abendiza huffed as she followed. "Mateo should have died trying to sacrifice someone he wasn't bonded to in the first place, but Tual did something I've never seen before—somehow he used his love for Mateo to sacrifice someone wholly unrelated, and it worked to an extent. It flies directly in the face of all my research. Perhaps because it was a shapeshifter who'd learned to love someone new, there were new ways to form a bond? Whatever the case, it still wasn't enough—Mateo ended up with a hole inside him."

"I don't need a lesson in shapeshifter theory!" Anwei picked her way around a prickly bush that reached for her as she passed.

But Abendiza continued musing, her eyes glazed as she ticked the facts off one by one on her fingers. "*You* may have killed your boyfriend by breaking your bond to him, but it shouldn't have put him into the *sword*. It's supposed to be a conscious sacrifice. A decision. You knew you were the only thing holding him together, but you weren't trying to take his soul. You didn't even *try* to stab him, and yet he's stuck in there."

"Go away!" Anwei yelled, dodging around a tree to get away from the shapeshifter. "You're just saying the same thing over and over."

"Souls trapped on the other side of the barrier grow corrupted, feeding on each other because they hunger after the lives stolen from them. Willow wasn't properly sacrificed, so she's jammed halfway through the hole instead of fully on the other side of it." Abendiza's voice rose as Anwei ducked around a tree, trying to escape. "All shapeshifters lose part of themselves to the sword when they put the one they love inside, but if someone tries to do it the wrong way, it should kill them. As near as I can tell, that's what happened, only Knox, who *did* love his sister enough to form some kind of bond, picked up the sword in time to forge some kind of two-headed link that stopped the hole in Mateo from killing him completely and also stopped the girl from being taken fully into the sword. She would have drained Mateo completely, and both of them would have died, but with that wholesome, *earned* connection to her brother, she had a source of energy that kept her partly in this world and stopped her from consuming Mateo entirely, I think?" The shapeshifter shrugged. "Which should be impossible."

"Who cares? It happened." Anwei gasped, looking for some sign Noa had come this way.

"Because it's breaking laws that I thought were unbreakable." Abendiza darted out in front of Anwei, blocking her way. "Half of *my* soul is in that sword. I did years of research trying to find a way to get it out and came up with nothing. Now there's a chance to destroy the sword once and for all, and you think I'm going to let the girl who can help me walk away? *Listen.*"

"I need to stop my friend from waltzing into danger for no good reason, so—"

"*You* are part of this web too, and you're more a danger to Noa right now than any of Calsta's little devotees." Abendiza grabbed Anwei's arm. "Mateo Montanne shouldn't exist. Knox's soul shouldn't have been sucked in without you stabbing him. And the ghost inside the sword shouldn't be able to speak so clearly to the wielder."

"Leave me *alone.*" Wrenching her arm free, Anwei fell to her knees, checking the ground, the trees, the bushes for hints Noa could have passed through. Wasn't that what Knox did when he was trying to follow someone whose aura was out of range? He looked for . . . she didn't even know. Broken branches. Footprints? There was no mud or dirt for footprints to be left behind, only dead leaves.

The shapeshifter's voice came out in a hiss, more snake than human. "The sword will suck you in too if we don't do something—"

"The sword is at the bottom of a lake!" Anwei roared.

"But if you help me, then we can get Knox out."

Anwei stopped, her madly beating heart going still. "You can get him out?"

Abendiza smiled, then strode into the trees ahead, weaving between plants and hopping over spots of ground as if she could feel the thin places around her. Anwei ran after her, swearing when her foot punched through the fragile earth, stone digging into her ankle. Abendiza walked on as Anwei struggled once more, leaving her behind in the trees. "Can you get him out, Abendiza? If I do what you want me to and try to destroy the sword, Knox comes back? Alive?" Anwei got her foot loose and limped after the old woman, ducking trees and crashing through a spider's web large enough to catch her. Swearing, she tore off the sticky strands, the phantom feel of spider legs crawling across her skin. "Abendiza!"

The shapeshifter hardly looked back when Anwei caught up. "I don't know. But I have hope."

"Hope?" The thin rays of light inside Anwei started to wither. Hope was for people without plans, for people with no answers, no end goal.

Hope was nothing.

"A *chance* isn't enough for you?" Abendiza laughed as she walked, that terrible gut-churning hiss. "Here's the only alternative I can see: you take the power waiting inside you where your partner used to be. Use it to save Noa before she stumbles into Calsta's camp with nothing but a pointy stick. Maybe you'd manage to save the Trib too—they might even love you for it, forget the people you've killed out of gratitude." She shrugged. "That's more hope again, I suppose. Not even magic can force people to forget the things they don't want to."

Anwei looked around, totally lost, tricked into following this woman for long enough that whatever bearings she'd had were gone. Her hands began to shake.

Abendiza whispered, "If hope isn't enough for you, then save the people you know you can. Kill Knox the rest of the way. Save Noa before she gets herself killed." She looked Anwei up and down. "Save *yourself* from being alone." Then Abendiza walked away.

The weight inside Anwei grew until she couldn't take another step. Panic unfolded inside her, and she could feel the ground crackling under her body, too much for anyone to hold. Her family dead at a god's hand—no, her *own* hand, the same way Knox was dead because she'd walked away, ignoring him when he cried out for her, choosing instead the snake-tooth man on his island, waiting for her now . . .

Only, the snake-tooth man, Tual Montanne, was *not* waiting for Anwei.

She was a fish he'd hooked without noticing, leaving her to flop along after him, gasping for air, unable to cut herself free. The earth beneath her trembled, the roar of underground channels, of the past, of the person Anwei was *supposed* to be waiting down there to wash her away.

If there was anything to take. Not even Anwei's own twin could remember her.

Knox beat inside Anwei's chest like a heart, every pulse a tiny bit dimmer. A heart she could eat to get back all that the nameless god took from her, and more. It was her way to save Noa, the only one who had stayed despite seeing the emptiness that was all Anwei had inside. To save Altahn, who dove into the water between Anwei and the snake because he trusted her. Knox's soul was a weapon full of storm and shadow and *power* just waiting—all she had to do was bite.

The ground beneath Anwei caved. She fell, hands scrabbling over roots and grass. Her arms screamed when she caught hold of a bare root, the spindly thing not near enough to hold her. Chest deep in the hole, her arms screaming, Anwei could feel the water snarling just beneath her feet, anxious to grab hold of her.

Knox glistened inside her, begging to be swallowed. Taking

his life would mean she would be strong like the snake-tooth man. Strong. Able to do . . . more. Enough to stop Devoted from hurting Noa and Altahn. Enough to find Lia out in the forest and convince her to put away her sword. Enough to destroy Tual. Enough to *make* Mateo remember her so she wouldn't be nothing anymore. Enough to get her out of this stupid hole.

But taking Knox would mean losing all of them just the way she'd lost him. Really, she'd already lost them. The thought of it felt more like *nothing* than any shapeshifter sword.

Tears ran like fire down her cheeks, and Anwei's arms began to shake, not strong enough to keep herself from being sucked down into the abyss. There was dirt in her mouth, and the stone beneath her arms and chest was beginning to crack, her fingers white from clenching at the world that wanted her to drown.

Because this was what it meant to be a finder, a fake goddess, a girl with a mixed tincture of death and revenge where her heart should have been. It meant dying here in the forest alone, having betrayed every person she loved.

Take it, and you can save Noa. The words were *hers,* not some god whispering what to do. *You don't have to listen to any god or keep any rules. Take him and his power. Become what you've always been, but with* power.

But what had she always been? Someone who put revenge before her friends? Before her own life? Anwei's chest was an iron cage, her soul hardened to flint.

But a voice seemed to whisper from the back of the storm in her mind. *Anwei.* Like Knox, every time he'd said her name. In anger, in fear, in panic. So quietly on the boat earlier that evening. What had she been so afraid of? That he'd leave? That he'd disappear? That he'd hurt her like everyone else she'd loved?

Could that possibly hurt more than him being *gone*?

Anwei could feel her muscles starting to fail, could feel the rush of water beneath her, the depth of magic waiting in Knox that could save her from any fall. But she couldn't let go. Wouldn't. Straining, crying, fingers bleeding, Anwei fought, her friends' lives somehow stacked against each other, because she'd set them in the scales that way.

But she wasn't going to choose. She refused to choose between them.

It always would have come to this; she just hadn't seen it before. Because she'd set them all opposite her, as if losing one or two would be worth destroying the man who'd been weighing Anwei down for so many years.

A man who couldn't even remember Anwei's name.

Anwei pushed the thought of the snake-tooth away, lost him, left him behind. She forgot *him* and the scales that needed to be balanced, because if she was going to die, she wanted the people she loved to be in her mind. The sharp smile Noa wore as she smeared her face with gray powder and practiced her ghostly caterwaul on the way to the tomb. Lia kneeling to take her hand as they'd sat at the bottom of the tomb, the world broken around them. Altahn diving into the water with nothing but acid, salpowder, and a stolen aura to keep him safe. And Knox. Fighting through everything he was and holding his hand out to her anyway.

She held tight to them, and the weight pulling her down seemed to fall away. Anwei dragged herself up inch by inch until her elbows, her chest, her waist, her hips, then all of her was on solid ground, and she rolled away from the hole.

Gasping, she forced herself onto her knees, cupping her hands to her chest where Knox beat inside her like a second heart. Onto her feet. And into the trees after Abendiza, after Noa, after Altahn and Bane and Gilesh, no plans, no tricks, no herbs, no magic, because her friends were the thing keeping her tethered to the world.

She wanted them more than she wanted any evil man to know that she was a poison of his own making that he was going to swallow.

She no longer wanted to be a poison at all.

When Anwei caught up to Abendiza, her heart was ablaze, her body aching, and her whole life boiled down to nothing that mattered other than the friends she didn't want to take from anymore.

Before she could say anything, something rattled the earth.

Anwei saw fire. And swords. And Noa surrounded by sparkle. And Anwei ran toward the fight with nothing but herself to offer. Like some hero.

⤙⤚

Noa wasn't walking aimlessly. The shapeshifter had pointed that gnarled finger of hers, and so Noa had gone, taking a second to twist her hair up and stick Falan's flower through it, a silent prayer to her goddess that luck would be with her as it always was. Her job was to sparkle, to be the distraction while the real work happened.

And now she was the one holding a bag with nothing but sticks coated in the last dregs of salpowder pitch Altahn had left in the belly of the ship.

He'd stopped, facing Noa while Anwei had stared into nothing and the shapeshifter woman watched. "You can come with us, if you like."

Gilesh had batted him over the shoulder with a lecherous grin, as if the rider couldn't feel the story spiraling out of control around him. Bane was trying hard to smile too. Maybe the two of them only survived because they pretended nothing was wrong. Altahn flapped a hand at them, telling them to go stand with the horses, Galerey chirping from his shoulder. As they went, the little lizard sprang off his shoulder and landed on Noa's head, her little claws soft points against Noa's scalp.

But Noa couldn't laugh. "Please don't go," she whispered. "We can figure this out. We can—"

"Calsta is not going to reward me or my clan with favor if I follow someone like Anwei. I don't know why I thought—" Altahn sighed, looking down. Then reached out and took her hand. "Come with me. You didn't know what she was. You don't have to stay."

Noa stared at his hand touching hers, Galerey clawing down through her hair to perch on her shoulder, pressing her warm little face against Noa's neck. "I knew she was a Basist, Altahn. Basists aren't—"

"No, I've gathered enough to know Basism isn't what's wrong with shapeshifters. You didn't know she was a *murderer*, Noa. Did you?"

Lips pressing together, Noa couldn't choke out the words, thinking of Belash Point, the magic gone wrong, the people stuck in trees. Of Lia's furrowed brow back when they'd been outside Rentara. *He doesn't know it was you?* Noa had thought they were talking about Anwei's magic, not what Anwei's magic had *done*. "The tomb . . . I think it was an accident. She lost control—"

"And killed my father. She lost control and then killed Knox, the person she's been mooning after the entire time I've known her. She loves you most after him. Does that mean the next time she loses control, you'll be the one to die?" He inched forward. "You told me to look closer, and I did—I thought she was more than Yaru. That all of us together were something special. A force that could change a past that went wrong." Then he looked over toward Anwei, still staring blankly at the rail, as if whatever had broken Knox had broken her too. "But she truly believes she is some goddess, that she's larger than the rest of us. That we're not worth as much. She could have told me what happened back in the tomb."

"And you still would have helped us?"

"Does it matter?" He turned back to her. "I'm trying to do what my father wanted."

Noa looked down. "I'm not trying to defend her. But do you really think any of this is what your father would have wanted you to do? Carting us all south, braiding your hair like a Rooster. Rigging a Basist fort with salpowder and fighting a snake with a Basist? What do *you* want, Altahn?"

Altahn breathed in slow. "My father would have killed her. He would have tried, anyway. I am not everything he wanted me to be. And I . . . . need to be more than he was too. Which is why I'm leaving." He reached out to take Galerey from her shoulder, the lizard squawking when her spines caught in Noa's hair. "I'll find another way to bring Calsta's favor. The more I learn about shapeshifter swords, the more I think the only benefit to taking ours back would be to destroy it somehow." He reached out to touch Noa's hand again. "Please come with me. When I was down in the water with elsparn all around me and that . . . woman . . . snake thing circling around looking for me, all I could think was I didn't want to die so far from home, and that maybe . . . some of this was worth it because I got to meet you."

Noa looked up at him, the trace of uncertainty in his face more appealing than any of the jokes, the silly banter, the last hints of that quiet smile. More appealing than any of her past beaus, the world to them nothing but a bauble to be taken. A perfect turn on a stage in a story that was more costume and fire than truth. Altahn was true though, heavier than the silver rounds and heavy silk that made up the life Noa had left.

But she looked away, because she'd found out she was real too, that the things she said, the promises she made mattered. "I can't leave Anwei."

Altahn started to laugh, taking her other hand so they were both clasped in his. "I almost think I'd like you less if you did come. Even if Anwei doesn't deserve you." Then he let go and started down the gangplank. Toward his riders, his horses, his life a path crooked before him. But at least *he* was walking it now instead of the version of himself he'd tried to divine from his father's last words. "Come find me some-day," he called.

"You'll be married and have eight new cows," she called back. "And you're a terrible dancer—you can't lie about it anymore. I've *seen.*"

"You just have very specific taste. I'm a fabulous dancer." Gilesh and Bane were laughing, catcalling Altahn as he took one of the horse's leads, and he even smiled—a terrible, stretched thing that showed all his teeth. It felt wrong. Suddenly it occurred to Noa that maybe all the other smiles—the ones full of calm acceptance of what was before him—*were* Altahn. None of them had been fake.

But it was the fake one he left with, turning away from her and not looking back, as if doing so would end in ruin. Now the trees were pink and yellow with Calsta's morning paint, and Noa was going to find Altahn much sooner than planned. The light had barely sunk down between tree branches, and everything was too dark. *Devoted.* Noa kept the thought in her mind as she strode forward. *That old snake lady said Altahn was about to stumble straight into their camp—*

A branch cracked behind her, and suddenly Noa could see it in her head as if she were watching from an audience. There would be four or five of them, all ranged out where she couldn't see them. One would distract her by making noise directly behind her to tease out a weapon, which would result in a fabulous dance of flames—

Noa turned, looking to one side, then the other, touching Falan's flower for luck. Pulling out the two strips of wood she'd coated in salpowder pitch, she started to run. It was the kind that would ignite on impact, so all she had to do was clap the strips together and—

"Noa Russo?" The voice spoke from the branches above her. Noa stumbled to a halt before swearing at herself because that was exactly what she *wasn't* supposed to do. She clapped the salpowder sticks together and began to run again. Maybe a sparkle would be enough if it meant distracting them long enough for Altahn to pass peacefully?

A man swung down from the tree in front of her, forcing Noa to pivot off course, but then a woman landed in a crouch down that path, and when Noa turned, there were five, just like she'd imagined, closing the circle around her until it was tight. "You *are* Noa Russo, correct?" The woman who had first called her name stepped up, the spitting, sparkling light of Noa's salpowder sticks catching in the double auroshe crest tooled into the leather over her chest. "I saw a performance of yours in Chaol before your father reported you missing. What are you doing in Forge?" Her eyes followed the length of Noa's arms, the splutter of fire making her look confused. "With . . . fire sticks?"

Noa tossed one up and caught it with a grin that hurt. "Would you believe I come out here to rehearse?"

The Devoted next to her laughed, his light cuirass hanging open with nothing but a loose tunic beneath it. "You came out to the waterways around Tual Montanne's house to rehearse . . . what?"

Noa gave a little spin, and the Devoted inched back from the fizzle of salpowder, their smiles sparking memories of her father not looking away from his ledgers when he asked her not to "dance around with all that cheap riffraff." As if she were *nothing* but sparkle.

"Miss Russo, I'm afraid we'll have to—"

Noa jumped into her next spin, twisting around to shove her salpowder sticks down the unarmored Devoted's tunic.

At least, that was what was supposed to happen. She turned in the air, driving them down at him, but he swatted them out of the air. Another Devoted grabbed hold of Noa around the ribs, pinning her arms. The sound of steel being drawn filled her ears—

And then the forest exploded.

⁕

Mateo stood across from Lia as if he'd somehow entered a new existence, one where an auroshe was snarling at his back to defend him. Rosie snarled again when Lia's sword twitched. Weeks ago Lia had come to him with her fists raised, demanding he teach her how he hid his aura so that the Warlord wouldn't find her.

He hadn't known then what he was. Now, she kept the sword pointed at his throat, reaching one hand out to take the rock he'd pried free from the tunnels, then tested on the Warlord's unmoving form in the courtyard before riding Rosie away from the island. Lia's aura fluttered around her like gilded petals, each so fragile that little more than a gust of air could scatter them.

Where is the sword? Willow's voice snarled up inside him, like a ghost of the backbone she was to him, but then she wilted, her touch soft and her voice echoing from far, far away. Thin and weak, as if even speaking those four words was taxing beyond her strength.

She left him as he was. Human.

Mostly.

Tual Montanne was human, mostly. A father fit for someone like Mateo. The only other person in the Commonwealth—in the world, probably—who believed Mateo deserved to live. He'd shown it over and over, taking him from the family that had hurt him, culling one of the many little girls the Warlord took in order to keep his heart beating. Joining the Warlord's circle when being discovered meant death. Tual was the only person who believed in him. The only person who had lifted a finger to help after Mateo did nothing but be touched by the wrong god.

And Tual was done hiding. Mateo had seen enough about shape-shifters of the past to know he didn't want to be one of the little skeletons at his father's feet, used up the way Cath had been. The way the Warlord had been.

Harlan. The guards. Maybe Hilaria.

Aria Seystone.

She'd been used up, the last flicker of life gone, even if she wasn't stiff and hadn't started to smell. She was exactly what Mateo would become if he didn't choose the correct side now: dead. Choosing Lia's side, running away, giving up . . . it had never really been a viable choice. But now, more than ever, it wasn't possible. Perhaps it had been Willow who had taken Aria Seystone's soul, but Lia would never, ever forgive *him* for it.

Lia snatched the stone, her fingers burning where they brushed his palm. The moment she touched the stone, the glittering crown of energy over her head winked out. He shivered, unable to look away from the way light dappled her copper hair, the touch of her eyes like fingers trailing across his cheek, down his neck, across his chest. Mateo knew what kind of lie he'd become. That there was nothing he could ever do to fix it. Lia would never, *could* never love him if she knew the truth.

She was an impossibility now. Not a choice.

The unfairness of it made him want her all the more.

"Where is my sister?" she asked quietly, the stone tight in her fist.

"On the island. I can't get her out myself. Not with my father . . ." Mateo licked his lips when her eyes narrowed. Rosie snorted, making him jump. "What reason could I have to lie? You'd know, wouldn't you?"

"Let's not pretend I'm stupid, Mateo."

Mateo swallowed, taking a step toward Lia. She didn't flinch, didn't run, didn't draw the sword. Just stood there, looking up at him. Her words itched, because Mateo had seen her aura was too small to be reading thoughts long before she'd seen him. If she'd been under a veil with Calsta opening minds around her, he never would have come within range. "I stayed with your sister—tried to make sure she was all right until I realized neither of us was safe there." Another step closer, hands outstretched. And he hated it. Hated it and wanted Lia to reach back all at once. "We have to get her out."

Still, Lia didn't move. "We were friends in Chaol."

"Yes."

"I liked you. I want to believe that's who you are."

"That *is* who I am. I never lied to you in Chaol. Not even once." He hung back, waiting for the sword to twitch toward him. "I just didn't have all the information."

She blinked, as if thinking back to every word that had passed his lips. They had been true. He hadn't needed to lie before. "If you want to help—"

The words froze in the air between them. Lia opened her mouth to say something after a moment, but suddenly she tensed, looking out into the trees.

"Lia?" He reached out—

But then the world was cracking open with the sound she must have heard moments before he could, a flash of fire and smoke in the distance, then a sound like a god's death attacking his ears. The ground began to shake, and Mateo was somehow on his knees, the forest floor *groaning* beneath him. Rosie screamed behind him, and Mateo turned to find her dancing back as the dirt at her feet seemed to drain into a hundred little fractures in the stone.

"Get back," he cried, fear for the auroshe filling him like she was his soft little Bella, ready to ride with him anywhere, rather than the broken creature snarling up toward the sky. "Don't fall!"

Rosie bowed her long, sinewy neck as if this were a command, then took off into the trees. Birds fled the branches overhead as he stumbled up from the ground.

"Lia!" he cried at her retreating figure. "Lia, you're going *toward* the explosion?"

Lia switched directions faster than a bird diving for a mouse, veering back toward him. For a moment Mateo was glad because she was listening to him. At least that was what he thought until she grabbed hold of his lapels and wrenched him to a stop. "If you want to help, you're going to do exactly as I say. Do you understand me?"

"Depends on what you say." He pushed back from her, grateful for Willow's preoccupation with whatever was going on with Knox at the moment despite the way his arms shook with weakness.

"The only person I know around here who can blow things up is my friend. And I can feel Devoted nearby. My friends are in trouble."

Lia's *friends*. A web of vines encircled Mateo's chest and tightened.

Lia was already running again, only pausing to call over her shoulder. "Do you have your drawing satchel?"

"No."

"Well then, we're going to have to make do."

⌒⌒⌒⌒⌒

The blast caught Noa in the chest, bowling her backward into the Devoted holding her so they both hit the ground. Noa rolled out of his grip and hopped onto her feet. She ran toward the blast, jumping downed trees and broken branches only to stumble to a crumbling edge where land had been only moments before. Now there was only a hole with water roaring at the bottom.

"Noa! What are you doing—" Altahn's voice rang out and she ran toward the hole, shouts chasing her faster. An auroshe scream needled down her arms, and then another, their beastly cackling racing toward her from the other direction. "Noa!" He yelled again, and she finally saw him hunched behind a tent, Bane next to him with a drawn sword.

"Leave it to you to walk straight into a Devoted camp!" She ran to him.

Altahn pulled her into the tent, Galerey chortling excitedly from his collar. Gilesh lay on the ground just inside the tent, his eyes closed and his face pale, the beginnings of a bruise at his temple and blood on his sleeve. "I didn't walk into their camp," Altahn hissed. "Gilesh was scouting, and they grabbed him. We barely managed to stay out of range. Thanks for distracting them long enough for Galerey to set off that last bit of salpowder I had."

Bane grabbed Gilesh's feet. "No time for chitchat."

Altahn took hold of Gilesh under the arms, and they pushed out of the tent only to find two Devoted standing outside, their swords drawn. Carefully setting Gilesh back down, Altahn put up his hands. "We only wanted to pass peacefully. Your goddess has no quarrel with my clan, and our treaty—"

He crashed into Noa's side, sending her tripping over Gilesh. She barely caught the flash of metal and moonlight, and the breeze of blade slipping through the air close enough to ruffle her hair. Noa fell to her knees, heart swelling up too large in her chest, quiet, as if it could feel the lack of applause in this particular drama. There was no stage, there were no tricks, no costumes—

"Stop!" And then Anwei was there, sliding to her knees before the two Devoted. "I know why you're here." Her hands rose in submission, showing she had no weapons. "We're here for the same reason you are. We're not a threat."

The Devoted who had tried to take off Noa's head paused. "I recognize you from—"

"Put your sword *away*." Another voice rippled through the other Devoted farther back in the trees. Noa gasped at the sight of the newcomer when she pushed into the little circle of open space between them and the Devoted. It was *Lia* . . . only it wasn't Lia. The shape of her face was wrong, and there were shadows spilling from her eyes like tears. Just like the wrinkled nightmare from the deep who had helped drag Anwei onto the boat.

"Of course you recognize us. We were all there when the tomb in Chaol collapsed," Not-Lia continued pompously, her hands stacked on the pommel of a sword Noa couldn't remember seeing before. The apparition shoved between the two Devoted and Noa, batting the swords away with her own. "And you are in danger of destroying my whole mission. I ran away on the Warlord's command to infiltrate the shapeshifter's household, and my friends are helping." As Not-Lia spoke, Altahn's hand snaked around Noa's wrist, pulling her back from the bristle of swords, as if somehow they could melt into the trees and the Devoted would forget them.

The Devoted was shaking his head. "The Warlord sent me herself to bring you in, Spiriter Seystone. Her orders were to dispatch anyone else with you and not to listen to anything you say because of shapeshifter corruption—"

"And the last communication the Warlord sent was to look out for a Beildan healer who was the real culprit, on the word of Mateo Montanne—" the second Devoted began.

"Mateo told you the shapeshifter was *me*?" Anwei stood, a motion that brought his sword to her throat. Her hands came up, her voice wobbling. "I came here with nothing. No weapons. No herbs. No help from any god. I'm powerless, with nothing but my braids to show what I am. I promise, if you listen to me, we can stop Tual Montanne from—"

"It's his *son* we need to stop. Mateo," the man gruffed back, pressing the sword closer. "Not the aukincer."

"Tual Montanne is very close to rising up and becoming like the shapeshifters in all the old stories," Not-Lia interjected importantly, her mouth stretching awkwardly with every word. "The Warlord is currently in his power, and you want to fight *me*?"

Anwei swallowed loudly, making the blade against her throat bob. Noa shuddered, her fingers tangled in the bit of hair now so much shorter than the rest. "I can help you get onto his island without being seen." Anwei's voice cracked. "There are waterways and rooms with. . . boats. . . ."

Noa tried to move forward, but Altahn grabbed her arm, holding her back. "We have to *help*," she said, her voice husky with tears.

"I suppose it might have closed," Anwei drew the words out too long. "But I probably could get it open. With some help. From you Devoted, and your swords, and *gods above*, would you just *run*!" The last she shouted toward Noa, Altahn, and Bane, Gilesh blinking confusedly on the ground.

Which was when Noa realized there was no plan. There was no grand distraction, no hidden doors or surprise flames, no decoy glass window. Anwei was standing there between them and the Devoted with nothing but her body to protect them. A surge of love for her friend rushed up inside her, Anwei sacrificing herself to save the rest of them.

Unfortunately, more Devoted had appeared from the shadows behind them, their swords blocking any hope of escape. Anwei stood firm, and Altahn rose to stand next to her, his hand reaching out to touch her arm almost like gratitude before he turned to face the new threat. Noa tried to fill the space next to him as if she would be some help in a fight.

She had no tricks to play, no sparks to distract with. There was no glitter under this kind of moon. "Can't *you* do something," she hissed toward Not-Lia, whose eyes had turned black.

"If I might interject before you all cut each other into little pieces?" a new voice rippled out over the bristle of tension and terror. Noa almost wanted to laugh at the polite interjection, but when she saw the speaker, she couldn't, new terror knifing through her. It was *Mateo Montanne*. Shapeshifter. The boy who held the other half of Knox's mad ghost. There were dark circles under his eyes, mud streaked across his extremely expensive coat, and a battered sun hat in his hands. He cleared his throat. "Um . . . *Lia* there is telling the truth about infiltrating our household. And about my father being the shapeshifter. To be honest, it might be too late to stop him. But there's a chance, if we all work together. . . I'm. . . I'm on your side."

Mateo Montanne was definitely not on their side. Bile rose in Noa's throat at the shadows pooling like sick all around him, just like the ones around his father. The air felt like a razor brushing soft down Noa's neck, at least until she felt Anwei hunch. The healer reached back toward her, fingers grappling until they found Noa. And all Noa could do was hold steady as best she could while Anwei stared at the boy who looked so much like her, down the freckles across their noses.

CHAPTER 26

The Root of the Problem

Knox's chest pulsed with pain and worry, and Anwei—whatever she was doing—was too far away. "Can't you see what's out there?" he asked his sister.

But she was in one of her dark moments, prowling at the edge of his circle of light, the shadow claws sunk bone-deep inside her. "This is some fool god's plan," she growled. "We have to keep your body alive or my connection to the world will break. It takes so much concentration, and we can't use Mateo's body without risking damage."

"It's you keeping me alive?"

"I can do it so long as Anwei doesn't *decide* to take your soul." Willow's voice broke, and for a moment she was swallowed into the darkness, a strangled cry wrenching from her lips.

"*You* want me alive?" Knox whispered.

Willow's face emerged from the shadow, and she wrenched herself free, brushing off her shoulders and arms as if she'd been coated in spiderwebs, a fanciful crown on her head like a little girl in a princess dream. "I do," she whispered. "But they think if your light goes out, then the hole will get bigger. If they take Lia, the hole will get bigger. Then Mateo, then everyone else. All the death in the world, that's what they want."

"They?"

The shudder that went through Willow, the way the darkness grasped at her wrenched at Knox's heart. He moved on, not wanting to make her explain. "What hole?" Knox stood and walked toward her, his light creeping over tentacles and claws and worms that skittered back to merge into the shadow hulking behind Willow. It seemed to reach around her toward him.

"What are you looking at?" Willow asked, looking up at him, the shadows both a part of her and something else entirely wearing her like a mask. Or perhaps she was wearing it. It seemed to be both and neither at once. Willow flashed, her fingers sharpening to claws. "*What are you looking at?*"

Which was when Knox realized that he *was* looking at something through the darkness. A spot of color on the not-walls. He stepped forward, forcing his eyes to focus on that one spot. Maybe it was a window, a *doorway* . . .

It tried to slide away from his attention, but he didn't let go, concentrating until the little spot took shape, sparking into reds and golds. It was a relief carved into what looked like stone covered in old, cracked paint, much like the ones that had been down in that shapeshifter devil Patenga's tomb. The lines of it resisted as they shuddered into being under Knox's gaze as if they'd broken some oath by letting him notice them. The markings were harsh, hewn with claws rather than tools. Knox took a step back, trying to look at the whole carving at once.

It was a tree.

There was a woman at its center, a twisted root carved around her body, her arms making branches and little flowers growing from the hair coiled around her head like snakes. Beneath her there were more roots, contorted and fuzzing in and out of focus. When Knox stared hard at them, they snapped into shape. The roots were *people*. They were all connected, a single body touching the tree's base, two below him, one below that, making a line of bodies. Some were twisted and broken, others doing the twisting and breaking. Knox's insides roiled, focusing on the woman who seemed to be feeding on them all at the very top. Only her legs were underground to the knee, the rest of her pressing up toward a dead sun in this dead place. Her roots connected her to every one of the awful bodies below.

Were they all shapeshifters? Shapeshifters and the ones they betrayed to become what they were? The more he looked, the more he could feel the violence of this place, the taste of death in his mouth, flickers of skeletons piled high at the edges of his vision, spreading out to make the walls, the darkness above, the floor beneath his feet, all of it connecting back to that *thing* wearing Willow's face. It was as if this place was all one being, manifesting as so many different things. He spun, trying to see it all at once, the bodies, the skeletons, the dead, but he could only see them from the very corners of his eyes where the darkness teased him most. Until he turned back toward Willow, who was taking hungry little steps toward him while he looked around. Her eyes had bled into nothing. The face and voice of whatever this place was because she was the last to be stolen.

Or because she was too big to swallow once she'd tied herself to him.

"Mateo wanted me to live, you know," Willow whispered, but her voice came out too deep, full of needles and knives. "Not like you. You just wanted me gone." Every word growled, her eyes glowing darkly at the edges, her skin going gray, and those claws about her shoulders growing roots and flowers from their knuckles so they looked like wings. No, *all* of her was growing, but there was still a ghost of little girl in the bloating monster. Even when she was the darkness, Knox could feel his sister inside it somewhere.

"Stay with me. Stay here, Willow. I didn't want you gone." Knox's chest grew heavy with the weight of her existence for so long in this place. He reached for her, trying not to cringe at the inky tendrils reaching back. "My whole life was dedicated to saving you from this place. It started talking through you, and . . . I didn't even know *you* were still in here."

"Don't touch me." Willow's voice was high and scared. "Don't touch any of the shadow—" She choked on the words, the darkness swirling closer to Knox, but not quite touching. Her voice lowered into a growl, rougher than a parchwolf's tongue. "Mateo knows what it means to be unfairly treated. To have life stolen away from you long before your first kiss, your first love, your first weapon, your first child . . ." The monstrous hand lifted from her shoulder, a single claw reaching toward Knox.

"I gave myself to Calsta for you, Willow," he whispered. The light around him glowed a little brighter, and the shadowy claw flinched back, Willow's eyes flicking up above his head.

And then Knox saw it. A boy next to the woman with her snakes for hair, her ribbons of souls spread around her like a war. He looked like Anwei. He had her same freckle-spotted, upturned nose, same light brown skin. His hair was cropped short, and he wore a jacket with lacy cuffs and ridiculous buttons that served no purpose Knox could see, only that they would get caught on things and would be easy to grab hold of in a fight. The boy wore the same half smile he'd seen on Anwei's face a thousand times.

Mateo. Knox put his hand on the wall next to the carving, Mateo's face staring blankly out at him. So much suffering over one boy.

"He's not as bad as you think." Willow's voice had turned soft again. "He's like me. But I don't know if he hears my voice any better than you did. The shadows make me say things all the time."

Willow was underground beneath him, like the other shapeshifter's roots. Her fingers were long claws that matched the ones still clasped around the real Willow's shoulders. But her carving was solid, whole, a pillar of strength rather than the twisted web of contortions making up the other shapeshifter's root system. One of Willow's hands had reached up to clasp Mateo's ankle, and the other had pushed free of the earth to grab hold of . . .

Knox's eyes fuzzed over the sight of his own form in stone.

He wasn't bent, dried out, *bloody* like the others, but his feet were firmly underground.

Above him, a new branch of the tree began to form before his eyes. The stone seemed to writhe as the marks formed a girl with long braids, little leaves and buds sprouting from her arms. Anwei. One of her hands was stretched down to grab hold of Knox, as if she were trying to pull him free. Her other hand reached for her brother.

Knox stared at that outstretched hand, Anwei's fingers crooked, distorted, *violent*. But she wasn't reaching out to strike him. She was reaching toward him.

Knox and Anwei were somehow joined to Mateo's tree, an unhealthy offshoot that crumbled and re-formed even as Knox watched, as if it were having a difficult time holding itself steady. And around the four of them, Anwei, Knox, Willow, and Mateo, the earth was cracked. Some of the other humans trapped underground twisted toward the fissures, their hands groping past Willow as if they meant to fight their way free.

"She's ruining everything," Willow said quietly. And all the victims in the reliefs began to writhe, some of them shrinking, being consumed by others so they became larger, only to be squeezed up close to the shapeshifter above, who took everything, no matter how much the victims below fought. Except for Willow—only partly underground, the roots close to her began to wind around her like ropes. Some curled up through the fractures to touch Mateo. Knox's carved form had scars on his legs, like those creeping vines left on buildings, but the mass of rooted bodies didn't touch him now. "All the others like her," Willow whispered. "They want to escape the hole we're making. Adding you in here just made it bigger. But adding you means I'll sink deeper. Like them."

"Was it like this when you first came here?" Knox whispered, turning away from the carving of his sister, wound around with rotting vines. "You always sounded like yourself at the beginning."

"I had light like yours at first. A bond burning bright that led back to the world. But it got thinner and thinner until . . ." Her voice was worried and small. ". . . until they got through it. They started to touch me, then to grow inside me. Don't let them touch you. It hasn't been me talking to you for a long, long time, and I've missed you *so* much."

"I've missed you too." Knox shrank back a little from the darkness layered all around him, his throat too dry to swallow. Over time he'd begun thinking of Willow as her rants and screams, the memory of her like this, the little girl he'd played with, mostly gone. She looked up at him, her face so, so sad. But she pointed to the gray thread connecting them, and it sparked.

Knox's other connection, the one to Anwei, seemed to pulse bright, the darkness shrinking back a fraction before pressing in close again. How long before she forgot him?

Before he sounded like Willow's anger, her hunger, her obsession with death.

But none of that had been Willow. It had been the sword. The darkness. The souls moldering in this awful place with nothing to remember but the betrayal of love.

He reached out without thinking, aching to comfort some of that sadness, but Willow hissed, scuttling back into the darkness. The sight of her bled inside him, still imagining herself in high khonin lace she'd made with her own hands and a little-girl crown. Everything she'd been before trying so hard to shine out from the shadows.

Knox concentrated on the bright light Anwei made of him. *Where are you?*

The steady pulse of warmth in his chest didn't feel like enough. When Willow spoke this time, it was the monster's voice pushing against the light around him. "Why do you hold on to her so tightly when she's the one who sent you to me?"

Knox closed his eyes. Anwei had picked him up off the street a year earlier despite the Devoted chasing him. She'd held on to him tight like some kind of miracle that should never have taken place—Anwei, the poisoner, the finder, the goddess, with a friend?

He hadn't known before what it had meant to her, but now he did. Now they were both taking turns holding the other back from the darkness. Willow ranged around the circle of his light, reaching as if she wanted so badly to enter, but the thing spread through her like rot could only endure so much.

Knox's determination to set Willow free was what had led him to Calsta. To Lia. To Anwei. Even to Noa and Altahn, their faces burning bright alongside the thin line still tethering him to a life outside this endless darkness.

Anwei had always been able to find what she wanted. And she wanted him. He *knew* she did. So she would find him. He had no doubt, the bond pulsing inside him like fire.

And the other bond, the one of gray and rot that ran between him and Willow—he concentrated on it, too, feeding it his memories of her with pink in her cheeks and breath in her lungs, twirling to make her skirt spin around her legs. He fed the bond his years of fighting, his obedience, he fed it *Calsta*, who had promised to help set Willow free. Because if a bond could free *him* from this place, then it could free Willow, too, just as he'd always promised.

He felt the shadows gathering closer around him as if Willow was the bridge to their next victim. Still, he reached, because through all his time with Calsta, Knox couldn't understand how he hadn't realized before that love wasn't what the goddess sought to limit.

Because he loved his sister. He knew there was light inside Willow to match his, not only shadows. And he meant to give her the chance to find it.

Lia watched from the trees as the Devoted dragged Anwei and the others to one tent, then Mateo to another, the rock Mateo had brought her hot in her fist. Not a single Devoted even looked her way, as if she were invisible.

The Basist rock really did block auras, then.

Devoted relied so much on auras to guard that, by the time she reached Anwei's tent near the center of the camp, all she'd gotten were a few confused looks past the smear she made in the air with Calsta's help.

The healer looked up as Lia slipped under the flap. She turned to find Gilesh and Bane pressed into the corner of the tent, as far from Anwei as possible. Altahn was next to them, glowering at nothing and everything as only an oldest son could. Noa sat halfway between the healer and the Trib, slightly singed and looking as if she wished she could mediate, but had only gone to dance school.

"You're here?" Anwei said faintly. "I was worried. When I saw . . . my . . . my brother—"

"What in Calsta's name is wrong with you?" Lia hissed at her. "Bringing Noa and everyone straight to a Devoted camp? This is a new low. What are you even hoping to get out of it? To keep away from me?"

"Aren't Devoted really good at hearing? We probably shouldn't—" Gilesh began.

"Devoted use sound dampening fabric for tents or no one would ever sleep," Lia shot back. "Where is Knox, Anwei? Fixed yet?"

Anwei swallowed, shaking her head slowly.

A form behind Anwei unraveled from the shadows, silence swelling out from the movement like ripples in a pond. Lia fell back a step, skin prickling all over at the sight of the woman, though she was thankfully no longer wearing a warped approximation of Lia's eyes, nose, and chin like a poorly fitted mask. The woman's features seemed to ooze into place as Lia watched, as if the moment no one was looking at her, the shapeshifter forgot to keep her face in the right shape. Anwei didn't look back at the old woman, but Lia could see the healer's shoulders tense, her hand pressed hard into her side where the medicine bag usually hung. The shapeshifter only looked calmly at Lia over the top of Anwei's braids, cocking her head. "Your aura is gone. Have you been to the caves, child?" She shifted forward, her movements too smooth, long habits from her accustomed form hard to break, apparently. "Did you bring more than Mateo here? Perhaps your sister in exchange for an entire camp of Devoted to taste—"

Noa bolted up from the floor, standing between the old woman and everyone else, though Lia could feel how much it cost her to be so close to the shapeshifter. The same as when she'd been near Knox before. "Would everyone calm down? Altahn, Gilesh, and Bane stumbled into the camp by accident, I tried to save them, then Anwei tried to save all of us, so you can stop saying she's all bad, Lia."

Anwei stood. "Lia's right to be upset. *Everyone's* right to be upset—"

Noa ignored her, turning to point a finger at the shapeshifter. "And you can stop being so sky-cursed creepy. Lia's here to save her sister, so don't bother insinuating that she brought Tual Montanne's entire household down on us."

The shapeshifter raised an eyebrow toward Lia. "Did you?"

"Mateo found me. He promised to help save Aria." Lia's fingers around the rock felt sweaty, an extra measure of confidence in her voice that she wasn't sure was merited. He'd come. He was the same butterfly, the same snark, the same boy.

The same boy. The thought was a glow inside her that felt as unnatural as the white of his aura, uncomfortable because she wanted so badly for it to be true. She wanted someone, anyone to be on *her* side, not on their own.

Altahn inched out from his corner. "He'd help me get the sword back, too?"

"I think he'd tell you where it's being kept, at the very least. We'll need it since Anwei *lost* Knox's sword."

"My sword." The shapeshifter's lips peeled back from her teeth in a constricted grin. "Mine."

"Mateo says Tual is gaining power and that this might be the only chance we have to stop him before he becomes like the old shapeshifters. Like the ones the first Warlord struck from all the records." Lia closed her eyes, concentrating on the flare of Devoted auras all around them, counting them one by one before turning back to Anwei. "Mateo was *scared*. With the Warlord still trapped on the island, we might be able to get the Devoted to help us. We might *need* them."

Anwei's eyes lowered. "Where did they take Mateo?"

A flare of anger crackled up Lia's throat, and she forced her shaking hands to calm before she pointed at Anwei. "I will not let you sneak out of this tent and poison him. Stab him. *Drain* him like you've done to the rest of us. If not of souls, it's only because you haven't learned how yet."

One of Anwei's hands snaked up to touch her forehead, her fingers shaking and her shoulders bowing forward. "I only meant—"

"That you're the planner? You need to be able to see the whole picture before you can kidnap your own brother?" The words stung on Lia's lips when the healer carefully sat on the ground, hugging her knees to her chest, but they tasted true.

"If you don't need me," Anwei whispered, "I'll go right now. I came to help."

I came to help.

Lia swallowed the rest of what she wanted to say, the acrid bite a familiar sick in her stomach.

"I want . . ." Anwei's eyes rose to meet hers, the black of them unwavering. "I want to remember who we were before."

The sickness began to blossom in Lia's stomach, little buds of worry unfurling their petals of bright warning colors. *Who we were before.*

That was all she wanted for Aria, wasn't it? That she would have something to remember? That she would have a *life*, one where Lia could be with her, the way they'd been as little children?

It's you who can fix this. Calsta's voice burned through her. *You and Knox and Anwei.*

But Lia couldn't force the words down her own throat now, not after everything. *Knox is already gone, Calsta. You want me to work with Anwei? The girl who killed him?*

And for once, Calsta seemed to draw closer, breathing like a gust from a fireplace on a cold day at the seclusions. Comforting. Expectant. There. *This is the right path,* she whispered.

Lia found herself staring at Mateo's rock, tight inside her fist. Slowly, she held it up to show the others. "We can use this to get everyone out after dark. It blocks auras. I think we can break it into smaller pieces, then everyone could have a piece. Without auras, it won't be as hard as you'd think to get past the Devoted guards." After a moment, she turned back toward Anwei. "But before we do that, I need to make sure no one is murdering Mateo. We'll need him. You know we'll need him."

Anwei's hand crept out to touch the rock, shivering when she did so as if there was more to it than stone. Her aura's white glow of light around her dissipated to nothing. "Do people often try to murder him?"

Drawing in a deep breath, Lia pulled up the back tent wall and waited for Anwei to follow. "Only the ones who have to talk to him."

"I . . ." Anwei's furrowed brow was painful. "I want to come with you. I won't hurt him. I won't do anything. I just want to see him."

The healer took Lia's hand, her fingers dry and cold where they clasped Lia's, the rock pressed between their palms. Lia wanted to shake her off, but she didn't. Anwei meekly followed her out of the tent as if she'd turned into someone new, keeping close every time Lia stopped behind a tent to let a Devoted pass. Mateo's was on the other side of the box the tents made, facing inward with Devoted watching from the center of camp and guards posted around the edges.

"He's not what you think," Lia said quietly when the tent came into sight, then realized how familiar the words felt. They were Knox's words once.

A burst of anger at the thought of Knox steamed up her throat. But she tamped it down. She needed to be in control of herself, because rage had no boundaries, no concept of a future, no goals. It only wanted to break things.

And Anwei did seem as if she was trying to be different. Like someone Lia could believe.

Unless this, too, was an act. Like Mateo. The two were more alike than they were different, both presenting a face Lia thought she could read when it would take Calsta's energy to pierce clear to their souls.

Anwei didn't answer, the beat of her heart growing louder and louder. Pausing just outside Mateo's tent, Lia reached out toward Calsta with a question. *Is this right? Putting Anwei in the same space as Mateo? Should I trust him? Should I trust her? Should I destroy him? Give me the power to see inside them as I could before. It's as much to your benefit as mine.*

The goddess's voice warmed in her mind like a fire on a cool night. *What do you truly want, Lia?*

The words jolted through her. A question her father had asked sitting there next to her dying mother, his hands clasped hard together. His little girl being in charge when it had always been his job.

What a mess she'd made of it.

Power is easy for some because they want nothing more than to serve me, Calsta whispered. *You and I can walk together a spell, but do you truly want a veil and sight? I could give it to you right now if that's your true desire. But you miss your sister. You miss these people who you thought were your friends. The only reason you want to see inside them is that it would prove them to you.* A beat passed, Lia's hand outstretched to pull back the tent wall. *That's not how trust works.*

What do you know about any kind of relationship? Lia asked. *All you do is take them away from people.*

From people who ask for it. People choose their own paths, and sometimes I help them find the one that suits them best. Master Helan showed you. If you do not wish for a veil, then stop trying to put one back on. If you want your family and friends, then trust them. Knowing what is in their heads won't give that to you. You have to believe what is in their hearts.

But Mateo! Lia protested. *And Anwei took Knox—*

Mateo is Mateo, the goddess breathed. *Anwei is doing her best to fix what happened to Knox, as she's said. No one is perfect. All of you are a bit confused. But I have hope again for humans. For myself. For my love. You, on your own, without my power, are enough.*

Lia's heart seemed to have stopped, Calsta's power burning through her a weapon. A shield. A way to hide. A way to fight even the people who were trying to help her. What would she be without it?

Power is not what will save your sister, Lia. She needs your heart more than I do.

Anwei nudged her shoulder, jolting Lia out of the conversation in her head. "What is it?"

It took three breaths. Then three more, Lia's heart rapping against her ribs as if it wanted to be let out. *You are enough.* She couldn't help but remember the feel of not being able to see when Ewan was chasing after her. Of not being able to fight.

And Noa stepping in for her. Vivi. Of Knox waking up and seeing her face, the smile on his face one that belonged only to her brother. Of Anwei holding both her hands, telling her to breathe when she couldn't.

"Lia?" Anwei's hands were holding hers now. "Please, I want to help."

Swallowing, Lia squeezed the healer's hands between her own, the pain of losing Knox, of Aria in so much danger, of a shapeshifter's death sentence over her head difficult to see around.

You cannot let rage corrupt you. The words were her own. Enough.

Lia breathed in deep. Looked Anwei in the eye. "You're going to help me get Knox back. And Aria, too?"

Anwei nodded. "Yes. I promise."

"You're not going to hurt Mateo?"

The healer swallowed. Then looked down. "Not unless he tries to hurt me. Or you. Or Knox. Or any of us."

The raw rage in Anwei's voice was all too familiar. But Lia could feel her telling the truth even without Calsta's power. So she pulled back the tent flap and let Anwei in.

❦

Mateo's hands wouldn't stop shaking, not even after the Devoted manhandled him into a tent, all completely unnecessary because he knew how to walk just fine on his own. He'd been doing it his whole life. He wasn't sure whether to be affronted or grateful that they'd stashed him in what appeared to be some kind of food preparation tent, as if the only guards he needed were a table covered in piles of green stems that looked even less appetizing than Bella's feed.

Golden auras were ranged around the camp like a compass, all of them pointing toward their queen on the island, frightened bees not knowing whether to save her or to hang back as they'd been told. Soon they'd come ask him questions, each one a sting. Because Lia said all her friends had to come. That she had to rescue them, as if she *liked* the weird flashy dancer girl and the Trib, who had swords instead of personalities, and the girl with the braids.

The braids. Mateo's chest tightened.

The tent flap rustled, and suddenly there Lia was at the far end of the tent, her aura blanked out by the rock from the tunnels. "Thank Calsta, I thought you were just going to leave me," he began to say, but Lia was drawing someone into the tent after her.

A girl with a hundred braids.

A girl with a hundred braids.

Mateo's knees wobbled, dumping him back onto the bench, and his mind began to unpeel, erupting with a murderous crack and pops of wood and bone in the place that was supposed to be his home, the smell of ocean and sand and blood in his nose. But behind it all, something else cried out to be seen. A quiet girl just his height waited patiently behind all the screams of pain and buckling bone as if she'd slipped in through one of the cracks in his memory. The girl before him bit her lip just as the little girl in his memory did, and Mateo saw a flash of his own fingers twisting the girl's hair and tying it off.

Something surged inside like scrabbling claws and teeth and shadow, as if Willow was straining toward him, but wherever she was, it was too far away.

"You really are alive," Anwei whispered—*Anwei*. The name slipped into his mind, not because his father had told him, not because Lia had said it. It rose inside him, a memory too sharp to hold between his fingers.

Mateo clenched his eyes shut, trying to stop the flood of his past. He didn't want to remember. His father had said *he didn't want to remember*—

The front tent flap blazed with an aura, and a Devoted stuck his head in the tent to look around. Mateo's heart was a snarl of thorns, and something was tearing at it from the center, trying to fight its way out—maybe Willow, maybe himself—

He slowly turned his head to look over where Lia had been when the Devoted didn't comment on her presence, but there was nothing to see but a shadow under the table, Calsta shielding Lia and Lia shielding Anwei.

Clearing his throat, Mateo sat up a little straighter, fixing the Devoted with a bored stare. "Did you need something?"

"Berrum will be in to talk to you in a few minutes." The Devoted looked around the tent once again, unsettled. But then he withdrew.

Mateo wrenched around to face the table, Lia still nothing but a shadow. "What is your plan, Lia?"

Anwei pushed out from behind Lia before the Devoted could answer, and Mateo couldn't look away because they shared a nose, and her hair was the same color as his. And his mind seemed to *bend*—

Not the violent, thought-splitting pain that had left him in a puddle in the Kingsol apothecary, but a slow widening, a whole world that belonged to him, waiting to be seen.

You didn't want to know. But he could taste it, smell it, feel the Beildan sun on his skin, his life of paints and charcoals and herbs. His life as one half of a whole.

He breathed in, scents of lilia and corta and bei hovering around Anwei like an aura, like a soul.

"Do you remember me?" Anwei whispered, taking a step closer.

And Mateo couldn't look, couldn't answer, the holes in his memory beckoning because he *did* want to know. He did and he didn't at the same time. He wasn't sure how to reconcile the terrible blankness where her aura should have been. He could only see the touch of gods, but she stood unmarked before him. "I can't see your aura," he rasped. "Is it the stone, or are you . . . like me?"

She flinched back, but she didn't break eye contact, cautious and . . . hopeful.

"Where's the boy who died?" The questions came faster, and Mateo wasn't sure they were his anymore, only glad they were blocking the ones unspooling from much deeper inside him, because Willow was swelling up cold like ice, like death, like teeth and claws—"Where's Knox? Where is he!" The words tore out of him in a growl, a scream that tore his throat. *"If he's not with you, then where is he? I want to live!"*

Knox looked up when Willow stopped midsentence and curled into a ball. One moment she'd been telling him about a trip she'd taken with their parents to the market in the next town over to buy special beads for a scarf, and the next, darkness surged around her, the claws that never left her shoulders digging in deep. Feelers burst out from the darkness toward him, and something began to lurch inside him—

Suddenly, Knox's connection to Anwei, to the life he still hadn't quite lost narrowed from a rope to a thread, then a thread to a hair.

"*Willow?*" He reached out toward her in panic, then drew back as shadows writhed across her like worms. "You're what's keeping my body alive, aren't you? Why are you stopping?"

◦◦◦✼◦◦◦

Anwei fell back when Mateo began to yell, the sight of her brother so familiar—thinner, and with cheekbones he seemed to be altogether too aware of, his muddy clothes covered in lace, his hair lopped off in short curls where his braids had been. But then he lurched toward her, his teeth bared and his hands contorted like claws as he reached for her neck.

All Anwei's hope flickered out as she grabbed for Lia, wrenching herself out of reach. There was nothing of Arun left in this boy. All the awful things she'd thought since finding him alive in the tomb, the words she'd wanted to yell, the poisons she wanted to brew for leaving her all alone to die on a beach and never think of her again . . .

It all disappeared when she saw how blank his eyes were. Mateo barreled forward, slamming into Lia as he groped for Anwei's throat. The stone wrenched from Anwei's hand as she ducked, wishing she hadn't come, because all there was to see was Willow squatting inside the body of a person she loved. It had always been the sword that had set Knox off before, but Anwei didn't know what would cause Mateo to forget himself. Or if there was a self left to forget. "Get away," she breathed. "We have to get *away*—"

Lia gasped, because the stone was on the ground, and Mateo was growling like some kind of feral beast. Planting her elbow in Mateo's ribs, Anwei kicked the stone out under the tent wall, terrified the Devoted would find it and confiscate it now that their auras were on display. She grabbed Lia's arm, dragging her out of the tent to find a circle of Devoted waiting for them outside.

Lia was pulling Anwei's fingers free from her wrist, sputtering about auras and something being wrong, and Mateo not usually being like *this*, but then the tent wall tore open, and Mateo's fingers were long and thin, his nails curling into claws. The Devoted were a mess of shouts and swords, falling back, which gave Lia time enough to grab the stone and for Anwei to grab Lia and run.

The bit of Knox still left inside Anwei twisted as if Willow was attacking from inside and out. Anwei's fingers found the packets deep inside her pocket. Sleeping Death.

Lia lurched to the side, dragging Anwei into another tent, then out the other side. Mateo crashed through the canvas after them. Digging a heel into the ground, Anwei pivoted to face him and had to choke back a scream that came stabbing up her throat. Her brother was on all fours, his body stretched long with knobby vertebrae bristling from his back. His hands had grown into paws, and his face—

Devoted burst through the tent, barreling into the supports and tearing at the canvas. Swords flashed, and there were cries of disbelief as the canvas roof collapsed atop them, and Knox kept flickering, twisting—

"We have to stop Willow! Her taking over Mateo is doing something to Knox!" Anwei yelled desperately, pulling the packets from her pocket even though they couldn't help. She had no way to make Mateo swallow them. And *breathing* the stuff would—

"No!" Lia broke Anwei's grip, slamming into a Devoted barreling toward Mateo, flipping his sword up into the air and catching it even as she drew her own. "The Warlord is trapped on the island, and Mateo's our only way to save her. You hurt him, she's *dead*, so back off!" She crossed the swords in front of her, doing some kind of menacing Anwei-didn't-know-what sort of form, forcing the other Devoted back. The ones closest to her began to gasp, hands to their chests, falling to their knees, and Anwei could almost see the energy spiraling out from them toward the thing Mateo had become, a body of parchwolf claws and narmaiden scales, lines like cracks up his fore-legs and spidering down his side.

He leapt toward her.

Dodging a broken tent pole, Anwei held the open packet close to her chest. Altahn was suddenly there at her side, Noa just in front of her, eyes wide. Anwei's insides were burning, her hope, her mind, her body, all of her lost because this thing, whatever he was, couldn't be her brother. The packets in her fingers felt slippery and skeletal, like a death in red splatters and cut fingers on the floor.

Arun *had* been murdered, just like she'd thought, leaving nothing but Willow behind.

"How did you stop Willow before?" Lia darted in front of Anwei, throwing a sword to Altahn as Mateo paced closer.

"I didn't. It was the sword—"

"He's going to *kill us*. If there's no god to stop him, no power, no weapon, then *we have to do it*. What about this? It put Knox to sleep." Lia swiped the Sleeping Death powder from her hand and threw the open one into Mateo's face.

"*No!*" Anwei was running before she could think, the world moving far too slow as the packet tore across Mateo's teeth. The powder bloomed out, the cloud enveloping Mateo's and Lia's heads.

Lia went still. Mateo went still. The whole world went still except Anwei because she was trying to stop it, like down in the tomb with calistet in the air racing toward Knox's lungs. But she had no power. She had nothing but hands to catch Lia when she fell.

Knox couldn't see the weight of something far too heavy pressing him hard against the shadowy floor. The thing roared and cried, and after a moment, he realized it was Willow, the shadows all around them and the connection between them scorching hot. Her pressing into his chest shifted from claws to feathers to hooves—

"You can't have Knox!" she screamed into the inky mist around them. "If you take him, it could kill me, and then where would you be?"

She already took him. It was a thousand voices, a thousand growls, a thousand screams, and Knox couldn't do anything but cover his ears and hold tight to the one line of light between him and the world even as it frayed. *But he's not all the way dead. Nothing is working the way it's supposed to—if we kill his connection to the girl now, perhaps we can take the boy's body and be the shapeshifter we're meant to be.*

The shadows rolled around Knox, but he realized they still weren't quite touching him, a faint glow from his skin holding them back. Willow was fighting them too, it seemed, as if the light belonged to him but the darkness was somehow under her control.

Or if it doesn't work—Knox shrank back from the sound of the thousand voices, a tendril of darkness jabbing toward his throat— *Mateo will be the only one left, and we can take him. But we need to get out before the hole closes again.*

Willow's weight disappeared from Knox's chest, and there was a scarce glow between them as Willow faced down the spears of shadow lancing toward Knox.

Everything went dark and then light and then dark, and when Knox's eyes stopped flaring with Anwei's light inside him, he was alone in his little bubble of light, the shadows quiet.

Willow was nowhere to be seen. But after a moment, he felt the shape of her prowling along the edge of his light, as if she was keeping a perimeter. Trying *not* to come closer even as the claws pushed her toward him. "Something happened," she whispered. "Mateo isn't moving."

"Why did the shadows get so much stronger?" he hissed, flailing to keep hold of his bond to Anwei. It was there. Brighter than ever, growing, as if she were reaching back toward him.

"Because they are swallowing me. We're spread too thin, out like a web, and I can't always make them do what I want. The bigger the hole gets, the stronger they are. I want to keep you alive here and your body alive in the world, and it takes so much of my concentration that they're getting through stronger than ever."

Getting through. To Mateo, the way they had before with Knox, taking his body and mind. He curled around the spot Willow had touched him when she'd knocked him out of the way, frantically reaching for the bond's warmth because he was suddenly cold. Too cold. Freezing.

It was the same spot he'd been stabbed by the sword, and it was icing over.

"I'm sorry, Knox," she whispered. "I was trying to help."

Hands over the wound, Knox finally forced himself to look at the shadows beginning to ooze up between his fingers.

<hr/>

It can't be for you. The echo of a terrible god's voice stabbed through Anwei's head as everything sped back up, Knox a glow of white fire that exploded back to life inside her, as if Willow didn't have enough energy to keep Knox alive and control Mateo at the same time.

Mateo pitched forward through the haze of powder in the air, his arms crumpling out from under him and dumping him onto the ground.

Lia was limp in her arms, her sword fallen like a dead thing on the ground. "No, no, no . . ." Anwei covered her nose with her sleeve, madly brushing away the white bits of powder from Lia's nose, mouth, and eyes, panic unfolding inside her because it wasn't enough. *She* wasn't enough. She couldn't feel the tick of Lia's humors, the flow of her breath, the slow pulse of her muscles and organs. She could only see the dusky gray of her skin, not a single smell to go with it.

The Devoted were a swirl of violence and color, and Altahn

crowded in next to her, his mouth and nose covered, and Noa was asking her what to do. The world was nothing but a giant high-pitched squeal.

It's not for me! Anwei yelled toward the nameless god as she tried to pull Lia up from the ground. *It's not for me. I'll do whatever you want. Please, she'll die.*

Lia's lips were turning blue. Altahn was on the ground next to her, Noa next to him, holding up Lia's head. "What happened? What is that *thing?*" Noa yelled, gesturing toward Mateo. "You have to fix this, Anwei!"

Anwei's fingers dug into Lia's loose shirt. She pressed her mind out hard, the bond with Knox pulsing gold and red and blue and all the colors as she begged for something, someone to help. *Please, any god, anywhere—*

And that voice, the one she'd thought was her own made of flowers and leaves, wind off the sea, powders, poisons, roots, and stone flooded inside her. *What do you want?*

"I can breathe into her mouth. Like Knox did for Noa. How, Anwei?" Altahn was yelling. "Tell me how to do it!"

Don't you see her? Anwei screamed. *I'll do what you want. I'll be the hero you want. You saw me come in here to save my friends. I could have taken Knox and been the terror you were so afraid of creating. I don't want that. Help me fix her. I can't do it alone, but I know we can together.*

We? The god grumbled. *That goes in two directions.*

Despair flooded through Anwei, Lia's limp body in her arms. The world was too small, closing in on her like a wave of the ocean, crashing in on all sides, pressing hard against her skin. Altahn was yelling her name and Noa was crying and she couldn't breathe, she couldn't see, she couldn't feel, but she could—

Anwei's eyes flew open because she could *smell.*

A sickly charcoal, cinnamon, and bone smell that slithered deep into her nose. Lia's head lolled to the side, her face gray, the smell of Sleeping Death coating her inside and out. Her humors were sluggish, fissures of *red* crackling through her. Anwei breathed in, and those lightning strikes in her brain electrified her bond with Knox, the thin string between them once again growing strong. She pushed Altahn back, settling Lia flat on the ground.

But the god inside her turned her toward Mateo. *Him first.*

Swearing with everything inside of her, Anwei crawled over to the thing her brother had become, inhaling until she could smell the terrible dust of death through his humors. Anwei chased every line of cinnamon red and burning orange the powder made, tearing it out of Mateo's lungs, up his throat, off his skin, and out of his eyes to hover in a cloud of gray above him.

Then she fell to her knees by Lia, searching for every last grain of Sleeping Death inside her and pulling them out to join the poison pulsing and wobbling in the air over her head. She sent it high over the trees, and wind scattered it past the camp in the branches. All around Anwei, Devoted were still shouting and drawing swords, but she could only watch Lia.

Her heart wasn't beating.

No! She scrambled to keep hold of Lia even as the Devoted dragged Altahn away from Lia. *No! She can't die.* Anwei pressed hard into Lia with her mind, as if somehow she could start everything flowing again with enough breath, enough energy, enough life of her own to share—

Something in the place where she and Knox were joined sparked, a single thread of lightning that lanced down through her fingers to stab at Lia's heart. It jolted like one last death throe, Lia's whole body twitching. But then it gave one sluggish beat. Then another. Her humors began to move out from her chest, down through her organs, into her arms and legs. Then, finally, Lia's lungs sucked in her first labored breath.

Chest heaving, Anwei collapsed next to Lia, fingers clutching Lia's too tight. Was this what the nameless god wanted? To name who she helped, how and when? To use her like a puppet to save or destroy?

Or perhaps it had been a test, to see if she'd obey and heal the monster in her brother's skin rather than the friend she couldn't do without.

That didn't seem fair.

It seemed like something Calsta would ask for. What Calsta *did* ask for.

Anwei twisted to look at the huddles of robes and armor on the ground that Mateo had left in his path, the occupants just now starting to come back awake, as if he'd sucked away their lives as he passed. Two Devoted had pulled Mateo's body up from the ground—he was human again, his face and clothes all powdered over with dirt. He looked like a boy, but the air around him still held the bitter aftertaste of *nothing*.

A Devoted knelt next to Anwei, and she flinched away, trying to calculate the space between tents and how fast she could run with so little energy left inside her, but the Devoted only bent to touch soft fingers to her wrist, checking for her pulse. Then up her arm to check her humors, as if Devoted cared about healing as much as killing. Where were the gods when Devoted made choices about who lived and who died?

Maybe all gods wanted their devotees body, mind, and soul. It was the gods who ate hearts, chewing them up and swallowing them down. But Anwei could still feel her heart beating in her chest. She could feel the nameless god watching her. Waiting for what would come next.

She didn't like it.

But she liked the idea of Lia dead even less.

And, much smaller inside, she didn't like the idea of Arun dead, and there had been much more powder inside him. So much, she wasn't sure if she could have gotten it all out of him if she'd helped Lia first.

Was that why? she asked quietly. *Not to torture me, but because it was the only way to save them both?*

The nameless god didn't answer her for a moment. *Those devoted to me ask before acting. They know I can see a much larger picture and how they fit into it.*

They ask for permission before healing?

They have to. No human can see as far as I can, and being able to ask and obey regardless of your own perception or loyalties—

Anwei sat up with a groan, pushing the Devoted's hands off her and gesturing to Lia. "She's the one who almost died." The nameless god was talking about an *oath*. Herbs and healing dictated by a god—

Oaths are required when gods-touched deal with life and death, Anwei. That's why so many of us are involved. It's never just one of us. Not you, not me, not just Knox or Calsta. Decisions like this take more than one mind.

Even when Anwei had worked in apothecaries, the owners had never wanted to be there next to her, pointing to which herbs she could use and which she couldn't. *This is ridiculous.*

Only for big things. Can you think of a better way to keep those who follow me from using my magic to stop hearts instead of start them?

I know how to kill people without your help. Anwei's thoughts stung even in her own mind. Partly because seeing Mateo run at her like a wild parchwolf, no limit to what he could do, made her see why. Even knowing all the things *she'd done* . . . Anwei could see why gods asked for so much before they gave.

If asking was what was required to bring Knox back . . . She closed her eyes hard, trying to imagine asking for permission like a little lapdog. Hoping the nameless god would only give what she wanted and not take any more back. But it was worth it.

It had to be.

Okay, she said.

When Anwei opened her eyes again, her brother was still there, somehow trapped inside the foppish, monsterish thing he'd become. His eyes were still shut just as tight as hers had been, as if he were waiting for a god to speak to him, too.

CHAPTER 27

Monsters Are the Ones Who Live

When Mateo's eyes blinked open, he was on the ground. His whole body felt stretched and sore, worn like an ill-fitting coat. He rolled onto his side, stomach heaving, but there was nothing inside him to come up.

Willow had raged to life at the sight of those braids, not looking for a sword or a soul, but to *destroy*. His fingers had grown, and she'd filled them. His teeth had cut where she bit. It was his body scraped and bruised, but it was Willow who had attacked Anwei.

Anwei.

He pressed his mind out to find her, to find Lia. Devoted were arranged around him like arrows, Lia on the other side of the camp with stars in her aura. Anwei was a terrible blank next to her, and he dredged deep inside himself for the sound of creaking branches and crunching bones. But the memory of broken trees and his sister's hands drenched in blood, had gone quiet, like it had never been real. A story someone had told him in the darkest part of the night, only now he'd woken up to see the truth.

Was the memory of her a story? Like Aria alive and not quite right in the tower? Shoved into his mind, like a trap closing the moment he stepped too close to the truth?

When Anwei had come into the tent, she hadn't come with a knife and a curse, ready to end him. She'd been something he knew well, an ache he hadn't known was deep inside him. It tasted salty and sweet, like the tears of a boy suddenly finding himself alone.

Worse than alone. Turned to something new. Something that shouldn't exist. Something *wrong*. Mateo tried to breathe, the last words he'd said—that Willow had said through him—like poison on his tongue. *I want to live.*

There wasn't much chance of that now. At least the Devoted were all staying out of the tent, hovering back where he couldn't snag them with claws and drag them to their doom. The question was whether Lia would stab Mateo before or after Willow had drained the last dregs of life out of him. Perhaps the Devoted would all come together and make a Mateo pincushion. If only he'd worn a clean coat. Something with bolder embroidery. The paintings people would do later of the last shapeshifter being destroyed would be so much more effective if he'd looked the part.

It wasn't until much later, the sky outside dark, and Mateo lying on the ground, trying to remember how to sleep without cushions and a blanket, that he saw Lia's aura wink out.

He closed his eyes, turning his face to the tent wall, the feel of the ghost's teeth in his mouth. Lia had seen him as he really was. He'd given her the stone—the one way she'd be able to hide from him, from the Warlord, from Calsta herself, probably. Mateo had given her a way to escape, and she was taking it.

Which was why he wasn't expecting the tent door to slip open and Lia to step inside. Mateo let his eyes drift shut, not wanting to see the moment she reached for her sword.

"They listened to me." Lia's voice was quiet, her feet padding closer. Not within reach, but much nearer than he would have ventured if their places were swapped. "About the Warlord being in grave danger. That your father isn't to be taken lightly, and that I left the order back in Chaol specifically to follow him undercover."

"They believed you? Not so surprising after you were the only one who expected me to . . . who could face down . . ." He swallowed, his whole body beginning to shake. The ghost had just . . . taken hold of him. Elbowed him aside and reached for Anwei as if she were a sweet roll Willow wished to eat and Mateo had been in the way.

Before, it had seemed like an inconvenience, a symptom of a sickness Tual Montanne would be able to cure. And then almost like Willow was a friend who understood. And now, more than ever, an emergency because there wasn't room for more than Mateo inside his own head and body. Willow seemed to know it too and was ready to take exactly what she wanted.

Him.

Don't I deserve to live? she'd said. It itched inside him, not a disease, but a *thing* that would destroy all that was left of him if he did not act. The way Anwei had looked at him in the tent before Willow had taken over had been the worst part of all: as if she'd come looking for a treasured painting hidden from the sun and found the canvas eaten away.

"Willow does it to Knox, too, you know," Lia whispered. "It's, like, a new thing because the sword is unstable. She's not supposed to be able to reach through, but she's not supposed to be connected to both you and Knox, either.

"She tried to use him to kill Anwei before, and Anwei says that . . . maybe she can fix it. That's how Knox and Anwei became friends in the first place—Knox was trying to get Willow out of the sword, and now Knox is . . ." Lia's voice broke. "Well, Anwei says she might know how to do it. Maybe it would fix you, too."

Mateo rolled over and forced himself to look up at her, surprised when he found her kneeling right next to him, the curls at the end of her braid brushing his shoulder. "What?" he asked.

"The Devoted are going to attack the house in the morning." She sat down, not quite meeting his eyes. "And they are probably going to try to put you somewhere safe before they do."

"If they ride over the bridge, they'll all die. You saw what my father did while you were at the keep." Mateo straightened, brushing off his coat front, the taste of stolen energy still in his mouth. It was impossible to face Tual Montanne. Not even Hilaria, keeper of all good food had been left face-down in the blueberries. "You saw what *I* did, and I don't have control. How many Devoted fell while I was . . . not myself?"

If he were Tual Montanne, he wouldn't have asked. He wouldn't have cared. He wouldn't have fallen to his sister's herbs, and Anwei would be dead. He'd have enough energy to live another few weeks or months. Maybe a whole generation, choosing who would have the great honor of giving up their life to feed his.

Mateo thought of the graves in the tunnel, their names carved into his thoughts. At least one per generation. The layers of rock and dirt over the room where they'd dug up Tual's lost love, hundreds of years' worth.

He'd suspected it already, but suspecting was different from knowing. From really believing that his father had eaten up at least one child of the old keep whenever he hungered, maybe feeding them the same thing he'd used to sedate the Devoted he'd stolen from Chaol. Changing his appearance every generation so no one noticed the boy, the teenager, the man, who came back to work for each and every family who took over the island.

Tual was the curse. Mateo whispered to himself, forcing himself to feel every word. *Tual* was the hand that dug those graves, one after another.

Do you really want to know? Tual had asked.

Even now, Mateo still didn't. He wished for his father's strong stomach. For Tual's ability to do what needed to be done.

"A few Devoted were sick, but they'll recover," Lia said it slowly. He knew she'd heard his whisper, but she was decent enough not to look surprised. Hopeful. To pry. "They want you locked away, but I know we need you, Mateo. We're going to use their attack tomorrow as a distraction. While Tual is fighting them off, I need you to show me how to find Aria. And Patenga's sword."

"You . . . still want my help?" Mateo's heart began to beat again ever so slowly, each pulse a jolt of pain.

Was there a chance the plan could still work?

But the thought felt like sick in Mateo's belly.

Lia was right there next to him, touching him, confiding in him—all things he'd thought were impossible, as if she could see him for who he was and valued him anyway.

And here he was thinking about shoving a sword between her ribs.

"I had to argue a little, but in the end Anwei and Altahn agreed," Lia continued. "He loves you—your father. If anyone could show us how to best him, it would be you."

"Anwei agreed? After what happened?" He shifted uncomfortably. "Why did she follow us for so many years? My father says he would have taken her too. Protected her. But that she fought instead. So why didn't she just leave us alone?" The last came out sharp as the pain inside him.

"Because she loved you, Mateo." Lia pressed a hand to her cheek, a flicker of anger crossing her face. He went very still, her fingers warm against his skin. "She gave up a lot to find you. Some things that weren't hers to give. But I understand now, I think, how it feels when someone you love has been taken away. How it can . . . change you." Lia's hand dropped, and she settled against the table next to him, her arm brushing his shoulder. She opened her fist to show him a bit of chipped stone, a tiny fragment of the one he'd given her. "We broke it up so we all could hide at once and sneak out of camp. But Anwei told me I had to choose whether or not you were coming because I was the only one who knew you. She thinks everything you were before is gone."

Gone. Mateo's gut twisted, glad Willow was still occupied because he was beginning to wonder which parts of him were his own and which were hers. "And you trust me?"

"It's not that simple," Lia whispered, her fingers closing around the shard of stone. "Calsta offered to give back my spiriter powers so I'd be able to see one way or another, but then she told me it isn't what I want."

A shiver needled up Mateo's spine, blossoming into panic. He couldn't let her see his thoughts. He couldn't let her see the hole inside him begging to be filled. He couldn't let her see his father going step by step over how Mateo could persuade Lia to trust him. To love him. And then—

Lia shrugged. "Calsta's *right.* I've always been used like a sword. I hardly know how else to be—swords were all I ever learned. But holding one hurts because I've been using it for things I shouldn't have." She looked over at him, and the panic arcing between his ears dulled to a muted hum. "I worry that if I saved Aria tomorrow, she'd be in just as much danger with me as she is on the island with your father."

"You think *you're* a danger to Aria?" Mateo couldn't hold the words back, couldn't understand why she was sitting there next to him, couldn't be what his father wanted him to be. The liar. The survivor. The shapeshifter. "Lia, didn't you see what I am?"

"Yes." Lia licked her lips. "It makes me want to believe there's hope for people like us."

Mateo blinked, completely lost. "What?"

"You left your father even though leaving might kill you. He can't heal you anymore, and you have . . . darkness waiting inside. All the Devoted saw—you knew I'd see, but you came because it was the right thing." She raised her eyebrows, cocking her head at him.

Mateo's throat wouldn't swallow, his hands beginning to shake. He wanted to be the person who was doing the right thing. The self-sacrificing, wonderful person she was trying to make him out to be.

But he wasn't.

Lia looked down at her hands again, shoulder against his as she traced the lines of her own naked fingers. "I *could* take back Calsta's power. Read all your thoughts to know if you're here to help or if you're here doing your father's bidding." She breathed in, her fingers slowly balling into fists. "But if I do that, I'll still be the sword. If I want to build something new, I have to *be different*."

Mateo couldn't make himself look at her.

"Your father loves you," Lia continued. "He trusts you. It seems like you're the only thing that matters to him, and . . ." She sighed. "I don't think I'll be able to find my sister without your help. And so I'm choosing."

The cracks in Mateo's head began to burn, all the things his father had taken from him waiting for him to notice them. Because he didn't want to be like Tual Montanne. He didn't want to be alone, sipping lives down every few years to keep the wrinkles from creasing his forehead. He didn't want to hurt Lia. He wanted to remember the person Anwei had been searching for when she'd come into the tent.

He had to look.

He didn't *want* to look. Because Tual knew how to save him. Tual was the one who'd saved him in the first place. Tual was the one who had told him to come here and ask for Lia's help to get her back to the island. Tual was the one who had tried to shield Mateo from Aria Seystone's murder, as if they spent enough time talking about the world and magic and sweet rolls then they could forget Mateo had been the one who had done it.

Tual wasn't the one who had sliced through two tents and attacked his own sister. Willow was in Mateo's head whether he wanted her or not, but he'd been the one to let her stay without too much of a fight.

She'd let him feel alive again and Mateo hadn't worried too much about who she was killing to let him feel that way.

"What is it?" Lia's voice made him jump, and she was searching the tent as if he'd found some threat she had missed, a snake or a sword or a sky-cursed narmaiden hiding under the bench, when the threat was *him*. It had always been him.

Mateo looked at her, really looked, Lia's eyes that sharp blue that flashed when she was angry. So much of her was hard angles and points. But her cheeks were smooth pink. She was alive, full to bursting with it, and he was near empty except for a scary little ghost who had learned to be big.

He had nothing. He was nothing. And the thought of Lia finding this out was worse than the feel of Willow's talons stretching out through his fingers, her teeth in his jaw. But when he met her eyes, she didn't flinch. "I just wish . . . everything were different."

Lia stared back at him, haloed in light, her aura masked by the rock in her hand, but he could imagine the golden halo it made around her, the touch of a goddess. And then she leaned toward him.

"What are you doing?" Mateo's heart began to race, a terrible beat that would kill him in seconds.

"I don't want to be the sword any longer." And Lia kissed him.

Mateo couldn't move because Lia's hands were pressed to his chest. Her lips were gentle and tentative against his, the one soft thing Lia had ever done in her life. And then Mateo wasn't frozen at all, the feel of her against him like a sigh of relief, and when he pulled her closer, she shaped herself against him, his arms around her waist.

She pushed away, her cheeks pink enough to put an entire batch of Hilaria's rose tarts to shame. He didn't let go for a second, then realized she was trying to step back, and he couldn't get away fast enough. "What . . . I'm . . . Lia—"

Lia didn't look away, her hands creeping up to press against her cheeks. "I get angry sometimes. Maybe all the time."

"What?" Mateo was having a very hard time caring, the shape of the words on her lips all he could take in.

"I could have put sugar in my tea, I suppose." She laughed, her cheeks going from pink to crimson. "But I had to break my oaths somehow. I can't afford to lose control tomorrow, which means I can't be the sword or I'll ruin everything. So I'm going to be myself. Calsta says I'm enough." She pulled a second shard of rock out of her pocket and placed it on the ground. "If you're coming, don't pick it up until the moon's at its zenith. That's when we're sneaking out."

Mateo sagged back, his head hitting the canvas wall. "I hate you so much, Lia Seystone."

"That may be, but it wouldn't have worked if *I* hated *you*." She smiled when he gaped at her. "All those weeks on the road, I kept hoping you'd . . . show up."

"But I didn't."

"You didn't. But you kept Aria safe."

Everything inside Mateo turned to bile. All he'd wanted was for Lia to believe him so that his father's plan could work, but her *choosing* to believe him was worse than an episode, worse than Willow's claws in his chest.

It was worse than *dying*.

She reached out to touch his arm, taking a hesitant step closer, then wilting a little when he flinched away. "Anwei might be able to help you, too. She's a really good healer when she remembers to care about the rest of us." And then Lia was gone.

Mateo stared at the open tent flap for too long, hating everything. So when an old woman burst through the doorway, all he could do was stumble back in surprise.

But she made no move against him, just settled on the ground, crossing her legs in front of her and looking up at him expectantly. Her eyes were glazed white, and he realized after a moment that she was staring at the spot just over his shoulder, seeing him but not with her eyes. She had no gods-touched aura, so she wasn't one of the Devoted there to kill him.

Clearing his throat, Mateo looked around, hoping for some clue. "Can I . . . . help you?"

"How many times has she tried to come out of you, Mateo?"

Mateo's cheeks stung. "Excuse me? Also, who are you?"

"The ghost girl inside you. How many times has she tried to crawl out through your bond and take your body?"

"Who *are* you?" he demanded again.

"You know me." She smiled, and her teeth were black. "I've been guarding your home for longer than even your father has been alive."

"You've been guarding—" Mateo blinked, coming out of a haze. "I've seen you before. You were with Lia's friends when I first came into the camp. And you looked like *her* . . . only not." He shivered. "Why are you old now? And I've *never* seen you at home—"

"Out in the deep, Mateo." She sang it, almost like a narmaiden. "In the lake, away from people who wouldn't understand us."

Mateo's chest began to contract, all the air bursting out of him as he tried to breathe. He sat down across from her, mouth gaped open a few times before he got the name out. "Abendiza?"

She gave a regal nod.

"You've always been . . . this?" he asked. "A person? A *shapeshifter*? Why didn't you help us? Why didn't you show me . . . ? You ate my *cat*!"

She licked her lips with that tongue. "We are going to destroy your sword. My sword. *Our* sword. But this ghost of yours worries me. No little girl could take control as she did this afternoon. What do you hear when she speaks?" Her eyes flickered closed, as if she could detect the thoughts Lia could not.

Fear pulsed in Mateo's chest. "I hear a monster. Death. Hunger."

Abendiza opened her eyes and nodded. "Your souls are all trying to come out."

"I'm very tired, and it's lovely to meet you like this and all—I always felt very safe with you . . . out there in the water." Mateo swallowed, drawing his knees up to his chest, trying to stay back from her.

"The souls on the other side of the caprenum plane are trying to use you to crawl out of their prison. Thousands of them, all shapeshifters and the people they killed. Bits of you are already trapped in the sword. Part of me, too." She looked down. "I saw in Anwei's memories that the ghost tried to come out through Knox, but he was too strong for her to take hold completely. But now things are even less stable. She took you easier than grabbing the ripest banana at the market."

"I'm feeling extremely uncomfortable right now." Mateo rose from the ground. "So if you don't mind, I'll go scare some Devoted by standing near them."

"I can't see into your mind, boy. I never could with other shapeshifters. Their blasphemy keeps me out. You've made your decision though, haven't you?" She grabbed both his hands, wrenching him back down. "Otherwise you would have told Lia Seystone that there's not much of her sister left. Your father put her to sleep while she died, just like he did to the Devoted he was using for power. Like he'll do to all the Devoted to keep them compliant while he steals their energy a little at a time, as needed. His own farm of bodies sleeping like death, unable to care that he's taking their souls." She jabbed two fingers to his collarbone. "Even he couldn't do more than draw out Aria Seystone's death. The last of her is there inside you, keeping her body from rotting until you use her final drop."

"You can see Aria's soul?" Mateo tried to pull his hands away, but her fingers were like claws holding him. "If Aria's still in there, can you take her out of me? Put her soul back inside her body? I never wanted to do it in the first place. *Please*, put her back where she goes!"

Abendiza didn't move, her eyes flickering past him. "I cannot justify taking from other souls. I can heal using the energy of one who asks me to fix them, but taking souls? I have nothing but regret for the years I spent stealing souls." Her voice cracked like earthquakes and ancient stone. "The world is cursed to bleed. I was the sword meant to cut out the infection. The maggots, the disease. But I only cut it deeper." She pulled one of his hands toward her, feeling along it until she found the pulse at his wrist. "We share a caprenum prison. Your life will be like mine if you choose the sword. Willow is waiting for you. They all are. Even if they couldn't crawl up out of you like locusts to spread their disease across the Commonwealth, it would be the same. The sword is worse than death."

Mateo knew what his father had tried to do to free him of it. He could still smell the blood, the splatters of it sticky on his father's fingers, the horror of watching the sword melt inside Knox. The boy had died, then hadn't. Just like the sword had melted, then had reappeared out there somewhere, waiting for him to find it. "I want to live," he said quietly like a plea.

"The sword will be destroyed regardless," she rasped, letting him go. "And despite what choice you think you've made, you're going to be the one who does it."

"I didn't have any choices. I never have." Mateo's voice rose, cracking over the words. "I didn't choose *any of this.*"

"I'll be a monster no matter what anyone else chooses. My future was written long ago by my own hand, and I regret it—all of us who did this to help were too prideful to see all we really wanted was power. Some of us connected to the sword will have to die to keep the others alive." She stood and walked to the tent flap to push it open, not bothering to hide herself, as if Devoted were nothing to be feared. "Those choices are still in front of you to be made, and I cannot watch you condemn yourself to an eternity of death for a few extra moments of life." She left without another look in his direction.

Mateo lay back on the ground, the taste of Aria Seystone's energy like bile in his mouth.

He already was a monster. There was no changing it. There was no saving him. Not unless he saved himself.

Something inside him twinged, the holes in his memory tearing wider as if to protest, to show him what he should have been, and Mateo closed his eyes, letting himself sink into the memories buried so deep inside him.

There were herbs, shelves and shelves of them, their smells sweet in his nose.

A young Anwei sitting next to him with a mortar and pestle, her hair in short curls. The flashes came faster the deeper he went, all the things he hadn't wanted to remember. His feet in wet sand, chasing waves and falling down to let them soak him through. An octopus laid out on a table as he sketched all its parts inside and out. Jars of paint in every one of Calsta's colors, colors that woke him in the night, that streaked through his thoughts and pushed him until he let them out. They'd made a mural that flowered out from his brush: a painting of his mother with her hair half braided and her wide, white smile. His father had come out in bold strokes next to her, his face looking toward the hands he used to heal, so much more important to him than the two children Mateo painted at his feet. That had been the part he'd loved most: quick flicks of his brush to make himself next to Anwei, their hands knit together, faces toward the sun.

And then Mateo remembered that a man had stopped to look. More than one, eyeing the paints smudged across Mateo's fingers.

Mateo curled away from the memory of the men and turned instead to a faded flash of Anwei laughing with purple frosting smudged across her face, only one or two curls left, the rest of her hair braided.

The images all pulled at him, stronger than Willow ever had, as if the ghost girl were only embedded in his skin and Anwei went bone-deep.

Mateo sank lower, and it was Anwei's smile that stopped him again and again because it wasn't the same as the one she'd flashed at the Devoted earlier, her edges sharpened to points. It was the differences in them both that hurt the most—who Anwei had been before and what she'd become, and the memory of a boy with more than paints struggling to break free.

A boy who wasn't the monster Abendiza could see inside him.

The boy he should have been. The one Lia could trust, the one his sister had loved. The boy who was touched by a god. A boy Mateo was not and could never recover, no matter how much he mourned the loss.

Because monsters were the ones who lived, in the end.

CHAPTER 28

A Bowl of Blueberries

oa looked both ways, hand latched tight around the shard of stone Lia had given her before she ran up the gangplank onto the boat that was no longer her father's. It almost felt like coming home, the railing familiar, the prow just waiting for a new house mark. Maybe.

If they lived.

She ran to the back of the boat to pull up the anchor as Gilesh, Bane, and Altahn followed her on board. She hissed orders as she ratcheted the anchor back into place, and by the time she went to the sails, Gilesh and Bane were at the oars and the boat was headed upriver. Altahn joined her, Galerey scolding Noa from her spot inside his collar when she slapped his hand away from the ropes that would send the sails tumbling down. "Falan's curls, do you know *nothing* about boats? Here, tie this one."

Altahn frowned when she reached out to scratch Galerey's head spines, and the firekey stopped chittering. "Hey, you're supposed to like *me* best."

Noa wasn't sure if he was talking to Galerey or her.

"Go on, get dressed!" Noa shooed him away toward the hold and the clothes Anwei had stolen back in Chaol to make them look like Devoted. When she turned to the tiller, her skin prickled at the sight of the little channel that would lead them back to the caves. Anwei and the others weren't far behind them, ready to return to the spot Abendiza had tried to kill them. Abendiza, who had disappeared in the middle of the night and never come back.

"If you try to put anything sparkly on my clothes, I'll have Altahn set Galerey on you," Bane informed her solemnly, his lips and fingers stained with something orange he'd been eating the whole way to the boat. "Fire isn't so friendly when it isn't at the end of a tether, you know."

"You concentrate on keeping our boat ready for us to get away." Noa caught sight of Altahn emerging from below, a sword hilt bristling out from behind his shoulder. "If you die, I'll visit your fiancée and her cows and tell her it was her name breathed out last." She furrowed her brow at him. "What's your fiancée's name?"

Altahn laughed, moving to stand at the prow. "I don't even remember. Only that she was from another clan and that there were no cows. If you die, I'll write your father an insulting letter every year."

Noa nodded enthusiastically. "Include ransom demands. And have Ellis send a bill to pay for that carom you lost him."

"*I* lost? You were the one who sank the boat. And he wasn't supposed to have it, anyway."

"*Knox* sank the boat." Noa waved her hand dismissively. The pool came into sight, and her whole body seemed to be made of wire, twisting tighter and tighter. It was all well and good to joke, but she didn't like the idea of disappearing into the darkness never to come out again.

But she loved Anwei. She was coming to love Lia. And Knox with all his shadows had saved her life, and she meant to return the favor. It was the other shadows, the ones dancing around Mateo, that she worried about. She went to join Altahn at the prow as the boat slid into the pool, silent and fast and perfect. Lowering her voice, she didn't quite look at him. "Do you think Mateo is really going to help us?" The plan, after so many weeks of chattering teeth and nights sleeping on the ground and elsparn and poison, had come down to something so simple. The Devoted would go with their swords and their magic, and Tual would try to talk to them, but Mateo said Tual was done hiding, so if they didn't want to talk, he'd fight. He *could* fight, a change no one had bothered to explain, as if Tual had spent years hulking in the shadows and had only just decided to step into the light.

A fight was a fine distraction for Lia to get her sister. Not as fine as the one Noa and Altahn would make, of course, because Devoted didn't know how to sparkle. The explosives from the caves would sparkle well enough, and though Altahn seemed to know more about breaking and burning things, Noa knew how to make a show that not even a shapeshifter could look away from, which would give Anwei enough time to take Patenga's sword and cover their run back to the boat, where Gilesh and Bane would be waiting to row them to safety.

She thought through the plan once, then again, to make it absolutely clear in her mind. Mateo had said that was the most important part. Thinking very clearly what was *supposed* to happen.

Noa shivered at the thought of trusting him, a true *belanvian*, the darkness inside eating at everything and everyone around him.

"I came to win Calsta's favor." Altahn's voice interrupted her thoughts. He was still looking toward the cave. "Let's hope that Mateo helping us is what happens instead of us sending the most powerful Devoted to their deaths so that there'll be no one left to stop two shapeshifters from draining the rest of the province. The Commonwealth. The *continent*."

"Look at the bright side." Gilesh squinted as he looked up from the oar. "Salpowder prices would rise clear to the sky. That's favor enough for me."

"The plan will work." Noa whispered it. Then said it again, running through it in her mind once more. When Altahn looked back at her, she smiled as brightly as she knew how. "Then, when we're through here, we can get to what we've all been wanting to do."

"We? I have *no* plans to kiss Altahn," Gilesh jeered. Bane sniggered, giving Gilesh a jaunty salute.

Clearing his throat, Altahn shrugged them off. "More like the first one to track down Ellis gets a prize. We need to get that carom back. Put some fear into all who take Trib treasures."

"I'd like a prize!" Noa went back to the tiller to maneuver them to the very edge of the pool and into the dark maw waiting for them. The boat felt small compared to the mouth of it, Noa hugging the tiller to her chest and looking up at the sails, the rail, the deck like promises of a future she didn't realize she could choose. "Having a carom has made trading down this river quite profitable for the Butcher. I might be in the market for one myself. Maybe I'll get to it before you do."

"Noa, you don't mean . . ." Altahn's brows creased, the darkness taking him first as they moved into shadow. "You wouldn't dare. Go pirate? It doesn't matter how prettily you smile, I wouldn't *let* you get your hands on that carom—"

"*Let* me?" Noa shivered as the darkness rolled over Gilesh, then Bane, then came for her, the cool air inside the cave like a grave. She reached up to touch Falan's flower and sent a quick prayer for the goddess to bless them with all her luck. Darkness was what came before the performance, the breath before the fire tethers ignited and the music began. The black before the spotlight. Noa clenched her eyes shut, feeling the brush of Falan inside her.

There would be an after to this darkness.

She believed it. She had to. You needed light to sparkle.

"You want to stop me?" Noa turned to grin at Altahn before the last light from the cave opening disappeared around the corner, everything around her falling into blacks and grays. "Who says you'll be able to catch me? I'm the one with a boat."

⚜

Anwei fingered the shard of stone Lia had given her as she sat at the very back of the canoe, Lia at the front and Mateo between them, a blindfold over his eyes. The long night of whispering together once they'd snuck out of the camp one by one hung like heavy shadows around her feet, no match for the brightness of the day. She'd gone back to the boat and sat in the room with Knox until the sun started to rise, reaching out to grab hold of his tunic as she always did. To keep him in this world so he didn't float away.

Which was what she was going to do.

The boat passed under the arch that led into the caves, and Mateo flinched at the sudden change of warm sun to cold, his fingers gripping the sides of the boat hard. Anwei kept silent, hoping it would be enough to stop Willow from using him to attack her again.

"Gilesh and Bane are already getting into place with the boats for when the Devoted storm up the beach," Lia was saying, her chin tipping up to look at the statue of the woman holding up the ceiling on her shoulders. "Altahn and Noa will set off the salpowder. Then, by the time you get to your father, Mateo, Anwei will cause a ruckus in the antiquities room where the sword is. That'll pull Tual's attention."

"Let's hope Willow stays put like a good girl."

The edge of his voice corroded with worry, the bite of it familiar. Anwei's hands stalled on the paddle, a memory she'd long forgotten of them sitting just like this with ocean waves pushing them up toward the sun, being grateful because it meant they weren't carrying them back to the apothecary and their father just yet. But there was something about the set of his shoulders, something that tasted different.

She looked away. It was almost harder, seeing him this way. Without Willow filling up all the cracks.

"I'll be there to help if Willow causes a problem," Lia said. "It'll be all the more distracting if she does. Once he's taken care of . . . You're sure you know where Aria is?"

Mateo nodded slowly, drawing his answer out a little too long. "Yes. My father . . . probably has her in his office." After a moment, he sat forward. "I remember Anwei now. I didn't before."

Anwei forced herself to keep paddling, her chest contracting. Lia looked over her shoulder to meet her eye. "And?"

"Father made her sound like a monster. Worse than anything we could ever be. But . . . I think it's like Aria down in the tunnel. She wasn't really there. She wasn't *herself*. She was what he thought we should see."

Teeth grinding hard together, Anwei dug in the paddle deep, Lia glaring at her when the canoe lurched too far toward the wall. They were almost to the tunnel where Abendiza had emerged from the lake, where the passage could take them onto the lake or into the monastery caves.

"This is ridiculous." Mateo's hands went to the blindfold, and it was off before Anwei could move. "It won't matter if I know how you got in and out—" And then his eyes set on Anwei. She froze, paddle raised before her like a weapon, her connection to Knox like a line of fire inside her. She could smell again, the sweat on Mateo's brow, the mud and bloody smell of auroshe on his coat, and something she hadn't smelled in years. Like . . . home.

Not herbs, not mortars and pestles or glass containers or wounds or pus, but *him*.

He stared at her, both of them still. And in that moment, looking at him, she could see that he wanted what they'd lost too. That his life had new things, things she didn't understand, but that deep inside, he could feel what they'd been so long ago. Anwei held tight to Knox's bond, thought of Noa, of Lia, even of the nameless god, the things that were both hers and kept her from turning into something else.

But then the nameless god breathed inside Anwei, letting the last dregs of *Arun* fill her. It smelled like sorrow and loss and a hurt she could never want to let go of. An ending that had whittled her down to her bones, and it was only now she could see how those bones let her stand. The nameless god sat with her as she explored it, making her muscles tense because she knew that the things they wanted weren't the same and the god wasn't above reaching through her to accomplish his own goals.

But he was rock and stone, solid inside her the way Knox and Lia were, as if he didn't mind being heavy enough to keep her from blowing away.

Mateo's eyes closed, tension flickering across his face, but then he forced himself to open them again and look her full in the face. "I remember a little. That's what you asked before."

Anwei's throat was made of blades, her arms and legs heavy as iron. But she nodded slowly, because now she was here for Knox, not retribution, or murder, or her life wasted away. Knox had to be what she fought for. "I loved you," she whispered. "I thought chasing Tual would fix it. You being gone. Our family and what they did. The whole town. What . . . I was."

Mateo leaned forward a hair, his hand reaching toward her, then going back to grab hold of the canoe's side. "I wish things were different. That I could be what I was before."

"None of us are what we were before," Anwei croaked. And then he was standing up, Lia helping him onto the dock that led up into the caves, and he disappeared into the darkness.

Lia held a hand out to pull Anwei up after her. "Are you ready?"

"No." Anwei searched for her calm, her center, her smile. For some reason, she didn't mind not being able to find them, relishing in the feel of herself crackling like a storm and not needing to be anything else. "But it's time."

❧

As Mateo walked down the passageway, the abbey walls felt like prison bars, the bodies encased inside with their weapons, their magic. None of it enough to stop the shapeshifter who had killed them, then pressed their remains into the foundations of this place they had built to rot. Not enough to stop Devoted burning every last hint of their existence away that they could. The walls seemed to breathe, and he started to run, hating the hole inside him that couldn't be filled with anything but blood.

He ran until he came to the stairs, then down to the platform where he'd broken the glass walkway and sealed the entrance on the far side, the glass on this side molded to close over the entrance somehow, as if the Basists had expected someone to destroy their creation and had instructed the glass to preserve the abbey in its last throes. Using the energy Willow had stolen from the Devoted, Mateo reached out with his mind and touched the wall.

It touched him back, the rock molding around his hands, then shooting out into the water like a wave of molten lava. The pieces all arranged themselves in his mind, to make a stone tunnel to replace the glass one he'd broken. When he opened his eyes, a passageway lay dark between the island and the caves. Where his hand touched the wall, a picture formed, a girl with curls made of stone, wide eyes, and her name in stark lines.

He hated the way it looked, hated looking at it. So he crossed, holding his breath until he was in the crypt. There, he couldn't stop his lungs any longer, breathing in the dead as he passed monument after monument to the people who had thought they could live.

Their names followed him out of the tower, across the courtyard, all the way to the kitchen where Hilaria was upright once again. The sight of something so normal as the cook sorting blueberries into three separate bowls calmed his nerves and made them worse all at once. Until he realized she was just staring at the wall, her cheeks still stained blue. She jerked to life when he waved a hand in front of her face, joy blooming in her like a little girl in a field of flowers. Then she frowned, of course. At least, one side of her face did, the other hanging slack. "Half the blueberries you brought me were unripe," she mumbled.

"Hilaria." Mateo grabbed hold of her arms. "Are you all right?"

"I *told* you I was going to make muffins." She tried to pull away from him, but she was too weak, her body trembling. "There's no need to grab me—"

"Hilaria. Gather the other servants. Can you walk? Is anyone out there . . . alive?" He peered out the window, the spot empty where Harlan had been lying. "Find anyone you can and hide them in the stables."

Hilaria's head tilted to the side, her eyes screwing up tight. "Is there something you want to tell me? Maybe about *stolen blueberries?*"

"I haven't stolen any blueberries. Hilaria, please! Listen. I need you to get everyone out—"

"Because your father's finally come for all of us."

"Hilaria—"

"We all knew something . . . was wrong . . . I was going to leave. . . ." Her words came in fits and spurts as if she forgot every other word that she was speaking. "I was going to hide. So he wouldn't come find me. But then he brought you to the house, you with your crying every night, asking for your sister—"

Mateo's hands pressed hard into Hilaria's arms, but the cook only trembled harder.

"I knew we could keep you safe." She reached up and patted his cheek, and he could feel the blueberry juice smearing across his skin. "You come with me now. We're going to the stables." Hilaria tried to wipe her hands, but she only managed to knock the towel onto the floor, purple dripping from her fingertips. "We'll protect you, Mateo. I'll bring the muffins from yesterday to keep you quiet, of course." She grabbed the half-mashed bowl of blueberries. "Unless you feed that horse of yours my good apples again. Then I'll let Tual have you."

Swallowing hard, Mateo's hands dragged down her arms to hold her free hand to his chest. But then he let it go. "I'll . . . I'll be there soon. Stay out of sight."

Hilaria blinked twice, but she toddled off when he gave her a push toward the stables, already muttering about Harlan and the maids. When she closed the door, Mateo stood for a moment, unable to move. But this wasn't a moment to be stuck between all the different paths in this world that he could take. The choices weren't real.

There was only one end to all this that he could make sense of.

So he went to the glass-walled office where his father sat, Tual's head in his hands.

"They're coming," Mateo whispered.

Tual peeled his fingers back from his cheeks, his eyes alight, and his smile made from bones and blood. The dagger was in his hand, the metal pressed against his cheek as if he couldn't be away from it. "Perfect."

❧

Anwei strode up the stairs, through a tunnel made of stone, past monument after monument to the idiotic families who stayed here despite Tual Montanne killing them one after the other.

Lia's hand darted out to touch her arm when they got to the door that led out into the courtyard. Peeking through, Anwei saw the Devoted in their boats, silent as any grave when they stepped onto the bank. The air warped around them, colors fuzzing to hide them from view.

Anwei stuck her head out the door to look for the little white-stone beach Mateo had mentioned and found Gilesh and Bane there throwing down the anchor just as they'd planned. Noa jumped onto the beach, her arms full of salpowder taken from the caves.

Lia squeezed Anwei's hand, and the two of them walked together toward the house. Anwei's stomach twisted, and she wanted to run because the pull of Tual Montanne was there, but she focused instead on the feel of Lia's hand in hers, Knox's guttering light inside her, and everything unfolding around them as if it was just another job.

Her last job.

They stepped into the house of marble columns. Anwei let go of the rock shard in her pocket, almost able to taste the hungry nights she'd slept on apothecary tables or outside under benches. These walls were carved in butter and sugar, icing and fruit, and they smelled of silver and magic.

Resisting the temptation to pocket one of the miniature paintings or the figurine of a horse by the stairs, Anwei slipped past what looked like a dining hall, Lia craning her neck to peer at the woman laid out on the table inside—the Warlord, shrunken and gray and too small for her armor. Across the entryway was a large set of doors set with bubbled glass: the antiquities hall Mateo had showed Lia on the map. Anwei pulled the door open, wondering how she would find the sword, then rolled her eyes at the sight of it standing on end at the very center of the room on a fancy display. The bronze-colored hilt glinted in the sunlight coming through the huge windows at the back, the shape of a horse's head.

Lia gave Anwei's hand one last squeeze before hurrying past the door toward the hallway where Mateo had said Tual's office would be. They were a little early, Anwei thought, because Noa hadn't come through the entryway—

A scream cut through the awful silence.

Anwei wrenched Patenga's sword from its display, hating the sticky feel of it in her mind. She grunted at the weight, the tip clanging against the floor.

Another scream curdled the air, and then another, neither so ominous as the dull rumble that began to shake the floor. Anwei dragged the sword toward the entry hall, the sharp point scraping along behind her. As she poked her head out the door, relief flooded through her at the sight of Noa prancing across the entryway. The dancer's teeth were gritted when she spun to a stop next to the grand staircase and pulled out the first of three salpowder packets to place at the bottom of the stair, as if she were telling herself this was nothing but a performance.

"Noa!" Anwei hissed, the dull rumble vibrating up through her feet, making her voice shake. But before Noa could answer, two Devoted sprinted out from the hallway Lia had disappeared into, no swords in their hands and fear in their eyes. A ripple in the black-and-white-checkered tile rolled after them.

Anwei gaped at the tile bending and cracking as it rolled past her, going faster and faster. It knocked Noa off her feet, then crashed around the Devoted's legs. One shouted, falling to the floor, and he sank into the stone, one arm and both legs encased in a swirl of tile. The other Devoted ran out the entryway doors, abandoning him there. And then there were ten Devoted. More. All running.

Anwei started toward Noa as the dancer frantically tried to tie down the bits of string linking the salpowder packages together, but the sword was too heavy, like an anchor holding her in place. Noa grabbed for a flint from her pocket as a terrible wail came toward them, growing louder and louder. Anwei's mind was full of blood, of the storm that let her escape the last remnants of her home, of sand and trees and the people who loved her not loving her enough. She breathed, trying to let go even as the walls twisted toward her, the floor lipping her toes as if it meant to swallow her next.

Tual was a panic inside her, the monster she'd hunted for so long, only to find he was a fight she never could have won. Her hands gripping the shapeshifter sword had begun to sweat, the bones in her arms grating as she tried to carry its weight.

"I can help," Anwei gasped, but she wasn't sure she'd be able to pick the sword back up if she let it go. Noa was already striking a little knife against the flint, her hands shaking, and then, in a blink, there was a man in front of the dancer, the air a crackle of lightning around him.

The floor around Noa bulged, and then she was gone, nothing where she'd been kneeling but a surprised gasp. The trapped Devoted was next, there one moment, swallowed down into the stone the next. Anwei froze, the sight of her friend there one moment, then gone the next like a kick to her gut. Something boiled inside her like a scream, building and building, but there was no way for it to come out.

"Quick, there are more in the courtyard." The man turned toward her, eyes glossing past her as if even now Tual Montanne couldn't be bothered to remember who she was. Then shock fizzled up Anwei's throat.

It wasn't Tual.

It was a boy wearing a new coat with long embroidery swirls down the back. His boots were capped in silver. "I've found them," he called over his shoulder, ignoring Anwei as if she were teash. "Just like I said, they came for the sword."

Mateo. It was Mateo.

❧

Tual strode after Mateo with a thunderous burst of energy roiling around him, as if he couldn't have asked for a more joyous event than the prospect of death in front of him. He'd never liked killing or pain before, at least not that Mateo had seen. *Everything* was changing.

"You said there were five—" Tual said.

"Eighteen Devoted, six others, and the boy who was supposed to die on the boat. We can take care of him once all these others have been dispatched." Mateo started for the door, sliding to a halt when Tual broke off. Because his father had seen her there in the antiquities room door.

Anwei.

Willow stirred inside him.

The girl who shared his nose. Patenga's sword was in her hands, but it was too heavy for her, Anwei swearing as she tried to pull the tip off the ground to point at them. The feeling of energy and life inside siphoned away at the sight of her, and death crept in, Willow's little-girl voice hardly hiding the warped croon of the thing she really was. *The sword. That one's not ours. Where is* our *sword?*

Mateo flinched when his father stepped forward, pity on his face. "That sword was built for a shapeshifter much larger than you, dear." Tual's eyes traced the line of her long braids, her cheeks pink with frustration, her eyes full of rage.

We can take her the way we did Aria, Willow sang inside him. *That would be much easier.*

"Mateo," Anwei croaked. "Mateo, you promised Lia—"

"I've been wanting to talk to you ever since the tomb," Tual interrupted, striding toward her. Mateo's stomach jumped, the murder on Anwei's face sharp enough to cut without the help of any sword. "You're practically family."

"Mateo!" she grunted, tears streaming down her cheeks as she tried to lift the sword, then dropped it dead on the floor with a foul curse.

Tual threw his head back, laughing at the sight of her and beckoning Mateo to join. And Mateo did because this was his fight, after all. Pulling the energy flowing through his father from the Devoted attack, Mateo touched it to the floor. It was easy, brimming with power like this—he couldn't hold it all himself, but Tual was a well that ran deep, sharing with his only son as if it were no more than water. The stone around him burst into colors, each different kind singing out to him to make them into something new. Mateo breathed in, then pushed the power out, sending a ripple of stone toward the sister he'd forgotten, knocking Anwei off her feet. The sword skittered away from her, the point slamming hard into the wall and sticking, inches deep.

Not like that. We need—

He cut off Willow as she tried to raise her head, the thought of Anwei lying still on the floor the way Aria had like a sickness inside him. The thought of his father taking Patenga's sword—

We need her, Mateo. And his fingers began to swell. Grabbing hold of all the power he could, Mateo drowned Willow out, focusing on Anwei as she rolled onto her knees, her teeth bared. "All I ever wanted was to avenge you!" she hissed.

"I didn't need to be avenged," Mateo said quietly.

The Trib came racing out from where he was supposed to be tying salpowder packs to the far side of the hall. Mateo pressed out with his power, and the world answered. Altahn dropped into the stone's clutches, not even a hair left from his head.

Anwei's scream turned feral as she fought the tiles gripping her boots. She fell forward again, scars peeking out from under her torn sleeve, and Mateo suddenly realized that it wasn't just his fingers that had been taken by their family.

He looked away from her. Not wanting to see her nose, her freckles, her anything as he closed his eyes and concentrated on the magic.

Mateo thought of what he wanted. Then the floor twitched, and the sword came skidding toward her, so when she fell, her head crashed into the hilt. Tual reached out to grasp his shoulder as if he meant to hold Mateo up when she didn't move. His sister. Limp as a ragdoll. Red dripping onto the tile and down the sword's blade. "Son," he started, "you—"

But Mateo couldn't think, couldn't do anything but turn to face the aura emerging from the hallway leading toward the office. Stomach twisting, Mateo tried to block the doorway before Lia could see what had happened.

But she had already seen, her eyes darting from Mateo to Anwei's body on the floor. And as he always knew she would, Lia drew her sword.

The sword! Willow surged up inside him, making his hands twitch, his chest inflate, his whole body strain at the seams. *The sword the sword the sword the sword—*

Panic jolted through him, unbelief and terror shaking through his hands even as they reached for the weapon that was supposed to be lost. Where had Lia gotten it? The same pockmarked blade he'd seen in the tomb. The blade that had killed Willow. Why had she brought it into the keep, why hadn't she told him— No one had mentioned . . . How was it *possible*—

Lia extended the blade toward him, the tip level with his chin. "You told me Aria was being kept in your father's office."

"Lia, it's not what you—"

"And Anwei?" Her aura was like a smattering of gold and silk as she pivoted to move closer to his sister even while she held the sword firmly between them. Her hair was all in curls, and there were scratches across her cheek, red to match. Her dusting of freckles with her bruised knuckles and torn shirt. She was perfect.

"You are everything I thought you were." Her voice came out low, in a growl. She lowered the sword so it pointed straight at Mateo's heart, the blade shaking because she was shaking, her whole face twisted in rage. "I trusted you—"

There was blood on the floor all around Anwei, and it colored the soles of Lia's feet, splashing up her boots as she walked toward him. Willow was a drumbeat in his mind to *take it, take the sword. Anwei's gone, and Knox will be too once the last of her drains out, and Abendiza will go easy enough when we find her, and Lia likes you, she does, you can take the sword, you can take her, and then we'll take you, we'll take you, and then we'll be free. What are you doing, why can't we take you—*

Mateo concentrated on Lia, trying not to look at the sword. Why *wasn't* Willow taking him? Lia's jerky movements had brought her past the pools of blood, and she stabbed the sword toward him until it pressed against his sternum. "Calsta take you, Mateo! *Where is my sister?*"

Why can't we take you? the voice inside him raged, and Mateo's eyes screwed shut as he thought of the plan, *only the plan*, his whole body quaking as the ghost battered against him. *I don't want what you want*, he whispered, as much to himself as to the monster. *I* don't.

Tual lashed out, striking the blade with his dagger, and Lia stumbled, the sword dropping a few inches and her arms going slack. "It's all right, child," Tual murmured, opening his arms as if he meant for her to collapse into them. Mateo could feel the warp of power coming off him, as if he were trying to burn away the thoughts he didn't want her to have. "Anwei wasn't your friend."

Face contorting, Lia pushed off the lie he was trying to feed into her mind and rushed toward Mateo, spinning at the last moment so the sword was against Tual's throat rather than Mateo's. The last sparks Calsta had left to mark Lia flitted back and forth over her head like mad. "I should have killed you in the tomb," she whispered.

"Your sister." The words ripped out of Mateo before his father could do something terrible. "She's—"

Lia jerked toward him, the sword leveling at his chin instead. "Tell me."

"You said you wanted to be someone different," he said quietly.

"Where is she?"

He drew in a deep breath and let it out. "She's *gone*, Lia. I couldn't . . . save her."

Lia's eyes went wide, and she froze. But then she was moving twice as fast, throwing the sword up and snagging it out of the air by the blade, driving the point toward her chest.

Mateo moved the same time she did, the terribleness of what she meant to do like a stain in his mind. But he wasn't fast enough. The sword was already sticking out from between her ribs. Mateo slid to the ground, catching her as she fell.

"I knew there would be only one way to stop you if you turned on us," she gasped. "I hope you die like all the Devoted you drained did.

In pain. Wishing death would come faster." She spat in his face with her last breath.

He cradled her even as her aura dissipated and her eyes glazed. A single drip of blood trailed down her chin, and he tried to wipe it away, but the red made an ugly smear up her cheek. The sword jabbed between them, sticky with blood.

The Devoted hadn't worn her armor. Her oaths were gone. She was nothing but Lia, the girl who had wanted a life of her own.

I want to live. A sob racked from deep inside his chest, and Mateo suddenly felt just how alone he was. His father rushed over, reaching for Lia as if somehow he could force her to stay. Force her to love his son, to fix everything like he'd planned. But Mateo sent power into the stones beneath her, prying them up and letting her sink into the ground before Tual could reach them. The sword somehow slid out of her, staying behind to stare at him, alone and bloody and *alive* on the floor.

Mateo turned away from it, batting back Willow's howls. At least he'd managed to tell her, Aria's death like a pall in the air around him.

All of Tual's plans worked.

Until they didn't.

Tual fell to his knees beside Mateo, his arms wrapping tight around his chest, his skin too warm and the air around him buzzing with power. Willow's voice had gone quiet in his head as he spoke to Lia, at least until now because it began to *scream* in a thousand voices, each of them fighting to overcome the next.

"We can fix this." Tual's voice wasn't calm any longer, almost as frantic as the terrible fight inside his head. "Bring Lia back up! I have so much energy, enough to fill a hundred people. Why not Lia? Son, I know you love her. Why didn't you—"

"It wasn't going to work," Mateo whispered. "You can't make someone like Lia love me. Not more than her family. Not more than the people we took. All she wanted was Aria."

"*You* didn't take anyone—" Tual faltered when Mateo looked up at him. "Aria was a mistake. You weren't trying to hurt her. That has to count for something."

Mateo shook his head. "I don't think it's loving someone when you have to hide most of what you are and the things you've done. What you actually want." He let Tual's arms pull him tight for a moment before the shouts of Devoted from outside curdled in his ears. Through the windows he could see some lying on the ground, barely any flicker of Calsta's touch over their heads. Some were trapped knee-deep in stone, and some . . .

Tual had gotten to some of them already.

"We'll try again." Tual's voice was rough but determined. "If Lia wasn't ever going to fit, then we'll find someone who will. I don't care how long it takes. We don't have to hide anymore. With Devoted so weak, we can help them change the rules about oaths and who has to become a Devoted—we'll find you a girl who won't fight so hard." He sighed. "Though I like the ones who fight. She suited you, son."

Mateo couldn't speak, his hands and arms where he'd been holding Lia were so cold. He reached up to wipe away her spit still clinging to his cheek, then didn't, not wanting to move. Willow was still inside him, her screams building louder and louder until it was all he could hear. He felt heavy, tired. Finished.

But he wasn't finished.

He looked up at Tual. *Father. Shapeshifter.*

"I can keep you healthy until we find someone better," Tual was saying. He pulled back to grip both of Mateo's shoulders, forcing Mateo to meet his eyes. "A gods-touched who can see there is more to be gained in this world than a god's favor. We can fix this. We can fix anything."

"More than Calsta," Mateo whispered. "Is that what we are? Will we have people Devoted to *us*, begging to be allowed to keep their own souls? Like the people in Patenga's reliefs."

"We can be anything, Mateo. No one can hurt us anymore. We'll never be nothing. We'll never be alone."

Us. Mateo wondered again what had happened in that room so high in the old abbey with the girl Tual had loved enough that they'd bonded despite the snake carved into his tooth. But Mateo couldn't see a future that wasn't like Patenga's—the deeper they went into the tomb, the more tragedy he saw. The more *regret.*

The tomb was made from despair. A warning to any who came for the sword.

Would Abendiza's end be different? He'd only seen her a few moments, but what shapeshifter full of power would spend five hundred years as a snake unless it was to forget?

Tual pulled Mateo close again. "It's going to be all right."

"You used Sleeping Death on the Devoted you stole from Chaol."

Tual's brow quirked. "Yes. I worried you'd relapse, and I needed power—"

"You used it on Aria."

He nodded slowly. "To try to save her life. I'm so sorry I failed. There are some things I haven't learned to do yet. But us together—"

"Did you ever use it on me?" Mateo thought of Aria's poor body, no way to fight, completely helpless. The Devoted who lived to fight, rolled up like rugs in the wagon to be used and disposed of as his father saw fit.

"I . . . Yes. I did. When you first arrived. You were injured. Afraid. And—"

"And I missed home. Until you took my memories. You put me to sleep until you could take my family away. Why did you do it?" Mateo hadn't planned to ask the question, the words hoarse as they scraped out of him. "How often did you put things into my mind like Aria?"

Tual's hands pulled Mateo closer. "I . . . wanted you to be happy. You've always been so fragile, son."

The answer felt like a hole inside Mateo. A hole to match the one his father had made with the shapeshifter sword. A hole to match the one in his mind where Anwei was supposed to be. Worse, he wasn't sure his father was wrong about him. "You did it again in the past few days. You made me see a memory I wasn't there for: my sister killing our village."

"It might not have been your memory, but it was still true. I worried that she . . . that Lia would persuade you to put yourself in her power. She was dangerous. You saw what she was trying to do here— she wanted to kill you."

"Maybe. Maybe I would have deserved it." Eyes clenched shut, Mateo slipped a hand into his father's coat to touch the caprenum hidden just over his father's heart.

Tual convulsed forward so fast, Mateo almost didn't understand what was happening until the dagger was in his father's hands, the metal pressing into Mateo's throat. Tual's eyes were wide, a burst of power rippling over him as he drew in even more energy, the Devoted, the people, everything on the island suffering, crying out. Mateo froze, Tual's fingers a fist in his hair pulling his chin back, the burn of skin parting and a hot drip of blood running down to pool in his collarbone. "Father . . . ?" he whispered.

"Father . . . ," Tual repeated, seemingly in a daze. "Mateo. *Son.* I don't want—" He jerked the blade away from Mateo's neck, but the fist in Mateo's hair only tightened, pulling his head back until Mateo was afraid his neck would break. "I don't want to hurt him," Tual rasped, and his fingers began to elongate. "I don't want to hurt *you.* I love you."

Mateo closed his eyes and thought of what *he* wanted.

A life he couldn't have.

Because he was supposed to have died years ago.

The rest of the world could have the life he wanted, but only if he stepped aside. Mateo knew he was no match for his father—couldn't hold even a fraction of the storm of energy churning around Tual

Montanne. But the small sip Mateo took from him was enough to jerk the stone out from beneath Tual's feet. Mateo drew in as deep as he could, wrenching stone blocks from the ground, groaning as they erupted out and bent to his will. The first caught Tual across the back of the head as he fell, knocking him forward across the second block. Tual's hand, still clenching the dagger, sank down into the stone, trapping it.

Mateo forced himself to stay back, growing the stone up to snatch Tual's feet, knocking him sideways onto the ground so the paving stones could slither up over his legs and torso, trapping him against the ground.

"Mateo?" Tual's voice was hoarse, but he did not lash out. Did not drain Mateo.

His expression was the worst part.

Unbelieving.

But then, even as tears streamed down Tual's cheeks, the whites of his eyes bled black, his whole body stretching and breaking into scales and spines and everything not human. Mateo clenched the stone together, sinking his father's hand the rest of the way through the rock so the dagger poked out on the other side, the fabric of stone crying out against the wrongness of what Mateo was doing to it.

"Son," Tual rasped, reaching toward him, even as the rest of his body convulsed toward the stone trapping the dagger, trying to wrench it free.

Stone was the one thing he'd always needed Mateo for.

After less than a second, Mateo felt his father lose control, claws of power ripping at his chest, stabbing into his humors, grasping for the energy he was using to trap Tual. It siphoned away faster than even Willow could take it, Mateo wilting down to his knees, so weak he could hardly hold his head upright.

But then it stopped, Tual straining against himself. "No," he croaked. "I . . ." His eyes pressed closed, his shout like a terrible clap of thunder, *"No!"*

The claws pulled back, and with the last breath of energy inside him, Mateo forced the stone to pry his father's fingers open. The dagger fell. Before he could think, Mateo caught the dagger, the caprenum burning hot in his mind.

He forced himself to look at the scales, the black eyes, the hulk of the thing that lurked inside his father. And at the tiny piece of his father left there that was still looking at him with love.

Then he opened the stone at his father's chest and stabbed the dagger into his heart.

Instantly, the scales and feathers, the claws, the teeth all shrank back to leave the man who'd hidden with Mateo under the bed. The man who had sat by while he painted, who had taken him to every dig he'd wanted to go to, given up his whole life to keep him safe.

Mateo collapsed, tears hot on his cheeks.

You don't want to kill until you do.

Mateo still didn't, despite the burst of hunger from Willow inside him, pressing him forward as if she could make him sip the last of his father down. Instead, Mateo let the stone holding his father captive collapse back to its natural state, relieved to be released. He gathered Tual close as his father had done for him so many times. The last beats of his father's heart like ink and shadows as the caprenum bubbled through his humors, mixing with his blood. "I'm sorry," he sobbed.

This *was* the only possible end. The end where everyone else got to live.

"I love you, son," Tual gasped, his arms wrapping around Mateo's back. He held him tight with human fingers instead of claws, his head falling to rest on Mateo's shoulder. "That much of me is true."

Mateo sagged under his father's weight, his arms buckling as he tried to hold him. "I love you, too."

But love wasn't enough when it came to monsters like them. They were too dangerous, too big for the world to hold. Lia had put herself in the same box as him, calling herself a monster, as if anger were enough to warp her into something so terrible as he was.

Maybe it was. Maybe it would, now that he'd told her the truth. But he didn't think so. She wanted to be something new.

The true monsters were the people who took. The people who blamed. The people who weren't willing to have anything less than everything they wanted, even when every breath they took cost two from someone else.

People who looked at their own monstrous selves and were somehow surprised when the claws came out even against the people they loved most.

You don't want to kill. Until you do.

The last of Tual's energy flickered, and his aura was so inflated and bright that even Mateo could see it condensed into a bubbling mass that sank down into the dagger instead of up into the sky.

Mateo bent over him and wept.

He didn't want his father to die.

He didn't want to kill.

He didn't want any of it.

CHAPTER 29

A New Way to Grow

Knox's connection to Anwei felt gray at the edges, shadows misting across his skin eating away at it. Willow was everywhere, her growls tearing through the prison. "The sword was right there. It was *right there*," Willow hissed. "He could have taken it. Why didn't he take it?" Her little-girl voice tore at the edges, contorting into the dark hunger waiting all around her. "We'll get into Mateo and *make* him take it. If we switch places—"

"I can't let you push me into Mateo." Willow suddenly shrank down, flickering and contorting. Her voice was her own again, not the hiss of a thousand monsters hiding in the dark. She was losing her battle without Knox's body holding her like an anchor to the world. "If Knox dies, Mateo will die, and the opening will snap shut," she pled. "You'll never get out again."

"Knox is dying." Her voice changed again to the one of teeth and hate, her body swelling up larger. "There's almost nothing left. But if we kill them in the right order, we'll be free."

Knox stared down at the shadow wafting up from the puncture in his side and closed his eyes. The bond seemed to flutter and twinge, as if the hole that let him into this place was twisting smaller every second. *Please, Anwei. Whatever you are doing, you need to do it faster.*

Willow's head pressed out from the shadow toward him, and he could feel an echoing press inside him where shadows had wormed their way out from his wound and were eating away at him from the inside. He bowed his head, reaching for Calsta, for Anwei, for anything. *All I wanted was to get my sister out.*

Please.

☙❦❧

Anwei didn't like being dead. She'd only done it once before when a crime boss over in the Elantin port had followed a trail of very sick minions to her doorstep and she'd had to do something drastic. Dying seemed to fit the bill. She'd shipped her own limp body out of the port city before he managed to murder her in whatever fabulously grisly way he'd planned to show what happened to people who crossed him. Even if he hadn't been satisfied with the outcome exactly, he'd let her go. A lifeless person nailed into a box being shipped north was much less fun to stab than a live one, and that was without considering what would happen if he had risked crossing the mail carriers to get her. Few were unintelligent enough to do *that*. Anwei hadn't much liked the part where she'd been there one moment, then gone the next, waking up days later to shiver over what could have happened to her while she had been sleeping so deeply.

Death, however, was required sometimes. And facing down a shapeshifter who would happily provide a proper death if you did not bring your own was one such case. She forced her eyes open, the stone around her smelling of a shapeshifter's touch.

Mateo had done it, then. Followed the plan.

Anwei and Lia had sat together whispering over the unopened packet of Sleeping Death for hours before calling him out of the camp, carefully making the little packets for each of their crew to hold in their mouths, ready to bite down the moment Mateo pretended to kill them one by one. Anwei had seen it work for Noa and Altahn as Mateo opened the floors beneath their feet. Tual Montanne could feel the tick of humors like a Basist and see auras like a Devoted, so both had needed to be stopped. Sleeping Death had fixed hearts and lungs, and the aura-cancelling stones had done for the other. The very picture of a quick death.

But there were tunnels under the island. Unlike the one lined with graves, the tunnel Mateo had dropped them into was stirring with life. Anwei could hear Noa laughing, Altahn grumbling, both of them trying to shake off the tiny dose Anwei had given them.

A voice, so tiny and weak, broke through the cotton stuffing her head. *Help.*

Anwei tried to sit up, her muscles water and her mouth made from sand. A hand gripped her shoulder, Noa's face appearing overhead. "Are you awake?" she asked. "Because you didn't warn me that coming back from the dead would involve wishing Mateo had just gone through with it."

Help. The voice broke, like shattered bone and burning hair. The bond. It was the *bond,* Knox's voice breaking through like it had that very first day in Chaol, panic like a fire inside him.

"Noa!" she croaked. "I have to get to Knox on the boat. Something's wrong—help me up."

Noa took both her hands to help her stand. "I'll come with you."

Anwei wobbled down the tunnel with Noa's help, the sickly, flushed smell of sugar beet paste sticky in her hair making her stomach turn as if it had been real blood. She forced her legs to move up the passage faster and faster until she was running, trying not to think of what she must have looked like, her death lingering enough for Tual to believe, with only Lia to protect her if Mateo went wrong.

The Devoted had taken her hand before going to get Mateo. *I will not let him take you.* Anwei had flinched at the sound of the words, because they were her own once, and she had not been able to fulfill them when Lia had needed her. But Lia hadn't blinked. *I don't think he will hurt you,* she'd said, *but I am prepared to stop him if he tries.*

It hurt, planning to be the distraction. The *sparkle*, when all Anwei's life she'd been the hands that did what needed to be done. The last moments of pure rage and *nothing* she'd seen in Mateo's eyes before her mind had gone blank rippled through her like the memory of a knife in her mother's hand.

They are not what make you. The nameless god's voice was almost annoyed. *Not any more than I am. Their choices don't make yours or Mateo's or anyone else's. You make your own.* The last words grumbled out, barely there. *That's the only reason we had a chance to fix any of this, you know. Hoping you little humans would finally listen to us and choose things that would help everybody, even if it hurt you for a little while.*

Anwei ignored him as she stumbled past a monument, her skirt catching a little statue of a cat curled at the base. She was almost glad to have him poke at her though, despite the way her scars still twinged.

You make your own choices.

Like her family on the beach. Her town, twisted in roots and branches. Like Knox, breathing when he should have been dead, even as the lash of her magic killed Shale in the tunnels. Decisions made in panic and without help, with outcomes she was both grateful for and would always regret.

Her scars were a testament to what could happen when people lost control to fear, anger, and hate.

Mateo had done some of what he'd promised—he hadn't struck Anwei down with the sword when Lia had brought it into the hall. He'd dropped her through the floor along with everyone else.

He'd chosen, just like Lia said he could. But now—

By the time Anwei pushed open the secret door into the tower's main floor, Knox had stopped crying out for help, nothing but a frantic pulse inside her. Her arms and legs began to shake with the feel of it;

part of her was draining away with each burst of light. Desperate, she flung open the tower doors, ignoring the shapes of fallen Devoted on the paving stones, their eyes empty as they stared up toward their goddess.

She could hardly spare a look for Tual Montanne's house to wonder if it would be him waiting for her at Noa's boat where Gilesh and Bane had left it tethered on the little beach. The two Trib were nothing but breaks in the earth where Mateo must have dropped them through to the tunnels below. Out of breath, tears running down her cheeks at the pain in her chest and the frantic silence inside her, Anwei waded out to the boat, her skirts dragging as she crawled over the rail and flopped onto the deck.

But when she stumbled down the ramp leading to the hold, she found *him* instead.

Mateo. His cheeks too thin, his eyes shadowed, and a pockmarked sword in his hands. Knox's body lay behind him, so, so still in the canoe where they'd placed him just in case they had to abandon the boat.

Knox's life thumped a rhythm in Anwei's head, like a heart on its last beats.

Mateo's fingers gripped the sword so tightly that blood was dripping onto the deck where he held the blade. It looked slick, oily in his hands, just like when Abendiza had appeared in the tent the night before carrying it.

She'd pulled Anwei away from all the others, a worried eye on the tent where Mateo sat alone. "Using Mateo Montanne is unsafe. It's *insanity*, child."

"We don't have another choice—" Anwei started to reach for the sword and had to pause, her stomach turning at the sight of it.

"You don't think the threat of dying will be enough to control Mateo?" Lia pushed between them, eyeing the sword with curiosity.

"This thing is unstable," Abendiza hissed, jerking it away from Lia when she reached for it, then immediately looking contrite. Swallowing, the old woman closed her eyes and held the sword out toward Anwei. Every movement was pained and mechanical, as if offering it was taking all the concentration she had. "We should destroy it here. *Now.*"

Anwei forced herself to reach for the sword, taking its awful weight in her hands. It smelled like death, like pain, like rage, like *nothing.* "You didn't seem anxious to get rid of it before."

"I didn't realize just how far out the broken souls could come. They *took Mateo.*"

"That's not normal? She's done that to Knox lots of times." Anwei walked back over to Altahn, Gilesh, and Bane as they went over the map traced into the dirt and set the sword down on top of her medicine bag.

"*No*, it's not normal. They used Mateo to attack *you.*"

"She's used Knox to attack me more than once."

"We thought it was so he could turn into a shapeshifter—" Lia followed her, reaching out to touch the sword, her finger trailing along the groove running the length of the blade. "All Willow ever wanted was to be fed. Souls. Energy. Knox couldn't take from other people, so she had to feed on him, and it wasn't enough. She took from Mateo too, and it still wasn't enough. But if she killed Anwei, the Basist Knox was bonded to—"

Abendiza was already shaking her head. "The dead souls shouldn't have so much control. I've never seen anything like this before, the dead reaching out to control the living. They whisper, they justify, they ask to be sustained in exchange for their advice and greater knowledge. . . ." Abendiza shuddered, pushing out of the tent to stand where she couldn't see the weapon as if it was still calling to her. Anwei set the sword down next to the map and followed, Lia close behind her. "But they don't *take.* Yet they chose to kill *Anwei* today, and that doesn't make sense. What would killing Anwei accomplish? The goal was always to kill you, young lady." She raised an eyebrow at Lia, who frowned. "And you were there, right in front of him. But he attacked her." She jabbed a finger at Anwei.

"Well, we aren't bonded, and he didn't have the sword . . . ." Lia began to tick the reasons off on her fingers.

"But why go after Anwei at all? They see the opportunity—they see how unstable the opening to their world is. I think they mean to destroy the sword too. To kill all of us holding the way between our planes open—but I think they plan to do it while they're *in Mateo*." She looked up at the sky as if there were something up there to appeal to for help, some combination of Castor, Jaxom, Calsta, and all the gods, all their magic and expertise, to stop what she could see happening. "If Willow comes out with all of them attached, we'll have something worse than the shapeshifters of old—Mateo would become a hungrier monster than the Commonwealth has ever seen. Hundreds of broken souls all taking from others. The victims are no better than the murderers after all these years. All they know is hunger. He would destroy everything in this country. In this world."

Anwei scrubbed at her palm where it had been touching the sword, the *nothing* still clinging to her hands like a foul itch. She'd seen Mateo's empty eyes. She could see the possibility of that future.

"How much of that is a choice?" Lia interjected. "Bonds are a choice. Oaths are a choice. Loving someone is a choice. So is killing someone. Mateo doesn't even remember who Anwei is. He's frightened of her."

"Knox was able to snap out of his episodes when I talked to him. More than once, actually." Anwei thought of the day in Knox's room when he'd been so frightened of Devoted finding him, then down in the tunnels the first time they'd gone into the dig.

And again when he'd fought Lia, trying to get to Anwei with Tual looking on. It had been his bond with Anwei that had saved them both, allowing Knox to push past Willow and retake control.

"We are outside of any researched conclusions." Abendiza wiped her hands on her long robes, looking toward the Devoted camp. "But Mateo is not a strong enough person that I'd be willing to trust him with my soul. Why do you think I brought the sword to you?" Her head swung toward Anwei. "You'll destroy it because what you want most is to bring Knox out."

"You still haven't told us how exactly we're supposed to do that," Anwei pointed out.

"Caprenum is at its weakest when it is in transition. You've seen it before—the way it melts when it's tearing a soul."

"You mean we have to kill someone with it." Lia's voice went flat.

Anwei's stomach twinged at Abendiza's matter-of-fact nod. "Not just someone. You have to kill one of you connected to it. While it's in that in-between state, we should be able to spread it out. Isolate the pieces so it can't re-form. Destroy the openings in the barrier for good." She pressed her hands to her chest. "It might let out those of us who still have a body and a life to come back to."

She was being very careful in the way she spoke. Anwei matched her matter-of-fact tone. "Or it might kill all of us?"

The old shapeshifter's mouth spread to a wide grin. "I suppose mincing words would be pointless. It's a better fate than being trapped inside the sword, child. How much are you willing to risk to save this boy you love?"

Anwei traced the feel of Knox inside her, his light guttering smaller for some reason. She reached toward him, wishing she could hear his voice. All she'd felt were rushes of panic, as if he were clinging to her like a rope suspended over an abyss.

She clung back, as she always had.

Sacrifice is power. That's what love is, after all, the nameless god whispered. *Knox won't live without you here. But there is great power in giving up yourself for those you love. That is what oaths are.* "We have everything we need right here to destroy the sword." Abendiza turned back to the tent, her sightless gaze fixed about where Anwei had left it inside. "I don't care about your fascination with Tual Montanne—let someone else go up against him. We need to take care of this *now* before Willow comes crawling out of the sword to trap us all inside and slam the door behind us."

"Who did you want me to kill so that you can live?" Anwei whispered.

Abendiza flinched. "I've lived on borrowed power for so many years that I doubt I'll survive. Besides, I'm an outside point on the web—hardly connected to any of you. A *sure* solution would be to—"

"To kill Knox? Or Mateo . . . or me." Anwei's palms began to sweat. "And whoever dies will likely end up trapped inside the sword because they *won't* be connected to this world anymore. They'll be dead. Like all the others inside there."

"Ideally that person won't be trapped for *long*—" Abendiza countered. "And if you were to choose Mateo, he'd probably count it as a boon."

"We are not killing Mateo," Lia whispered. "He's the only one who knows where my sister is."

"That's true enough," Abendiza snorted.

Anwei reached out and took Lia's hand. "I'm not going to kill anyone. Killing has been the answer people keep reaching for over and over, and it hasn't served any of us very well. Shapeshifters. The Warlords. Tual. You. Abendiza. Me." She shook her head. "We can find another way to destroy the sword."

Abendiza's lips curled back, her hands in fists. "You will doom us all." But she turned and walked away into the forest, control tight across her shoulders as she melted into the darkness. Not willing to destroy anyone else even if it meant she might be able to go free.

Noa's head peeked out from the tent. "She scares me very much."

Anwei let Noa pull her back into the tent, her mind running. If the sword was so unstable, maybe she could brew and burn and magic the sword into pieces with the nameless god's help. But he didn't say anything, his words from before echoing back. *Sacrifice is power.*

Lia's hand in Anwei's squeezed as they walked back toward Altahn and the others to finalize their plans. "Mateo has done the right thing over and over. He's stronger than you think."

Noa settled between Altahn and Gilesh to trace a little flower next to the little rock that represented their boat on the map. "Runs in the family."

Anwei flinched, almost as if Noa had accused her of something. She'd been so focused on what she wanted that she'd somehow tried to let go of the things she loved to get it.

"He is a lot like you, Anwei." Lia moved to pick up the sword, Altahn, Gilesh, and Bane looking up as she tested the balance, then pulled off the empty sheath at her back and slid the sword inside. When she looked back at Anwei, her eyes were hard. "You really think that old creature is telling the truth? That you can get Knox out of here?"

Choices. What she wanted. What she loved. They all mattered. Anwei pressed her hands to her chest, feeling the steady *tick, tick, tick* of her own heart. If it came to it, she knew what she was willing to give up. So she nodded.

"What about Mateo? Can you get the part of him that's stuck in there out?"

"I don't know," Anwei whispered. But she thought of the boy she'd been so angry over for the last eight years, the boy with braids, his face smeared with purple frosting.

For that little boy, she'd do anything, though she wasn't so sure about what he'd become.

Lia set the sword back down and went to the tent flap. "I'll go talk to him then, Anwei." She paused, looking back. "I won't let him take you."

The words still hurt. But as Lia snuck out into the darkness, Noa pulled Anwei back into the tent to look at the maps again. Huddled between Altahn and Noa, Anwei felt as if both her feet were on solid ground instead of crumbling through to the rushing water beneath. Maybe for the first time since standing on that beach with blood running down her arms.

Because that was what she'd hated the snake-tooth man for taking from her. Love.

And now, back at the boat as she faced her brother, she felt the weight of Lia, wherever she was, of Knox mostly dead where he'd been placed in the canoe to protect him while they rowed, of Noa and Altahn, even Gilesh and Bane, all there because of one another.

The words echoed in her mind as Anwei walked toward Mateo. His face, his voice, all so familiar except for those long, terrible fingers made from stolen souls.

Mateo is a lot like you.

Anwei hoped not.

Slowly, painfully, Mateo set the sword onto the deck. "If you make me wait, I'll get bored and go order a new coat or something." His face contorted with pain, and his fingers began to stretch. Mateo clenched his eyes shut, hunching over the sword. "Please. I can't hold on to her much longer. I know how this thing gets broken. And I know what's holding it together: I am. *We* are."

"You're stopping Willow from taking you," Anwei breathed. "You stopped her when I had Patenga's sword. Why?"

"Listen to what I am saying. I can't—" His hands, those long fingers that were claws and then fingers and then . . . not, shrinking down as if there were nothing there. "I remember you. Not very much, but I . . . . understand now why you followed me so long. And I wish I'd known so I could have . . . I was scared. I was angry. And my father loved me, so I just . . . didn't look back. And I wish I had." Tears were running down his cheeks. "I wish I had, because even if he loved me, it wasn't fair to separate us."

Anwei's throat was like a vise, holding her voice fast.

"We both know—" The words came out in spurts, his fingers growing long again. "We both know it needs to be destroyed. And that to do it, someone has to die." When he opened his eyes, they were the wrong color, the pupils stretching to slits. But she could still see him, the boy who had tied her last braid. "I want you to live."

He kicked the sword toward her.

Stronger than you think. The words pulsed in Anwei's mind alongside Knox's. *Please, Anwei.*

And the nameless god. *Sacrifice is power.*

Mateo's arms had begun to stretch, his teeth curving down to press into his lip, blood running down his chin. "Do it." The pockmarked blade was there at her feet, absorbing sunlight instead of reflecting. Mateo's coat was streaked with burns.

He looked hollow, as if every last bit of what made him up had already gone. But it wasn't. The sword stinking of *nothing nothing nothing*, reached out for him as it always had with Knox, but Mateo was reaching for her too. That's what bonds were made of. Choices.

"Just . . . do it," Mateo's voice croaked. "I know there isn't enough soul left for me and Knox both. You don't need to pretend you came here for anything else. Please. Just do it. This is my gift to you. My recompense."

Recompense. Just like Anwei had always wanted. For her not believing anyone would love her enough to stay. For not being worth remembering when all she'd ever been able to do was remember, stuck in that one awful moment where everything went wrong. Knox's connection to Anwei pulsed like acid and corta and calistet and poison and hopes and dreams and terrible nightmares. She grabbed hold of the sword.

One of us will have to die, Abendiza said.

One of us.

Anwei couldn't believe it. The old woman thought in calculations of souls on a scale, moving grains between the dishes to even them out. But all this had come about through killing—the sword hadn't even melted when it had taken Knox. It had sat there, firm between her shoulder blades, as if every breath it took now made it more solid.

Killing only made everything worse.

The thought sat inside Anwei even as her hands gripped the sword, Knox still as death. *I need him. I want him back. I have to fix him.* Her hand twitched toward Mateo, sitting there with his throat bared.

He hadn't forgotten her on purpose. Arun hadn't become Mateo to spite her or leave her behind. He'd done it because he had been led, following in the footsteps of a monster who professed to love him more than Anwei could.

But that was a lie.

Inside her, she could feel the truth of it, the burning image of Arun, who she'd wanted so badly to save. Because somehow it would have saved her, too.

But killing Tual Montanne never would have changed what had happened to the people she loved. It would have just been more blood spilled.

Anwei grabbed hold of Knox with one hand, focusing on the sick beat of *nothing* coming from the bond in time with his light dying in her head. Setting the sword down next to him in the canoe, she offered Mateo her hand. "Help me," she rasped.

Mateo's hands twitched forward as if he wanted to take it. "Help you?" he moaned. "I'm *trying* to help you. Is my life not enough?"

"No." Her voice broke, her hand shaking as she held out the sword. "You betrayed me, you forgot me, and you left me to die." She couldn't stop her voice from whittling down. "I shouldn't have to help you fix things now! I want to *live*, so something has to change. What is it *you* want, Mateo?" She grabbed his hand, linking her fingers through his, warmth spreading up her arm as she realized how familiar it felt. "Lia says you're stronger than we think. Stronger than *you* think. I didn't believe her before, but I want to now. I *have* to. Help me save Knox instead of giving up. You owe me more than that."

Mateo looked at their hands joined together, his face panicked.

"Remember who you are," Anwei demanded. "Who you were before and . . . and the good parts of who you've become. Who you *want* to be."

She took Knox's limp hand, Knox only a shadow in her mind. *Please*, she thought she heard his voice say. *Please.*

Mateo started to shake, and Anwei could feel the shape of the ghost inside him, of the unfairness, of wanting to live. Willow pressed out through his skin, swapping between Knox and Mateo, Knox and Mateo, the energy running faster, hotter, building up inside Mateo to stretch his fingers long, the ends blacking to claws.

She reached out and covered one of his hands on the blade, hope a razor inside her. "Your name was Arun Ruezi."

⁂

Mateo's hands were on the sword, and the world was going dark. Willow was hunched in the darkness, squeezing tighter and tighter around him, only it wasn't just her; it was hundreds, thousands of eyes and hands, their skeleton fingers pressing out through his skin until he thought he would break, each one trying to grab hold of the sword. But Anwei's hands were on his as if she knew he didn't have the strength to do it alone any longer. "Your name," she whispered, "was Arun Ruezi."

And in the storm of bones and death and *nothing* inside him, Mateo could see her face looking up at him from his memories.

Her voice shook. "We took turns taking the blame when Father got mad because something wasn't clean enough, or ground fine enough, or the right color."

The memory of her was like an eye in the terrible hurricane of magic and hatred and wanting. Darkness peeled back from her voice, Mateo breathing through their rage that was his own. Of unfairness, of a world that didn't want him to exist, of death waiting inside him and the bridge Tual had built time and time again to let him wander back into life.

He pulled back, because the bridge was made of bones, made of compromises, made from death and hurt. The bridge was made from those who'd had as much right to live as he did.

The ghost inside him was desire, it was hate, it was power taken for reasons that could be explained away and reasons that couldn't, its roots strong in the places left hollow by the things Mateo had thought should be his.

But Anwei's voice brought a new calm up through the places the ghost had claimed.

"You earned your hundredth braid six months before I did. I didn't understand that I was different until you were gone," she whispered, her fingers pressing hard against his, and she didn't let go, not even when blood ran from his claws and dribbled onto Knox's shirt. "You gloated about it every single day until my ceremony was scheduled. We were going to open an apothecary that sold cupcakes. You were an artist, and the things you made were beautiful." She took in a shuddering breath, so quiet and yet louder than the winds battering him like a storm off the sea.

The boy she remembered wasn't who he was.

It was too late for him.

But when he opened his eyes, Anwei was looking at him as if she understood, the color of her eyes the deepest brown he'd only found in raw umber and squid ink. "You were saved by a man who loved you, and he named you Mateo."

The ghosts' howling inside him seemed to quiet just a little. Not because they had stopped trying to steal his soul, but because she could see him too.

"You are still the boy I knew with all the colors in the world flowing from you." Her voice broke like the cracks inside him, the ghosts swirling larger as they tried to take him over to destroy this girl who spoke the truths they didn't know how to twist. "You just lost your father, who you love, and it isn't fair. You hurt people, and it wasn't fair. But that doesn't mean you wanted it to happen. You still deserve to live."

Mateo sagged, his hands around the sword going tight. And it began to bubble and melt between his fingers in a black mass, the liquid streams of it running down the front of his coat, because he didn't want Willow anymore.

What is it you want, son? Tual had asked.

Mateo wanted *himself* back, and he could feel his own truth there inside the sword. The last dregs of Aria rolled inside him, straining to go free. He could feel the things he'd been so willing to take as long as it let him keep going.

He remembered the life he'd thought he wanted. Of Lia, and how easy it had been to plan her death in exchange for his continued existence. The dull certainty that his father must be right if it meant Mateo could have what he wanted. And the unfairness that he shouldn't have had to choose between himself and everyone else. Mateo thought of what he could remember of the life he'd had before, the tiny dregs he could bring back. Of Lia and her smile. Of Aria, wanting nothing more than to make an adventure out of a terrible injustice, and how he'd let Willow take her. She hadn't had to ask, because he'd already made the decision to *live.*

He'd let her do it.

The ghosts, with their terrible claws and teeth, told him to take. To take was to live.

And Mateo let them all go.

⤷⤶

Anwei refused to let go of Arun, of *Mateo* because that's who he'd become, refused to give up, even as metal melted between her fingers, burning her skin. She could feel the ghosts inside her brother showing him the terrible picture of all his wrongs and tried to give him the good she remembered instead, tried to remind him of his soul that half belonged to her the same way she'd belonged to him.

She thought of Knox taking the sword and holding it, protecting it to keep his sister from being lost, even when it had hurt him. Holding fast to the oaths he'd made even as Willow grew heavier and heavier on his shoulders.

They were the web Abendiza had described, she and Knox, she and Mateo, Mateo and Willow, and Willow and Knox, but instead of tearing a hole open to darkness, she stood firm, holding the darkness back.

Mateo pitched forward into the canoe, taking her with him.

Please, she whispered toward the nameless god as everything tangled together. Burning metal, Knox's shirt, Mateo's blood, her braids. *Please.* In her chest she could feel the violence of magic wanting to take control, vines waiting to strangle and crush, trees, flowers, bushes, seeds ready to crack open the ground. Breathing in deep and slow, she didn't have to let go of the rage and anger that had lurked in her heart, because they were somehow already gone. Instead, she felt the nameless god flex inside her like another support under her feet. Not a weapon, but a part of who she was, if she wanted. *Please,* she thought. *I don't know how to fix this. But you probably do, right?*

Knox felt something stab through him, and the air began to warm, his connection to Anwei like vines growing into his stomach and up through his chest, only they were on fire.

The blackness leaking out from him in a terrible cord wrenched one way, then another, and suddenly began to spool out of him like a fishing line being reeled in. Willow reared up from just outside the web of darkness, her tears like little flickering flames. "Don't—" she cried. "Don't leave me!"

Knox crashed through the darkness and grabbed hold of her even as the shadows surged around them both, hammering against his skin and hers. Anwei pulsed brighter and brighter inside him as he tore claws and teeth and bones away from his sister's skin, holding her close even as darkness burrowed into him. Anwei's bond to him turned hot, and the gray line of connection between him and Willow sparked in the black haze churning around them. Knox's body grew and shrank and twisted and broke, and Willow was crying because of the shadows in her own skin and bones. The air around him seemed to condense, pressure hard in his ears and his eyes blinded—

But then he was lying in a boat, his arms gripped tight around something bright and warm that bled away, like a sigh of relief, then was gone.

He lay there, heart hammering, feeling around for Willow inside his head. The line of connection between them sparked one last time, then evaporated in a flare of light.

It is done, Calsta said. *She is free.*

Knox's arms and hands flailed to touch his own body, once again made from skin and bone and muscle. There was a wooden floor hard beneath his back and a fist twisted into his tunic, Anwei's Still holding onto him as if she was the only anchor he had. The bond hung like a question between them—a question he could somehow say yes or no to, power hanging over them in a haze.

But when he opened his eyes, she wasn't looking at him, her other fist gripping a fancy coat. A boy with freckles like Anwei's, his skin a shade lighter and his hair in messy curls. And for a split second, he could feel something like a web of bonds, as if he were connected to the boy too.

The boy collapsed onto the ground, his fingers ending in gristly, bloody ends, his aura streaming up toward the sky. Knox sat up, tears on Anwei's cheeks as she screamed out, not letting go of Mateo's coat. *"Stay here! You already left me once!"*

Knox grabbed her hand, the bond between them like liquid gold, her eyes full of auras and her muscles full of his strength, his nose full of herbs and the sharp obsidian jab of broken humors. Everything between them was a mix of color.

The boards under their feet groaned, knots and branches sprouting from the old wood and growing up to circle Mateo as Anwei concentrated. Knox felt her borrowing from him as she burrowed into Mateo, asking him to *grow* like a plea instead of the command that had given Knox the scar on his side and broken the tomb.

A hand touched his shoulder, and suddenly Lia was there too, though her aura had diminished down to a calm glimmer at the edges. Her other hand touched Mateo, and somehow she was a part of their circle too, her soul, untarnished by the sword, a connecting force that completed them as she gave herself over to finish the pattern of purple, gold, and white settling over Mateo. Lending herself to their bonds because she loved them all too.

After a moment, the growing stopped, and everything was far, far too quiet. Knox gripped Anwei's hand, not able to move.

Lia slowly extracted herself and gently knelt next to Mateo. She grabbed hold of his ridiculous lapels and wrenched him up from the bottom of the boat. "*Where* is *Aria?*"

Mateo's eyelids flickered, not quite opening.

She hauled him up from the deck. "Where *is* she?"

"Abendiza said . . ." His head lolled back. "Some of her was still inside of me."

"You *ate* her?!"

"It was my fault," his voice croaked. "And I didn't want to believe she was gone, so I didn't. Until I made myself face it. Made myself go look. But now I'm . . . letting . . . her go."

"I pretended to stab myself to stop your father like you asked, and now you're telling me that you *killed my sister?*"

"I wish—" He gasped. "I wish it were different." And he crumpled into the canoe as if he were made of ash. One last breath sighed out between his lips, and his chest went still.

Anwei's hand crushed so hard around Knox's fingers that tears sprang to his eyes. She grabbed hold of Mateo, but her brother began to sink into the slick oily black coating the bottom of the canoe. It felt like shadows, like the empty places the sword had punched through Knox, leaving a hole for the darkness to reach through. They'd taken and taken and taken, and he could feel the same gaps in Mateo, but the sword, the holes, the *nothing* sucking away at him were all gone, the feel of the life he'd always clenched so tight in his fists suddenly a miraculous thing of beauty he didn't need to clasp so tightly.

Anwei was calm itself, her eyes shut as a tree's branches grew up over the boat's rail. A branch circled them with the canoe, gently lifting them up from the deck. Knox gulped as the trunk beneath them thickened, roots fingering out into the water and down into the sand. The light from Calsta burned too hot in Knox's chest, and even Lia was beginning to gasp and sweat, but all of them stayed still, the branches high above the beach, casting everything in light of blues and greens.

Finally, Knox felt Anwei release, her aura of ropes and nets and webs and swirls slipping down from around her like sand. The roots had grown up over the canoe's edge, new-sprouted flowers waving in the breeze to touch Mateo's cheeks and forehead, the last of the oily slick of shadows beneath him finally gone.

Only, Mateo was gone too.

Lia let go of Mateo, the last hope in her like a fizzling wire. She climbed down from the new-formed branches and ran up the beach and across the courtyard. Noa and Altahn dragging Gilesh out from the kitchen. She ran past a Devoted up to his waist in rock still trying to reach his sword. Her heart raced faster than Calsta had ever let her run, faster than the clouds in the sky or lightning blasts because that was all she could see or feel on this awful blue day. She ran because there was nothing left she could do. If Aria was gone—

As her feet hit the bridge, something out in the middle unfolded. A pinkish beast with broken horns and long, cracked teeth. Rosie's mane was a snarl where there should have been jaunty braids and her rosy hide stained with mud and blood. The creature raised her head up with a bottomless keen that echoed through Lia like the *nothing* Anwei had spoken of in whispers.

The auroshe struggled up to her feet and limped toward the tower. Lia didn't move until Rosie gave a blistering screech and charged the doors, butting through them. Running after her, Lia leaped stair after stair until they were at the very top of the tower, Rosie nosing her way into the room where Lia had found Aria hiding with Mateo.

But it had been a trick. A fake aura. A belief Tual had managed to turn into a fantasy of Aria alive in Lia's brain.

Steeling herself, Lia followed the auroshe into the room, Rosie snaking forward to bite at the bedclothes. The window had been covered, and the bits of glass and wood Lia had broken had been brushed off the bed and floor into a neat pile. And there, sitting at the head of the bed, was Abendiza. Aria's shock of red curls burned like fire against the old woman's skin as it went slack, dripping and crumbling even as Lia watched.

"What are you—" Lia started forward, Rosie's hackles rising, but Abendiza hummed out a long tone, almost like a lullaby, that filled the air.

The old woman faded, her aura draining like Calsta gathering a sunbeam back up to her bosom even as Abendiza cradled Aria's head. "He asked me to take her out of him," the shapeshifter crooned. "The last little seeds of her were inside him, not enough to bring her back. There's not enough of him, either, or he wouldn't have let Willow take her. But as for me . . . I took so much life to fill the emptiness where my soul was, more than I ever needed." Her voice dulled to a whisper. "It made me wonder if, after so much breaking, I could fix something instead. Seeds grow if you plant them. And energy given freely is different from what we steal. . . ."

Abendiza melted with the words, her hair unknitting to fall in clumps onto the bedcovers, her cheeks and chin puffing away in a cloud of dust. Though Lia's aurasight was gone, she could feel the burn of energy sparking out from Abendiza, but instead of pouring up toward the sky like every other death Lia had seen, this energy lanced down, branching into a fork, half striking Aria and the other half lancing out the window toward the beaches.

Lia leapt forward to catch her sister's head as the last of Abendiza's energy dissipated, and the woman with it. She crawled up onto the bed, cradling Aria close, her sister's skin cold, her body limp . . .

Until she felt the faint rumble in Aria's chest, a stolen heartbeat put back where it belonged. *Tick . . . tick . . .*

Tick.

CHAPTER 30

What We Choose

When Noa loaded the last of the candlesticks and herb packets and fancy chairs she'd taken from Montanne Keep, she began to hum. Mostly because she wasn't actually the one loading things since she had Gilesh and Bane to do it for her. Right as they lined up the last load of crates of the deck, Lia came calling from the house.

"Gilesh!" she yelled, sword in her hand. "Are you ready for me to destroy you?"

Gilesh gasped, both hands clapping over his mouth. "My sword. Where is my *sword?*" Bane chortled like a little girl, darting into the hold and coming out with both their blades, and the two of them ran happily down to meet Lia on the grass. Altahn frowned from the far end of the deck where he was rigging sheets of wood stolen from the house into safe stalls to transport the horses and came to the railing to stand beside Noa as Gilesh faced off against the former Devoted.

Both of them flinched when Lia disarmed him before he'd managed to even attack her. Crowing something about not following rules, Gilesh convinced her to let him pick up the sword, and was only a little grumpy when she suggested Bane join in to give them better odds.

"I don't think I can watch," Altahn breathed. "Oh good, Anwei is coming, so I don't have to." Galerey came crawling out from behind his neck to see what was causing the strain in his voice, but when there was nothing to see, consented to a few pets from Noa.

"How did you end up bonded to a firekey, anyway?" Noa asked, pulling his attention away from the healer as she approached. "Is it like Lia and Vivi, where he seems to know when she's mad and sometimes he bites things when she wishes she could?" The auroshe was still quartered in the stables, Lia sneaking off to feed him treats of bloody meat. Rosie had opted to stay out in the forest, visiting often enough to give the servants nightmares.

Altahn's brow furrowed, reaching up to run a finger down Galerey's side. "She was sick when I found her. I helped her, and she stayed with me." He twitched when the lizard climbed down his back and scrambled onto Noa's shoulder instead. "Traitor."

"Good taste is what it is," Noa countered, nuzzling Galerey's cheek.

"I don't really know why she chose me. Or why she added you to her very short list of acceptable modes of transportation." Altahn fixed Galerey with a perplexed stare. "There aren't any other bonded firekeys in my clan. Usually when we find wounded ones, they're killed for the wet salpowder in their guts. It's more potent than the bones and fossils we dig up."

"You saved her, and she loves you for it." Noa smiled, liking the story.

Anwei walked up the gangplank, Knox behind her. He had lost his *belanvian* darkness, his body just blocking light from Calsta's sun rather than casting hungry shadows behind him.

Galerey jumped back to Altahn as Noa ran to wrap her arms around her friend, not sure what to say in parting. She was grateful to have been pulled away from everything she hated so much in Chaol, but also grateful to no longer feel eclipsed by her friend. Anwei didn't speak for a moment, holding her just as close, as if she couldn't bear to stop.

Finally, Anwei pulled back, her smile a little too tight. "So you're leaving me to take these ridiculous hangers-on back to Trib land." She shot a playful glare toward Altahn, who smiled, though he looked away after a moment, the past between them something not so easily forgotten. Anwei closed her eyes a little too long before turning back to Noa. "I feel like I'll never see you again."

"You have to keep an audience wanting more," Noa said, nodding sagely. But then she lunged forward, hugging Anwei close again. "It won't be hard to find you. I'll just look for signs of Yaru—rich people happily stabbing one another in the back."

"I never stab." Anwei squeezed her tight. "But I'll miss you." Lia came on board to hug Noa goodbye as well, softer somehow than she'd been before finding her sister. Anwei and Lia waved as they headed back down the gangplank, Anwei pointing a finger at Gilesh when he passed the two of them, sword heavy in his hand and a dejected set to his shoulders. "Don't think I didn't notice you skipping that tincture you were supposed to drink this morning. I can *smell* your humors clotting around the bruises those Devoted gave you. Don't slack just because it tastes funny."

"Like dead caterpillars and thistles," he muttered through his teeth, setting his sword down to pick up one of the crates he'd abandoned on deck.

Knox waited until Anwei was a safe distance away before giving Noa a tight smile. "I don't think I'll miss you."

"You'll do more than miss me." Noa grinned. "Don't think I've forgotten about what happened in the rowboats after that whole bathtub incident."

He blinked. "You mean when you almost died and then I saved your life?"

"That time you almost killed me, then got your mouth all over mine? Yes, that's what I mean. And if that's what you count as kissing, I mean, poor Anwei." She couldn't help the laugh that burst out when his cheeks turned rosy. "Don't worry, I'll be back to help."

"I'm not—*you're* not—I didn't . . ." Knox couldn't seem to get the words out.

"Go on." She waved him off toward the gangplank. "I don't have time to show you right now."

"You offer classes?" Gilesh's head popped out from the hold. "I mean, I remember you saying you went to the university in Chaol, but I didn't realize it was as an instructor. I guess that explains why you tolerate Altahn hanging around—"

"Gilesh—" Altahn looked out from behind the load of boxes. Galerey snarled from her perch on his shoulder.

"It's nothing to be ashamed of, Altahn," Bane chimed in. "We all heard the rumors back home about how you need all the help you can get. Otherwise your dad wouldn't have had such trouble finding you a wife—" He whooped with laughter, dragging Gilesh behind him down the gangplank. Altahn swore, dropping a box to chase after them.

Once the horses were settled and the gangplank was up, Noa didn't like the feeling of pulling apart from Anwei and the others. But as she eased the boat down the now-open channel to the main river, the promise of seeing them soon was nothing to the feel of water beneath her and wind in her hair because she didn't have anything to run from any longer.

Altahn came up from tending the horses, watching as Gilesh and Bane moved when Noa told them to untie things, then retie them mostly because she wanted to see how long it would take before they realized what she was about. She grinned at him. "I want to put a new house mark on the prow. And the canoe, of course."

"You don't want to keep your father's mark so Ellis stays away from you?" Altahn grabbed hold of a rope with a humorless chuckle. "The *Butcher.*"

"Oh, *I* need a good nickname!" She pulled his hand off the rope to stop the sail from turning. "Maybe I'll come up with one when you're finished sanding my father's house mark off the canoe. I'll put out flyers or something so people know to be frightened of me. Go on." She pointed to the canoe when Altahn shot her a less than enthused look. "You didn't think I was going to take you clear to Trib land for nothing, did you?"

"Don't you want it to be perfect?" He shot back. "If *I* sand it—"

"Oh no, I'm captain. I can't get sawdust all over me." She tapped her lips, squinting at the little vessel. "What house mark would suit me? Something like that window we left for the First Scholar, perhaps? Hands so soft you can tell they've never done any sanding, and your face."

Alarmed, Altahn looked up from Galerey sending sparks down his collar.

"What's she talking about, boss?" Gilesh called from the bench.

"A man who obviously knows his way around the bilges—"

"Fine, I'll sand it!" Altahn's face flushed. "Just . . . don't put my face on any windows. Or house marks. Or signs, or . . . flyers—"

Bane stood up to help Altahn pull the canoe onto the small, unoccupied bit of deck between the benches. "Why do I get the feeling that Altahn's been rejected again?"

"Again?" Noa dug deep for her most scandalous voice.

"You didn't even properly ask her, did you?" Gilesh sighed, setting down his oar. "Remember? We talked about asking for a nice meal. A stroll by the water." He waggled his eyebrows at Bane, who shoved something into his mouth and chewed noisily. "Girls outside the clan don't know they're supposed to pay their way into the kynate's family, Altahn. Can't have hard feelings that the poor girl didn't throw herself at you like you wanted. You knew sailing down here to catch her attention was a ridiculous venture. Just look at how shiny her hair is. You thought that girl was going to follow you back to Trib land?"

"We both *know* I didn't—wait, *what is this?*" Altahn threw down the canoe properly glaring at Gilesh. "Aren't you supposed to be on my side?"

Gilesh shrugged.

"Fine," Altahn said. "We all like Noa, but no one ever thought she was going to sparkle her way north. She likes throwing fire around and teasing boys until they cry. So as much as I would like—" He looked around, as if suddenly noticing Bane waggling his eyebrows.

"You can't say it like that." Gilesh sat down with the sandpaper and began to scratch at the purple house mark carved into the curled nose. "You have to start with a question, like 'Miss Noa, when we get to Trib land, would you like to meet my fiancée's eight cows?'"

"I did not agree to—" He was actually frustrated, his cheeks even redder than before. But then he started to laugh. "Miss Noa." He gave her a bow far too deep with a flourish that was probably meant to mock Mateo's ridiculous fluttering but actually looked quite handsome. "Would you like to sail straight into our side of the bay and sell my extended family some of the stolen candlesticks you've got in the hold? I have a cousin who likes stealing things too, you know."

"I don't take cows as payment," Noa said haughtily, going to the bench where she'd seen paints. Looking them over, she picked up the dark green. "You think I haven't noticed you mooning around after me like some kind of lovesick narmaiden, which coincidentally also happens to be your dancing technique."

She laughed when Altahn started toward her, his placid smile unfolding larger as he scooped the paint away from her and picked up the brush. "You can teach me."

"I don't *want* to teach you. Laughing at you is more fun."

Bane moved to help Gilesh with the canoe, the two of them squatted at the prow with a bowl of sand she'd brought from the beach. Altahn dipped a rag into the bowl while Noa tended the sails, wondering at the sight of her father's house mark being rubbed away so easily as if it had never been more than a bit of paint. When they were finished, she took some paint and went to examine the blank new space, full of possibilities.

"Green?" Altahn cocked an eyebrow. "I thought you were joking about going pirate."

Noa dipped the paintbrush and put it to the wood, starting with a swish that looked like a skirt, another that made raised arms and a head, then a third a bit of flame. A fire dancer. "Green matches my eyes."

"I think those are sails upriver," Gilesh called. "What do you want to do?"

Setting down the paint and brush, Noa went back to the tiller, liking the way Altahn watched her for a moment with that calm smile on his face. She made a show of shading her eyes to peer into the distance. "We'll meet them head-on, of course."

⚜

Lia sat on the floor in the study, holding a terrible, terrible book that seemed to be the only one Noa had left behind: *One Thousand Nights in Urilia*. She held it away from her to turn the page, flinching at the words and quickly flipping to the one after that. "You *read* this?"

"He read it to me while I was . . . asleep, or whatever that was. Why do you keep stopping?" Aria's voice was still a little faint, her face pale where she was propped up on the couch.

Lia turned to look at the formless lump of blankets huddled on the couch opposite. "Mateo Montanne, what is *wrong with you?*"

"I didn't do it," he mumbled, his hand flopping over the edge to grab for the sweet roll Hilaria had brought. "I'm damaged. I need lots of rest, a good helping of pity—"he took a bite, chewing noisily—"and lots of sustenance before we have this conversation."

He *was* damaged. Anwei still wouldn't say anything when she looked at Mateo or Aria, just kept mixing herbs and powders and other things she'd raided from Tual's office. But every day the healer looked a little less blank, as if maybe it was as Abendiza had said when she sent out the last of her energy to plant the seeds of her stolen life in Mateo and Aria. They'd started growing again.

Lia snapped the book shut. "If this is the kind of book your father read to you, then I'm beginning to understand why you are such a terrible person."

"At least I'm entertaining." Mateo took another bite. "Are we going to talk about the fact that you totally kissed me?"

Aria's hands went to her mouth. "I *knew* it."

Lia stood up. "I think both of you have had enough excitement for one day. No, you can't have this." She tucked *One Thousand Nights* under her arm, dodging Aria when she tried to swipe it on her way to the door. Aria stuck her tongue out before Lia shut the door on her.

It was odd, staying in Tual Montanne's house. It was even more odd the way Aria had asked for Mateo right after she'd woken to find Lia at her side. The color in her cheeks was returning, and Mateo seemed to like needling her as much as she needled him back, though Lia had still found him sitting in a corner with his hands over his face more than once after talking to her. But then Anwei would come sit next to him and let him tell her a story about copying tomb reliefs, or Knox would bring out a hand of cards, and it was almost as if the four of them hadn't nearly killed one another.

Lia walked out into the hall toward the dining room, where most of the cots had been set up. There weren't as many as she would have liked, only eleven of the Devoted who'd come to claim Tual clinging to life. They'd taken Anwei's tinctures and powders without complaint, the reality of their lives being saved by a Basist making the dining hall where their cots were all set very quiet.

The Warlord hadn't survived, and a new monument to her and the Devoted who had been with her, Cath, had appeared in paint that felt like Mateo alongside the memorials in the tunnels below the island. Lia hadn't asked, but she was fairly certain Mateo's affinity for stone hadn't returned.

When Lia entered the dining hall this time, the Devoted all looked up to her as she went to the head of the table. "Anwei says most of you will be well enough to return to Rentara within the week," she said quietly.

"Anwei is planning to let us return?" Berrum's voice held a note of bitterness. Lia wondered if he still felt awkward about being left tied in a boat by a healer.

"You're not prisoners." Lia fiddled with her sleeve. "I've had too many people tell me where to sit and how to do it properly to want to start dictating things myself." She sighed and sat down. "But all of you saw what happened here. The Warlord was keeping Tual next to her like a pet, and he sipped her down with his tea. He did it to all of you, and no one noticed. It was Anwei and Mateo—both Basists—who managed to stop him."

None of them said anything.

"The way Devoted do things right now isn't healthy for the warriors who follow Calsta. Or right. Basists aren't any more corrupt than Devoted I've known." Mateo's words came back to her, said in a moment of quiet as they looked at his painting of Calsta and the nameless god reaching for each other in Chaol. "It's not power that's good or bad. It's what we do with it."

One of the Devoted near the doors eased himself up from his pillow and set his feet tentatively on the floor. A plate of plain bread sat next to him on a table, and Lia wondered how long he would last before Hilaria tore through the room and forced him to eat every bite. "I knew a girl who was touched by the nameless god when I was young. She used to feed birds, making little houses for them that would stay up. Like castles. She would sit and watch them for hours, and . . ." He looked down. "It never sat well with me what happened to her. Even after I took the oaths. Hunting for the Warlord didn't feel the same because . . . the people I found were angry. Dangerous. I never got to see them tending birds."

Lia nodded. "How many of you even wanted to leave your families for the seclusions?"

None of them answered, because Devotion was silent obedience. Giving things up for the goddess meant pretending you hadn't wanted those things in the first place.

Finally, she shrugged. "I'm not saying I have a solution. But I hope that maybe if we all went back to Rentara together with the Warlord's body and explained . . ." She stood and started toward the door. "The first Warlord erased even how shapeshifters are made because she was so afraid of anyone doing it again. Not only did that cause us to lose many innocent and valuable lives, none of us had the education we needed to spot an actual shapeshifter in our midst. In dispatching him, we managed to destroy a caprenum sword. Something the first Warlord certainly never managed." She stopped at the door. "What if we went to the scholars and helped research? Tried to figure out what was lost when we decided it had to be a choice between Calsta and the nameless god? The one Basist and two shapeshifters I've known had vastly different affinities for magic—Tual couldn't move a single stone. Why? Do Devoted have similar affinities? If so, what are they, and why have we been so focused on *war*?" Shrugging, she turned back toward the hallway. "I think Calsta would approve of us trying to get a more complete picture."

When Lia left the room, she heard their voices begin to murmur. It was difficult to know what to do to fix five hundred years of pain and bloodshed, but it wasn't only her choice. Devoted listening to her despite her diminished aura was something. Even beginning the conversation was something. But it wasn't enough.

Back in Aria's room, Lia found her sister was sleeping, her freckles stark against her pale cheeks. Mateo seemed to be asleep too, at least until he rolled over to look at her, head lolling a bit to the side when he rolled too far. "Do you really mean all that?"

"All what?"

"There are air passages here that let out in the dining hall. You want to do research? To find the things we lost?"

Lia lowered herself into the chair by Aria's bed. "Isn't that what you were trying to do? Maybe Tual would never have become a shape-shifter if he hadn't been so afraid, or . . . the person he killed hadn't been afraid—"

"I'm not sure exactly what happened. Only that . . . fear was part of it. My father wasn't a Basist to start with. I think he focused so much on herbs and healing because . . . whatever had happened before, whatever he'd done, he couldn't fix it. So then he tried to fix everything. Including me."

"In all the wrong ways."

"Right." He tried to prop his head up on his hand. "Gods above, there are two of you."

"Your worst nightmare." She chuckled.

"Exactly." He let his head flop back down. "I want to help you, Lia. Can I help?"

Her eyes pinched shut for a frustrated second. "I'm glad you're not dead, Mateo, but that doesn't mean I want to—"

"Wait." He put up a hand. "Before you say anything else, can I make a request?"

Lia frowned. "You can request anything you want so long as you realize I probably won't give it to you."

"Fair enough. I just hoped that . . . if you're going to say, 'No, thank you, Mateo, I've seen your soul and I don't think the color of it matches my eyes,' could you maybe hold off rejecting my offer to sit next to you and take notes on how to save the world until, I don't know, tomorrow?" He rubbed a hand tiredly across his face. "We were friends enough before for, say, a twelve-hour grace period, right?"

Lia snorted. "You need twelve hours before you're willing to face whatever I was going to say?"

"It's been a difficult few weeks." He slumped back to stare at the ceiling. "I've even found myself being grateful for how slow Aria's recovery has been, because she's the only one around here who knows how to properly murder someone." When Lia didn't laugh, he tipped his head toward her, sighing. "Too soon, I suppose?"

Lia looked away.

"It *was* an accident. But . . . she should never have been here in the first place. I never should . . . There were a lot of things I did wrong, that ended in . . . *wrong*." He tried to sit up again, and Lia suddenly realized that with Aria asleep, Anwei off brewing something, and Knox out in the courtyard doing forms, she and Mateo hadn't actually talked alone since the night in the tent.

When, as hed so helpfully informed Aria, she'd kissed him.

He was slurring a little, trying to speak too quickly as if he were afraid Lia would run away before he could finish. "I never should have sat in that carriage and let my father drive us away knowing she was with us. I didn't know about what he did to your family, but I didn't know a lot of things because it was easier not to know." Mateo sighed, his eyes slipping shut. "You know I'm a terrible person."

"I do." Lia nodded. "But I guess it's hard to stack that up against the fact that you were raised by . . . well, not exactly a paragon of virtue." She turned toward Aria, smoothing a curl back from her forehead. "It makes me wonder what I've already done wrong."

"She loves you." Mateo's eyes opened. "Maybe that's why she talks about stabbing things all the time."

Lia sat back in the fancy chair, the windows so tall she could stand in them and see over the tops of the cliffs to the bones moldering inside. What she knew she had to say next felt like a boulder perched at the edge of a cliff waiting to fall. A decision she both wanted to fight for and didn't all at once. "I think your perspective would be helpful in Rentara," she finally said. "If you ever manage to focus your eyes again, I mean."

He laughed, but it was a little strained. All of him was, as if he didn't feel like he fit into his body, his mind. After so many years of fighting to live, he wasn't sure he deserved it anymore.

If that was a thing. *Deserving* to live. That was part of the problem the Warlord had set rolling through the Commonwealth, dictating which people lived and which died, no better than any shapeshifter.

"Do you remember that time you pulled the scarf off your face like some kind of Tanlir dancer?" Mateo's voice was quiet as he stared up at the ceiling. "And then I almost died of shock?"

Lia went still, the question in his voice one that made her feel wary. "I think you tried to swallow an entire sweet roll whole and then proposed to me."

"I didn't *propose*. I'm not stupid. Usually." Mateo turned to look at her. "I've always wanted to paint you. Just like you were that day."

"You make it easy to forget who you are, Mateo." Lia stood up. "I like talking to you. Just you and me."

He didn't move, cheek digging into the couch's arm and his hair in knots. "Who do you think I am?"

"I shouldn't like you. Aria shouldn't like you. None of us should." She swept a hand through her hair. "But I do. I didn't really expect that after everything."

Mateo blinked twice. "Am I really so bad? Would it really be so bad if . . . ?" He closed his eyes, pressing his cheek harder into the bright upholstery, and Lia's stomach turned a somersault. It was a nightmare sitting here waiting for Mateo to say something she wasn't sure she should want to hear.

But wanted to hear anyway.

"You make it easy, too," he finally said.

Lia slid out of her chair and sat on the floor, her back against his couch, his knees curving around her and his head pressing forward to see past her shoulder. And they sat, Aria snoring quietly across from her.

"Things are going to change," she said quietly.

"Calsta above, I hope so."

❧

Anwei stood at the back of the turquoise boat as the sun went down, the wind playing with her braids as she stared out at the southern horizon, all of it gray like the underside of a storm. Beilda. Home. She toyed with a braid for the first herb she'd learned, the one her brother had sectioned off and tied before he'd shorn off his own and become someone new. She'd had it rebraided many times, re-oiled and waxed, but still his touch seemed to be there.

He's not a different person. The nameless god's familiar rumble no longer sent arrows of discontent and anger stabbing into her humors as it had just a few days earlier.

Are you? she whispered to herself and to him both, his voice stronger now than it ever had been.

Probably. It's hard to remember after being so quiet for so long.

She thought for a moment, remembering her medicines brewing, the Devoted in the dining hall, and the promise of what them existing in the same space she was in could mean. *You'll get stronger, won't you, as more people are allowed to believe and make oaths—*

There are more oaths for you. He almost sounded like an instructor at one of the universities, ready to give her a list. After a beat, he added, *If you want them, I mean.*

She was already supposed to only use her smell for others. Then to use the larger healing and moving of matter only with the nameless god's approval. Or maybe that was just in bodies. Or maybe—

Anwei frowned. *I hardly know what I've already agreed to. Don't push it.*

How about you don't push it, he blustered back.

She felt Knox approach, and she turned to meet him as he came out of the shadows. The bond between them felt less like light and more as if it had been forged in iron, stronger every day. "You want to go back?" He pointed out to the ocean. Toward Beilda.

"Maybe." She twisted to look at him, his jaw still tight, hair a collection of loose ends that never could stay in their tie. "I'm surprised you didn't start running the moment you got out of the sword. Since the moment I met you, you were set on bribing your way over the Lasei border. Was that Calsta's idea?"

"No, it's just where I thought I could work on letting Willow free. That was all I wanted—to let her go. Well, then I wanted to not have to take care of your spiders for you."

"I still want you to deal with the spiders." Anwei shivered.

Knox breathed in slow and let the breath out like a prayer, as if he'd shed a weight that had been riding inside him and could finally fill his lungs all the way. "Calsta is still bugging me about Devoted and things. I guess Lia's going to start working with them, but she no longer has her oaths. Something about swords not being the way she wants to do things anymore."

"I honestly can't imagine that."

"I can't imagine anything." He took Anwei's hand, staring out into the sea. "I'm glad to be done, but who are we without Willow and the snake-tooth man?"

Anwei looked down at their hands clasped together, as if *he* were trying to keep *her* grounded for once instead of the other way around. "I could open an apothecary."

"Where the goddess Yaru answers prayers to those truly heavy in purse?" Knox sketched a hand across the horizon. "Maybe with a few gaming tables where we can pick up any gossip. Three khonin knots at least or you're out."

Please spare me this nonsense, the nameless god groaned.

Anwei grinned. "It's the lower khonin who know all the secrets. In Lasei I think high khonin wear their hair free like Trib."

"Well, with Noa stealing up the river on a boat, you behind the apothecary counter, and Altahn with all his salpowder and contacts through Trib land, I feel there may be some potential benefit to us all working together, don't you? You never could devote yourself to healing full time. So maybe there's room for a little side business I could help you with?" Anwei's stomach twinged when Knox squinted at her. "Healing hurt you, didn't it? Almost as much as it hurt *not* doing it."

He was right. Healing was one of Anwei's many pieces that made her both sharp and smooth with no way to separate them. "You want to go back to stealing things at night and trying to pretend you weren't terrified by little jars of dead plants during the day?" She couldn't quite look him in the eye. "Knox, after everything that happened—"

His hands were on her shoulders, and suddenly she was looking up into those dark eyes, and for the first time, he felt *there*. Solid and secure, as if he'd chosen to stay all on his own, despite the fact she wasn't holding on to him. "What about it?"

"I *killed* you. I chose all the wrong things."

"And then held on to me just like you always have until you could bring me back. I couldn't have saved my sister if I hadn't gone into the sword. And you . . . held steady. Just like you always do." Knox leaned closer, and she could feel the heat of him trilling down her arms, her neck. "I know what you did to get me back out. You chose me instead of everything else."

"And you're choosing me now?" she breathed.

Before the words were properly out, he was kissing her, lips soft against hers, and Anwei couldn't remember what it felt like to be alone.

Later, much later, they walked toward the house, Knox's hand in Anwei's as if it had always been there. "If you want to work at my apothecary slash den of thievery, you'll have to carry my bags. And learn how to do sutures."

He grinned down at her. "All my favorite things."

You could do more. You have a name that could mean something.

You do too, don't you? Anwei thought for a moment. *Why haven't you told me your name?*

I don't remember it anymore. And I've changed since it was last spoken. My old name would probably be wrong.

Names hold power. You need a name. Anwei thought for a moment. *I think I'll call you Potato.*

You will not! The god's voice rose inside her. *Anwei Ruezi, you will not destroy what little pride I have left—*

Potato is a good name. Earthy. Like you.

And, with the rumbles of a less-than-content god in one ear and Knox at her side, Anwei couldn't help but feel that instead of her finding something, her life had finally found her.

⁂

Mateo couldn't sleep, especially after Lia left him to stew in the room alone, confused and full of hope and electricity and worry. Brushing crumbs from a day's worth of sweet rolls from his shirt, he limped out of Aria's room toward his own. He stopped when he got to his own bed. It was made, the blankets tight, and there were still snakes carved into the woodwork. After a moment, he knelt down and crawled underneath.

Spine pressing into the floor and the scent of wood and wool rug in his nose, Mateo closed his eyes to the underside of his bed. When he breathed in, the air felt close, his thoughts even closer. He could almost feel Tual there beside him, the echoes of the silly stories he told until Mateo was no longer scared making it feel all the more empty.

After a moment, footsteps quietly entered the room and bare feet appeared by his bedside, white scars across the tops of her feet. Anwei.

She bent down, her snaky braids pooling on the floor, some large, some small, some short, some long. Some tied with leather, others with twine. Mateo moved over to make room when she slid underneath to lie next to him. "We used to do this when we were little," she said quietly.

"When we were scared?" he asked.

"No, it was where we went to find each other. It was a secret— maybe our parents knew, but they'd let us sit under there to make all our plans and . . . just be. It was our spot."

Mateo closed his eyes, trying to remember, but so much of it had gone. Blocked out for so long, he couldn't find it again. But somehow, his body had known. His mind. That when he'd come here, he'd wanted to find her. Swallowing the feeling down, he pointed to the braid closest to him on the floor. "Why are there a hundred?" he asked.

"You don't remember?"

"Only that purple frosting was somehow a part of tying them."

Anwei snorted, one hand going to her mouth. "You were the one who was so sure the frosting had to be purple. Mostly because then Father wouldn't know which of his extracts we'd stolen to flavor it. We were going to open an apothecary bakery combination."

Mateo flinched. Fathers. Every time he uncovered more about the man who'd actually brought him into the world, he felt as if he'd pulled up a bit of bark from a rotten log and the sight underneath wasn't for the weak of stomach. "Will you show me?"

She took the braid in her hands, holding it up. "This one was for the first herb. Calia. We use it to treat sore throats and . . ."

Mateo breathed in as she spoke, trying to remember why the salty, herby smell of her was so familiar, echoing in the blank spaces of his mind as he strained to find the memory that went with it. Propping his head up on one hand, he thought he could remember something about the way his bones and humors were supposed to fit together, his neck to his spine, his spine to his ribs, humors cradled inside their cage. Every word Anwei said as she picked up her next braid were like parts of a story he'd been told as a child, the words coming into his mind even as she spoke. His bones seemed to hold him steady despite Willow's absence, as if she hadn't been his skeleton at all.

Perhaps he'd grown a new one.

All Mateo knew was that now he couldn't smell death.

Acknowledgments

I'm so sad to be leaving this world behind. Some books feel more personal than others, and these characters and this place were in my head a long time before I actually got to write them down. So, thank you for descending into my mind weirdness to read it. Thank you to all the readers and booksellers who have gotten excited about these books and forced them on their friends and relatives. You are the real stars!!

This book was an exciting one to write, and I'm so grateful to my editor, Sarah McCabe, for the time and effort she put into slicing to the heart of this story—Abendiza is a hundred percent cooler because of you (to name one of a thousand things), and it's a privilege to work with you. To the fabulous people at McElderry: I couldn't ask for a better team, and I know exactly how lucky I am to work with so many smart, thoughtful, wonderful people. So many people had fingers in this book—some of whom I got to work with closely, others who I never met: Justin Chanda, Karen Wojtyla, Anne Zafian, Eugene Lee, Elizabeth Blake-Linn, Greg Stadnyk, Chrissy Noh, Caitlin Sweeny, Alissa Nigro, Lisa Quach, Bezi Yohannes, Perla Gil, Remi Moon, Amelia Johnson, Ashley Mitchell, Yasleen Trinidad, Saleena Nival, Emily Ritter, Amy Lavigne, Lisa Moraleda, Nicole Russo, Mitch Thorpe, Christina Pecorale and her sales team, and Michelle Leo and her education/library team. I do the writing, but the rest of it, the hardcovers and the paper ordering (which is more complicated these days than you'd think!), the designing, the publicity and marketing, and . . . everything. All I really know is that I only have the barest idea of how much work goes into producing a book once I'm done with all the words. You all do real-life magic.

Thank you, Carlos Quevedo, for the stunning cover art (just look at it!!).

As always my writing group aided greatly in preventing this story from being set on fire and thrown off a building; I knew where I wanted to go, but they helped me figure out all the ways not to get there. As always they managed to cheer me on and ask for my best in the same breath. Kristen Evans will always be the number one Mateo apologist, Cameron Harris will always catch everything that doesn't quite make sense, and Aliah Eberting always knows exactly where to swoon. Thank you.

More than anyone else, thanks go to my family. They are the most supportive, lovely humans even when we all have to juggle to make everything fit. Thanks especially go to Allen, not only for pushing me out of the house to go write when there were maybe actual fires being set by the children, but for knowing to be very, very quiet when I asked him to help me work out plot points, and for being the best cheer-leader a girl could ask for. Also, he says to put in that he's stunningly attractive, which is true, so there you go.

I'm so grateful to be able to write books, grateful for all the people who make it possible, and just . . . grateful in general.

About the Author

Caitlin Sangster is the author of the Last Star Burning trilogy and *She Who Rides the Storm,* and the founder and cohost of the *Lit Service* podcast. She grew up in the backwoods of Northern California; has lived in China, Taiwan, Utah, and Montana; and can often be found dragging her poor husband and four children onto hikes that feature far too many bears. You can find her online at CaitlinSangster.com.